POWER
IN THE
BLOOD

POWER
IN THE
BLOOD

GREG MATTHEWS

Aaron Asher Books
HarperCollins*Publishers*

HarperCollins books may be purchased for educational, business, or sales promotional use. For information, please write: Special Markets Department, HarperCollins Publishers, Inc., 10 East 53rd Street, New York, NY 10022.

FIRST EDITION

Designed by *Claudyne Bianco*

Library of Congress Cataloging-in-Publication Data

Matthews, Greg.
  Power in the blood : a novel / Greg Matthews
    p.   cm.
  ISBN 0-06-017969-4
  I. Title.
PR9619.3.M317P68   1993
823—dc20   92-53350

93 94 95 96 97 ❖/RRD 10 9 8 7 6 5 4 3 2 1

FOR ZENON, LAURA AND RYAN

For they eat the bread of wickedness, and drink
the wine of violence.

Proverbs 4:17

PART ONE

THE
BREAD
OF
WICKEDNESS

1

It was Zoe who found their mother dead. The boys were still asleep, wrapped in blankets in their corner of the room. Zoe slept alongside her mother in the only bed, and the first light of morning told her Nettie Dugan was dead. She was already cold, so it had happened in the night.

Zoe didn't want to touch her mother again after that first hesitant poke, just a fingertip against the sharp cheekbone; her finger had jerked away as if burned. Mama's eyes were open, her bluish lips slightly parted, the familiar gaps of missing teeth visible. It was almost a smile. Zoe hadn't been so close to death since she'd seen an old man fall down directly in front of her on Union Street last winter, so near to her a coin in his hand had rolled and hit her shoe. She'd picked up the coin before anyone else saw it, and hurried away. Only a nickel, but it was hers. Zoe had considered spending it solely on herself, then reconsidered and presented it to Nettie, who told her she was the goodest girl there ever was.

Drew was stirring. The youngest, he usually woke first. Zoe was three years older, and Clayton was three years older than her, plus a month. Despite this, Zoe knew she was the one in charge whenever Nettie got sick, no matter how Clay might insist he was the boss. Now that Nettie was gone, who would be the leader? It worried Zoe almost as much as her mother's passing.

Zoe sat up and beckoned Drew over. He slid from beneath the blanket covering himself and Clay and approached the bed, squinting the way he always did when he first got up. The squint pulled his round face into a smile that indicated nothing more than semi-wakefulness. He was already clutching the tip of his penis under the grimy shirt he wore day and night; Drew always needed to pee immediately on rising. He pulled the pot from beneath Zoe's side of the bed and deposited more urine in it. Today was Clay's turn to empty it. Zoe assumed her mother's death wouldn't change that.

"She's dead ...," Zoe whispered.

"Huh?"

"Mama died. Look at her if you don't believe me."

Drew lowered his shirt and walked around to the bed's far side. He stared at his mother for some time. "No she's not," he said.

"She is, because there's no breathing. Touch her, I dare you."

Drew's fingers reached, felt the cold skin and were pulled back. Zoe saw with satisfaction that he believed her now.

"Why did she die?" Drew asked.

"She was sick," Zoe reminded him, "and she must've gotten sicker, so she died."

The squinting smile on Drew's face grew inappropriately broader. Zoe knew this meant he was close to tears; everything about Drew was backwards, but he was only seven after all. "Make her come back," he whispered.

"I can't, stupid. She's *dead.*"

Sure enough, tears began rolling down Drew's face. He was beyond speech, beyond understanding. Zoe felt more sorry for him than for Mama; at least Mama would have understood the fact of her dying, the irreversible nature of it. Drew's tears were contagious, though, so she found herself crying too, and their combined sobbing finally woke Clay.

Scowling, he came to the bed. "What?" he said, conveying in one word his authority and annoyance. He appeared not to notice Nettie's unnatural stillness at all. His sister and brother, now that Clay was awake, allowed themselves to howl unashamedly, irritating him further. "What!" he demanded. Zoe's glance at their mother made him look closer at the head on the pillow, and then he knew.

The effort required to keep from crying himself made Clay feel sick. He'd been expecting this thing, this death; Nettie had warned him of its approach and drilled him on what to do when it happened. Clay knew he had to tell Mrs. Smalley down the hall, and that is what he did.

Having been deserted by her own husband, Mrs. Smalley regarded herself and Nettie Dugan as sisters in suffering. They had worked in the same mill for several years, then Mr. Smalley had died and left his wife a small insurance policy, which enabled her to stop working and ease the pain in her failing legs. Nettie had continued at the mill until she became sick.

The death was not unexpected, and Mrs. Smalley resolved to waste no time in unproductive mourning but to concentrate on the problem of burial, and the greater issue of what to do with Nettie's children.

She could not take them into her own room, not with her drunkard son and his wife there, so she told Clayton to keep his brother and sister inside their mother's room while she arranged a five-dollar funeral through Schenectady's lowliest church.

That took two days. She escorted the children to the graveyard and stood behind them as Nettie was lowered into the earth. Heart failure, the death certificate asserted, but Mrs. Smalley knew it was sorrow over no money and no man that had done it. The cheap wooden marker would last no more than a few years, and they'd likely bury some other pauper on top of her then. But that was of less concern than it might have been, for Mrs. Smalley was a planner by inclination, and although her planning had borne no fruit within her own family, she was determined that her talent for organization should benefit the three souls Nettie Dugan had left behind. If all went as intended, the children would be far away before the mound had settled on their mother's grave.

In answer to prompt inquiries launched by Mrs. Smalley, she was informed by a letter from the Children's Aid Society in New York City that places had been found for Clayton, Zoe and Drew on the next orphan train, scheduled to depart Albany for points west on May 19. The children would have less than a week to prepare themselves for something Mrs. Smalley convinced them would be an adventure, the answer to their need for family and a place in the sun.

"They'll be children such as yourselves," she assured them, "and with unhappiness the same as you've known just recent, or maybe worse. There's some of 'em been running around in the big town without a mother or father for years, and now you'll all be taken together to the west, where there's folks as have had their children took from 'em by sickness, like you've had your ma took the same way.

"They're wanting new children in Ohio and Illinois, so you'll be appreciated by folks out there. You're the lucky ones, you should know, getting a chance like this to start over, and all because my cousin's married to a good man on the railroad as knows about these things. A prayer answered is what it is, so now we'll bow our heads and give thanks for God's mercy on us all."

Clay was not ungrateful for Mrs. Smalley's help. He knew that in the west everyone rode a horse and carried a gun to shoot wolves and Indians and buffalo. That sounded all right to Clay; he just hoped the places Mrs. Smalley mentioned were far enough west. It would suit Drew as well, and they would find someone to marry Zoe so she could be happy too. Her husband would stand by Zoe and be good to her. That was definite. Clay wasn't going to let his sister suffer as his mother had. Zoe's husband wouldn't run off and leave her the way Mama's had done, or Clay would go after him and kill him. He'd be sure and make that point before the wedding ceremony, just so everyone knew how matters stood.

Drew appeared content to believe Clay's promises, but Zoe demurred; as usual, Clay was running things to please himself. Zoe was troubled by an apparent lack of sadness among all three children since the burial. Somehow they seemed to have put Mama behind them too soon. Zoe herself was guilty of this, yet she knew she had loved their mother. The boys' talk of ponies and pistols was annoying, and so she was not disposed to reward Clay for his self-serving plans by appearing interested, or even anxious to be away from Schenectady, a place she'd despised all her short life. In the days remaining until they entrained for the west, Zoe kept herself to herself, and was dismayed that the boys accepted her aloofness without comment.

Mrs. Smalley organized the hiring of a cart to take them to the station at Albany, and stood with them on the platform. An hour before noon, an unruly herd of children, at least fifty of them, crowded into the station. They had marched in ragged file from the riverfront, having been brought up the Hudson from New York City by overnight steamer. In charge were a rather stern young woman and a one-armed man who, despite this disadvantage, carried a large wicker basket on his back.

Mrs. Smalley had been expecting fewer children under broader adult supervision. She introduced herself and her charges to the custodians, who in turn gave their name as Canby, Mr. and Mrs. Then it was time for stilted good-byes.

"These nice people will take care of you till you find a home. You be sure and heed them, and be good always, promise me now."

"Yes," said Zoe.

The boys simply nodded, their attention on the newcomers flocking around. Clay was already testing with his eyes the resolution of anyone who cared to match his gaze. He liked the idea of being top dog of this so called orphan train, even though it was obvious from all the grown-up passengers milling around that orphans would constitute only a small portion of the payload.

Tall for his age, Clay was disappointed to note at least a half dozen boys older and bigger than himself; he hadn't thought there might be such things as orphans over the age of thirteen, and felt a fool for it. The trip was not shaping up as he'd anticipated, so he scowled and said as little as possible to Mrs. Smalley, wishing he could blame her somehow for his displeasure. While she lectured on good behavior and obedience, he stared at the soot-encrusted walls round about, allowing her voice to be drowned by the station's din.

Clay had heard that in the west there was no soot, at least not enough to accumulate on streets and buildings. A clean place, he told himself; new and clean. He had heard that less than two weeks ago the nation was linked by a continuous set of rails built simultaneously from east and west; they had met and been joined by a golden spike somewhere in Utah Territory. What was to prevent the Dugans from riding all the way to the Pacific? he asked himself. All they had to do was refuse the entreaties of anyone wishing to adopt them along the way. It would be easy.

The orphans had a car entirely to themselves, the oldest and least comfortable available, the seats little more than narrow wooden benches set close together. "The most seats for the littlest money," Drew heard the man with one arm say, but the man didn't sound pleased that they had the most seats.

Leading the first wave of boarders, Clay shoved Zoe and Drew against a window and sat beside them. "That boy!" Mrs. Canby cried, pointing at him. "There will be no pushing and shoving, do you hear!" Clay loathed her instantly. "There is room for all!" she called over her shoulder. "Once seated, remain there, all of you!

We will not hold up departure of this train through rowdiness!"

Several boys who had sneaked away to admire the snorting locomotive were rounded up by railroad staff and brought to the car for inclusion among the swarm already aboard.

"Settle down!" roared Mr. Canby, and the effect was immediate; all unnecessary movement among the seats was stilled. Clay admired the man's ability to control so many with just his voice.

Despite relative calm inside the car and a full complement of orphans, the train did not leave for a further twenty minutes. Zoe, crammed against a window, could see Mrs. Smalley on the platform, clearly unwilling to call a halt to duty until the train was gone. Zoe remained invisible behind the grimy pane. She pointed out Mrs. Smalley to Drew, but he was more interested in a knee-bumping contest with the boy seated opposite him.

Clay refused to look out the window; Schenectady already belonged to the past. He stared at the back of Mrs. Canby's tightly bunned and bonneted head further down the cramped aisle and willed the train to begin moving. When finally the whistle blew and the cars lurched forward in a rattle of couplings, he found he'd been holding his breath.

Within a very few minutes, the station and Mrs. Smalley, the edge of the town itself, all were gone, left behind. Clay resolved to remember his life up until this moment only in the broadest terms. There had been too much unhappiness in that place receding behind the red caboose, too much hunger and desperation, too little laughter. When he recalled their lives in Schenectady without sentiment, he saw there had been no real hope for them at all.

2

During the day and night it took to leave New York State and enter Pennsylvania, Zoe learned that Mrs. Canby was without humor or warmth, and seemed in fact not to like children. She had made sure the newcomers knew her rules soon after the train left Albany. "Remain seated at all times. Hold up your hand if you require attention. Do not leave the car without permission. Do not make unnecessary noise or create disturbances among your fellow travelers."

Her husband, the one-armed man, was more approachable. He would tell anyone who asked him how his arm was lost at Shiloh. Zoe had heard the story several times already. Mr. Canby didn't change so much as a word of it each time, so it must be true. The part about the rebel ball that shattered the bone was interesting, but best of all was his description of the hospital tent, with arms and legs stacked outside.

"And then the surgeon picked up the saw," said Mr. Canby, "and he started in on me with just a stick between my teeth and not even a shot of good whiskey inside me for the pain of it, and he didn't quit sawing till that arm was off and the flapping piece of flesh they left all nicely tucked and stitched over it. Then came the hot pitch— slapped on the stump like a mud pie it was—and didn't I howl, you bet I did, howled like a pup. But you know what the strange part was?" Everyone did by then, but his audience leaned forward anyway. "I still felt the arm," Mr. Canby said in hushed tones, "felt it joined to my shoulder, just like the other one, with the fingers wriggling all alive still, even if the whole thing was gone. A phantom arm ..." It never failed to produce an intake of breath.

Drew was fascinated by the openness of the countryside. During the hours of daylight he stared through the window at an endless series of neat farms and tiny hill towns. Sometimes the train would stop to let passengers off from the other cars, and new passengers would step aboard to be drawn westward through the long afternoon and evening.

He talked occasionally with the boy seated opposite him, Kerwin (who pronounced it Care-win), but found conversation difficult because of Kerwin's peculiar big-city accent. "Eeeehh, fuck yez," Kerwin eventually said, when it became clear he was not understood, so Drew returned to watching the world roll effortlessly by.

He'd been unprepared for so many trees, so great an expanse of sky, and they'd only just started. Clay said everyone would be on the train for days, getting west. It was a shame Mama couldn't be there to enjoy the newness of it all with them. Mama would have sat with the bonnet lady and talked with her like she'd always sat and talked with Mrs. Smalley back home, back in that place none of them would ever see again; even Mama, who'd stayed there, would never see it again. Drew wept silently, then fell asleep, and woke up to find still more countryside sliding by, late afternoon sunlight lengthening the shadows of the trees. He was terribly hungry.

At sundown the orphan car was detached from the train for transfer to a string of boxcars behind another locomotive, which would continue hauling westward through the night. While the car was switched onto a siding, the children were ordered to stand in an orderly fashion along the station platform to receive their first food since breakfast. Mr. Canby opened the wicker basket he'd wrestled with literal single-handedness from the car, and his wife dispensed a meal of bread generously spread with lard. This was followed by two dried apricots for each child. It became clear the basket was not intended to feed so many for very long.

"What's needed here," said Mr. Canby with a grin, "is a miracle of the loaves and fishes, maybe." Mrs. Canby frowned darkly, and he stopped grinning.

The new train having been shunted onto the main line, the

orphans' journey resumed. Reinvigorated by food, they could not fall asleep as ordered by Mrs. Canby. The distraction of a passing landscape no longer available to them, the children found renewed interest in one another, and the car soon was filled with a continuous babble of young voices raised to their highest pitch to overcome the grumble and clatter of rolling wheels and the more immediate din of their neighbors.

"Cease!" cried Mrs. Canby. "You must be quiet!"

Zoe wished it were possible to change seats temporarily, just so she could talk to some of the other girls, or even some of the boys. It was wearisome to be forever in the same place, looking at the same faces arranged opposite her, not one of which she liked. It had been interesting at first to listen as Kerwin held whispered swearing contests with the boy beside him, an Irish youth named McIlwray, who could not, despite coaching from Kerwin, learn how to pronounce "fuck" correctly. It became a laughing matter in the immediate vicinity of the swearers, and McIlwray grew irritated. "Fock yew," he said with genuine feeling, and Kerwin responded in kind.

But that sport had become boring through repetition, and Zoe chafed at her immobility. Occasional rearrangements of seating were made by Mrs. Canby, usually to terminate cases of harassment, verbal or otherwise, conducted by boys against girls. Mrs. Canby even threatened to separate the sexes, girls on one side of the aisle, boys on the other, if such despicable behavior did not cease upon the instant. The threat was not carried out, to Zoe's relief. For all that she wanted to sample friendship throughout the car, she would have felt lost without her brothers on either side. Mr. Canby slept throughout the worst of this crisis, his snores the object of much stifled giggling.

Migration among seats being forbidden, the one place anyone could visit, after raising a hand, was the crude privy built onto the car's rear platform. In daylight it had been exciting to watch the crossties flashing past under the hole in the plank; it caused a delicious shiver to imagine oneself falling through, to be cut in half by the wheels. After nightfall some of the girls preferred using the privy in twos, comforting each other beneath the inadequate light of a swaying oil lamp while they relieved themselves onto a roadbed made invisible by darkness.

Sleep was difficult on the unyielding benches. The children sat as they had throughout the day, the next shoulder along providing a bony pillow as the night lengthened. Girls used each other's soft laps, but the boys were denied this comfort, with the instinctive rejection of physical closeness among their kind. Drew was just young enough to avail himself of Zoe's thighs without embarrassment. Zoe in turn leaned against sturdy Clay, upright as ever despite his closed eyes, behind which he slipped in and out of dreams that showed him Mama beckoning him further west, further west, until he came to a place where the sun lay like a molten ball of gold, a brilliant puddle on a desolate plain, and Mama was nowhere to be seen. Waking, he allowed himself a brief moment awash with tears that went unobserved in the dim car, now quiet as it swayed along rails into the Pennsylvanian night.

Breakfast came from the same wicker basket: bread and chicken fat, plus two dried apricots apiece. Mr. Canby, a large man despite his incompleteness, was seen to stare at his portion for some time before eating it, his expression doleful. Lunch saw no change other than the Canbys' having to reach deeper into the basket. Mealtimes had already become less rowdy, almost sullen occasions.

In the evening, when the train reached Pittsburgh, there was a treat for all—dinner in the station restaurant. The menu was lengthy, but everyone had soup, Mrs. Canby having protested at the exorbitant price of every meat dish. Mr. Canby spooned soup under his mustache, his face darkened by unknown forces within. Glaring at his emptied bowl, he insisted there be a dessert. Over his wife's objections, he ordered pie, and then pie again, not one belly having truly been filled. Mrs. Canby refused to look in his direction as they herded their charges back to the car, now hitched onto yet another train. The benches seemed less uncomfortable, an advantage of repletion, which Mr. Canby referred to as "intestinal fulfillment, like a live human's supposed to feel at least once every twenty-four hours for good health."

The morning of the third day revealed Ohio, and now there was real excitement in the car. This was the first state in which it was possible to be selected for adoption. Orphans wondered, silently or aloud, at their chances. Clay was scornful; he told Zoe and Drew they had to hold out for more westerly regions. "Ohio's just not far enough," he said.

In the afternoon it happened. The car was detached from the

train and shunted onto a siding at the edge of a sizable town. A council representative approached smilingly to speak with the Canbys and suggested bringing all orphans to the town hall, where a crowd had already gathered in anticipation.

The Children's Aid Society was in its fifteenth year of good work, having begun in 1854, and a larger than usual turnout of prospective foster parents had assembled to survey the spring crop of adoptees. A diphtheria epidemic of unprecedented virulence the previous winter had sharpened interest in the children.

"Plenty of families lost their little ones just recent," the councilman whispered, keeping his voice from the straggling line of painfully hushed orphans following behind. "These here'll be snapped up in double-quick time, I guarantee. Folks have come in from a hundred miles around, farmers mostly. They'll be eager for the younguns, all right."

Inside the town hall, arranged on a long bench covered by cloth, without a single chair to impede access, a feast was waiting—a communal celebration of the orphans' arrival. Anxious adult faces were everywhere, yet these were thrust into the background by the endless table of food, real food, present in variety and abundance. There were cold meats and cakes; fresh bread and pies; an assortment of dried fruit, notably apricots (these would be ignored); jars of preserves with their melted paraffin seals dug out; butter molded into rough blocks of tantalizing yellow; crocks of milk still smelling of the udder. Not a feast—a banquet.

"Fall to and take your share," commanded the councilman, and not an orphan hesitated. Surrounded by questing eyes and subtly pointing fingers, they attacked the fruits of central Ohio and set about gorging themselves. The councilman, a student of human nature, gently pushed the Canbys toward the food. "Have at it, one and all," he urged.

Mr. Canby held back several seconds more for propriety's sake, then joined in under the guise of supervisor. "You, boy! Take less of a handful than that! Manners! One mouthful at a time there, laddie. Don't be eating too fast now, or the cramps'll follow ... No need to shove! Plenty for everyone! Pass me a slice of that ham, missie ... thank you kindly."

His wife resisted in agonized decorum for several minutes more, then slid among the tempting array, sampling here, ingesting there, all dignity set aside in pursuit of sustenance. This was her third trip west with orphans, and the Society, despite its fifteen years' experience, still had not properly victualed the party, obliging Mr. Canby and herself to abandon decency before an audience of strangers. It was an unforgivable oversight, and she was determined, as prune pie overwhelmed her soul, to insist on adequate provender should she and Mr. Canby be selected for a fourth sojourn. Next time it would be different, or she would know the reason why.

Bellies filled, the children became aware of the scrutiny that had attended their meal. As the last of the food disappeared, self-consciousness took hold, and they began studying the ground. Some of the older boys glared at the surrounding faces, daring them, whether to select or ignore them the boys themselves could not have said. The business of the day was at hand, and everyone inside the town hall knew it.

The process had no formal beginning; men and their wives simply began moving among the orphans, as wary of what needed to be done as were the children they sought.

Often the topic of introduction was the food that had been consumed during the time of silent appraisal that now was ended. "That peach cobbler, my missus made it. You kin have more, you come home with us. Be good to you. Lost our own girl, and we need another'n for the family. There's a sister an' two brothers for you to be with."

Or it might be a dare: "You strong? Look perty strong to me. Got work for a strong back. Figure you're up to that, boy? Welcome to climb in the wagon and come on home. Decent home. Christian."

Or cajolery: "There's a swing in the chinaberry tree. My husband here made it special for a special someone. Could that be you? I been wanting a nice little girl since ours got took. The Lord taketh. Did he bring you? I suspect he did. You think he might've done that, brung you to us? We're Sullivanses, from around here. Biggest chinaberry tree in the county. Mr. Sullivan's grampa, he planted it. Got the swing all set, and there's dresses, real pretty dresses. You'll grow into 'em right soon. What's your name?"

Or painfully casual: "Plan on going further west, boy? It don't get no better than around here, that's a fact. That's why they stopped here and give you a chance to stay. First choice is best choice, they say. Had my eye on you, me and my wife. She's sayin' she likes the look of you, and I won't say no if that's what you'd like, to come with us. You think about it and don't rush or nothin'. We weren't lookin' at no one else, I'll tell you. Whereabouts you from, son?"

The answers came quickly, or not at all; a smile and nod were often enough for "yes," a nervous sideways glance or lengthy boot-studying as good as "no." There was little coercion, no real bribery other than the promise of good food and hand-me-down clothing kept like holy shrouds in the closets of the dead, awaiting resurrection. The smiles behind beards or hidden in the shadows of calico bonnets were genuine.

Sometimes an orphan didn't know for sure if the people stooping down for an answer were indeed the right ones, but agreed to go with them through instinct, or a calculated loathing of the railroad car's harsh benches. Some thought Ohio must be pretty far west already, so why go further? Deals were struck with a look, a wink and a smile, an awkward handshake between man and boy, the placing of a woman's hand on some girl's narrow shoulder.

Clay kept his family close by him, flanked himself with sister and brother. His knowledge of geography was scanty, but he knew Ohio was below Lake Erie, and that was nowhere near far enough west. He held Zoe and Clay beside himself and challenged them all, the farmers and townspeople in their Sunday best, with unmistakable sullenness.

Mr. Canby noted the look. There was one like this boy on every trip, resentful and proud and difficult, made that way by reasons Mr. Canby didn't really want to know. He hadn't informed himself of any orphan's circumstances since the first trip, when the stories, told with matter-of-fact directness, had made him weep after dark. The boy holding on to his own was defying kindness, hedging against selection, building a wall with his eyes. Mr. Canby had seen it all before, and knew who the last orphan on the train would be; the fact was stamped right there on his young brow like the mark of Cain. But Mr. Canby said nothing, offered no advice, knowing this was not the time or place. He would talk with the boy later. Mr. Canby turned away, bit into the last pastry and licked the flyaway crumbs from his mustache.

They drifted by, those needy couples, and more than once cast interested eyes on the Dugans, but three mouths to feed were many, and above the purely practical considerations of investment in food and clothing and bed space there was the knowledge that three children linked by blood would never be wholly assimilated into a new family. No, they would have to be separated, one from another, to be made dependent upon their benefactors, especially the tall boy with the eyes that dared anyone to come closer and make an offer. No one did.

3

His wicker basket was replenished by the town, but Mr. Canby found his charges uninterested in food that night. Their car coupled onto the rear of a new train, the orphans found their number whittled by fully half; there was room for the remainder to sprawl as they wished. Ohio always got the most winsome; those less pleasing in appearance continued west.

The hundred or so miles after that first stop in Ohio passed quietly, as the unselected asked themselves why it was that they were still on board the train. Even if they had chosen to avoid adoption for some reason, they felt the implicit shame of having passed through that first sieve, the net that gently snared. They felt, with undeserved passion, that they were rejects of one kind or another.

Most, Mr. Canby knew, would brood over their feelings and submit to whoever invited them home at the very next stop. It would happen on this trip as it had happened before, and the sadness of it made him despair in ways he could never communicate to his wife, whose opinion was that orphans couldn't afford to be choosy. Mr. Canby felt toward the leftovers the same kind of commiseration he used to feel for himself over the loss of his arm. It made no sense, but that was how he felt.

When Clay came out of the privy he found Mr. Canby smoking his pipe on the moonlit car platform. Behind them the rails formed a gleaming set of parallel lines receding into darkness and infinity. "Nice night," offered Mr. Canby, before Clay could escape.

"Yes."

"Fresh air. Shame to cloud it like I do, but nicotine's a powerful habit. Don't you be taking it up."

"All right," said Clay.

"Did your sister and brother tell you how they feel?"

"No." Clay thought he meant how they felt about tobacco.

"They disappointed about not getting picked back there?"

Now Clay understood. "No," he said.

"In my experience, the chances of all three of you getting taken up by a family are pretty hopeless, but I guess you already thought of that. You can hold out forever like you did today, but we only go as far as Missouri, and not even all the way across. Sometimes we don't even get that far, everyone getting picked before we get there. Don't be hoping to hold off what has to come, boy. It won't work. I've traveled this line before and seen the direction these things take. Sooner or later you'll have to tell your brother and sister good-bye. I'm telling you as the oldest, and you need to be passing it on, so they'll know and be prepared when the time comes. None of my business, you're thinking, but it is. You think about it now, and tell them tomorrow."

Mr. Canby knocked out his pipe against the platform rail and went inside. Clay remained staring into the night, hating the friendly man who'd spoken the very thoughts that had filled him since the car resumed rolling. He stayed on the chilly platform until a girl came out to use the privy; she wouldn't do so until Clay went away.

"I don't want to," said Drew.

"He says we have to," Clay told him.

"He can say it all he wants," Zoe stated, "but he can't make us do it."

Mr. Canby's advice had been passed on next morning, and rejected.

"Go tell him," Zoe said.

Clay didn't want to but as the eldest, had little choice. He stood and moved along the car.

"Mr. Canby, sir?"

"Yes?"

"Uh ... we don't want to. We decided."

"You won't split up?"

"Nossir."

"You're sure?"

Clay nodded, not trusting his voice. He hadn't gone against the wishes of an adult male since before his father left Schenectady, four years earlier. His defiance then had earned him a badly wrenched shoulder and lacerations from a heavy belt buckle. He couldn't remember the exact nature of the offense, but its punishment was probably Clay's most indelible memory.

"I guess I can't make you," said Mr. Canby. He knew someone who could.

Clay returned to his seat. "I told him."

"What did he say?" Zoe asked.

"He said he can't make us if we don't want to."

"There, I told you!" Zoe felt vindicated. "We just have to stay together and someone will take all of us."

Clay wasn't so sure anymore. Mr. Canby had experience in the orphan business, and if he said it wasn't wise to stick together, it was probably true. Clay didn't know if he liked Mr. Canby or not, but he didn't think the man was a liar. It was disturbing to consider any option other than that which they wanted, terrifying to think they might have to.

He kept the fear to himself. Zoe and Drew had recovered their spirits immediately; it would be a shame to make them sad again by talking out loud. Clay made Drew surrender the window seat so he could stare at the countryside instead of at his sister and brother; that way he could pretend he was by himself, which would certainly have made life a lot simpler were it so.

"Andrew?"

Mrs. Canby was hovering over them in the aisle. She was smiling, a rare and unsettling sight. "Andrew?" she said again, revealing even more gray teeth.

"We call him Drew," corrected Zoe.

"Drew, then. Would you come with me, Drew?"

"Where?" Drew asked. There was nowhere to go but the privy out on the platform, and his mama had quit taking him on trips of that kind a long time ago.

"Just to share a seat with me," said Mrs. Canby. "We'll just be a minute," she told the other two.

Drew went with her.

"She'll try and change his mind," Zoe predicted.

"Well, he won't listen."

They craned their necks but could see and hear nothing of what transpired on the Canbys' bench. Mr. Canby, curiously enough, had gone out to the platform, presumably to smoke his pipe. The fact that the man was prepared to walk away and leave the business of persuasion to his wife was shocking, so unexpected it unnerved Clay completely; he simply didn't know what to make of it, and was not surprised when Drew returned in tears.

Zoe ignored his distress. "Well? What happened?"

When Drew could finally talk, he said, "Mama's watching from heaven, and we shouldn't do what Clay says or she'll be sad up there. ..." He wiped snot onto his already grievously soiled cuff and looked at Clay and Zoe for consolation, or acceptance, guidance of any kind.

"Don't you listen to what she says," Clay told him. "She doesn't know a goddamn thing, that lady."

"She said ..." Drew wiped more snot onto himself. "She said for you to go see her too, Zoe."

"Well, I won't! I don't have to!"

"She *said*. You'll get in trouble."

"She'll only come and get you," advised Clay. "Go and listen and nod your head, then she'll leave us alone."

"I'm not going near her. I *won't*."

She went anyway, and returned with a face like wood. The boys waited, but Zoe wouldn't speak. Mr. Canby came back from the platform then, and Clay wondered how he'd known exactly when to do so. Probably he'd been watching through the rear door window, like a sneaking spy. Clay was suddenly bitter; the man had disappointed him badly, letting Mrs. Canby do what she'd done to Zoe and Drew.

There were forces conspiring to separate them, Clay saw it now, and in the deepest part of himself—the part that recognized truth without pressing it through the filter of emotion—he knew that the plans being made by the Canbys would succeed, and the Dugans' defiant scheme would stand no chance, as Mr. Canby had foretold last night on the platform. Any hope of staying together had vanished right there, been borne away on the night wind. The Dugans were wishing wishes, dreaming dreams, but the physical world would tear these apart.

Staring out the window again, ignoring Zoe as a punishment for her silence, Clay drove all thought from his mind. To think, to use the brain, was an act that somehow had no effect on what was bound to happen. There existed an inner world, one without actual substance, and over it there towered the outer world, consisting of everything that was not Clay himself. Both places, the small and the large, seemed to exist independently of each other, but it was clear the physical world, the one you could touch and see and hear things in, was more powerful. People like the Canbys ran that place, and people like himself and Zoe and Drew were no match for them, probably because adults had been in the place too long, and knew exactly how it worked. Of course, Mama had been an adult, but it seemed she had never learned the secret of manipulating the real world to her advantage; maybe Mama had been flawed in some way. The helplessness of the young was cruel, unfair, but there was no getting around it, and Clay saw for the first time just why it was that orphans were the weakest of the weak: they had no grown-up person to protect them and steer them gradually into the real place where strength and power lay.

Clay realized he had experienced a revelation of a kind, but it didn't make him feel any better. It was the lowly wisdom of the clam, the learning of rocks and stones that had been revealed, and he was not at all sure it should be valued.

Halfway across Indiana, in a river town, Zoe surrendered. She took Clay aside and told him, "Someone has to be first. It can't be Drew, he's too young, and it won't be you because you're too stubborn, so it has to be me. That's them over there, the ones next to the wagon. They seem like nice people. I have to go with them, or with someone. You and Drew have to as well. Remember the name of this place, and the place Drew gets picked in, because he'll be next, and someday you have to come back for us."

"You don't have to go with them! You don't. ..."

"I do. Mrs. Canby said if we didn't let ourselves get picked, we'd just be left in the middle of nowhere, and we'd starve right there."

"She's a liar! They wouldn't do that. Mr. Canby wouldn't let her. "

"She told me he would. We have to be made examples of, she said. I hate her. I want to get off the train. I can't look at her anymore."

Clay felt his anger slide into despair. Zoe would do it, he could tell. He was no longer in charge, eldest or not. Zoe had done the thing that should have been up to Clay; she'd made a decision, a choice, and had proved herself stronger than him. He was ashamed.

They went to find Drew, who had drifted from Clay's side. When he was found, Clay stood back and said nothing as his sister talked to and comforted and hugged the boy. Drew was still crying as Zoe announced her choice to the Canbys, then left the station yard with the man and woman who wanted her, perched between them on their high wagon seat.

Clay felt a humming inside his head. The main street of Wister's Landing became leached of color and substance. Clay had to sit down on the plank sidewalk, from which position it was easy to hang his head and weep more tears than he had shed even for his mother.

"Why'd she do it?" Drew sobbed.

"She told you, didn't she? We all have to. There's no other way— now quit making so much noise!"

In Illinois Clay tried offering himself along with Drew in several towns, hoping against hope there was a significant difference between three and two, but there was not, and so he told Drew to stand away from him at the next town, and to come tell him if some people he liked the look of offered him a home. Drew didn't want to, but Clay told him all over again why it had to be that way, and finally Drew agreed.

Separated from his brother at the next stop, Drew, with his look of disconsolation and loss, held such appeal he became surrounded within minutes. He came to Clay for approval of what he perceived as the nicest people. To Clay they were indistinguishable from the rest of the child-seekers he'd seen, but he told Drew he had chosen wisely, then went to inform Mr. Canby, having waited until his wife was elsewhere.

"Good," said Mr. Canby, and strolled over to talk briefly with the couple.

Clay took Drew aside. "Listen," he said, "I'll come back here as soon as I can to get you, then we'll go back and fetch Zoe, too, and be together again, all right?"

Drew nodded. It didn't sound like anything that might really happen, but he appreciated Clay's saying it. Then he began crying. Clay had to guide Drew over to the people he had selected.

"He's my brother," he explained.

"We'll look after him," said the woman.

"Depend on it," her husband added.

Clay watched another wagon take a part of himself away.

Mr. Canby knew very well what Clayton Dugan was up to. The number of orphans had been reduced to seven, not enough to warrant the hiring of an entire car for themselves, so they occupied several seats along with regular passengers. Then six of those seven also found homes. One had been selected by a woman riding the train.

That left Clay, and Clay didn't want to be chosen by anyone. He made that clear when they stopped at the first big town across the Missouri line. At least a dozen couples were on hand to claim the last orphan, but the boy was pretending he found them unacceptable. He refused them all, politely but pointedly, looking at the Canbys while he did it, letting them know his performance of rejection was for their benefit.

Mr. Canby didn't like that at all, even found himself beginning to dislike the boy. He knew what Clay planned—a fruitless continuation of the journey west, just himself and the Canbys, and at every town he would find the people wanting him unsuitable. The Society couldn't afford any wasteful extension of the trip, not so much as an extra mile beyond what was required.

The gathering of prospective foster parents was in confusion, each couple believing itself in competition with the rest for the boy in their midst. None of them found his murmured regrets convincing, and so thought he simply couldn't make up his mind, probably because the poor lad was unused to being the center of attention.

"Folks," Mr. Canby announced, holding up his arm, "our young friend here is having a hard time picking out a ma and pa from among so many that's suited for it, so I'll just be talking to him for a minute alone, if you don't mind. Thank you kindly, one and all."

He beckoned Clay to him. "Now you listen," he said, his voice low. "I'll just say it once. I know your plan, and it won't happen like you want it to, because I don't aim to let it happen that way, see? You get back there among those good people and you pick someone, I don't care who, it's your choice, but you make it right quick or by God I'll wring your scrawny neck. You understand me, boy?"

"Yes ..."

"Go do what I said. I'll be watching. I was you, I'd take the feller with the shaved face and his wife, she's wearing blue. They look like righteous folk to me, but like I say, it's up to you. Don't be making fools of good people that's suffered enough already from their loss. You're no better than any of them here, and that's a fact. Now go."

Clay wandered hopelessly back among the smiling faces. He'd intended making the Canbys take him still further west, then he'd jump from the train one night and make his own way to the Mississippi and get work on the riverboats. He knew now it wouldn't happen. Mr. Canby had outsmarted him.

It seemed easiest, considering his inner turmoil, to take the advice of the man who had proved himself smarter, and go with the couple suggested. Their look of surprise and relief as he approached them was pitiful.

Clay gave them a lopsided grimace and was embraced.

4·

He usually tried to surprise her in the barn, while she gathered eggs hidden there by the hens. The eggs were always in the same place, and so was Hassenplug. "Got 'em all?" he'd say, and Zoe would nod, the basket held between herself and her foster father. Both knew that broken eggs would be questioned by Mrs. Hassenplug, so the basket was Zoe's only defense.

It had started when her breasts came. They were not particularly evident beneath her blouse, but they were there, and Hassenplug's interest in her had escalated overnight, it seemed. First he'd pressed his hands over them in so casual a fashion Zoe thought it natural. "They have to be kept warm to grow," he'd said, massaging the shallow mounds. This made sense to Zoe, who had often placed her own hands over her developing breasts in exactly the same way whenever they were sore, but Hassenplug's smile alerted her to the incident's unnatural overtones. After that first time, she backed away whenever his hands reached for her. It happened only when his wife was nowhere around; this made Zoe aware that her breasts (and presumably the monthly bleeding that had accompanied their arrival) had not only changed her, they had altered Hassenplug beyond all understanding.

As a farm girl, Zoe knew that male creatures were equipped with

a rod of flesh for the penetration of female creatures, and the principle applied also to humans. Until now, she had assumed the difference between animals and people lay in the state of matrimony that
existed only in the latter, but Hassenplug was married to Mrs. Hassenplug, not to Zoe, so why did he want her to lift her skirts for him
every time she gathered eggs? Wasn't he able to lift Mrs. Hassenplug's skirts? It was mystifying, and she hated going to the barn,
previously one of her more enjoyable chores. Her father had spoiled
the quiet business of egg gathering for Zoe, and it was for this, as
well as the confusion his actions aroused in her, that she began to
resent his existence.

Zoe liked her mother well enough, although Mrs. Hassenplug had
never paid much attention to her new daughter beyond teaching
her those things that needed to be taught—needlework; cooking;
putting up preserves; yardwork; cleaning house, and so forth. It
was Zoe's impression that Mrs. Hassenplug wanted a boy, if only to
please her husband, but had accepted her foster daughter as a useful substitute.

"He's still wanting a boy to pass the place on to," her mother told
Zoe. "Still trying, he is," she lamented. It was some time before Zoe
realized that Hassenplug's "trying" meant mounting Mrs. Hassenplug and penetrating her private parts with his rod of flesh. Zoe
knew that a son was considered superior to a daughter, in that
property could be passed along down the male line, whereas a
daughter was simply a burden to be employed domestically, until
such time as she could be married off to some young man who
wished to use her for the purpose of siring a son to whom he could
pass along his property. It was the cycle of human affairs, as such
things were understood in Indiana.

Zoe's breasts had placed her already precarious position within
the household in jeopardy. She knew her mother would not approve
of Hassenplug's gropings in the barn, since Zoe wasn't married to
him. What if someday he should actually force her to lift her skirts,
and she had a son! Would she then be considered married to her
father in the same way that Mrs. Hassenplug was, in the manner of
the Mormons? It seemed an unlikely arrangement this far from
Utah, and anyway, the Hassenplugs were Presbyterians, even if
they never attended church meetings. Having the son for Hassenplug that his wife seemed unable to provide would not result in any
new arrangement of benefit to Zoe, that much was obvious, and so

she held the egg-laden basket before her like an armored breast-plate, to ward off the man beneath whose roof she lived.

In the first year, she had waited for Clay to ride up the road to the farm. He would be mounted on a fine pony, and carrying a pistol. She would know him even from a distance, because he was her brother. When he was close enough, he would smile and say, "Sorry I took so long. Pack your things; we have to go fetch Drew now."

The dream sustained her well into the second year, then died. No one came riding up the road but an occasional neighbor. Hassenplug never took his wife or Zoe to town, just twelve miles away. "You want something, you tell me and I'll get it," he said. He hadn't considered buying a dress that fit Zoe properly until his wife mentioned how foolish the girl looked in clothing too small for her. When two new dresses of the least expensive kind finally were brought home, they were several sizes too big. "She can grow into 'em gradual," explained Hassenplug, "so we don't get no more of this whining about clothes that's too small. Using the brain, see?" He tapped the side of his narrow head and grinned. Zoe tried on the dresses and wept. He had done it deliberately, to humiliate her, and she couldn't guess why.

By the time the new dresses fit, she no longer thought of rescue by Clay, scarcely thought of him at all, except in dreams of Schenectady. And when the dresses that were too large eventually became tight across her expanding chest, her father's disposition changed so abruptly she was caught by surprise—in the barn, with the eggs.

He tried bribery when direct requests for the lifting of her skirts were ignored. Dresses seemed an appropriate commodity for barter. "Just a little piece of loving" was all he wanted in exchange for stitched cloth. Zoe could choose the pattern, the style, even try the dress on beforehand to make sure it was exactly right for her. He would take her to town for a fitting.

"You take me there," she said, "and I'll think about it."

Her nerve amazed Zoe, flabbergasted Hassenplug. His little orphan girl was turning into a wily vixen. He laughed and said *he'd* do the thinking. For a week he gave no sign, then offered her a ride to Wister's Landing with him on the monthly trip for supplies.

Mrs. Hassenplug was outraged. "Why her and not me!" she demanded. Her husband thought about it, then smacked her once across the face with force enough to send her reeling into the kitchen corner. "Because I say so," he said.

The trip to town was still three days distant, but the slap that preceded it spelled the end of the casual relationship between Zoe and her foster mother. Mrs. Hassenplug, long since reconciled to being the mate of a churl, would have accepted the slap (it was not the first) if the reason for it had not been Zoe. Her man intended carrying this young female in his wagon a distance of twelve miles to town, and another twelve miles home again, just so she could get a dress that fit right. That privilege hadn't been granted Mrs. Hassenplug since the early years of the marriage, in fact she suspected her husband enjoyed the time spent away from her, actually experienced greater happiness in her absence. Mrs. Hassenplug remembered very well the things she'd been required to do back then in exchange for a trip to town, so it was natural for her to assume the same quid pro quo applied to Zoe.

Hassenplug's wife had endured much in pursuit of male progeny. Hassenplug had forced himself on her times beyond number for just that purpose, and she had no choice but to submit, that being her duty; the cornerstone of any marriage was the transfer of property to a son. But her suspicions had been nudged when Hassenplug chose from among the orphan train offerings of 1869 a girl instead of a boy. She had seen him approach several boys, it was true, but these had panicked when he described for them his need of a strong back and willing hands to work the finest little farm in the county. They'd be city boys, his wife warned him, but he insisted on presenting himself as some kind of slave driver, and every boy had shaken his head.

Then he'd gone to the girl, an unremarkable female to be sure, but at least she'd be able to assist his wife. Mrs. Hassenplug had thought her husband was being generous at the time, getting her someone to help out around the house. Four years later, she saw that the unremarkable female had been an investment, not a gift. It was a grievous insult. No woman who had endured as she had should have to fight against something as ubiquitous, as callow, as younger flesh. Mrs. Hassenplug had attempted to halt the course of events by protest and been slapped silly for her trouble. Now what would happen would happen. Mrs. Hassenplug hadn't been driven to church since her wedding day, but she knew the situation was in God's hands. No one could have greater need of His help than herself.

The day of the trip to town dawned fair and warm. Zoe had not heard a civil word from the lips of her mother since Hassenplug announced he would take her with him in the wagon. Zoe was afraid, and already ashamed; she had encouraged the man by saying she would think about his offer, and now that he had followed through with an invitation to town that didn't even include the presence of his wife, Zoe felt she'd stepped off a cliff, and in so doing made an enemy of the woman who'd been reasonably good to her for a long time.

She considered reneging on the arrangement, simply staying home, but that option smacked of weakness. Only fourteen, she had a quotient of the Dugan blood that had been strong enough to survive desertion and poverty (Nettie's blood, that was, not the craven stuff that flowed in the veins of Zoe's true father, the coward who'd left them nothing but his name). No, she'd go to town and choose a dress, and the devil take what happened. She was careful, though, to slip a small paring knife into her sleeve before joining Hassenplug on the wagon seat.

Mrs. Hassenplug refused to come out into the yard to witness their departure. As the wagon crept away she raged at her helplessness, her inability to change anything in her life, but before long her anger turned to tears, as it always did. Now she took up the long and bitter weeping of the irredeemable victim, knowing that by the time her husband accomplished what it was he planned, her face would be dry, set like stone with the salt of her misery.

Surprisingly, Zoe remembered some of the landscape from her passage in the same wagon four years before, on the long drive from town with her new parents. She was now a different person, and didn't feel at all that she was moving back into her own past. The station where she had said good-bye to her brothers would still be there, but her brothers would not. That was the saddest thought for Zoe, sadder than knowing the man beside her had plans no father should have.

"Not saying much," Hassenplug commented.

She looked at him, at the smile beneath his mustache. He imagined things would go the way he wanted, but Zoe knew they would not. Her plans did not extend beyond hiding the knife, but as she looked at Hassenplug's mouth, an alternative to stabbing him flashed into Zoe's head. The knife would not be necessary after all.

"I don't have much to say," she said, and turned her face to the road again.

Hassenplug laughed. "That deal we made, that what you're thinking about? Remember the deal?"

"Yes. I said I'd think about it when I got a dress."

"That ain't the way I recall it. Straight trade, that's how it'll be. You get what you want after I get what I want."

"That isn't what you said."

"Don't get a notion to wriggle out of it, not after you made a deal. Anyone makes a deal with me, they stick to it."

His voice had turned ugly, the smile had soured. Zoe glanced at him, then away. She saw he meant what he said.

"Afterwards," she reasoned, "after you get it for me. Then ... then you can."

Zoe intended leaving the store by its back entrance, assuming it had one, or by any available window if it did not. She would go to the station and get aboard the first westbound train that pulled in, and when the conductor asked for her ticket she would admit she didn't have one; the worst he could do was put her off at the next stop, where she would wait for another train. In this on-again, off-again fashion she would go west, where Clay and Drew led unknown lives. The new dress, with its perfect fit, would give her the confidence to step inside the first of many cars.

"Shoes," she said, picturing herself aboard the train. "I want shoes too, real shoes, nothing like these." She looked down at her clumsy boy's boots, graceless as buckets.

"Anything else?" Hassenplug asked. "Diamonds and pearls, maybe?"

"Just the shoes, and the dress ... and a new petticoat."

"Petticoat! What you think you are, a goddamn princess?"

He laughed again, the same ugly sound, and flicked the reins. "You don't know a thing, girl. You don't know nothing, you hear?" Zoe wouldn't look at him. "You hear me!"

"Yes ..."

"Don't be telling me what you'll get and when you'll get it. I'll be the one does the deciding, not you, hear me?"

"Yes."

"A thing's only worth what it's worth," he said, and nodded in agreement with himself. "It ain't worth no more than that. I'm a fair man," he continued, softening his tone, "and a fair man makes a fair trade. Don't you worry, you won't be sorry about a thing, not a goddamn thing."

They drove another mile, then Hassenplug said, "Right here'll be about right," and steered his wagon off the road into a thick stand of dogwood.

Zoe stiffened with alarm. Hassenplug's schedule for the trade was the reverse of her own. "No," she said, "after the dress ..."

"Get down, and don't be running away. I know how you figured it to be, getting to town and then running. Well, you won't run, not in town and not here neither, because you won't go to town. Think I'd let you? I know better, see. You'll get your dress, a real pretty one. You be nice and I might even get you some regular shoes, with them little bows, maybe. Just you be nice and you'll get what you want. Now get down like I said."

Zoe did as she was told. Now everything depended on her willingness to use the knife. It made her sick to think of jabbing the blade into Hassenplug, even sicker to think of what he intended doing if her gumption failed and she froze instead of defending herself.

Hassenplug was getting down from the wagon on the same side as Zoe, unwilling even to give her the chance of a head start, should she decide to run. His face was creased by an openmouthed smile, the lips wetted by his roaming tongue. He had never looked uglier. She could never let him touch her, let alone place himself inside her. Even his breathing had been coarsened by his sense of power over Zoe, and his eyes were unnaturally bright with wanting.

Zoe reached inside her sleeve, found the paring knife, pulled it out and held it before her. Hassenplug's face fell, then his confident smirk returned. Without taking his eyes from the blade, he felt behind him for the horsewhip in its metal socket, yanked it free and lazily unfurled the lash.

"Better not," he advised, flicking the tip toward her along the ground. "I can take a fly off old Beulah's ear without she feels a thing. You put that down now and you'll come to no harm. We made a deal. Can't blame me for holding you to it, now can you, huh? Set it down. Set it down or by God I'll make you sorry. She know you took her knife, the missus? She'll skin you with it for stealing. Lay it down now and she'll never know it was gone. You hear me!"

Zoe turned and ran. The lash caught her around the throat.

When bitterness had given way to resignation, Mrs. Hassenplug rose from her kitchen chair and went into the yard. Watching chickens scratch the earth around her feet, she failed to notice Zoe's return until the girl was almost to the gate. At first Mrs. Hassenplug thought it was some old neighbor woman mysteriously arrived on foot, suffering some kind of ailment maybe, all bent over that way. Then she recognized the dress, the old too-tight dress that had caused all the trouble. She'd had no idea Zoe's hair was that long, since Zoe tended to it herself; it hung over her face like a curtain, but the bruising beneath was not entirely hidden.

Mrs. Hassenplug took several nervous steps toward the gate Zoe clung to, then stopped. Why should she help? The girl had put herself in harm's way, and harm had come to her, closer to the farm than to town. That fact was welcomed; the hussy hadn't even completed the trip's first leg before the harm came. It would have been unbearable to know she'd seen the streets and houses and people denied Mrs. Hassenplug all these years. There was rough justice at work here, she could see that, and it cheered her up considerably. With moral satisfaction bolstering her mood, Mrs. Hassenplug felt herself capable of approaching Zoe with something like charity in her heart.

Lips pursed, she unlatched the gate. Robbed of support, Zoe almost fell into the yard at her foster mother's feet.

"He went and did you, then," said Mrs. Hassenplug. "I knew he would. You asked for trouble and got it, I reckon. He's a mean man when the mood's on him, I grant, but he never would've done you harm if you minded yourself and kept out of his way. There's the blame. You get in the house and clean up this instant. Look at you!"

Zoe went indoors and dabbed at her face with a cloth and water from the kitchen tub. He had punched her several times, slapped her more times than that. Her face hurt, her vagina hurt, but the sharpest pain came from a deep cut on her shin, where a nail in the thick sole of Hassenplug's boot had penetrated as he stepped clumsily away from her after the rape. He'd staggered as his foot rolled on the narrow bone, caught himself in time and kicked her in the side of the buttock for almost tripping him up that way. She had watched from beneath tangled hair as he climbed back onto the wagon and returned to the Wister's Landing road as if nothing of importance had taken place. He hadn't looked at her once the wagon started rolling.

Why she had come back to the farm instead of continuing on into town to report what had happened to her, Zoe herself could not quite understand. It was more than a question of fewer miles to cover on her sore leg, but the inner component of her choice eluded Zoe until she put down the cloth and saw Hassenplug's rifle on the wall. It was his most valued possession, a Henry repeater kept in perfect working order, fully loaded at all times for the kind of native uprising that hadn't occurred in Indiana for a generation.

Zoe made herself look elsewhere; Mrs. Hassenplug was in the kitchen with her, and must not be alerted to the train of thought that suddenly had made clear to Zoe why she had returned to the farm. In town, she wouldn't have known where to find a loaded gun, and would probably have had trouble locating Hassenplug among all those streets. At home, the rifle was in its appointed place, as if hung there by fate for Zoe's purpose, and her target always approached the house from the barn after putting up the horses. Zoe's window upstairs overlooked the yard, a perfect sniper's roost.

"I'm ... I'm going to lie down now."

"You do that. You lie down and think on what you did, you silly girl, leading him on with all that nonsense talk of dresses. You be thankful he didn't hurt you bad like he could've. You stay up there till you're told you can come down again!"

Mrs. Hassenplug went outside to sit under the willow tree beside the pond, where she spent the afternoon hours fretting over what attitude to strike when her husband returned. Should she pose as the champion of maidenly virtue now plundered and gone, or as betrayed wife, the loyal spouse wronged by male carnality? Or should she let Zoe shoulder all responsibility for the incident? This last option would be easiest, given that Hassenplug usually returned from town drunk. Maybe he wouldn't want to talk about it at all, which presented the best possible chance for a peaceful evening. In the morning it wouldn't bear thinking about, let alone discussion. That would definitely be best. She wouldn't say a word when he arrived, would simply heat up his supper, if he proved capable of eating it, and wait on him in silence until he climbed the stairs to fall asleep with clothing and boots still on, as was his way.

Her decision made, Mrs. Hassenplug went back to the house and began to prepare the makings of her husband's favorite treat, pig knuckles in gravy. As she worked, it seemed to her that something was amiss in the kitchen, some familiar thing misplaced, but she could not identify it. The sensation eventually was lost in her greater concern for the kind of life that would be lived under Hassenplug's roof in future. Now that he'd had the girl, would he do so again? Everything in life became easier the second or third time; that was a fundamental law of nature. Should she be surprised if it happened in her home? Would Hassenplug be so cruel? She knew he would.

It spelled the end of everything she had known. Her married life had been a bed of bent and rusting nails, but it was the only bed she had known as a woman, and the thought of being usurped by the bruised slip of a thing upstairs was torture. What if she bore him a son! He'd send Mrs. Hassenplug away and marry Zoe ... marry their foster daughter! It was too harsh, too biblical.

"No!" she told the walls, and that was when she realized the Henry rifle was gone from its usual place. Had her husband taken it with him to town? He'd never done so before. Hadn't it been up there on its pegs while the girl dabbed at her face? And after Zoe had gone up to her room, Mrs. Hassenplug went outside for a long time. ...

She mounted the staircase at a run, lifting her skirts high, panting with alarm. Zoe's door was closed. Mrs. Hassenplug opened it slowly, quietly. A chair by the window presented its back to her. Zoe was sitting in it, and did not turn around when her name was hesitantly called. A closer look revealed Zoe asleep, breath whistling faintly in her nose, hands entwined in her lap. Zoe's swollen face seemed peaceful enough if the mottled patches of blue on her cheek were ignored. The rifle lay across the chair's armrests at chest level, like some imprisoning device. Had the girl been preparing for suicide? How could she sleep, following the events of her day?

The window's lower half was raised, the curtains shifting languidly in a late afternoon breeze. Mrs. Hassenplug stifled a gasp, crammed several fingers into her mouth and stared at the girl, the rifle, the window. If she tiptoed out, leaving Zoe undisturbed, the act would very likely be committed; her husband would be shot dead in the yard like a sheep-killing dog.

More disturbing than her awareness of Zoe's intent was Mrs. Hassenplug's consideration—mere seconds long—of leaving quietly to let it happen. How could she have allowed such an idea to enter her mind! To protect herself from the consequences of unfettered thought, rather than out of love of her husband, she plucked the rifle from its resting place and hurried away. When her husband returned, he would find the rifle where it should be, his victim secured upstairs where she could do him no harm.

The farmhouse, formerly a place in which few words were spoken, became monastic in its ritual observance of silence. The thing that had happened was never mentioned, but the more intense the silence, the louder it became.

For Zoe, the weeks that followed her rape were skewed, unreal, her chores performed in an undersea world of dragging slowness, the burden of an unnamable, crushing weight. She was a tiny fish in a set of rooms on the ocean floor; two larger fish swam carefully around her, blowing bubbles of nothingness, avoiding her eye. Every day she became slower still, until she knew the reason why. It was too big a secret to tell the other fish, but in time they saw for themselves, and were even less pleased than Zoe.

"She is."

"She ain't!"

"Look at her! Just look!"

"She ain't!" insisted Hassenplug.

"Think she got that way on what we eat? You can pretend all you want, it won't change a thing. Don't think I'm fooled. You wanted it this way all along, don't think I don't know. She can give you what I can't, isn't that so? Isn't that the way you planned it?"

"Quiet!"

The life inside Zoe was growing at a fearful rate, and she wished herself rid of it, but her wish was not granted. Her belly continued to expand, and now she truly did need a new dress. Mrs. Hassenplug gave her one of her own. The hem dragged at the back but was lifted clear of the ground in front. Zoe was still expected to do her share of work around the place.

Hassenplug approached her with an incredible offer one afternoon in the barn. "Listen here. You make a boy and I'll get you that dress you been wanting. This time I mean it. You make a boy and I'll get you that dress for sure, and the shoes too, by God. The missus, she can't make one. This boy, I'd like him better than some adopted boy. He'd be mine, a genuine son. I'd be good to you, you make me a boy."

When he left her, Zoe cried. To bear Hassenplug a son, the very thing he wanted, would be the final insult to her. The irony was insupportable. She prayed for a girl. Her god would not have been acceptable to any churchgoer, being female, very much akin to Nettie Dugan in appearance, but fifty feet tall. The avenging angel at her side, the one who would take care of Zoe's secondary prayer—the death of Hassenplug—bore a definite resemblance to brother Clay.

5

He actually enjoyed digging
postholes. The fatigue he brought to bed helped ease the pain of his
growing bones. Almost eighteen, Clay stood six feet four inches on
naked feet, and he continued to grow. Despite his alarming height,
Clay weighed only one hundred fifty-nine pounds. Beanpole, they
had called him at school, until he quit.

His departure was prompted by being cast in the school play (a
radical enterprise from a new and enthusiastic teacher) as Ichabod
Crane, the gangling dupe of Sleepy Hollow. Being called Ichabod was
no better than being called Beanpole. Clay had squared his books on
the minuscule desktop before him, risen and said to his teacher,
"Excuse me, ma'am, they need me at home," and walked out.

Explaining himself to his father was another matter. Edwin
Delaney owned ninety-eight acres west of Tamsen, Missouri, and
considered himself something of a gentleman farmer. He was educated, erudite, no friend of fools.

"Why," he asked Clay, "did you do this thing?"

"I don't like it there."

"Because they mock your height?"

"Yes!"

"Please moderate your voice. The measure of a man is often the
limits to which he allows himself to be pushed. I find it hard to

believe a flock of schoolchildren has pushed you to your limit, Clayton."

"Well, they did. Them and the teacher."

"You don't think you've taken their name calling too hard?"

"No."

"Observe my nose. Do you see its distinct leaning to the left?"

"Yes."

"In school I was made fun of for that small defect. I rose above it, and I recommend you do the same. An unlettered boy becomes an ignorant man, or do you disagree?"

"No, I just ... I can read books by myself. I don't need school to learn things anymore. I don't like it there. I like helping you here."

Edwin had noticed Clay's preference for farmwork over study. The boy's hands and feet were huge; he was lantern-jawed, and his ears stood out like jug handles. He already looked like a farmer.

"A lifetime of physical labor is your ambition?"

"No. I don't know yet. For now ... yes. Labor."

"If I beat you, would you return to school?"

"No."

"You're sure?"

"Yes."

Edwin Delaney stared for some time at his son by adoption. The act had officially been recorded at the county seat, and Delaney was proud, in an undemonstrative way, of the boy he had brought into his home. There were, however, aspects to Clayton's character that puzzled him. The boy's phenomenal growth was to be marveled at, the manifestation of an unusual physical condition, but it was the stealthy workings of Clay's mind that prompted a subtle disquiet in the man.

"Very well. I intend working you hard. If you find you've had your fill, you will return to school. The choice will be yours, do you understand?"

"Yessir. Thank you."

"I wonder, Clayton, if you'll thank me a week from now." The boy had always been willing to help in the fields but, apart from extended assistance at harvest times, had never truly been pushed. Edwin employed a man named Chaffey to work the farm with him, and Clay was handed into his care for a tough assignment. "Don't give him any slack," Edwin ordered. "Use him hard."

"I will, Mr. Delaney, you can bet on it."

"See that you do."

Clay was introduced to the new regimen by being ordered to dig postholes for a new fence. He made no complaint at all, even when his hands began to blister. Next, Chaffey and Clay began felling trees on land Edwin had recently purchased, thirty-three acres adjacent to his own. The former owner, a keen hunter, had left an extensive section timbered for game cover, but Edwin had no need of sport. The trees were all to go, and Clay was to perform more than his share of the work required to be rid of them.

Chaffey reasoned that anyone so tall and skinny wouldn't have the muscle necessary for reducing woodland to farmland, but the boy surprised him, chopping with a will, manhandling the mule team with a natural talent Chaffey found intimidating. No one should work that hard, or make it look that easy. The boy was showing him up, obliging him—in the beginning anyway—to work beyond the usual parameters simply to maintain his pride. He began to resent Edwin for having placed Clay in his charge.

"Heard you never wanted no more schooling," Chaffey said, as they shared lunch. Conversation between them was stilted, engaged in only during the daily half hour when both stopped working to eat.

"That's right."

"Never felt the need for it either. Had a cousin went to school, though. Fell in a horse trough drunk one time. Drowned. You'd have to be a fool, ending up that way. Learning," he said, and shook his head. Several minutes later he added, "They ought to learned him to swim, I reckon!"

For Clay, the work was balm, the lunch torture. Chaffey was a stupid person, in Clay's estimation, and a lazy one to boot, allowing Clay to do more than his share of the work.

"My brother, now, he never went to school, same as me. He does just fine. Works over Jeff City way."

"What does he do?"

"Turns his hand to this and that. Could do 'bout anything, purty much. Never went to school, not one day. Proves my point."

Clay always stood up to resume work before Chaffey, who liked to linger while his stomach digested the food prepared for them both by Mrs. Delaney. The boy just wouldn't sit still for a minute like a normal person would have, just had to be up and raring for more sweat. Chaffey made it a habit to delay a minute or two longer each

day, following their lunch, to let Clay know he had no intention of
imitating his example. It infuriated him even more that the boy
seemed not to mind in the least. Chaffey almost bit his pipestem in
two, watching Clay set about hitching the mules to yet another
obdurate stump. Clay's enthusiasm for work was an aberration,
against human nature. Somebody ought to teach him to slow down
and not be showing off that way.

"Clayton, Mr. Delaney has such plans for you."

"He told me, kind of."

These plans were of the vaguest, hinting at the possibility of
political office in the state for a young man who wanted such a
thing. Clay wanted no such stature in the community, but hadn't
said so outright.

"Then you are aware of the high regard Mr. Delaney holds
you in."

Clay nodded awkwardly. He could never bring himself to call
Edwin's wife anything but ma'am, just as Delaney himself was
always sir. They accepted this; each addressed the other, in company or in private, as Mr. and Mrs. Delaney even after nineteen years
of marriage. They were his legal parents, and Clay liked them well
enough, but they were not of his blood, nor could they ever be.

"Would it not be better to do as he wishes and return to school?
Nothing is accomplished in this world without knowledge."

"I know."

They were good people both, and it hurt him to go against their
wishes. Only his respect for the Delaneys had kept Clay on the
farm for so long, but the duration of his stay was the worst kind of
thorn, pricking him every day. He had promised Zoe and Drew to
return for them, and so far hadn't taken a single step eastward to
fulfill that promise. He was ashamed, didn't understand why it was
that he shied away from leaving the Delaneys. Was it nothing more
than a need to remain as far west as he'd already come? Was that
reason enough for betrayal?

He could, if he wanted, go east only for as long as it took to locate
and sweep up his brother and sister, then all could go even further
west together, to places Clay truly yearned for. The one lesson he
had studied assiduously in school was the location of Missouri in
relation to the continent; it wasn't even halfway across.

The life he led was tolerable enough to hold him in stasis, divided by westward hankering and eastward obligation. Clay inhabited the narrow margin between indulgence and responsibility, and found it an uncomfortable place. The dichotomy was persistent, insoluble, forgotten only when Clay worked his gangling body to exhaustion. He wished the stand of trees slowly succumbing to his efforts were an endless forest, a magical wood wherein he could lose himself forever, beholden to no one. The illusion might have been possible, on a daily basis, if not for the grating presence of Chaffey, with his inane conversations and casual approach to the work Clay wished could be more Herculean a task.

"Then why, Clayton, do you resist?"

Mrs. Delaney's round, sweet face could be irritating in its warmth, its quality of eternal forgiveness and understanding. Clay acknowledged she was a woman deserving of a son's love, but he did not want to be that son, nor did he want to fulfill Delaney's expectations of him. Wasn't Delaney himself no more than a farmer with high-flown notions of himself and his place in the world? Who was he to be planning a life for Clay? Neither of the Delaneys knew of Zoe and Drew's existence. Clay held that secret close, a kind of talisman against falling under the spell of the Delaneys' cozy concern for him, their careful planning and obvious affection, the very things he would need to overturn when the time came to escape their gentle prison.

"I just don't want to, not right now."

"Is Mr. Chaffey working you hard?"

"I don't mind. I like it."

"But not forever. You could do so much more."

"Yes, ma'am."

"You know our own boy was clever, like you. He could have gone on and made himself into something if the Lord had seen fit to leave him with us. You could do that too, with just a little effort in your heart."

He hung his head and felt ashamed. She was right, but Mrs. Delaney's correctness existed in a world different from Clay's. There was no bridge between these worlds.

"Good night, Clayton."

"Night, ma'am."

"Ever take your toby out?"

Clay looked up from his food. "What?"

Chaffey gave him a conspiratorial smile. "Your toby, your thing, ever take it out and handle it, you know?"

"No," lied Clay.

"Boy your age, you don't know about your toby? Never felt it stiffen up, kind of? That's when you got to take it out and grab ahold and squeeze it, kind of."

Clay turned away from him, blushing with anger and disgust.

"Course, it's better with a friend," Chaffey persisted. "You trade tobies and do the squeezing part. I could show you how."

Clay stood up so fast his lunch flew from his knees. "Don't you ever touch me. ..."

"Just a friendly offer is all," Chaffey protested, a look of bafflement on his face. "No need to get huffy."

Clay was already walking away. Chaffey called after him: "I don't believe you never done nothing with no one!"

Clay ignored him. Chaffey hated him then, his dislike finally changing to something darker. He was disappointed too. Several times he'd seen Clay's cock when the boy relieved himself, and it was long as the boy himself, just the kind Chaffey liked to fondle and suck. It was pretty harsh rejection, and he decided he was justified in being offended. Clay Delaney was as high-handed as his father. Both of them needed taking down a peg.

"How is the work progressing, Chaffey?"

"Coming along good, Mr. Delaney, real good."

"Is Clayton working as hard as yourself?"

"Oh, he's a devil for it, yessir. Good worker, that boy."

"No sign of him wearing out? No lamenting his lot?"

"Nothing like that, nossir, not as I've heard. He don't talk much."

"Well, keep hard at it, both of you. I'll be asking you again about him."

"Yessir. Mr. Delaney?"

"What is it?"

"My brother, he'll be coming by here in the next few days. I got a letter says he'll be over to see me, so is it all right if he stays with me just one night? Ain't seen each other in must be three, four years now. He could use my bed. No need to feed him. Bill generally brings his own provisions."

"Very well. One night only."

"Thank you, thank you, sir."

Delaney watched him walk away. Something about Chaffey left him feeling unclean, even after so short an encounter as this. At least the man was a good worker, worth keeping for that reason alone. It was a pity, though, about Clayton. How could so ungainly a body sustain so extended a period of punishment? The clearing of trees had gone on for almost a month now, with no sign of Clayton bending under the pressure of a man's work. He seemed, in fact, to be thriving, the long cords of muscle in his arms thickening almost daily; his chest, although still painfully narrow, was now layered with enough lean meat to hide the washboard bones there before. Edwin's plan was not producing the desired results, but he would not call a halt just yet; something could still happen.

The horseman came on Sunday, while the Delaneys were at church in town. Returning home, they saw a sorrel mare hitched outside the cabin Chaffey lived in. "That'll be the brother," said Delaney, and drove on by to the barn. "Clayton, you'll tend to the buggy and team."

Clay got down, unharnessed the horses and curried them in their stalls, then pushed the buggy deeper into the barn to its appointed place. Everything had a special place on the Delaney farm, even the simplest of tools; nothing ever went astray.

He was wiping the buggy's painted bodywork with a damp cloth to remove the dust of the road, when a shadow fell across him. A man stood in the barn doorway, a short man wearing a striped vest.

"You the boy?" asked the man in the vest.

"I suppose," Clay said.

"You suppose? Ain't you the boy around here, then?"

The man's voice was similar to Chaffey's, but deeper, with more of a drawl. To Clay's ears the man sounded lazy and insolent, so he chose not to reply.

"Someone don't know who he is," the man went on, "I don't know as I'd want to trust my horse to him. Likely he'd forget all about the horse and do nothing. That what you'd do?"

Again, Clay said nothing.

"Well, are you the boy or not?"

"I'm him."

"Glad you remembered. I expect you seen my mount. Needs taking care of bad. I rode a long way getting here. Bring her over, boy, she's gentle."

"Bring her yourself."

"Say what now?"

"Bring your own horse, I said."

The man paused before laughing. "Had a banty rooster like you," he said. "Stood tall for what he was, but skinny. Strutted considerable, but he was no scrapper. Had to wring his chicken neck one day when he pecked me. Never drew blood, but I twisted his head clean off for it."

Clay turned his back and resumed work on the buggy. When he glanced over his shoulder the man was gone.

Some time later, his chores completed, Clay left the barn and went to the house. The sorrel mare stood as before, dusty and untended. Chaffey's brother hadn't even bothered to loosen the cinch. Conscientious by nature and training, Clay had to make himself ignore the horse and go inside.

Edwin was not happy about the new arrival. "Not once since we arrived home has Chaffey brought the other fellow over. Common politeness would have him do that. The man has no sense of what's right."

His wife asked, "Do you really wish to meet Mr. Chaffey's brother?"

"That is neither here nor there, Mrs. Delaney. Common politeness brings the guest before the host. Chaffey is not the host here, even if the fellow is his brother!"

Clay said, "I talked to him."

"You?"

"He came into the barn and said to take care of his horse. I said no."

"Did you now. Well done. Does he think we're here to wait on him? Damn that Chaffey for bringing him here!"

Mrs. Delaney hurried away before further profanity could reach her. Edwin was angrier than she'd seen him since the day he found the sow had rolled on her litter, killing eight of the ten. She couldn't see why the hidden guest should arouse his temper so, and was secretly glad the Chaffey brothers had seen fit to isolate themselves. Mrs. Delaney had always found Chaffey peculiarly repugnant, even though Mr. Delaney swore he was a better than average worker. She occupied herself with embroidery.

When evening came, Edwin's mood darkened. "This has lasted long enough." He left the house and went to Chaffey's cabin. Clay watched from the window as his father knocked and was let inside.

The grandfather clock beside him ticked away less than two minutes before Edwin reappeared and stamped across the yard to the house.

"Drunk!" he raged. "They're both drunk, flat-out devil-take-me drunk!" Clay watched him march twice around the room. "I won't tolerate this tomorrow," Edwin said. "A Sunday drunk is bad enough, but if Chaffey can't perform his work come morning I'll send him away, brother and all."

He didn't tell Clay that Chaffey's brother had told him to either pour himself a drink and join in the merrymaking, or leave them in peace. Chaffey had looked a trifle sheepish at seeing his employer humiliated that way, but had said nothing. Edwin had already made up his mind about dismissing Chaffey, whether he was capable of work on Monday morning or not; the qualification was for Clay's benefit.

"I ... regret placing you in his hands, Clayton. Do you have any complaints to make about the fellow? I'm prepared to listen."

"No."

"You're sure? A closed mouth is an admirable thing more often than not, but I want the truth now."

"There's nothing."

Clay could not bring himself to speak of Chaffey's advances. Delaney seemed content with silence, and began filling a pipe, muttering of ingratitude and low breeding. Clay excused himself and went to his room.

Morning saw the stranger's horse still untended, and little improvement in Edwin's disposition. Immediately after breakfast he went to Chaffey's cabin and entered without knocking. Less than a minute passed before a gunshot was heard. Clay and Mrs. Delaney ran to the cabin. Edwin lay dead on the floor. Chaffey's brother stood by the far wall, lingering wisps of smoke still issuing from the barrel of his pistol.

"Never did get acquainted," he said, his voice slurred by liquor. "Bill Chaffey's my name, and I don't like for to be told my business."

Chaffey was standing openmouthed in the corner, staring at the dead man. Mrs. Delaney moaned once and fell upon her husband to cradle his head.

"Won't do no good, lady," Bill assured her. "See where I got him? Don't many men live with a bullet in the chest. He's gone. I told him to quit yelling, but he wouldn't, so I made him, and be damned if I say I'm sorry. He brung it on himself."

Clay turned and left the cabin. He knew where Edwin kept his gun, a heavy cap-and-ball Colt of Civil War vintage; even hands large as Clay's had trouble lifting the brute. Halfway across the yard, he heard a second shot. Instead of continuing on to the house, he turned and ran back inside the cabin. Mrs. Delaney lay across her husband, a patch of blood darkening the back of her dress.

"You be still there, boy," Bill warned. "I'm in no mood for folks that don't do what they're told, so help me I'm not."

Clay stared at the bodies. He felt paralyzed. He should have kept going to fetch the Colt from Delaney's bedside table. Even now he could have been aiming it from the upstairs window, waiting for the murderer and his accomplice to step outside into sunlight. He'd made a terrible mistake, acted like a fool, and very likely would die for it. Vomit welled up inside him and gushed from his mouth, some of it reaching as far as the dead couple.

Bill watched him, not without sympathy. "Well," he said, addressing no one in particular, "now what?" He seemed calm, even a little bemused by the situation. Chaffey hadn't moved since Clay came in. A sour reek of bile filled the cabin. Clay began to hiccup with fear. Bill would have to shoot him too, as the only witness.

"Outside," Bill told his brother. He had to push Chaffey's shoulder to start him moving toward the door. Clay listened to the low buzzing of their voices. There was no other door to escape through than the one they stood near, discussing what to do with him. He heard his name twice before Bill came back inside.

"Boy, is there cash money on the premises?"

"No ..."

"You sure?"

"He ... he never kept money ... not here."

"I better not find any, or I won't be happy about how you lied."

He went out again, talked for several minutes, then was replaced by Chaffey, nervously holding Bill's pistol. "He's gone to see. I told him Mr. Delaney, he always paid his bills monthly in town. He's gone to see anyway."

"Let me go ...," Clay said.

Chaffey shook his head. "I can't. He'd kill me too. He's mean."

"Before he comes back ... we can both go! You didn't do anything bad yet!"

Chaffey wagged his head violently from side to side, pressed his lips together to keep himself strong.

Clay used the word he'd been saving till last. "Please ...," he said.

The gun was lifted. "Bill says ... he says I got to, so we're both in this together. I swear, he'll kill me if I don't. I'm sorry, truly. ..."

He thumbed back the hammer and took aim. To Clay the muzzle opening seemed impossibly large, big enough to swallow him whole. He heard the shameful sound of his own voice begging, begging as the seat of his pants filled with a fetid brown froth, and all shame was subsumed by the need to talk his way out of dying.

Chaffey's eyes told Clay when the moment had come. They closed against the anticipated blast. Clay turned to throw himself away from the yawning muzzle's line of fire, but he moved too late. The shot's deafening sound was merely the aftermath to what felt like a skewer rammed through his face from one side clear through to the other. The bullet had passed through both cheeks, missing the teeth and gums only because Clay's mouth was wide open in a scream he couldn't hear. He fell, more from shock than any conscious plan to play dead, then lay still, his mouth filling with blood.

Clay heard Chaffey's boots moving across the floor, and had the presence of mind to stop breathing. His face was buried against the surprisingly firm flesh of his mother's side. He could feel blood gushing from his ruptured cheeks onto the cloth of her dress. Chaffey's breath rasped a few feet above him for a long moment, then the boots moved away, and he heard Bill's voice coming from over by the house.

"You get him?"

"I got him!"

The combined sound of their voices moved in the direction of the barn. Clay drew breath and lurched upright. He hurried from the cabin and crossed the yard, glancing at the barn door—no sign of the Chaffeys—then upstairs to the bedroom of his parents, a room he had never been inside. Delaney had told him once that the pistol was kept near to hand in case robbers should enter the house at night. Had Chaffey searched the upper floor during his brief time inside?

Clay yanked open the drawer of the bedside table. There lay the gun, smelling of oil. He picked it up. The Colt seemed to possess a weight beyond its own metal and wood.

Delaney's two best horses had been taken from their stalls to the yard. The only saddle was placed on the first, then Bill went to fetch the saddle from his own inferior mount to put on the second. Unbuckling the girth, he hesitated, then turned. The last thing he saw was the boy standing in the house doorway, aiming a pistol at him. Bill heard the first chamber misfire, but the second killed him with a bullet to the chest. In the few seconds it took him to die, he cursed his brother for a fool.

Chaffey came hesitantly from the barn. Had that been Bill's gun he heard? It sounded louder than Bill's. The boy he thought he'd killed was already halfway across the yard, a pistol held before him in both hands. Chaffey felt his knees give way, and he sank to the ground. The gun grew larger as Clay approached to within a few feet of the kneeling man.

"He made me ...," Chaffey said.

The hammer went back. He watched the trigger squeezed. The dull click of a misfire was too cruel. The following chamber also granted him a few extra seconds, but the next did not. Chaffey felt his skull fly apart, then felt himself leap out of his own demolished cranium.

Clay watched the body crumple sideways into the dust of the yard. Both men were dead by his hand. The fact stunned him, elated him. How had any of this happened? How could Chaffey, who had worked alongside him this past month, aim a gun and try to kill him? The fact that he had done so made Clay's reciprocal aiming and more successful killing acceptable. Clay didn't doubt it, even if his body was beginning to twitch, even as the instrument of retribution fell from his hands. It had been right, right and good, to do the thing he had done.

He washed his mouth free of blood, then changed his fouled pants before mounting the horse that would take him to town. His face was on fire by then, the pain so bad he couldn't keep himself from crying.

6

Hassenplug paid for a doctor. It was worth two dollars to be sure his son was born right. His wife could have organized the assistance of area midwives, but Mrs. Hassenplug was in no mood to cooperate, wouldn't go anywhere near the girl or fix her food, hadn't even spoken to Zoe after her belly started to balloon.

It was jealousy, pure and simple, Hassenplug could see that, but he didn't interfere; best to leave his wife out of things till the baby was born, then he'd put her in her place. Zoe might even change her mind and begin showing respect for the father, might even consent to be his real woman, a second wife, like the kings in the Bible had. Yes, he'd keep Mrs. Hassenplug away from the baby, before and after its birth, just in case she was jealous enough to do the boy harm. She'd been acting very strange of late, and couldn't be trusted.

The doctor earned every cent of his fee. It was a night birth, protracted, noisy, troublesome. He very nearly lost patience with the girl under his care; she didn't seem to be trying hard enough to push her baby out, reluctant to experience the ultimate pain of passage. He encouraged her, instructed her, shouted at her, and finally the thing was done, another soul received into the world of men. The doctor went downstairs to inform the Hassenplugs their erring daughter (or servant girl; the doctor had not quite fathomed the relationship) had delivered herself of a healthy female.

Hassenplug paid the fee, but his two dollars felt like lead weights. A girl! What use had he for a girl! It was a colossal betrayal of trust. He'd wanted a boy, told Zoe many times to concentrate on making it so, exhorted her to prayer, if that was what it took. And she'd let him down with a girl as useless as herself. When the doctor's buggy departed into the night, Hassenplug uncorked a jug and proceeded to get drunk.

No one visited Zoe to inquire after her needs. When her chamber pot was filled, she tipped it out the window. When she felt hungry, she ignored the feeling, too proud to call downstairs for food—an act of begging, in that house—and in time the need for food seemed to pass. She drank from a bucket of water kept standing by for the doctor's use in the delivery; the doctor had used little, and Zoe calculated it would last her at least another day.

Her baby ignored Zoe's various deprivations, insisted on and was granted as much suckling as she desired. Zoe had been convinced she would give birth to a boy, despite entreaties to otherworldly forces, and her delight in a girl was sufficient to quench much of the hatred and misery that had been growing inside her along with the child. A girl was not what her rapist wanted; this alone was a major triumph for Zoe. By a process she could not have defined, Zoe eliminated Hassenplug's role in the pregnancy. Her girl had come to her by accident, as it were, and was in no way connected to anyone or anything on the farm. She was Zoe's alone, a projection or extension of herself, and so doubly precious.

On the second day after the birth of her daughter, Zoe came downstairs. The Hassenplugs drew away from her as she placed herself and her baby on a kitchen chair. "I need to eat," she stated. She had rehearsed the words many times, perfecting the tone to her own satisfaction; it sounded less like begging, more like a demand. The Hassenplugs looked at each other, then Mrs. Hassenplug complied, setting down a chunk of dry corn bread.

Zoe broke off a morsel and nibbled daintily, not wanting to gratify the Hassenplugs with a display of voracious hunger. When the edge was taken from her appetite, she unfolded the blanket from her baby's face and said, "Her name is Naomi. She's mine."

Mrs. Hassenplug's confidence in reclaiming her husband had been strengthened by the doctor's report of a girl, and she was disposed, now that the issue of a male line for the Hassenplugs had been scuttled, to be more amenable to Zoe's needs. This did not mean she would have been the first to venture upstairs, had Zoe not come down, but now that the baby was before her, she could not help herself; she had to lean forward and inspect the thing that had threatened her marriage.

"Why, there's a mark on it. ..."

Hassenplug himself came forward, made curious. The baby was indeed marked; from the outer corner of her left eye there streamed a cloud of inky blue that swept around the side of her head to wrap itself about the ear, itself completely blue, almost purple.

Whatever universal empathy Mrs. Hassenplug might have allowed herself to feel vanished utterly at the sight of the birthmark. She knew such things were, if not the devil's work, at the very least indicators of inferior blood. The child would very likely turn out to be an idiot, even if her face was sweetness itself. It was a sign, a definite sign that all was not right with the circumstances of the birth, and should anyone be surprised that it had turned out so? This was no product of love or sanctified marriage. Her husband had forced himself on the girl, and the act was transferred to the face of the child she bore. There it was, for all the world to see, a massive blue tear leaking sideways from that innocent eye.

Mrs. Hassenplug stepped away, and her husband joined her in that backward step of condemnation. Not only was the child not a boy, it was marked by permanent ugliness. It was no child of his. Zoe must have tricked him into thinking it was from that day when he'd taken her partway to town. The little whore had clearly been lifting her dress for some half-witted farmhand in the area, then led Hassenplug to believe the swelling was due to himself. Such gall! Any child of Hassenplug's, even a girl, would never have been so disfigured. The entire episode was a trick, but he had no intention of playing the dupe for long.

Zoe got her trip to town. Mrs. Hassenplug and baby Naomi (already called Omie by her mother) also went along. Hassenplug bought Zoe a new dress and shoes, then she was taken to the station where the Hassenplugs had chosen her almost five years before. A ticket was purchased and placed in her hand. "This'll take you far as Springfield, Illinois," she was told, and a five-dollar bill was tucked into the baby's shawl. "That's for the things you'll be needing," Mrs. Hassenplug advised.

To Zoe, none of this was surprising. The Hassenplugs had been hinting she might be better off elsewhere, in a big town. In a way, it gave her satisfaction; this was the very plan she'd concocted for the day Hassenplug had raped her. Now it was happening. The difference lay in the ticket, the five dollars, and Omie.

She said nothing, had said virtually not a word since being informed she would be going to town that day. She was being sent away, mailed by locomotive to a distant place where she could not bother her erstwhile parents.

They stood on the platform, together yet separate, waiting for the train. Zoe looked at her baby, at other travelers standing about, at the rolling stock in a siding, anywhere but at the people who had taken her in, her betrayers. It was best to be gone from them, and yet she felt a certain inexplicable sadness. The paradox depressed her even further, and Zoe spent her final minutes on the platform staring into the air, seeing nothing she could name.

When the 2:20 westbound rolled in and came to a clanking halt, she stepped up into the nearest car without a word and took a seat on the far side, away from sight of the Hassenplugs who, for their part, departed the platform before the drive wheels began to spin and grab at the rails. Wister's Landing receded, and Zoe did not look back.

Within minutes the woman she had seated herself beside began making conversation with Zoe.

"Now, that wouldn't be your baby, would it?"

"Why not?"

The unintended brusqueness of Zoe's reply made the woman hesitate to continue. "Well, it's just you're so young."

"She's my baby sister," Zoe said. "We're going to Springfield to see our ma. She sent the money. We were at Aunt Lucy's, but now we're going home."

"That's a long ways for a young girl to go alone, and with so little a baby. How old is she, two months?"

"Three."

"How is it that your ma's all the way to Springfield, and this little one's just been born? Why isn't she with your ma?"

"She's sick, our ma is. She sent us away so we wouldn't catch it too."

"She sent a slip of a thing like you all the way to your aunt's on your own?"

"No, ma'am. My brother Clay, he came too. He went back yesterday."

The woman believed not a word of this. She peered more closely at the baby, looking for a resemblance to the plain-faced girl at her side, and noticed the birthmark.

"Now, there's a shame, but you know, blemishes and suchlike respond to lemon juice applied two times weekly till it goes away. I had a second cousin, Rosalie, with a strawberry mark on her chin, and it went away by the time she was nine years old. Well, almost. You could still see it in direct sunlight, but not so's you'd notice unless you looked. She didn't care a bit. Lemon juice, fresh squeezed, just dab it on. Of course, Rosalie's mark was smaller, and not so dark, more of a deep pink than blue."

"It's her blue tear," Zoe declared, "for all the sadness in the world."

"Oh, my, but that's so poetical! I can tell you're a girl who's been to school."

Zoe didn't contradict her.

"I'm Mrs. Ringle. Don't you have any baggage at all? You must have a bottle at least, for the baby."

"No, ma'am, I've got nothing."

"Well, didn't your ma provide you with such things before you left? Or your aunt, for the trip home?"

Zoe shook her head and looked out the window to avoid Mrs. Ringle's eyes. Mrs. Ringle knew she had encountered a small tragedy in the making, or more likely the second or third act of that tragedy. "Little girl," she said, leaning closer so the nearest passenger, a gentleman apparently asleep against the window frame, couldn't hear. "I want you to know I'm your friend in need, if that's all right with you. Everyone needs a friend, someone to trust. If you feel the need, you can tell me anything at all, and I'll listen and tell you what you're maybe needing to know."

"Yes, ma'am. Thank you."

Less than an hour later, Zoe rose from her seat with crying Omie and took herself away to the car platform for some time. Mrs. Ringle knew she was out there with the flying cinders and scenery, giving suck with her little girl's titties to her own little girl, and it made Mrs. Ringle sad to think of such things happening in a Christian country.

Stepping down in Springfield the following day, Zoe waved to Mrs. Ringle, who had taken herself out to the platform to say good-bye. Mrs. Ringle was continuing on to Saint Louis, where her brother owned a draper's; she had been asked to join him when her husband died back in Chillicothe, Ohio.

She passed Zoe a scrap of paper bearing her brother's address, and told her to go there "if things don't work out the way you expect, with your ma being sick and all." Zoe thanked her, and the wave she delivered as the train began moving was sincere. She would not, however, place her trust in grownups again, no matter how concerned they might seem.

Zoe had made up her mind, on the moonlit ride across the state line from Indiana to Illinois, to be her own mistress from that night forward. Her sole concern would be to care for Omie and move westward in hope of finding Clay and Drew. She knew this last aspiration was near to impossible in so vast a land, but what else was she to do with her life, if not attempt reunification among the carriers of Dugan blood?

Zoe hadn't attended sufficient Sundays in church to believe with any certainty in the accepted God, but she placed great trust in a concept more ancient than Jehovah; she trusted in fate, the inexorable grinding of wheels within wheels. Her need, her passion, was for her brothers. Since so strong an emotion as hers could not simply fly away into an empty sky, the thing she desired must eventually come about. She knew it with the certainty of all believers. It was the rock of her soul, excluding all others.

The wide streets of Springfield intimidated her with their neatness and order. A general air of prosperity gave the people on those streets a quality Zoe could never hope to imitate. Where could she and Omie possibly fit in? The answer was clear; they simply wouldn't try to fit into this bustling town. Springfield would be the place where they transferred from railroad to something else in their journey west. Clay would never have settled hereabouts, only one third of the way across America.

A nearby restaurant wafted the tantalizing odor of food to Zoe's nostrils. She approached it, examined the menu hung in the window, and was shocked at the prices listed beside each dish. Made aware of her hunger and her limited resources, she passed along several more streets, to an area less salubrious in appearance, and entered a chophouse.

The place was nearly empty, the lunchtime trade having departed, the dinner regulars yet to arrive. Zoe chose a corner table and set her baby down. She had never entered such a place before, but was aware someone would eventually come and ask her what she required. The person was a young man, and Zoe selected plain chops with a side dish of potatoes; she declined a pitcher of beer. Her waiter went off with the order, then returned for conversation. His oiled hair was parted in the center and arranged in two remarkable wings over his temples. His mustache was similarly spectacular, reaching almost to his ears.

"Your kid?" he asked.

"Yes."

Zoe knew Mrs. Ringle hadn't believed her denial, and so had decided to speak the truth.

"How old are you?"

"I don't see why you need to know."

The waiter smiled. He knew people, could judge them by their face, their hands and clothing, above all by their voice. He calculated the girl before him was fifteen, appealing in a half-starved, elfin kind of way. The waiter had recently left his wife for just such a toothsome waif, only to have her taken from him by a peddler passing through to Kansas City. His wife wouldn't have him back, but the girl might be replaced, if he kept up a smooth flow of words. The fact that his customer had a child would make the waiter's seduction of her that much easier; no girl so young and in need would think to question a helping hand. The waiter had been abandoned only a week ago, but restitution was on its way, if only he trod lightly enough.

He fetched Zoe's chop and set it down with a flourish. "You'll be wanting pie after that," he said.

"No pie. I'd like some water, though."

He supplied a brimming glass, and a generous wedge of pie. "It's on the house."

Zoe looked up, her mouth full. "On the house?"

"No charge. A gift, see?"

Zoe didn't see. "Why?" she asked.

"Because, excuse me for saying so, you look real hungry, more than just pork chop and spud hungry. Your little baby there, he won't eat right if you don't."

"She."

"She. Babies, you have to be careful. Have to give babies what they need or they get sick, so the pie, that's for her, see, even if it's you that eats it."

"Thank you."

"I know about babies. I had one, and a wife. They both were lost last year, taken away by sickness, so don't you be getting sick, you hear?"

Zoe's chop had already disappeared. Without pause, she tackled the pie. The waiter watched her eat his gift. He wouldn't charge for the chop either; it would all come out of his pocket, but he considered it a worthwhile investment.

"Tully's my name; what's yours?"

"Zoe Dugan."

"And the baby?"

"Naomi. I call her Omie."

"I expect you'd tell me to mind my business if I asked where you're headed this fine day."

"West."

"West? Now, that brings to mind a mighty big picture. How far west?"

"I don't know. I need to find my brother Clay, and Drew, he's my brother too. They're out west somewhere."

"I hope you find them," Tully said, his voice somber. He could tell Zoe was admiring his mustache. It was the mustache that first attracted the other girl, the one who'd run off to Kansas City with a man who hadn't half so fine a set of handlebars. Tully bet she'd be regretting her choice by now. He bet if he showed up in Kansas City and found her, she'd fall into his arms and stroke his mustache and say what a fool of a girl she'd been. She was so pretty, much prettier than Zoe. Her name was Lovey Doll Pines, and Tully had to admit he was still in love with her. There could be no real substitute for Lovey Doll.

Tully had heard there were jobs aplenty in Kansas City, so much bigger a place than Springfield. He knew also that bold moves were not a part of his nature. He wouldn't mind striking out for Kansas City if there weren't the possibility of disappointment when he got there; he needed to be sure ahead of time his attempt to win back the runaway would be met with success, and Tully was intelligent enough to know such things are never guaranteed.

Of course, if he went there with another girl in tow, and never did meet up with Lovey Doll, or found her and was rejected all over again, he'd have the second girl right there to comfort him. His mind was working quickly now. In Tully's boardinghouse there was a man named Aspinall, a stonemason by trade, bound and determined to go west. "There's folks dying out there by the score," he maintained, "and nothing but wooden markers to show where they lie." Aspinall didn't doubt there was a place for him beyond the Mississippi, and Tully didn't doubt the man could accommodate in his wagon passengers such as himself and the little mother wolfing down cherry pie.

Several families invited him to live with them, including that of the doctor who sutured his cheeks. Clay used the lattice of horsehair stitches on either side of his face to resist answering them all. He would tap his mouth and shake his head, like a dumb person. Some people in town thought Clay's tongue had been shot off, but the doctor assured anyone who asked him that no, the boy's tongue was intact; it was only the flesh of his cheeks that was disfigured.

Clay took a room at the hotel while recuperating, and it was there a lawyer came to inform him that the Delaney farm and all stock, equipment, dwellings and furniture thereon belonged to him; Edwin had made a new will just ten weeks before his death, stipulating that his son—he referred to Clayton throughout the document as his son—be the beneficiary in the event of Edwin's wife predeceasing the boy.

"It's all yours, Mr. Delaney," the lawyer said, genuinely pleased for him; the entire county was talking of nothing but Clay's grit in tackling and killing the murderous Chaffeys. At the Delaney funeral, many complete strangers had shaken his hand and wished him well. Clay wondered how they would have felt had they known he shat in his britches. His small but potentially embarrassing secret made Clay cynical.

So the farm was his. What earthly use did he have for it? He was no farmer. At best, farmwork was a distraction from himself, from his guilt over having made no move to go back for Drew and Zoe. It occurred to him that he could do that now, go fetch them from the towns where they'd been taken in; Wister's Landing, Indiana, for Zoe, an even smaller place in Illinois called Dinnsville for Drew. Clay's course of action was obvious, largely because of a lack of alternatives.

The lawyer was watching his face. Clay's lips parted. The lawyer leaned forward in anticipation.

"Sell it," Clay told him.

"The farm?"

"Sell it fast."

"Is that the right thing to do, Mr. Delaney? That's a real nice farm you've got there, practically a showplace."

"I don't want it. My name's Dugan."

The lawyer was offended by the last remark, but didn't allow himself to show it. "Would you like some time to reconsider?"

"No."

"My fee for real estate transactions is five percent of the sale."

"Ten percent if you get rid of it before the end of the month."

"I'll return tomorrow with a contract."

"Return this afternoon."

"I ... very well, this afternoon."

The lawyer had changed his mind about Clay. The boy was cold clear through. The lawyer didn't think Clay felt any real sorrow over the death of the Delaneys. He was just a tall bag of bones with a face like a skull and hands that looked as though they could crack rocks the way ordinary boys cracked pecans. The patchwork of black stitching under both cheekbones gave his face a desperate, haunted aspect, but the eyes were calm, unflinching. He seemed a great many years older than a youth almost eighteen.

The lawyer earned his ten percent, and Clay boarded an eastbound train with a thickly wadded money belt around his waist. On the first leg of the trip, to Dinnsville, he felt himself becoming excited at the thought of seeing Drew again. He'd be twelve years old now, and probably still walked with his feet pointed in: Mr. Pigeontoes, Nettie had called him (Clay, whose feet were planted at a forty-five-degree angle to each other, was Mr. Duckfeet); and he'd probably have that same big smile, the kind Clay had never had, the kind that made people want to be Drew's friend. These simple recollections made Clay weep as he watched the countryside roll by, and the crinkling of his face with the small grief of remembrance caused his cheeks, recently released from their stitches, to hurt.

In Dinnsville he asked around the town for two days before learning that the Kindreds, who had taken Drew in, had moved west about four months before, to an unspecified location. Reeling, Clay boarded the next train east, bound for Wister's Landing. Zoe had just better be there, or he didn't know what he'd do.

* * *

Hassenplug was pitching hay into the barn loft when someone rode into the yard. He recognized the horse as belonging to the livery stable in town. Even at a distance the rider's face looked strange, hollowed out somehow. Hassenplug climbed down from the hay wagon and approached him.

"Something I can do for you?"

"Mr. Hassenplug?"

"That's me."

"I'm looking for my sister, Zoe."

Clay watched the man's face cloud over.

"Say who?"

"Zoe. Dark hair, thin build. You took her off the orphan train about five years ago."

"Well, she's gone, sorry to say."

Clay dismounted. "Gone where?"

Hassenplug raised his hands in a helpless gesture.

"Why'd she go?" Clay asked.

"Never told us. Never said a word, just upped and left, must be four, five weeks ago now."

He stared at the stranger's face. There were two holes in it, filled with new, pink flesh, as if someone had driven a stake clean through his cheeks. It was an ugly sight, but he looked at the scars rather than into the eyes of Zoe's brother, because those eyes were also holes of a kind, unblinking as a snake's. Hassenplug realized he was a little scared, and wished he hadn't left his pitchfork on the wagon.

"Anything else to tell me?" Clay asked.

"No, reckon that's about all."

Clay took several steps closer. "Now you listen. I spoke with some people in town, a lot of people, including a doctor who said Zoe had a baby. You don't remember the baby?"

"Oh ... the baby. Well, there's things that's not polite to mention."

"Who gave her the baby?"

"Never told us. Never said a word. Could've been anyone around here; no way to tell, if the girl won't say, I reckon."

"I heard stories," Clay said. "There's talk it was yours."

"No ... nossir, not mine. I got a fine wife right here with me as can bear witness. I never touched her; paid for the doctor to come, even—he tell you that? Cost me money to let her have the baby safe and sound."

"She got on a train. They say you were at the station with her, you and your wife."

"That's right, that's correct, we seen her off. She wanted to go, wouldn't listen to us when we said she can stay here. The missus, she begged her to stay on. We were hurt bad when she left that way, real bad, it's the truth."

"The truth."

"That's what I'm saying."

Clay stared at him for a long moment. A woman came out of the house, carrying a rifle. The window was open; she'd probably heard every word.

"You believe in judgment, Hassenplug?"

"Like the Bible says? I reckon so."

"That's good to hear. I believe in it too."

Clay mounted and rode away. Mrs. Hassenplug joined her husband and let him take the rifle from her. "Ought to've killed him," he said. "See the face that feller had? Like a dead man."

"Well, he's gone now."

Shaken, Hassenplug took to his jug for the rest of the afternoon and evening. He was in no condition to act when his barn caught fire after midnight. Animals were milling in the yard, the entire loft was ablaze, and all he could do was stare at the conflagration and feel the tears on his face evaporating in the heat.

The conductor on the express run saw a curious thing just west of Wister's Landing that night. He saw a horse and rider racing alongside the train, keeping pace in the moonlight till the rider grabbed the rear platform of car three and swung aboard. The horse immediately slowed and veered away from the train.

The rider entered the car and sat in a vacant seat. Every other passenger was asleep under the dimmed oil lamps. The conductor approached him with a mixture of curiosity and professional outrage. He slowed when he saw the rider's face with its riven cheeks.

"Ticket?" he inquired.

The new passenger produced several large bills and handed them to the conductor. "End of the line," he said.

"You mean Indianapolis?"

"That's what I mean."

"You've given me too much, sir."

"No I haven't. I got on back in Columbus, yesterday."

"Columbus?"

"Yesterday. If anyone asks, understand?"

"Yessir. Columbus through to Indianapolis. Correct change, sir. Can I get you a blanket?"

"And a drink, unless it's extra."

"Nossir; a stiff belt comes included in this amount."

The conductor left Clay alone, then returned with a glass and a blanket.

"There you are, sir. Should be getting into Indianapolis just about sunrise."

"Thank you."

The conductor hovered a moment longer, but was ignored. He left to count his small windfall in private. Clay sipped at his very first whiskey, pulled the blanket up around his chin and wondered what in the world he would do now.

All three, himself and Zoe and Drew, had been uprooted within the space of a few months, as if there existed a fantastic plot to ensure that they never came together again. Only God could have arranged such a thing, and since Clay didn't believe in God, he was left with a numbness that bore no name.

Morgan Kindred had religion. It was not a matter of regular Sunday churchgoing, or even the commonplace practice of Bible readings taking place within the home; Morgan had an entirely different appreciation of God. He knew for a fact he was to play a personal role in some act God had hinted would soon take place.

The revelations had begun even before Drew's adoption by the Kindreds. Morgan and Sylvie had produced five stillborns in a row before accepting that they were not to be blessed. The first revelation was an instruction to Morgan that he be present at the Dinnsville station two days thence to receive into his heart a special child. Sylvie was unconvinced until she laid eyes on Drew Dugan standing disconsolately beside his older brother; then and there she accepted the instructions from God, and thanked the Lord for having sent them such a handsome little fellow, even if his face was swollen by crying.

No further commands were received from the heavenly realm. For Sylvie it was enough, but Morgan was disappointed. He moped over the brevity of his communications with the highmost. In time, he accepted that Drew had been the sole reason for God's intervention. The voice had spoken to end their childlessness.

Drew's proud new parents ran a store in town, supplying the county with necessary dry goods. The business gave them a fair living, but Morgan had always imagined himself aspiring to a more exalted plane. The store was inherited from his father, a man devoted to money. When his mother died, Morgan took her place behind the counter, and stayed there, bringing in Sylvie to assist him when old Kindred died and the store became Morgan's. He was tempted to sell out and move on, pursuing some kind of life more attuned to his inner need for spiritual truth; but Sylvie, a practical woman, persuaded him against making so rash a decision, and under her more intense style of management the business prospered to a degree that eventually offended Morgan; earthly riches were a dreadful trap, and he dreamed often of the needle's eye.

A short while after Drew turned twelve, the second revelation came. The same disembodied voice woke Morgan from restless sleep with an instruction of awesome simplicity. Morgan sprang from the bed, sweat streaming from him, the words ringing still in his ears: *Go Thou to a desert place.*

He wakened Sylvie and conveyed the message to her. A deep sleeper, slow to comprehend when woken abruptly, she nodded and lay down again, no wiser than before. Morgan understood he would have to try again after breakfast.

Once Sylvie realized what had transpired, she let Morgan know the strength of her resistance. She told him a move to some uninhabited region would be madness. She would not do it—never! Morgan pleaded, but Sylvie stood firm.

Drew was in favor of the move once he learned the likeliest place was somewhere in New Mexico Territory, an area swarming with redskins, he was told at school. Drew's latent urge for adventure in the west, a thing he'd assimilated from Clay without fully remembering the source, was awakened. Drew thought of nothing but deserts.

Sylvie believed she had turned her husband away from his ludicrous scheme, but Morgan was not to be diverted from God's business by any woman; he announced he had found a buyer for the store. When he told Sylvie the price agreed upon with a rival merchant down the street, she went immediately to the man and declared the sale would not go through unless he increased his offer substantially. Since no formal contract had been signed, the would-be buyer had little choice but to agree on an equitable sum. His revenge was to spread around town the idea that Morgan was a fool, dominated by his shrew of a wife.

* * *

The Kindreds left Illinois, telling no one in Dinnsville of their destination, since they had none in mind; God would direct Morgan at the appropriate time. A hint was dropped to the new owner of Kindred's store that the family was headed "southwest." The townspeople assumed Morgan, or possibly his wife, was suffering from consumption and required the drier air of the territories that offered such remedial stuff.

By rail and stagecoach they made their way to Santa Fe. Their arrival was early enough in the day for Morgan to bypass the hotels and search instead for a small open wagon and team. He located these by midafternoon, paid cash and drove back to the depot, where Sylvie and Drew were dozing in the fierce heat. He loaded their baggage aboard the wagon, drawing attention to the fine condition of both vehicle and mules. Sylvie refused to speak with or even look sideways at her husband. Drew, despite an unquenchable thirst, was excited by the strange adobe dwellings around him.

Morgan bought food supplies and a small tent, then followed the road out of town, heading west. The desolation ahead lifted his spirits, made him euphoric. Sylvie was despondent. Her faith in the voice of God was dwindling, and it had never been great. She hoped a few days of extreme discomfort would bring Morgan to his senses.

It wasn't until Santa Fe was well behind them and darkness falling that she realized they were without a gun.

"Supposing there are Indians?" she said.

"They won't be hostile. In any case, we have divine protection."

"Supposing we don't?"

"That's foolish talk. We *have*."

"Will they be real Indians?" Drew asked. The native Americans he'd seen in Santa Fe seemed as sleepy as himself, their long hair like coarse wigs. He wanted Indians on horseback, feathers streaming in the desert wind. "Let us hope not," said his mother. Drew was quiet after that. He was aware Sylvie didn't see things in the same light as himself and his father; she had done nothing but carp and snap at them both for weeks, ever since Morgan heard God.

Drew believed in God because Morgan did. Anything Morgan did was acceptable to Drew. His father had always been kind, even though he was often distracted by the workings of his own mind. Drew respected Morgan's ability to sit and think, doing nothing outwardly, yet living an entirely private life behind his eyes. Drew had this ability also, but only in limited bursts of introspection; the physical world was so distracting, so richly furnished with interesting objects and situations to be experienced by the senses. Drew had never known a moment's boredom, but the events he was now taking part in were of an altogether superior kind; it promised to be an actual adventure, and Morgan had made it possible, with some help from friendly old God. It was a shame about not having a gun, though. Clay had always wanted a gun. It was one of the few things Drew remembered about his brother.

They ate from cans around a cheery campfire. The road they had followed until dusk had become little more than a set of ruts meandering west among sage and cactus. Morgan prepared and served the food. The air had become surprisingly cool.

Even when the tent was properly raised and pegged, Sylvie wouldn't set foot inside it. "I'll sleep in the wagon," she said. "Hostiles will go directly to the tent and take your hair, while I have a chance to make my escape. It'll be your fault, Morgan. They'll take the boy and raise him a heathen. They do that all the time. No scalp for you, and no salvation for Drew. Is it worth such risks?"

"Why, yes," was all Morgan could say in reply to such bitterness.

He found there was little room inside the tent for himself and Drew, despite the absence of his wife. He should have bought a larger size; if Sylvie changed her mind there wouldn't be room enough for them all in anything resembling comfort.

Next day, the road simply disappeared beneath them. The mules continued plodding toward the Jemez Mountains, unconcerned. "Have we arrived at the chosen place?" Sylvie asked.

"Not yet."

"Are we perhaps nearby?"

"I can't be sure. I'll know when we arrive."

"Oh, good."

Drew couldn't understand Sylvie's bad humor. Losing the road was the most exciting development so far in what was turning out to be a fairly uncomfortable expedition. The air was much hotter than he'd been expecting, and Morgan sometimes refused him water from the barrel. "We must think of the animals too," his father said. "They have their needs, just as we do, and they have to pull us all along. Wait until you truly need to drink."

Drew felt the need constantly, but forced himself to deny his thirst for the sake of his father's wishes. He developed a severe headache. The lurching of the wagon suddenly became intolerable, and he began to cry.

"Stop!" commanded Sylvie. "Stop this instant!"

Morgan hauled on the reins.

Sylvie turned to her husband. "Turn around."

"We've come so far. ..."

"Turn around and go back."

"Do you doubt what has been revealed to me?"

"Look at our son, already sick with heat. I feel it myself. Take us back."

Morgan shook his head, genuinely regretful. "I cannot."

"You can, and will."

"No," he said, barely whispering, and Sylvie saw he meant it. There was nothing in his voice or posture suggestive of strength, yet he would have his way. It was foolishness, the entire venture. Sylvie had never thought it would go this far. She got down from the wagon seat.

"I begin walking from here, back to town."

"No, Sylvie ..."

"Yes, and Drew will come with me."

"He couldn't possibly walk the distance, nor you. This is not sensible talk. We may be closer than you think. Today may be the day our desert place is shown to us. It may be among the hills you see as we speak."

"Then give him water when he wants it. I won't have him suffer because of your ... dream."

This last word truly offended Morgan. Had his wife always felt this way about his revelation, and kept her thoughts to herself? She had been reluctant to sell the store, but he forgave her, attributing her mood to the natural caution of women regarding their home; but she had not until now disparaged outright the quest God had directed him to follow. He cared greatly for her good opinion of him, and it hurt Morgan deeply to hear her speak her mind.

Using Drew's discomfort to make Morgan feel worse was another low blow. Not for the world would Morgan have his boy suffer needlessly; it was just that the storekeeper in Santa Fe had advised him to go easy with the water barrel. The storekeeper had in fact advised him against going to the mountains with a woman and a child, had been almost abusive in his comments, but of course, the man could have no conception of the special business Morgan was about, else he would never have called his customer a fool to his face. It was fortunate that Sylvie and Drew had been nowhere near at the time, or such talk might have discouraged them.

"The place is before us, near or far. That is where I go, and I beg you to stay by me. The place is there."

Sylvie turned away from him. She had always believed that God had spoken to individuals in the Bible lands all those thousands of years ago, and wondered now if their spouses doubted them as she doubted Morgan. Was God alive and in charge of the universe even in these modern times, as she had been brought up to believe? If he was not, was it because people like herself doubted the visions of people like her husband? Was Sylvie contributing to the death of God by not believing?

Theology had not concerned her overmuch till Morgan claimed God had directed him to place the Kindreds in Drew's path, intercepting him as the orphan train moved west. He was a wonderful son, and she could fully accept that he was sent by God to fill her need, and Morgan's. Did she doubt the truth of Morgan's second communication because it caused physical discomfort? Because it required actions that seemed to fly in the face of common sense? These objections could be overcome by Christian will. It was a simple enough choice—to believe, or not believe. She need only set her mind to it, and the thing might well come to pass as Morgan predicted. She must allow him his chance. God's presence on the earth should not be whittled away by human doubt, certainly not that of Sylvie Kindred.

She climbed back onto the wagon. "We will continue, but we will drink whenever we please. God will provide."

"He will," Morgan assured her, and himself. He flicked the reins, and his family moved deeper into the barren, broken land ahead.

On the third day they drank the last of their water. Unused to animal husbandry, conscious of his responsibility to God's dumb creatures, Morgan had allowed the mules far more water than was necessary for their continued health. They were in prime condition, while the Kindreds were already suffering the onset of dehydration. All had thudding headaches, and found the simple business of staying on the wagon increasingly difficult.

Morgan guided his team along the path of least resistance, followed winding gulches to their confluence with weather-eroded ravines, turning back often when his chosen route terminated in a box canyon or impassable crevasse. This was a wilderness of suitably biblical harshness, unrelenting in its heat, its aridity, unforgiving of foolishness. Morgan had bought no maps, no compass; he relied solely on God's favor in completing the enterprise begun in Dinnsville. They must persevere until the designated place, that unique spot in the midst of nothingness, was chanced upon. It could be over the next rise, around the bend of a narrow dry wash, or days distant, somewhere in the shimmering air ahead, or behind, or to the left or right. It made little difference; all places were under God, all equally accessible to the faithful.

Morgan saw now what he should have seen much earlier. The first communication from God—the instruction to select Drew from among the orphans—had been easy to follow, but this search for a particular location in the desert was a task of far greater consequence, hence it could be achieved only after much suffering had been endured by the Kindreds. Morgan had been chosen as conduit between heaven and earth, but his family would pay a stiff price for the privilege.

It saddened Morgan that they must feel the pain that should be his alone. Maybe he shouldn't have brought them along, but the thought of journeying to find the desert place on his own simply had not occurred to him; Morgan wanted his loved ones to share the joy of discovery. He suspected also that Drew, having been delivered into his hands by God, had some crucial role to play, once the place was found. Morgan's instincts told him there was ethereal linkage involved, its significance as yet beyond his understanding.

And so they kept on, Morgan encouraging his wife and son with campfire readings from the book of Exodus. On the fifth day he released the mules from their harness, determined not to further their suffering. The mules made use of their freedom to follow their noses; less than an hour's amble from the Kindreds they located a trickling spring and drank deeply, then began to nibble at the ground-hugging succulents round about.

Sylvie collapsed not far from the useless wagon. "Now we die," she announced through cracked lips, her throat a tube of dust. Her hair hung in limp horsetails from her bonnet; her hands were coarsened by the sun, the nails packed with fine desert grime.

"No ...," Morgan croaked.

"Drew will die first," insisted Sylvie. "The young have less resistance."

"We are almost there. I would not have released the mules ..."

"Almost dead, yes."

Drew leaned against his mother and passed out, as if to prove her correct. Morgan nudged at his son, and Sylvie pushed him away. "Leave him! Let him pass away in peace."

"No one will pass away. God will not allow it. ..."

"Don't you see? Are you blind to what has happened? You have killed us."

Morgan shook his head, too dispirited to argue. The place was near, he knew. The lord of all creation would not permit his servant to come so close, only to let him die. This was the ultimate test of strength, of belief. Morgan was determined to reject all sense of personal misery in order that he might acquit himself in a worthy manner. God would forgive Sylvie's capitulation to despair if only Morgan stood firm, even as he faced death.

The Kindreds had fallen in the shadow of an earthen wall, the southern side of a small ravine that bore the signs of once having channeled running water between its crumbling banks. Morgan imagined a sudden return of that blessed moisture, an opening of the ravine floor, a great spewing forth of water, a rushing torrent to ease their agony. If God could create a dry pathway through the Red Sea, then could he not, for the sake of His emissary and his family, produce at least a rivulet of life-giving liquid?

For the first time, a sliver of doubt entered his thoughts. Could Sylvie be right? Was he guilty of leading two precious people on a fool's errand? He dismissed the temptation to think that way. Satan was whispering in his ear, dribbling his filthy skepticism into Morgan's brain. Suffering was his righteous lot for the moment; there might even be worse to come; the test of his endurance most likely would be bottomless, from Morgan's purely human perspective. He might even have to face losing his wife and child to prove himself. That would be the harshest test of all, but he would confront it if need be. To be resolute at such a time was difficult, but to his own surprise, Morgan achieved it.

The sixth day passed in hellish torment. Morgan watched his family dying. He expected Sylvie would be proved right; Drew would be the first to go. They were still within sight of the wagon, hadn't even attempted to continue on foot. Morgan supposed they must all be weaklings, but he couldn't have reached the wagon without assistance, let alone walked in search of civilization. There were no buzzards overhead, to his disappointment; the creatures were an integral part of death in the wilderness, according to the illustrated periodicals.

Where was God? Where was the desert place? He lacked the strength even to crawl on hands and knees over the next hill. It might be waiting there, resplendently empty, a hallowed spot where the spirit of God met rude earth, but Morgan wouldn't see it now. Keeping his eyelids raised was more than he could accomplish. He slept.

In the evening an angel came. Morgan saw it standing above him on the far rim of the ravine. The angel's hair was long and white, its clothing loose, stirring slightly in a rare breeze. A peculiar package was cradled in its right hand. The light of the setting sun was behind the angel, preventing a more detailed inspection of its face and form. It was enough for Morgan to know that mercy had arrived.

He watched the angel disappear from view, then suddenly materialize at his side. Morgan felt water pass between his parched lips. The angel was older than expected, an ancient soul with wisdom in its eyes, but where were its wings? He asked the angel to give water to his wife and son. No words passed from Morgan's mouth, but the angel understood, and moved across the intervening ground in a distinctly earthbound lope to administer life from what appeared to be a leather bag. Morgan had been anticipating a silver flask, but was in no condition to voice a complaint.

The water, far from reviving him, sent Morgan into a deep sleep from which he did not awaken until the morning of the seventh day. Where was the long-haired angel? He turned to his wife, and was devastated to find her dead. Scrambling to Drew's side, he saw the boy's eyes open. If Morgan and Drew had survived, why had Sylvie been taken from them? His conscious mind would not admit it, but he hated God at that moment, hated with a passion so intense he swooned and fell back once again to the dust.

Drew knew his mother was dead, just by looking at her. His father was still alive, but with eyes closed in the painful half-sleep Drew had just woken from. His first thoughts, knowing Sylvie was gone, were of sadness for himself; without her he couldn't possibly be happy anymore. For his father, Drew felt a kind of bafflement that almost turned to anger. He recognized that Sylvie's death was Morgan's fault, for having led them into the desert, but Morgan was a good and loving man, so Drew could not allow himself the easy pleasure of hating him for what he had done.

There had to be another culprit, someone equally culpable. The only suitable individual was God. It was God's fault. Drew opened himself fully to hatred of the Almighty, and his anger thrust him up from the ground, onto his feet. He took several steps in search of God, and tripped over a leather water bag. The sloshing of its contents erased all notions of revenge; Drew fell to his knees and pulled at the crude wooden stopper, tipped the bag and inundated his burning throat with tepid water, choked, drank more and fell back beside his father, carefully holding the bag upright to avoid spilling a drop. Where had it come from, this miraculous thing?

He shook Morgan to consciousness and pressed the water bag to his lips. Morgan drank deeply, coughed some of it back up again, then passed out anew.

Drew continued sipping from the bag. He looked again at Sylvie, then away. She hadn't been his real mother, he told himself, so it was all right not to cry; he doubted his dried-out body could make tears anyway. If he kept telling himself she wasn't his mother, then this thing that had happened to her could be lived with. Drew wanted above all else to continue living, and he reasoned, bit by bit, that living was best accomplished while a person wasn't crippled up with sadness. So she was not his mother. And the man lying with mouth open a short distance away was not his father.

Moments before, Drew had wanted to blame God for everything, but staring at Morgan rekindled his original anger, the anger he had stifled. No gun, no compass, no map or guide, and not enough water. The man was a fool. And yet Drew loved him. He tried again to summon hatred for God, but God seemed less substantial than the afternoon heat waves dancing over the wagon, and so Drew was left with nothing but despair and a great hunger to live, even if living meant being aware at all times of this same unresolvable despair.

His head hurt even more now, from the effort of thinking. He turned from his parents, and decided to walk away from this place on his own if Morgan didn't agree to give up the search for whatever it was he thought was out there. Drew decided also he would take the water bag with him when he went; if Morgan didn't quit searching, he was crazy, and Drew wasn't about to let a crazy man drink his water.

It was night again when Drew next opened his eyes. A campfire was burning close by, Morgan hunched over it, turning a rabbit carcass on a stick. Drew reached for the water bag, and in lifting it discovered the impossible—it was heavier than it had been earlier. He decided he must be wrong about that.

Morgan was smiling at him as he drank. "It'll be ready soon. Are you hungry?"

Drew nodded, and came closer to the fire.

"How'd you catch it?"

"I didn't. The Lord provided, or should I say, His angel."

"Angel?"

"I saw him once. He was old, not like you'd expect from pictures. He must have made the fire as well. It was already burning when I woke up, and the rabbit was on the stick."

"An angel did it?"

"Without doubt."

Drew did not accept this. He would eat the rabbit, enjoy the fire's warmth and light, and drink from the water bag, but he would do so without believing these things came from God. There had to be another answer.

"We need to bury your mother. We'll do that directly after we have partaken of the manna."

"It isn't manna; it's a rabbit."

"Its purpose is the same, to sustain us in pursuit of our goal."

"It's a rabbit!"

"Please don't upset yourself. We're both too weak for argument. We have only each other. Come to me."

Drew moved around to Morgan's side of the fire and leaned against him, tucked under a fatherly arm. He instantly forgave Morgan everything. It would be better to leave with his father too; that was far less frightening than his plan to walk out alone. He loved Morgan still, even if Morgan loved God too much. The arm tightened around him. Morgan was crying; Drew joined him. They had enough water in them now for tears.

Food and water came by night for two nights, their deliverer silent, unseen. "We are blessed," said Morgan. Drew said nothing.

Sylvie was buried, the grave dug with wagon strakes, the mound piled with rocks to keep off coyotes and cougars. Morgan spent an entire day scratching her name and the dates of her birth and death onto one of the digging boards, then set it up as a grave marker. He preferred to do this unassisted. Drew was inclined to let him, having no knack for woodworking, but it disturbed him to hear Morgan holding a conversation while he worked.

He thought at first his father was talking with Sylvie, addressing her spirit or some such, but the tone of the conversation lacked the sense of intimacy Drew had grown used to between Morgan and his wife. The man was talking to someone else entirely. Realizing this, Drew became scared, and his fear assumed the shape of bad temper.

"Who are you talking to!"

Morgan turned to him, a slightly dazed look on his face.

"Talking?"

"You're talking all the time. Whisper, whisper ..."

"With God."

"You're not!"

"Why do you not believe?"

"You're not talking to God! Stop it!"

"I talk with the one who has saved us both."

"He never did! It was someone else!"

"Calm yourself. I know now where the desert place is. Have you forgotten our purpose?"

"Where is it?"

"Here. This is the desert place, where I have buried my wife. This is the place because she is here, and we are here."

"That's ... stupid!"

Morgan smiled tolerantly. "There is much I don't understand. He speaks in riddles. Something is being revealed to me, some vast thing. I'll share it with you when I can."

In the following days Morgan showed no inclination to leave the wagon and grave site. His conversations with God continued; he did more listening now than talking, it seemed to Drew.

"Aren't we going to leave here?"

"When the time comes. We have suffered terribly just finding the desert place, and we'll remain until I'm told we may leave."

"Did you ask God what we need to wait for?"

"One does not question; one listens."

"So we're staying here."

"For the time being, yes. The angel brings us all we need. Why are you not satisfied?"

"It's not an angel; it's an old man. I think he's an Indian. I saw him last night, sneaking away. He's got a bag over his hand."

"A bag?"

"Like a big glove with no fingers. He's got long white hair. He left that pile of firewood over there."

"You're mistaken, Drew. That was an angel of God. It's possible that such beings appear in different guise to different people, so as not to frighten them. You expect to see an Indian in this region, so an Indian is what you see."

"He *is* an Indian."

"Why would anyone, even an Indian, wear a bag over his hand?"

"Maybe he uses it to bring water, and tips it into the bag that's always here."

"That is ridiculous."

Drew could only frown angrily. His father wasn't the same man he'd been back in Illinois. Drew thought maybe the sun was cooking Morgan's brain, even if he always kept his hat on. Morgan didn't even go near Sylvie's grave anymore, too busy listening to the whisperings of God.

Drew seldom approached Sylvie himself. The last time he sat by the marker he found himself talking out loud to his mother, complaining about how Morgan was turning into a crazy man for sure; if he hadn't been when he led his family into the Jemez Mountains, he was now, with his muttering and head-nodding whenever God made a point that Morgan agreed with. Drew didn't want to be a talker with invisible presences, and so avoided the grave.

He revived his plans for escape. The ravine was becoming a prison without walls. Morgan's behavior continued to deteriorate. One night by the fire he ordered Drew to recite in order the books of the Bible. Drew began stumbling badly after Ecclesiastes. When his guesses ran down to a sullen silence, Morgan leaned over and slapped him hard across the face. "You, sir," he said, "do not deserve a savior!" He shoved his Bible into Drew's hands. "Study it! That is the book of all things!"

Drew flung it into the fire. Morgan roared and thrust his hand among the flames to retrieve it, was burned along the wrist and jerked back. He used a stick of firewood to flip his Bible out onto the ground. Drew moved away while Morgan did this. They glared at each other across the fire. Morgan's face twisted lopsidedly with pain as he clutched his wrist. "Unbeliever ...," he growled.

Drew almost felt guilty. He'd thrown his father's Bible into the fire, the very book Morgan and Sylvie had entered his name in on the births-and-deaths endpaper, to show they considered him a true member of the family. He could see naked loathing in Morgan's eyes. With firelight illuminating him from below, the man looked like a demon. Walking backward, Drew took himself away into darkness to avoid him.

For several hours afterward, as Drew hid among shadows, he could hear Morgan moaning, whether from the pain of his burn or from some particularly intense dialogue with God, Drew couldn't tell. He was determined to stay awake that night for two reasons, the first being a genuine fear of being found and murdered by Morgan, the second being a wish to catch the old Indian in the act of bringing them what they needed. Why would an Indian be doing this? It was almost as worrisome as Morgan's escalating madness.

His vigil faltered through drowsiness. When Drew woke after dawn, he rose and came closer to the fire. Morgan was still asleep, the charred Bible in his hands. Drew saw a freshly skinned jackrabbit by the embers. Drew preferred rabbit to the strange long-legged bird their benefactor had twice left them; he always skinned the rabbits, but apparently couldn't be bothered plucking the birds. The water bag had also been replenished. Drew decided today was the day he must escape. He would leave the jackrabbit, but take the water bag. It was a fair division of resources.

"Good morning, son."

Morgan was awake, smiling at him. He looked like the old Morgan, kindly and sane. He stood and stretched himself, but made no move toward Drew.

"I know now what must be done here," he said. "The answer has been given to me. When we accomplish what must be done, there will be no need to linger."

"What is it?" Drew asked, his expression guarded.

"We must build a fire."

"A fire?"

"In the wagon; pile it high with brushwood."

"Why?"

"Because that is the wish of our God. I ask you to believe me. Will you help?"

He sounded like the old Morgan, quietly explaining himself.

"All right."

A fire in the wagon seemed foolish to Drew, but if Morgan was prepared to leave that awful place afterward, then he would help build a fire Morgan could be proud of. Despite everything, it would be better to walk out of the desert with his father, instead of alone. Maybe Morgan's crazy talk would pass with time, as his grief over

Sylvie's death eased. They would build a fire (for Drew, it would be lit in Sylvie's honor, not God's), then leave, to be father and son again.

"Do we start now?"

"Gather every stick, every twig, but don't wander far in case you become lost."

The gathering lasted several hours, and resulted in a pile of dead sagebrush. It came nowhere near to filling the wagon as Morgan had specified. Drew thought it would probably all burn away in just a few minutes, too quickly to set the wood beneath and the wagon itself ablaze, if that was what Morgan wanted. He didn't ask. Asking questions might cause his father to begin spouting nonsense again. This way the fire would be over and done with that much faster, and they could be on their way.

"Enough," said Morgan. "Rest."

He drank, then passed Drew the water bag. They inspected their work, the wagon's insubstantial load. Morgan seemed content. "Do you have faith in me?" he asked, turning to Drew.

"Yes," Drew said, not wishing to provoke him.

"That is good. That is as it should be. The severest test will be mine, but yours is no easy task, I admit. Your trust in me is natural, since I am your father, but the trust I must place in the father of us all is a true act of faith. Fetch me a rock, one that will fit in my hand. The choice shall be yours."

"A rock?"

"A rock, a rock, an everyday rock! Don't waste time!"

Drew searched a short distance along the ravine and returned with what he thought would be acceptable.

"Perfect! Into the wagon with you. Hurry now."

Drew climbed onto the seat, worrying a little by then; why get in the wagon when the mules were no longer there to pull it?

"Among the brush, if you please."

"What for?"

"That is where the sacrificial fire will be lit. Place yourself in the middle. Did not Abraham prepare such a fire for his son Isaac? Did he not prepare to sacrifice his child for the glory of God when called upon to do so? Did not God stay Abraham's knife a breath away from spilling blood on the sacrificial pyre? All this will be done as it was in ancient times.

"I see alarm in your face. Did not Isaac trust his father, as you trust me? This rock found by your own hand will be my knife. I know in my heart as I raise it high, our father will command me to halt. You need fear nothing. Share my faith. What has happened before will happen again. We, you and I, have been chosen ... and Sylvie will be returned to us as our reward: I have the promise of God himself, if we only show to him our faith. ... Stay there!"

Drew had vaulted from the wagon seat and was running for the water bag. He snatched it up without pause and ran on. Morgan's outraged screeching followed him along the ravine. Drew scrambled up the nearest bank and dashed among the rocks, seeking cover. He fell, panting with fright, and listened for Morgan.

There was no sound other than himself. He should have grabbed the jackrabbit too. Morgan was crazy after all, but not so crazy he didn't get Drew to help build his own funeral pyre, and even go pick out a rock to crush his skull! The deceit behind Morgan's behavior upset Drew even more than the pathetic madness directing Morgan to do it.

When he was certain he had not been followed, Drew stood and began walking. He chose a direction he believed led directly away from the wagon, and as he walked, he wept for what had happened. Now he was without a mother and father for the second time, and he wondered if this was maybe the natural order of things, the way it was intended by God that his life should be. But what did God have to do with it? Wasn't it God who had brought them to this place? And now Sylvie was dead, Morgan insane, and Drew an orphan again, even if Morgan still lived; Drew wasn't having any crazy man for a father.

He was alone, would probably die himself when his water ran out; dead like poor Sylvie. At least he wouldn't go mad like Morgan, who had listened to and believed what God told him. God had never talked with Drew, and he suspected Sylvie had also been ignored by the heavenly presence. That was all right with Drew; any being that caused the catastrophe he had witnessed was someone he had no use for. He'd never really liked church anyway; the only good thing about Sundays in the white clapboard box in Dinnsville had been the chance it afforded to look at Betty Pulvermiller in her best dress and bonnet, just the prettiest girl in town. Of course, she always stuck her tongue out at him whenever she noticed him looking, which was discouraging, but Drew figured that with time and patience he could have married her someday. Between them, Morgan and God had ruined that plan too.

Doubts about God had surfaced in Drew's mind a long time ago, when he tried many times through prayer to alert Clay and Zoe of his desire to see them both again. Neither of them ever came, so it looked as though God had ignored his prayers. It was another good reason not to believe in or need such a thing as God. It was all hooey. There probably wasn't even a heaven. If he was wrong about that, he hoped Sylvie was there already, sipping cool sweet water from a little pool all her own. Morgan could go to hell.

Walking on, Drew wondered if Clay and Zoe were still alive. They were too young to be dead, surely, unless they got very sick and gave up the ghost, but it would be very unfair if that happened before he got the opportunity to see them again. Prayer hadn't worked, hadn't summoned them to Dinnsville, so now he'd go find them, his brother and sister, so they could be their own family, without grownups. It made him slightly sick to think they might be perfectly happy with the families they'd found after stepping down from the orphan train. That would fix his plan all right, having Clay and Zoe wanting to stay right where they were, wherever that might be, so happy there they never once thought about coming to find him all these years later. Clay said he would, but it was pretty clear Clay had forgotten his promise.

Well, if Clay wouldn't come to Drew, Drew would go to Clay, and Zoe too. He'd find them both, without using a single prayer. He'd just search and search until he found them, and after he told them both off (especially Clay) for not coming to fetch him, they'd all laugh and cry and be happy together, the Dugans again.

He stopped to drink, and while water trickled like life itself down into him, he saw the Indian, and dropped the bag in surprise. Drew snatched it up again before more than a mouthful had belched from the spout, then looked hard at the Indian to make sure he was not imagining him. The Indian was even older than Drew had guessed by moonlight, old and cracked in the face like sun-dried mud. He wore a loose store-bought shirt made for a larger man, and deerhide moccasins; his skinny legs were bare. And he wore a bag over his right hand, just as Drew had told Morgan.

He gestured for Drew to come closer, and when Drew did so, the Indian turned and began walking. Drew followed, his trust in the old man immediate. He stumbled in the wake of the Indian—a man of considerable sprightliness despite his years and stooped spine—having no knowledge of their direction or purpose; it was enough to be with another human being. Drew was allowed to catch up with

his guide at the top of a low rise. The Indian held a finger to his
lips, then beckoned Drew forward until they lay side by side. The
Indian slid forward on his belly, and Drew followed.

They were overlooking the ravine where Sylvie lay buried. Drew
realized then how utterly lost he must have been when the Indian
found him. He saw Morgan stride from behind the wagon, buttoning his pants. It was fascinating to observe, unseen, the man who
had intended killing him for God. Morgan picked up his Bible from
the wagon seat and began declaiming to the sky.

Drew recognized passages from Deuteronomy, but couldn't understand their significance in these surroundings. Maybe to Morgan's
crazy mind the words he spoke made sense. Morgan began to walk
as he read, following a wide circle around the wagon, his voice rising and falling, sometimes failing altogether; without the water bag
Morgan's throat must be awfully dry, Drew thought, but he had no
intention of returning it.

He looked sideways at the Indian, who happened to be looking at
him. "He's crazy," whispered Drew. The Indian said nothing. Drew's
eyes went to the leather bag covering the Indian's right hand, and
stayed there. The bag was more interesting than Morgan's madness; Drew really wanted to know why it was there, and the Indian
understood his curiosity. He began unpicking the rawhide knot at
his wrist that held the bag in place, then slid the bag free.

Drew stared. The Indian's hand was held in a closed fist, and had
been held that way for many years, because the fingernails had
grown clear through the palm and out the back of his hand, long
gray nails that curled like streamers of pointed ribbon frozen in the
air. The thumbnail had grown in a wide, looping curve around
knuckles that stood up like a row of burial mounds. The Indian was
smiling, proud of his hand. Drew couldn't see why; it was the ugliest, most awful thing he'd ever seen in his life.

The proximity of that pierced hand to the ranting madman just
over the rise produced in Drew a sense of disbelief. The things that
his eyes and ears told him were real could not be. The world was a
colossal joke of some kind, an unreal place. Everything the Kindreds had ever taught him about God's place in the affairs of men
was nonsense, a trick. The smiling Indian, himself unreal, was
revealing to him another way of seeing. Drew felt he had stepped
off a cliff and was tumbling in the air, unsure even if he was falling.
Even Clay and Zoe were robbed of meaning, of reality; they

belonged to another time, another place, another life. The world was being made over in seconds as Drew stared at the cruel hand. The boy called Drew was becoming someone else, someone without identifiable features, an entity Drew might not even recognize when next he looked into a mirror. Drew knew it, and Smart Crow Making Mischief knew it too.

Dazed, Drew allowed himself to be led away from the ravine to a place nearby where two familiar mules grazed, one with a rawhide halter and reins, the other without. Drew was ordered with a gesture to mount the first, while Smart Crow sprang onto the broad back of the other and grabbed a handful of mane. Drew hadn't known it was possible to ride like that, and found himself even more impressed once he learned how difficult it was to stay aboard his mule without benefit of a saddle. He mastered the technique soon enough, and was well pleased; it was one more new thing in this new world he found himself living in. Nothing was the way Drew had always held it to be, and realization of his error made him light as air.

They rode toward the mission at San Bartolomeo. Smart Crow had been headed there to see his grandsons when he was diverted by the antics of the madman and his family. The delay had been worth it; he would use the white boy to persuade Bleeding Heart of Jesus and Nail in His Feet to abandon the appalling religion of the Dead Man Flying on Wood and return with him to the true life for which they had been born.

8

Aspinall's stonecutting equipment was wrapped in burlap, but no matter how carefully he arranged it, a part of some tool always managed to find a reciprocal part of another tool, and together they produced a *chink, chink, chink,* to rival the steady tinklings of bridle and bit. Aspinall preferred to handle the two-horse team himself, since the wagon was his, and that meant Tully had much time to spare for Zoe, who had none for him.

"The baby, she's a real little traveler. Not a peep hardly."

Zoe knew he complimented Omie as often as he did because he was aware that Zoe loved her. Omie was a convenient handle by which Tully attempted to grasp her mother. Zoe ignored most of what flowed from him. It was annoying, though, to have to climb into the back of the wagon whenever Omie required feeding. Zoe had tried baring her breast while seated up front with the men, but although Aspinall was sensitive enough to keep his eyes elsewhere, Tully always ogled her nipple before it disappeared into Omie's reaching mouth.

Tully's crassness was the only blemish on an otherwise pleasant journey. The road from Springfield to Saint Louis was well traveled. When they reached the Mississippi and were ferried across, Zoe thought of Mrs. Ringle from the train, but decided against visiting;

Mrs. Ringle would certainly not approve of her accompanying two unmarried men. The wagon passed through that great town without pause, Aspinall eager as always to be moving west. The road to Kansas City was arrow-straight in precisely that direction.

They avoided hostelries and wayside inns; Aspinall was a tight man with a dollar, a keen appreciator of campfires and starry skies. He would not share the wagon's limited floor space, however, which placed Zoe in closer proximity to Tully than she would have chosen. For the first few nights Tully had not violated the several yards separating their blankets, but well before they reached Saint Louis he had come creeping to her side to whisper words of love into her ear. A small blade entered his vision; Zoe had purchased it in Springfield for just such a use as this. She told him, "Don't you touch me ever, or I'll poke your eye out." Tully was intelligent enough to believe her.

On a lonely stretch of trail halfway between Saint Louis and Kansas City, they made camp by a shallow creek. During the night, Zoe incorporated Tully's voice into a dream, then woke up. He was calling her name, softly and insistently. When she saw him moving closer, she found the handle of her knife and gripped it hard.

"Zoe ... Zoe ..."

He was close, but not within stabbing distance. Zoe watched with a barely opened eye as he wriggled closer in the moonlight.

"Zoe, can't you see how I'm paining? You've got me loving you. Soon as I saw you that day, I said, That's the girl I want to marry, swear I did. You know me by now, Zoe, you know the way I am, all in love with you. I know how it is, with the little one and all; you'll be wanting a man steady as a rock to be providing for you both. That's me, it is. I'll be good to you and Omie both. Are you listening? You're a funny one, Zoe, I swear. Are you awake, are you?"

He came closer. "You're the girl I've been wanting all my life, so help me. I don't care if another man had you. No one's perfect in this world. I'd be a true husband, my oath on it ... only let me in with you, in there under the blanket. Just a little kiss and I'll tell you the things I bet you've been wanting to hear from an honest fellow, which there's very few of us about, Zoe, very few indeed. Let's have a little kiss, just a little kiss to show I care, Zoe ..."

Mistaking her silence for acquiescence, Tully slid closer. Zoe opened her blanket, just the way he wanted. Tully couldn't believe his luck; she thought he truly wanted to hitch up with her and her bastard, and was willing to receive him into herself to speed the marriage along, the little trollop. He'd keep up the pretense until he found Lovey Doll Pines, then let Zoe down with a bump that might make her think twice next time she offered herself. He'd be teaching her a necessary lesson in life, Tully told himself as he moved toward Zoe with a grin on his face. She was a sweetie, and the next few minutes should be worth the considerable effort he had expended to get this far with her; perseverance was a lover's asset, along with charm and an impressive mustache.

As he reached for her, Zoe's blade jabbed Tully just below the jawline. For a brief moment he was unsure what had happened, then saw the knife in her hand rushing at him again. He rolled over to escape it, blood spraying from his neck. Tully was angry. He lunged at her, avoiding the blade as it whizzed by his head in a tight arc.

Grabbing her wrist was easy; subduing the rest of her was not. She twisted like a pinioned snake, and hissed like one. Tully was in no mood for gentleness; it was open war between them now, and the fault lay with Zoe for rejecting him, the ungrateful little bitch. Who had arranged for her to be on this trip west, if not Tully? Who had shown her every respect, even to the point of proposing marriage, if not Tully? And what had his kindness got him but contemptuous looks? She thought he was dirt beneath her dainty feet, and that angered Tully, who was used to success with women. It was to redress the harm done to this picture of himself that Tully decided to make a painful example of Zoe Dugan. He'd show her with his cock that what she'd done was not acceptable, not to a man like him, and after it was done she'd very likely come around to his view of things, as was right and natural. Once she learned her lesson Zoe might be enjoyable company for a while, but first she needed the hard lesson. Tully would be her teacher.

He began hitting her with his closed fist, the other hand occupied with keeping Zoe's knife away from him. Zoe attempted with her free hand to scratch and claw. Tully could feel her nails sliding off his face; was he sweating so much? It was soaking his shirt, soaking him all the way to his waist. Suddenly he felt weak, and began to worry that his grip on Zoe's wrist might give out; she could stab him again. She had already stabbed him once; that was why he was so angry, he reminded himself, and knew then that it was only the anger that had allowed him to hold her off; he was weak, so weak his breath wouldn't come. She had stabbed him, and it was bad. The sweat was not sweat, but blood.

Tully's head began to swim, his ears to hum, and the hum deepened to a low droning, like wind echoing through a cavern. He was unable to see clearly. The girl beneath him was shining, shining with blood, her body as drenched as his, and seeing her that way, Tully knew he was dying. It didn't matter now that her knife hand finally pulled away from his fingers; he couldn't even feel those fingers anymore, or his feet. He fell back, hearing someone close by breathing hoarsely, then realized it was himself, a panting beast, slaughtered, dying quickly now, the sound of his slowing blood a distant rushing noise. She had killed him with one poke of her stupid little knife, and all because he asked her to marry him. Tully wished he had the strength to snap her neck and take her with him to hell, but it was too late for revenge against Zoe, close as she was; he couldn't move a muscle, could do nothing but lie in a widening pool of blood and feel the life gushing from him with faraway metronomic thuddings, the dying heartbeat that became everything for a short while, then was gone.

Zoe hadn't made a sound throughout Tully's dying, and was afraid to open her mouth even when it was over. The thing she had done was too big, too awful to encompass with her thoughts. Zoe's predominant emotion was not regret, however, but fear for herself. Murderers were hanged by the neck, and she had murdered Tully, even if he deserved it for ignoring her warnings.

She had somehow to remove herself from proximity to the deed, had to be far away when the body was found, but first had to clean the blood from her dress, her blanket, the very earth around them both. When it was done she would sneak away into the darkness ... no, she would bury Tully first, so no one would even know he had died. It was incredible to her that Aspinall was still asleep despite what had occurred mere yards from his wagon. Zoe remembered then how very silent a struggle it had been, no more than gruntings and pantings while they wrestled each other for control of her knife. Tully hadn't said another word after she stabbed him. Zoe didn't wish to recall any more of the event. She must concentrate—bury the body; clean up the blood; escape.

It was too much. She could never hope to accomplish it alone. Zoe knew what she must do. It was not so much a choice as a surrender to circumstance. She went to the wagon and called Aspinall's name until he woke.

"What?" he asked, his voice thick with sleep.

"I killed him."

"Who?"

"Tully. I cut him and he bled. I told him not to touch me."

"You cut him?"

"He's dead! Get up!"

"You killed Tully? Do I hear you right?"

"I don't know what to do. He's dead. He came over to touch me. I warned him not to a long time ago."

Aspinall dragged pants over his union suit, pulled on his boots and climbed down from the wagon. He lit an oil lamp and turned up the wick—the sudden splash of light revealed everything.

"Jesus God Almighty ... You did this?"

"I *told* him not to touch me. ..."

"You're sure he's gone?"

Zoe nodded. The area seemed to have been sprayed with blood, buckets of it; her own hands were red and sticky, her face and hair plastered with blood. Aspinall squatted to examine Tully. "Neck artery, looks like. Must've emptied like a spigot." He stood. "You never led him on?"

"No!"

He studied her face, the lamp held close.

"Well, then, you get in the creek and wash yourself down, and your dress. Take the blanket too. Wash everything." He gave her the lamp. "Go."

Zoe hurried away. Aspinall piled wood onto the fire's embers, then fetched a shovel from the wagon. Omie had slept through the entire incident, and was sleeping still.

By dawn it was done. Tully was buried a short distance along the creek. Aspinall left no mound, carried the excess earth back to camp and spread it over the bloodied ground beside the fire. Zoe—naked, nursing Omie—was wrapped in a dry blanket inside the wagon. Her wringing wet dress and underthings were suspended on hooks from the wagon hoops, and her damp blanket was spread over the canvas cover outside to dry in the sunlight already creeping across the sky. Aspinall had the team harnessed, the fire covered, before full daylight arrived. He inspected the scene carefully, then climbed aboard and set his wagon moving along the road to Kansas City, while his stomach growled for breakfast.

"You stay back there till you can get dressed again," he told Zoe.

"I wasn't going to do anything else," she said.

Zoe resented the hold Aspinall had over her; having been assisted in disposing of Tully, she was in his debt. She supposed his actions made Aspinall her accomplice, but this gave Zoe no comfort. It was distressing to be beholden to the man.

"Was he your friend?" she asked.

"Tully? Acquaintance, I'd say. Never had much time for him. He paid ten dollars just to come along. Five was for you."

"I told him to keep away from me."

"It's been done now. He's been judged. I believe he brought it on himself, so just quit talking about it now. I don't want trouble holding me back from where I'm going."

"Nor me."

It seemed an appropriate basis for understanding between them. By afternoon, when Zoe was able to dress, the atmosphere of panic had been replaced by awkwardness. Both parties to the crime were confirmed noncommunicators, had barely spoken to each other since the trip began, except through Tully, who had also filled the extended silences with his prattling. Tully had been the grease enabling them to rub along day after day; without him, Zoe and Aspinall grew cautious of each other. Aspinall did go so far as to ask Zoe if she wouldn't call him Bryce, just to ease their mutual anxiety. Zoe said she would, but found no opportunity to do so for another hour.

"Bryce, I'm hungry."

He stopped, and they prepared their first food for the day. This commonplace act brought them together as no amount of argued justification for their predawn collusion could have. Bryce revealed that he liked to cook, and was a better than average hand at it.

"My ma ran a restaurant in Cleveland. She taught me how. A man that doesn't cook, he's a useless man, that's what she said. She didn't want me to be a cook for a living, though. It's not a man's work, she said. She got me to being a stonemason's apprentice. There was a fellow used to come in and eat there regular, and he took me on. She died before I finished the apprenticeship. I'm twenty-seven. How old are you?"

"Eighteen," Zoe lied. She had assumed Bryce was at least forty because of his receding hair.

"Tully," said Bryce. "I thought you and him were together, you know. He begged me to take you along. I didn't want to, then he gave me the money. You don't hold that against me, I hope."

"No."

"It's a long way to go, just by yourself."

Bryce slept on the ground, leaving the wagon for Zoe and Omie. He did this night after night across western Missouri, and during all their days together asked not one question regarding the baby's father, or Zoe's own origins. It was not that he lacked interest; Zoe could see curiosity backed up behind his eyes whenever he looked at her. Bryce Aspinall's glances in her direction were always fleeting, and it dawned on Zoe the man was shy. She hadn't encountered this quality in a male before, and its discovery made her shy herself, deepening the silence between them.

They paused in Kansas City only for necessary supplies. Zoe contributed her few dollars. "Thank you," was all Bryce said, but she could tell he was grateful. The man Tully had called stingy was simply poor; beyond his wagon, team and tools, he had little of worth.

She had never disliked Bryce, but Zoe was disinclined to trust any man. She was not aware of consciously waiting for Bryce to stumble and reveal his true nature—she was fairly sure she'd already seen that—but she was not actively seeking his friendship, nor anything else. There was room in Zoe's life for Clay and Drew and Omie, and that was all. She was not unappreciative of Bryce's help, acknowledged he was indeed a good man, but there her contemplation of Bryce Aspinall ended. There was no point in going further. It would have made little difference had he been taller and more handsome, possessing a full head of hair; Zoe had her itinerary, her need, and it seemed unlikely that a man with a trade like Bryce's, requiring a permanent workshop, could ever fit into her overall plans.

Zoe knew Clay wouldn't have lingered in Kansas; mountains were the thing he'd always wanted to see. But the mountains were a long time coming. The plains were endless. Twice a day, and again at night, trains swept by their plodding progress beside the railroad tracks they now used as their guide west. Bryce worried about buffalo. "They roam in herds of thousands, and if they stampede they run down everything in their way." They saw occasional herds in the distance, never numbering more than a few hundred. Bryce was surprised, even disappointed. "There should be more," he said. He knew they were killed for their hides, but was unaware of the slaughter's full extent. They saw no Indians; not one.

Zoe asked him, "Are you going to stay in Wichita or one of the big towns to get work?"

"I might just go through to Colorado. There's plenty of stone there to work with. Headstones are my specialty."

She had expected, since killing Tully, to be haunted by the memory of that deed, but Zoe experienced no guilty dreams, no regret. This prompted her to question whether she lacked a conscience. Could she really be so incomplete? Even her self-doubt lacked conviction, because it had no useful role to play in her plans.

The guns were at eye level, a matched pair of .45s, the metal deeply blued, the handles plain, beautifully marked with a natural wood grain. Seeing them behind the glass, Clay knew he must have them. He had wandered around Kansas City for three days, never thinking to visit a gun store, but the window display drew him that morning like a magnet. He had known even before he was close enough to see the twin Colts that something awaited him behind the sun's reflected glare. He went inside.

"Help you today, sir?"

"The Colts in the window—I'd like to see them."

The presentation case was lifted out and set before him. He picked up the first gun, then the second. They felt like extensions of himself. Edwin Delaney's old cap-and-ball pistol was a thing from antiquity, a blunderbuss compared to these finely balanced beauties.

"Finest we've ever had in stock," said the salesman. "Very handsome appearance. Twelve-inch barrels. Not too many of these around."

Clay cocked the hammers, sighted at various objects out in the street, lowered the hammers again and set the weapons down. "I'll need a gun belt," he said.

"Yessir, twin holsters. We have a fine selection available right over here. You're probably thinking of the regular open-ended model to accommodate those long barrels, but then you face the problem of the front sight getting caught on the edge when you draw your pieces. That won't occur if you select a specially crafted long holster set with closed ends. No snagging, and it keeps dirt from drifting up your barrels. Leg ties for hard riding, and hammer ties too, so your guns won't go bouncing around and fly right out of the holsters. Comes the time you need to use them, just pop the ties off and you can whip them out fast. We have unadorned leather, or a fancy hand-tooled Spanish style—a work of art, I think you'll agree, sir. Or if you prefer, we have the cavalry model, with complete over-the-top flap to keep your gun in and grime out."

"The other kind, the open holsters. Not the fancy ones."

"Yessir, I believe this is definitely the one for you, or should I say two, ha ha—just my little joke for the day, sir."

Clay knew his holed cheeks were being studied throughout the sales talk. "How much?"

"Forty dollars even. These are special weapons."

"Take off five dollars for the box the guns came out of. I don't need it."

"That's genuine cherrywood, sir, finest display box available, and real velvet, soft as a damsel's touch."

"I don't need it. Take five dollars off or I won't buy any ammunition from you. I need a thousand rounds.

The salesman fetched boxes of ammunition down from the shelves behind him and placed them on the counter, then watched Clay draw a money belt from beneath his shirt, open it and count out cash.

"Wrap it all up," Clay said.

"Wrap it up, sir?"

"When I know how to use them, I'll wear them."

"Yessir."

"Keep it here for me. I'll be back in an hour."

He bought a horse, a tall gelding with a coarse mane and tail, an unkempt-looking animal, but deep in the chest. Edwin had taught Clay about horses. He bought a saddle and bridle, then rode his new horse to a haberdashery. "A big hat," he told the salesman. "Wide in the brim."

"Heading west, are we, sir?"

"We are."

He had realized it himself only that morning, after buying the Colts. There was no surprise in the decision; Clay simply intended doing at last what he'd always planned on doing, and today was the day.

He left the haberdashery with his latest purchase casting a shadow across his shoulders, picked up his guns and rode west out of town, came to his senses several miles beyond the outskirts of

Kansas City and turned back to spend more cash on a packhorse and supplies. Angry with himself, he set out again late in the day, and lost himself on the prairie to learn the art of the shootist.

An insufficiency of suitable targets became his first problem. He shot at clumps of grass, and managed to miss them more often than not. Clay persuaded himself his bullets were actually hitting their mark, but grass yields no sign of impact; he needed hard things, objects that would fly apart when hit. In time he came upon a meandering creek, its banks held together with willows and cotton-woods, providing dead branches for target practice. To Clay's dismay, he was unable to hit them more than one time in twelve. Even the trees themselves seemed to dance sideways when he pulled the trigger. Were his beautiful Colts defective?

He loaded and fired, reloaded and fired again, and again, then faced the truth—he was a dreadful shot, an appalling shot. Clay changed his tactic, concentrated now on drawing the guns from their holsters, ignoring for the moment the inconvenient fact that, once drawn, his weapons wouldn't hit anything Clay wanted to hit. Even this simple operation, the extraction of the gun from its holster at speed, proved impossible. Clay's big hands fumbled and missed; his thick fingers had to search before locating and worming behind the trigger guard; his thumbs failed to haul back the narrow hammers without slipping, and often left the guns dangerously half-cocked. His hands were so large his little fingers found themselves tucked under the butts, with nowhere to take hold.

The guns had felt so good in the store. How had they changed, out there in the open air? Clay practiced till his fingers were sore, and when all one thousand rounds of ammunition were gone, he forced himself to face the unsettling fact that he could neither draw his weapons with alacrity nor hit anything at which he aimed. Even when he rested the barrels on top of a fallen trunk and took his time about aiming, he still missed the rocks, the branches—he doubted he could even hit the sky. Clay felt humiliated.

It was the hands, those big stupid hands of his, the farmer's hands that could snap a branch like a twig. He felt like a clod, a dunce, a clumsy bonehead. All those years of dreaming about handling fine weaponry had been wasted time; he just wasn't cut out to be a gunman. Expertise with six-shooters would never be his, thanks to the big fumbling hands and a general lack of coordination.

He knew now why it was he'd wanted so very badly to prove himself adept at shooting; it was so he could kill bad men, human scum like the Chaffey brothers. Killing those two had been a wonderful experience, the only flaw being the ill-timed misfirings of Delaney's old pistol. New pistols, Clay had reasoned, would facilitate his ability to remove bad men from the face of the earth, but he had to reconsider that plan now, in light of his ineptitude.

Clay packed the Colts away and returned to Kansas City. He sold his gunslinger's rig to a firearms store as far away from the site of their original purchase as possible, and recovered two-thirds of the cost. Turning to leave, he noticed a rack of shotguns, and saw a way out of his dilemma.

When he left Kansas City for the final time, Clay cradled a shotgun with the last two feet of its twin barrels expertly removed. Around his waist he wore an ammunition belt, the stitched leather loops accommodating twelve-gauge shells. He used his new toy often, blowing bushes to smithereens even when firing from the hip. He never fumbled a draw, since the gun was always in his hands, ready at a moment's notice to be aimed and fired. Clay was happy.

9

Lovey Doll was almost stepped on by a horse as she crossed the street. The rider didn't even notice her, a circumstance Lovey Doll was unused to, so she studied him hard as the horse carried him by. Even mounted, he was obviously tall, a long and lanky man with a face to match that of his horse, and a sawed-off shotgun in his arms. Lovey Doll found him repellent. She liked handsome men, well-dressed fellows with plenty of money to spend on her. The tall man's packhorse also came close to treading on her little button boots.

"Watch where you ride, why don't you!"

The horseman turned to look at her. His scrubby beard couldn't hide the holes in his face. The scars were ugly enough to make Lovey Doll sick, but the eyes above the holes were even more compelling: black pools without expression of any kind—a madman's eyes, she thought. It was a relief for Lovey Doll when he turned away and continued on down the street. It was one of Kansas City's main streets, and it led directly to the westbound road, so she felt she wouldn't have to face the ugly man again. The road was for poor people who couldn't afford an easy ride west on the train from Independence, or for sodbusters with their heavy wagons filled with stoves and seed and children.

Lovey Doll entered a narrow doorway and ascended the stairs to the topmost floor of a four-story building. She was very late for her appointment, but was not troubled by it; the man waiting for Lovey Doll was very much in love with her, and would forgive her quickly if she just batted her eyes a little at him. He was a fool, like most men. Lovey Doll sometimes thought if she ever found a man who wasn't a fool, she'd pretend to be a virgin, make him fall in love with her and get married. Of course, if the man wasn't a fool, he'd never believe she was a virgin. It was a problem, but in any case, the chances of finding a man who wasn't a fool were slimmer than Lovey Doll's tiny waist.

She entered Dunnigan's room without bothering to knock, this being her way of letting him know she didn't care about being so late. His easel was set up in readiness beneath the skylight, his paints laid out, the podium laden with enough pillows to ensure her comfort without concealing with their bulk the pillowy softness of Lovey Doll herself when naked.

She began immediately to undress. Nevis hadn't said a word since she flounced in, and now was pretending not to watch as her clothing fell away. Lovey Doll deliberately slowed her disrobing to tease him.

"Would you please hurry a little," he finally begged.

"Well, *I am,* so don't be snippy with me. Someone almost squashed my foot with his horse just now, the ugliest man I ever saw. You could paint a picture of him and call it a portrait of the devil."

"Please, Lovey Doll..."

"I'm hurrying," she assured him, wiggling with exaggerated slowness out of her camisole. Nude, she was at her most powerful. No man had ever seen her thus without exhibiting interest, or trying hard not to, like Nevis Dunnigan. It amounted to the same thing, and was even preferable from Lovey Doll's perspective, since the confusion her body aroused in such men made them far more pliant, more maneagable, than those coarse brutes who simply admired her shape and wanted, in the most forthright manner, to penetrate her private parts with their own.

Lovey Doll referred to the male appendage as Moses' rod, for just as that patriarch's wooden staff was turned to a snake and back again, so the one-eyed worm of maleness could be at one moment a sluggardly drooping thing of comical unloveliness, and the next rise to attention like a ship's prow, aimed always at Lovey Doll's snug port of call. She had, when first encountering the phenomenon, assumed men carried such hardened rods at all times inside their pants; the discovery that its capacity for change was an essential characteristic of the organ fascinated her. Lovey Doll's naïveté at fourteen had long since turned to semiscornful bemusement; she was now just one month shy of seventeen.

"Your position, please," Nevis said.

Lovey Doll turned and strode to the podium, aware that Nevis watched every enticing jiggle of her buttocks as she mounted the steps, aware of his eyes on her bosom as she lay down among the pillows and propped an arm behind her head. Her hair was still up, but Nevis liked to do the unpinning. It was remarkable, the things men liked to do, apart from the actual act of fornicating. They were like children, really, and Lovey Doll still had not divined the reason why they chose to be that way.

Feeling Moses' rod inside her was uncomfortable at worst, a sweaty bore at best. The attraction she felt for men lay not in their foolish probings and pantings, but in their ability to buy for her the things she truly wanted: fine things, expensive things, clothing for the most part, and trinketry to adorn herself with. If a thing was not of direct use to Lovey Doll, she had no interest in it. Nevis's painting-in-progress, for instance: she saw that he was talented with his brushes and colors, and was developing a fine likeness of her on canvas, but it was nothing Lovey Doll could ever use, nothing she wished to touch with her fingers, her body; she couldn't wrap a painted canvas around herself and admire the result in a mirror, couldn't draw pleasure from the feel of it against her precious skin.

She failed to see why art had monetary value at all, since its purpose was nothing more than to be hung on a wall and be gawked at by men Lovey Doll wouldn't touch with the longest of poles. It was one more example of the stupidity of males, of their pathetic infatuation with female flesh. It was ridiculous, but apparently it was the way of the world, and Lovey Doll would use it to her advantage. She didn't doubt she would one day marry a rich man, a very rich man. She deserved no less.

Nevis was approaching her, his long fingers literally twitching with anticipation. "I'll just let down your hair," he said, a trifle breathlessly. He proceeded, with care and delicacy, to do so. Lovey Doll tried hard to contain her impatience. Such protracted fussing

as this infuriated her after more than a few minutes. Nevis's hands
fluttered hither and thither like moths, accomplishing little with
their excess of motion, their nervous tremblings. She could feel his
breath on her face and shoulders, and was unaccountably irritated
by it.

Eventually she rejected Nevis and his infatuated bumbling.
"Back!" she ordered, and completed the unpinning herself. This
brought Nevis close to her again, for the purpose of arranging the
long swatches of hair in such a manner as to emphasize, rather
than conceal, her roundly audacious breasts. The grand finale to
this traditional rite was approaching. This was Lovey Doll's seventh sitting for Nevis Dunnigan, and she knew him through and
through.

"Oh, Lovey Doll...," he moaned, collapsing beside her, his heavily
oiled head sliding between what Lovey Doll insisted on calling her
bubbies. This was Nevis's favored resting place. She had to inhale
the scent of his cheap pomade for several minutes at the beginning
of every sitting, before his professional instincts dragged him away
to the easel and his work. She knew the application of paint to canvas would be anticlimactic for Nevis, following contact with her
skin, her odor, her aura of utterly approachable yet frustratingly
distant sensuality. The next hour or two would be without interest
for Lovey Doll also. The high point of each sitting was the ludicrous
positioning of Nevis's head on her chest, a tableau maintained for
only a short while before work on the canvas commenced.

The painting was titled "Venus Revealed." Lovey Doll thought it
appropriate that she represent the goddess of love. She had never
loved anyone, but love, at least in the abstract, was an important
thing, the thing that made the world go around, she'd heard, so
Lovey Doll was pleased to personify so essential a cosmic ingredient. Her true name was Griselda, but she had always known she
deserved better.

As he worked, Nevis forced himself to be less concerned with
Lovey Doll as a female; she was a model, *his* model; a collection of
planes, masses and lines, an exercise in chiaroscuro, in draftsman-
ship and painterly execution. She was himself, or a part of himself;
there was just as much of Nevis Dunnigan on the canvas as there
was of Lovey Doll Pines. He thought his efforts worthy of comparison with similar studies by Ingres and Delacroix; Rembrandt's
nudes, and Rubens's, were far too fat. Lovey Doll was perfectly pro-

portioned, despite her shortness of stature (she barely reached his shoulder, and Nevis was by no means tall), a real little pocket Venus. He would never find another like her—never.

It hurt him to love her as he did. Lovey Doll had made it clear she believed herself destined for the bed of a rich man. She made no bones about finding and winning such a millionaire, be he old or ugly or senile; the money was the thing. "Everything could be wonderful," she told him, "with lots of cash to spend." It was a deplorable philosophy, but he forgave her, as he forgave her lack of interest in him. She knew nothing of art, could read only with difficulty, was ignorant of most things in the world, yet very pleased with herself nonetheless.

It distressed Nevis to know she would probably get exactly what she wanted, and would in all likelihood enjoy to the utmost the riches she sought and found. Lovey Doll was without morality or scruple, was not even terribly intelligent, but the shape of her luscious little body, the perfect Cupid's bow of her upper lip, these things alone made him love her. It was humiliating, this love he had for a girl far beneath him intellectually and spiritually, but Nevis couldn't help himself.

He had heard that in Paris, artists routinely made lovers of their models; it was *de rigueur,* traditional, an indispensable part of the artist's life. Even in New York City it happened, but not to Nevis. He had studied himself in mirrors and made innumerable self-portraits in an attempt to discover why it was that women, especially young and pretty women, had no wish to be his partner. Even proposals of marriage had never advanced his cause beyond thwarted gropings and sweatily nervous hand-holding. He tried impressing females with his talent for painting, showed them everything he had ever produced, from charcoal sketches to oils the size of a dining room table. They always murmured polite phrases of appreciation, but he could tell they wanted to be gone from his studio, gone from the painful, anxious nearness of him.

In time, he saw he must do something different to win female companionship. He must leave New York, leave the civilized world and go west for inspiration, depict the crude characters and imposing landscape beyond the Mississippi. Catlin and Bingham had done it, and so could Dunnigan. He would become famous, and fame would bring its own reward. He had faint hope that this might be achieved before Lovey Doll found and wed some cattle baron or railroad magnate, but didn't such gentlemen reside in New York or Chicago or San Francisco? Lovey Doll was stranded far from these marital hunting grounds, for the moment at least.

Nevis had been in the west almost four months, and the work before him now was his first commission in all that time: a likeness of Venus to be hung in a smoke-filled barroom in Kansas City. Nevis felt his talent was deserving of a place in the Louvre, not the Plainsman Saloon, among brimming cuspidors and the ubiquitous smell of beer. No customer in such a setting would appreciate what he had accomplished. The common reaction would be a silent wish in the mind of the cowboy critic to be lying beside Venus, fondling her bosom, the very thing Nevis wanted for himself, he had to admit.

Nail in His Feet and Bleeding Heart of Jesus took a particular interest in Drew when their grandfather brought him to the mission. They sat beside his bed until Father Zamudio shooed them away, as he had shooed away Smart Crow Making Mischief without allowing the old man access to his grandchildren. Smart Crow was forever creating a disturbance at the mission, trying every other month to lure the boys away with him.

Drew had been delivered after sundown, was placed immediately in the dormitory and promptly fell asleep, watched over by the silent boys. He awoke the following afternoon, and found himself surrounded by empty beds. An elderly Indian woman seated beside him fetched Father Zamudio, who brought to Drew's bedside a bowl of steaming broth, or soup, Drew couldn't figure out which; he gulped it down anyway, watched by the priest.

When the bowl was empty, Father Zamudio asked, "What things do you remember before today?"

To Drew's ears it was a nonsensical question; he could remember his whole life, practically, given enough time. He said nothing.

"Before this time," the priest said, "do you remember how it is you came to be at San Bartolomeo?"

"I never heard of it," Drew said.

"That is this place. You remember nothing?"

"No," Drew told him. He didn't want anyone going out into the mountains to look for his father. Drew preferred Morgan dead, unable to betray him again. It was simpler that way. He felt no shame about the lie.

"You do not remember how it was the Indian found you?"

"No." ·

"Your name?"

"John."

"Your family name?"

"... Bones."

"Bones?" Drew nodded. The name had sprung into his head from nowhere, and he found he liked it.

"You came from Santa Fe?"

"No."

"You remember this?"

"From somewhere else. Not there. I don't remember where, though."

He didn't want anyone asking questions in Santa Fe, prompting recollections of the family that came to town on the stagecoach and left again the same day in a wagon. Someone would recall the Kindreds, and Drew wanted that name removed from his life. It was a lie to protect himself from his immediate past. It was no one's business but his own. He was quite proud, in fact, to have lied so readily and convincingly to the man with the doleful face and long black skirts. The priest had very dark eyes that seldom blinked. Drew knew he was being studied, evaluated, and this made him nervous. He made up his mind the man would never learn anything from him. It would be a kind of game. He knew he had to match the gaze of the priest, not glance guiltily away from those darkly probing eyes. It was important to win this game of looking and looking back.

Father Zamudio believed nothing the boy told him. The boy had not suffered greatly in the wilderness surrounding the mission, was neither starving nor perishing from thirst. Wash the dust from him and he would be no worse for his experience, whatever that might have been. He lied well, without fear, and it was this strength in untruth that Father Zamudio found disturbing. Something bad must have happened, something the boy felt had to be kept hidden. Perhaps Smart Crow should have been invited inside just this once to explain the circumstances, but that would have resulted in the old man haranguing his grandsons and Father Zamudio himself at close range, something everyone but Smart Crow wanted to avoid.

The two grandsons were already curious about the young stranger Smart Crow brought in from the mountains, and this

might prove advantageous. A boy might talk to other boys, where
that same boy refused to answer an adult, or lied, as this John
Bones did.

"You are strong now? You can walk?"

"Yes."

"Come with me."

He led Drew around the mission. San Bartolomeo was a hollow
square of adobe brick to the west of the Jemez range. A heavy wood-
en gate beneath the arch in one wall lent the place a fortress air.
One side of the square was a chapel, the second a classroom in
which another priest, Father Dominguez, was teaching a lesson in
Spanish. A kitchen and a dormitory formed the square's third side,
and flanking the gate on the fourth were a storeroom and the quarters of Fathers Zamudio and Dominguez. These two were the only
whites; everyone else was Indian.

Drew was taken through a small door in the gate and shown the
gardens of corn and squash. A short distance beyond lay several
rows of adobe houses such as Drew had seen in Santa Fe, with Indians moving among the deep shadows inside, most of them women,
Drew noted. Everyone but the priests wore simple cotton garments
of white, and all the males wore their hair cut short, like white
men. Drew didn't think they looked like Indians at all, certainly not
like any he'd been expecting. The sole exception so far had been the
old man who had rescued him, the one with the fingernails growing
through his hand. Drew asked Father Zamudio about that, and
learned the name of his savior.

"His hand is this way because it is the hand of a murderer. With
this hand he killed his own son. He holds it so, in the fist, to punish
himself. Many years now he has done this, but the nails still grow.
His regret is sincere, I think. How many men would do this to their
own flesh for what they have done?"

"Why did he kill his son?"

"Why? Because his son became a follower of Christ, and brought
his own sons here to learn our ways. Smart Crow is too proud of his
past to accept this. He was in his youth a warrior who killed many
men, Indians and whites. He is Apache. You have heard of these?"

"They like to fight."

"He tries to win his grandsons from us, to teach them the old
ways of his people. They do not wish to leave, so this makes him
angry, with them, with me, with things he cannot make different.

Soon he will die, without finding Christ, but we have the boys. You will meet them and talk. They have English."

"All right."

"Smart Crow has never come with mules before. Where did he find them?"

"I don't know," Drew lied. "I thought they were his."

"He will come back and ask again for at least one of his grandsons. He thinks he has paid for one by bringing you here. That is the Indian way, one soul exchanged for another, like clay pots."

"Oh," said Drew, disappointed to learn he was just an item of barter.

He was left alone for the remainder of the afternoon, free to wander at will inside and outside the mission. Drew's explorations revealed little that Father Zamudio hadn't already shown him, and he realized he would have to leave. Drew didn't believe in God anymore, but found it unsettling anyway to be within a Roman Catholic institution. Morgan and Sylvie had never said a good word about Roman Catholics. Drew understood all Catholics were the servants of a man who lived in a big town called Rome in another country across the sea. This man, a powerful king of some kind, was called the Pope, and he slept in a huge room filled with dazzling treasure given to him by his servants worldwide, who feared they would be excluded from heaven if they did not contribute wealth to the Pope's vast palace of marble and gold.

Drew couldn't see any gold at San Bartolomeo; presumably it had all been given to the Pope. Morgan had always said Catholic churches kept some of it back to gild their multitude of images and statuary, but the life-sized crucifix in the chapel was carved from wood, the Christ figure painted in very realistic colors; there wasn't even any gold paint that Drew could see.

The Indians encountered on his wanderings around the mission either stared at him expressionlessly as he passed them by, or smiled, but the smiles were largely confined to the very young. He definitely did not belong there, and would have to leave as soon as he possibly could.

Father Dominguez, short and round, with a beard far exceeding in length the beard of Father Zamudio, fetched Drew to supper late in the day. He was escorted to the kitchen and given a place at one of the crude benches, seated between two Indian boys. Grace was given in Spanish by Father Zamudio. Drew understood nothing but the name John Bones, mentioned twice; apparently thanks were being given to God for his safe rescue from the wilderness. The name of Smart Crow Making Mischief was not mentioned, so far as Drew could tell.

There was a peculiar flat bread to eat, and corn, plus a kind of cornmeal mush that Drew found uncomfortably hot, but he was hungry enough to eat two bowlfuls, his mouth quietly aflame. The boys on either side of him, obviously twins, began talking, their manner excited yet shy.

"I am Nail in His Feet. This is my brother."

"My name is Bleeding Heart of Jesus."

"Our father named us. Our grandfather killed him because he found Christ. Our mother was already dead."

"She died putting us in the world," Bleeding Heart of Jesus explained.

"Grandfather was angry with the names and killed our father," Nail in His Feet said. "He says we must go with him and learn the old ways, but Father Zamudio will not let him inside the gate."

"He would never leave if he got inside," Bleeding Heart of Jesus assured Drew. "He is a very crazy old man who will never take Christ into himself."

"We feel very sorry for him."

Drew said, "Well, he wasn't so crazy he didn't save me."

"It was to make Father Zamudio give us up to him," Nail in His Feet insisted. "We know this about him. Many times he has come with deer, but Father Zamudio never gave us back to him for the meat."

"We will not go outside the walls, or Grandfather would take us away with him to the mountains."

"We would never see this place again."

"It was very funny to see Grandfather lose his deer and not get us," Bleeding Heart of Jesus said, politely hiding a smile behind his hand.

"Why were you in the mountains?" asked his brother.

"I don't remember," Drew said.

"Your name is Bones, truly?"

"Yes."

"That is *huesos* in Spanish."

"What is it in Apache?"

"We do not know," Nail in His Feet said proudly.

"We have never learned it," Bleeding Heart of Jesus stated. "It is the tongue of unbelief. We do not want it."

"No," agreed Nail in His Feet; he added, "You are a believer?"

"Yes," Drew said, sensing the need for another lie. "It was God that told your grandfather where to find me."

The twins nodded in unison. "Yes," said Bleeding Heart of Jesus, "that is what happened, but even such a thing as this does not make grandfather seek our Lord, which makes us sad."

"Very sad," emphasized Nail in His Feet.

"It's a shame," Drew agreed.

He liked the brothers. They were several years older than himself, the handsomest boys he had ever seen. Their hair hung straight to a line above their ears and eyebrows in a bowl snip, the kind of trim Sylvie had given Drew when he was little. Bleeding Heart of Jesus and Nail in His Feet gave the impression of being very young and very old at the same time. It was a pity they accepted so wholeheartedly the teachings of the church; Drew would have liked to have them as his friends, but such a thing was not possible in the light of his atheism. Drew took his nonbelief very seriously, suspecting it was the key to his new feelings about everything. The chasm between himself and the twin brothers was wide enough, they being Indians, but their piety made it wider still.

"Father Dominguez and Father Zamudio say we will take the word of God to our people one day when we are old enough," said Nail in His Feet.

Drew didn't see how this was possible, since neither boy spoke Apache.

"We wish that day to be soon," Bleeding Heart of Jesus declared, his voice bright with conviction.

Drew ate, not knowing what to say.

"Will you be here with us a long time?" asked Nail in His Feet.

"I don't know. I don't know anything anymore."

"God will show you what you must do. He has protected you for a purpose. The reason is not known yet."

"You will know one day," Bleeding Heart of Jesus solemnly assured him.

"I hope so," Drew mumbled.

They dogged his steps the following day. Drew couldn't understand the brothers' fascination with him. Both boys were friendly, cheerful, clearly somewhat in awe of his fame as a person of mysterious origin, and they seemed eager to explain their own exclusive status within the mission.

"We are Apache," Bleeding Heart of Jesus told Drew.

"Mescalero Apache," amended Nail in His Feet.

"The worst kind." His brother sighed, clearly ashamed.

"Then what kind are the rest of them here?" Drew asked.

"They are not Apache; they are Pueblo."

"They do not like us."

"Grandfather has killed many of them a long time ago."

"Grandfather was a war chief. He was very bad."

"They will not let us forget."

"No one will talk with us but Father Zamudio and Father Dominguez."

"We are being tested. We see this and forgive them."

"We are being made strong by their silence. We have English, Like Father Zamudio. He teaches no one else this. We are special."

"Special for the work that will be ours."

"There are no other Mescalero Apaches anywhere like us."

"No, there are none."

"We will make the others become like us when we are ready."

"Except Grandfather. He will never become like us."

"No, not Grandfather, but he will die soon."

Drew smiled at them both. He liked them very much, and felt sorry for them.

In accompanying him everywhere, at all times, they were able to avoid classes others their age were obliged to attend. Drew attributed this apparent privilege to the brothers' unique position as a pair of ecclesiastical teachers' pets, until Nail in His Feet said, "Father Zamudio has been angry with us today."

"Why?"

"Because you will not tell us things he must know."

"But I don't remember anything," Drew protested.

"That is what we said to him, but he is angry."

"He makes a big anger," Bleeding Heart of Jesus said, turning down the corners of his mouth.

"He told you to ask me about who I am?"

The boys had indeed been pestering him to try and recall his life prior to arrival at San Bartolomeo; it was Drew's only real source of irritation with them, apart from their prattling about God.

"Yes, many times. He must know the truth, he says. Father

Zamudio believes you have not told him the truth. We do not say this."

"No, we do not say this," echoed his brother.

Drew was insulted that Father Zamudio doubted his story. It had been an excellent lie, in Drew's opinion, and he further resented the way Nail in His Feet and Bleeding Heart of Jesus were being used as spies. It wasn't right. It was low-down, sneaky behavior, altogether typical of a religion that made people give their money to the Pope. Even a madman like Morgan had been correct in his assessment of Roman Catholics.

"I already told him I don't remember, so he's got no call getting mad with you two. You tell him that."

The twins exchanged a fearful look.

"He makes a big anger," Bleeding Heart of Jesus reiterated.

During the silence that followed, Drew wondered how Clay would have handled a situation like this, and was shocked to discover he had no idea what Clay would have felt, said or done. Clay had become an abstraction, a face and a voice made less distinct with the passage of time. Drew had known, ever since leaving Morgan to rant at the sky, that he was on his own, but now he knew exactly how lonely his position was. Zoe and Clay were far away, probably no more capable of recalling his features than he was of recalling theirs. Watching the brothers shake their heads over the prospect of confronting Father Zamudio, Drew was even more certain than on his first day that he had no business at the mission.

"The road outside," he said, pointing to the gate. "Does it go to Santa Fe?"

"Yes, to the east is Santa Fe," Nail in His feet said, his features brightening as the subject was changed.

"But it is less far to a place the other way."

"What place?"

"We do not know its name," Bleeding Heart of Jesus said. "It is just a place."

"How far?"

"We do not know. Sometimes wagons pass by from there."

"If it's less far than to Santa Fe, how far's Santa Fe?"

"We do not know. We have never been there."

"Could I walk it?"

"To Santa Fe? I think you could not."

"No, the other place."

"We do not know."

The twins appeared a little shamefaced by their ignorance. Drew smiled at them both. "That's all right. I was just asking. It doesn't matter."

They sat together that evening to eat as usual, but no one spoke. Bleeding Heart of Jesus and Nail in His Feet knew that in revealing Father Zamudio's request for information they had lost their friendship with John Bones, yet keeping the truth from him another day would have caused them even worse torment. The brothers were without guile or cynicism; they would not blame Father Zamudio for their sadness, so it must be they who had done wrong and caused such dejection at the table.

Drew found it easy enough to remain awake after the dormitory lamps were extinguished. Sheer excitement over what he proposed doing that night kept him alert. He was not bored while the hours passed; there was too much to contemplate, too many possibilities were invading his thoughts. The mission had been a way station, a place along the pathway to his future. He had not asked to be brought there, and he would not ask to leave.

When he judged the hour to be around midnight, Drew rose and silently dressed himself. He stole through the dormitory and crossed the square to the kitchen. There was no need of locks within the precincts of San Bartolomeo, and he crept inside. He emptied a sack of beans onto one of the tables, then began filling it with such dry foodstuffs as could be hauled away and eaten without need of pots and pans. Most of his supplies could be located by touch; Drew had inspected the kitchen pantry closely late that afternoon, until chased out by an Indian woman. He filled two goatskin water bags and slung them over his shoulder, then picked up the bulging sack.

Fully laden, he crossed the moonlit square and carefully lifted the bar across the gate's small door. Stepping through, he found himself face-to-face with Smart Crow. Drew should have felt surprise, but somehow did not. Smart Crow held out his bagged hand. Drew thought he was trying to shake hands with him, like a white man, saying good-bye maybe, but that was not Smart Crow's intent at all.

The drawstring holding the bag about Smart Crow's wrist was sliced with a long-bladed knife. A jerk of his arm shook the bag free, and Smart Crow held the pierced hand before his own face for inspection. Apparently satisfied, he knelt by the doorway and set his curling nails against the lower sill. Drew watched without breathing as the four fingernails were hacked off with one blow to each, then the curved thumbnail which, since it penetrated no flesh, could be removed at the thumb tip.

Smart Crow stood up and showed his hand to Drew, who continued to watch as Smart Crow's fingers began to flex. Without assistance from his other hand, Smart Crow withdrew his truncated nails through the hand they had punctured years before. Released, the nails were set against the sill as before and shortened further. Smart Crow twisted his hand this way and that beneath Drew's nose, making sure he saw it well. There was surprisingly little blood. Then the Indian passed through the doorway and closed it behind himself.

Drew heard the bar being replaced, and did not know what to make of the wordless ritual he had seen. He assumed Smart Crow Making Mischief wished to see his grandsons, a need Drew could sympathize with; it wasn't right, the way Father Zamudio had kept them apart. Drew hoped Smart Crow understood Spanish, or his visit would be wasted. He wondered how Smart Crow would find his grandsons in the darkness of the dormitory, then decided there was no point in worrying about that; it was none of his business after all. Smart Crow had done him a favor by saving him from Morgan, and now Drew had returned that favor by allowing Smart Crow access to his own flesh and blood. That must be why he had withdrawn the fingernails from his hand—the importance of the occasion: reunification with his family.

Drew was almost envious, and had to make himself turn away from the gate. He began walking west, down the road to a place without a name. He wished he had a gun, but acknowledged you couldn't have everything.

Smart Crow stood in the square and watched his own shadow, consulting with it. He would find his son's sons with the help of his shadow self, which would lead the way, but first he must open his mind to the many presences in so confined a space. He wished to know where the blackrobes slept. These men, the tall thin one and the short fat one, had corrupted his grandsons, continuing the damage already done to them by their fool of a father, whom Smart Crow suspected of having secretly become a woman himself when his wife died giving birth. Only a woman would have surrendered sons that way.

Smart Crow was able to tell from his distant glimpses of the boys over the years that the blackrobes were turning them to women too. They would grow breasts, and their penises would fall off. It was a shameful fate, but it could be avoided if only they were taken from this place of unnatural magic. There was a sickness here, the sickness of the Dead Man Flying on Wood, which had plagued Smart Crow's people for many generations; only recently had some of them begun to yield, his own son-who-became-a-woman being among the first. Smart Crow wept at the memory of such perversion. It had been necessary to kill his son in order to save him from the blackrobes, and then he had made himself suffer the pain of nails growing through his hands, since no man could kill his own son without himself suffering, even if the killing had been just.

All the suffering and perversion would be undone this night. His shadow told him in which direction the boys lay sleeping, and the blackrobes too. Smart Crow felt the spirit of his son stirring in the new hand held before him, the hand that would turn the world right side up again. It was Smart Crow's luck to have as his destiny this righting of a great wrong. The sun tomorrow would shine upon a different world.

Smart Crow lifted his knife, a white man's knife, admittedly superior. It would spill blood from the opened throats of the blackrobes without even waking them.

10

Bryce and Zoe reached Pueblo, Colorado. Bryce spent a day ascertaining the availability of stone from a local quarry, then set up a store in the back of his wagon at the edge of town. On his first day of business he took in three orders: headstones for an infant death from unknown causes, a victim of heart failure, and the unfortunate loser in a drunken gunfight. It was clear the area needed Bryce Aspinall's professional services.

He would journey no further, he said, then he asked Zoe to be his wife, adding, "You don't have to answer right this minute, you can think about it awhile. I'll wait."

Think about it she did. Zoe's capacity for honesty with herself obliged her to draw up a mental list of her suitor's strengths and weaknesses. She felt no guilt over this; a decision of such magnitude required hardheaded calculation, plus and minus.

First, the good things: Bryce had never attempted to touch her, unlike Hassenplug, unlike Tully. He appeared to care for her baby, had never expressed a disparaging remark over the blue birthmark, even took the time to cradle Omie in his arms when Zoe's attentions were elsewhere. He did not drink. He seemed intent on working hard in a respectable field of employment, with every likelihood of success. He promised he would build her a real home when this became possible. He seemed genuinely to care for her and Omie both. She was indebted to him for the way he buried Tully without condemnation and carried Zoe away from the scene of that incident. And he was the first man ever to ask for her hand.

Against this powerful current drawing her to him stood two mighty rocks. The first was her need to find Clay and Drew. If she settled in Pueblo, what chance did she have of ever finding them? She could only trust to fate and hope the nation's westering winds sooner or later would bring her brothers to her. The second obstacle to acceptance was, if anything, even larger: she did not love him. Zoe didn't know why this was so; if ever a man was deserving of love, it was Bryce Aspinall. She set aside his homeliness (Zoe would never again trust a handsome man such as Tully) and tried instead to isolate that aspect of Bryce which told her this was not a man she could love. Zoe devoted considerable thought to it, but could arrive at no specific answer. She simply did not love him, or see how love might develop between them. She felt affection, and no more than that.

To arrive at a decision, therefore, Zoe ignored her own needs. Her choice would be made for the sake of Omie; whatever was best for Omie would bring with it the resolution to Zoe's dilemma. Viewed from this perspective, her options were reduced to just one. Seven hours after hearing Bryce's proposal, Zoe accepted. She did so without any sense of compromise too large to deny her a measure of happiness. There was no reason, in Zoe's opinion, why the marriage should not be bearable. She resigned herself to it not with regret, but with a feeling of relief at having made a decision. Once and for all, she would sever ties with an unsatisfactory past, without binding herself to some risky or unpredictable future. Bryce was a good man, and Zoe didn't doubt she was a good girl. Despite everything, it would work.

After the wedding, Bryce located a small house for them to rent not far from the wagon-workshop. Zoe found herself happy enough with life, but she had formed the habit of mentally checking over her shoulder for approaching calamity. None came, and she wondered if maybe she was free to enjoy the new life that was hers, because she had earned it with pain. It seemed an appropriate attitude, so she embraced it, and became happier still for most of her waking hours.

Bryce worked hard and gave every cent to Zoe. "You go ahead and hold the purse strings and apron strings both," he told her, "and leave the hammer and chisel work to me." She often watched him marking with chalk the names and dates and floral edging that every headstone, even the simplest, required. Zoe admired the way Bryce tapped lightly but confidently at the flat surfaces with his tools, flawlessly executing the commonplace inscriptions of death and remembrance. Bryce had no time to set up fake stones as examples of his skill; business was so brisk his works-in-progress were the best recommendation he could have placed before the public.

In the evening he walked the hundred yards or so to their home, and was served the plain fare he preferred, a fortunate circumstance, since Zoe's culinary talent was limited, even for that time and place. When darkness came, Bryce read to her from the tales of Sir Walter Scott, or Zoe read to Bryce, alternating chapters of this rip-roaring stuff. *Ivanhoe* was far and away Zoe's favorite of the several volumes they had shared since marrying. Her own affection for Bryce in no way compared with the love between Ivanhoe and Rowena, but she was content; Zoe would not let niggling doubt mar her first enjoyment of living since she was very small.

When Bryce approached her in the marriage bed she allowed him the one simple thing he wanted satisfaction in. The act was over with soon enough not to interfere with her overall peace of mind. He always fell asleep before her, and it was during the hiatus between Bryce's first gentle snore and the final closing of Zoe's eyes that those doubts, the few and formless kind that still bedeviled her, came and stood about the bed to express misgiving.

The marshal of Keyhoe, Kansas, was Grover Stunce, and he oftentimes felt himself inadequate for the task. He was forty-one years old, and did not like running up against drunken cowboys. He found the work repetitive and pointless, since the same fools always showed up, drunk again, after a night in the cells. Once, a cowhand on a spree had resisted arrest and blown a hole in Grover's calf with his .45 before being cut down by the marshal's own gun. The killing bothered Grover for many weeks afterward. He was neither a brave man nor a coward, but he saw the need for civil order, and in Keyhoe there were few men seeking after his job.

Grover had a powerful sense of communal obligation, but he also had a wife. Mrs. Stunce had refused to let him touch her since the day of the shooting that brought him home with bloodied pants.

"Why should it be you that does this filthy work!" she wished to know, and Grover could only repeat that no one else seemed to have the stomach for such a calling. "Then share it!" she instructed him. Grover was prepared to admit she had a good point, so he hung in the window of his office a hand-lettered sign offering gainful employment to anyone prepared to wear the badge of a deputy marshal. The sign remained in his window for eighteen days, then was brought inside late one evening by a tall individual cradling a sawed-off shotgun.

"This offer still good?" he asked.

"It is."

"I'll take it."

"That depends. It's not a job for just anyone."

The light in Grover's office was poor; only after close scrutiny of the face before him did it become apparent there were badly-healed-over holes through both cheeks. It was not a pleasant face, the jaw hanging like a bucket, the eyes like pistol bores, cheekbones like a hungry Indian's, and all of this framed, as it were, by the dark halo of a wide-brimmed preacher's hat supported on two jugged ears. Grover reminded himself that handsomeness was not a requisite for the position.

"I'll take it anyway," the applicant said, and Grover didn't argue.

"That your only piece?" he asked, nodding at the sawed-off.

"Yes."

"Revolver's the standard sidearm in law work."

"I'll stick with this. My name's Dugan."

"Been on the right side of the law at all times, Dugan?"

"Yes."

"I like to set an example. I won't take on a man who's been convicted of any felonious activity. A clean slate is what I ask for, and honest ways, also I can't use a man looking to make a pile of cash from doing what we do here. It won't be a stepping-stone to riches, this office."

"Didn't think it was," said Clay. "Am I hired?"

Grover let him wait a moment longer. He was not altogether happy with the situation. "Got your own horse?"

"Got a good one, and a spare."

"Go on over to Merton's Livery, just across the street. Tell them you're working for me and he'll put up your mounts, care of the county. The same doesn't apply to room and board. There's a num-

ber of rooming houses that charge a reasonable rate and are clean.
You take your pick."

"What's wrong with here?"

"Here?"

"That's a bed, isn't it?"

Clay aimed his eyes at the rawhide-sprung frame and mattress in
the office corner, under a locked rifle rack.

"That's just for when we have to guard a prisoner overnight if
there's a lynch party wants him out and hung. You can't live here
full time, it's an office. There's no amenities."

"Where do the prisoners shit?"

"In a pan, generally, and you empty it in the outhouse next door;
they don't mind."

"Then I'll just skip the pan."

Grover felt that matters had been settled far too quickly, but was
not inclined to delay official approval of the would-be deputy. He
outlined briefly the responsibilities of the office, then added, "You a
drinking man, Dugan?"

"No."

"That's one thing I won't tolerate, especially on duty. A position of
authority in a fair-sized town like this one, you need to watch out
for public opinion and stay on the good side of it, hear me?"

"I said I didn't drink."

"Well, all right. There's just certain things have to be spelled out
clear so there's no misunderstanding."

"I didn't misunderstand."

"All right, then. Now, there's supposed to be a piece of paper you
sign after I swear you in, but I don't believe I can lay my hand on it
right this minute, so we'll take care of that another day and go
ahead with the swearing in. Raise your right hand."

Clay repeated the oath Grover spouted, and lowered his hand.
Both men looked at each other. Clay raised an eyebrow.

"Badge?"

Grover went home with something approaching a spring in his
step. This was the second-best news he could possibly have conveyed to Mrs. Stunce; first best would be a declaration that he
intended returning to his original line of work, as a wheelwright.
That was the work he had done when he married Sophie. She was
his second wife, quite a bit younger than himself. His first, and
their two children, had been taken by cholera.

"Deputy?" said Mrs. Stunce with some disbelief.

"A real deputy, looks mean enough for two."

"You're sure now."

"Of course I'm sure. I hired the man. You can walk down and meet him tomorrow if you like."

"You should have invited him home for supper. That would have been the decent thing." Mrs. Stunce was becoming quite excited. "I could have dished up something extra for a real deputy!"

"He might not be the inviting-to-supper type, Sophie."

"What type is he?"

"Well, he's ... standoffish. Not one for socializing is my guess, but I'm sure he'll be just fine for the job. Dedicated, by God. Wants to sleep right there in the office. I think I got us a good one, Sophie, I do."

She permitted extensive intimate fondling that night, but would not allow full coitus until such time as she had seen for herself the caliber of this new deputy.

Clay took himself to the Ambrosia Eatery for a meal, and attracted considerable attention by placing his shotgun among the bowls and cutlery. A waiter asked him to remove the offending item, but Clay declined. "No, I'll just leave it there, thank you," he said, and proceeded to order from the menu. The waiter decided not to press his complaint; the man with the holes in his face had an intimidating air, and besides, he wore a deputy's badge.

His belly full, Clay strolled up and down Keyhoe's main street, inspecting his beat. There were fourteen saloons, so he would earn his pay. He visited each one in turn with his truncated shotgun, and introduced himself to the bartenders, most of whom tried to curry favor with the new deputy by offering drinks on the house. Clay refused politely.

He found his reaction to these establishments interesting. Clay's own intermittent encounters with alcohol since burning down Hassenplug's barn in Indiana had shown him liquor's appeal. The fact that scores of men chose to congregate in rooms reeking of tobacco and sweat and beer struck him as sad. He learned also that the whores who encouraged men to spend money on drink and themselves made him angry. Clay was a virgin still, and intended remaining that way until some virtuous woman who could ignore his appearance should cross his path.

His opinion of saloons and their floating populations was judgmental, puritanical in its overall condemnation. The trick to his playing a representative of the law lay in Clay's conviction that he was superior, in the moral sense, to every person inhabiting such places as were found along the street. If any one of them gave him the least amount of trouble, Clay felt fully capable of arresting that person, and in the case of armed resistance, would shoot dead the offending party without a qualm.

It was not to happen that first night. When the bars finally closed, he marched himself up and down the street one last time before returning to the marshal's office to divest himself of coat and hat and lie down on the prepared mattress, not the most comfortable he'd ever slept on, nor the least. He set his weapon beside him, both barrels loaded as always, and turned out the lamp. In the ceiling above him, Clay saw projected no future, no past, no hope or joy. He was, in his way, content.

Mrs. Stunce came to evaluate her husband's choice. She chose subterfuge over directness to accomplish this, arriving at the office around noon with a basket of food for both men. Grover happened to be absent at the time, and Mrs. Stunce took this as good fortune. She wished to run her eye over this new associate, with a long-term view to encouraging him in notions of replacing her husband rather than continuing as his deputy.

She introduced herself with a smile, and the smile broadened as she began to appreciate how unusual Dugan's appearance was; the holes in his cheeks were positively mesmerizing in their ugliness and the questions they raised concerning their origin. Dugan's face registered neither pleasure nor annoyance at her presence. He nodded as she gave her name, and thanked her quietly for the lunch.

Mrs. Stunce shook her gaze free of his pierced face and settled on his weapon, lying before Dugan on the desktop. His shotgun had the uncompromising bluntness of an implement of slaughter. It was made for cutting men in half, nothing else, and caused her a moment of extreme discomfort. Guns of any kind made her nervous; those without the adornment of scrollwork or ivory handles to soften their look of deadliness were the ugliest of all. A tall ugly man with a short ugly gun was her firm impression. She could not have guessed his age, but sensed he was far younger than his face and manner suggested.

"May I ask where you're from, Mr. Dugan?"

"Schenectady."

"That is in the east?"

"New York."

"A fascinating city, I'm told."

"New York State."

"Oh. And you have chosen law enforcement for your career in the west."

"You might say, or it chose me. One or the other."

"I see," said Mrs. Stunce, but she did not see at all. Grover had become marshal only because two highly skilled brothers had set up a wheelwright's shop in competition with him a year ago and quickly stolen his business away. She could not understand why any man would willingly choose such work, if there were alternatives to so dangerous a field. The marshal before Grover had been killed while trying to arrest a thief, who seconds later was gunned down by a bystander anxious for justice and a reputation for man-killing. This person then left town without a hand being raised against him, since he had justifiably avenged the shooting of a lawman.

It was everything Sophie Stunce loathed, this policing of the town, and it was clear to her, looking into Dugan's dark yet cold eyes, that he, not Grover, should be in sole charge of such work.

"Is it your intention to become marshal yourself someday, Mr. Dugan?"

"Not necessarily."

Mrs. Stunce decided she would assist Dugan to replace her husband. Once out of law work, Grover would never return, not even if the office fell vacant again; Sophie would see to that.

"You have a very determined air about you, Mr. Dugan. I believe you'll do very well."

"I believe you're right."

Sophie chose to ignore the possibility that she was being mocked. Despising the man would not serve her plans.

"I won't wait for Mr. Stunce. Please tell him I dropped by."

"He'll see the basket and make that conclusion anyway, ma'am, even if I'm not here."

"Good day to you."

"And you, ma'am."

She slammed the door behind her. Clay wondered if he'd met an enemy or a friend. Either way, it didn't matter. Somehow he felt impervious to all influences working upon him, for or against. The job he held was exactly right for Clay Dugan. He didn't know why he felt it was so, assumed in a lazy fashion it was evidence of destiny at work, or some such. His sense of invulnerability, whatever its source, would serve him well in Keyhoe. There were bad men in town, inferior persons who sooner or later would step over the line and challenge him, if only to see if his ugliness masked a devil or a poor, tortured soul. He would show them which. It worried Clay not at all that he anticipated his first professional kill with serenity and certitude. If his life had any higher purpose than the one that naturally felt right, Clay couldn't see it, and had no use for it. He practiced loading and unloading his gun until Grover Stunce returned. Clay was very fast, his huge thumbs capable of cocking both hammers simultaneously.

11

On the first day, he ate and drank as he pleased. On the second, day he was more prudent, recalling the fate of the Kindreds. From the moment he saw his first dawn away from the mission, Drew had felt himself charged with a new-found sense of freedom. He wished he could have taken Nail in His Feet and Bleeding Heart of Jesus along with him, but they were probably better off with Smart Crow Making Mischief, who would knock the Christian stuffing out of them lickety-split, Drew bet.

He was on his own, and would make the best of it. He was again in the wilderness without a gun, but this time felt there was no danger. The ruts of the road were clear, obviously used every now and then; he might even be overtaken by some travelers who would allow him to join them. For the moment, though, he preferred to be alone. The twins had dogged his steps at San Bartolomeo, doing Father Zamudio's spy work. It was better to be as he was.

The third dawning found him less sure he had made the correct decision in simply walking away from the mission, instead of waiting for a passerby to invite him along. The road was less frequented by traffic than he had thought; maybe the ruts stayed looking fresh because there was never any rain to wash them away. He might keep going for days and still never hear the sound of hooves or wheels. It was an unsettling notion, and Drew didn't want to lose his brave face so soon. He still had food and water left—the second goatskin was about half full—but he couldn't deny that by the evening of the following day he would be in trouble. Until then, he would march on without a backward glance.

The fourth day passed slowly. The path wound among eroding hills speckled with low brush and cactus. The band of Drew's hat, formerly dark with sweat, began drying out. The water was gone, his supply of tortilla bread now a sack of crumbs, difficult to swallow without spit. He was covered from the crown of his hat to his shuffling boots with a fine dusting of alkali; the backs of his hands were gray with it, and his face; his eyes were redly rimmed, fiercely squinted against the omnipresent brightness. He wondered, for the first time, if he might die. It had not seemed a real possibility when he had Morgan for company, however demented he had been, but Drew's solitary state made it more probable, somehow.

That evening, lying by the side of the road as the sun set, he wanted to cry for himself, but was too dry for tears. He had not thought to steal matches from the mission, and so had no comfort or warmth from a fire; he had also neglected to steal a blanket. Each morning found him waking stiffer than the morning before from cold nights without covering. Drew decided that next time he stole, it would be with considerable forethought. If a crime was to take place, it should be well planned, a thing to be remembered later with pride. He kept the idea with him as something to entertain himself with in the deepening twilight.

Before the Kindreds left Illinois, the newspapers had been filled with reports of the James brothers and their exploits as robbers of banks and trains. Morgan and Sylvie had expressed contempt for such rogues, and Drew had imitated their attitude, but now Morgan and Sylvie were dead, killed by their belief in something they held dear, so it was natural for Drew to set aside his earlier condemnation of Frank and Jesse and their gang, and see such desperadoes in a new light. It was only a game, this sudden acceptance of robbery as a legitimate exercise in boldness and intellect, but Drew toyed with it for a long time, wishing himself an associate of the Missouri men, a prime contributor to their next escapade. He would carry many guns and make off with lots of cash. It was an exciting fantasy, and it kept him awake long after the coyotes began to howl. It must be a great thrill, Drew rationalized, to see your name in the newspapers, and have such poor fools as Morgan and Sylvie tut-tut over the adventures detailed in black and white for all the world to read.

The fifth day was brutal. Drew convinced himself it was not necessary to continue carrying the sack with its remaining morsels of food, yet he had no clear recollection of having dropped it by the wayside. He stumbled west by south, toward the place without a name Bleeding Heart of Jesus and Nail in His Feet had told him of. Had they lied, those holy Apaches, or simply been misinformed? Their talk of a place along the road would very likely be the death of him. Drew would never have started out in that direction had they not told him of the place. It wasn't fair that he might die because of a genuine belief in something that was not there.

He should have corroborated the existence of the place with father Zamudio, but that would have alerted the priest to Drew's plans for escape. If he died, it would be just too bad. He would laugh a very dry laugh, since he couldn't cry, in the moments preceding his death. Drew was very proud of his ability to consider things in this enlightened manner. He felt old and wise, even as his head threatened to separate from his neck with dehydration.

When he came in sight of an adobe dwelling that afternoon, he did not accept it as real. Not content merely to snatch him away from the world, death was teasing him with false hopes of survival. It was too cruel. He sat down in the road, as he had done several times already that day, and waited for the dwelling to fade from view in a ripple of heat haze. He would continue on, one tortured step at a time, after the mirage had disappeared. It was a contest of sorts, to see which would give in first, the boy or the apparition.

It was a perfectly ordinary house of mud brick, tempting the observer, with its mundane appearance, into believing it really was there. That belief would be turned mockingly aside if the place was approached, so Drew wasn't going to fall for it. His dignity and his physical weakness kept him in the middle of the road, and it was there he passed out, his eyes filled with the approaching figure of a woman as she moved from the deep shadow of the doorway toward him. He refused to believe, even as he heard the approaching slap of her sandals in the dust.

Drew's impressions of returning to the world were similar to his first moments inside the San Bartolomeo mission. There was a woman sitting nearby, a Mexican or an Indian woman, he wasn't sure, and he was in a bed, a very uncomfortable bed with a thin and scratchy mattress that rustled at the least movement. A man's head came into view behind the woman, a face with a high forehead and sweeping mustaches.

"You all right now, boy?"

These words came from somewhere beneath the mustaches. Drew asked himself what he might say in reply. He wished to be truthful, but was not sure what the answer should be, so he said nothing. Both man and woman faded from sight, growing smaller as he watched, until they were tiny, remote as figures in a tintype.

His second awakening came an indeterminate period of time later. The man was there alone, and he said to Drew, "More water, boy?" Drew could not recall having had any in the first place, but he nodded, unwilling to deny himself a chance for more. It occurred to him, as he felt tepid liquid poured into his open mouth, that the things surrounding him were real. I won't die now, he told himself, and slipped away again into welcoming darkness.

"Boy! Wake up there, boy!"

Drew woke up. He felt weak, able to move little more than his eyes. The man was back, his thick mustaches inches from Drew's face. Drew could smell tobacco on his breath.

"You need to be getting on your feet. Lying in bed, that's how you stay sick. Get up now."

Drew was hauled upright. He wore only his shirt. The man helped him step inside his pants, and tied his bootlaces. Drew's hat was placed on his head. "Outside now," he was told, and he headed for the brightness of the doorway.

In the dusty yard he halted, struck blind by sunlight pouring from a furnace wide as the sky. The man caught him as Drew slumped against a wall, then steered him to a split-log bench on the shady side of the house. The man fetched a dipper of water and made Drew drink all of it.

"What's your name, son?"

Drew really couldn't recall for a moment; was it Drew Dugan, Drew Kindred, or John Bones? His brain seemed incapable of the simplest function. "Drew," he said finally.

"Yancy Berdell."

The man extended his hand. Drew pumped it weakly. Berdell said, "Care to tell me how come you're where you are, in the shape you're in?"

Drew considered various lies and half-truths, and fell back on what he felt was becoming for him a tradition of caution. "I don't remember."

"The sun'll do that to a man, wipe his mind clean as a dinner plate. It'll come back to you, though, unless you got knocked on the head. Did that happen to you?"

"No."

"So you remember that much."

"There's no bump," Drew said, "that's how I know."

Yancy Berdell was grinning. Drew could tell the man saw right through him. "Mind your business," Drew told him.

Berdell's smile widened. "You know," he said, "just about everybody's got a secret or three tucked way back in their head. Me, I've got a bunch, all squirming around back there like a nest of rattlers. Most of them aren't for sharing, that's a fact, but I tell you what I'll do, Mr. Drew No-name, and that's share a secret with you, if you'll share one with me. I'll even go first, how about that? Are you game, boy?"

Drew nodded warily.

"Step along behind me," Berdell said, and began walking away. Following him, Drew saw the woman emerge from brush nearby, and formed the impression she had been attending to a call of nature back there. She watched them both until man and boy were beyond sight of the house.

Yancy Berdell stopped and pointed to a long mound of earth between two low piñon pines. "Take a guess," he invited.

"It's a grave."

"Yessir, it is. Care to say who might be in it?"

"George Washington," said Drew, and Yancy laughed.

"Not correct. Huntzucker's the name of the deceased, known hereabouts as Hump, on account of spinal deformity. The lady you saw back there's his wife, name of Maria. Now then, Drew boy, how'd he die?"

"I don't know. The sky fell on him."

"One step away from his sickbed, and the boy shows humor. Wrong again. I shot him is how."

"You shot him?"

"You heard right."

"Why?"

"He made an attempt on my life, just because I paid attention to his lady wife. This was an ugly man, so he got jealous, being that

I'm tolerable handsome. Pulled a gun on me from behind, but he missed. Then it was my turn, and I did not disgrace the Berdell name. Dug the hole myself, to make amends. Look at this."

He showed Drew two blistered palms. Drew looked again at the mound, unsure what attitude to strike. He liked this Yancy Berdell, and there appeared to have been justification for the deed. Yancy seemed quite unashamed, and Drew admired that.

"Let me tell you, the widow did not grieve, not for a minute. I believe I did the lady a favor—at least she tips me the glad eye—so I'm not about to waste my time feeling low over the death of some back-shooter."

It all sounded reasonable to Drew. He looked at Yancy, and Yancy's face told him it was Drew's turn to share a secret, so he told of Sylvie and Morgan and Smart Crow and the mission. When he was done, he hoped Yancy would approve of every decision Drew had taken, and it appeared he did.

"Interesting," was his verdict. He produced a cigar. "Do you indulge?" Drew shook his head. Yancy struck a match on his boot and puffed with obvious delight.

"So you're all alone in a sea of strangers, all thanks be to God. Religion's a peculiar thing. It can fill you up or drain you dry. I see before me a young man painfully dried right down to the bone. Listen here: you haven't done a damned thing wrong, not one. I like your spunk, and I don't lie. Now I'm saying to you, what next? Where does Drew No-name go from this desolate spot?"

"I don't know."

"What man does? We take what comes, and avoid what misery we can—you take my meaning? From pillar to post, that's been my path, and I'm no slave to shame. I'll step right up on Judgment Day along with the rest and take what's coming, if anything is."

These sounded like brave words to Drew. He liked the way Yancy talked.

They strolled back to the adobe house, which, Drew now saw, was located at a crossroads. The place was not so much a dwelling as it was a trading post or store. The front room, which he'd stumbled through without really noticing anything about it, was in fact lined with shelves of trade goods. There was another person there as well, a Mexican; Drew must have blundered right past him earlier without even seeing the man.

"One of Hump Huntzucker's customers," Yancy explained. "He's been happy these last few days. He owed Hump money, and he knows the widow won't ever be able to collect off him. He thinks I'm a great and wonderful fellow for wiping out his debt. Buenos días, Julio."

"Buenos días, señor."

"The full extent of my Spanish," admitted Yancy. "With the widow Huntzucker I speak only the language of love, you understand?"

Drew did. The widow was staring at Yancy Berdell with an intensity that would have made Drew nervous had he been its recipient. He assumed it was the look of love. He had never noticed Sylvie looking at Morgan that way. Yancy made him aware, with his breezy ways, that the world was half female, and even the married ones apparently had no qualms about falling in love with men passing by. The whole business suggested great excitement and intrigue to a virgin like Drew.

"Siesta time," Yancy said.

"I know. They did it at the mission."

"Then you know to find a shady place and nap."

Yancy left him standing by the plank counter supporting Julio's drink, and walked by the widow, who turned and followed. Drew felt abandoned, he wasn't sure why. Julio stared at him blearily and spoke a few words in Spanish. Drew smiled and nodded awkwardly in response. Julio beckoned him nearer and pointed to a barrel seat beside his own.

Drew sat. There was a bowl of lemons in front of him, a paring knife, a salt shaker and a bottle of pale liquor. He watched Julio perform the tequila ritual. Julio wanted him to join in, so Drew obliged. The stuff was foul, like drinking turpentine, he thought. Drew ate an entire lemon to scour the taste from his mouth. Julio found that very funny. Drew went outside to fetch another dipper of water from the well nearby, and on his way back heard the unmistakable sounds of intercourse from a window shuttered against the heat. He rejoined Julio, and became aware of the same sounds indoors. Julio could hear it too; he made several obscene gestures with his hand, and laughed. Drew didn't want to be near him anymore, nor within hearing of the widow's cries.

Outside was a crudely timbered corral, with two horses and a mule standing disconsolately by an empty manger. Drew found some hay in the stable loft and threw it down for the animals. Eventually they wandered over and began chewing listlessly, whisking flies from themselves with tail and mane. He watched them for a while from the loft, then lay down among the remaining hay and slept.

In the evening Yancy drank a fair amount of tequila and played cards with a man named Ogden who happened by late in the afternoon. He came from the east, along the road Drew had traveled on foot. Drew personally attended to his horse, at Yancy's request, then stood around while the men played. He didn't know the game they became so engrossed in, or any other game; cards had been forbidden in the Kindred home, called "the devil's pasteboards" by Morgan. Drew ate lemons while he watched, and nibbled stale tortilla.

"Hear about the commotion yet?" asked Ogden.

"What commotion's that?" said Yancy.

"Back along the road a piece, this mission place. Some Indian come in and carved up the priests. Blood all over, I seen it myself. They reckon Apaches done it. That's the one word I could understand—Apache! Apache! Place had nothin' but Indians in it anyway, and the two dead Mexes. I disbelieve it, though. Apaches would've killed more'n just two, and stole the women besides. Whole place was just tame mission Indians. They never knew what to do about it, just weeping and wailing and tearing their hair, and it happened a couple days before, already. Like chickens with their heads off, every last one. It was never Apaches done it, though. They would've killed more'n just two."

"So you said." Yancy turned to Drew. "Think it was Apaches?"

"One Apache."

Yancy laughed. "With an accomplice who opened the gate—am I right, Drew?"

Drew nodded, feeling his stomach lurch. He had thought Smart Crow would simply take the twins away with him.

"What's he know?" said Ogden, frowning. "He weren't there to see it."

"That's right, friend. He doesn't know a thing, but he's an opinionated boy, so I like to consult him once in a while."

"What the hell for?" Ogden said, torn between concentrating on his cards and following the difficult conversation.

"Respect," said Yancy. "This boy saved my life a short while back, shot a cougar that jumped me. Shot it clean through the eyeball with a pistol."

"That ain't true," scoffed Ogden.

"Pardon me, sir, I was there, under the weight of that dead cat, and the bullet hole in its eye was inches from my own. I know what I saw, and I know the debt I owe this boy, this sharpshooter here, so kindly don't contradict a witness to the event."

"I reckon I'll contradict who I please," Ogden said.

"Indeed you won't, sir, if I'm the contradictee."

"Speak plain or shut your mouth."

"Excuse me; I forgot I was addressing an illiterate."

"What say there? Say what?"

Yancy spread his cards across the table. Ogden studied them, then laid his own cards down. "Too bad," he said, smiling.

Yancy inspected the greasy boards. "I don't believe it's possible for you to have had that hand," he said.

Ogden's chair fell over as he stood, mouth open in outrage. "You goddamn snake! Take it back!"

"Take it back yourself," Yancy told him, and began scooping up the meager pile of dollars.

This action sent Ogden racing for his saddle, which Drew had brought into the room after corraling Ogden's horse. He had noticed at the time a fine repeating rifle in the saddle scabbard, and it was this weapon Ogden lunged for now. He had half its length cleared when Yancy flung the table aside and advanced on Ogden with a small pistol in his outstretched hand. The first shot from it was loud, solely by virtue of being first, and the four that followed had the reduced impact of firecrackers. Ogden collapsed across his saddle at about the same time that Julio, until then a seemingly permanent fixture at the plank counter, ran on bow legs through the doorway and into the night.

Drew still had a wedge of lemon stranded in midair near his mouth. Ogden's body slid and met the floor solidly; it was clear he had died on the way down. Yancy stepped close to the corpse and made sure all his bullets had found their mark. He then ejected his spent shells onto the floor. "Drew," he said, reloading, "go out to the stable and fetch back the shovel there."

Maria Huntzucker came flying to Yancy's side, talking loudly in Spanish. He pushed her away and pointed to Ogden. "That's the one to be yelling at," he said, but her eyes wouldn't leave him. The man on the floor might as well have been a sleeping dog.

It required more than an hour to dig a grave by lamplight and haul the body over to it. Drew gave assistance as directed. He spoke only once, as Yancy gave the mound, a short distance from that of his previous victim, a final patting down. "Did he really cheat?"

"Drew, I would never shoot a man for less. A simple apology and forfeiture would have seen him breathing at this hour. Bring the shovel; my hands are sore as blazes."

Inside again, Yancy poured himself a drink, then set before Drew a letter. "This was in our friend's pocket. Seems he was on his way to Arizona Territory to meet with his brothers, ranchers just over the line and not too far from here, by what he says. Now then, if they're expecting him, which the letter suggests they are, and he doesn't arrive, they may well come this way to find out what happened. Julio and the lovely Maria wouldn't hesitate a moment to let them know, if dollars were dangled before them, I think. So you and I must vamoose before that time arrives. You may have his saddle and horse. Yes, and his rifle also. Are you with me, Drew? If not, stay here and wait for them."

"I'll come."

"Good. I suggest a southerly route, away from Ogden's direction of travel. Ever seen the gulf by moonlight?"

"Gulf?"

"Gulf of Mexico."

"No."

"Then you shall."

Maria Huntzucker screamed a good deal at Yancy while they saddled up. She was screaming still as they rode away.

12

It was more than a week before someone had the gumption to ask Clay what had happened to his face. The question was posed in a saloon one night. The questioner was drunk, and had requested the information bluntly.

"How'd you get them holes?"

Clay looked at the man, his expression mild. "Pardon me?"

"Them god-awful holes—you chew 'em out, or what?"

"Disease," said Clay.

"You mean to say pox?"

"A disease of the tongue. The tip is where it starts."

"Tip of the tongue?"

"And spreads to the cheeks."

A considerable audience was listening now.

"Hell, I'd shoot myself first, before I got to where I looked like that."

"Poke out your tongue," Clay suggested.

"Huh? Why?"

"So I can tell if you're infected."

"Oh, is that right?" The man tipped his drinking friends a wink. "Better do what the doc says, hey, boys."

He poked out his tongue, crossing his eyes at the same time for maximum comic effect. Clay brought the butt of his shotgun up hard, directly under the man's chin. His teeth met, severing the tip of his tongue completely. As the man staggered back, howling with pain, Clay looked down at the scrap of pink at his feet.

"Good news," he said. "No sign of infection."

It was inevitable that the man should reach for his Colt, pain and humiliation together overcoming prudence. Clay allowed the gun to partway clear its holster before he fired. The man before him seemed to implode in the region of the gut. Clay and others were spattered with tissue as the blast drove the man back several steps. A massive welling of blood gushed from him as he fell. Powder smoke eddied in the air.

"For the public record," said Clay, "they're bullet holes. I killed the man who did it, and I killed the man with him when he did it."

He walked out.

Grover Stunce caught up with Clay shortly after.

"Dugan! You can't do that! There wasn't the justification for it!"

"I'd say a gun halfway to killing me is justification."

"The barkeep says all you had to do was answer the question straight and none of it would've happened."

"He was pulling his gun."

"Because of what you did!"

"He asked for it, and he got it."

"But it didn't have to happen, is what I'm saying. You can't just shoot someone because he's a fool."

"He was an armed fool."

Clay was not so nerveless as he seemed. He had already vomited twice in alleyways, and Grover couldn't see his face well enough in the darkness to observe its waxy pallor.

"This happens again," he said, "and I'll be taking back that badge."

"All right."

"Don't act so unconcerned. I know you now, know your type. You like it, don't you, pulling the trigger."

"If I believe it's the right thing, why not?"

"Because it wasn't the right thing!"

"In my opinion it was."

"The badge. Now."

Grover put out his hand. Clay unpinned the badge and surrendered it.

"You can sleep tonight in the office, same as usual," Grover told him. "Tomorrow you find some other line of work, and not in this town, you hear me?"

"Yes."

"Be out by morning."

Grover became entangled in argument with Mrs. Stunce that night.

"You tell him first thing in the morning he's hired again," said Sophie.

"Why should I do that?"

"Because he did you a favor. Now those saloon rowdies will think twice before they open their drunken mouths after what happened. You tell him he's got the job again."

"I won't go back on what I've already done."

"Nobody knows you did it, just him and me and you."

"That makes no difference. I told him, and he'll leave Keyhoe tomorrow."

"You told him to leave? Oh, what's the matter with you? Don't you understand he's exactly what you need here, to keep things calm? Can't you follow that simple fact? People will be scared of him, and because he's your deputy they'll be scared of you too, and scared people behave themselves, Grover, it's human nature. He's made everything different overnight, with this one thing he did."

"It wasn't a thing, it was a killing. He started the whole mess himself."

"I thought you said the other fellow did, asking that thoughtless question. Why shouldn't Mr. Dugan get upset over something as personal as his appearance? I don't blame him at all."

"Sophie, he shot a man clean in half, practically, and before that made him bite off his own tongue! What kind of behavior's that for a deputy marshal! It won't do! It isn't professional conduct, and it's just plain not right."

"You need him."

They glared at each other.

"Look," said Grover, "I'm not even sure anymore he isn't crazy. He didn't turn a hair when he did what he did, everyone says. What kind of man could do that and walk away without feeling a thing? He's not a regular man, I'm sure of it now. Taking him on in the first place, I kind of wondered, but I said to myself he makes me uneasy on account of the way he looks, that's all, but it's more, something behind the eyes. ... I never should've hired him."

"Yes you should, and you'll have him working for you again before anyone finds out what you did."

"I won't!"

"You must!"

When Clay awakened to the light of dawn behind the office blinds, he saw Grover Stunce seated behind the desk. It disturbed Clay that Grover had entered the office without waking him. He must have been very deeply asleep. He recalled having slept with profound depth on the first night after his killing of the Chaffey brothers. Did it mean something, this unnaturally deep sleep that followed a death at his hands?

"Don't know how you can rest so easy on that bunk," Grover said.

"I'll leave soon."

Clay threw back the blanket. His body felt like lead.

"Wait up."

Clay looked at Grover, who fidgeted with the badge in his hands.

"I've been thinking," Grover said, "and I'll admit I might have been hasty, saying what I said."

Clay pulled on his boots. He stood and began buttoning his vest.

"Don't you walk out till you've heard what I've got to say," Grover told him. Clay lifted his jacket from the back of a chair and put it on. He walked to the elkhorn rack by the door and picked up his hat.

"Take it back, the badge," Grover said. "You've still got a job here if you want it." He saw Clay hesitate. "With a seven dollar a month raise in wages." Clay put the hat on his head. "Ten dollars," said Grover.

Clay turned to face him.

"Sure about this, are you?"

"Dugan, the one thing I'm sure of is there's a long box waiting for us all under the ground. I need a deputy. Seems like that's you, rightly or wrongly. I'm asking you to stay on, only don't do what you did last night again. That's not law enforcement, that's just terrorizing the citizens. That's my opinion. I'm not saying you have to agree."

Clay looked at the floor. Grover continued fiddling with the badge. He'd been told by Sophie not to bother coming home without Clay Dugan on the county payroll again. Now Clay was approaching him, taking the badge, pinning it on.

"One more thing," said Grover.

"What?"

"You can't sleep in here anymore. It's not civilized, gives the wrong impression. There's a shack in back of my place, not big, but it's weatherproof. A man your height, he'd have to stoop some, getting through the door, but you're welcome to it."

"No rent?"

"Ten dollars a month, including meals."

Clay smiled crookedly. Grover saw that his teeth were a curious gray, most of them misaligned. He'd never seen them before, since Clay talked with barely a movement of his lips, probably due to the scarred stiffness of his holed cheeks.

"I'll take that deal too," he said.

Grover was relieved. Sophie was his again.

The domestic element of Clay's closer acquaintance with the Stunces proved less intolerable than he had anticipated. His decision to join them as a kind of backyard renter had been made to keep the peace with his employer, and Clay admitted the office was an uncomfortable place to live full time. The wisdom of his choice would be proven, ultimately, by the cooking provided at the Stunce residence, and he was not disappointed. He had expected a certain frostiness from his landlady, given their unfortunate first encounter, but such was not the case. The woman was positively effusive in her welcome of the new tenant, lavish in her cuisine.

Clay was suspicious at first of such unwarranted friendliness, but saw soon enough it was Sophie Stunce's way of rewarding him for having provided her husband's office with a measure of backbone it had not previously possessed.

Proof of this came from the lady's lips the next day, as she delivered what had become the traditional lunch basket. Clay was alone, as on the first occasion, and Sophie told him with a smile, "Our credit has been extended."

"Pardon?"

"At the store. Our credit."

Clay nodded warily. What did this have to do with him? Divining his confusion, Sophie explained that her husband's salary was not large, nor was it made available on what might be termed a regular-as-clockwork basis, which necessitated the running up of a credit sheet at the store where Sophie did most of her shopping for essential foodstuffs and basic items of clothing. That day, on entering the establishment to increase the Stunces' debt even further, Sophie had been taken aback when informed by the proprietor that her husband's line of credit had been doubled. "And the reason," said Sophie, "is the way things have been so quiet around town this last week. Mr. Simmons, that's the owner, he said it was thanks to you and Mr. Stunce there hasn't been hardly a peep from the rowdy element. Mr. Simmons took his wife for a walk down the street last night, and he hasn't done that for a long time, nor plenty of others, believe me. It just shows how appreciative folks can be when you give them something to appreciate."

Clay understood; the Stunces were better off in their community because of what he had done to the fool he'd killed. Clay didn't begrudge them their newfound propriety, but didn't wish to share in it, even if he was actually its cause. He had killed because he felt justified in doing so, not in order to inflate the social prestige of Grover Stunce and his wife. He felt uncomfortable. Clay fully intended killing more stupid men who dared to cross him, but this future winnowing of society's fools was to take place in an aura of personal judgment and retribution, not out of some moral or legal code acceptable to the majority.

Clay's itinerary was his own, conducted by himself, for himself, under the convenient aegis of state-mandated law enforcement. It had nothing to do with the Stunces, or with Keyhoe, or the price of silk in China. Sophie's triumph was something Clay found objectionable, a trivial thing clinging to the coattails of his act, his ridding the town of an inferior human being. Did she understand? It was unlikely. He felt a little sorry for her, despised the obvious joy she was trying to bring him with her great news of extended credit. Sophie Stunce knew as little of what went on inside Clay's head as she did of the moon's dark side.

He knew better than to reveal his thoughts. Clay was politeness personified that evening, an avid listener at Sophie's dining table as she held forth on whatever took her fancy. The subject of her choice was usually culled from newspaper articles. Grover was not a great reader of newsprint, and relied on his wife to supply him with tidbits while he ate. He seldom commented on anything she quoted, a frustrating reaction to a woman of such gregariousness as Sophie, so she aimed her reading and commentary in equal measure at Clay, in hopes of a conversational partner.

Clay played his part with reluctance, feeling that any response to another man's wife, in full view and hearing of that man, had of necessity to be both circumspect and uninflammatory. While he agreed with some of what she said regarding the political news, he had to remain silent when Sophie ventured opinions contrary to his own. Clay reminded himself it didn't matter what she thought, or what he thought; neither of them, or Grover Stunce, mattered a damn in the wide world. She could spout and opinionate as much as she pleased; the planet would turn at its own speed and life proceed as if none of them was there. His rejoinders over supper were therefore of the tamest.

He sensed Sophie's frustration with him, and ignored it. Heated debate with Grover's wife under the nose of Grover would have constituted a gross breach of etiquette, Clay felt, and he was not about to antagonize the man who had given him a job in which it was Clay's legal right to eliminate those persons who stepped from the narrow path of righteousness. Such was Clay's chosen work, and he would jeopardize it for no woman. He had a sneaking admiration for her anyway, if only because Sophie was a handsome individual despite her faint mustache.

The town was indeed a quiet place for more than a month following the shooting. Then, as the incident receded from the common experience of Keyhoe's transients, and a fresh wave of cattle herders swept into the saloons, boisterousness and gunplay were heard on the streets again. Clay had known it would be only a matter of time before new targets were set up before him.

He felt no disquiet, no misgivings over blood that would soon be spilled in the course of his self-appointed task. The merits of every man within range of his scattergun would determine how well or badly he fared in Keyhoe. Clay genuinely felt the thousand possible outcomes of every evening were determined not by himself and his readiness to kill anyone deserving of it, but by some vast web of fateful influences, a flux of events that could snare a man unaware of its invisible workings. Clay's job was to pick off those foolish enough to put themselves in harm's way.

He did not imagine himself to be some custodian of society, a guardian of public morals; Clay didn't even like people very much. It was something more personal than that, a part Clay had cast himself in without consultation. He chose to be this person, this haggard angel of death, and thought it was kind of funny the way folks believed he did it on their behalf.

He hauled drunks to the jail every night, then became sick of having to clean out the cells next morning. Far better for these men to vomit in the streets and fall asleep under wagons; Clay wanted nothing to do with them. Only when a drinker became careless with his gun did Clay consider intervention justified. His manner in these arrests was always civil, smilingly calm despite his readiness to turn the simple matter of a request to hand over the offending weapon into a life or death confrontation. He was neither glad nor disappointed when, time after time, the cowhands looked at his face and slowly realized they should do what he said. There would come a time when one would not.

While he waited, Clay became aware of tension in the Stunce household. Grover was an uncommunicative man, at home or at work, and Clay was not about to ask for details concerning a man's trouble with his wife. Clay knew most men would have liked to side with their companion against a woman, but Grover was no companion of Clay's, in fact Clay had determined that Sophie, not Grover, was the stronger of the pair, therefore more deserving of his support. He said nothing, did nothing, gave no indication he was aware of enmity between the two. Sometimes it was a relief to leave the house and retire alone to his shack in the yard.

Clay thought more often about marriage than he used to, and supposed this was a result of having lived in proximity to a married couple. So far he hadn't seen anything to recommend the institution, nor any specific reason to reject it. The Stunces appeared no more or less happy than anyone else, including Clay. It was a fact, he admitted, that he often felt lonely, even if he had just that moment left Grover and Sophie in the middle of another burst of silent warfare. Was he perhaps missing out on some essential human experience?

He often pictured the couple in bed together, not necessarily engaging in sexual intercourse, just lying there. Clay's understanding of sex was a limited commodity; he remained a virgin, no matter how often the hurdy-gurdy girls and flat-out whores propositioned him on his beat. He knew a lot of them by their first names, and was unfailingly correct in his treatment of them, but Clay could never have assented to intercourse with any such creature.

There was in Keyhoe a well-known character called Captain Switchback, a middle-aged syphilitic whose spinal disks, so Clay was informed, had been eaten away by the disease, thereby allowing the vertebrae to grow together into a single inflexible rod. Captain Switchback couldn't bend an inch, and had to turn his entire body rather than his trunk or neck alone. His unfortunate condition obliged him to walk with a comical throwing-out of the feet and frequent jumps to correct his path along the sidewalk. When the Captain turned a corner with legs flying and head bobbing, he reduced small boys to fits of howling, which only served to make him spring in circles, trying to identify and kick his audience. Captain Switchback was fast becoming senile as well, the syphilis having affected his spine as far up its stem as the brain. No, Clay would never risk such a possibility for himself. It was bad enough having to endure the stares his scarred cheeks brought him.

Sophie began to think she had done herself and Grover a disservice in encouraging Clay Dugan to remain in town. True, he did an excellent job of maintaining law and order with his ugly face and his shotgun, but the result was an increasing laxness on the part of Grover toward his duties. He often wanted to stay at home when he should have been out patrolling the streets with Clay who, for his part, made not the slightest protest. This indicated to Sophie that Clay considered her husband an untrustworthy partner, useless in a dangerous occupation such as theirs. His lack of complaint was an insult in disguise. She who had originally encouraged Grover to abandon the field of police work now wished he would distinguish himself in the public eye, and not leave most of the daily sidewalk strolling to his deputy.

One morning Grover returned home less than an hour after having left, and suggested to his wife that they go upstairs to engage in the marital act. Sophie had been married to him almost eighteen months, and this was the first time he had ever made so outrageous a suggestion. Had the first Mrs. Stunce consented to intercourse in the hours of daylight? Sophie had no idea how to cope with the situation, and so collapsed onto the kitchen floor she had been engaged in scrubbing when Grover returned home with his contemptible proposal.

Grover immediately rushed for the salts of ammonia to revive her, and when Sophie appeared to recover, he begged her forgiveness. "Forgiveness?" said Sophie, apparently still dazed. "For what, pray tell?" Grover said nothing. The shock of what he had done had driven recollection of his words clear out of Sophie's mind, and it was as well to leave the moment lost.

He hurried back to work as soon as his wife had regained her feet, and vowed never to insult her virtue in so shameful a fashion again. It was maddening, though, the way she had lately taken to refusing him access to her body. He knew of instances where men had divorced their wives for such acts of selfishness, but Grover loved Sophie too much to do that. He tried to analyze her behavior, track down its beginnings and see if some event at its inception might possibly have caused her to change. It required only a few minutes to realize that Sophie's impatience with him in general, and her lack of inclination to couple with him in bed, had worsened with the arrival in Keyhoe of Clay Dugan.

Could there be a connection? It seemed unlikely, Dugan being as unattractive as he was, but then, Grover had heard tell that women sometimes overlooked an ugly face if there was something else about a man, some indefinable aspect of personality or character to make up for the lack of physical comeliness. Did Clay have any of that, maybe? Grover couldn't see where he did, but that didn't necessarily rule him out as having found favor in Sophie's eyes. He would have to watch and listen for the clues that would reveal, if anything could, the game going on behind his back, assuming there was such, which he didn't believe for a moment.

Awareness of a fundamental change in his relations with Grover came slowly to Clay. Whereas the marshai had been content to allow his deputy free rein to patrol the saloons alone at night, when danger was most likely to unfold, he now accompanied Clay everywhere. Clay had assumed until then that Grover recognized his own ineptitude when dealing with the drunken element, which constituted the bulk of their arrests, and was content to let Clay do what Clay did best, without interference. The sudden change of tactic puzzled him for a while, then he reasoned that Sophie had been nagging at Grover to get out and show himself around town, as he used to before Clay came. Clay didn't like the way Grover stuck to him up one street and down another; it made them both look cowardly, too afraid to enter the bars alone.

"Why don't you handle this side of the street and I'll take the other. It'll be twice as fast that way, then we'll trade sides later on for another go-round."

"No."

Grover offered no explanation for his rejection of a perfectly sensible plan, and Clay didn't push him for one. The new regimen was clearly of domestic origin, and Clay was still inclined not to mess with whatever anxieties were at work inside the Stunces. It was none of his business, but maintaining order was, and Grover was jeopardizing, with his unwanted presence, the ambience of subtle menace Clay had built around himself of late. He was ruining everything, and for no reason.

Grover kept it up night after night, to Clay's irritation. They never spoke to each other, and Clay managed always to keep one or two steps ahead of the shorter-legged Stunce, just to let the man know he didn't want or need him along. Grover was undeterred, and their dual footsteps became a recognizable pattern on the wooden sidewalks. "Here comes Boney and Phony again, boys," was just one of the comments Clay overheard.

At last he had had enough, and steered the marshal down an alley for a whispered confrontation.

"You quit it, this dogging me all over."

"You work for me, so you do what I say. You don't give orders. ..."

"Like hell I work for you. We both work for the state. Now quit following me around like a lost kid."

"I go my own way, Dugan."

"I just wish you would."

"I bet you do, then you could double back home and I'd never know the difference."

"What?"

"You can get out tonight, so far as I'm concerned. I want you out of that shack and into a room somewhere else. Don't fool yourself I haven't got eyes. ..."

"Mind telling me just what it is you're saying?"

"Out by morning, and you can damn well turn your badge in too, first thing tomorrow."

"Again? Is this something you do every full moon, Grover? Just tell me, so I'll know when to expect it next time." Clay was almost laughing, the conversation was so ridiculous. He really didn't know what was eating at Grover, but was fairly sure it had something to do with whatever problems the man was having with his wife. Clay was glad at that moment he wasn't married, not if matrimony turned men into fools on a regular basis.

"You get!" Grover hurled at him, and Clay began walking away, not so amused anymore. He wondered if Grover was working himself up to some kind of brainstorm that would require doctoring and a long spell in bed. That would be fine by Clay, who would then be able to resume his customary progress around the town alone.

He would take Grover's order seriously for the present, though, in order to avoid any further confrontation when both men arrived back at the Stunce house. Clay planned on being gone by the time Grover came home.

When he entered the house and walked straight through to the backyard, Sophie was puzzled; Clay had never come home in the middle of his evening patrol before. She followed him out to the shack, and found him packing the few things he owned into a leather satchel.

"Why are you doing that?"

"Grover doesn't want me here anymore."

"For what reason?"

"When you find out, I'd like to know."

"He wouldn't tell you?"

"Not in words that made any sense. Anyway, he wants me gone, and I'm not about to argue."

Sophie felt unfamiliar panic take hold of her chest. He was going, the ugly young-old man who lived in the yard and ate his silent meals without ever complimenting her cooking unless Grover did so; the man who listened as she talked, but never offered a contrary opinion, although she could see plenty behind his eyes; the man who had single-handedly established respect for the office of marshal. Grover was jealous, she saw it immediately, and could not hide from herself her own part in making much of Clay's accomplishments to Grover when they were alone. What a fool she'd been, to do that, and now he was leaving!

"Clay!" she barked, and he looked up from his packing, as surprised at the tone of her voice as Sophie was herself.

"Clay ... this is not at all sensible."

"I'm in agreement, but it's his place."

"No; as a matter of fact, it isn't. This house is mine, left to me by my father. You're my tenant, not Grover's."

Clay was struck by the novelty of this, but not for long. "I can't stay if he wants me out, not if you want peace and quiet in your house, Sophie."

It was the first time he had ever used her first name, and he had only done so now because he was leaving. It was a last-minute intimacy that made her quite faint. She actually felt a little sick at this sudden development. She could have kicked Grover for his insensibility and childishness. Clay mustn't go from her, not now, not because of Grover.

"No," she said, and felt herself step up to the edge of a cliff.

Clay looked at her, unsure what to do or say. Did the look of resolution on her face mean she had a plan of some kind? He wasn't all
that interested if she did; after what Grover had said, it would be
impossible to share a meal again, no matter what Sophie did. He
closed the satchel, turned around to pick up his gun, and on turning
back to leave found himself chest to chin with Sophie Stunce. He
was so alarmed at her abrupt proximity he took a step back, but
Sophie followed. "No," she said again, her voice lower, softer this
time.

She was so close he could smell her. Clay couldn't have said if it
was a good smell or bad; to him she smelled simply of woman. It
began at his nose and traveled clear down to his boots, filled him
like smoke in a jar, and he knew he was in trouble now, because
this was what Grover had been talking about—Clay and his wife: it
was clear as day, only he'd been too stupid to see, and within a half
hour of his hearing the unfounded suspicions, they were coming
true.

He couldn't breathe for the woman smell of her invading him,
flooding him with a kind of slow quaking. He could even feel the
push of her heavily corseted breasts against him. No female had
been this close to Clay since Nettie bathed his cuts and bruises. He
heard the heavy satchel fall, and had the presence of mind to toss
his shotgun onto the bed. With both hands free, his arms seemed to
curl of their own accord around the woman pressed against him,
and as soon as they had her fully encircled she softened and sagged,
obliging him to hold her even tighter or drop her to the rug. Her
entire body appeared to have become limp. He could tell which
parts of her were flesh, and which parts whalebone, and the small
bulges of woman where they met in conflict were under his fingers
no more than a moment before those same fingers began clutching
and tearing at the back of her dress.

Grover worried that he hadn't been firm enough with Clay. He
hadn't been fooled by Clay's pretense at not understanding the
hints Grover threw down like cards. It was perfectly obvious there
was something between his lodger and his wife, at least it was perfectly obvious to Grover. He stopped walking, realizing he'd gone
and sent Clay home to pack up and get out, and home was where
Sophie was. Grover didn't doubt that there had been many clandestine visits during working hours, before he started accompanying
Clay everywhere, but it was intolerable that there should be one

more meeting of the two betrayers, especially at Grover's request. He'd slipped up there, because of his anger. It had been a mistake, but he could go home himself and make sure the farewells that took place were no fonder than they needed to be.

Or maybe he wouldn't. It was unlikely they would do anything, now that they knew Grover was onto their game. Clay would just breeze in and breeze out again, most likely. Grover didn't really want to be there with the both of them allied against him. This was the second time he'd told Clay to go elsewhere, and if Clay refused, right there in front of Sophie, Grover would look a perfect fool. No, he'd stay away and let events sort themselves out. He was on duty in any case, and the town would go to hell without at least one peace officer in evidence to hold back the ungodly.

When Grover entered a saloon called Minnie's Place he did so with a worried mind. He knew as soon as he set foot inside that he should never have come. A silence laden with contempt descended as the drinkers saw who he was. Someone at the back of the room, a coward hidden by tobacco smoke, bleated like a sheep, and the sound produced guffawing that swept across Grover like a cold wind.

He couldn't understand why they hated him. Before Clay came to Keyhoe he had managed to keep the place pretty much on the rails, even been complimented occasionally by ladies on the street for the way he kept things quiet, or as quiet as a Kansas cow town had a right to expect. What had he done wrong? It was Clay's doing, somehow. Clay had shot a man, and by so doing had made Grover look weak, despite the fact that Grover himself had killed a man in the line of duty not so very long ago. By what convoluted logic did these cattle punchers and whores assume he was inferior to his own deputy. It was an insult, personal and direct! He couldn't let the moment pass, or the last scraps of his dignity and professional standing in the community would be torn away. Having no other choice, Grover went to the rear of the bar where the bleating had come from. There were at least eight men there who might have been responsible, all of them staring at him with faces like stone.

"Which one of you made that sheep sound?"

There were no volunteers. The men were together, had driven a herd of beeves from Texas up to the railhead at Hays City, and now were returning home to do the same thing over again. None among them had made the sound. They all knew it was a skinny drinker a short distance from them who had done it, but they were disinclined to turn him in, especially to a lawman as foolish as this one. They would say nothing and hope he went away again, so they could resume their drinking and plan further entertainment. Any town in which the locals openly made fun of their own marshal would likely turn out to be a wild place where they could really let rip over the next day or so. The Texans awaited the next development with interest.

"Well?" demanded Grover.

"Tolerable," said a cowboy, and Minnie's Place erupted with laughter again.

This time Grover knew his man. "You," he said, pointing to the joker. "You're under arrest."

"Me?"

"Come here, and put your hands inside your belt."

"Haven't finished my drink. You go along without me and I'll follow on later."

More laughter, lacking the previous level of hilarity, rippled by Grover's burning ears. "You do what I say, when I say it," he said, feeling his throat begin to close with fear. He should never have gone in there, should have gone home to be with his wife whom he loved, but Clay was there, so he couldn't, which was another mistake he'd made already that night, and the result of all his confusion and misery and miscalculation was this—an unwanted confrontation with some stranger who had done nothing more than mock him gently in front of an audience that already mocked him day after day. The whole thing was Clay's fault.

"You get over here now," said Grover, but his voice had to squeeze past the fear clenching his throat, which made him begin to cough, so his words came out raspingly, without the least authority, and the cowboy stayed right where he was. To have responded to so feeble an order would have made him look foolish in front of his friends.

Grover stifled his coughing. He desperately wanted to be somewhere else, far from Minnie's, and far from his wife as well; she wasn't worth it. The faithless hussy probably had done a terrible job of hiding her marital treachery from the neighbors, which would account for the way everyone in town was laughing at him lately. Far from Sophie, that was the place he wanted to be, where he wouldn't have to listen to any more snickering, or see the kind of smirk the cowboy in front of him wore, the kind that said Grover was a pathetic fool who couldn't be taken seriously, an opinion so grossly unwarranted it made Grover angry, and so he did the only thing he could have done under the circumstances fate seemed to have arranged for him that night. He drew his gun to arrest the one who smirked, the one who had provoked unjustified laughter, and then, without fully intending it, Grover pulled the trigger.

His tormentor took a bullet in the abdomen, but managed to draw his own gun and fire before beginning to slide along the bar and onto the floor. The others already had their guns out and pointing at the marshal, but it was not necessary to fire a shot; their friend had put a hole in Grover Stunce's chest, a surefire dead shot, and the fool with the badge was dying as he fell, the pistol dropping with a clatter beside a rolling spittoon his foe had overturned.

It took almost an hour to locate the deputy. Someone finally caught sight of Clay on the street and dragged him to Minnie's. Both parties to the shooting were dead by then, the cowboy having had time to dictate a succinct will that disposed of his few disposables. Several of the Texans were unashamedly tearful, and in no mood for interrogation by someone as biased as the dead marshal's deputy was bound to be. They were surprised when Clay listened, rather than gave orders. When he had talked with others who witnessed the event, Clay declared that no charges could be pressed against any living person. He further told the cowhands that their dead companion would be buried at the county's expense.

The town was not greatly surprised when, two months after the death of Grover Stunce, Clay Dugan married his widow.

13

It was the heat, rather than the flies, that exasperated Drew so much. It never went away, even at night. It had taken Yancy and himself a month to reach Galveston, and in that time they passed from the dry heat of the desert to the humidity of the Gulf of Mexico. Yancy had promised cool ocean breezes, but Drew had yet to experience any such thing. The air, when it moved, was like molasses: heavy and thick, tasting of salt tang and fish. Clothing pasted itself against his body within minutes of his dressing, and his socks became damp as bar cloths inside his boots.

"My hometown," Yancy said with pride. He had already told Drew he was born in Arkansas, but Drew was becoming used to his lies. Drew reasoned that the information Yancy provided could be divided into two categories—things that mattered, and things that didn't. It didn't matter if Yancy wasn't born where he said he was born, so Drew didn't bother challenging him over that and similar contradictions. Hard facts were alien to Yancy, but he had offered good advice on how to handle the frisky mare and powerful Winchester Drew had taken in New Mexico Territory.

Yancy's "embellishments," as he unblushingly called them, were reserved for details of his personal life. Drew thought maybe the truth was too sad to tell of, so he forgave Yancy's lying, because he liked the man. He considered himself a kind of plodding older brother to an immature sibling who just couldn't help but tell whopping fibs, try as he might to curb the habit. It was a minor flaw, made harmless by Drew's understanding nature.

It was clear that Yancy was not a man of any permanent or legal trade, but Drew simply accepted this aspect of him along with the rest of his charming defects. Yancy seemed genuinely to like him, and at no time condescended to Drew in the usual manner of men toward boys.

"All I ask of you, Drew, is that you never deliver me into the hands of my enemies."

"Who are they?"

"Anyone at all, at any time, and I sure don't lie. Being independent as I am, I do things to please myself, but the world oftentimes won't accept a fellow that does what he likes. Ever been around the army at all?"

"No."

"Worst kind of hell. The army life is for dunces who don't know if they should pull their boots on or take a shit without the sergeant tells them to. Cavalry's bad enough, but infantry's worse. To be an infantryman you have to be certifiably stupid. They know right away if you are, because only a certifiably stupid person would ever voluntarily offer his body for purgatory in uniform."

"Were you in the army, Yancy?"

"Do I strike you as being stupid in any way?"

"No, you're smart."

"And there lies your answer."

Which meant that he had been in the army, by the topsy-turvy logic Drew was becoming accustomed to when dealing with Yancy's past. He couldn't imagine Yancy taking orders from a sergeant, but he was learning that the world was bristling with things he had never been able to imagine.

The place they lived in, for example, was tenanted mostly by young women too lazy to dress themselves even in the middle of the day. They were very friendly for the most part, especially Winnie, who was just a few years older than Drew, although she practiced the same mode of undress as all the rest. Drew knew she was friendly because she kept winking at him. He had thought at first it was some kind of nervous twitch of the eyelid, the kind a young man back in Illinois had, that everyone said he never had before he was in the war. That young man's eye had twitched constantly, but

Winnie's seemed to flicker only when Drew passed her in the hall-way on his way to the outhouse. They hadn't spoken as yet; it was Yancy who told Drew her name, and the names of some of the other lazy women.

"Why don't they get dressed? Is it because it's so hot?"

"That's exactly right, Drew boy. These ladies are sensitive to a fault, and can't abide the conditions of humidity this part of the world inflicts on them."

"Why don't they go somewhere else to live?"

"Because Vanda won't let them, not until they've paid for room and keep. Vanda's put a lot of cash into these females, and they owe her plenty. They're hers, so don't you be talking with them over-much and distracting them from their work, or Vanda'll take it out on my hide."

Drew was left puzzling over the nature of the ladies' work, since none of them ever seemed to go anywhere or do anything. Of course, he was confined for the moment to his and Yancy's room on the top floor of Vanda's big house. Vanda was a friend of Yancy's, so Yancy said, and wouldn't mind them staying with her for a while, but Drew had to remain cooped up for a little while yet. It had already been two days, and Drew was becoming bored.

On the third day he waited until Yancy left the room, then went out into the hall. There weren't any ladies around to tell on him, so he went down to the floor below, where two of them were talking together. They turned to look at him, and one said, "Hello there, sugarpie. He let you out today?"

"I let myself out," Drew said. He didn't like the way their smiles seemed to be making fun of him.

"'Scuse me," said the lady, and resumed the conversation with her friend.

On the next floor down, Drew bumped into Winnie, who quickly steered him into a room and sat him on a chair by the window. He could see the ships in the harbor from there, and kept glancing out-side while she spoke.

"Does he know you're out?"

"I can do what I like."

"You're supposed to stay upstairs, Mrs. Gentles said."

"Who's she?"

"Only the person who owns this whole entire building you're sit-ting inside of, that's who."

"It isn't. That's someone called Vanda."

"Well, that's her first name, peckerhead."

"Oh."

"She doesn't want you here, that's what they're saying."

"Who is?"

"The heavenly chorus, who do you think? Does he get in the same bed with you?"

"Who?"

Winnie rolled her eyes upward in exasperation. "Handsome Yancy, that's who. Well, does he?"

"Why would he do that? There's two beds."

"Are you telling the truth? I'll hurt you if you're not."

"I am."

"Good; that's fifty cents I won. I said you weren't his little pooter boy."

"What's a pooter boy?"

"One that spreads his butthole for gentlemen."

Drew didn't understand that at all, but thought he might look a fool if he asked for further definition.

"So if you're not," said Winnie, "what are you?"

It was a tough question. He decided to be straightforward. "I'm Drew Kindred ... no, Drew Dugan."

"And I'm the Empress Josephine. No, I'm Cleopatra. No, Queen Victoria, that's who I am."

She found this funny, for no reason Drew could see. He was beginning not to like her, even if her face was kind of pretty. "Why do you wear half your clothes?" he asked, to steer talk away from himself.

"Why? Because that's the way they want you to look."

"Who does?"

"The customers, donkey. They want to see what they're getting before they pay, give us the eye before they buy, that's what they do. I made that up myself. Mrs. Gentles laughed when she heard. She's fancy Yancy's mama."

"His mother?"

"Everybody's got one, or had one. Mine's dead. You still got one?"

"No."

Drew was a little dazed. Yancy had said Vanda was a friend. No one could mistake his mother for a friend, so it was another one of Yancy's colossal fibs. He should have expected it to be untrue.

"Are you his sister?" Drew asked.

"You're a stupidhead. Why would I be his sister, for heaven's sake?"

"I don't know," Drew confessed.

"You're certainly not very smart, are you?"

"You shut up."

Winnie jumped up and smacked him across the face. Before he was aware of it, Drew had smacked her back, but not very effectively. They glared at each other, breathing hard.

"Pooter boy!" Winnie accused.

"Pooter boy yourself!"

Again, he'd said something hilarious. Winnie fell across the bed, giggling. Drew realized this must be her room, the way she rolled around on the covers. Finally Winnie stopped, and sat contemplating her guest for a minute or so.

"Come here and kiss me this instant and I'll forgive you," she said.

"I didn't do anything. You hit me first."

"Just you quit arguing and do like I say, or I'll tell Mrs. Gentles you came down from upstairs."

"She can't be his mother or her name'd be Berdell, so you told a lie."

"I didn't, and it doesn't matter a damn what their names are, punkinhead, because she was never married to the man that put Yancy inside her, so you don't know as much as you think you know!"

Drew absorbed this, and was silenced. Winnie tossed her hair and patted the bed beside her. "You come here," she ordered, and Drew took himself away from the window and its view of masts and spars to place himself gingerly beside her. He half expected another slap, and was ready for it. The talk of kissing was obviously a trap.

"Well, what are you waiting for?"

Drew shrugged, beginning to experience embarrassment. Winnie apparently was sincere in her request; her mouth was puckered and ready. He stared at it, then decided he'd better do what she wanted. This would be his first kiss that wasn't given to a mother. When it was over with he pulled back fast.

Winnie shook her head. "You were supposed to kiss me on the lips, stupid, not the goddamn cheek like your granny does. Do it again."

He did it again, and was startled when her mouth opened like a pit and seemed to draw him inside. His entire body felt completely different from the way it had felt mere seconds before, especially his toby, which began thrusting against his pants in an insistent manner.

Winnie broke off the kiss and grabbed at his crotch, then smirked at him in a way Drew didn't think he liked, but couldn't actually dislike, not with the blood pounding through him that way, and her hand being where it was, kneading him with a practiced deftness that made him ashamed yet exhilarated at the same time.

"Well," said Winnie, "I take it back. I guess you're not a pooter boy after all."

"I told you," Drew gasped.

Winnie jumped up and pointed to the door. "You better get, before someone finds out you came down here."

He didn't want to leave, but could think of no good reason for staying that would not have sounded like some kind of begging. Winnie had done something to him that made him want to do whatever she told him to, so she'd like him and maybe later on invite him to kiss her again.

"All right."

He stood up, stooping a little.

"Bye-bye now," Winnie told him. "Don't strangle it, will you."

This enigmatic farewell accompanied Drew upstairs.

In the afternoon Yancy returned. "Come and meet Vanda," he said. "What's the matter? You look blue."

"Nothing."

"Well, put a smile on. Vanda likes happy souls."

They descended four floors, and Drew saw that although the upper stories were divided into many rooms, the ground floor consisted of just three large chambers. The first and biggest was occupied by the women and a few men, mostly sitting around on small sofas, the like of which Drew hadn't seen before. The second he knew was a barroom, because of all the bottles and glasses.

The smallest of the three rooms had the fanciest wallpaper of any of them, and the biggest desk Drew had ever laid eyes on. Behind the desk sat a woman much younger than Drew was expecting, and fully clothed. He wondered if Winnie had told him the truth about Vanda being Yancy's mother. There was no resemblance between them that he could see.

"Vanda, meet my intrepid pard from out west. Drew boy, say how-do to Vanda, only you'll call her Mrs. Gentles."

"How do you do," the woman said, smiling just a little.

"I'm very well, ma'am, Mrs. Gentles."

"Sit, please."

Drew perched himself on the edge of a plush armchair facing the desk. Mrs. Gentles studied him, then asked, "Will you tell me about yourself, Drew? Yancy says you have had quite an adventure."

He told her everything, excluding the siesta noises between Yancy and Maria Huntzucker, and Yancy's two killings at that desert location.

When he was finished, he was told, "You are a boy with grit, I think, to have come so far alone."

"Yancy helped me."

"And rightly so. Where will you go now?"

"Go, ma'am?"

"If you could be taken to any place you chose."

"I don't know," Drew said, and hung his head, knowing it was an inadequate response.

"Look up. I ask because I wish to know what I should do with you. Have you any suggestions?"

"No, ma'am. Ma'am?"

"Yes?"

"If this is where Yancy lives, I'd like to stay here, ma'am, if you don't mind."

"No, he does not live here."

"Oh, I thought he did, you being his ma."

"Who told you this?" demanded Mrs. Gentles.

He had to protect Winnie. "Yancy did, ma'am."

"That's not so," Yancy protested. "As if I would ..."

Mrs. Gentles lifted a hand to silence him. Drew was impressed by the way it made Yancy shut right up, which wasn't like Yancy at all.

"Drew, I have a question for you."

"Ma'am."

"What is this place, do you know?"

"This place?"

"Is it a baker's shop, or a bank, or a dry goods store?"

"No, ma'am, it's a ... a whorehouse."

He had concluded this after much thought upstairs. Whorehouses

had never been discussed in the Kindred home, but a few tantalizing morsels of information had reached him in the schoolyard back
in Dinnsville. Winnie's brash behavior and the state of undress of
the other women made it obvious, and he felt a fool for having
taken so long to become aware.

"That is correct. What is your opinion of such places?"

"I don't know, ma'am. I was never in one before."

"You will have noticed that apart from the gentlemen customers,
and yourself and Yancy, who are guests, we are all women here.
How would you fit in with so many ladies all about?"

"Ma'am, do you live here?"

"I? No, I have a small house for my own use, next door."

"Well, I could live there."

"Could you indeed. And what if I say I have no use for a boy."

"If Yancy isn't your son, then ... I could be."

Mrs. Gentles looked across Drew to Yancy, and it seemed she
smiled a little.

"Tell me, Drew," she said, "what is the function, or shall I say the
duty, of a son to his mother?"

"Oh, well, he's got to study hard on his lessons, mainly, and ... uh
... do chores when she says."

"Is that all?"

"Kiss her good night and not get in trouble."

Mrs. Gentles burst out laughing. When she was calm she asked,
"Should he wander the country seeking after he knows not what?
And come visiting with a smile and an outstretched hand once or
twice a year?"

"He ought to come more often than that."

"Much more often," confirmed Mrs. Gentles. "Indeed."

Drew could hear Yancy stirring restlessly behind him.

"And if I allow you to share my house, will you be the kind of son
a son should be, or will you go your own sweet way as the notion
takes you?"

"I'll do my best," Drew promised. "I can already read and write
and figure better than most, my teacher said."

"Then I shall give you the chance to prove her correct."

"He was a man, ma'am."

"Yancy will return you to your room. Good day, Drew."

"Yes, ma'am. Thank you, Mrs. Gentles."

She smiled, and looked again at Yancy. "You may call me Mother, if you wish."

Having few possessions, he moved quickly and easily into the small house next door to Mrs. Gentles's brothel. Yancy insisted on helping him, which meant carrying Drew's rifle, leaving Drew empty-handed. Drew allowed this peculiar assistance, curious to see Yancy's reaction to the house.

They ran into trouble at the door, when a handsome Negro man asked Yancy kindly not to set foot inside, as per instruction from Mrs. Gentles.

"You just step aside now, Meggs," Yancy told him, "and go take the matter up with her yourself. Or you could just not tell her I was here, in which case she won't shout at you for not doing what she wanted."

Drew was dragged past mildly protesting Meggs. Once inside, Yancy released him and began prowling from room to room, as if in search of something. Drew trailed along behind, and was in turn followed by Meggs, who wore a deep frown of consternation. In the kitchen. Yancy greeted a black woman who was preparing supper. "Hello, Sukie. Long time gone."

She looked at the rifle in his hands. "You aiming to shoot me, Mr. Yancy?"

He laughed. "No, I'm not. That'd get me in trouble, now wouldn't it."

"Guess you'd know 'bout that."

Yancy laughed again. Drew heard the annoyance in it, and knew Yancy didn't like to be spoken to that way by kitchen help. He knew also that these two black people worked for Mrs. Gentles, and so were safe. Yancy was afraid of his own mother, which struck Drew as nothing less than amazing, given the man's behavior to date. He had killed someone for allegedly cheating at cards, without batting an eye, yet was obliged to grin while his mother's cook sassed him.

"That the boy she told about?" Sukie asked.

"This is him. He's my pard, so you feed him up good and be nice."

"She already told me."

"Which room's his?"

"Reckon you know the one," said Sukie, and turned to her chopping of vegetables.

Drew saw Yancy's face harden. "This way," Yancy said, turning and pushing past the hovering form of Meggs. He led the way to a small room at the rear of the house, flung Drew's Winchester onto the bed and shut the door firmly in Meggs's face. Drew didn't like to look at Yancy, knowing as he did that this had once been Yancy's room. He felt guilty somehow.

Yancy joined the rifle on the bed, lay back and looked at the stamped tin ceiling. "Drew boy," he said, "you're smart for your age, so tell me what you make of all this."

"I don't know."

"A diplomat. I'm proud of your sensitivity."

Neither spoke for a short while, then Yancy swung his feet onto the floor and looked hard into Drew's face. "I won't be staying here for long—Galveston, I mean. She's not partial to long visits from me, and that's a fact, so I'll be paying a few calls around town and then be going."

"I wish you wouldn't, Yancy."

"I wish so myself sometimes, but we take the hand that's dealt us and play it as best we can. Don't despair, we'll meet up again, seeing as I can't stay away for long, not anywhere as long as she'd have you believe. See, a woman such as her must have her little piece of the respectable, which seeing as she's in a profession that won't permit it, has to come from somewhere else, namely myself. Politician, state's representative, that's what she had planned. She'll have it in store for you too, don't worry, so better you make up your mind early to be respectable, or else get out like I did. There's nothing in between, I'm telling you."

Yancy stood, clapped Drew on the back and strode out. Drew considered following, then stopped himself; the front door could be heard closing in any case. Yancy had fled his past once again.

Vanda Gentles lived in two worlds, allowing Drew access to only one. He was not permitted to mention in her presence the existence of the brothel next door, nor to speak the name of Winnie, its only occupant whose name he knew. Meggs and Sukie would not discuss their mistress's line of work with Drew, but he sometimes overheard them referring to the premises of ill fame as "over there." Mrs. Gentles was not available for the greater part of each day and night, barring Sundays, because she was "over there," or, as Meggs preferred to phrase it, "minding her business."

Between the adjacent backyards of Vanda's home and her business was a lengthy trellised walkway festooned with creeping vines. She could pass from each of her worlds to the other without effort, or the inconvenience of having to submit to neighborhood staring. Every householder on the street was aware of her profession, yet accepting of it; all Vanda Gentles was required to do was appear to live the life of a middle-aged recluse, and present herself in public as little as possible.

Provided her business caused no untoward noise or traffic, and provided she contributed generously to the local political apparatus, she would be left in peace to practice her sinful but necessary calling. Her girls were never to be seen leaving the brothel by way of the front door, and a special alleyway had been created for their few social excursions. Every window facing the street was kept shuttered at all times. The two worlds were a large and silent house, and a small and silent house, side by side, communicating nothing of their purpose.

Drew's horse was stabled nearby, and he was free to ride every day but one. On Sundays, he was instructed to don an uncomfortably stiff suit of clothes and accompany Mrs. Gentles on a ride through Galveston and along the coast some four miles to a small beach, where it was customary, weather permitting, for them to partake of a picnic lunch. This ritual took place beneath a canvas awning erected by Meggs, who drove the carriage and performed those various small chores requiring male strength.

A young woman usually accompanied Mrs. Gentles and Drew on these pleasant excursions to nature, a slender creature named Clara, whom Vanda described as her companion and secretary. Meggs advised Drew to treat Clara with respect, because Clara was Mrs. Gentles's "diddy woman." He would not explain this curious term, but Drew accepted the advice and was unfailingly polite in Clara's presence.

There were discoveries to be made in the hushed and secretive existence Drew found himself immersed in. The first of these was the realization that Clara lived in the same house as himself, although he never once saw her there. Clara's presence was no more tangible than the sound of her voice in a distant room permitted. He expected he would have seen her at mealtimes, but there were no shared breakfasts, lunches or dinners in Vanda's house. Drew took these meals alone, waited on by Sukie, who proved herself aggressively uncommunicative on the subject of Clara, her employer, or the big house next door. "You just eat," she advised him, "and keep your nose clean as your plate."

Once, gripped by curiosity too great for containment, Drew asked

Vanda outright if Clara lived there with them. Vanda had stared at him for a moment before replying, "That is none of your concern, Drew. You are my son, not my keeper, and you will occupy yourself with the tasks I assign you, and no others."

This was a reference to Drew's intense schooling each day for several hours by a mournful individual named Sheldon Babb. Vanda required from Drew a detailed account of each day's lesson before he went to bed after a solitary snack at nine o'clock. It was obvious to Drew that the area of the house he was forbidden to enter, virtually half the lower floor and all of the upper, was the domain of his new mother and her companion/secretary. He suspected this had something to do with Meggs's cryptic designation of Clara as a "diddy woman," but the fullness of the mystery eluded him still.

The second discovery was the alleyway by which Vanda's whores were permitted egress to the outside world. Drew, in the course of his daily neighborhood perambulations, had several times noticed young women entering the street behind Vanda's home from the entrance to this alley, but thought they were simply using a shortcut from one block to the next. He realized his error when one of the young ladies was recognizable as Winnie. She was alone, and he approached her at a brisk trot, smiling in anticipation of a conversation with the one person besides Yancy who had expressed a personal interest in him since his coming to Galveston.

He was bewildered when she looked up, saw him approaching her and turned abruptly around. It almost seemed that she was consciously avoiding him, but Drew knew he must be mistaken; no one who had placed a hand intimately on his person would spurn him so, even all these months after their original encounter.

"Winnie!"

She hurried away from him at a faster pace. Drew broke into a run and caught up with her while Winnie was still several yards from the alley entrance, which she clearly was attempting to escape into. He blocked her path, his confusion laced now with anger.

"What's wrong with you! Didn't you see it's me?"

Winnie looked around them to be sure they were unobserved. It was a little past midday, and the street was empty of everything but a mongrel dog, but it was possible they were being eyed from behind any of several sets of curtains closed against the heat.

"You'll get me in trouble," she said.

"With who?"

"Her. She'll get me. I'm not supposed to talk to you or even look at you. None of us are."

"Why?"

"Because of *her,* stupid. Go away and let me alone."

Drew took Winnie by the arm and began steering her from the alley entrance. She resisted at first, making small sounds of exasperation, then fell into step with him, knowing that a peaceful young couple would attract less attention. She planned on breaking suddenly away from him before they reached any of the more populous streets, a block or two distant.

"She wouldn't hurt you," Drew assured Winnie. "That's just silly. She's very nice, really."

Winnie snorted undaintily to express her disbelief.

"I live in her house," Drew insisted, "so I know."

"You don't know your cock from a door handle."

"I do too!"

"Oh, excuse me, the door handle would be bigger, wouldn't it. If you get me in trouble with her, I'll kill you, little boy. She most likely knows already. She's got spies and lookouts everywhere."

"She hasn't," he protested.

"What would you know, little mister stupid."

"Stop calling me little."

"Big mister stupid. I'm not taking another step. If you try and make me, I'll kick you."

Drew fell back a few feet, still keeping pace with Winnie's furiously swishing skirts. "I'll stay back here, then no one'll think we're together."

Winnie abandoned her plans for a long walk alone, one of her few genuine pleasures in life. She led the way to a small public park a short distance from the waterfront. Its only occupants were several drunks arguing among themselves. She sat on a bench and allowed Drew to seat himself at its furthest end. She would not turn to face him, and instructed him to do the same for her. Drew watched the drunks instead. One of them was wrestling weakly with another for control of a bottle.

"Why won't you please leave me alone?" asked Winnie.

Drew thought hard. "I love you," he said. He wondered briefly if he meant it, then decided he'd better; Winnie didn't strike him as the kind to take such a declaration lightly. The least display of insincerity on his part and she'd very likely kick him hard. She seemed to be taking quite a while in responding.

"I do," he insisted, ignoring Winnie's instruction not to face her. He was not sure what expression to anticipate upon her face, probably something wry or contemptuous. What he saw instead, as Winnie broke her own rule and turned toward him, was a peculiar blend of pity and regret.

"Poor little boy," she said, not unkindly. "You really don't know anything at all, do you?"

Drew defended himself. "I know plenty," he said, sounding feeble even to himself.

"Listen, you: I'm a whore, and whores don't have anyone fall in love with them, just fall on top of them, which you haven't even done either, and I wouldn't let you anyway because you're a silly little boy that doesn't know anything! Don't you know you're her little doggie? She did the same with Yancy—did he tell you? She doesn't like boys, or men either, so she makes them into dogs to follow her around and do whatever she wants, even if they don't know they're doing it. We all know about her. Us, we know, so you can believe me. Even Clara's her little dog. Did you meet her yet?"

"Yes."

"Then you know *something* at least."

Drew was not so sure. Winnie's words seemed to be directed at someone else. He admitted that it was possible he really didn't know very much at all. Winnie seemed so much older, almost as old as Yancy, who Drew suddenly wanted back in Galveston so he could discuss with him this harsh talk against their mutual mother.

Winnie stood up. "Don't you follow me. Don't you ever come near me again," she said, and walked away. Drew watched her leaving. The drunk who had lost the bottle yelled incoherently as Winnie passed from the park to the sidewalk and was gone.

Drew felt like a fool. He'd gone and made Winnie, whom he felt a genuine fondness for, despise him for being a son, or dog or some such, in the house of Vanda Gentles. He was unsure why his circumstances, which were not of Drew's doing, should prejudice her against him. Could Vanda truly be as awful a woman as Winnie indicated? Drew sensed the worst had not been revealed, out of fear.

Two days later, when he was told to prepare for the usual Sunday picnic at the beach, Drew informed Vanda he would prefer not to attend.

"And why not?"

"I just don't want to."

"That is not a reason. You will come."

To his own chagrin, Drew did. He was determined, as he rode beside Vanda in the carriage, to assert himself more forcefully on the sands. The exact nature of his rebellion was unclear, even to himself, but he had to do something that would reach Winnie's ears, something to convince her he was no house pet. As witness to his protest he would have to rely on Meggs, since Clara had inexplicably been left behind in town, her first such absence from the beach picnics.

When Meggs completed setting up the awning and chairs, Vanda took her seat facing the Gulf of Mexico, as usual, then became aware that Drew had not placed himself in the chair beside her. She saw him some distance off, and sent Meggs to fetch him. Meggs returned with Drew's regrets; Drew would prefer to be alone.

"Tell him to stop this nonsense and come here directly."

Meggs delivered Vanda's message. Drew ambled back to the awning in his wake, deliberately dragging his boots through the sand. He sat in his accustomed chair, but refused to look at Vanda. He had obeyed only because he didn't want to be responsible for Meggs's tramping back and forth under the hot sun, relaying commands and refusals.

"Must I ask for an explanation?"

"For what?"

"Your ridiculous behavior."

Drew set his mouth in a line to match the horizon.

"You have nothing to say?"

"No."

"Perhaps I should ask Winifred for an answer."

He managed to stifle a reaction, knowing she watched him from the corner of her eye.

"Yes," she continued, "a short conversation with Winifred should clear up the matter. I have had occasion to chastise her before, so this will be nothing new."

"You leave her alone."

Vanda's head swiveled atop the stiff lace collar of her blouse. "Repeat those words if you dare."

"It was me. I went up to her. She told me to go away, but I didn't. It's not her fault."

He was appalled at the cringing tone in his voice. Winnie had been right; Vanda had spies everywhere. What kind of resistance could he muster against a woman like that? He felt his body packed tightly inside his Sunday clothes, like meat crammed into a sausage skin. It was intolerable that he should have to sit beside this woman he suddenly realized he hated, and hear someone he was fond of threatened with nameless punishment. "It wasn't her fault," he said again, knowing it was probably too late to alter whatever course Vanda had set her mind to.

"So she said," murmured Vanda, and Drew understood the interview had already taken place. She had been playing with him, deceiving him, waiting to see if he would step into some trap she doubtless had laid.

"What did you do?" he asked. It was inconceivable that she had done nothing.

"Winifred has departed our fair town."

"Where did she go?"

"Is that important? I hardly think so. You are well advised to learn a lesson from this. You are a part of my household, and for as long as you remain, you will abide by my wishes, my rules. I am not a cruel person, but I will not have my rules denied. You were told, were you not, that there should be no communication whatsoever between yourself and any of my employees. You did not do as I asked. Even Winifred could not dissuade you from wrongdoing, and now look what has happened. This girl you sought to attach yourself to has gone away as a direct result of your foolishness. You have only yourself to blame. Do you accept your role in this? Do you?"

"Yes," he said, defeated. He was glad Meggs was some distance away, unable to observe his humiliation.

"Then we shall talk no more of it. You will tell me instead what you have learned this week from Mr. Babb."

"I told you last night."

"You will tell me again."

Drew related some snippets from his latest lesson. Vanda nodded her head. "Excellent," she said. "You have the ability to absorb learning. Mr. Babb informs me you are a brighter than average boy. I'm pleased by this. A bright boy becomes a smart man. No other kind will accomplish anything in this world." She smoothed a crease from her bombazine dress. "You know, Drew, I have some small influence in Galveston. I am on friendly terms with a number of important persons who would be willing to accommodate you among their ranks when the time is right. For a special kind of man, there are no limits to his achievement. A special man could one day become governor of Texas, and from there, who knows, perhaps even aspire to the nation's highest office. Does such a notion attract you?"

"No."

"But it will, I assure you."

"Did Yancy get attracted?"

Vanda faced the gulf. "No, he did not. He was, however, not as clever at your age as you appear to be. Some are learners and some are not. Yancy is as Yancy does. You will not follow in his footsteps, because you are nothing like him."

Drew resented this comparison. What Vanda said was true, but he chose to see it as untruth, simply because he liked Yancy—gone no one knew where—better than he liked the woman beside him. It was very nearly a challenge; was he like Yancy, or wasn't he? Drew knew his own preference, but couldn't concentrate on it. The biggest shock from this stilted conversation beneath the awning was the disappearance of Winnie from his life. He had caused it, forcing himself upon her in public the way he did, despite her warnings. He didn't hold himself responsible for the loss, though; it was Vanda's fault.

What she had done was unforgivable. Winnie's picture of Vanda as a manipulator of lives had been borne out by events. Too late, Drew appreciated the power she held, and her willingness to dispense it at will, confounding her enemies, real or imagined. Why Winnie should have been counted among these was a puzzle to Drew, but he knew how to regard the woman responsible.

His moral obligation to hate Vanda was obvious, so he hated her with a purity of purpose that frightened him a little. She had done something she ought not to have done, and in so doing had freed Drew. He need no longer feel gratitude for the way in which she had accepted him into her home. Winnie had also been right in characterizing his life inside Vanda's house as that of a pet. He was indeed a weakling, incapable of the least heroism. Winnie's scorn had been earned within days of its delivery. He felt like a worm. Vanda had done it to him, and he had done it to himself. He was the lowliest of creatures. Even Meggs, as unctuous a servant as could be found, was staunchly resolute by comparison with Drew.

"What do you have to say for yourself?" Vanda asked.

Drew could give voice to nothing that was inside him.

In the week that followed, Drew's attention to his lessons wavered. Mr. Babb persevered, unwilling to lose so gratifying a student to the malaise of disenchantment he detected in Drew. He had seen it before, and always in boys approaching manhood. The distractions were substantial, but a professional like himself knew a way around them.

Mr. Babb abandoned for the moment any form of rote learning, and began reading to Drew from translations of Apuleius and Boccaccio, stopping often to explain the societies in which these chronicles of excess took place. Drew was captivated by the rampant sexuality of the tales, and absorbed more ancient history than would have been the case had his tutor been of conventional mold. Relishing his success, Mr. Babb decided to broaden Drew's horizons beyond the Roman-Italian world; he would approach Cervantes by way of Rabelais, then proceed to the moderns. It was a shame there were no equally earthy works of American literature through which to interest Drew in his own land, but Fenimore Cooper would do in a pinch, by substituting adventure for lust. Mr. Babb's practice of imparting knowledge through fiction (he referred to it as his "novel approach") had never found so willing a recipient, and he considered writing a small manifesto proclaiming its virtues, in hopes of raising controversy and perhaps some dollars.

The happy state of communion between teacher and pupil was called into question when Vanda happened one morning to enter the small back room set aside for lessons. She browsed among the books carelessly left behind by Mr. Babbs. Vanda had received an extensive education herself, and knew a legitimate school text when she saw it; instead were arrayed several volumes of filth, the worst offender being the illustrated Boccaccio. Such pictures were available in the brothel for the titillation of customers, but Vanda was outraged to find them in her home. She went directly to Drew's room, intending to confront him alone before Mr. Babb's arrival, but Drew was not there. A quick search revealed he had been doing his homework, as evidenced by a bookmark halfway through *The Golden Ass*.

In the afternoon Drew arrived at the lesson room to meet with Mr. Babb, and found himself facing Vanda. "Sit down," she told him. Drew sat.

"Where's Mr. Babb?"

"No longer with us."

Drew's heart lurched. "He's dead?"

Vanda was tempted to use this mistaken notion to avoid another lecture of the kind prompted by Winifred's departure. She did not enjoy confronting the boy over poor choices of association; in this instance, of course, the choosing had been her own.

"Mr. Babb was not the right man for the task. Education is a serious undertaking, I'm sure you'll agree. Mr. Babb clearly did not take the position seriously. We must admit to our mistake and find another tutor, someone without Mr. Babb's unfortunate flippancy. You may use the remainder of the day as you choose."

Drew left without a word. She had done it again, stolen away someone whose only crime was to be his friend. The woman was horrible, awful, a cruel and heartless monster! She must hate him as much as he hated her, to have done what she did. Why had she taken him in as her son if she only wanted to torment him? What sense was there in his even being there in her house if the both of them were locked in some kind of muted battle for supremacy over the living of Drew's life? The worst part was knowing he had fought poorly, if at all, in his own defense.

Drew had won for himself a reprieve from death at the hands of Morgan Kindred simply by running from him into the desert. Had the time come again to remove himself from harm's way? The harbor was jammed with ships; some of them must be in need of cabin boys. He had no particular wish to go to sea, though, and it would mean leaving behind his horse and gun; he didn't think sailors carried Winchesters. Vanda had at least allowed him to keep it in his room, so long as he promised never to load it with bullets. He had a dozen or so in his chest of drawers. He supposed he could shoot Vanda and be rid of her that way, but the complications that would follow murder dissuaded him; he doubted in any case that her wickedness was deserving of the ultimate punishment.

Although he had already ridden that day, Drew went to the stable down the street and saddled his horse again. He rode to the northern edge of town, taking this direction for no particular reason, and traveled for several miles along the Houston road before stopping to rest his horse beside a huge cottonwood tree. He dismounted and stared at the sky, asking himself if flight was the answer. There was nothing to stop him from continuing on to Houston that day, if he wished, but it would be better to return first for his gun and a change of clothing.

A rider was visible to the north, a mile or more distant across the flatlands. The only moving object in view, this individual occupied Drew's thoughts as he came slowly nearer. Drew decided to ask him how long it would take to reach Houston, just in case that was the plan he chose. He soon became impatient with the rider's dawdling pace and rode out to meet him. The rider's broad hat concealed his face with shadow until Drew was just a few yards away.

"Yancy!"

"I thought I recognized that nag. Who told you I was coming?"

"No one! I just came out here to ... I don't know ... Are you going to stay this time?"

"For exactly as long as it pleases me, Drew boy, and not a minute longer."

Their horses fell into step. Drew couldn't erase the grin from his face. Yancy's appearance at the very moment Drew needed him had the magical resonance of a wish granted. He even looked a little like a prince returning from faraway regions of excitement and danger, his hatbrim and belly holster canted at the same rakish angle, his handsome face lightly smeared with the road's romantic grime.

While they rode toward Galveston, Yancy told a rambling tale of women and cards and high times on the Mississippi riverboats, clear up to Saint Louis and back, followed by more of the same in New Orleans, culminating in yet another gambling house dispute that sent Yancy fleeing to Texas with a murder charge riding his coattails. Drew was unsure how much of it was true, but it hardly mattered; he was too happy over Yancy's return to care.

"Take me with you when you go," he begged.

"I'm not even home yet, and you want me to be planning another leavetaking already? You sound to me like a desperate fellow, someone not content with his lot."

"I want to go away. You better not go without me this time!"

"Ah-hah! Threats! Has it been so terrible?"

"Yes!"

"Tell me all, and I'll stop you when I hear something that surprises me."

Drew spilled his tale of resentment and woe. Yancy interrupted only once, to ask if Drew had managed to have his way with Winnie before the girl was dispatched elsewhere by Vanda. Drew admitted he had not, and Yancy shook his head.

"Drew boy, the longer you linger hereabouts, the more miserable you'll become, and so will Vanda. I told you, the lady craves respectability, but knows it'll never come to her, being what she is. A son's the thing that's supposed to bring it to her, but I'll confess I was made of weaker stuff than she requires. Her cronies are all politicians, and powerful folk in their own right. I truly believe she could push a suitable fellow to the top, with their help, but it won't be me, and I see by your face it won't be you either. Correct?"

"Correct."

"Then you'll come with me. You're too young a piece of fruit to wither on the vine, I think. Correct again?"

"Correct again!"

"Now listen. You go on ahead and don't tell a soul you've seen me. We don't want you-know-who to think we're scheming together over your escape. Sometime tonight I'll make an appearance at sweet Mama's, but when I do, you behave toward me like you'd treat a leper, and I don't mean with a samaritan's kindness. Fool her, or she'll have you tied down with chains until I'm gone. Can you do it?"

Drew said yes.

He waited that night for Yancy's entrance, and was still awake and dressed after midnight, when Yancy arrived at Vanda's door on a plank supported at either end by newfound friends. He had several deep knife wounds to the stomach, and was already unconscious from blood loss. He did not revive before dying on Vanda's parlor floor, ruining her Turkish carpet in the process.

Drew remained in Galveston until the funeral, to which Vanda invited no one of importance. As soon as he was able, Drew left with his horse and gun. The things Yancy had given him were precious, even if they were stolen from a dead man killed by Yancy's hand.

In Houston he sought out the lowest section of town and began asking around for friends of Yancy Berdell. Some people said they had never heard the name, and others were immediately suspicious, and denied knowledge of Yancy in a way that made Drew aware they were lying. He didn't know why they would do this, since he clearly was not a lawman.

"Yes you do know him," he said to the latest of these liars, a very fat gentleman in a seedy cafe, "and you better know he's dead. That's all I'm trying to tell you. He's dead and buried in Galveston."

"Yancy's dead?"

"And buried. He got stabbed."

"Some woman's husband?"

"He was gambling."

"Aah, so even Yancy's lucky streak ran out. Sit down, boy. You'll take coffee with me. Are you by any chance the one he rescued from Apaches in the desert west of here?"

"He didn't save me from anything. He was a big liar."

"That's true, and I guess you're the one. It was never a convincing tale, not one of his best. I forget the name he gave you."

"It's Drew, and it was always my name. What he gave me was a horse and a Winchester."

"So he said. There was always a kernel of truth in Yancy's tales. So you've flown the coop of mother Vanda's chickens for sale."

"I wanted to tell his friends what happened. She never would've."

"Indeed no, she would not. Yancy was the blackest of sheep."

The fat man extended a well-manicured hand. "Marion de Quille," he said. "I do hope we'll become friends. Are you in need of friends, young Drew? Don't be too proud to say so. Everyone on this earth needs a friend or two."

"Yes."

"Now tell me this: are you Vanda's boy, philosophically speaking, or Yancy's? Think about the question before answering."

"Yancy's."

"You're sure? Someone young as you is maybe not ready to be Yancy's boy, spiritually speaking, or do I mean morally? You take my meaning, though. Yancy was not an honest, hardworking citizen, now was he?"

"Nossir."

"Please, call me Marion. We have Yancy's acquaintance in common, so that puts us on friendly terms right away. Now then, Drew, have you thought about what it means to be Yancy's boy, and to choose the life Yancy chose?"

"It's better than the other lives."

"What lives are those?"

"The ones I already lived."

"Aah, yes. We all have led lives we would prefer to have avoided. And so you wish to be a gambler."

"Yes."

"You know, don't you, that poor Yancy was not a clever man with the cards. He wished himself better, but never achieved that wish. I myself hold several hundred dollars of Yancy's bad debts. When

Yancy lost, he tended to fling lead at his opponents, which is not the way of the professional. Are you sure you wish to follow in his footsteps?"

"I thought he was a good gambler."

"Alas, no, but he did have other talents he might not have shared with you. It may be that you have the nerve to be what he was after all."

"What talents?"

Marion de Quille told him.

14

The first odor to greet his nostrils every morning was that of slightly damp socks. Most of the men washed their socks outside the cabin, then brought them in and hung them over the stovepipe that ran below the roof for several yards before angling up through the shingles. There were never less than two dozen pairs of socks draped over the pipe, scenting the cabin's already foul air, a fetid brew of sweat-soaked clothing that somehow never merited the attention given to socks, of tobacco smoke, seldom-emptied spittoons, kerosene lamps, bad breath lightly disguised by whiskey, and lastly, since no window graced the cabin walls and the door was kept shut all night, the overpowering odor of stale farts. Altogether, it was enough to force a man from his bed even before Bruno the cook began pounding with his iron bar on the wake-up triangle outside.

Slade prided himself on being able to greet Bruno as the cook plodded toward the triangle. He knew it irritated the man that someone should be up before he had the opportunity to beat and bash the metal, jerking the camp into wakefulness. Slade knew he could never have risen before Bruno, since Bruno's duties obliged him to be up and preparing breakfast for sixty men a full hour before the triangle woke everyone. It was satisfaction enough to be up and mobile before the clanging and banging began. Bruno went

to bed early in any case, long before anyone else, so Slade felt his
point was made, simply by his standing there with a smile when
Bruno came across to the triangle with his iron bar. It was a ritual,
and as all rituals are designed to do, it renewed Slade's faith in
himself and what he did.

Slade cut down trees; not ordinary trees—the largest trees in the
world. They stood around the camp, dark titans looming in the
morning mist, and he never failed to appreciate their size and their
implacable stillness. The first branches of the redwoods began well
over a hundred feet up the trunk. When the mist was thick, as it
usually was, these lower branches were completely hidden till midmorning, so the trees stood like massive pillars in a chilly temple of
air. Slade had heard that the largest redwoods were between two
and three thousand years old. It was hard to credit such antiquity,
but he believed it, and never approached one to bring it down with
less than the respect he felt it deserved.

His fist was always the first to smash through a scum of ice that
formed in the water barrel. A frigid splashing of the face was
enough to bring about instant alertness. Slade was always waiting
in the cookhouse when Bruno returned to sling his bar into a corner
beside the massive stove.

The Northern California Timber Company was not niggardly
with its fare. Every man could eat as much as he pleased at every
meal, and loggers were not known for their lack of appetite. Ham,
scrambled eggs, bacon, flapjacks: they were waiting by the plateful
as the men straggled in, hitching suspenders over their shoulders,
some still yawning the sleep from themselves. There was little conversation to mask the clattering of heavy-duty cutlery as they sat
on the split-log benches and began serving themselves. Many of the
men were foreigners with little English, and even these were disinclined to speak among themselves at so early an hour. The business
at hand consisted of fueling the body for a day's hard labor, not communication; that could wait for the evening, for the pipe smoking
and harmonica playing and stilted camaraderie of the logging
brethren.

Slade ate and ate. He was approaching middle age, but had never
felt so strong, so powerful. This was truly the prime of his life, a
time of intense happiness, and it came from the straightforward
task of felling gigantic trees. Slade had toppled Douglas fir and
Sitka spruce and Ponderosa pine up and down the Pacific coast, but

he believed himself fulfilled only as the agent of destruction for the redwood. This was the giant, the tree of trees, and he felt he had earned for himself a place at the bole of the earth's mightiest living thing, ax in hand.

It was the apex of his work among the limitless forests of the far west, this bringing down by sweat and toil of the high and mighty. Slade was a proud man, smart enough to base his pride on actual accomplishment. He pictured himself among these ancient colossi forever, or until such time as an accident took him. He could not conceive of himself as old, infirm, incapable of performing the work that made him a king within the limited realm of his kind. It would be a mercy, he sometimes thought, for a dislodged bough to come crashing down and crush him instantly, rather than to endure the humiliation of physical weakness, the gradual degeneration of his notion of himself.

He doubted that his fellow workers brooded on such topics. Slade knew his thoughts were of a far more complex nature than those of his fellows. He had never fit in, wherever he worked, and this fostered in him a sense of his own uniqueness. He ate his ham, wolfed down his bacon, drained cup after cup of gritty coffee like a god quaffing ambrosia.

Slade always walked ahead of the rest. The current felling area lay almost a mile from the camp, more than three from the mill. Morning was the best time, with mist still thick around him, and sometimes the faint salt smell of the ocean at Mendocino. If he got far enough ahead of the rest, he could barely hear their few words of talk.

The forest was capable of swallowing just about any sound man could make. Even the biggest sound, when a tree came crashing down, would reverberate for only a short time, then be gone. The sound of axes was puny, the bellowings of the oxen that hauled log sections down the skid road to the mill were as nothing. Slade's voice was considered the loudest of any tree faller, but as it warned of another giant's imminent collapse, it was only a squirrel squeak in the deep woods.

Every tree required two fallers working as a team to bring it down; every tree except the one Slade chose to work on. He worked alone, the only man in the company allowed to do so. He could not topple a redwood in the same time it took two men to do so, but he was never more than a day or so behind any regular team, and this in a field of work that often required a week's solid work per tree. One man, performing the work of one and three-quarters men, but paid only one wage; it was an arrangement that made fiscal sense to Slade's employers. He was too arrogant to be made a bull of the woods, or logging boss; Slade neither gave nor accepted orders. He would work in the same general area as lesser men, but never consent to be one of them. It was not company policy to allow exceptions to their rules, but in Slade's case they relented; he was, after all, a legendary figure in the industry, therefore something of a bristling feather in their cap.

Slade's tree of the moment was a monster of around two hundred feet, not the biggest he'd ever felled, nor the smallest. He had worked four days already on the undercut, the huge wedge-shaped bite taken from the bole near the redwood's base. An ordinary team would deepen its axed-out undercuts with double-length crosscut saws and wedges before tackling the backcut, the smaller chunk, taken from the opposite side, that would cause the tree to topple. Not Slade; he required nothing but his double-bladed ax for both cuts.

Today he would begin the backcut. He had already directed the layout crew to prepare a long bed of boughs leading away from the trunk, in the direction Slade intended it should fall. He had placed a stake in the ground for them to work toward, and if his calculation and skill were of the usual order, this stake would be driven into the ground by the upper reaches of the descending redwood. The crew had done a good job, he saw, arranging the lopped boughs and covering them with great swaths of bark peeled from previously felled trees, to make a soft landing bed for Slade's latest conquest. With a little luck and several buckets of sweat, it would hit the earth before daylight was done.

The work was performed as art, as self-expression. Slade poured himself into every swing of the ax, working with rhythm, no movement wasted, taking each bite from the precise spot he aimed for. He was aware at every moment of what he was about, allowed no thought to distract him, not even the simplest. He knew this ability to empty his mind completely was as important to his skill as the superior strength in his arms and back. He knew of men who had died horribly because of wavering concentration. To Slade's way of thinking, those men had betrayed themselves, revealed their inferiority, and paid the price. He had no sympathy for them, nor would he have sympathy for himself if he should ever let his attention wander. That was a fate for others. If he should die in the woods, it would not be any fault of his own; the tree that killed him would be brought down by almighty God, no less.

He drank often from the two-gallon jug that accompanied him each day, felt the water flood through him and out his pores minutes later, a constant irrigation or oiling of the engine within. When the sound of other axes was stilled around noon, Slade drove his blade lightly into the trunk below the narrow springboard he stood upon to work, jumped to the board below that, and from there to the ground, where his lunch pail stood beside the jug. Inside were the usual two-inch-thick beef sandwich and the heavy oatcake or sweet bread Bruno and his assistant prepared for the pails that every faller collected on his way out of the cookhouse. It never varied beyond the oatcake/sweet bread alternate, but Bruno received no complaints.

When he was done with eating, Slade contemplated his place in the universe, and found it satisfactory. His primitive state of bliss renewed, as it was over every lunch, Slade allowed himself a brief nap, into which no dream intruded. He awoke at the first thud of a distant ax, raised himself up and stretched like an animal well content, without enemies, a creature belonging body and soul to its time and place in the natural order of things. He leapt to the first springboard, and to the next, yanked his ax from the tree and drew it slowly back for the first of the final series of blows that would bring it down.

He worked without pause until the backcut had been deepened to a dangerous extent, then cupped both hands around his mouth and bellowed at his loudest, "She faaaaaalls ...!" This was a phrase of Slade's own invention; let the rest of them holler "Timmmm-berrrrr ..." like so many echoes of each other; Slade had his own holler, because he had his own way of making a redwood fall. The cry he gave was a summons to anyone in the vicinity to come see an event such as they would see nowhere else in the tall woods, the thing that had made the name of Slade synonymous with daring and bravado and—the ingredient guaranteeing legendary status—a touch of magic.

They were already running through the trees to be nearby when the tree came down. It gave Slade pleasure to see them flocking toward him this way, like so many ardent followers answering his call from the tower, adherents to the creed of Slade. Soon there were three dozen or more, standing at a respectable distance from Slade's tree.

He jumped down from the backcut boards, marched around to the undercut and launched himself up the boards remaining below it until he could stand in the cut itself, the sloping roof of the missing wedge several feet above his bushy head. He stood with hands on hips, his back to the narrowed waistline of wood still supporting the two hundred feet of tonnage above. The redwood could begin to fall at any moment, depending on the winds, and the recess in which Slade chose to stand was the most dangerous, since a toppling tree could shatter at its narrowest place and drive splinters ten feet long into the region cleared by the faller's ax, or if it did not, the ragged end of the separated trunk could spring back into that same space when its upper branches hit the ground so far away and sent a reciprocal, gargantuan twanging back along its own length to the point of injury and despoilment.

Nonetheless, Slade chose to stand there, smiling at his audience, and when he judged the moment was right, he looked up at the partial vault of wood above, its sap bleeding in droplets onto his beard. This was the time of Slade's magic, the conjuring of the right wind from just the quarter he required, a gentle stirring among the high treetops that soon was causing his redwood to groan and squeal like a mast bent on unstepping itself before the elements. The wood behind Slade began to splinter. Another faller would have jumped for safety then, but he remained as before, beaming his rigid smile, and moved his boots not an inch. If the wind shifted, if it happened to reverse itself then, he stood a fair chance of being caught in the undercut's closing maw: but the breeze favored Slade as always, and pushed his ailing giant in precisely the direction he wished.

The massive trunk began its protracted fall, the fulcrum of its descent mere yards behind Slade's heedless back. Now the length of it was quivering as if in pain, as the crown arced downward past the tree's own offspring, gathering speed at the forty-five-degree mark, accelerating from there to the forest floor, where it smashed itself down along the prepared alignment of boughs and bark, its arrival tossing earth and matter into the air, the ground itself buckling and recovering itself in a series of shudderings that were felt through the boots of every onlooker. Their eyes were on the jagged splayings of wood at the trunk's end, horizontal splinters liable at a second's notice to spring backward, impaling him. But they did not, and while the dust of impact hung in the air still, and the earth seemed to vibrate inside their legs, Slade's admirers watched as he executed a stiffly mocking bow to their faces.

Tomorrow the peelers would strip the giant's foot-thick bark: then the buckers would attack it with their crosscut saws, dividing the trunk into manageable lengths; the choker setters would follow in turn, to lash the truncated sections with cable so the bullwhackers could harness each section to their teams of oxen and haul it down greased skid roads to the millyard.

There the redwood would be further reduced by an assortment of screaming metal blades, its bulk halved and quartered by endless bandsaws; then would come the series of belittlings that rendered a colossus into squared railroad ties, or so many board feet of planking; at its most humbling, the tree's great bulk became roofing shingles a mere twelve inches long. All of this, tie or board or shingle, would be dumped into the stream-fed flume that would carry it to the coast along forty-three miles of man-made water road, a narrow rushing rivulet contained within banks planed from the most serviceable lumber around—redwood.

Slade knew little and cared less about this end result of his handiwork; the sawing and dicing of timber was a task for little men. Once the living tree was down, Slade's part in its termination became an event from yesterday, a thing to be proud of, surely, but not to be contemplated overlong. Slade knew the men who owned the mill, and others like it from San Francisco to the Canadian line, were millionaires, but he could never bring himself to consider them more important than himself. They were puny fellows, he supposed, with whitened skin and dry coughs; one strong breath from Slade's lungs would have knocked the lot of them off their pins. Slade had no wish to earn vast sums of cash; no amount of wealth could have brought him the one thing he already had, a reputation as the best faller in the western woods. He had earned it. It was his, and he wore it like a crown.

Hartley and Hubert Louther owned the Northern California Timber Company. Hartley was the older brother by six years, and made a habit of reminding Hubert of his inferior status. Hartley tended to make the larger business decisions on behalf of them both, but was prepared to leave the bookkeeping and accounts entirely in

Hubert's hands. Hartley was content with the arrangement; Hubert was not. Transplanted New Englanders, they ran the tightest and most profitable logging operation in Mendocino County.

Neither their admirers nor their detractors were fully aware of the bad feeling that existed between the Louther brothers. Their mill and lumber shipping concerns had been developed by their father, Hartley Senior, and his firstborn had always known himself to be the true heir. Hubert might disagree, and often did, but was silenced each time by an offer to buy him out. Hubert didn't want to leave the company or the Louther mansion outside Ukiah; he wanted to own it all and throw his bullying older brother out on his pompous ear.

The rift between them widened when Hartley married a young lady who happened to conform almost exactly with Hubert's notion of the ideal woman. Susan was not perfect, of course, since she had accepted a boor like Hartley for her spouse, when she could just as well have chosen Hubert instead, but Hubert forgave her; Susan was very young, hardly responsible for the magnitude of her error.

Hubert made love to his sister-in-law with his eyes for months before confessing his feelings toward her. Susan stared at him, then laughed at the expression of anguish on his pudgy face and said, "Oh, Hubert, you are such a silly boy. Now I won't say a thing to Hartley, because he may not understand you were only making a joke, but just you keep your silly jokes to yourself in future, or I might change my mind, and then where would you be." She capped this with a lighthearted laugh.

Crushed, Hubert slunk into Ukiah to find solace at his favorite den of low vice, an unpretentious brothel run by a Mrs. Clancy. After sobbing onto the breast of Mrs. Clancy's newest girl, Hubert went downstairs to get very drunk.

Toward evening, he looked up from his mug to see before him the largest man God was capable of assembling without recourse to the term "giant." He was alarmingly, stunningly, unavoidably large, and Hubert could not help but stare at the fellow's sheer massiveness. He watched as this Goliath began climbing the stairs behind a girl who appeared quite inadequate for the work in store, and heard the woodwork groan beneath his Brobdingnagian boots. What a creature! It could only be a logger.

Hubert fell to musing, suddenly uninterested in his beer. Several years earlier, brother Hartley had hired a man with the reputation

of being able to perform the work of two ordinary fallers, a muscular but otherwise unremarkable-looking axman by the name of
Slade. Hartley had done it because he wanted the Northern California Timber Company to have on its payroll the acknowledged best
in the business. Slade hired on, and had stayed in the logging
camp all this time, never coming down from the mountains with the
rest of the men to blow off steam in establishments such as Mrs.
Clancy's.

He was considered something of a mystery man, this Slade, one
whom no amount of questioning could tempt to answer the simplest
question. It had been a sharp move on Hartley's part to bring Slade
into the fold, even Hubert agreed, since Slade's mere presence
granted the falling team a glamour it might otherwise not have
had. Contenders for the woodsy laurels Slade wore had come forward from time to time, and what Hubert referred to as "hacking
contests" were held to determine which was the better man. Slade
had won all of these without real effort.

Hubert knew, as if the fact had been whispered in his ear by
angels, that the hulking creature whose footsteps could at that
moment be heard above was a foe worthy of Slade, just as Hubert
was himself a worthy successor to Hartley at the company helm.
The unrelated nature of these clashes was already blurring in
Hubert's imagination, becoming as one.

He ordered a fresh beer, in a celebratory mood, but ignored it
when it arrived; he must keep his head clear for the bargaining and
cajolery that undoubtedly would be required to convince even so
large a man as the one directly above him (Hubert could hear the
bedsprings now, and changed tables) that he could beat the company's reigning champion.

A whisper traveled up-country to the mill, and from there to the
camp: a new man was coming, a big man, a veritable giant, and a
mean master of the double-bladed ax. When every ear had received
the rumor, and every mind digested it, every eye turned to Slade for
his reaction.

True to form, he said nothing, although it was clear he had heard
the whisper around him, and was mulling it over in his own imper-
turbable fashion. The team would have been disappointed had he
spoken of this topic that seemed to fill the cabin. Slade's response
was the appropriate one: say nothing, wait and see. It could well be

that the whisper had exaggerated the new man's size and prowess, as whispers often did.

Bruno noticed, next morning, the increased appetite of nearly everyone. The logging team scoffed their food and looked at each other often, as if sharing some obscure joke among themselves. He knew it was the whisper that had done this, stimulated them to eat more than their usual heaped portions. For the first time since he could remember, he was obliged to make second helpings of almost everything, and that did not sit well with Bruno, for whom the art of estimating in advance the needs of the communal belly was a source of professional pride.

There had been other whispers, other new men who came with the specific intent of besting Slade. Bets were placed, axes sharpened; wood chips flew like angry bees, and closely tallied scores were kept, sometimes for days on end, as the contender kept pace with Slade. But in the end these aspirants faded, their strength gone, seemingly sucked from them by Slade, who never once appeared to tire. There had been a close-run thing some years ago, when a big Swede came closer than any man before him to breaking the magical hold Slade had on winning, but even that one had given out in the end, in a most spectacular manner; gouts of blood had suddenly spewed from his mouth, and he fell from his springboard to the forest floor, stone dead before the nearest man could even reach him. Slade had continued hacking until his tree came down, then wandered over to witness the sorry fate of the Swede. Naturally, he said nothing.

It would have been gratifying, Bruno thought, if Slade could be brought to his knees just once, to teach him a lesson in humility. Bruno had experienced a great many of these lessons in his life, and resented Slade's apparent ability to escape the vicissitudes, great and small, that bedevil the affairs of ordinary men. Slade's reputation appeared bulletproof, a permanent fixture around the man, like the unearthly glow Bruno had seen around holy personages in illustrated Bibles.

Slade was unworthy of being singled out thus by fortune, in Bruno's opinion, but there was nothing he could do to upset the divine balance Slade seemed to enjoy. It irked Bruno that Slade somehow knew of the animosity directed at him by the cook. What else could have explained the morning ritual of finding the big man waiting by the triangle every time Bruno went out with his iron bar to bash and jangle the camp to wakefulness. It was a stupid act, without meaning, and the faint smirk that accompanied it occupied much of Bruno's thoughts for the rest of the day, every day.

There had been a time when he considered murdering Slade. When everyone else went down to the town to get drunk and fight and fornicate with whores, Slade always remained behind, as did Bruno. For the cook, Ukiah represented Sodom and Gomorrah, and probably a few other cities of iniquity besides; his mother had warned him of the dangers, moral, spiritual and physical, attendant upon consorting with loose women. She had given him many pamphlets, with such titles as " Carnality's Poisonous Secret" and "A Rake's Descent" and "A Doctor's Earnest Advice to Christian Men." Bruno understood from an early age that the body is the temple of the soul, sacrosanct in the eyes of the Lord. He couldn't abide to see so many temples sullied by unworthy tenants who insisted on visiting the pustulant harlots of the lower valley. Bruno intended to remain pure all his days, despite the ribbing this earned him from the fallers whose food he served.

His celibacy was his pride, the thing that had granted him uniqueness in the camp, until Slade came. It quickly became apparent Slade also shunned the fleshpots, but Bruno saw no evidence of piety influencing Slade's choice. It was irritating to have to share the camp on Sundays with this silent unbeliever. His presence was an intrusion, a distraction; Bruno couldn't concentrate on his Bible studies with the dedication that had come easily from being surrounded by nothing but the greatest of God's trees. Slade tended to prowl restlessly, like a caged brute suddenly freed, but directionless in his freedom. They saw each other often each Sunday, always at a distance, and never spoke, didn't so much as nod. The morning ritual by the triangle had been their most intimate contact for several years, and seemed likely to continue.

Three days after the whisper arrived, its subject came to the camp after quitting time, brought up from Ukiah in the fancy surrey of Mr. Hubert Louther himself. Such a thing had never happened before. Even Slade had been hauled from Ukiah on an oxcart filled with supplies. From a distance it was obvious who was who, the new man having caused the near collapse of the vehicle's springs on the right-hand side. Mr. Louther went straight inside the cabin of the camp boss, leaving his passenger to disengage himself from the tiny seat that had withstood his bulk up the narrow pathway from the mill.

As he stood clear, it was with a practiced slowness calculated to draw attention. The giant stretched his arms as if to embrace the world, then placed both ham-sized fists on his corduroyed hips and smiled at the gathering he faced.

"Been expecting me, boys?" he asked. "Or maybe you was expecting the circus, huh?"

He laughed when no one responded. His audience felt Slade should have been there with them to witness the new man's arrival. The two could have strutted around each other like prize roosters, each sizing up his opponent, but Slade was nowhere around.

"Name's Chason, but mostly they call me Chase. You men here, you do that, call me Chase. That's the way I prefer it, friendly like."

His smile was made ugly by tobacco stains. Chason was taunting them with a false display of openness, every man could see it. Chason knew very well why he was there, and felt he had already scored against his opponent through the latter's nonappearance.

"This all of you, right here?" he said.

"Except for Slade," someone offered.

"Slade? I heard of someone called that. Little man, plays with his pud, that the one?"

"I don't reckon."

"Sure, that'll be him. You see him hiding out, you tell him there's a new man here to work alongside of him."

"Slade, he don't work with no one."

"Well, he does now, orders of the big man in there."

Chason jerked his thumb at the door Hubert Louther had disappeared behind. Raised voices could be heard from within the camp boss's cabin. Looks were exchanged among the men. Hubert must be sick and tired of his big brother's man ruling the roost, and had brought the new contender up from town himself, so everyone understood exactly how matters stood. It was an unthinkable violation of the camp boss's authority to instruct him, as Hubert clearly was doing, that Slade and Chason were to work together. Nothing could better have been calculated to antagonize the champion than this invasion of his professional domain. Slade's work practices had until that day been of his own devising. The men were anxious to see if he would submit to working with a partner.

Hubert Louther came outside, climbed into his surrey and

departed without even a glance at the man he had brought. The camp boss came out a moment later, and indicated that Chason should accompany him. The entire team fell in behind as Chason was led to a cabin and told to find a vacant bunk. It was not the cabin Slade used, Bruno was disappointed to note. The boss obviously wasn't wanting to cooperate in Hubert's plan to thrust Slade and Chason up against each other as soon as could be arranged. Bruno happened to know there was a vacant bunk in Slade's cabin the new man could have used, but it didn't really matter; Slade and Chason would confront each other soon enough, over Bruno's cookhouse tables.

The evening meal of mutton was served in an air of muted apprehension. Neither of the two men had arrived to eat, and heads that usually were lowered to their plates were constantly twisting toward the door in expectation. When Chason entered, a hush fell. What happened next was foreseen by a prescient few; Chason went directly to the one available space left at the table—Slade's. As he lowered himself to the split-log bench, a collective sigh could be heard. Now there would be hell to pay when Slade came in. No one ever sat where Slade wanted to; one man had tried it a year or two back, and been thrown across the room.

"How's the grub in this hole?" Chason asked. "You men all look healthy enough." He examined the heaped plate awaiting Slade. "Sheep," he said. "I like sheep." His first mouthful provoked another sigh. The confrontation to come as a result of this would be savage. Chason was bigger than Slade, much bigger, and seemed already in the mood for confrontation.

Where was Slade? Was he going to let the camp down by not showing up for dinner? No one capable of walking had ever not shown up for dinner, so his absence, if it continued, would be construed as cowardice. Slade a coward! It was inconceivable that this should be so, but the occupation of Slade's place by the usurper was a powerful blow already to those who, even if they had no personal liking for Slade, supported him in the challenges that periodically were mounted to bring him down to the level of other men. He belonged to them all, even if he never had a word to say, a story to trade, even if he never accompanied the rest down to the dens of Ukiah every Saturday night.

The men ate more than their usual share, drawing out the dinner in hopes of witnessing some kind of development, but Slade disappointed them all by staying away. It was established that he had returned to the camp along with everyone else but had not been seen since. No one could say for sure if Slade was even aware of Chason's arrival, but the two things, seen in relation to one another, seemed inescapably linked. Slade's behavior was mystifying, even when he was discovered fast asleep on his bunk. He had never missed a meal through exhaustion before, and it did not bode well for his ability to compete with the newcomer, but at least it put to rest the notion that he had avoided the cookhouse out of fear. The good news was spread to every cabin before the lamps were turned out.

Approaching the triangle next morning, Bruno half expected that Slade would not be there with his usual smirk, his inexplicable look of triumph at having beaten Bruno to the place once again. Bruno had never fathomed the meaning of Slade's morning ritual, and was unsure if it conveyed a personal hatred of himself, or some general, abstract motive beyond understanding. It could even be that Slade was a mild kind of madman; it was impossible to tell with someone as silent as him.

He was there, but the expected smirk was not. Slade appeared angry, or possibly confused. He was staring at the ground when Bruno approached the triangle with his iron bar, only looking up as Bruno raised his hand to strike metal upon metal. The movement of the raised arm triggered in Slade a primitive reaction. He came suddenly to life and shoved Bruno hard in the chest, causing him to fall back onto the ground, the bar flying from his hand, the breath knocked from his lungs. Slade glowered at him for several seconds, then strode away.

Bruno picked himself up, panting with anger. He was not a large man, and considered Slade's unprovoked assault an outrage. He would not complain to the camp boss, however, since that would make him appear a weakling. Any man in the camp who could not take care of his own affairs was not fit company for loggers, even if he occupied the lowly position of cook. He would get his revenge in his own way, his own time. Bruno was not completely upset by the incident, since it revealed, as yesterday's nonappearance and early slumbers had not, that Slade was cognizant of, and severely rattled by, the arrival of Chason. Events from that morning on would definitely be of an interesting nature, and Bruno felt himself a part of it all, since Slade paid more attention to him than to anyone else.

Slade was already waiting in his usual place at the breakfast table when the rest of the men began trickling in from the water bucket and the latrine. They looked at him without talking, knowing that to ask questions would be futile, possibly dangerous. Chason drifted in with the rest, noted the individual seated where he had sat for dinner, and found another place for himself by nudging one of the smaller men aside with a broad hand and broader smile. "Mornings, I need to set right down and commence to eat," he said, "not waste time looking for no seat."

The displaced man went elsewhere. Slade was eating by then, his back to Chason's seat, but the silence was such that he could not have helped but overhear the intimidation occurring behind himself. He gave no sign, offered no reaction, another disappointing letdown for the men. The game between Slade and Chason was a long time getting up and started, they thought, but at least life was being made more interesting by the rivalry, which already had extended beyond mere competition concerning who could bring down the biggest trees in the shortest time. This was some other kind of confrontation, more serious than any of them could have foreseen.

Shouldering his ax and springboards, Slade began walking into the woods. He would start work on a new tree today, always a satisfying task, but as he walked ahead of the rest, Slade was aware of a vague disquiet within himself. The evening before, he had gone for a stroll before dinner, just a short walk off among the redwoods, far enough to isolate himself from the sounds of the camp, but not so far he wouldn't hear the dinner bell. Slade often did this, having no need of companionship. He expected his stroll to be uneventful, and was surprised, therefore, when he found himself lying on the ground in darkness, when his last thought before finding himself there was of being upright in the pleasant light of day. What had happened? His head had throbbed wildly as he retraced his steps to the camp. He avoided crossing anyone's path, went straight to his bunk in the empty cabin and threw himself down, hoping to stop the pain in his skull by remaining still.

Sleep had followed with merciful swiftness, but he had awoken that day with an inexplicable anger in his heart. He had knocked the cook to the ground for no reason other than that the sight of the little man had intensified his anger beyond endurance. Even now, after a full breakfast, with anticipation of a rewarding day's labor ahead of him, Slade felt a lurking darkness within him. It did not help his mood at all when he realized he had forgotten to pick up his lunch pail before leaving the cookhouse.

More confusion followed when a large man Slade had never seen before approached him. Slade was at the base of a redwood of his choosing, carefully chopping out a gash to insert his springboard into, when the man said to him, "I'll take this side, you go on around to the other and start again."

Slade stared. The words had reached him, but their meaning had not. He turned away from the man, whose face he was unfamiliar with, and resumed cutting.

"You hear me?"

Slade looked at him again. Why was this person annoying him? Didn't the whole camp know he wasn't to be approached while working, unless he indicated he wished for a gathering of witnesses, as he had yesterday? This tree was barely begun; he had work to do, and didn't want to be bothered by some new man who had not been told that Slade must be left strictly alone. He turned away again.

"I said, you go work on the other side, you deaf son of a bitch." Slade faced Chason, suddenly hating him. He didn't like the face before him, or the voice spitting words at him. This new man's arrogance at telling Slade what to do was beyond belief. Slade decided it was beneath him to answer such a fool, but he would allow the fool to withdraw from his company before any more insulting words came out. He pointed to the fool, then pointed off into the woods, a clear indication he wanted the fool to quit his company immediately.

The fool seemed not to understand. "You dumb as well as deaf?" he asked, thrusting his face closer to Slade's. Chason was a master of intimidation; usually his physical presence alone allowed him to get his way in all things. He had been told by Hubert Louther to make himself as obnoxious as possible to Slade, in order to rattle Slade's confidence in himself as king of the woods. He was not impressed at all with Slade's lethargic reaction to his goading. The man appeared to be simpleminded, which might complicate Chason's assignment to bring him to his knees.

"You hear me, huh? Get around the other side there."

He saw Slade's ax lifted, saw the blade arcing with surprising speed, saw it begin its descent toward him without understanding that he was about to die for his words. The blade edge, honed to hairsplitting sharpness, sliced into the thin layer of skin and flesh across his forehead and continued on through Chason's skull and brain until the haft met resistance from the nasal bone and lost momentum. Chason sank to the ground with Slade's ax standing from his head like a peculiar growth. He toppled silently sideways, eyes still opened. The ax handle's end tapped lightly against earth.

Slade looked at what he had done. He was very angry that he had been obliged to silence the fool. Someone should have informed him that Slade was nobody to order around, but no one had, and this was the result. It was maddening to think of the trouble that would result from the fool's pestering. Slade might even be blamed for what had happened, and be obliged to explain why he had done it. They would want him to talk and talk and talk, which wouldn't be fair, since none of what happened had been his fault.

No other faller was working sufficiently close to have seen or heard anything. This cheered Slade a little. He picked up the fool's ax and flung it far away into the woods, then he lifted the dead man by the belt at the rear of his pants and carried him some distance away and dumped the body in a tangle of brush, extracting his ax before he scattered some loose twigs over the dead man to conceal him even more. Then he went back to his tree. There were a few drops of blood en route, and he took care to scuff these over with his boots. At the spot where the new man had fallen there was a small pool of red that had leaked from his cranium, and Slade similarly disposed of this, then wiped off his ax and resumed work.

He was well advanced with the undercut when the camp boss approached him and began looking around. Slade ignored him until the camp boss asked, "Seen the new man?"

Slade shook his head and kept on working. The camp boss went away, but came back several times through the morning. Slade didn't stop to eat at noon, since he had forgotten to bring along his lunch, and the sounds of his ax brought other fallers, most munching on their beef sandwiches, to see why he was not taking advantage of the break. Some asked him the same question the camp boss had, and Slade shook his head for them. Eventually work resumed and he was left alone.

It became apparent he was not working to full capacity when the undercut did not proceed at the pace Slade was accustomed to. He was unable to concentrate fully, kept seeing before him the body of the new man as it collapsed, kept wondering why he had lost several hours of memory during the previous evening, kept asking him-

self why it was that he had struck the cook that morning for no reason. It was all extremely bothersome to Slade. His ability to empty
his mind completely while chopping had been impaired by these
sudden events. He hadn't asked to be involved in any of it, and felt
his anger of that morning return, now compounded by stirrings of
alarm over what would happen if the body should be discovered.

At the end of the day he waited until he was sure everyone else
was headed for the camp, then checked on the body. It was as he
had left it, well hidden, so he was probably safe unless people kept
on asking about the fool. It puzzled Slade why anyone would want
to know the whereabouts of someone so ignorant and downright
rude. The woods were a better place for Slade having got rid of him,
whoever he was. He left the springboard in place for an early start
next morning, picked up his ax and began tramping toward the
camp, hungry for the food he had not enjoyed at noon.

Bruno saw him coming, and knew what he was looking for. The
one lunch pail left behind that morning had been emptied by Bruno
and his assistants after it became clear its owner was not going to
return for it. The pail was now only one among many ranked along
the wall where the logging teams deposited them at the end of
every working day.

Bruno found it pathetic that Slade should begin poking among
the many dozen identical pails, picking them up and rattling them
in hopes of finding his lunch. He must have forgotten to take it with
him because he was worried about the new man, threatened by
him. That this should be so was a surprise to Bruno; he didn't like
Slade, and hoped he would be ground into the earth in some kind of
contest with Chason, but still, it was not like Slade to go to pieces
so fast, before the new man had so much as breathed on him.

"Where is it?"

Slade was looking at him. "Where's what?" said Bruno.

Slade thrust an empty lunch pail at him. Bruno pretended not to
understand. "Where is it?" Slade said again. "I want it."

"It's gone," Bruno told him.

Slade looked at the stacked pails beside him, then began hurling
them around the room, pulling down the clattering tin boxes, even
kicking and stamping on some of them in his fury.

A lunch pail in flight almost hit the camp boss as he entered.
Slade stopped and glared at him. The boss was carrying a pail.
Another audience might have found this amusing. Slade, and

Bruno and his assistants, all looked at the pail; even the boss looked down at it before offering the thing to Bruno. "Found this," he said. "Still got food inside."

Bruno accepted the pail and opened it. A beef sandwich was inside, still wrapped in greaseproof paper.

"What's the problem here?" the boss asked, looking at the mess Slade had created.

"He was looking for his lunch."

"Well, that's it there. I found it near where he's working. This your pail, Slade?"

Slade nodded. He knew it was the new man's pail, and was annoyed with himself for not having spotted it earlier and enjoyed a good lunch.

"You never saw the man I sent out to be working with you? Never seen him once?"

Slade shook his head. He wanted to hit the camp boss for having sent the fool out to pester him. It was the boss's fault the man was dead. The boss was a fool to try and make Slade work with someone when he knew very well Slade worked alone. It was too late to tell him that now, though. Slade wanted to eat something, but it would have made them suspicious if he demanded food before supper, when he apparently hadn't even bothered to eat his lunch. The best thing would be to go away, and that is what he did, and lay on his narrow bunk to try and ignore the pain in his stomach. It was a long while before the dinner bell clanged.

While he ate, Slade was aware that everyone was looking at him. He pretended not to notice. Soon everyone would quit wondering where the new man went, and life would be the same as it had been before the new man arrived to change things with his stupid bullying. He'd picked the wrong man to push around, that was for sure. Anyone talked like that to Slade, he had to expect trouble, and that was what he got, all right, the new man. It served him right. ...

"He asked for it!"

Slade looked up. The cookhouse was silent, everyone staring at him again, more intensely than before. He realized he had spoken out loud. Would they know who he was talking about? Would his face give him away? He looked down at his plate and continued eating. If he concentrated hard, everyone would forget the words he had shouted. It had been a foolish mistake to let the words out that way, but no harm would come from it if he just concentrated hard enough to wish away the day now almost done, erase it and everything that had happened in it, leap from yesterday to tomorrow with a fierce clenching of the brow and be done with fear.

He was afraid. The admission was frightening in itself. Slade could not recall ever having been afraid before. The newness of this emotion almost returned Slade's dinner to his plate. He was afraid. What might happen now that his heart understood what other men felt; would he become weak, as they were? Was that what fear did, even to someone like himself? He would defeat fear, beat it down, choke it off. Fear was not for him, not now or ever. He looked up at the men, still watching him, and made himself laugh in their faces. If they expected his fear to show, he would disappoint them all, and their staring be damned!

When Slade suddenly stood and left the cookhouse, the buzzing of opened conversations followed him out into the night. He began walking to the cabin where his bunk lay waiting. Slade felt very tired, and his stomach hurt because he had bolted his first food since breakfast, too hungry to restrain himself. He would pay the price for that without complaint, but he would never admit he had done something wrong to the new man the camp boss had flung at him. That was none of Slade's doing, and he wouldn't confess to a thing, not a goddamn thing, nossir, not him, not to a soul, not while he lived.

His bed no longer held appeal, so Slade took himself into the shadows at the edge of the camp to watch what might transpire. Before long, it was obvious a search party was being assembled to look for the man Slade had killed. The teams were assembling in front of the supply shack to pass out lamps, and soon had dispersed among the trees in the direction taken by Slade that morning. He didn't doubt that they would find the dead man before daybreak, maybe a lot sooner than that, and he knew with a cool burst of self-appraisal that no matter how hard he might deny being the one who had done the murder, they would see the truth in his face.

He knew also that they wouldn't bother taking him down to Ukiah for trial; they would lynch him right there in the camp. They would do it not because they had any love for the new man, who was a stranger among them, but because they had a powerful resentment of Slade. He had been the king for too long, he saw, and now they wanted him uncrowned, dethroned, beheaded by their sense of common resentment against him. They would do it if he let them, but he decided he would not let them.

Cleaning up after dinner, Bruno was faced with more than the usual mess, since his assistants had joined the crowd out searching the woods for Chason. Not a man seriously doubted that Slade had done something bad, and their collective blood was up. Bruno knew they would devour an enormous breakfast because of their night-time exertions, an even larger meal if they found the body, but would be too excited to eat at all if they were lucky enough to capture Slade himself. The man had walked out of the cookhouse like a fugitive, but no one had made any kind of move to halt him. Even as they suspected him of murder, they had allowed Slade the privilege of escape.

They knew they were cowards, but would take their revenge for having been made to feel that way; Slade, when captured, would be unlike Slade the faller. No one would be afraid of him then, at least not while they surrounded him as a crowd. Before they killed him, they would make sure no individual spent time alone with Slade. The administering of justice would be a community affair, as it had to be. Bruno would be there at the end, along with the rest. That very morning, Slade had pushed him over without the least provocation. Watching the perpetrator die would be sufficient compensation. It was difficult, though, to imagine life at the camp without Slade around.

Movement in the corner of his eye made Bruno turn. Slade seemed to have drifted like smoke from his thoughts, to coalesce as flesh and blood by the door. They watched each other for a moment. Bruno felt the hair along his neck standing up. "You'll be wanting food," he said.

Slade nodded, and came closer. Bruno began backing toward the pantry. "Fix you up with something good," he said, his voice surprisingly firm. Slade was still approaching. "Nobody here but me," Bruno assured him. "They're all out looking for you, you and the other man. You can get clear if you go now. You take some grub and go, and chances are you'll get clear."

"You said to them I never took my lunch. That's why they know. You told."

"No I didn't. I never said a word to anyone, I swear. I'll get you something to eat. I'll fix it now, a couple roast beef sandwiches, huh? Easy to take along with you, not like soup."

It made Bruno feel cowardly to be talking that way, but his humiliation would be worthwhile if he was the one who brought

about Slade's capture. He pictured, briefly but intensely, the looks
of appreciation that would be directed at him if he could only hurt
Slade enough to delay his escape. There was a selection of knives
near to hand; all it would take was some nerve and a skillful thrust
or two. Slade was unarmed. Bruno told himself to wait until he had
finished making the sandwich; he would have a legitimate reason
for having a knife in his hand then, and Slade would be used to seeing it there. He could surprise him.

"I'll make it now, all right? The beef sandwich?"

Slade was still moving toward him very slowly, never taking his
eyes from Bruno's face. "You got them started thinking," he said,
"about that lunch."

"No, I never mentioned about the lunch. I didn't even know it was
yours that got left behind. How could I know? They all look the
same, those company pails. ..."

"Hadn't been for that," Slade continued, still approaching, "they
never would've known, I bet."

"It's not my fault. You shouldn't have come in here and kicked
everything around like you did. That's what got them started,
not me...."

Slade lunged for him. Bruno grabbed for a knife, but missed;
before he could reach again, Slade's fingers were around his throat.
Bruno immediately felt behind himself again for the knives, but
Slade was drawing him away from the table, and the ease with
which he did it told Bruno that physical resistance was not going to
save him. Instead, he went limp. He had heard that this was the
thing to do when attacked by a bear, so it might work with an unin-
telligent brute like Slade. He realized within a few seconds that it
would not, and was still conscious as his windpipe collapsed, producing a steam-whistle sound inside his head as oxygen was cut off
completely from his lungs. As the screaming in his ears intensified,
Bruno knew he was dying, the sour smell of Slade's breath hanging
around his face like an invisible mist. He wondered how he could
smell it if he could no longer inhale, and died with the question
unanswered.

The body was hidden beneath a pile of empty potato sacks, far
back in Bruno's pantry. Slade knew he had done the right thing,
killing him. Bruno was linked somehow with the camp boss and the
new man, all of them trying to do him harm, when all he wanted
was to be left alone to be the best faller anyone in the woods had

seen. Maybe he should have been less of a show-off; his trick of standing on the stump as a tree fell, daring the trunk to spring back and crush him, was probably too much for some men to take without getting jealous. That was at the heart of what had happened, but he couldn't quite figure out the exact sequence that had led to his murdering two men. He recalled having thought, at some time during the day, that Bruno had most likely put something in his food to cause his blackout the previous evening. He'd never liked the cook; Bruno looked exactly like one of the guards in the territorial prison at Yuma, where Slade had served a number of years; a hateful little man. It was probable that Bruno and the guard were related, maybe even brothers, so it was good to have killed him after so long a time.

He left the cook house and began walking across to the sheltering trees. No one saw him, and Slade saw no one; every man was out looking for the first one he had killed. He kept on till he came to the skid road, a raw gash cut through the woods, leading down to the sawmill. There was really only one direction he could take if he wanted to get away.

When he reached it, the mill was in darkness but for a lamp in the watchman's shack. Slade worked his way around to the flume, guided by the sound of its rushing waters. Its entire length of forty-three miles would be free of planks at that hour. He searched around for the flume boats, wishing he could remember where he had noticed them when he first came up through there to the logging camp. After some minutes' blundering around, he found them with his shins, three narrow, V-hulled craft just inches less across their beam than the width of the flume's wooden banks.

He set the first two boats into the stream and watched them being whisked away by the strong flow. The third boat he set carefully in the water, then flung himself inside as he felt it snatched from his hands. The sense of acceleration was immediate, an intoxicating rush of water against wood, the slap and gurgle of the four-foot-wide channel inches from his ears as he lay sprawled along the flume boat's length. The sheer speed of it frightened Slade for some minutes, then he raised his head to look over the flume's low sides at the moonlit country flying by, and forgot his fear in the novelty of such dramatic conveyance.

He sat up, being careful not to upset the boat, and squatted on one of the boards bracing the hull, to travel in some semblance of dignity. Mile after mile flashed by, and Slade began to appreciate the great work required to set up the flume. Its shallow bed of redwood snaked among the hills, supported on wooden trestles of lattice construction, their spindle legs and crossbeams appearing impossibly fragile. It curved and swooped, following the landscape, angled always downward by several degrees, sometimes plunging abruptly for a half mile or so where the engineers had calculated it could be done, and the flume boat fairly hummed along, with Slade clutching its sides, moving faster than the fastest train.

No one would ever catch up, not with the only other boats racing ahead of him. He caught glimpses of them sometimes as they rounded a curve made silvery by moonlight, two darting sticks of blackness. He would arrive at the company's lower mill at the end of the flume before they even found the first body back in the mountains. The planing sheds and drying yards where the timber was stacked were a stone's throw from the ocean, the loading docks an easy route onto whatever ship lay waiting. Slade knew most of the lumber went south to San Francisco, a big enough town to lose himself in without fear of apprehension by the law. If no ship was loading, or he felt he couldn't stow away without being discovered for a day or two, he would simply turn south and start walking along the coastline. It was a simple plan, and it would work.

He was not afraid anymore, was even a little ashamed at ever having been. He could not bother his head with memories of what had occurred in one short day; it already seemed far behind him, a jumble of events that had happened to someone else, and been told to Slade by way of a third party. It meant nothing. He was speeding toward another future than the one he'd planned, but that was not a bad thing, he decided, not if it left him breathless with the rush of air against his face, his narrow craft like an arrow flying straight and true along its predetermined path, the target ahead a new life. Slade had begun a number of new lives, so the thought of doing so again held little regret. He could not recall in detail any of those previous lives, but knew he had done this several times before, cut and run to begin anew in some other place. It was a shame to leave behind him the redwoods, since his work among them had been the most satisfying of his many lives, but it was always possible that whatever lay in store for him would bring with it similar rewards. Slade knew he deserved them.

15

Omie learned her letters with a swiftness that put Zoe in awe of her ability. At five years she could read all the labels on the packets and jars in the pantry, and by the time she was six, Omie's favorite exercise was reading the headstones her father inscribed. The family had their own house, and the yard at the rear was Bryce's area of business. The slabs and tablets of stone were strewn around by the dozens, propped against each other in the open during the warmer months, stacked in regimental rows inside a stove-heated shack for the winter.

Omie's visits with Bryce during working hours were not a cause for vexation, since she never interfered with the projects in progress. She was content to wander among the stones, reading aloud, with surprisingly few mispronunciations. Bryce was proud of her. His own boy was not more loved than Omie. Patrick was two years old now, and nowhere near an understanding of the alphabet.

"Emily Jo ... Johonson," said Omie.

"Almost," Bryce encouraged, "but the *h* is silent, so it's Johnson."

"Johnson."

"Very good."

"Eighteen fifty-one, eighteen eighty. 'She Shall Weep No More.' Why was she weeping?"

"I don't know. I put the words on the stone that the customer says to put. They don't always tell me what they mean by it."

She went on to the next. "Henry Rickers. Eighteen thirty-three, eighteen eighty. 'At Peace with the Lord.' That's Jesus, isn't it?"

"That's right."

"Wendy Orm ... Ormagast. That's a funny name. Eighteen seventy-eight, eighteen eighty. She was only little."

"Yes. It's a shame when someone dies so young."

"Will I?"

"No, you'll get to be ninety-nine and a half years old and have long white hair down to the ground and fifty-seven grandchildren."

Omie giggled and moved on to the next stone. She stared at it while Bryce resumed his work. He turned around some time later to find her staring at the same stone.

"Is that an interesting one?" he said, smiling. The stone was perfectly blank.

"Patrick Aspinall," said Omie. "Eighteen seventy-eight, eighteen eighty. 'Beloved Son ...'"

Bryce stood abruptly, as if charged with electricity.

"Don't make silly jokes!"

She turned to him, her face so ashen the blue birthmark seemed almost black. "It says it, Papa...."

"There's nothing there! You stop this! Go in the house, and don't you come back out here till you're invited."

Omie was weeping as she went inside. Minutes later, Zoe came out and approached Bryce. "Why is she crying?"

Bryce explained, too upset to resume work.

"I'm sure she didn't mean it, not seriously," Zoe said.

"She *was* serious. I know when she's joking; there's a little grin she puts on. She was serious, or pretending to be. What kind of a thing is that to say to me, that my son's going to die? Is she jealous?"

"She loves Patrick. You've seen the way she dotes on him like a little mother."

"Then why would she say it?"

"I'll talk to her."

Zoe returned to the house, then came out again.

"She says those are the words she saw on the stone. I don't think she's lying. She's very confused, and not just because you shouted at her. She wants to know why Patrick's going to die so young."

"He isn't! Stop it!"

"I'm not saying it's true; I'm only saying what she believes."

"I don't care! It's gone beyond a joke. I don't want to hear another word about it. Bring him here. I want to see him."

Zoe fetched Patrick from the house. Bryce could see Omie watching from the kitchen window. He ignored her and made a great fuss over the boy, a handsome fellow with a fine thatch of curls. Until now Bryce's only concern for his son was the possibility he would one day lose that curling crown, as Bryce had.

Patrick picked up a chisel and lunged inexpertly at some scraps of stone. "Like father, like son," Zoe said, and made herself laugh. She'd never seen Bryce so distraught.

Zoe left the boy with his father and spoke again with Omie, telling her never again to mention what she imagined she saw on the stone. Omie said she wouldn't, then cried some more, because they really had been there, those words and numbers, and it upset her awfully that Papa would carve them, then get angry when Omie saw what he had done. None of it made any sense. She wouldn't go near his horrible tombstones ever again, to punish him for being so mean to her.

Nine days later, Bryce was backing his delivery wagon out of the yard. He had a good team that responded well to his commands, even the difficult backward maneuvering required to get the wagon into the alley. He suspected nothing until the broken body of Patrick appeared below the wagon tongue. Bryce let out a cry that brought neighbors into their yards. Zoe came running. Bryce was on the ground beside the nervously stamping horses, cradling Patrick. Both wheels on the wagon's left side had passed over him. Patrick had died without a sound. Bryce hadn't even been aware he was playing in the yard.

Zoe couldn't make him talk, not in the days preceding the funeral or in the days that followed, when Bryce did nothing but work on the blank slab of stone, chipping out the words Omie had seen. He would not eat, would not look at his wife or stepdaughter. The stone was everything. Zoe's own grief at their loss seemingly meant nothing to Bryce; he acknowledged no pain but his own. Zoe and Omie began finding subtle ways to avoid him, rather than suffer the rebuff of silence and averted eyes.

"Why won't he look at us, Mama?"

"He thinks what happened to Patrick was his fault."

"But it was an accident."

"I know, but he's such a gentle man, he can't bear to think he was responsible. He can't cope with talk now, so we'll just wait till he can. We won't bother him, all right?"

"Yes, but he's been working on the other stone."

"It's Patrick's stone. When it's finished we'll all go and help place it in the cemetery."

"No, the other stone, the one with Papa's name on it."

"There is no such stone!"

"I saw it, Mama. It says Papa's name, and the year he was born, and this year. I *saw* it."

"Like you saw the stone with Patrick's name?"

"Just exactly like it, only with Papa's name."

"Promise me you won't tell anyone about it."

"Why not?"

"Just promise me."

Omie promised. While Bryce slept that night, Zoe took a lamp and inspected every stone in the yard. Patrick's headstone was almost completed. There was no sign of anything bearing Bryce's name, yet Zoe believed Omie's statement to the contrary. On top of her misery over Patrick, Zoe had to deal with a mystery, and the anguish of anticipating its repetition. She knew she mustn't blame Omie, who clearly had no inkling of the strange thing that had transpired.

Zoe was not unfamiliar with such phenomena. When she was small her mother had several times experienced moments of fore-knowledge. Nettie Dugan had been semiliterate, not given to extended conversations, even with her children, but there had been times when she would describe for them events happening at that very moment, she insisted, far from Schenectady. For the most part these were mundane enough, usually involving members of her family in New England. She was especially sensitive to their deaths, one by one, over the years. She even described their funerals. None of what she related could be verified, since her family had disowned her following her marriage to James Dugan.

All three children had accepted their mother's visions as a kind of storytelling, taking her seriously on only one occasion, when she suddenly fell down in the street and began depicting with her limited vocabulary a terrible train wreck, paying particular attention to the fact that the respective engineers of the two colliding trains were, by remarkable coincidence, brothers. It was too fantastic a story for belief, but they read the newspapers for several days, waiting for reports of the event Nettie had described. It had not taken place for another two weeks, and the engineers were indeed brothers. The children were impressed, and Nettie herself began to wonder if the various deathbed scenes and funerals she had seen inside her head had in fact taken place long after she pictured them. The notion disturbed her greatly, suggesting as it did the pre-destination of events, a concept alien to Nettie's mind. Thereafter she never spoke of such things or shared whatever visions might have visited her still.

Zoe had not given that aspect of her past a thought in years. Might Omie somehow have inherited her grandmother's gift of fore-sight? It was an alarming prospect. The gift, if that was what it was, had never benefited Nettie in any way, had even driven a wedge between herself and her husband on those occasions when he learned of the things she had seen. Dugan had been a superstitious man, and he called his wife "a sister of Satan, been touched with his fork."

Zoe promised herself that if the gift had truly been passed on, she would not allow it to come between herself and Omie. But in having tacitly accepted the reemergence of the gift, she granted Omie's vision of a gravestone for Bryce a kind of legitimacy, and having done that, Zoe had also to accept that it was only a matter of time before the stone would actually be carved, and that was too much for her to embrace without a fight.

Bryce installed Patrick's headstone himself. When the family returned home, Zoe sent Omie on an errand to the store, then con-fronted her husband.

"Listen to me. You mustn't do this thing I know you're thinking of. Do Omie and myself mean nothing at all to you?"

His eyes, for five days now focused on some spot in the distance, narrowed a little, and Zoe saw her suspicions were close to the mark.

"You mustn't," she said. "If you love us, stay and be with us. What happened was not your fault. No one can say it was. Why do you tell yourself it was? And this other ... matter. That will never bring him back. You may not even meet him ... over there. They say there's a different place for those who ... who take their own life. Don't you leave us, don't you dare, just because you're feeling too sad to live. It wouldn't be right. Don't you dare!"

She hadn't meant to shout, but the eyes that looked briefly into her own quickly clouded over, and shifted from her face to a corner of the room. She took hold of his shoulders and shook him, a thing Zoe had never imagined herself doing to any man. Bryce resisted not at all, simply ignored her, even when Zoe delivered a stinging slap to the side of his face. "Damn you!" she screeched. "Wake up and be with us again!" But he would not.

The following day he began work on the second stone, and when she saw the name forming beneath his chisel, Zoe felt her hopes slide into a trough of despair. Now the unthinkable had become the seemingly inevitable, and she was obliged to ask herself if she loved him enough to do everything in her power, practice every conceivable stratagem to persuade him toward life, or else accept that her affection and respect for Bryce (never really love, she admitted with less reluctance than usual) had weakened considerably in the face of his unmanly surrender to absolute misery and self-pity. She did not blame him for the tragedy of Patrick's death, but saw no way to avoid holding him responsible for what he planned to do next.

Zoe's family was on the verge of being reduced to herself and Omie again. The more letters that were added to the stone, the less Zoe believed she could alter the path Bryce seemed bent on following. She begged the preacher who had buried Patrick to talk with Bryce, but the man's earnest efforts came to nothing. Neighbors, getting wind of events, advised roping Bryce to his bed and spoon-feeding him like a child until his malady passed. "Melancholy, seen it before plenty of times," was the general diagnosis of what ailed him. "Keep him inside and away from guns and knives. He'll get over it soon enough."

But Bryce was unchanged. Zoe was aware that interest in the manner Bryce would employ to do away with himself had become a topic of open speculation in the area. A reporter from the *Pueblo Chieftain* arrived for an interview, and was quickly shown the door. He penned an entertaining article anyway, under the headline:

GRIEVING PARENT PLANS OWN END
WILL JOIN BABY BOY ON NETHER SHORE
WIFE FAILS TO INFLUENCE COMING TRAGEDY

Someone slipped the paper under Zoe's door. This was the most humiliating moment so far. She was tempted to confront Bryce with it in the yard, but the fence was lined with curious onlookers, most of whom were prepared to wait all day, watching the grieving parent perform the final duty to himself by carving his own headstone. Some shouted advice, encouraging Bryce to add all manner of

scrollwork and curlicues to the piece, in order to delay its completion, but Zoe knew the finished stone would be bare of ornamenta-
tion, as Patrick's had been. Omie had described its exact appearance, and Bryce was nearly to that stage already with his delicate
tap-tap-tapping.

Finally it was done. Bryce wiped the stone clean of chips and
dust, then went indoors. A low moan escaped the crowd gathered
along three sides of the yard, then they debated among themselves
the likelihood of having had their last glimpse of the sorrowful
stonecutter, as Bryce was now universally known. There was some
argument over the possibility of drawing straws to see who among
them might win a chance to stand vigil inside the house, along with
the unfortunate wife and daughter. A bystander offered to make
this suggestion to Zoe. He knocked on the door and haltingly outlined the proposal. Hearing it, Zoe knew beyond all doubt that the
tragedy had turned to farce.

"No," she said, and closed the door firmly.

All potential instruments of death had been removed from the
house and deposited with a sympathetic neighbor. There remained
not a knife or fork. Shortly after Bryce came in from the yard, Zoe
went out, to collect and count his stonemason's tools. Every chisel
was there, from the heaviest to the finest. She bundled up the lot,
including all sizes of mallet, and passed them across the fence to
her female cohort next door. This lady rented gawking space along
her side fence for fifty cents per person, but Zoe forgave her.

Now the waiting began. Bryce had selected a comfortable armchair for himself, and appeared content simply to sit. Staring at
nothing, he did not speak. Zoe sat nearby and took up some knitting.
For two hours they sat together, in different worlds, then Zoe heard
voices somewhere in the house. Investigating, she found Omie chat-
ting with the reporter from the *Chieftain* through her opened bedroom window. She turned guiltily as Zoe entered the room.

"Explain yourself," Zoe demanded.

The reporter tipped his hat and was gone. Omie chewed her bottom lip and looked at the floor.

"What did you tell him?" Zoe asked.

"Nothing."

"I heard you talking."

"I didn't tell him anything. He just wanted to know if Papa ever
said anything to us, and I told him no, that's all."

"Are you telling me the truth?"

"Yes."

Zoe didn't believe her.

"Shut the window. You can come in the sitting room with me." It would not have sounded right to have said, "in the sitting room with your father and me." Bryce wasn't really there, not in spirit anyway. And was he still there in the flesh, or had he run madly from the house the minute Zoe turned her back. She hurried to the sitting room and found Bryce exactly as before, his expression vacant as a statue's.

Zoe hadn't the least doubt now that her husband fully intended dying. The stone with his name stood waiting, as Omie had predicted. Of course, her seeing the stone was not the same as seeing her father dead. Maybe Omie wasn't able to see that far ahead. It was an encouraging thought, but Zoe dismissed it; Omie's vision aside, she felt that Bryce was already gone, his courage nowhere in evidence, his spirit dwindling by the hour. There was a special kind of darkness in the house, an atmosphere of inexorable doom. She could do no more than wait, Omie beside her, Bryce across the room. They were all in a prison cell bounded by lush wallpaper and the ticking of a mantel clock.

Bryce neither ate nor drank, so it was not to be wondered at that he did not budge from his armchair to visit the outhouse. Zoe and Omie had to, and each time ran a gauntlet of townspeople now openly tramping around the backyard. An illustrator from the *Chieftain* was rendering the fateful stone in India ink for posterity on page one. It was some consolation when evening came and the crowd departed.

It was an insult, the way Bryce had chosen to ignore the needs of Zoe and Omie, and brought down on all their heads the humiliation of public fascination. She still could not understand why he was as he was. The pain of Patrick's death, harsh though it assuredly had been, did not require such extravagant sacrifice to ease its passing. Bryce's life in exchange for Patrick's was a bargain no god could sanction, and Zoe certainly didn't. She recognized a growing resentment inside herself, a bitterness at having married this man and borne him a child, in expectation of a life filled with the usual joys and hardships. Nothing had prepared her for this. It was more than a disappointment; it was a betrayal. The cause of Bryce's grief did not justify his extreme reaction to it. He had seized upon their misfortune in order to exorcise himself of some other, darker secret, or so it seemed to Zoe. There was no means of knowing what thoughts swam in his mind.

Zoe remained in the sitting room with Bryce throughout the night, sending Omie to her room when the clock struck nine-thirty. She slept fitfully, kept the lamp burning low in order to see at a glance if her husband was still there whenever she woke up. He always was. If she could have been sure of his immobility, Zoe might have spent the night comfortably in bed. It was one more unnecessary annoyance.

Next day her neighbor delivered to Zoe a copy of the *Chieftain*'s morning edition.

GIRL FORESEES TALE OF WOE

UNCANNY PREDICTIONS BY YOUNGSTER

TOMBSTONE INSCRIPTIONS REVEALED

DAYS IN ADVANCE

Zoe took it directly to Omie. "Did you tell that man about what you saw? Did you?"

Omie hung her head. "Yes."

"Why! Why did you! Now they'll never leave us alone!"

"I didn't mean to. He said Mrs. Grimes next door told him her little girl told her I told Lucy I saw the words on the stone before Papa put them there. He asked me was it true. I didn't want to tell a lie."

Zoe sat beside her and put an arm across Omie's trembling shoulders. "So you know you saw a thing that hadn't happened yet."

Omie nodded. "I thought at first he really was making the words but saying he wasn't. Then I believed him, but the words were there anyway, like they were waiting to come out of the stones. ... I didn't mean to do it."

"I know you didn't. It's something you have inside you, a kind of gift."

"Gift?"

"An ability, so to say. You can ... see things happen before they really happen, because you have ... a special eye, I suppose you'd call it. It's a very unusual thing, but you don't need to be frightened by it."

"I'm sorry I told the man."

"It doesn't matter now. Have you seen anything apart from the words on the stones? Have you seen us ... burying Papa in the ground?"

"No. Why did I get the thing inside me, the special eye?"

"I don't know why, but I know where it comes from."

She told Omie of her mother's faculty for seeing events of the future. Omie was particularly impressed by the story of the brother railroad engineers who ran into each other and died along with so many of their passengers.

"Will I see something like that too?" she asked, excited at such a dramatic prospect.

"I hope you never do. I hope you see only good things, happy things that will happen later on. It isn't fair for a little girl to have to see bad things."

"Is it because of my blue mark?"

"No, no, it has nothing to do with that. It isn't a punishment, either thing, the special eye or the blue mark. They're both just things that you happen to have. They're part of what makes you ... you."

Omie considered this, then said, "Is Papa still in the chair?"

"Why don't we find out."

He was, but Bryce's immobility was the only calm aspect of that day. The newspaper article on Omie's clairvoyance caused a sensation, and the crowds around the Aspinall house doubled. Soon people were at the door requesting that Omie give them an estimate of their own mortality, or that of a sick family member. She was asked also to diagnose various maladies the town doctors were unsure of, and to prescribe a cure for these. Several young women wished to know if their young men were fated to marry them, and some begged Omie to describe in detail young men as yet unmet. Zoe allowed Omie to talk with none of them, fearing that a single interview, however disappointing it would assuredly prove for the one who came wishing for knowledge of things to come, would open the floodgates to even more comers than had already knocked upon the door. It was an impossible state of affairs.

To put a stop to it, Zoe allowed a reporter, the one Omie had talked with through her window, into the house. She had schooled Omie in her statement and the responses she would be obliged to make to his questioning. Omie shuffled her little boots and told the man she had lied about seeing the names on the stones. It was a big fib, she said, and she was sorry now for having said it. When the reporter began badgering Omie, hoping he could get her to admit she was lying about having lied, Zoe showed him the door.

"You did very well," she told Omie.

"He didn't believe me."

"No one likes to believe things that sound sensible and everyday. They prefer to believe things that are silly and can't happen."

"But it did happen," Omie reminded her, and Zoe could only nod ruefully.

Another night in the chair. In the early morning hours Zoe grew angry at her discomfort and took herself to bed, leaving Bryce on his own in the dim lamplight. She was sure he would still be there come morning, and her own increasingly nervous condition required a decent night's sleep. The bed was wonderfully roomy and accommodating without her husband in it, and Zoe drifted off with ease. Her rest was deep and untroubled, and this caused her extra guilt when she discovered, on rising next day, that Bryce was gone.

He was not in the house, not in the yard, not even at the cemetery, where Zoe fully expected to find him lying across Patrick's grave. Word quickly spread, and a good number of Pueblo's citizens began a search of the town. By evening it was generally accepted that the man in the chair had vanished completely, just walked away while no one, including his wife, was watching.

The incident received much coverage in the newspaper, which had yet to print a word about Omie's retraction. Zoe couldn't decide if this was a good thing, or bad. At least this way her daughter was not branded a liar. That might have been preferable, though, to having been labeled a prophetess. For the next three days the *Chieftain*'s editorial asked, encouraged, and finally dared Omie to locate her father by means of her unique ability. Zoe considered making trouble for the paper by telling the dwindling crowds around her house that Omie had already admitted her story was untrue, but Omie begged her not to.

"I don't want to lie again. I hated telling that man a lie!"

"Very well, we'll cope with matters as they are."

In the following week interest in mother and daughter waned slightly, then was revived by the *Chieftain*'s revealing at last that Omie had confessed her second sight was nothing but a hoax perpetrated upon the gullible citizenry of the town. The article was cleverly worded, creating the impression that Omie had only now admitted her prank, and it was further hinted that the disappearance of Bryce Aspinall might very well have been similarly planned to excite public interest, with a view to winning sympathy for the family, and possibly monetary support.

Zoe was outraged, but knew there was little she could do. When a rock came through the window she decided to sell the house and move on. The sale was quickly accomplished, bringing renewed attention to what the *Chieftain* called "a saga of deception not yet ended." Zoe's last act of interest in Pueblo was to install Bryce's headstone in the cemetery. Even if Bryce was not known to be deceased, he might as well have been, so she wished his stone set up next to that of their son. The sexton objected to such an unusual request, maintaining that a gravestone should be raised only when there was a body to accompany it. He obliged her, though, when Zoe gave him ten dollars over the common fee. It was a bargain, since he didn't even have to dig a hole.

The two remaining Aspinalls (Zoe made up her mind to resume the Dugan name as soon as possible) bought tickets on the Denver and Rio Grande Railroad and journeyed north by west, into the mountains that supplied the ore for Pueblo's smelters.

Traveling through the magnificent cleft of the Royal Gorge, the sky a mere strip of blue far above, Zoe asked herself if she had mourned enough for her son. It seemed there had been no time for prolonged grieving. No sooner was Patrick dead than all attention had been turned to Bryce and his peculiarities. Patrick's demise had been overtaken by events begun by Bryce, expanded by the newspaper, and finally ended by Zoe. Every hour since Bryce climbed down from his wagon had been unreal, an exaggeration of misfortune, without room inside its coils for true feeling. And now it was somehow too late. She had wept for Patrick, but not enough, and now could weep no more. Zoe felt numb inside, could barely recognize as her own the girl beside her with the blue birthmark swirling from her eye. Bryce had destroyed a part of her, she felt, and into the hollow place left behind, Zoe could pour nothing of herself that was not required elsewhere.

Omie was attempting to see the top of the gorge, high above. The train was a toy winding through the narrow defile, buried deep in noonday shadows.

"Will the cliffs tumble down on us, Mama?"

Zoe shook her head.

16

When their son was born, Clay and Sophie named him Silan. He grew to be a sturdy boy, with his father's powerful hands. Both parents were relieved to see that his face resembled Sophie's, rather than Clay's. He was a handsome boy, and they were proud of him. Silan was the center of their marriage, its cause, and the reason for its continuation, but the parents allowed no hint of that to pass their lips when the boy was within earshot.

It had become clear even before Silan was born that Sophie and Clay had nothing in common but their shared sense of guilt for having betrayed Grover at the hour of his death. It was not enough to build love upon, barely sufficient for mutual respect. Sophie had another lawman in her life, and Clay made it clear he liked the work; he would not be persuaded to quit. He had been elected marshal without opposition, and took pride in not requiring a deputy to assist him in keeping things tamed in Keyhoe.

He had killed another man shortly after assuming the office. That man had refused to set down a rifle he walked out of a store with, after declining to pay the proprietor. For all Clay knew, in all the shouting, the rifle was loaded, so when the thief refused to release his hold upon it, Clay counted down from three. Incredibly, this was accepted as some kind of dare by the thief, who died with a show-me smile on his lips. He was not a local, and no one laid any blame at Clay's feet for his death. The rifle, it turned out, had not been loaded, and this reinforced Clay's belief that stupidity, in conjunction with conscious lawbreaking, had resulted in the demise of an individual no decent person need shed tears over.

He gave much of himself to the work of making Keyhoe safe, and was on first-name terms with most of the citizens. Clay could muster what it took to make small talk on the main street with storekeepers and passersby, but always felt more like his true self when silent, unaccosted by people he had no real interest in. He sometimes thought of them as cattle he had been hired to protect. His aloofness, a handicap in any other field, was Clay's ally in law enforcement. News of the tall preacher-like figure, with a sawed-off shotgun he didn't hesitate to use, spread throughout the county and beyond, and Clay learned that a reputation is as powerful a weapon as anything from a gunsmith's forge.

He was capable of appearing at any time of the day or night, in any part of town. Some people spoke of having entered Clay's office and found him staring at them from his upholstered chair, but they formed the impression his eyes had been closed a fraction of a second before their hand rattled the doorknob. Though no one ever caught him with his eyes closed, it was said that the marshal catnapped frequently, conserving himself for the endless hours consumed by his duties.

Sophie saw him with closed eyes often. Clay seemed to fall asleep whenever he came home, which was generally only a few hours in the early evening, for a meal and a pipe. After eating, he used the sofa to stretch out on while he digested and smoked, and when his bowl of tobacco ash was knocked out, he would sigh deeply and fall into a profound sleep not even Silan could penetrate with his squalling. For his wife, Clay had little time and less conversation. He occasionally mounted her, but never with sweet endearments to ease the ritual of penetration.

Sophie often stood by the sofa and stared at him as if he were some embalmed object of ancient times, interesting enough in its features, but so remote from everyday life as to arouse no emotion whatsoever. This was her husband, this sleeping man, and she felt nothing for him that a wife should feel. The frustrations of their first year together had slowly yielded to an understanding, on Sophie's part, that Clay saw the marriage as something he had been forced into by circumstances, a regrettable compromise in a life otherwise unblemished by concession. It baffled her still, his utter lovelessness.

The cruelest aspect was his revelation of a tender side, reserved exclusively for short periods spent with Silan. Let Sophie so much as enter the same room, and Clay's playfulness was stuffed back inside himself with alacrity. It was a miserable marriage, a miserable household, and Sophie dreaded the day Silan was old enough to comprehend the sterility around him.

In March of 1880, when Clay was twenty-four but looked a decade older, the second-largest bank in Keyhoe was robbed of a sum in excess of seven thousand dollars in easily transportable folding money. While someone rode to fetch the sheriff from the county seat, a full hour's gallop away, Clay decided to organize a posse of his own and set off in pursuit while the trail was still hot, hoping the sheriff and his own posse would join them before too long.

Seven armed volunteers presented themselves and were hastily deputized. Witnesses told Clay he couldn't possibly mistake the robbers when he caught up with them, because one of the men rode a horse unlike any other. This animal seemed to have as many descriptions as there were witnesses to its gallop through town, but was generally acknowledged to be swirled in colors not commonly associated with horsehide. The two riders were rendered in nondescript terms. Look for the horse, he was advised.

The robbers had fled south, heading for the Indian Nations between Kansas and Texas, where lawlessness was the norm. This land, set aside for the use of native Americans, was within the far-flung jurisdiction of the Western District of Arkansas, and was known to be a haven for desperadoes, a land beyond the rule of law. The federal marshals of Judge Isaac Parker's court in Fort Smith, Arkansas, were permitted entry to the thousand untamed bolt holes of outlawry inside the Nations, but Clay, as the members of his posse pointed out several times while they rode nearer to this ill-favored area, was no federal marshal. He held no official power outside the town of Keyhoe, and that had been left behind. Even the county sheriff, should he ever catch up with them, had no legal right to penetrate further south than the county line bordering the Nations. Word would have to be sent to Fort Smith, over two hundred miles away, for any further action against the robbers.

Confronted with the dwindling enthusiasm of his posse, Clay

ordered them home. When they turned their horses, Clay dismounted and began examining the front left fetlock of his gelding.

"Trouble?" he was asked.

"Getting lame. I'll follow on."

There were offers to wait with him. Clay refused them all and
soon was alone, a state he found preferable to the short-lived excitement of heading a posse. He filled his pipe and smoked awhile, considering his next step. Sooner or later, probably later, the sheriff
would happen along with men of his own, and likely tell Clay to get
back where he belonged, in the restricted bailiwick of Keyhoe. He
would probably even escort Clay back there, eager to turn the whole
affair over to Parker's men from Arkansas, even if delaying pursuit
meant losing the trail altogether.

Clay didn't want to do that. He wanted to catch and kill the men
who had robbed a bank in his town. It didn't matter that they had
harmed no one in the course of the robbery; that was sheer good
luck, in Clay's opinion. They were robbers, and deserved to die for
doing what they did. It was a personal insult, their choice of Keyhoe
to ply their trade. It meant they didn't fear him, or else had never
heard of him, or, if they had, didn't believe what they'd heard. Clay
wanted to stretch their ears and shout death into them. Two dead
men and a sack of loot, that's what he wanted to take home, and to
hell with the county sheriff and Judge Parker's federal marshals.

The tracks of his prey were clearly visible, even to a nontracker
like Clay; two swaths cut by galloping horses through the long
prairie grass lying heavy from rains the day before. They wouldn't
be too difficult to follow if he kept hard on their trail and didn't quit
till he caught up. He mounted and rode on.

The landscape he passed across was featureless for the most part,
an extension of Kansan anonymity expressed in an abundance of
flat sky and equally flat prairie. It was the lack of geographic diver-
sity, perhaps, that caused Clay to begin ruminating on his lot. He
asked himself if he was, if not actually happy, then fulfilled in his
deepest part, and had to admit that he was not. His duties as marshal of Keyhoe had become routine, were tedious in their change-
lessness. This hunt for robbers was the most exciting event to have
overtaken him in a long time, and the illegality of his continued
pursuit beyond the bounds of his jurisdiction did not bother Clay
one bit; rather, they enhanced his pleasure, his relief in at last finding a worthwhile task for himself.

He decided, quite suddenly, that after apprehending and executing his quarry, he would contest the next election for county sheriff. Assuming he won, and used his enhanced powers to the fullest in ridding the locality of lawbreakers, he would then be in a position conducive to selection as a United States marshal, allowing him access to virtually every nook and cranny between the two oceans. These thoughts of a field large enough to prove himself upon lifted his spirits.

Clay continued south as the sun completed its arc and sank at last below the long line of the horizon. In the dusk he could not follow the trail with any certainty, but stopping to wait for the night to pass seemed pointless; he had brought along no food, could not have risked a fire to cook it in any case, and had not tied a bedroll to his saddle before riding out of town. He'd behaved like an amateur, in fact, not a leader. Since rest was not possible, he decided to keep going in the same undeviating direction the trail had indicated all afternoon. The robbers just might be foolish or confident enough to announce their presence with a campfire somewhere ahead.

It was so unlikely a scenario that Clay, less than an hour later, was startled to see ahead of him the unmistakable flickering of a small blaze. Filled with self-congratulation and a low opinion of his prey for their predictability, Clay rode slowly closer, and dismounted when he calculated he was a quarter mile from the fire; much closer and there was a chance the horses might smell one another and create a fuss. He took from his saddlebag a lead weight, attached it to the reins and set it on the ground, then took his shotgun and began making his way carefully forward, feeling for each step, wary of gopher holes and matted grass that might trip him.

The night was near moonless, few stars visible behind the clouds gathering for another storm. Clay could scent rain on the light wind, and wood smoke. Where had they found anything to burn in that treeless place? As he came closer, he saw by the firelight what at first appeared to be low brush. A few steps more and he realized they were treetops. The fire had been built along the rim of a sunken creek bed. The men he wanted had built a fire of willow wood, in plain sight of any posse that cared to follow them this far. Why hadn't they taken the obvious precaution of locating the blaze down on the creek bed, where it would not have been so glaring a signal across miles of open plain?

It was an obvious trap. They were waiting for anyone stupid enough to rush the fire, probably had their rifles resting along the

rim, just beyond the firelight's reach. As he watched, Clay saw a
chunk of wood come sailing from the darkness and land in the
flames, followed by another. At least one man was on watch, feeding
the fire from behind cover, waiting for any arrivals.

Clay felt a quiet rage. They, the perpetrators of a crime, were laying for him. Did they know for sure he was tailing them, or were
they just being cautious, if setting up such an unmistakable
ambush could be termed caution? He would assume they were
expecting him, and make his approach accordingly.

It required a half hour to worm his way through the grass until
he found the creek bed, several hundred yards east of the fire. Clay
slid carefully down the eroding banks, wishing he had just a few
minutes of moonlight to show him the way upstream. In the pitch
darkness all around, he had to pause before every step. The stream
bed was dry, but littered with branches and debris deposited when
the water gave out during last summer's heat; soon the spring thaw
would fill it again. Before setting his boot down at every step, he
had to be sure there was nothing underfoot to create the least noise.
Progress along the creek, following its serpentine curves, was frustratingly slow.

Eventually he could make out the fire along the rim, some twenty
yards further on. Of the men, or man, who fed it there was no sign.
Clay cocked his shotgun's hammers and waited for the men to make
a move that would reveal their place of hiding. The fire was burning low, in need of replenishment. Even at this distance Clay felt
uneasy. He needed to know where they were, couldn't do a thing
until they revealed themselves.

He heard a series of soft nickerings, brought to him on the wind
from south of the dry wash. Their horses had been staked or hobbled away from the fire in case of gunplay. He bet the money was
with them, ready for a fast getaway if something went wrong, the
arrival of a sizable posse, for instance. But the setup before him had
all the earmarks of having been arranged for just one man. It irritated him, this lack of knowledge about the situation he was stepping into. Each of his previous killings had involved a set of known
parameters, the whole thing laid out before him, its various permu-
tations evident in advance. Clay preferred it that way, not skulking
in darkness. He was actually beginning to shake with the tension of
waiting for developments, and had to make a conscious effort to
stop. No more wood was flung onto the fire, and the extent of Clay's

field of vision was narrowed as the open flames degenerated to embers.

He couldn't wait any longer. Ten more steps along the dry wash failed to reveal anything he wished to know, but his eleventh step resulted in the cocking of a hammer close by on his left. Clay whirled and fired, once, twice, the brightness that flared from both barrels blinding him, but before darkness swamped his eyes he saw someone rammed backward by the blast, a fool too dumb to get behind cover before taking aim.

Clay ran for the nearest tree, scrabbling for fresh shells from his belt, shoving them home, snapping the barrels into place and cocking the hammers again, expecting momentarily to hear or feel bullets from the gun of the dead man's partner. He dropped behind a fallen trunk and opened his mouth to breathe, his pinched nostrils making too much noise. There was nothing to hear, nothing to see but the dark outline of willow trees against a lesser darkness. He wanted to call upon the remaining man to surrender, but didn't dare risk revealing his own hiding place. It was to be another waiting game, and against all his instincts, Clay prepared himself for it.

"You out there!"

The voice came from above, on the northern bank, probably the fire feeder. Clay said nothing.

"Don't you be shy," called the voice. "I know where you're at, can see you pretty good."

Clay doubted it; if he was visible, he would already have been shot at.

"No sense in waiting till daylight. Why don't we settle this with a deal right now?" suggested the voice.

Clay took a chance. The other man's voice gave no clear indication of his location, and any sound Clay might make would be made useless for targeting by the slight echo down there on the stream bed.

"What deal?" he said.

"You stay where you are and I go lose myself. My partner, he's got most of what you're after tied around him under his shirt. He ain't going nowhere, so you stay here with him and you'll get back most of it. You come after me and I'll have to shoot you down."

"Don't believe a word," Clay said.

"That you, Dugan?"

"It is."

"Knew it was, soon as I heard that boomer. You ain't got any kind of range with that cane cutter, Dugan. I got a long-barrel repeater here, better you know right now."

Clay was surprised that his identity was known to the other. "Who are you?"

"Lonnie Baines Marshal."

Clay knew him; Baines worked at the livery stable in Keyhoe, a colorless young man with an obsequious manner, the last person Clay could have imagined robbing a bank.

"You must've known I'd come after you, Lonnie."

"Well, no, we never did. A little ways out of your yard, ain't you?"

"Only as far as you made me go. Why don't you come out where I can see you and lay that weapon down? I'm duty-bound to take you back. You can ride your horse or get slung over the saddle; I don't care. You make your choice, Lonnie."

"Well, I already did, I have to say."

A fusillade of shots whined past Clay, one striking the trunk a yard or so from his face. Lonnie Baines wasn't bluffing. Clay realized he should have given a cry to simulate a hit. Lonnie would have come down sooner or later to make sure of it, and he could have blasted him then. He wasn't thinking fast enough.

There was no point now in denying he was still alive. "How is it no one in town recognized you, Lonnie?" he called.

"New coat, Marshal, new hat too. Had on a handkerchief as well. They never told you that?"

"Who was your friend? I know him?"

"Don't believe so. Henry Pulvermiller?"

"Never heard the name."

"He's from out to Colorado way. Well, he won't get home again now, I reckon."

"You want to get home, Lonnie? Throw that repeater out where I can see it, and come out after it."

"No, no, I sure can't do that. Let you have the money Henry's got wrapped around him, though. You take that and let me go, how about it?"

"Not tonight. Get yourself out here and be sensible about this, Lonnie."

"I won't do it, no, I sure can't. See me going back there without the money I took, and a prisoner and all? They'd laugh at me. Nossir, can't do it."

"It's better than dying, Lonnie."

"I ain't dead yet. Might happen to you, not me."

"No, Lonnie."

A long silence followed, then Clay heard the scuffling of boots. He swung the shotgun up, fingers tightening around the stock, expecting to see Lonnie making a suicidal rush for him. But the sound was already receding along the rim. Lonnie had decided to make a dash for the horses. Clay knew he would go a little way along the creek, then cross it to the south side, then double back to where the horses were waiting. He'd be keeping a check behind him as he ran, in case Clay was following, but Clay wasn't about to.

Lonnie spent almost fifteen minutes doing what Clay surmised he would, and found the horses at last only because one of them whinnied softly when he came near enough for it to recognize his scent. Lonnie looked over to the creek bed, a vague line of darkness fifty yards away. He hoped Clay was still there, or better yet a long ways upstream looking for him still. Now he saw the horses, the white shoulder of his own and the less distinct outline of Henry's. It was a shame about Henry, and a bigger shame about the money that would get left behind with him, unless Lonnie found the nerve to go strip it from the body. It was a good idea, if Clay Dugan was indeed still on a cold trail further along the creek, searching in the dark, but a bad idea if Clay hadn't fallen for it and was lying right there just a few yards from Henry and the cash. Lonnie hesitated.

"Don't you move, Lon."

It was Dugan's voice, close by. He'd come looking for the horses, and found them. Lonnie hadn't thought of that possibility, and felt angry with himself for slipping up so bad. Henry had slipped up, and now Lonnie had too, and it seemed like all he could do now was try and hit the marshal with a lucky shot. He fired it, and received both barrels in reply. Blown backward, already dying, Lonnie was thankful he wouldn't have to hear any laughter after all.

Both horses had tried to escape the noise and flashes, lunging away into the darkness, prevented by their tight hobbles from fleeing. Clay approached and gentled them with soft words for several minutes before attempting to lead them to the creek. He tethered them near the fire, now not much more than embers. Clay tossed wood from a pile prepared by Lonnie, then waited for the wood to catch before going out to retrieve the bodies. After hauling them both to the blaze, he went in search of his horse, and returned with it.

The money had been divided, half of it wrapped in a sash inside

Henry's shirt as Lonnie had said, the rest in Lonnie's saddlebags. Some of it had been made unusable by buckshot and blood. Clay tied the dead men securely across their saddles, kicked dirt over the fire and mounted up for a return to Kansas by night, riding slowly, leading the other horses. He was not tired, could ride until Keyhoe came in sight sometime tomorrow morning. He wanted to amble, and think about what he had done, while the miles quietly passed him by.

The two stiffening men trailing behind were low caliber specimens, and Clay took no great pride in having killed them. He doubted that Henry had any reward money posted against his capture or demise; only a first-time bungler would have taken Lonnie Baines for a partner in robbery. There would be a general shaking of heads in town when the story came out, the usual pious consternation over why someone like that had chosen the left-hand path to perdition. Clay never asked himself any such thing. He assumed individuals made the choice consciously, having weighed the potential rewards against the likelihood of a short life. They knew the risks in advance, these acolytes of crime, and Clay was not about to ponder their stupidity. He wondered how many of them truly repented as the rope snapped tight against their ear, or the bullets came smashing into them.

Toward dawn, back across the Kansas line, Clay fell asleep in the saddle. He awoke as the sun rose, and stopped to watch it push above the horizon. When it had separated completely from the plains, he turned to assure himself that his dead men were still tied aboard their mounts. They were, and as Clay stared at the horse under Henry Pulvermiller he recalled the advice of witnesses to the robbers' escape: Look for the colored horse.

Last night in the firelight it had seemed a common enough beast, its hide randomly splotched with different hues, none standing forth from the rest. Clay admired pintos and paints for the clear separation of their patches, and had thought the horse before him, with its unaesthetic smearings, a disappointing animal.

The sun, however, changed his mind. Sunlight did for Pulvermiller's horse what firelight somehow obscured. The light of a new day burnished its hide to a coppery brightness, but that tint was only one of many present; there was a subtle shade of what Clay wanted to call purple, but was in fact closer to lavender, and there was indigo, and a gray so vibrant it defied grayness, even a startling undertone of rose pink. All of these were splattered and streaked and swirled together, their edges melding, forming colors Clay could not identify. The mane and tail were a curious mixture of deep brown and gray and blue—Clay swore there were actual blue hairs among the rest—and the legs below the knee were dark, in four differing shades.

It was a remarkable sight. Clay made up his mind then and there to have the horse for his own. He felt he had earned it. No one would argue with him if he impounded it as evidence and later released it for his personal use. He simply had to have it, because it was a horse unlike any other.

He noticed, as the morning wore on, that its hide became somewhat dulled as the sun rose higher. There had been something special about the first unspoiled light of morning. That was the time Clay's new horse had revealed itself fully, unreservedly. He would call it Sunrise.

17

Drew was asleep when Marion de Quille entered his cell. The clang of the steel door closing woke him. Marion looked around at the cell's bare walls, and at the young man sitting up on his narrow bunk.

"Drew boy, you don't look good."

"I don't feel good."

"How they treating you here?"

"They feed me and take away the shit bucket once a day."

"Can't ask for more'n that, now can you."

"You going to get me out, or just stand there admiring the furniture?"

"Believe I'll stand, just for now," said Marion. "We have us a little problem this time. Feller you shot wasn't just any feller. He's the cousin of the state representative in Congress, no less, so there's folks that want a piece of your hide for what you did."

"He started it."

"I believe you, but the point is, he's had to have the arm you hit taken off above the elbow, and it's his right arm. What'd you use, a forty-four? Smashed the bone all to pieces, so they had to take it off. You can see how that'd tend to make the man a little bit peeved."

"You've got me out before, Marion."

"I have, when it's no one special you got mixed up with, and there

wasn't too much blood spilled. This time it's different. This time
there's lawyers involved, and I can't even get you bail. What all
were you fighting over anyway?"

"A girl. She didn't want him, but he kept on grabbing."

"So you had to be Sir Galahad and rescue her."

"As a matter of fact, she started screaming at me after I shot him.
His gun came out first, I want you to know. He was drunk, so he
missed."

"So you're in the pokey because you tried to get a congressman's
cousin off of his favorite whore. I wonder sometimes if you aren't a
fool, boy. How old are you now—eighteen? You should know better
than to argue over loose women. There's not one that's worth it."

"Next time I'll mind my business. What do they want from me,
this congressman's cousin's lawyers?"

"I'd say about a year behind bars for doing him grievous injury. A
real good lawyer might get you off with six months."

"Then get me one, why don't you."

"Can't," said Marion. "There's not a lawyer in Houston wants to
touch you, not even your money, if you had any, which I guess you
haven't."

"Nope. You don't give me enough work to earn any."

"Oh, so it's my fault, I guess." Marion snorted. He was genuinely
upset to see Drew in jail. Drew had outgrown boyhood while working for Marion as a general factotum, assisting in all manner of illegal activities. Marion smuggled imported materials of all descriptions up from the gulf, and arranged for their dispersal across
Texas. Drew had begun, as Yancy had, at the seafaring end of the
operation, but discovered, like Yancy before him, he had no sea legs
at all. Marion moved him back to Houston to help oversee the dis-
tribution of the untaxed booty, and Drew had used his sharp brain
to fulfill whatever directive Marion gave him, then abandoned his
mentor in crime to wallow in the usual troughs young men were
drawn to. He was in danger of becoming a wastrel, like Yancy, and
that would have been a shame, since Drew possessed greater potential for success than Yancy ever had.

"There was one thing I did," said Marion, "but you won't like it if
I tell you."

"Tell me and be sure."

"I sent a telegram to your mama down in Galveston. She's got
influence down there, and a parcel of it stretches up this far."

"Did you get an answer?"

"I got one, all right. No, is what the lady said. I guess you don't visit home like you should. He's made his bed, is the message she sent, so now he can lie in it. Not a whole lot of sympathy there. Would you have taken help if she offered any?"

"I'd take help from the devil if it got me out of here."

"Haven't seen old Nick in the area, but I'm not one to let down a friend, Drew boy, so I came prepared. You can bet they're not about to let you out of here till your trial's due, and then it'll be straight into the wagon and down to the courthouse, and directly from there to prison. Seeing as your mama won't help, you'll have to bust out of here on your own, and get clean away from Texas for good. That is, unless you figure you need to serve the time they give you for the good of your soul, and to make restitution for the bodily harm you did to that leading citizen. That how you feel?"

"Can't say I do."

"Thought as much, so like I said, I came prepared. Get over to the door and keep a watch out for that dumb guard brung me in here."

Drew got up and stood watch while Marion slipped his suspenders and lowered his pants.

"Are you in love with me by any chance, Marion?"

"Keep your tongue in your mouth and your eyes where they'll do the most good."

"Mind telling how you intend helping me by showing your butt?"

"This big old butt is what'll save your hide, son. They searched me pretty good when I came in, patted me down every which way to make sure I'm not carrying a weapon in concealment, but there's one place they never cared to venture."

Marion bent over and extracted a tiny derringer from between his buttocks. "Been in a nervous sweat about that thing ever since I jammed it in there. Man could do himself serious harm with a misfire in his pants. There you go, and I don't make any apology for the way it smells."

He handed the derringer to Drew. Its breech contained just one bullet. "I tried to carry loose ammunition alongside of it," said Marion, "but it all kept falling out. You'll have to get by with what you've got."

"Marion"—Drew grinned—"you're like a father."

"Don't accuse me of being a father to someone dumb enough to get in trouble over some other fool's female. Now listen, you wait at least a full twenty-four hours before you use that thing. I'm leaving town tonight for a long spell, and I don't want you busting out five minutes after I walk out of here. The longer you wait, the less sure they'll be it was me that gave you that peashooter, so you hide it good, and wait, you hear me?"

"I will, I promise."

"You better."

They talked some more, then Marion called for the guard. While he was escorted out, another guard entered Drew's cell and began searching in every corner.

"Looking for something, Herb?"

"That old crowbait de Quille, he's sly enough to get something in here as would help you get out, so I'm lookin' for it."

"He wouldn't do that, Herb. He's getting me the best lawyer in the state, but keep on looking if it makes you happier."

Drew had wedged the bullet into a crack between the bricks, up near the ceiling, and dropped the derringer into the bucket containing his own shit and piss, thrusting it down out of sight. Herb took the time to examine the bucket, but didn't touch it, and appeared satisfied that no weapon had been smuggled into the cell.

"Herb, can I ask you a favor? Send a preacher in to see me, would you?"

"Preacher? You?"

"Marion gave me a lecture about mending my ways, but he didn't have any practical advice to offer, so would you get the preacher from the church just down the street? I believe his name's Appleton."

"I'll ask, but I don't say it'll happen."

"Thank you, Herb."

Reverend Appleton was allowed into Drew's cell the following afternoon. His humor had been sorely tested by the search he was subjected to before being allowed access to the prisoner, and he was curt to the point of rudeness.

"You wanted my advice?" he snapped, refusing Drew's offer of a seat on the bunk.

"All the advice I can get, Reverend."

Appleton provided what he could, as quickly as he could, the smell from Drew's latrine bucket upsetting him even more than the indignity of the search. The derringer had been retrieved, dried and placed under the straw-tick mattress before the bucket was emptied first thing in the morning, then hidden again in its original place as soon as there was enough fecal matter in the bucket to conceal it. Drew knew the cell would be searched after the preacher left, and so it was.

"See the light?" asked Herb, as his partner escorted Appleton from the building.

"What light's that, Herb?"

"Holy light—what the hell else?"

"No, I can't say I did, but the man did his best, I'll give him that. I don't regret asking him in, nossir."

"Waste of time for someone like you, I reckon," said Herb, nosing suspiciously around the cell.

"You may be right, Herb, but anything's worth trying once, don't you think? Are you really looking for a gun left by a man of God, Herb? That's kind of farfetched, wouldn't you say?"

"I got orders. Anyone sees you, they get treated the same, I don't care who they are. You're in deep trouble this time, boy. They're out to get you good. You stepped on the wrong toes this time around, I reckon."

"A man without enemies, Herb, he's got to be a pretty poor example of spunk, probably a scared little fellow that never says boo to anyone. I wouldn't want to be that kind of a man."

"You ain't any kind of a man, so how would you know?"

"Always glad to hear your opinion, Herb."

"You're keepin' me up nights. My wife, she don't like it, that's my opinion."

"Sorry to inconvenience you. Why don't you take the night off? I promise I won't saw my way out of here before morning."

"Damn right you won't. I'm gonna be right out there, keepin' watch. They pay me extra, see, for the nights."

"That's good to know, Herb."

Herb's sleep was intruded upon that night by cries from Drew's cell. He went to the door and looked inside through the peephole.

"What the hell's that racket!"

"Appendicitis ...," Drew gasped. "Get a doctor. ..."

"You've just got a bellyache is all, now hold down the noise."

"Doctor ...," Drew pleaded. "Please, Herb ... oh, God! Get a ... get a doctor!"

Herb swung the keys from his belt and unlocked the cell door. He wasn't about to leave the prisoner alone in the jailhouse while he went running for a doctor the prisoner didn't need. Anything could happen while he was away. He'd check the boy's forehead, and if it wasn't sweating a stream the way it should if he was genuinely sick, he'd smack him good for disturbing his sleep and maybe even plotting escape.

"You just better be real sick. Hold still now. Quit that squirmin' around, I said!"

"Herb ... it hurts so bad. ..."

Herb's fingers brushed against Drew's perfectly cool and dry forehead, but before he could summon outrage to his voice he found a tiny pistol resting its muzzle against the skin of his eye socket.

"All right now, Herb, you do what I tell you. First thing we're going to do is walk out to the desk, nice and slow. Come on, Herb, out we go."

Made speechless by surprise, Herb allowed Drew to take his pistol and holster from the desk drawer. A pair of handcuffs were tossed to him. "Try these on for size. Pass the chain around behind the pillar."

Tears of humiliation at the shame to come were already welling in Herb's eyes as he fastened himself to a pillar of brick in the center of the room. His wife would never let him forget this, nor would anyone else. "Sorry, Herb," said Drew, and hit his jailer across the temple with the barrel of Herb's own gun.

Drew passed from the jail through the rear door, the pistol jammed into his waistband. He proceeded at a fast walk to the livery stable where Marion had arranged for two good horses to be waiting. A boy was waiting with them, and Drew wondered if this one would become Marion's new protégé. He mounted up without a word and led his second horse through the streets of Houston to the plains of darkness beyond.

The quickest way out of Texas was south, to the gulf, but Drew was not disposed to take the obvious trail, in part because it was too obvious an escape route, primarily because Vanda's sphere of influence lay in that direction. He supposed he couldn't blame her for not wishing to assist him in his hour of need; he had proved as wayward an excuse for a son as Yancy, returning to Galveston only on business for Marion de Quille, and only visiting with his would-be mother three times in five years. He couldn't resent her lack of concern, nor expect assistance onto a ship. These would be prime targets in any case, since the whole of south Texas knew he worked for Marion, and Marion's trade at the receiving end was merchant shipping of dubious registry.

No, he would have to leave Texas the hard way, the longest way, by heading west until he crossed the state line into the territory where he had wandered alone and been found by Yancy Berdell a lifetime ago.

18

Leadville was the last and most illustrious stop on the line, but within minutes of arriving there, Zoe and Omie learned of a newer, potentially richer discovery further into the mountains, which had transformed a high valley without a name into a rip-roaring camp among the clouds. This abode of bighorn sheep and bears near the great divide was now called Glory Hole.

Its discoverer was a longtime miner by the name of Gumpe, whose luck in the lower mining towns had never brought him more than a meager living. Following a dispute with his partners that prejudiced him against human company, Gumpe had set off on his own toward the monumental skyline of central Colorado. He panned and probed along remote creek beds for ten weeks without result, and grew lonely in the process. He asked himself if maybe he was prepared to forgive humanity its faults and rejoin the community of miners downstream, but could not make up his mind.

Made angry by his own indecision, Gumpe kicked at the ground with his scuffed boots, and unearthed a nugget, dull and ordinary in appearance, yet to Gumpe's trained eye, unmistakably gold. He promptly forgot his misery and began digging. Within minutes he had enough nuggets to fill a tin cup, and within the hour had reached, at the remarkably shallow depth of four feet, a veritable

treasure trove of nuggets clustered together in so tight a formation
he thought they must constitute the biggest lump of gold in creation.

The cluster broke apart as he worked around it, and as he raked
out the separate chunks, Gumpe felt his heart begin to gallop all
over again as yet more nuggets were revealed beneath those
already dislodged. He had in truth stumbled upon a glory hole, the
work of years culminating in one furious hour of digging, the riches
of several lifetimes revealed in a space no larger than a hip bath.
Gumpe had his reward, and the anonymous place he had wandered
into had a name.

Glory Hole was as yet beyond the reach of rails, was not even at
the end of any established road, but even as Zoe stepped from the
train at Leadville, men were packing up possessions and equipment
and streaming up toward the higher peaks to become part of the
rush to Gumpe's valley of gold. With the naïveté of the newly
arrived, she thought at first the pandemonium in the streets was
an everyday occurrence. Only when Omie was knocked over, and
the perpetrator stopped for thirty seconds to lift her up and explain
by way of apology, did Zoe learn of the need for haste among the
hundreds of men swarming by.

So pervasive was the atmosphere of optimism and excitement
around her that Zoe thought briefly of joining in, then reconsidered.
She had in her tote bag a little over three hundred dollars, proceeds
from the sale of her home in Pueblo, and had concocted while on the
train from there to Leadville a scheme for its practical investment.

One of her few domestic accomplishments while married to Bryce
Aspinall had been the art of cookery. Unable to do much more than
peel potatoes and shuck corn in the beginning (these having been
her primary tasks in the kitchen of Mrs. Hassenplug, back in Indiana), Zoe had quickly earned the stilted praise of her husband
through the purchase of a common cookbook, followed by assiduous
application of the recipes therein. If Bryce, with his nonadaptable
palate, had found satisfaction at her table, then others would presumably do the same.

Zoe had no grand notions of establishing a fancy restaurant; an
ordinary eating house would suit her modest talents. She even had
a name for it—The Cornucopia—borrowed without compunction
from a thriving store in Pueblo. Zoe's eatery would dispense food fit
for miners, and plenty of it. She had been convinced it would work

long before the locomotive ceased its toiling and set herself and her daughter down among the thin air and thinning population of Leadville.

She would ignore the new strike, and sink her money into a community already established in national importance. This place called Glory Hole that men were stampeding toward would in all likelihood prove to be a flash in the pan, as so many of the new strikes did. She and Omie would have no part in it.

Finding accommodation was not difficult, given the sudden surge of humanity toward Glory Hole, and within a short while mother and daughter were established in a rapidly emptying hotel that offered Zoe's two basic requirements: cleanliness and cheapness. Their bags unpacked, they went downstairs again to watch from the sidewalk as tidal waves of activity swept back and forth along the street. They were joined by the proprietor, who shook his head at the spectacle of energy and movement before them.

"It's hopes of finding their own strike," he explained. "Around here it's all been claimed and worked over till there's only the big fellows can afford to sink mines for the stuff deep underground. No one wants to work for someone else when there's a chance he'll find his own lode under the sky and not have to crawl like a mole for some big fellow that's already made a pile of money. Chasing dreams, that's the reason for this. Most of them'll be back inside of three, four months, asking for their old jobs, and most likely getting them too, for less wages. It'll be a lesson for them, ma'am, but you can't tell them beforehand. I've seen it in Nevada, and I've seen it here."

The proprietor had only glanced once at Omie's birthmark, just enough to settle his curiosity, not stared and stared at it as many people did, so Zoe was inclined to open a conversation with him. "You must have been drawn to a dream yourself," said Zoe, "to have experience of both places."

"That I was, and never regretted it, but I'm no miner, so it's different for me. So long as there's precious stuff coming out of the ground right here in Leadville, I won't be moving up there to Glory Hole, not unless it turns out bigger than this town, which isn't likely. Is your man coming to join you, ma'am?"

"No, he is not."

"Excuse my asking. See, I've got the habit of looking at my guests and figuring just who's here for what, if you see what I mean, and you strike me as a lady that's here for a definite purpose. Committed, you might say. No offense."

"None taken," Zoe assured him; she continued, "I have a notion to open an eating house. I wonder if you could advise me as to my first steps in that direction."

"Eating house? We've got plenty of those, right on up to the kind of place you can get yourself just about anything the human stomach'll accept, and mighty expensive too. Larks' tongues—ever tried 'em?"

"No, I haven't."

"Me neither, but if you care to try, there's a place just a block and a half away'll set it down in front of you on a dish you can just about see through, and charge you a week's wages."

"I have in mind a more practical place, with ordinary fare."

"We've already got as many as is needed, ma'am, and I'd say there'll be too damn many for the population that's left at this rate, begging your pardon."

"You're saying I have arrived at the wrong time?"

"Exactly the wrong time, ma'am, I'm sorry to be the one that tells you. You stay around, though, and most of them'll be back, like I say, but that'll be a while yet, right about when the cold weather starts. Nothing like a cool breeze coming through the holes in his clothes to make a man see good sense again and go find himself a paid job."

"Could it be that with so many leaving, there are eating establishments up for sale by owners with the gold-mining fever?"

"Ma'am, I just don't know. This rush only got started yesterday, so you'd have to be finding out for yourself. Me, I need to be asking around if there's hotels in the same condition, and finding out if I'm in the same bad situation I recall from Nevada."

"I do hope not, for both our sakes."

"Me too, ma'am, but I'm not hopeful, not after the last time."

"Mama," said Omie, "will we go where the men are going?"

"No, I think not. That is, I hope not."

She was no longer sure of anything. The plan hatched en route to Leadville seemed foolish in the light of events taking place before her eyes, events based on the mercurial nature of human activity when meshed with news of a fresh strike. Not even reports of plague or imminent flood could have caused so many men to move so quickly in one direction. Only the siren song of gold in the mountains could have accomplished this anthill scurrying, as men rushed for the newest place where the oldest song was heard.

Zoe felt the tugging of panic at her sleeve. This was not what she had been expecting. It was unkind of fate to have stolen from her a reliable husband, then whipped from beneath her trusting feet a plan to make up for his disappearance. Maybe she should have gone back east, instead of bringing her daughter further into the regions of uncertainty Colorado seemed built upon. It was too late now for regret, however; she would just have to find out at first hand what options were available, and make a choice accordingly. She would do this with a view to whatever was best in the long term for Omie who, although possessing the ability to see future events and report on them to her mother, had not done so in this case.

"Is all of this surprising to you?" Zoe asked Omie, knowing the hotel proprietor would not understand the question's deeper meaning.

"Oh, yes," Omie said, smiling with great enthusiasm.

Zoe knew she could not rely on her daughter to provide warnings in advance of disaster or sudden change, a circumstance she found ironic, given Omie's proven powers.

By evening the rush had dwindled to a smattering of late starters setting out on foot or on horseback for the new diggings. Zoe felt the time had come to assess Leadville's need of her dream, and so commenced to stroll about the town. Every commercial enterprise appeared to be flourishing; there seemed little chance of the community's becoming deserted, despite Glory Hole's allure. On every street she found movement and noise enough for two towns.

Omie was with her, having protested at being told she should stay in their room until Zoe's return. She held tightly to her mother's hand as they passed from one block to the next, surrounded by the cacophony of miners drenching their throats at the end of a day's shift, crowding the sidewalks in front of every saloon, shouting to each other of Glory Hole. It was all so fascinating, this clamor and clatter; Pueblo had never known such commotion.

As the windows and street lamps began to come alive with light, Omie grew excited, then restless. Something was pulling at her awareness, some unidentifiable thing that had no place on the street, a presence inside her, becoming more familiar to her senses with every visit. It was without personality, faceless and voiceless, yet it commanded her attention as surely as if invisible hands had grasped her face and turned her eyes toward whatever the thing demanded she should notice.

"Omie, keep up or you'll get lost. Omie!"

She had slipped her hand from Zoe's, an almost frictionless sundering of contact, and stood now before a dance hall's double doors, which beckoned to the lonely with colored flames in sconces mounted overhead. To Zoe it looked like hell's doorway, with Omie an innocent about to be swallowed by it forever. She hurried back and took her hand again.

"The blue-eyed man ...," murmured Omie.

"Come along, and keep up."

Men entering the place stared at Zoe in passing. Loud, jangling music spilled briefly from inside as the doors were opened, then closed.

"Only one eye is blue," said Omie firmly, recovering herself. "The other one is brown."

"What eye? What man?"

"The man with the blue eye. In there."

She pointed at the dance hall doors.

"Well, he has nothing to do with us, and we have nothing to do with him, or this place, so please come along."

Zoe had to drag Omie for several steps before she consented to be led away down the street. Zoe glanced at her each time they passed a lighted window, and felt a moment's exasperation at the dumbstruck expression on Omie's face, almost as if Omie were not there behind her own features.

"What is it?" she asked, stopping. Omie stared resolutely beyond her, lips slightly parted, eyes unblinking.

"It's gone ...," she said.

"What is? What's gone?"

"The ... the money."

"What money? What do you mean?"

Then Zoe knew. She had hidden her three hundred dollars beneath the carpet in their room at the hotel, thrusting it far from the edge, spreading the bills with her fingertips so no trace of a bulge could be detected. It was not possible that this was the money to which Omie referred, but she felt coils of apprehension begin to tighten around her heart anyway.

"Ours ...?"

Omie nodded slowly, her face without identifiable regret or alarm. She still was not looking at her mother.

"Hurry!"

Zoe began to run, hampered by her long skirts and Omie's unresponsive weight on her arm. "Hurry! Please hurry!"

The desk clerk was made curious by his newest guest's panic-stricken face and hoarse breathing as she collected her key.

"Has ... has anyone been up to my room?"

"No, ma'am, not even the maid, not till tomorrow. Something wrong?"

She ran for the stairs, the little girl dragged along behind with a perfectly blank expression on her peculiar face. The desk clerk decided the proprietor should know about such goings-on, and sent a bellboy to notify him at the restaurant across the street, disturbing his supper with a woman who was not his wife. Annoyed, the proprietor sent back word that the desk clerk should investigate for himself, and report on what he found, if anything, the following morning.

Receiving his instructions mere minutes after Zoe had flown with her key to the stairs, the desk clerk trudged up to the second floor, where he found Mrs. Dugan sitting with head in hands on the edge of the bed, while her little girl stood looking at the carpet between them.

"Ma'am, has something happened?"

Her head lifted. The desk clerk had witnessed grief often in the course of his work, and was able to recognize her distress, but he could see no cause for it.

"Ma'am?"

"My money ..."

"Money, ma'am?"

"He took it ... someone did."

"Someone took your money? Where was it you kept this money, ma'am?"

Zoe nodded at the corner. "Under the carpet," she said, the words leaving her like tired breath.

"Oh, ma'am, you shouldn't have done that. Leadville's got plenty of banks that'll take care of your cash just fine. That's just awful. Was the door locked?"

"Yes."

"And the window?"

"I ... don't know. I didn't look."

The desk clerk went to the window and found it unlocked. The newfangled fire escape was bolted to the bricks outside, a perfect escape route for any thief. There was a notice on the inside of every door in the hotel, warning guests to lock their windows when absent from their rooms.

"You say someone took it, but do you know who?"

"He had ... one blue eye, I think."

The desk clerk began to doubt her immediately. "One blue eye, you say?"

"I believe so."

"You saw this man?"

"No, my daughter did."

The desk clerk squatted down in front of Omie.

"Was the man with the blue eye coming out of this room?"

"No."

"Well, where did you see him, exactly."

"In the place with the colored lamps."

"And what place might that be?"

"She means the dance hall nearby," said Zoe.

"Ma'am, I don't think I can see a connection between the fellow with the blue eye and what's happened to your money, I really can't. Is there something more you can tell me?"

"He might still be there, at the dance hall. Where can I find a constable?"

"City marshal's office is just down the street. Turn left at the lobby entrance."

He wanted no further part in whatever scheme the woman was trying to work. Her acting was better than most, and the girl's contribution was well rehearsed, even if her delivery was a trifle stiff and unconvincing. They should have concocted a better story between them, though, if they wanted to collect money from the hotel as compensation for allowing some blue-eyed or one-eyed thief into their room to rob them of their nonexistent savings. It was a shame the mother was training her daughter in such criminal arts, especially since the little girl was already saddled with a physical affliction no amount of ill-gotten cash could rectify. The desk clerk found himself without any sympathy for the woman.

When they were alone again, Zoe asked Omie to try and remem-

ber just what the man with the blue eye had to do with the disappearance of the three hundred dollars. Omie squinted and frowned,
and could tell her nothing; she could no longer recall with any clarity the vision that had struck her outside the dance hall doors. Seeing Zoe's disappointment, she began to cry. Zoe enfolded Omie in
her arms and assured her she had done nothing wrong, and was not
responsible for their loss. "I know," was Omie's slightly offended
response.

"Stay here," Zoe told her, "and don't open the door to anyone but
me. I have to go and find the man, if I can. Will you be all right on
your own?"

"Of course."

Zoe did not go to the marshal's office. She had seen the change
that came over the desk clerk's face when he heard of the man with
one blue eye. A marshal would be even less likely to waste time on
such a case, and Zoe could see why. She would have to take care of
it herself.

The place was in full uproar when she arrived. Zoe noted for the
first time its sign in letters of gold: GODS OF THE DANCE. The clientele
spilling in and out were anything but godlike, most of them already
drunk despite the early hour. She pushed open the doors and went
inside.

Almost immediately, a large man barred her way. "No women," he
said. Zoe barely heard him over the din. A band of musicians was
pounding, sawing and scraping with vigor on a rostrum at the far
end of a cavernous space aswirl with men and women in close
embrace.

"No women," the man repeated.

"I have to find someone," Zoe explained.

The man leered knowingly. "All of us got to, lady, but we got all
the someones we can handle inside here right now."

"I don't want to dance. I'm looking for someone ... a certain person. I'm sure I saw him come in here."

"Someone you know?"

"I ... yes."

"What's his name?"

"He has one blue eye."

"Say again?"

"One blue eye. Has anyone like that come in here?"

"With an eye patch, lady?" Her interrogator was clearly enjoying
himself.

"No, he has two eyes, but only one of them is blue. Please tell me if someone like that has come here tonight."

"I guess I would've noticed a feller like that."

"He's a thief. He stole some money from me."

"Oh, he did? You come with me, lady."

The man beckoned a colleague of equal size to take over his position by the door, then led Zoe around the edge of the crowd lining the walls. The smell of liquor and tobacco and perfume was overpowering. Zoe was feeling quite faint by the time she was ushered along a short corridor marginally less noisy and smoky than the main hall, and brought to a halt outside a closed door. Her escort knocked, then went through, indicating with an impatient gesture that Zoe should follow. She entered a small office. A man with oiled curls of hair pasted to his forehead sat behind a desk, writing in a ledger of some kind. "What?" he said, without bothering to raise his head or cease writing.

"Lady here says we got a thief come in."

The man looked up. His cheeks were smooth and plump, his features boyish.

"What thief?" he asked.

"I don't know his name," said Zoe. "He has one blue eye. The other eye is brown, I think."

"What did he take?"

"Three hundred dollars."

"Know him if you saw him?"

"I would know the eyes."

"Would you mind waiting outside for just a minute, ma'am."

Zoe stood beside the office door until the large man emerged. "He says to take you around and look at everyone. If you see the feller, you tell me. Does he carry anything?"

"Carry?"

"He got a knife, a gun, blackjack maybe? I need to know before I tell him to hand over what he took, see."

"I don't know if he's armed. I'm sorry."

"Just go ahead and pick him out, and I'll handle it."

They returned to the echoing hall. Zoe saw now that every woman present wore a dress of bright coloring that revealed as much as possible of the shoulders and bosom. Arranged like furniture along one wall when not actually dancing, these women never, to Zoe's eye, turned down a prospective partner, drunk or sober. She had not understood until then that the women were employees of the man whose office she had visited, not casual visitors like the men, whose price of admission presumably entitled them to lurch around the floor with any female of their choosing. Zoe found the concept vile.

Her eyes were beginning to weep in reaction to the smoke-filled air, and she found it difficult to concentrate on the faces, whiskered or clean-shaven, that swam before her. Some were too bleary-eyed to even notice her scrutiny; others registered surprise at the presence of a modestly dressed woman in their midst. The lighting was dim, and she was obliged to thrust herself close to every man whose eyes she checked. Several times this uninvited closeness was misinterpreted as lewd invitation, and the men concerned attempted to embrace Zoe, only to be thrust away by the large figure at her side. She looked and looked, but saw no eye of blue that was not accompanied by another of the same hue.

"No," she said, sick at heart. "No more."

"He ain't here, you reckon?"

"No."

"Come on back and see Taffy."

"I would prefer to leave, thank you."

"Taffy said come back when we're done, so we will."

Too dispirited to argue, Zoe accompanied him again to the office. This time she was ushered into the presence of the owner alone.

"Mr. Taffy, thank you for your help, but I must go back to my daughter now."

"Just a few minutes of your time, ma'am. The name's plain Taffy, by the way. Take a chair, do."

Zoe sat on a comfortable settee by the wall. Taffy swiveled his padded armchair to face her. Zoe thought his artificially arranged hair was effeminate in the extreme, but she could not deny he was polite.

"This thief, he took everything you've got, am I right?"

"Yes."

"Mind if I ask what your business is in Leadville?"

"I came here to ... to open an eating house."

One eyebrow lifted itself among the oiled curls. "With three hundred dollars? Ma'am, you're not serious."

"Would that have been too little? I confess I'm not an expert in these matters."

"I would say not, if you'll pardon my frankness. So you have a little girl to take care of, and no money."

Zoe nodded. She felt unbearably tired, and her clothing reeked of tobacco smoke. Her dream, such as it was, had died among the gods of the dance.

"So you'll be needing employment directly."

"I'll find something," she said.

"Well, maybe. Then again, maybe not. It's men that's gone tearing out of town this last day or two, not women. If you're a miner you'll find an empty job to fill, but I just don't know what else there'd be for you, ma'am. Would it be an impertinence to know your name?"

"Dugan, Zoe Dugan."

The name caught Taffy's attention. He had that very morning read a Kansas newspaper that had arrived wrapped as protective padding around some panes of glass ordered to replace those repeatedly smashed during drunken fights on the sidewalk outside. The account he read over his morning coffee had told of one Clay Dugan, marshal of Keyhoe, Kansas, who had single-handedly pursued a team of bank robbers into the Indian Nations and brought them and their loot home again, the bandits having been rendered beyond any need for legal counsel. Dugan sounded like the kind of man Taffy admired. The newspaper was several months old. He knew there was no connection between that Dugan and the one before him now, but the mere coincidence of their name made him look kindly on the woman who had lost everything to a man with one blue eye.

He examined her from a professional point of view. The look of respectability about her meant little; some of his most popular girls had looked like Zoe when they sat on that very settee and asked for a job. With the right dress, this one could prove to be every bit as successful as his best earners. She was not too plain, nor too pretty, which often made men leery of demanding a dance, let alone an assignation in the back rooms. With a smile painted on her, she just might work out fine.

"I have a position open here," he said. "You probably saw how things work while you were out there. The men buy tokens, little brass arrowheads—I thought up that idea myself—and they hand them to the ladies every time they dance. The one with the most tokens at the end of the evening gets paid more than those with less. Pay for merit, that's the term."

Zoe hadn't noticed the exchange of tokens, but what she had seen was enough to negate Taffy's self-satisfied picture of the enterprise.

"Thank you, no."

"Think about it. Look around, then come back."

"I will. Thank you."

Zoe had no intention of wasting a moment to even consider such work. She stood, thanked Taffy again for having allowed her to inspect his clientele, and departed.

Omie was fast asleep when Zoe returned to the hotel. She had paid in advance for just three nights, thinking this more than enough time in which to launch her plan for an eating house. How lamentably inadequate her preparations seemed now.

Stifling her fears, Zoe set out early the next morning to find work. She applied at every hotel, hoping there might be need for someone to change the sheets or assist in the kitchen or clean the floors, but there was not. She was similarly unable to interest the owners of the very eating establishments she had hoped to supplant. Even a position as waitress was impossible to find. She returned to the hotel twice during the day, to be sure Omie was not distressed in any way over having to remain cooped up in their room for so long. Omie understood what Zoe was attempting to do, and knew the presence of a child would make success even more elusive. She appeared content to play with a favorite doll while Zoe went out again to try her luck.

On her second day she applied at those places she had avoided on the first, but the meaner hotels and hash houses were as uninterested in her plight as their more prosperous competition. Zoe returned to Omie with dragging feet, and together they went out to eat a cheap meal in silence. This was to be their last night at the hotel. Zoe rehearsed her story, hoping to find the proprietor in a charitable frame of mind come morning. He had seemed friendly enough on Zoe's arrival, and might countenance a rent-free period of several days, just until she found work.

This hope was short-lived. The proprietor listened with sympathy, but could offer Zoe nothing more than a promise to hold her luggage and effects in the back room until she found somewhere else to stay, rather than subject her to carrying these possessions with her around the town. Zoe asked if he could find work for her, however lowly, on the premises. He regretted he could not.

Futile as it might be, Zoe went out to comb the streets again for some kind of employment, this time taking Omie with her. She would even have considered a position as laundress, truly a back-breaking profession, had one been available, but Leadville's laundry was monopolized by Chinese, and Zoe found their appearance and alien chatter intimidating, and so did not apply among them for a job she would not have been given in any case.

As if directed by fate, she found herself in the afternoon standing outside Gods of the Dance, inspecting with resignation its unlovely facade, the cheap gilt of its sign and the tawdriness of the colored lamps awaiting the evening to be made bright and beckoning. She had known even as she turned the corner that the dance hall was her destination. It took all her strength to push open the doors. The sight of Omie walking through under her arm gave Zoe gooseflesh; a child had no place inside such a den of vice.

The place seemed unnaturally quiet without music or dancers, and the smell of tobacco smoke was considerably less. She approached a middle-aged man sweeping the floor, and for one mad moment considered begging him to relinquish his broom, hand it and his job to her that she might avoid the pit yawning to receive her. No mother should have had to be in that place with her daughter, simply to pay for food and rent. The world was a heartless place, if something or someone did not intervene to prevent Zoe from taking the step she intended taking.

"Help you?" asked the man, pausing to look up.

"Is ... Mr. Taffy here?"

"In the office. Know where that is?"

"Yes, thank you."

Zoe went to the door and knocked. Taffy's voice ordered her in. She allowed Omie to enter first, perhaps as unconscious emissary of goodness to ward off what was to come. Taffy, however, expressed no surprise. "Good afternoon, ladies." He beamed. He offered Omie the use of his swiveling chair to distract her while he directed Zoe to the settee. "You don't look well, Mrs. Dugan," he said, taking his ease at the settee's far end.

"The weather is warm."

"For hereabouts, yes."

Zoe stared at the floor, unable to explain her presence there, knowing no explanation was required.

19

Clay's quest for further authority in the region was aided by an act of God—the county seat was struck by a devastating tornado and demolished almost completely. Rather than rebuild, most of the inhabitants packed up their few remaining possessions and moved to Keyhoe, which, with the sudden influx of population swelling its electoral rolls, became qualified virtually overnight to assume the mantle of county seat. The former county sheriff having been literally borne away on the wind (his body was identified some weeks later, much gnawed upon by wildlife, recognizable only because of the badge still pinned to a remnant of shirt), it became clear to the citizens of Keyhoe that Clay Dugan should inherit the late officeholder's powers of arrest and enforcement.

A hasty election was held. There was no real competition against Clay, and he won an easy victory. Some townspeople were disturbed, in the days that followed, to learn that Clay Dugan had no intention of relinquishing his other badge, that of town marshal, simply to accommodate the newer piece of metal sharing his vest. It was clear he considered himself capable of handling both jobs from the one office, and banking both salaries. "Neither one's what you'd call princely," he explained.

When a newspaper editorial suggested there might be something unconstitutional about one man wearing two badges, Clay made it known he didn't give a damn what the editor thought, so long as the arrangement was acceptable to the people of Keyhoe and to the state government that paid him to maintain the law and strike down or otherwise apprehend those individuals caught flouting it.

Most people thought Clay's attitude showed gumption, and a rival sheet, newly arrived to set up its presses from the ruins of the former county seat, seized upon the local man's gaffe and proclaimed its endorsement of Clay Dugan for sheriff, marshal, chief alderman, tax collector and dogcatcher. Readership loyalty shifted from one paper to its fledgling rival overnight, and Clay's unusual position was confirmed by public opinion.

To his wife, however, Clay was less than a hero. Sophie was convinced that only she could see him for what he was—a meanspirited man who thought only of Clay Dugan, to the detriment of all others, principally herself. It was true, he appeared to dote upon their son, but Sophie suspected he did this only because Silan was an extension of himself, a kind of mirror in which to admire his own reflected glory.

It irritated her beyond measure to see people nodding to her husband on the street, as if they were his proud owners. His nodding in return to the men, or smooth touching of fingertip to hatbrim for the benefit of the women, struck Sophie as the quintessence of hypocrisy. She knew for a fact that he despised almost everyone in town for a fool or weakling who could not stand up to a stiff breeze without the assistance of hired help. That was his puzzling description of his twin professions—hired help—yet he made no secret of his enjoyment in their practice.

Sophie concluded that this was because the work allowed him to be a bully. He enjoyed his dominance over others in a way her first husband never could have done; Grover Stunce may have been a man of extensive personal limitation, never truly comfortable with the power that was his to wield, but no one could ever have characterized him as a bully. Sophie felt it should be possible to make people do what the law obliged them to, without smashing the side of their head with a sawed-off shotgun, or emptying its barrels into the more obstreperous of them. No, there should be a method somewhere between Grover's benign fumbling and Clay's remorseless administering of public order.

An even greater source of Sophie's anger was his behavior at home. Clay did not love his wife, probably never had, and took no pains to hide this unpleasant truth from her. He never bothered to approach her as a wife anymore, and spent his sleeping hours alone on the sofa. It was the final insult, this rejection of her flesh. She heard no whisper, saw no evidence of another woman, but such a figure began stalking her thoughts more often. Was Clay so inhuman as to have no need of the marriage bed? His purely masculine needs should have directed him to her, whatever the state of their love. His abstinence was wholly unnatural, and Sophie saw herself as its victim. She had her needs, and not one of them, apart from being maintained in a comfortable home, was being met by her husband. He spoke seldom, and would not respond when she cautiously broached the subject of their life together.

Sophie's only comfort was Silan. He was a loving boy, still too young to be aware of the gulf separating his parents. When he was with Sophie, he enjoyed following her from room to room as she performed the domestic chores, and even offered to assist her with them. That endearing habit ceased when Clay came home unexpectedly one afternoon, to find Silan happily washing dishes. Clay ripped the apron from him and said, his voice heavy with controlled anger, "Don't you ever do that again, boy. That's women's work, not something for you to be getting into, you hear me?"

"Yessir."

Clay looked forward to teaching Silan the things a boy should know: riding and shooting. Silan told his mother he wanted to be the sheriff and the marshal himself when he grew up, just like Papa. Sophie gave him a sickly smile and informed him that there remained plenty of time in which to find his own path in life. Silan's expression indicated that he didn't see the need for being anything other than what his tall and famous papa was. Sophie felt heartsick for days afterward.

Clay rode Sunrise as often as his official capacity allowed. Being responsible for the entire county, he was able to ride its length and breadth whenever he chose, and would often take the time to serve legal papers or collect small fines from the county's furthest corners himself, rather than send one of his two deputies. Clay knew why he did this; it was simply to escape from his wife and the town of Keyhoe for a while. Alone beneath a sky so broad it appeared curved, he could appreciate what it meant to be himself. Not husband or father, not lawman: just plain Clay Dugan.

The feelings that invaded him on these extended rides among the badlands of his inner self disturbed Clay. He could not quite get a handle on precisely who he was. The things that defined him—his twin badges, his shotgun, his horse of many colors, which had become every bit as much of his popular image as the healed-over holes in his cheeks—were not enough to reassure him that he was indeed the person everyone accepted as their custodian, their guardian. Was anyone standing guard over Clay? He felt something missing, some essential part of himself that was nearby but separate from him: a key; a dislodged brick from some wall around a secret.

He wondered if the missing part of himself was so obvious a thing as the brother and sister he had thrown away hope of ever finding. Could the answer be so simple? The clearly limned portraits his memory had retained of Drew and Zoe were blurred now, reduced to a few facial expressions and bodily or vocal characteristics that he was aware were being steadily eroded by time. Once, alone by a campfire, he felt a presence so strongly beside him he snatched up his weapon and turned to the darkness in fear. He thought he saw a girl standing just beyond the firelight's reach, a girl with some kind of partial mask over her eyes, but then she was gone, probably a fragment of a waking dream Clay had not even been aware was taking place within his mind. Shaken, he built up the fire, then found himself crying, his mustache soaking up the inexplicable tears.

One of Clay's pleasures on these lonely rides around his county was the sight of his horse cropping grass in the shining moments just before and just after the appearance of light in the sky. So aptly named, Sunrise glowed like a spectral creature from an earlier time, a fairy horse stripped of wings, confined to earth until some magical spell be broken. The sight always moved Clay in ways beyond his understanding.

He found cause for sorrow in the fact that his senses were never so moved as when he saw Sunrise at the special time of dawning. He should have felt such wonder when looking at his wife and child, but he did not. Even Silan could not provoke in Clay's chest the same elation, the same sense of perfection, as Sunrise, a dumb beast. The fault for this misplacement of emotion lay in himself, he was sure. He was an incomplete man. Those parts of himself that were present were arranged in all the wrong places, and it seemed there was nothing he could do about it.

* * *

Silan always expressed admiration for Sunrise. He begged Clay often to let him share the saddle on the colored horse, and was always refused. "He's too tall for you, boy. When you're older I'll get you a pony of your own."

"You could hold me on. Why can't I, just for a little while?"

"Because I say. He's my horse, and I'm your father, so you heed what I tell you if you don't want a switching."

"You never switched me yet, so I don't believe you."

Clay laughed. He knew he indulged his son. "Comes a first time for everything, so you watch your tongue, you hear?"

"But can I ride on Sunrise with you?"

"No, and don't be pestering me again about it."

Sophie overheard this exchange in the yard from the kitchen window. There was never awkwardness between Clay and the boy, the way there was between husband and wife. Inside the man there was a small wellspring of affection, but none ever ran in Sophie's direction. She was herself loving toward Silan, but only when Clay was not present. Like him, she felt it was not appropriate to fuss over the boy while under spousal scrutiny. The family spent so little time together in one room that the tension between Sophie and Clay, and the mutual ignoring of their son, never became obvious enough to cause embarrassment.

On a day in midsummer when he found his duties irksome, Clay finally relented, and agreed to take Silan up onto the saddle before him while he rode Sunrise from one side of town to the other. There was no real risk, since his arm was around the boy at all times, squirm though he might with excitement at finally being allowed onto the horse he considered the most wonderful in the world.

Together, father and son reached the edge of town and turned to amble back to the livery stable. That was when the dog, someone's mongrel, rushed from a yard to attack the horse. Sunrise reared to his highest reach. Clay grabbed with both hands at the reins to control him, and Silan, panic-stricken by the commotion and sudden elevation, fell backward against Clay's stomach, rolled sideways without encountering the supporting arms he was expecting, and slipped from his perch. He was gone from the plunging saddle in an instant. Clay made a futile grab at his receding jacket, then had to concentrate on reining in Sunrise before he was thrown himself from the horse's back.

When he had control again, Clay saw Silan's body lying still on the ground. He leapt from the saddle and allowed his horse to gallop away down the street. Scooping Silan into his arms, he murmured the boy's name over and over, a low babbling of sound that came directly from his heart. The back of Silan's head was caked with dirt and blood. The dog had followed Sunrise along the street. A crowd was gathering around the two figures in the dust.

Silan was carried to the house and set down on the parlor settee. Dr. McNab bathed his head to expose what appeared to be a minor laceration of the scalp at the base of the skull. Sophie wandered in and out of the room, dazed. When Silan suddenly emptied his bowels, she attended to him without a word, first making the men leave the room.

"The wound's in a bad place," McNab told Clay. "A blow to the head can be a serious shock to the brain. That's likely the reason for him not responding to anything. He's unconscious, but with his eyes wide open."

"How long will it last?"

"I've heard of cases that continued for several days, others that lasted just an hour or two. It could be he'll come around before suppertime, with nothing more than an aching head to show for it. Or it could take longer; I just don't know. When Mrs. Dugan has finished in there, you may as well put a nightshirt on him and put him to bed. At least he'll be more comfortable."

Silan did not come to before suppertime, on that day or the next. There was no perceptible change in his condition. He would eat, if food was thrust into his mouth, and drink water poured into him, but his eyes would not close. Not a limb, not so much as a finger, showed any inclination to twitch. Silan lay utterly still, his mouth gaping slightly, eyes fixed on the ceiling.

Sophie stayed with him most of the day and evening. Clay slept in a chair beside Silan's bed at night, following his rounds of the town saloons. He would enter Silan's room, rouse Sophie from the chair and take her place. For a long time he would stare at the boy's wan face with its staring eyes, then he would arrange himself for the hours of sleep that refused to come until near dawn. He spent several hours each day asleep in a cell at the office, while his deputies took care of business and kept things as quiet as they could.

Silan's twilight state persisted for forty-seven days. Dr. McNab instructed that he be turned, like a side of beef on a spit, four or five times every twenty-four hours, to prevent the onset of bedsores, and this operation was carried out with diligence by the parents. Silan's body did not waste away, since Sophie fed him as much as his champing jaws could accommodate, in fact he became heavier than a boy his age should be. Sophie cleaned up his bowel movements without fuss, and seemed not to expect Clay to participate in this, the least acceptable sickbed task. On the one occasion when Clay was obliged to perform it, in the small hours of the morning, he did not communicate to Sophie his outrage that anyone other than a baby should require such treatment. Whereas Sophie's attitude toward Silan's condition remained essentially unchanged from the beginning, Clay was aware of a fundamental alteration in his thoughts.

He asked Dr. McNab, "Can he go on this way?"

"I've heard of such instances, yes. The patient is sometimes able, with constant care, to maintain the bodily functions for considerable periods of time."

"But without getting better."

"No. It's my understanding that once the comatose condition has been entered into for more than a week or two, there is no return to normalcy. I don't say that my knowledge, or lack of it, is the last word in such instances, but I won't hold out to you any false hope. I know you for a man who appreciates the unadorned facts, and these are what you have. Mrs. Dugan is perhaps not ready to accept them."

"Thank you for being honest."

"A great many things are in the hands of God, probably more things than we know of."

Clay nodded, doubting it.

Clay was temperamentally disinclined to allow a situation beyond his control to persist indefinitely. It was against his own nature, and against nature in general, that a boy five years old be allowed to lie like a log in his bed, eating and excreting without the slightest indication that he was aware of his own humanness. It wasn't right that such a thing be permitted to continue, without any end in sight, without hope of restitution or redress. There lay Silan, a wonderful boy about to enter the stage before manhood, now reduced to a form Clay could not bring himself to recognize as that of his son.

He began to drink, guardedly at first, then with an openness that surprised his deputies and shocked Sophie.

"That isn't the way," she said. "You won't help him by getting drunk."

"Is that so. And how *will* I help him? Tell me that."

"By believing."

"In what?"

"The strength and mercy of God."

Clay's braying laughter made Sophie realize just how far her husband had strayed from the path of righteousness. He never did anything more than silently mouth the hymns in church every Sunday, never discussed religion with her, or prayed, or read the Bible. He was an unbeliever, and it was likely that his sin was in part responsible for Silan's tragedy. The laughter was unforgivable. Sophie hated Clay more intensely at that moment than she had at any other time, and recognized her hatred as the kind that left a permanent mark on the memory, a hatred from which there could be no returning.

"You are an evil person," she declared.

His laughter stopped immediately. "Say that again."

"You have no love inside you for anyone, even your son. You won't make the least effort to bring him back to us."

"Bring him back? What the hell can I do? Oh, you mean *believing,* am I right?"

"I mean you should get down on your knees this instant and beg the Lord for mercy! Beg with all your heart, and Silan may yet come back to us! I have! Why should you not!"

He stared at her, feeling some sympathy for her plight. Here was a woman who expected divine intervention because she had prayed for it. There could be no further conversation between them that would mean anything. They might just as well have attempted communication in different languages. He felt sympathy for his wife because she would never get the thing she wanted, for all her efforts. It made him only slightly irritated that she would blame him, not the absence of God from the world, for the continuing farce of Silan's death-in-life existence.

"I'm sorry; I can't."

"Then on your head be it," she said, and swept from the room. Clay picked up his whiskey, the little shot glass twinkling merrily in the lamplight. "My only friend," he said, and then saw himself as an unbearably pathetic individual, smart enough to understand he could do nothing to alter things, cowardly enough to cope with his sadness through liquor. It had been a long time since he felt so weak, so maudlin. Another drink would fix that, and another one or two would allow him to forget anything he wished to.

After sixty-one days without a change in Silan, Clay made a decision. He drank nothing all day, and his deputies exchanged dour expressions; was Clay Dugan about to climb out of the hole he'd dug for himself and start acting like a lawman again? They had protected him against too much public scrutiny since the accident, knowing his pain, but it was about time he took control of himself, whatever the misery in his private life. Keyhoe and the surrounding county needed a drunk running things the way it needed more mud in winter.

When Clay returned home to assume the nightly watch over Silan, Sophie left them alone without a word. Husband and wife had reduced their domestic exchanges to the barest minimum of words and glances. Most tasks could be accomplished in complete silence. Clay found he preferred this stunted intercourse to the pointless arguing that would have resulted from actual conversation.

He waited for more than an hour, to ensure that Sophie was fast asleep, then lifted Silan from the bed and carried him outside. Sophie's house was near the edge of town, and Clay was able to carry his boy away from the streets and buildings, out to the empty prairie and the long horizon of Kansas, a ruler-straight edge to the canopy of stars. He set the boy down and knelt beside him. The evening was cool; fall had come.

"That's quite a sky, don't you think? No one can ever count the stars, there are so many, like dust in the air. You asked me once how many there were, and I said I didn't know, and you looked at me like I should have known. Well, I didn't. I don't know much about anything, as a matter of fact. I know you won't ever get better, though. That I do know. And I know it isn't right to let you be the way you are. It isn't your fault, but it isn't right either. I mean to change the way things are. I have to. There's some who wouldn't let me, so we have to do this together, just you and me, so it can get done like it should. I always loved you. You're my darling boy. That ... that's why I have to do this. If there's a tiny part of you way deep inside that can hear me and understand what it is I'm saying, please forgive me. This is the only way, Silan, the only way out. If there's a hell, and I have to burn there forever for this, I'll do it gladly, anything but look at you day after day, turning into something that isn't even you anymore. It isn't right, and so we're out here, you and me, to put it right. Good-bye, son. I love you."

Clay took from his pocket a large handkerchief folded neatly into a square. He lifted Silan's head, cradled it tenderly with his left hand, and pressed the handkerchief firmly against the boy's mouth. Soon the body that had moved not a muscle since being thrown from Sunrise began to thrash feebly, its jerkings without coordination, the instinctive response to oxygen starvation. Clay hugged him close, and held the handkerchief tighter. An end to movement came with surprising swiftness.

When all movement had ceased, Clay lifted the boy in his arms. The walk home seemed endless. Clay had to stop once in the shadows while a drunk staggered by. He was sure no one had seen them as he returned Silan to his bed.

The lamp was brought closer, its wick turned up for an inspection of Silan's face for telltale marks around the mouth. There was none that Clay could see. It was not that he considered the suffocation a criminal act; he simply had no wish to share knowledge of the event with anyone but the dead boy. It was too personal an episode to allow outside his heart.

Clay returned the lamp to the dresser and settled himself into his customary armchair. He wanted a drink very badly, but would deny himself, he wasn't quite sure why. It seemed important to maintain sobriety, so he would, clear through until morning, when he would break the sad news of Silan's release to his wife. He would definitely need a drink after that.

Dr. McNab pronounced Silan dead of natural causes arising from his unfortunate condition, and a funeral was held as soon as could be arranged. Many townsfolk attended, out of respect for their leading lawman and his grieving wife. The parents conducted themselves in public with stoicism and dignity, and the community wished them well in their hour of loss. It was hoped that they would have the chance for another son, but Sophie's three miscarriages following Silan's birth did not augur well for a continuance of the Dugan line.

Clay kept his drinking to a tolerable level. Those who were aware of its subtle effect on his work made no comment, allowing him more time for his personal grief. At home, he was able to tolerate the presence of his wife only by way of whiskey, and spent as little time there as he possibly could.

Sophie had embraced religion with a fervor he had not suspected she was capable of. When he married her, Clay thought Sophie a fairly hardheaded woman who gave the church its due as a force in the land, without subscribing overmuch to its tenets of belief. Silan's accident, and then his death, had brought out in her a penchant for mysticism he found alarming. She would not leave him alone, and insisted on convincing him that the error of his ways was based on the twin evils of alcohol and atheism. The harder she proselytized for his salvation, the deeper Clay plunged into both.

"I don't want the comfort of the Lord," he told her, "and I don't need it, because it isn't there, so I'd be a fool to be wanting it and needing it, now wouldn't I."

"Then you must think that I'm a fool."

"Just let me alone, and believe what you like."

"Aren't you the least bit concerned that Silan is watching, and feeling anguish in his heart over the way you refuse to see what must be seen?"

Clay performed an elaborate inspection of the corners of the room from his chair. "I don't see him."

Sophie sniffed. "He is with us anyway. You would be aware of his presence if you would only allow yourself to turn in the direction of the light."

Clay turned to face the oil lamp on the table and squinted fiercely at it. "Still don't see him."

"Playing the fool does not become you."

"Woman, I'm not the fool in this room. He's gone, and you and all the preachers in the world don't know where he went any better than I do, so don't be telling me you know what you don't."

"You simply will not be guided."

"Not by you."

"There's a darkness in you, Clayton Dugan, that will eat your heart."

He lifted his glass. "Here's to its appetite."

Sophie dashed the drink from his hand, her face twisted with sudden fury. "You monster! You blind fool! He sees us! He sees everything, hears every word ...!"

Clay was out of his chair and shoving her against the wall, shouting, "He sees nothing and hears nothing! He went where I sent him because your precious Lord didn't have the mercy to send him there from the start! He's dead and gone, and *I'm* the one that spared him, not God or Jesus Christ!"

Sophie's mouth dropped open. She stared at Clay's face, inches from her own, and stopped trying to wriggle out from between him and the wall. Watching her eyes, seeing in them a horror he had not anticipated, Clay realized he had said too much in anger. She had never looked upon him like that in their entire married life. Her face was screwing itself into a knot of loathing, her lips attempting to shape themselves around the words to condemn him. Clay released her and stepped away. He kept an eye on his wife, as he would a dog he half expected to attack if he turned from it. He needed to be out of Sophie's house, as far from her as he could get, and he needed a drink as never before.

Sophie watched him leave the room, heard him pause in the hallway to pick up his hat and shotgun, then open and close the front door. She sagged to the floor, slid down the wall Clay had pinned her against, and allowed her body to find its own position against the skirting boards. She felt the side of her head touch the edge of a rug. It felt comfortable there, so she made no further move to adjust herself; she could not feel the rest of her body in any case.

Clayton Dugan had killed her son. It was too awful a confession to be a lie, something designed solely to hurt her. She had seen the will to hurt her in Clay's eyes for years, and known he would one day do so, just to relieve himself of the need; but this thing he had spoken of, this murder ... It was an unspeakable deed, the act of a madman. No—Clay was anything but mad. He had done it with his eyes open, his mind unclouded, convinced of his own justification. That was how Clay conducted himself in life, and she saw no reason why he would not have done what he did with exactly the same ruthless calculation, the same unyielding stubbornness of spirit. He would be punished for it, since God would never allow so great a sin to slip past His omnipotent eye; but Sophie, lying crumpled in a heap on the parlor floor, demanded of God that she be His instrument, that she play a part in the downfall of the murderer. She would avenge herself for her loss, and do so in the full light of day, before a legion of witnesses, so God's retribution—administered by way of herself—would not go unrecorded on earth or in heaven.

While he walked, Clay cursed his mouth for having opened when it should have stayed shut. It was not that he was ashamed of having released Silan from his suffering—in fact he was proud of it—but he had known, even before pressing the handkerchief to Silan's face, that it was an act he could never share with anyone, least of all the boy's mother. Sophie would have persisted with looking after him year after wasted year, in the name of God's mysterious ways, and Clay, for all that he no longer loved his wife, if he ever had, didn't wish to see her lose what was left of her youth in the service of unmoving, inhuman Silan. Clay had heard an old tale about a man condemned to roll a large stone up a hill and let it roll down to the bottom, only to repeat the task again, forever. That was how he had seen Sophie's nursing, and he had delivered her from it, but was unable to claim credit for having done so, not while she believed the things she believed. He should have stayed silent, and been content to know, deep within himself, that he had done the right thing by his boy. He had allowed anger to sweep away prudence, and now there would be hell to pay.

He entered a saloon and ordered a drink. The bartender set it down without a word. Clay knew there were whisperings about his drinking, knew also that he still had the sympathy of the town over Silan. It wouldn't last much longer. He had to get on top of the drinking before commiseration with his troubles evaporated. No town or county wanted a drunk in charge of its law enforcement. He would begin tomorrow, after it became clear which way Sophie would jump. If she did the sensible thing and kept her mouth shut, he would be able to lick the drinking without too much trouble. If, on the other hand, she insisted on making a fuss, his lot would be intolerable without a bottle to ease the burden of cohabitation with a vengeful shrew. Sophie was at heart a practical woman, he told himself, and would keep quiet about his revelation. In time, she might even see things his way, and admit their son was better off away from his useless body. It might happen. He could hope.

He stayed in the bar for over an hour, drinking steadily. He asked himself, as solitary drinkers often do, if he was a happy man, and was honest enough to admit he was not. No part of his life to date had afforded him the kind of intense satisfaction he considered should have been his; not his marriage, which was probably no less comfortable than many another, or his profession, which had elevated him at a comparatively early age to a position of considerable authority in the community.

Clay wondered if maybe he was demanding too much from life. Maybe the man pushing the stone was not so unusual a figure after all, and had eventually grown used to his eternal task. Clay had never considered himself a philosopher, and so was unprepared for questions relating to such weighty matters as an ultimate purpose behind the living of one's life. He made a conscious decision, as he tipped another glass of whiskey inside himself, to make peace with his wife, and attempt to accommodate their differences in a new marriage that would begin once he was sure the business of Silan was behind them.

He had admired her once, when she was still the wife of Grover Stunce, and could admire her again, if only she would let him. Clay had no desire to begin his life over again. If he and Sophie persevered, they might even have another child, despite the string of failures. All in all it was worthwhile to attempt rebuilding the marriage. He drank again, to celebrate the beginning of something.

"Marshal? Better come down to the livery."

Someone was standing by his side, a townsman Clay could not put a name to, drunk as he was. He smiled at the man and said, "What the hell for?"

"Your wife just shot your horse."

Clay hadn't heard any shot, and the stable was only two blocks away. He guessed the shooting must have taken place inside the stable, muffling the sound. He was aware, in a befuddled kind of way, that the structure for a revived marriage he had been busily erecting as he drank was collapsing around him as he stared at the messenger's worried face. He smiled and said, "I'll push that stone till I die."

"You better come see what she did. She's shouting and hollering all kinds of things about you, Marshal, I better warn you right now. She says the next bullet's for you."

"She does? Well, you know she hasn't been in her right mind since what happened to our boy."

He hated himself the moment the words escaped him, and recognized the lie for what it was—a means of self-preservation in the storm that was approaching. Sophie had shown her hand with remarkable swiftness. He really should have anticipated such a reaction. He'd been a fool to hide away in a saloon and drink himself into a state of hopefulness, a true fool, but he was fully awake now, and not about to compound his stupidity by going down to the livery stable while his wife was still there.

"Listen," he said. "You go along to my office and tell Jeff or Elgin, whoever's there, to go take my wife into custody. I can't do it myself; you can see why. You go do that for me, would you?"

"Sure, I'll do it, but you better hear what she's saying about you."

"I know what she's saying, and it's a crazy lie. You go get the deputies working on this, and I'll have something to say about what she's accusing me of later on. You go do that, then come back and tell me when she's under lock and key. Thank you.".

The man left. It disturbed Clay that he couldn't remember the fellow's name. It didn't really matter, since Clay was all washed up in Keyhoe anyway. No matter how hard he might deny what Sophie was bawling at the top of her lungs, the story would stick, and be believed by more and more people as time went by. To a holder of elected office, it spelled disaster. Either he was a child-killer, or he was the husband of a madwoman. His career in Keyhoe was already a thing of the past, and he hadn't even seen the carcass of Sunrise with his own eyes yet. Thinking of his wonderful horse made Clay want to cry. Sophie didn't need to do that. It was revenge, personal revenge against Clay. Everything had been turned upside down. He had only himself to blame, for telling Sophie what he had done. Now he would pay the price. He poured himself another shot of whiskey.

When informed that his deputies had taken Sophie to the jail behind his office, Clay went down to the livery stable. He saw Sunrise in his stall, blood on his neck from the bullet hole behind one ear. At least Sophie had killed him outright, not left him to suffer from a shot to the belly. Clay assumed she had used Grover's pistol. He needed to be gone from this town where everything had suddenly gone wrong for him.

He asked the livery stable owner, "What's your best horse, and the price?"

"Sorrel, yonder. Forty dollars."

"Thirty."

"Thirty-five'll get your dead animal taken care of too."

"Get the sorrel saddled up."

Clay went home to collect some cash and a few articles of clothing, then returned to the stable. His new horse stood waiting.

"Lighting out, Marshal?" the livery stable owner asked.

Clay didn't bother to answer. He handed the man his money and mounted up. Outside, he could see a crowd gathered around his office down the street. Sophie would give them an earful, and continue doing so until they all believed her. His riding out of town without any effort to defend himself would be construed as guilt. He was finished in Kansas forever. Somehow he didn't care.

20

They always pressed as close to her as she would allow, and all the girls were under instruction to allow their partners as much closeness as they wanted, no matter how smelly they might be, or how drunk. Inside the walls of Gods of the Dance, the customer was king.

Zoe was a popular attraction, solely on account of her newness, and soon learned of the propositions she would be subjected to by almost all of her partners. No one had told her of the back-room trade before her first evening. Several of the girls had made cryptic reference to "dancing without music," but Zoe understood nothing until her second partner suggested they retire "out back for some privacy." Thinking his suggestion a request for conversation, she had willingly gone through one of several doors leading from the dance floor, only to find herself in a squalid bedroom, already used despite the earliness of the hour.

"Two dollars," said her partner, smiling.

Her partner groped for Zoe's breast, at which time she broke from him and ran from the room. The girls on the dance floor nearest the door she burst through gave her hard-faced looks of pure delight, and Zoe realized she had been kept in ignorance in order that she might go through this initiation. Her partner came through the door behind her, his face dark, his words drowned by the music until he was beside her. "All right, then—three."

Zoe slapped his face, and instantly became the center of attention in that corner of the hall. The man was at first shocked, then sheepish. "Well, now," he said, recovering his good humor, "I guess I'll make it five, like I should have all along." He could not understand why the little miss he'd paid good money to dance with suddenly turned around and walked away from him. A regular patron, he knew she had no right to do that to him.

"Hey! You come back here!"

Zoe was halfway across the floor, heading for Taffy's office to tell him she could not work as a dance partner if the work included having carnal relations with the customers, when she was spun around by a strong grip on her arm. She expected it to be the man who had first ushered her into Taffy's presence, an individual she had since learned was named Tyler, but it was a girl who had hold of her. "Don't waste your time," she said. "He'll only say you should have known, and he's right."

Zoe pulled away from her and continued on, then slowed to a stop by the corridor leading to Taffy's door. The girl was right; she should have known. Zoe leaned against the wall, made sick by the noise, the smells of drink and tobacco swirling around her, and above all by her discovery of the dance hall's other face.

"You don't have to go with them."

The girl who had taken hold of her arm was by Zoe's side again. She looked very young, but had a knowing air about her. Zoe knew this girl had gone to the back rooms, but only when she chose to. "You'll make more money if you do," she added.

Zoe nodded, unwilling even to thank her for the advice.

"You'll get used to it," she was told.

"No ..."

"It's easy enough. Just let them do what they want, and you think of something else while they do it. It never lasts for long. They're too drunk most of the time to even do it."

Tyler loomed beside them. "Back to work, both of you," he warned. "You," he said to Zoe. "I got my eye on you."

"So's half the men in this hole," said the girl, "so you be nice to my friend, see."

Tyler gave the girl a look that expressed a tolerant contempt, and Zoe formed the opinion that these two had more knowledge of each other than their respective jobs could have accounted for.

"Back to work," repeated Tyler, and left them.

"He won't be so polite about it next time," said the girl. "Are you all right? Can you do it? You get through this first night, and the rest will be easy as can be."

"Thank you."

"If you get in any more trouble, you ask for Winnie."

She was gone from Zoe's side, snatched up immediately by a passing man in search of a partner. Zoe panicked; should she walk out, or continue as a dancer? She was apparently under no obligation to do anything more than dance, unless she became desperate for money. A rough hand took her by the shoulder and spun her around to view a whiskered face inches from her own. "Dance," said the miner. It was a command, not a request. Zoe danced.

In time she recognized Winnie for a friend. Winnie shared a room with two other girls, one of them a fellow worker at Gods of the Dance, the other a waitress who slept regularly with her employer. "Just to keep hold of her job," Winnie explained, "and he's a big fat brute, but what else can she do?"

Having heard of the cramped conditions these three lived under, Zoe invited Winnie to visit the small room she shared with Omie in a cheap boardinghouse. Winnie accepted, and brought with her some cold cuts of meat and bottled beer for a shared supper. Zoe declined the beer, and Winnie proceeded to drink the lot, without exhibiting the least sign of inebriation. After Omie had gone to bed, the women talked of personal matters, and Winnie hinted to Zoe of an extensively checkered past, despite her youth. "I've lost count," she said, referring to the men she had known.

Zoe was appalled at her casual attitude. "How can you do it, knowing they don't love you?"

"Oh, some of them did, for a little while anyway. There was one boy, I didn't even sleep with him, and he said he loved me. He meant it too, I could tell."

"Do you hope to be married?"

"One day, when someone who isn't a filthy drunk asks me, or someone who isn't a miner. I'd never marry a miner, not after dancing with our rough crowd, not me. What happened to your man?"

"He died. A tumor of the brain, they said." It was an easy lie.

"You've got your little girl to remember him by."

"Yes."

"She's a funny little thing. When you were down the hall in the jakes, she said to me, 'Do you know where my brother is?' Did you lose a baby?"

"She's never had a brother. I had two myself, a long time ago."

"Are you looking for another man to wed?"

"No."

"Good, because you won't find him where we work. No man worth the name would set foot inside there, I don't care how lonely he is."

Zoe agreed.

In her third week at Gods of the Dance, Zoe admitted that the money she earned by dancing with the customers was not enough to keep herself and Omie fed and boarded. She was already tardy with her rent for the week, and had been informed by the boardinghouse proprietress that the cash must be forthcoming in the next twenty-four hours, or she and her daughter would be out on the street, with their few belongings held in lieu of payment.

There was only one way out of her predicament, and knowing it made Zoe feel so ill she could not eat all day. When she arrived at work, her condition was noticed by Winnie, who asked what was wrong. Zoe told her. Winnie promised to help, without specifying what it was she could do; Zoe knew Winnie was herself low on money, even though she regularly went with men to the back rooms. Zoe suspected Winnie's wages went for drink.

Halfway through the working evening, Zoe still had not taken the irrevocable step of selling herself. She had not been asked so far, since it had been well established among the regular clientele that Zoe did not do anything but dance. Winnie had not told Zoe that her nickname among the rest of the girls was Ironpants. Her lack of opportunity to compromise herself did nothing to ease Zoe's mind, and she began to wonder if Winnie's promise of aid had been sincere.

"It's all set."

Winnie was at her side, pointing across the room at a small man who was ostentatiously pretending not to look at them. "You go back with him, he won't hurt you. He doesn't even want to put it in, just have it pulled. I think he's scared of catching something. Go over there and tell him you will. I've done him plenty of times. He'll give you five dollars."

"Five dollars," Zoe repeated mechanically.

Winnie gave her a gentle shove. "Go *on*."

Zoe drifted awkwardly through the dancers, trying not to look at her client-in-waiting, trying to postpone the moment when she would have to speak with him. When she stood at last beside him, the little man smiled and said, "Which room?"

Zoe noted one door without a thigh garter draped over the handle, a sign it was unoccupied. "That one," she said huskily, and had to say it again when the little man leaned closer and bellowed "Huh?" in her ear.

She led him inside the room, took the purple garter from a hook on the inside and hung it over the outer handle, then locked the door. The music outside came through anyway. Turning, she found her client had already unbuckled his belt and allowed his pants to drop around his boots. The fly buttons of his union suit were opened in a trice, and the man stood with legs apart, hands behind his back. His stance, with belly thrust forward, reminded Zoe of a statue, some minor political figure perhaps, captured at the instant of greatest confidence and self-satisfaction.

"What are you laughing at, girlie? What's there to laugh at, hey?"

"Excuse me."

"You aren't here to be wasting time like that. My time, my money. You come over here and get down on your knees, and hurry up about it, see."

Zoe approached him, unhappy that his tone had turned so abruptly to impatience. "Come on, come on," she was told. "On your knees, on your knees. How else you going to get at it, hey? All right now, fish it out, fish it out, come on."

Zoe reached inside his underwear, and found a warm and shapeless lump she vaguely recognized as male genitalia. The little man was little all over, and probably required the service Winnie had described because he was not capable of inserting so puny a morsel of manhood into anything more commodious than a tightly closed fist. The tiny penis was coaxed from hiding at Zoe's hesitant touch, and sprang from its flannel cave like an angry mouse, all pink and quivering.

"Yes, yes," encouraged the little man. "Go on, go on."

Zoe attempted to grasp the thing, and smothered it completely with her hand. With a feeling of numbed resignation, she pumped at her client in a lackluster fashion he evidently found stimulating in the extreme. "Yes ... yes ...," he muttered, eyes clenched shut. Zoe pressed on, grateful that he appeared to find no fault in her execution of the task, and concentrated her attention on the man's fly buttons, one of which seemed on the verge of separating itself from the cloth. Several others had been sewn with a clumsy hand and mismatched thread, probably by the straining client himself. He was producing a variety of ecstatic sounds now, and Zoe could feel his little member begin to swell and palpitate inside the tube of her fingers. She moved her head aside just in time, and daintily blotted semen from her bare shoulder while the man buttoned and buckled himself up again to face the world.

"There you are," he said, and dropped a five dollar bill on the floor. "Just be more quick about it next time."

He unlocked the door and left. Zoe picked up the money. She wanted to shred it into tiny pieces, but could not afford such self-indulgence. The piece of paper she had humiliated herself for was folded several times, and wedged down inside her dress. She stepped outside, paused to return the garter to its hook behind the door, and made her way over to the wall of girls awaiting fresh partners.

A dull shame covered Zoe like a cloak. She wished herself invisible, but had already seen the other girls looking in her direction and smirking. She had finally become as they were, despite a lack of true sexual intimacy in her transaction with the little man. She wondered how soon it would be before she accepted a man inside her. The thought of it brought back the queasiness she had been experiencing all day. For a minute or two she felt she might vomit in front of the hundreds of people around her.

Winnie appeared. "A real horsecock, isn't he?" She began to laugh, and Zoe found herself joining in. She was the next thing to a whore now, and she could either laugh about her fall, or slink away and die, and she would not do that while Omie needed her.

Acceptance of her lot brought about changes in Zoe. She began keeping Winnie company while Winnie drank. Zoe's room was the venue for these beery sessions. "I never drink hard liquor," Winnie explained, "because that makes you a real drunk. Beer just makes you a tippler, that's how I see it." Zoe was willing to agree. Being a drunk as well as a whore would have been too much to bear.

She had not yet consented to intercourse, but knew she would soon have to decide if that final step needed to be taken. She and Omie barely subsisted on the wage she brought home. She had several times agreed to perform the sexual service her first back-room customer required, but would not use her mouth to satisfy anyone, no matter what price—sometimes as high as ten dollars—was offered. Complaints from the clientele circulated among the other girls (Zoe's nickname was now the Handmaid) and reached the ears of Taffy, who summoned Zoe to his office.

"Are you happy working here?"

An honest answer would have been ludicrous. "Of course," she said.

"Word comes to me that you're a woman of fastidious persuasion."

"I suppose I am."

"My business is legitimate because I don't offer anything on these premises but dancing partners. I charge more for admission than other dance halls, and men are prepared to pay that extra cash, because they know that dancing is only where the evening starts. You're aware that I take no cut from any gifts of cash made to my girls. That means I'm not in the whoring business, and I don't have to pay unofficial license fees to certain persons who run this town. This is a small outfit, yet it works, and the big fellows leave me alone, but I need every man who comes in here to go out again with a smile on his face and a kind word on his lips for my little dancing establishment. Some miner goes out and tells his pals he got turned down by some snooty piece down at Taffy's place, that's bad for business—catch my drift?"

"Yes."

"And are you prepared to play your part in keeping our customers smiling?"

"Yes."

"Then go out there and prove it to me."

Zoe returned to the dance floor, ashamed of herself for not having told Taffy what a hypocrite he was. She had been unable to do so for the sake of keeping her job, borderline whoring though it was. That she should have to do what she did, simply because she had no money, was not fair. Zoe had never dreamed of great wealth for herself, but saw now that only riches could enable a person to do exactly as she pleased. Wealthy people did not have to guard their tongue, but could say whatever they wished. She suddenly hated the rich for their power, their ability to step over any problem, their chosen pathway paved with silver dollars and golden ingots. Zoe's helplessness was an outrage, a crime against her human potential for advancement.

Winnie approached her. "What happened?"

"He says I have to fuck them."

Winnie saw how upset Zoe was; she had never used that word before. Zoe's mouth was turned down at the corners with anger and shame; she was close to tears.

"What are you going to do?"

"Fuck them."

"Maybe you should get out now."

"And do what? There isn't anything. Even if I went somewhere else, I'd need money for a train ticket."

"I'll give you some. I've got a little set by."

"I can't take what's yours. I'll have to do what he wants, it's as simple as that."

"Listen, you've already started to drink because I do, and you play five-fingered Mary for the clods who come here. Don't be like me and go full-out whoring."

Zoe was taken aback. Winnie had never claimed to be anything but reconciled to her work, yet here she was, telling Zoe not to follow in her steps. Her expression was more serious than Zoe had ever seen.

"You ladies nailed to the floor or something?"

Tyler was beside them, displeased at their absence from the throng of paying customers.

Winnie said, "Tyler, go put your cock in a skunk's ass and freshen up."

He looked at her, then nodded. "Sure, I'll do that, little chicken, and then you're gonna suck it, or I tell the boss you need to get the boot, same as this one." He jerked his thumb at Zoe.

"I wouldn't suck yours if you poured sugar over it," Winnie sneered.

"Think about it first," Tyler advised, not in the least put out by her insults, and left them.

"You shouldn't have said that to him. He's always in Taffy's office. If he says you have to go ..."

"He won't. I'll give him what he wants. It wouldn't be the first time. But you should go. Get out, I mean it, or he'll have you sucking it too, just to be kept on here. We all do it, except you, so far. Get out, Zoe, *please*. ... Nothing's worth this. Do you want Omie to know what you really do in this pigsty? Do you?"

Winnie had taken hold of Zoe's arms and thrust her face close to hers, imploring her with eyes squinted almost shut with anguish. Zoe had never seen Winnie this way, without any of her usual brashness. The young woman before her now was the real Winnie, a soul descending, clever enough to know it, sincere enough to warn a friend away. Zoe could not refuse so nakedly heartfelt a plea, and surrendered with a sense of relief.

"I will," she said, and Winnie burst into tears.

Tyler made a swift reappearance, angered by something he could not comprehend. "What goes on?" he demanded. "Get moving, both of you, and don't let me see you talking to each other again, or it's the boot, I'm telling you now."

"Oh, Tyler," sniffed Winnie, "you big stupid galoot, go put it in a knothole, why don't you."

Tyler jabbed a finger in front of Winnie's scornful mouth. "That's gonna cost you, I mean it."

"Lick my toes," responded Winnie, and Tyler backed away, shaking his head, his smile pitying.

"Come with me," begged Zoe.

Winnie shook her head. "I'm already a whore. I can pretend I'm not, but I am. There's nowhere else for me that I haven't already been, and been thrown out of too. You go, before it's too late, and be a mother to Omie. Go on."

Winnie turned away, suddenly wearied by her outburst, and lost herself among the clumsily cavorting dancers. Zoe watched as she was whirled off in a sea of brightly colored dresses and drab miners' clothing. Winnie did not want to be pursued; Winnie wanted to be left alone, having spoken her piece and gone. Zoe saw Tyler watching her, his expression one of gloating contempt, and wondered if all men wore this ugly mask beneath their everyday face. She knew she hadn't the experience to pass judgment. Winnie had, but Zoe suspected that the truth according to Winnie would be too ugly, too despairing to be borne.

She went to the dressing room, stripped off her purple gown and stepped into her own nondescript clothing. When she stepped outside, Tyler was waiting. "You'll be back," he predicted.

"No," she said, "I won't. And you are an ugly man, down to the bedrock of your soul."

She left him speechless, and passed from the building through a rear door. The evening had barely begun. She would go back to their room and relieve Omie from her solitary existence after dark. She should never have chosen as she did. Winnie had made her aware of that, and Zoe would be forever grateful. Winnie, she now knew, would not prize herself free from the life she had followed since breasts grew on her. Zoe had been raped at that age, but only by one man, and the result had been Omie, blameless, blue-marked Omie, with her grandmother's inner eye that saw more than should be allowed to anyone. Zoe would resume her role as parent and custodian. Omie's life lay ahead; nothing should be allowed to jeopardize her future. Zoe wondered, as she passed down the street, away from Gods of the Dance, if Omie could see what was in store for herself, or only for others.

She passed the sign before its message impinged upon her thoughts. WOMAN WANTED. HONEST JOB FOR HARD WORKER. Zoe turned and went back to be sure it read as she thought it did. The sign was carefully hand-lettered on a square of cardboard propped inside a store window. Zoe stepped closer to read a smaller message along the bottom: *Apply Leo Brannan—Roelofs Hotel.*

She knew the place, and went directly to apply. The desk clerk directed her to room fourteen, with a look that told her she was not the first to arrive.

"How many have there been so far?" she asked.

"Dozen or so, maybe. It's early yet."

She knocked on the door to room fourteen, and was told to enter. Zoe closed the door carefully and turned to meet her interviewer. She saw him in profile, since he was staring out the window. When he faced her, Zoe saw an unremarkable man in his early thirties, neatly dressed in brand-new outdoor clothing, with a very recent growth of beard sprouting along his jaw. There was something not quite right about the way he looked at her, and Zoe decided he was slightly walleyed; it was difficult to be sure in the lamplight. She made a point not to shift her gaze from one eye to the other, in case he was self-conscious about his defect. He had the look of a man unused to mining, or any other kind of hard labor.

"Good evening," he said, without enthusiasm.

"Good evening."

"Can you cook?"

"I happen to be an excellent cook."

"Is that so."

"It is. I would not have said it otherwise."

The man made a wry face. "Then I must believe you, I suppose."

"That would be the correct response," said Zoe, aware of the asperity in her voice, but unwilling to control it. She was not in the mood to be patronized by yet another inferior male, even if he had legitimate work to offer her.

"No doubt you're a seamstress beyond comparison."

"I would not make that claim for myself. I am adequate for straightforward sewing and stitching. If you need a wedding dress, I can't help you."

He seemed to find this amusing. "I'm in no danger of marriage, ma'am. Are you possessed of a healthy constitution, by any chance?"

"I am seldom sick, and I recover quickly."

"What line are you in currently?"

"I am without employment, and have been so since my savings were stolen from me."

"Leadville is riddled with thieves, to be sure. My partners and I are of a mind to leave, and try our luck at Glory Hole. Are you able to walk with us to that place, carrying a fair share of our load?"

"I am. Is it a cook and bottle washer you're after?"

"And nothing more. We have no interests other than finding a fat vein for ourselves. We are honorable persons, I assure you. I won't offend your ears with descriptions of most of our applicants. You've doubtless noticed this place is a small piece of Sodom. Your duties are to be strictly domestic. We want to waste no time performing any task not directly associated with our search. Preparing food, maintaining an orderly camp, keeping the fire supplied with wood, that'll be your job. Assuming I choose you, of course."

"What wages are you paying, may I ask?"

"You may, and the answer is five dollars a week, and a bonus of some description if we make a strike."

"Give me two dollars more, and my daughter will help me. She's a very intelligent girl."

"How old?"

"Six."

"Strong?"

"As I am myself. She'll be no burden at all."

"Assuming I choose her mother."

"As you said. When might you be making up your mind, Mr. Brannan?"

"Oh, I should say sometime tonight. We're anxious to be away. Are you able to conclude your affairs by morning?"

"I have none to conclude."

"Very good. Your name, ma'am?"

"Zoe Dugan."

"And your husband is where?"

"In a better place, I'm sure."

He laughed. "I like your style, Mrs. Dugan. I believe I can recommend you to my partners. Are you positive this is the job for you? I want no backing down at the last minute."

"You'll get none from me."

"Then pack your bags, and welcome aboard the limited company of Brannan, Brannan, Chadbourne and Yost. We call ourselves the El Dorado Engineers. Our approach to mining is strictly scientific."

"How interesting. Should I present myself here in the morning?"

"You should, and must, if you're to come with us. Is five o'clock too early for your girl?"

"She can rise at any hour."

"Then we'll meet, one and all, in the lobby."

"Thank you."

"And thank *you.*"

He came forward to shake her hand, and she saw his face more clearly. He had one eye of brown, and one eye of blue.

21

Before he could leave the state, Drew fell in with low company. He had no wish to become involved with Cecil and Carl, the Rucker boys. He changed his mind, at least temporarily, when they told him he was a dead man if he wouldn't come with them to rob the stage near Croker Flats.

"It's your horses we want, to tell the truth," said Carl. The brothers rode sorry nags. "We could take 'em from you easy, but you can make the choice for yourself, I guess. There'll be money in it for you."

"Why not just trade your worst horse for the best of mine and leave me out of this," reasoned Drew. The Ruckers had introduced themselves in an open and friendly manner before suggesting he join them in their proposed criminal act. Drew judged them to be several years older than himself, but not particularly bright.

"Could do it that way," Cecil admitted, "but with the extra man along we can keep 'em covered much better. There's a mean dog rides shotgun on this line."

"Be better with three," agreed Carl. "What's your name anyway?"

"John Bones."

"Bones? Naw, not Bones, not truly."

"That's my name, and I wear it with pride."

The Ruckers were laughing softly.

"Heard of a dog one time, had that name," Cecil recalled.

"Skinny dog," said Carl. "Dave Mullen's dog, weren't it?"

"Naw, his cousin's, and it was called Boney, not Bones."

The conversation took place on a stretch of west Texas, a land-scape without feature or scale. Drew had seen the brothers coming toward him for an hour or more before they finally met under a sky that bore on its invisible currents no trace of cloud.

"Hell," said Cecil, growing impatient, "are you gonna throw in with us, you and the horses, or do we lay you out right here and now?"

He pulled a pistol from his belt for emphasis, and aimed it in Drew's general direction.

Drew sighed. "Care to tell me more about the plan?" he asked.

The stage route lay two hours' ride north of the place where he made his bargain with the Rucker boys. They rode together in ami-able company, Cecil's temper having improved the moment Drew agreed to participate.

"Got plenty of time yet," said Carl. "She don't come through till near about noon."

Neither of the Ruckers possessed a watch, and Drew hoped they might arrive too late at the place designated for their attempt at robbery. There was no sign, when the stage road was reached, to indicate any recent passage of wheels, and Drew accepted the situa-tion. He could always hope the Ruckers were cut down fast, leaving him to turn tail and gallop as far from the scene as he could. The road itself was nothing more than a dusty trace cut through a plain peppered with low sagebrush.

"Anyone on the stage will see us a long time before they get here," he said.

"We thought of that," declared Cecil.

"We come prepared," Carl said. "You watch this."

The brothers dismounted and made their horses lie down on their sides. "See? When it gets near the time, we throw a little dust over 'em too, and won't nobody see 'em at all."

"We'll be right down on the ground alongside," added Carl. They both looked to Drew for approval, and he saw they had, after coerc-ing him into their little band, unconsciously made him their leader. A headache was beginning to gnaw at his temples.

"Boys," he said, "I bring you bad news. My horses won't lie down like that, either one of them."

Drew had no idea if the animals Marion de Quille had provided would lie down on command or not, but the Ruckers apparently trusted his word to the extent that they didn't consider trying to prove him wrong. Watching the consternation on their faces, Drew felt there was a reasonable chance he could dissuade them from their plan.

"You'll have to do this some other day," he advised.

"No, we sure can't. We need money, don't you?"

"Everyone needs money, but if my horses won't lie down, we're not going to be able to hide ourselves before the stage comes along, now are we?"

Carl's face was made sad at the thought of abandoning their scheme for fast riches; Cecil's face registered bafflement and anger. "Well, there's got to be a way," he said, talking loudly to reassure himself.

Drew shook his head and assumed a doleful expression.

"I know!" Carl shouted, and began to perform a shuffling, kicking dance in the dust.

"What the hell idea you got there, Carl?" demanded Cecil. "Quit that and tell me!"

Carl tripped himself and fell. He sprang up again and began knocking dust from his hat.

"It's real simple," he said. "Boney here waits by the side of the road with his horses, only he won't be mounted, he'll be standing next to 'em, like they're lame, see, and when the stage comes along he lifts his hand like he wants it to stop for him, and when it does, we come up out of nowhere and take 'em by surprise!"

Cecil's look of doubt faded instantly. "By God, Carl, that's right! That'll do her! Hear that, Bones?"

"I heard."

The Ruckers grabbed each other's forearms and began a whirling dance, shouting and whooping in celebration. Their horses, made nervous by the spurs being whipped past their noses, regained their feet without being told to, and stood shaking dust from themselves with rapid twitchings of their hide. Drew wished they were nervous enough to dash away toward the horizon, obliging him to set out after them.

Allowing his eyes to wander in the direction of his wishes, Drew noticed a distant plume of dust to the west; the approaching Croker Flats stage. He nudged his horse sideways, so the plume lay behind his shoulder. With luck, the Ruckers would fail to see it until too late, and wouldn't be able to blame Drew for lack of attention.

"Lookit!" Cecil broke off dancing and pointed. "Here she's comin'!"

"Too soon!" howled Carl. "I bet they seen us already!"

"Maybe not," said Drew; from his higher elevation he could make out the top of the coach and the two flyspecks of its driver and guard. They, being higher still, could certainly see him.

"Shitfire!" Cecil spat. "Now what do we do? They seen us yet, Bones, you think?"

"Well, I'd say so. Thing to do now is pretend like we just happen to be on the same road as them. You'll have to cancel your raid and set it up again some other time—that's what I think."

"We already set it up for right now," Carl whined. "Hell, now we're gonna have to do it all over again."

The brothers mounted their horses and slapped dust from themselves while the stagecoach drew nearer.

"See Middlebusher?" asked Carl, whose eyesight was less keen than his brother's.

"He's up there on top, same as usual," said Cecil. To Drew he said, "Man's the next thing to a rattlesnake, just pure bad through and through. Loves to kill ordinary folk if he can. Stage line keeps him on so's no one tries to rob 'em. He got Rufe, that's our friend, jest a couple months back. Deserves to die, Middlebusher does."

"But not today," Drew suggested.

"Anytime atall," corrected Cecil, his face hard.

The stage was slowing as they spoke, and came to a dusty halt directly in front of the trio. Several passengers stared at them from the windows, one of them a woman. Drew looked at Middlebusher, the one with the shotgun, and was surprised at the man's bland appearance, just a skinny fellow with a long mustache, nobody to look at twice.

"Ho there, boys," called the driver. "We thought you was laying for us till we seen who it is. How's your mama, Carl—still got the misery?"

"Doin' real poorly, thank you."

Drew knew then, with a sinking heart, that he had been coerced by something even worse than amateurs; the Rucker boys were local amateurs. Their stupidity was beyond belief. They would have had to kill everyone on board the stage to avoid being identified as the perpetrators. Drew felt himself break into a light sweat at the thought of what had been avoided. It had been the narrowest of escapes for them all, and it had been accidental, nothing more than a misjudged sense of time.

"Middlebusher!" Cecil yelled. "You sorry turd, when you gonna lay down and let a wheel roll over your goddamn yellow back!"

"Afternoon, Cecil," responded Middlebusher, seemingly unfazed by the insult. The woman inside was heard to gasp at Cecil's language.

"You better run next time I see you, you sorry piece of shit."

"Got a lady on board don't want to hear you talk that way, Cecil," said Middlebusher. "You mind your tongue now, boy, or I might have to mind it for you."

It was a mild enough warning to Drew's ears, but Cecil chose to be insulted. He snatched up his pistol and aimed at Middlebusher. "Throw down the shipment!" he barked.

"Awww now, Cecil, don't be making the same mistake Rufus done," advised the driver. "Just you cool off about that."

"You shuddup, Will. What you think we're doing out here— huntin' jackrabbits? You throw it down directly."

"Don't have no shipment this trip, Cecil. The express box went yesterday, and I ain't lying."

"You are too!"

"He isn't," said Middlebusher.

"I believe I'll kill you right now," Cecil told him.

"All right," said Middlebusher, leaving Cecil confused.

The driver said, "You boys cool off now, and don't make this any worse'n it is already."

"This is between him and me," Cecil insisted.

"Not if I say it isn't," said Middlebusher, sounding tired. His shotgun was aimed nowhere near Cecil, Drew was glad to see, since he was right beside him.

"He's just joking," Drew said. "Cecil, put the gun down, please, and quit this nonsense."

"Nobody asked you!" Cecil shouted at him, taking his eyes from the stage, and it was in the split second when Cecil turned to look at Drew that Middlebusher raised and fired his shotgun, blowing away the side of Cecil's neck. The second barrel was discharged into Carl's chest. Both the Ruckers were on the ground before Drew was aware of the sharp pain in his upper arm. Looking down, he saw three small buckshot holes in his sleeve. The blood had not had time yet to soak through the cloth. If the shotgun had had more than two barrels, Drew would also have died, important parts of himself mangled or removed by Middlebusher.

"Throw that piece down, son," the driver advised Drew.

Drew lifted his Colt slowly from its holster. "I had nothing to do with this," he said. "They told me if I didn't come with them and let them use my horses, they'd kill me."

"Expect us to believe that!" screamed the woman inside the coach. "Get him!" she instructed the men in the driver's seat. "Get him before he does it again, like those Ruckers!"

"Calm down there, Mrs. Christy. ..."

"I won't be! I won't! Get that one too, why don't you!"

"Boy," said Middlebusher, carefully reloading his weapon, "you drop that pistol and get off the horse."

"Better do it," the driver said.

The days he spent behind bars at Croker Flats were not uncomfortable, the regimen being considerably more relaxed than that of the Houston jailhouse. Drew's wound was slight, and adequately dressed. He was allowed whatever reading material was available, principally a series of school readers and a battered Bible. He surprised himself by browsing among the passages he had rejected following the attempt on his life by Morgan Kindred. It helped pass time that would otherwise have moved with the speed of dripping molasses.

His jailer was not unfriendly, nor overtalkative. Drew was awaiting the arrival of the circuit judge, who would decide his guilt or innocence on the charges brought against him by the stage line. A number of citizens had paid him visits in his cell, curious to see the well-spoken boy accused of attempted robbery. Most of them went away convinced by his cherubic face, his earnest manner and his story of intimidation by the Rucker brothers, who were known as misfits and troublemakers and plain fools. Drew's prospects for dismissal appeared fair to middling, and he did not despair at finding himself again in the circumstances he had so recently escaped from. Judge Craven, he was told, was not an unreasonable man.

Middlebusher came to call, and smoked his pipe awhile.

"Reckon you'll get away with it?" he asked Drew.

"I'm not looking to get away with anything. I haven't done anything wrong."

"You say."

"That's right—I say."

"Won't work."

"Why not?"

"On account of I say different."

"I'm telling the truth."

"That's another lie just come out of your mouth."

"You sound very sure about that, Mr. Middlebusher."

"Got good reason to." He pulled a sheet of paper from his pants and held it up for Drew to see. "Happened to see a few of these posted up around Fort Stockton. That's where the line ends up, in case you didn't know."

Drew recognized himself in the drawing reproduced under the banner REWARD. It was worth a hundred dollars.

"Got nothing to say?" inquired Middlebusher.

"No."

"Drew Dugan, otherwise known as Drew Gentles. Says here you shot a man's arm off."

"I shot him, then a doctor took the arm off."

"Is that right. Figure you'll stand much of a chance if I show this to Judge Craven? He's a tough old son. Hates to ride the circuit on account of his piles. Bad-tempered feller because of the pain. No time for outlaws at all. Hangs 'em outright, generally."

"Does he hang innocent people?"

"What's that to you? You're guilty as hell."

"You say."

"And I'll say it to old Craven, sure."

"I can't stop you."

"That's right, you can't."

Middlebusher left, and Drew began to worry. With his true identity revealed, he would almost certainly be found guilty, and even if he wasn't, he would be returned to Houston to face charges there. Drew began trying to think of ways in which he might escape, but without a friend like Marion de Quille on the outside, there seemed little hope.

Three more days passed, then Judge Craven arrived in Croker Flats. He disposed of petty disputes first, then ordered Drew brought before him. Drew was fetched from his cell and brought across the street to the hotel that substituted for a courthouse, where he found a considerable audience gathered to witness his trial. Several young ladies among the audience gazed at him with open sympathy. He took his place on the chair of the accused.

Testimony was taken from the stage driver and from Middlebusher, and the woman passenger as well, since she was a local citizen, therefore still available for an appearance in court. Drew wished some of the other passengers were present to offer a potentially less damaging version of events, but they had all passed through to Fort Stockton.

Middlebusher and the woman told the judge it was abundantly clear that Drew was in cahoots with the Rucker boys. The driver was less sure, and ended his testimony with the unverifiable claim that "The boy looks honest to me."

All relevant witnesses having been heard from, the judge allowed Drew to tell his own story, which he did with succinctness and not a little humor, directed mainly at the Ruckers' stupidity. The judge had to call for quiet several times during Drew's testimony. While defending himself, Drew had to avoid distraction in the form of a girl in the front row of chairs, who insisted on waving her fingers at him, despite her mother's frequent slaps on the wrist.

When Drew was done, the judge eased himself back and forth on his chair, adjusting the cushion he sat on, then cleared his throat to address the room.

"I find the defendant not guilty by reason of everyone in this county knows the Ruckers. They're mean and dumb enough to do exactly what the defendant described. This young man is a victim of circumstances, and lucky to be alive, being as Lew Middlebusher is a more than fair hand with a scattergun. Case dismissed."

The girl in the front row swooned. There was general whistling and applause. Drew stood up, dazed with relief. The judge beckoned him over.

"Son, you and I have to talk in private. Go through there."

He indicated a door nearby. Before leaving the room, Drew noticed Middlebusher scowling in the direction of the judge. Drew waited less than a minute before he was joined in what appeared to be the hotel proprietor's unused front parlor. The judge produced the reward poster Middlebusher had given him before the trial began.

"Son," said the judge, "is this you?"

"It is, Your Honor."

"So you aren't John Bones at all?"

"Nossir."

"Well, now, Mr. Dugan, or Gentles, or whoever, that puts a whole different complexion on the case, wouldn't you say?"

"I would."

"This crime you're accused of, dismembering an individual in a gunfight—you did that?"

"Not exactly, Your Honor. A surgeon took the fellow's arm off after my bullet smashed the elbow to where it wouldn't have worked again, and infection would've set in fast, so he took it off."

"Says here he's related to the state's congressman."

"Yessir, but he pulled his weapon first."

The judge studied the poster in his hands, then looked at Drew for a long moment. "I have to tell you I regard politicians as the lowest form of life. This congressman is a liar and a cheat and as crooked as a snake's backbone, I know it for a fact. You shot in self-defense?"

"Yes I did."

"Swear it."

"I swear he pulled his gun first."

"Son, you're a good boy, I believe, but you've strayed from the straight and narrow path. I'm going to let you go, but before I do, I'm going to extract from you a promise. Will you keep the promise I ask you to make, in exchange for freedom?"

"Yessir, I will."

"The minute you get back on your horse, you ride for wherever you were headed, which I presume is anywhere outside of Texas, but as soon as you get clear, you go to the nearest army post or recruiting office and get yourself enlisted. You serve your country for a few years, and this incident can be put behind you. Do you so swear?"

"I so swear."

"God heard you, and I did too. You do it."

Drew saw Middlebusher once more, as he rode out of Croker Flats. Neither spoke.

A urinating dog greeted the stranger at the outskirts of Poloma, Wyoming. The dog inspected its puddle, then turned to the rider and two horses approaching. Its barking attracted the eye of Poloma's mayor, taking his ease on the porch of his brother-in-law's general store. From the cane seat of his favorite chair the mayor could take note of anything that happened, since his view extended about a hundred yards in each direction, which effectively encompassed the entire town. A war veteran, he was used to unusual sights, and counted what he saw ambling along the town's only street as worthy of attention.

The rider looked like Abe Lincoln, so tall his legs were bent, even with the stirrups set at their lowest. His face was hollow, like Abe's, and about as sorrowful. The mayor had seen Abe Lincoln up close at Gettysburg, so he knew. This rider coming along the street slow as Sunday even wore a shabby suit, like something Abe would have woken up in after a three-day drunk, but the illusion was spoiled by the hat; Abe habitually wore a tall stovepipe, and the long man coming nearer all the time had a hat wide as a wagon wheel. The rider was interesting stuff, but the load on his packhorse was even more so. The packhorse carried two dead men across its back.

The mayor decided it was time to exercise his authority, and so lifted himself from the chair, stretched pleasurably and stepped down from the porch, planting himself alongside the rider's projected path. He could see a sawed-off shotgun cradled in the man's arms now, and deep craters or scars in both cheeks; it was these that had created the lean and hungry Abe Lincoln look from afar. This fellow was really nothing like Abe, now that he had arrived.

The mayor raised his hand. "Afternoon to you."

The rider reined in his horse. "Law," he said, or rather croaked. His face was dusty, his throat doubly so.

"Pardon me?" asked the mayor.

"Sheriff, marshal, either one. Deputy'll do."

"Well, now, we're a little on the small side, so we don't have any of them. Got a mayor, though. That's me."

"I've got two men here, wanted on federal charges made out in Denver. Bank theft, murder, also rape, one of them."

"Mister, you're in the wrong place. Denver's about two hundred miles due south."

"I know where I am. I can't take them anywhere near the Colorado line, let alone Denver. They're two days dead already, and ripening nicely. You have a boneyard hereabouts I can plant them in?"

"Got one, but it'll cost you three dollars apiece."

"That can come out of the reward money, two hundred for each man."

"I'd do that, I sure would, but I don't see the actual money in front of me."

Clay suppressed a sigh. His teeth hurt him, every single one of them, it felt like, and he was not in the mood for bargaining and explanations, but the smell of his quarry made such things necessary.

"Here's how it'll be, Mr. Mayor. You see to it that these flyblown sons of bitches get buried at county expense in your pleasant little town here, but first you verify they're who I say they are, which won't be any kind of a difficulty seeing as I've got official descriptions, right down to the scars and tattoos. You write a letter stating they're the ones, all right, and you sign it and put the mayoral seal or some such on it, and I go to the federal marshal's office in Cheyenne and collect my cash money for apprehending and disposing of these aforementioned dead fellows. When it's in my hand, sir, I'll mail the burial fee, plus twenty dollars for you personally, as my way of appreciating your trouble in this matter."

"What you're saying is, you want me to trust you."

Clay nodded.

"Well, I might," said the mayor. "Let's see the descriptions."

Clay dismounted, pulled some much-folded reward fliers from his saddlebags and handed them over. The mayor gave them a cursory reading, and attempted to match the drawings on paper with the upside-down faces of the men tied to the packhorse. They were swollen and blue, their eye sockets infested with flies, tongues protruding from blackened lips. They smelled so bad the mayor cut short his inspection and stepped back.

"Peel back the big one's sleeve," Clay told him. "There's a tattoo in bad taste on his arm, same as in the description."

The mayor decided to accept this bounty hunter's word. If he didn't, the man would simply dump his kill somewhere out in the wilderness, and the mayor would get nothing. If he allowed a double burial and corroborated the hunter's claims to the identities of the dead men, there was a chance for reimbursement, if he was dealing with an honest man.

"All right, sir, you'll get your burial."

"I thank you. Any place in this town I might find a drink of water?"

"Step right inside here. Water and a little something else to cut the dust, on the house. You can tell me how it was you came upon these outlaws and got the drop on them."

Clay took his water, and watered whiskey besides, but the mayor couldn't get him to elaborate on his success beyond a terse "Tracked them, warned them to give up, had to kill them when they wouldn't."

Put out by this churlish display, the mayor rounded up two volunteers for the gravedigging and, when they were done, suggested to Clay that he hand each of them three dollars.

"Burial fee?" asked Clay. "I'll be sending that to you, like we arranged."

"Diggers' fee," corrected the mayor.

"I guess I can't just add it to the bill?"

"Nossir. These boys have already gone and done half their work under the noonday sun and need their payment now, in hard cash. That's right, ain't it, boys?"

"Worked for it," said the first man.

"Worked damn hard," said the second.

Clay decided he didn't like the mayor after all, but if he didn't do as requested, the letter of certification he needed would likely not be forthcoming. He dug in his pockets and produced a five-dollar bill.

"Gentlemen, my worldly wealth, and I don't lie. Take it, and be happy in the taking. The other dollar will have to wait until your leading citizen here collects from his Uncle Sam."

"Sounds like a righteous deal to me, boys," said the mayor, and the bill was plucked from Clay's fingers.

The dead men were hastily rolled into their graves and covered with dry soil. Clay asked for, and received, a note of certification from the mayor:

To whom it may consern,

Owner of this note, Clay Dugan, did bury in Poloma semetery Wyoming Teritory two dead outlaws, Jerome Deidsheimer & Bob Zweig which are wanted by law and are the same, with obsene tatoo on one and horse on other as per federil flyer for same. I sertify this is a true statemant of actuel fact this day, septembr 21 1880

Douglas Onderdonk
Mayor, Poloma Wyoming T.

On his way out of town in the afternoon, Clay passed by a picket fence overgrown with milkweed. The desiccated brown pods had split to reveal the white seed-bearing spores within. Clay thought he was looking at a flock of headless sparrows with fluffy white chests, until he was close enough to make out the pods.

He had been aware for some time that his eyesight was deterio-
rating, along with his teeth. A world in which a hunter of men could
mistake milkweed for decapitated birds was a dangerous one; he
would have to eat his pride and get himself a pair of eyeglasses, like
some spinster schoolmarm. His body's betrayal of its youth made
Clay angry, and anger made his teeth hurt even more.

The mayor watched him leave. Poloma's first visit from a bounty
man had left two more bodies in the graveyard, and a lingering
smell of death in the air.

22

The El Dorado Engineers were Leo Brannan, who had hired Zoe; his cousin Lewis, and John Chadbourne and Sell Yost. All four were from California, and all were educated men with considerable experience in mining, although to Zoe's eye they looked too smooth, too clean to be miners. Leo told her, as they trekked uphill to Glory Hole, leading their pack mules laden with equipment and supplies, "The day of the grizzled forty-niner with his lowly pan is gone, Mrs. Dugan. The esteemed Gumpe, who has sent us scurrying to his discovery, is likely to be the last of the breed. Science, not the blessings of Lady Luck, is the way of the future. My colleagues and I will use our combined learning to make our fortune."

"You seem very confident, Mr. Brannan."

"And I am what I seem. You've heard of the Little Dollar mine?"

"I'm afraid not."

"The third-most-successful operation in California. We have all worked there in one capacity or another. Now we have the opportunity to find our own Little Dollar."

Zoe admired the zeal of the El Dorado Engineers, but could not bring herself to trust their leader. Leo's mismatched eyes were a source of confusion and doubt. Zoe had taken Omie aside and asked her if this man with the eye of blue and eye of brown was the man in her vision of the loss of Zoe's money on their first evening in Leadville, the thief Omie had indicated was somewhere inside Gods of the Dance, but now Omie had no clear memory of what it was she had seen, let alone said. "I think he's very handsome," was her only confirmable opinion. Zoe was left with her suspicions. Leo seemed an unlikely robber, equally unlikely as a habitué of such low places as dance halls. His implausibility in these roles made Omie's assertions at the time of the theft appear less credible, but Zoe could not forget the precision with which she had delineated the gravestones yet-to-be in Pueblo.

All in all, Zoe's feelings toward her employer were confused. The man's companions comported themselves as earnest, no-nonsense types who, if far too shy in their dealings with Zoe and her daughter (a typical day's conversation consisted of a morning greeting and a "Thank you, ma'am" for each meal Zoe dished up), were certainly courteous and uncomplaining. If an individual could be judged by the company he kept, it seemed likely that Leo Brannan was honest and true blue. Still, she wondered.

Many hopeful souls had preceded them up the arduous mountain trail, and many more followed behind. Glory Hole was the nation's newest mining Mecca, word of its riches already inflated beyond the realm of the possible, already causing upheaval among the restless of the planet. Anything was possible if a body could just get to the fabulous camp in the clouds and plunge fingers into the gold-laden soil, kick over those few worthless rocks hiding the wealth mere inches beneath, and scoop an instant fortune into one's shabby pockets. Glory Hole's allure lay in the color of its bounty; whereas Leadville was mined for its namesake and for silver, Glory Hole was a repository of the earth's most favored metal, and so shone more brightly in the minds of men.

The journey required four days. As the crow flies, the party traveled fewer than twenty-five miles, but those miles were elongated by the Rocky Mountains to a number approaching fifty, most of them a series of thigh-torturing ascents that seemed endless. The groves of aspen at that altitude already were turning to their own kind of gold, and the nights were chilly enough to set teeth chattering well before dawn.

At midmorning on the fifth day, the party was able to overlook the high valley enfolding along its single stream the antlike activity of Glory Hole. All timber adjacent to the water was gone, stripped away to build cabins and to reinforce the shafts boring down through rock and soil in search of a golden seam. The much-used trail leading down to the camp was of the same reddish mud that scarred both sides of the creek and polluted its waters. Even at a distance, the enterprise below appeared excessive, so many men crammed together along so short a stretch of land, jostling for nearness to the site of Gumpe's original strike. Each hundred-foot-long claim had already been divided into subclaims and leased for a percentage of the profits to come, in order to finance the firstcomers' own continuing efforts to duplicate Gumpe's phenomenal success.

The Engineers set up camp at some distance from the stream, their object being to locate a likely claim by way of their professional expertise well in advance of the general run of miner, whose method consisted for the most part in working as close to a confirmed strike as possible, on the assumption that where gold had already been found, there was sure to be more gold nearby.

Leo instructed Zoe and Omie not to mention anything of the Engineers' occupational history, for fear of alerting their competition for whatever gold remained to be found in the vicinity. "One wrong word and none of us will be able to take two steps without being shadowed," he warned.

"I understand."

"You'll certainly be questioned. I haven't seen another female in the entire camp. My partners have agreed to spread the mistruth that we are all former shipping clerks from San Francisco, come to try our luck like all the rest. I hesitate to ask that you propagate this lie, but it may be crucial to our success."

"I have no qualms, Mr. Brannan."

"I have to tell you, it's also been decided that you are my sister. I feel it's necessary to keep tongues from wagging."

"Thank you for informing me."

"I believe we should begin addressing each other on first-name terms, to maintain the fiction of our relationship. One never knows who is listening."

"Very well, Leo."

"Can I too?" asked Omie, when she learned of the arrangement.

"Certainly you may," said Leo, "in that you're my niece, so to say."

"Why are your eyes that way, Leo?"

"Because my mother and father couldn't decide which color they should be, so in the end I was given one of each."

"Oh."

Leo picked up his equipment; his three partners were waiting. "We'll return before sundown," he said. "Please have a substantial meal prepared."

"I will, Leo," said Zoe. She could tell he was unsettled by her immediate and casual adoption of his name.

"Until then," Leo said.

The men left, and Zoe began arranging their supplies inside the two small tents that had been erected in a clearing among the pines. "Which one will be ours?" Omie asked.

"I don't know; perhaps neither."

"I want a tent. It's too cold at night."

"The decision belongs to Leo and the others. You and I are hired help, nothing more. We must do as we're told, like it or not."

"Well, I don't, not if we don't have a tent. I'll tell Leo we want one, then he'll give us one."

"And why should he do that, just because you want it so?"

"He talks to me all the time. Well, sometimes."

"I haven't noticed the two of you conversing."

"He's the one that talks. I just listen. He doesn't really talk to me, it's more like he's talking to himself."

"Leo doesn't strike me as being that kind."

"Not talking out loud. Talking inside his head. Thinking."

"You know what he's thinking?"

"Sometimes. Once he thought it was sad about my blue mark, but he thinks I'm pretty anyway. He thinks about you too."

"Me?"

"He thinks you're very brave for never looking down, even if Papa is dead. You fibbed to him about that, Mama. He likes the way you hold your head up so high. He thinks you're pretty too."

Zoe considered this, then asked, "Can you see the things in my thoughts?"

"Only sometimes. When we were on the train you were hating Papa for what he did that made us go away like that."

"Is that the only thing you've seen inside my thoughts?"

"There was a man with blood coming out of his neck, but I only saw him for just a little bit. Who was he, Mama?"

"A bad man. You don't need to know more. What else does Leo think about us?"

"Nothing else. He thinks about his cousin a lot. Lewis is not very well. Leo didn't want him to come, but he wanted to, so Leo let him."

Zoe had noticed that Lewis often became red-faced and short of breath on the trail to Glory Hole. "Will he be all right?" she asked.

"Oh, no, he's going to die very soon. It's a shame, Mama. Leo is very fond of him."

"You must say nothing of this to anyone."

"I know."

The Engineers returned at dusk, talking excitedly among themselves. Their conversation halted as soon as they were enclosed by the firelight. Zoe was irritated by their clumsy secretiveness. "Well, gentlemen," she said, in a manner so pointed it could not be ignored, "were you successful?"

"We believe so," said Lewis, after hasty glances at his partners. "There's a spot not far from here no one has thought to claim, despite its attractions."

"We'll do so tomorrow," added Leo.

"So kindly be quiet about it till it's all signed and legal," said Chadbourne.

"Who would I tell?" asked Zoe. "The chipmunks?"

"Just in case someone comes snooping around, that's all."

"As you wish," Zoe told him, looking Chadbourne so fiercely in the eye he was obliged to look away from her.

Sell Yost said, "We all know what to do, even Omie."

"I'm just making sure, that's all," Chadbourne insisted. "Something as important as this can be said twice, can't it?"

"Enough, John," said Leo. "Mrs. Dugan ... Zoe ... knows full well what we're about. Her discretion may be relied upon."

"So you say, but I can spell it out again for the lady and the girl, no harm done."

"Mr. Chadbourne," said Zoe, "I am not a fool. I wish you every advantage, even if it means avoiding the truth."

"Good," he said. "Now we want to eat."

Zoe waited for one of the men to comment on this particular rudeness of Chadbourne's, but no one did. She realized then that she had come to expect a modicum of chivalry from Leo; she should have known better than to expect anything resembling consistent behavior from any man. She was a paid servant among these prospectors, and her only friend was Omie. It was disappointing to have to remind herself of this, but then, Zoe was more or less accustomed to disappointment as the prime ingredient to the living of her life. What was, was. She could do little to change anything to suit her own sense of justice. The men had all turned from her and gone about their business, real or pretended, to avoid the look on her face. Only Omie was looking directly at her mother. Zoe smiled at her.

When the meal was done with, and Zoe cleaning the dishes at the stream some hundred yards from the tents, she was approached by Leo. His embarrassment was obvious despite the darkness.

"John expresses himself bluntly. I apologize."

"None is necessary, and if it were, Mr. Chadbourne could surely deliver it himself."

"We've come a considerable distance, Mrs. Dugan, to chance everything we have. Every dollar we own has been invested in this enterprise. You can see why good manners are sometimes left by the wayside under circumstances such as these."

"No, I cannot see. I have also invested all of myself in this venture, and am capable anyway of civility, even to such a one as Mr. Chadbourne. I expect there will be other incidents similar to this, unless you become millionaires overnight."

He laughed. "Little chance of that. In any case, I ask for your indulgence."

"You have it. Will you help carry dishes for me?"

"If so instructed." He began picking up the tin plates. "One of the tents is at the disposal of yourself and Omie."

"Thank you. Who will have the other?"

"John and Lewis. Sell and I are hardened outdoorsmen."

"Good. Your cousin requires comfort."

"Canvas over his head is scarcely that."

"You must take care of him. I believe he is not at all well."

They began walking back to the camp. Leo said, "Lewis becomes short of breath at this altitude, nothing more."

"But you are aware that he has difficulties."

"I am, and I don't make light of it. Lewis is my cousin, and I care a great deal for him."

Sell Yost appeared before them. "The little girl," he said, "she's behaving ... strange."

Zoe hurried ahead. As she reached the firelight she could see Omie at its furthest edge, staring fixedly into the pine-scented darkness. Zoe went directly to her side.

"Omie? Omie!"

Omie opened and closed her mouth several times.

"What is it?"

"A deer," said Omie, "only bigger ..."

"Bigger?"

"Than a deer ..."

Leo and Yost had caught up with her. "What does she say?"

"A deer," said Zoe. "She saw a deer, that's all."

"Plenty of them around," said Yost. "They're almost tame."

"Digger ..." intoned Omie.

"She may mean an elk," suggested Leo. "We saw one ourselves this afternoon, further up the mountainside."

"Shiny beautiful ..." murmured Omie.

Zoe knew the men were looking at her, waiting for an explanation. Chadbourne and Lewis had approached them.

"She sometimes gets very excited by things," offered Zoe, "... anything unusual."

"An elk," Leo pronounced. "If it was bigger than a deer, it was an elk."

"They don't shine, though," suggested Sell Yost.

"Perhaps the firelight made it seem so," said Zoe.

"It was golden ..." Omie said, her words barely audible.

"Well, then," said Yost, "it must have been an omen of good fortune. Golden elk, you don't see them every day."

The men were laughing among themselves. Chadbourne said, "Ask her to guess its troy weight," and the laughter increased.

Zoe shook Omie gently by the shoulder. "Omie?"

"Yes, Mama?"

"Do you still see it?" asked Zoe.

Omie turned to face her. "See what?"

"The golden elk."

"What's one of those?"

"Like a deer," said Leo, "but bigger."

"Where?" asked Omie, turning to the darkness in sudden excitement. Zoe saw the men exchanging glances.

"It's nothing," she said. "It's gone, and you and I must go to bed."

"Where dreams are supposed to happen"—Lewis laughed—"but not before you get there."

Zoe saw he was trying to ease the awkwardness Omie's unusual behavior had caused. She guided Omie to the tent Leo indicated was theirs. For some minutes afterward, she heard through the canvas a whispered conversation concerning Omie, in which the word "touched" was given prominence. If only you knew, she thought wryly, and prepared herself for sleep beside her daughter.

The El Dorado Engineers filed claim and began to dig, erecting a sizable A-frame above their shaft, building a mule-driven whim and sheave wheel to haul the buckets to the surface as they drove deeper into the earth. Zoe seldom visited the site, since the men returned to camp for their midday meal, begrimed but optimistic, their enthusiasm for the task infectious. "Any sign?" Zoe would ask, and be told, "Not yet, but we can almost smell it," or, "Any minute now, just you wait."

Two things concerned Zoe more than the likelihood of the Engineers striking gold; the first was the weather, daily becoming colder, and the second was Omie, who began spending longer and longer periods of time away from the immediate vicinity of the tents, where Zoe could see her. On those occasions when Omie returned, Zoe would ask her, "Where have you been? Didn't you hear me calling?" To which Omie would reply with a disingenuous "No, Mama."

"You need to dress more warmly, with a shawl."

"I'm warm enough, Mama."

"I saw your footprints in the frost first thing this morning. Don't you dare wander barefoot on ground so cold. You put your shoes on first thing when you get up. You put them on before you go outside, do you hear me?"

"Yes, Mama. Mama?"

"Well?"

"He hides, but not so I can't see him."

"Who does?"

"The gold elk. He's a stag, Mama, because of the big horns. That's the man elk, isn't it?"

"Antlers, not horns. Yes, that's a male, but Omie, there are no such things as golden elk. Elk are darker in coloring than deer, and even deer are nothing like golden to look at, beautiful though they are."

"But he is, Mama, he's shiny and golden, especially when the sun shines on him. He owns a special place."

"What place?"

"It's his, all for himself. He stands there and turns into a statue so lovely to look at, Mama."

"Does he have one blue eye and one brown eye?"

Omie considered the question. "No," she responded, "His eyes are both yellow, like the rest of him, goldy yellow. I can show you the place. He stands so still and proud-looking, I'm sure he'd let you sneak up and see him there."

"Very well, show me where."

Omie led her far from the camp, far from the stream and its persistent din of humanity, up the valley wall. Soon Zoe was panting from the climb's exertions, despite the chill morning air. "How much further?"

"It's near. He's there now, I think!"

Zoe struggled higher, following Omie's darting skirts up and up, deeper among the pines swaying and whispering in a wind from the north, which bore the promise of snow.

"Almost there, Mama!"

Breathing hoarsely, her face glistening with sweat, Zoe caught up with Omie halfway to what appeared from that angle to be the summit of the world. Omie stood at the bottom end of a small mountain meadow invisible from below, an area perhaps twenty yards across, a ragged oval hemmed in by a dark wall of trees thrashing their needles in a continuous sigh. Three deer occupied its center, each with its head to the ground, unaware they were observed. They seemed to be eating, but there was no grass at the spot where they stood. Omie was casting her eyes about for the golden stag, distress clouding her face.

"He's not here. ..."

The deer lifted their heads as one, and bounded instantly away to the perimeter of the meadow, then stopped out of curiosity to watch as Zoe and Omie advanced to the place they had vacated. Zoe examined the patch of open ground, with its many imprints of deer hooves, and the larger impressions of what she presumed must be elk. Creatures clearly were attracted to the location, despite its apparent lack of sustenance, and when Zoe knelt and raised a pinch of the earth to her tongue, she understood why.

"It's a deer lick," she announced.

"A what, Mama?"

"The deer come and lick the ground to get natural salts in the soil. You can taste it."

"No, it's dirt!"

"It's clean dirt. You can taste the salt. That's what a deer lick is.

Animals like salt, just the same as we do, so they gather in places where the soil holds it, and lick it up. I dare you to taste it. It isn't awful, I promise."

Omie scooped up a modest handful of earth and cautiously lowered the tip of her tongue into its moistness.

"Thhhhhpppthhh ...! It's horrible, Mama! You fibbed!"

"And didn't you? Where's your wonderful gold elk, might I ask?"

"He wouldn't come on account of you—that's why he isn't here!"

"Are you sure he isn't just a lovely thing to think of on a lonely day with nothing to do?"

"No! I *saw* him! I did!"

"Please don't shout. I believe you."

"He lives here. He stands looking that way."

Omie gestured to the empty sky above the valley containing Glory Hole. The broad trough of dark green was bisected along its length by a winding line of silver. From the deer lick's height the diggings were barely in evidence. The gash of mud and men and their auxiliaries was being gouged ever deeper, dwellings spreading up the slopes on either side. Here one could forget the ugliness and confusion below. Zoe supposed she would like to have gold, just as the men clawing for it did, for the avenues of choice and decision it would open for herself and Omie, but as she gazed across the valley to its far rim, the need for such stuff as gold seemed remote. Zoe felt stirrings of pity for Leo and his associates and their dream of riches, then caught herself in her superiority. Easy enough for the servant to despise the master, she thought, and gave her mouth a twist wry enough to suit her mood.

For five weeks the Engineers worked their claim, sinking a deep shaft without finding what they sought. Since they operated at such a distance from the other miners, there was curiosity in the camp over their choice of location. Questioned, they would laughingly insist they had thrown dice to determine where they should dig. The questioners, dissatisfied with that answer, would approach Zoe, who acquitted herself of the prearranged lie with considerable talent. "I suppose they're hopeless," she would say, "trying to accomplish anything that way, but it isn't any of my business how my brother and his friends choose to waste their time and money."

The alleged dice-throwers came up empty-handed, day after day, and jokes about them were passed around the camp. A spirit of despondency settled over the Engineers, in keeping with the grayer skies more frequently blanketing Glory Hole with darkness and rain. Each morning found the earth covered in frost, and everyone began to complain of the extreme cold at night, which prevented adequate sleep. It was decided that Sell Yost and Lewis would quit work on the shaft for as long as it took to build a cabin big enough to shelter them all, and a rude stable for the mules. This plan was pursued, but the cabin rose too slowly, and progress on the shaft was even less productive, so it was decided that all hands would work on the dwelling, snow having fallen that day. When it was completed five days later, a full complement of workers was able to resume digging.

In mid-October a blizzard struck Glory Hole, making outdoor work impossible. The men stayed huddled in the cabin for three days, debating the wisdom of sinking a second shaft in pursuit of a gold vein the first had not encountered. Tempers became short when Leo and Sell favored a new beginning, and John Chadbourne insisted the existing shaft should be given another chance. Lewis was unable to make up his mind; his health had become enfeebled by the coming of winter and the strenuous nature of the digging. Zoe was in no doubt they had all expected to strike at least a trace of gold much sooner, and she wondered if their much-vaunted learning in the geological and metallurgical sciences was truly advantageous to the enterprise, or if throwing dice would have been just as effective in producing nothing at all.

When quarrels erupted between the men, Zoe retired behind the blanket curtain that screened off a section of the cabin's interior for the exclusive use of herself and Omie. There was no avoiding the sounds of dissent, but being on the curtain's far side was defense enough against the ugliness of their bickering. Omie often joined her there, or else was already shielding herself from the men when her mother lifted the curtain aside and eased herself into their shared seaman's hammock. Leo had accepted five of these in exchange for two mules from a merchant newly arrived in Glory Hole, rather than waste more time constructing bedframes of pine and obliging Zoe to create mattresses. The trading of the mules for the hammocks, which were extremely comfortable once the trick of entering and exiting their capricious folds was mastered, enraged Chadbourne to the point where he threatened to knock Leo down.

"Why not get rid of her instead?" he said, pointing to Zoe. "She doesn't do enough to warrant the money you pay her, and the other one does nothing but eat and stand around looking at nothing! Aren't we capable of making the kind of grub that gets dished up? Where's the need for her?"

"Zoe and Omie remain," Leo stated, "and if you need to fight with me, man to man, I'll oblige." Chadbourne had backed down from actual fisticuffs, and later apologized to Zoe, but the harm had been done; the El Doradans were thereafter a sorry crew, kept from the physical labor that might have drained some of their frustration, jammed together in a space that would have been uncomfortable for half their number.

Omie began spending more time enclosed in her canvas cocoon in the corner than she did in the cabin at large. It was sometimes possible to forget she was there at all, and it was this invisibility by choice that fooled Zoe, one bleak afternoon, into believing her daughter was inside the cabin when she was in fact elsewhere. When Zoe went to the hammock herself to escape the usual wranglings of the men, she found it untenanted, and tried to think where Omie might be. Had she gone to the privy dug a short distance from the cabin? When time passed and Omie did not return, Zoe visited the unsavory pit herself to ensure that no mishap had occurred, but Omie was not there either.

Alarmed, Zoe hurried back and requested that the Engineers begin an immediate search for her. They seized upon this as reason enough to go alone into the afternoon for relief from one another's company. The blizzard had passed, leaving everything under a deep layer of snow. Not one of the Engineers was equipped with snowshoes as they scoured Glory Hole, tramping through a ramshackle collection of shanties and cabins scattered among the claims, their frigid breath hanging in the air as they asked at each doorway if the occupants had seen the little girl from the upstream claim, the one with the blue mark on her cheek. No one had. Reporting back to Zoe, they shamefacedly admitted their failure, and Zoe felt herself beginning to panic. That was when the only answer to the mystery, albeit the least likely to be understood, came to her.

"Up there," she said, turning to face the darkly wooded slope above them. "She went up there, I know it."

"For what purpose?" asked Lewis.

"She has a favorite place. Help me find it, please."

"Why would she go there in weather like this?" Leo asked as they prepared to leave.

"When she wants to, she goes," snapped Zoe.

Lewis was obliged to abandon his place in the search party before long, breath whistling noisily through his lungs. The others pressed on, led by Zoe, who cast about for the telltale footprints that would confirm her hopes. She found them a third of the way up the slope, a meandering trough dragged through the deep snow by Omie, without a doubt. It angled up the valley wall in the general direction Zoe recalled.

The trees were heavily weighted with whiteness, and new snowfall began sifting from the sky as they climbed, a powder so light it appeared to hang in the air like mist before coating the eyelashes or beards of the searchers with tiny spicules of ice. Halfway to the sloping meadow, the air suddenly was filled with denser flakes, chunks that dropped with deceptive slowness onto a snowpack at least a foot higher than at the lower elevation. Zoe, throat rasping, sides awash with sweat despite the cold, forced herself to an even faster pace. Leo was fifty feet behind her, Chadbourne and Sell Yost even further back, lost to sight among the trees and swirling snow. Now Zoe's breath was bursting from her in harsh sobbings. If Omie should die, there would be nothing left to live for, no part of herself in all the world she could be close to.

The meadow, when reached at last, was occupied only by a small herd of deer, noses down to the salty earth exposed by their hooves. Their heads were raised as one when Zoe blundered from the trees, and they turned tail to bound from her unwanted presence with the silent grace of birds in flight. There was no sign of Omie.

"No ...," said Zoe. "No ..."

She sank to her knees, staring at the scuffed area of the deer lick at the center of the clearing. She could not think what she might do next, what other place to rush toward in expectation of finding her daughter. She was utterly spent, numb with exhaustion, but the panic within her spun on like some uncontrollable gyroscope.

Leo caught up with Zoe and stood over her, breath whistling past his lips. Zoe waited to see if he might suggest what they could possibly do now, and was unprepared for the words he spoke. "There she is. ..."

Zoe lifted her head. Omie stood at the meadow's upper edge, a few feet back among the trees, as if wishing to remain unseen. "Omie!" Zoe called, her voice an unlovely screech. She got to her feet, ignoring Leo's offer of assistance, and ran across the clearing to the small figure partially hidden by snow-laden boughs of fir.

Dropping again beside her, Zoe threw both arms around Omie and hugged her close. "He melted away," Omie said, as if this was explanation enough for her being there.

"Don't you ever go away by yourself again! Don't you ever, do you hear me!"

"I had to see him be melted."

"On a day like this you could have died from the cold. How could you be so foolish!"

"I had to. ..." Omie sniffed, the corners of her mouth turning down in the usual preamble to tears.

"Had to come here for what? What melted?"

"The elk," offered Omie, "you know, that I told you about that time."

"That's no excuse for doing anything so foolish. Everyone has been out looking for you and getting bone cold in the looking, I might add."

Omie guiltily lowered her eyes as Leo approached. "Safe and sound, young lady?" he asked. Omie nodded briefly, avoiding his face. Chadbourne and Yost had finally reached the lower end of the meadow. Zoe could hear their voices, sounding very far off despite their nearness; she supposed it was the thickly falling snow that made them sound that way. An educated man like Leo could probably explain it to her. She wondered why her thoughts were becoming vague, disoriented, and realized she was about to faint. Zoe resisted the impulse with all her will, knowing she would be ashamed to succumb to any kind of weakness in front of the men. They must never be allowed to believe she was, as they would have expressed it, only a woman. She took several deep breaths, then stood, blood pounding in her head.

"Home," she said, for want of anything better.

Omie began meekly to retrace her path down the slope toward the other men, who had paused there, seeing that the child was already found. "All's well that ends well," observed Leo.

"No, it is not," countered Zoe. "All is not well. We have very few supplies left, and Lewis grows sicker by the day, or haven't you noticed?"

"I have, and Lewis has agreed that if we make no significant progress by Christmas, he'll return to California until he has recovered."

"That will be too late."

"Do you have medical learning, Zoe?"

"You know I don't, but anyone can see how Lewis fails a little more each day. There isn't enough air in these mountains to fill his poor lungs."

"If his condition persists, I'll insist he leaves for a lower elevation at the end of the month. Does that satisfy you?"

"My satisfaction is not at stake. Your cousin must go immediately."

"Surely that is his decision to make."

"Please, Leo, tell him today. Make him leave before he dies here."

The night before, snuggled against her mother in their hammock, Omie had whispered of the Christmas to come, and described in detail how the El Dorado Engineers would sit around the fireplace with gloom on their faces. Zoe and Omie would be there also, but Lewis would not. Asked if Lewis was merely gone from the cabin, Omie whispered back, "Gone from the world, Mama, and he's a nice man. It should be Mr. Chadbourne that dies."

"Hush. No one here deserves to die. Say nothing of Christmas to anyone."

Zoe asked herself now if Leo was capable of accepting what it was that lived in Omie, the omniscient presence without identity or personality that used her eyes, her voice, in ways beyond comprehension. If Omie saw, by whatever means, that Lewis would be dead by Christmas, then it would be so, unless Leo could be persuaded before then to insist that his cousin depart for the warmth of California.

Omie was joined by Sell Yost and Chadbourne as she passed them by, and all three entered the trees together. Zoe hung back, obliging Leo to do the same. "I have something to tell you," she said.

When she was done, Zoe waited for the mild scorn she expected from him, but Leo was genuinely intrigued by her story of things unseen and little understood.

"I've always felt there was something ... different about Omie, and now I see why, but I must ask you not to mention this to the others. I'm a man of science myself, but the spirit world has fascinated me from time to time. My partners, though, follow the material school of thought. Logic, pure and simple, that's the way. Lewis will be faced with a choice he's already aware of—he goes home, or he dies. Leave this to me."

"That was my intention in telling you."

"And I thank you for it."

The sky was already darkening as the cabin was reached. Entering ahead of the rest, Omie saw Lewis resting in his hammock. She had been told that he had turned back soon after joining in the search for her, because of his poor lungs. Approaching him, Omie prepared an apology for the trouble she had caused, knowing this was what Zoe would expect of her. Lewis appeared to be asleep, eyes closed, his lips slightly parted, but no breath came from those lips, and they were an unusual shade of blue. Omie told herself this was because he had allowed the stove to burn low while he slept, but the motionless chest beneath its blanket told her otherwise. She had killed him by running up to the golden elk's secret place without telling anyone first, killed him just as surely as if she had chopped off his head. Omie felt awful. Punishment of some terrible and inescapable nature must follow such naughtiness. She was responsible, and she would have to pay. She fought back tears as the grownups clumped with their heavy boots through the doorway to witness the full extent of her crime.

It required all of Zoe's patience and forbearance that night to convince Omie she had not caused Lewis to die, just as she was not the reason little Patrick had died and her stepfather had run away from them. "You see these things, but that doesn't mean you make them happen," Zoe explained several times over, and eventually was able to steer Omie toward guiltlessness.

Long after the men were asleep, Lewis's body having been taken outside, where the cold would preserve it better than any undertaker's skills prior to burial in the morning, Omie explained for Zoe her expedition up to the deer lick.

"He told me to go where he was, the gold elk, so I did, because ... he told me, and when I got there he was standing like he does, looking at the sky, but then he melted, Mama, like a piece of ice, just melted away into the ground."

"How disappointing for you, after you went all that way."

"Yes, but I could see him still, under the ground, still all shiny bright even if he wasn't an elk anymore, just lumpy and golden way down under my feet, and there was more down there too."

"More elk?"

"All his friends and neighbors and family," said Omie. "He showed me them all."

"That was nice of him; now you try and sleep."

Omie shifted her weight against her mother's breast in a way that brought them both deep comfort in their physical closeness, and began promptly to snore. Listening to her daughter's nasal stutterings, Zoe counted herself among the lucky of the earth. It was difficult to experience any pangs of sadness over the death of Lewis, when her mind was still flooded with the relief of finding Omie alive and safe. She supposed that what she felt was selfish, but she had done her best to pass on Omie's fateful prognosis for the man, and could not apportion blame to anything less abstract than the workings of fate. It had happened sooner than expected, and most likely could not have been averted even if Leo had been allowed time to remove his cousin from harm's way. She consciously absolved herself of any wrongdoing, as she had done for Omie, and felt her body softening, preparing itself for sleep, and when that sleep came, Zoe dreamed of golden herds prancing beneath her, buried by mountains, yet lively and joyous. It was a pleasant fantasy, and, as dreams do, it left her head in the same stealthy manner by which it had arrived.

Lewis Brannan's funeral was held the following day, on a morning so fair it was difficult to recall where the masses of snow, fast reducing the pathways of Glory Hole to mud, had come from. Miners attending the service were torn between two possible means of celebrating the return of sunshine—a thunderous wake for the dead man, utilizing all available supplies of hard liquor; or a return to the work that the blizzard had delayed. Compromise was the route chosen by wiser heads, and whiskey was consumed camp-wide for several hours before the drink ran out and the drinkers turned to their chilly holes in the ground, and proceeded to dig out the snowfall still frozen in their lower reaches.

Several heads were hit by buckets lowered too hastily or without warning, and a number of toes came near to mutilation by pickax as the day wore on and the whiskey wore off, but it was generally agreed that a good funeral and its aftermath was what everyone had needed to get their spirits up after being confined for three days indoors.

At the Engineers' cabin, condolences for their loss were not sufficient to cancel knowledge of a potentially greater loss—their confidence in the location of their claim. Thus far, the earth extracted and washed had produced not the faintest indication of gold-bearing ores. It was useless to remind themselves of their professional expertise, since this had clearly failed them. Dunces galore were finding gold further along the stream, simply because they had filed claim on the nearest hundred-foot stretch of land the law allowed them. There was no system of calculation and deduction to their method, no carefully considered choices made; they simply filed and dug and, more often than not, found what they sought. The death of Lewis was, in a sense, symbolic of his companions' dismal prospects for success. If direct application of scientific knowledge and practical experience did not produce the expected results, then the Engineers' faith in themselves and their techniques had been a pipe dream. It was a humbling moment.

Omie kept to herself in the days that followed, and although Zoe knew her daughter was not burdened by guilt over what had occurred, it disturbed her that Omie seemed content with her own company for so much of the time. Attempting to draw her out, Zoe asked, "Is the golden elk still under the ground?"

"Of course," said Omie, "until someone digs him up and makes him into an elk again."

She turned her back on Zoe and resumed her silent contemplation of a corner of the cabin. Omie would have been puzzled by her mother's next act, consisting of a sudden drop onto one of the crude stools beside the fireplace, and the placing of both hands on her thin cheeks. Zoe held herself in this fashion for a moment, then composed herself to ask, "Are you quite sure he is under the deer lick?"

"Yes."

"I see," said Zoe, and took herself off to the claim, where she called down to Leo, digging in its depths, that she must speak with him. The mule-powered whim raised him to the surface in a trice, and he shivered as the cold air touched his flesh. "Hot as Hades down there," he said, smiling awkwardly. Zoe avoided staring as he covered his torso with a flannel shirt and heavy jacket. Sell Yost stripped and was lowered down into the shaft to work with Chadbourne. Leo began spading earth and gravel into a wheelbarrow for transportation to the rocker cradle at the water's edge.

"What is it you need to talk with me about?"

"Gold."

"My ears are pricked."

"First, do you believe that Omie foretold what would happen to Lewis?"

"She may have. On the other hand, she may not. There's no evidence to prove it, either way."

"Then perhaps I shouldn't go on."

"No, please, tell me what it is you're thinking of."

Zoe hesitated, then said, "Omie has seen gold."

Leo dropped the wheelbarrow handles and turned to her.

"She has? Why didn't you say so before now? Where?"

"She has not seen it with her eyes ..."

His face fell. "Oh," he said, and resumed wheeling the barrow.

"She has seen it with her inner eye, directly under the deer lick."

"What deer lick?"

"The place she went to when we thought her lost. Deer go there to lick salt from the ground."

"What of it? I think little Omie may be a poet in the making, but a prospector? No."

He ran the load up a plank incline and dumped it directly into the cradle's commodious hopper, then brought the barrow down again and opened the sluice from the hand-built water tank a short distance up the slope. Water gushed over the new earth, and Leo began rocking the cradle back and forth, back and forth, as he watched for gleamings among the riffle slats. He concentrated on the job, Zoe saw, in order not to look at her.

"You said, just a short time ago, that you are fascinated by the world of spirits, those things that baffle us."

"I did, and I was truthful, but Zoe, how can you expect me to believe that Omie can detect gold deep underground? Gold is metal, with weight and properties. Gold is real, not the product of dreams. Gold is found by effort and intelligence, and yes, sometimes by plain luck, but never by dreams. There is no gold where Omie led us. The rock strata are not suitable. Please, forget this."

"You won't investigate?"

"I will not. You might approach John and Sell with this nonsense, but they're harder-headed men than myself."

"So you don't believe me."

"I can't. We made ourselves objects of ridicule by digging where no one else would, and finding nothing for our pains. Now you want us to abandon this claim and go mountain climbing? We'd be laughed at."

"And so? Let them laugh. There is gold where Omie says; I'm certain of it."

"But I am not. File your own claim if you believe so much in Omie's visions. I'm sorry, but I can't begin to consider this notion seriously."

"Very well," Zoe said, and turned from him.

On her way back to the cabin, she fought against resenting Leo for his reluctance. It was no fault of his that he could not accept what she told him. But she did truly believe it herself, and not to act according to her belief would have been foolish. She would do as Leo had suggested, although his words had been flippant.

Omie was still staring at nothing. Zoe took her purse, marched to the claim registration office and asked how she might stake out a particular section of the mountainside above town.

"You mean next to where those fellers you're with have got theirs?" asked the registrar.

"No, somewhere else. Up high."

"High?"

"I would say halfway up the side of the valley, on the eastern slope."

"Way up there? What for, ma'am, if you don't mind my asking?"

"For mining, what else?"

"Mining."

"Yes."

"Ma'am, that area hasn't even been surveyed. I'd have to send someone up there special, just to get the claim recorded right."

"And could that be arranged for today? I want to start mining as soon as possible."

"Ma'am, are you absolutely sure about this?"

"Absolutely."

"Ten dollars," said the registrar, "and ma'am, I'm going to have to charge you an extra ten for the inconvenience."

"Of course."

Zoe laid her money down.

She announced her claim at dinner that night, and was met with expressions of amazement. Leo said nothing as Yost and Chadbourne asked for an explanation.

"I simply feel there is gold to be had up there," said Zoe, her manner perfectly self-contained.

"Just ... out of the blue?" Yost inquired, smiling as one would when questioning a simpleton.

"So to speak."

"Woman, you're cracked," was Chadbourne's response.

"Perhaps. May I borrow a pick and shovel from you, gentlemen? I'm afraid I spent almost all I have on registering my claim."

"Certainly," said Leo, overriding Chadbourne's protest.

He watched Omie for her reaction, but the girl simply looked from one adult face to the next as they spoke, as if the conversation were held in some exotic language beyond her comprehension. Leo wondered for the first time if mother and daughter were afflicted with some kind of mental disease that made such ridiculous goings-on appear sensible. It was a depressing thought. He was very fond of them both, but further involvement with such types would be impossible if his suspicions proved to have foundation. An uncle of Leo's had once married a woman who at the time appeared quite sane, but within two years had developed the habit of speaking with invisible entities and sleeping on the floor like a dog. Séances and table rappings were interesting phenomena, but illnesses of the brain were something else entirely. He felt very sad for the Dugans, and a little sad for himself.

"If you're thinking of going into business on your own," said Chadbourne, "you've drawn your last wage from our pockets."

"I can do for you as I've done, and still find time to work my claim, Mr. Chadbourne."

"Oh, really? That means you must have been doing considerable amounts of nothing until now. Maybe we should be reimbursed for your wasted time."

"That will do, John," warned Leo.

"I've said all along that a woman to cook and clean is a needless expense, and here's the proof of it, from the lips of the *lady*."

"I said that's enough!"

"I meant," said Zoe, her voice rigid with distaste, "that with a great deal of *extra effort* I will be able to spare an hour or so each day on my claim."

Chadbourne snorted, his expression sour. "I guess you don't know the other reason friend Leo hired you," he said.

"No, I do not."

Leo interrupted. "To have a civilizing influence on us all," he said, glaring at Chadbourne. "Men alone are apt to degenerate without the presence of a decent female."

"Such low beasts we are." Chadbourne smiled.

"Well," said Zoe, "I hope I may have aided you, or at least some of you." She stared pointedly at Chadbourne, who sneered in return and looked away. Zoe could willingly have shot him at that moment, if she had had a gun to hand.

Sell Yost proposed that the new arrangement, incorporating Zoe's efforts on the slope above, should go into effect the following day, to ascertain its worth. "If it turns out to be impossible, which I believe it will, given the time spent getting all the way up there and back, then we can reconsider our options, one and all."

"Mr. Yost's plan is fair," said Zoe, and all talk thereafter, until the lamp was turned out, was of the most banal and inoffensive variety.

Zoe found out soon enough how correct Sell Yost was. It required three quarters of an hour to reach the deer lick, and a half hour to return. While there, she dug for a solid hour, but managed to accomplish little. Deer watched her from the trees as she attacked their salt lick with inexpert swingings of the pick. Her laborious spadings of loosened, partially frozen earth were accompanied by clouds of exhaled breath that disappeared immediately into the crystalline air. She exhausted herself several times, and had to sit on her meager pile of displaced soil to regain her normal heartbeat. She must ask Omie how deep the golden elk lay. With luck, it would be just beneath her boots.

For more than a week Zoe struggled to maintain work on her claim. Omie was unable to say how far below the surface her golden elk lived. Leo offered Zoe the use of one of their two remaining mules, but Zoe refused. She changed her mind the very next day, when new snowfall made struggling up the slope with her tools even more difficult than usual, but learned, on arrival back at the cabin, that Chadbourne had sold one animal that afternoon to pay for supplies; the remaining mule would, of course, be kept hard at work raising the still-barren earth from the Engineers' claim.

Zoe knew the timing of the sale was not coincidental. It made her angry at first, then more determined than ever to prove them all wrong, especially Leo, whose initial rejection of her plan had hurt the most. His attitude toward herself and Omie had changed since then, becoming more distant, apart from the offer of the mule. She could not tell if he wished her to fail so that he and the others should be proven right, or if he hoped somehow to have his former opinion of Zoe restored, by an admission on her part that the mountainside mining scheme had been pure foolishness. She felt herself being judged, and did not like it. The El Dorado Engineers had been cockily proud of having chosen to stake their own claim where no other cared to join them, but in doing the selfsame thing, Zoe had earned their scorn. She supposed this was because they were men of education, while she was neither male nor learned. Leo had still not told his colleagues the reason for Zoe's having chosen the spot she had, and she felt some small gratitude to him for that; word of Omie's gift would only complicate matters.

Late in November it became impossible for Zoe to continue; the air was simply too cold. For all her effort, she had barely been able to lower herself into the ground to the depth of her own shoulders. The hole was surrounded by a ring of its own material that froze solid each night, as did the earth to be taken from the bottom. Zoe had to swing her pick against a substance more akin to rock than soil. She would have to wait until the spring thaw before resuming her attempt to unearth the golden elk and its attendant herd. They paraded like carnival creations through her dreams, gleaming like creatures of sunlight, led by the elk that seemed always to bound just beyond her reach, its antlers gaudy as a Christmas tree.

Her reward for abandoning temporarily the highest claim in the valley was to be informed by Leo that the Engineers could no longer afford to pay her for taking care of their food and washing needs. He told her reluctantly, knowing that if he did not, it would be John Chadbourne who broke the news of their new state of impoverishment, and John would have dismissed Zoe with a kind of glee. "You and Omie are welcome to continue sharing the cabin with us, and we'll share what food we have, in return for your usual duties. All back wages will be made up when we make our strike, naturally."

"I accept your offer," said Zoe, mustering what dignity she could. Whichever way she chose to look at it, she and Omie were now charity cases, cared for directly by the Engineers, who could scarcely meet their own requirements.

Unable to work her claim, smitten by guilt over Leo's benevolence, Zoe took herself to the general store in Glory Hole and paid fifteen cents for a square of cardboard and the use of a brush and paint. She then stood on the main thoroughfare, exhibiting in her mittened hands the result: SEEKING HONEST WORK. SEW, WASH, CLEAN. The results were fast in arriving; Zoe was invited to put her talents in these dreary fields to work almost immediately, and the miners in need of her services were generous in their payment.

It became apparent from the start that one area of commerce she had not listed was what the miners required most of all—the sound of a female voice. While she worked at whatever task she had been hired for, Zoe was kept company by her new employer and a hasty gathering of his friends, all eager to watch and listen as she performed her menial assignments. She was offered life stories by the dozen, opinions on every subject under the sun, and was requested to say a little something about herself, including her reasons for staking a claim where she had. All this was for the sole purpose of hearing her speak. Zoe had only to open her mouth and the room she worked in would fall silent. It was as if she had become some great and wise leader of men, whose every utterance was treated with respect. Intimidated at first by this ludicrous status, Zoe quickly found herself enjoying the attention. She took particular delight in telling her audience that the claim she had staked was the result of a dream in which her dead mother appeared and spoke of the location in terms of golden salvation. The more sensitive among the listeners were prepared to accept this as reason enough to do what she had done; the rest decided it was pure bunkum, but were happy to hear it anyway, so long as it came from the throat of a respectable woman.

In less than a week of similar performances around the gold camp, Zoe was able to earn what would otherwise have taken her two months. She washed and ironed, darned and sewed, swept and cleaned; but above all, she chatted. Her only moment of alarm came when a man, considerably drunk despite the earliness of the hour, accused her of being "one of Leadville Taffy's dancin' whores, by God!" The drunk was ejected after a brisk pummeling that left him senseless. Apologies were offered Zoe on behalf of "the feller that had to leave just now, sudden-like." Zoe accepted with a grace that did not sit well alongside the urgent galloping of her heart. If another man should identify her, general suspicion would likely follow, and Zoe's lucrative reign of humble domesticity would be punctured in an instant. It had been the narrowest of escapes, accomplished only because the man had been disgustingly inebriated; a sober accuser would almost certainly produce different results. She jabbed herself painfully with the dull needle her latest employer had smilingly provided for the reattachment of his shirt buttons.

Her proceeds were spent not only on herself and Omie but on the remaining El Dorado Engineers. Zoe's generosity was prompted in

equal parts by her naturally sympathetic character and by a need
to thumb her nose at the men who allowed her to stay on as their
servant in return for food and shelter. Now she was able to support
their needs for a time, and her satisfaction at their embarrassed
acceptance made the financial sacrifice worthwhile. Chadbourne in
particular was affected by the changed circumstances in the cabin;
he would not look at or speak with Zoe unless in answer to a direct
question from her, and even then would give only the briefest of
replies.

Chadbourne began spending time at the drinking shack that
passed for a saloon in Glory Hole. Work on the diggings had become
sporadic, dependent entirely on the weather, and that was generally cruel at so high an altitude. Zoe visited her claim once in late
December, and discovered almost a dozen elk licking at the ring of
frozen earth around the hopelessly shallow hole. They bolted, abandoning the lick so quickly their bodies collided with and rebounded
from each other with solid thuddings, and their blundering passage
through the deeper snowdrifts sent up showers of whiteness. They
were the first elk Zoe had seen, and although their size had been
impressive, she thought them less appealing than the daintily
bounding deer; the former were heavy, substantial creatures of the
earth, the latter almost a part of the air.

Christmas Day found the cabin exactly as Omie had predicted,
the atmosphere so unrelievedly glum Zoe was obliged to leave, just
to escape the tension inside. She took Omie with her, and asked if it
gave her daughter pleasure to know she had foreseen exactly how
the day would transpire. Omie said no, because she had liked Lewis
almost as much as she did Leo.

"And do you still like Leo?" Zoe asked.

"Yes," said Omie, "but he's very sad now, and wishes you were
someone else."

"Someone else? Who?"

"You, but different."

"I see," said Zoe, and they walked on through the forest beyond
Glory Hole, in the crackling cold of the afternoon. Sunlight was all
around them, refracted through the billion prisms of ice hanging
from the trees. The valley walls shone with a whiteness so intense
it glittered and hurt the eyes. Zoe thought it the most beautiful
scene she had ever witnessed, and said so to Omie.

"It's ugly," Omie replied, her tone matter-of-fact.

"How can you say that? See how the sun shines off every tree."

"There aren't any trees, Mama, they've all been cut down. There's a town all over, a dirty town with lots of smoke from big chimneys like they had in Pueblo."

Zoe knew she was referring to the refining smelters.

"And what else do you see?"

"Houses, all up and down the sides, little houses all squeezed together and smoking."

Zoe tried to picture the scene described by Omie. The effort was similar to passing folds of black silk across a brilliant mirror, obscuring its light.

"How sad for our little valley in the clouds."

"Yes, Mama."

On the first of January, Chadbourne declared himself at the end of his rope. "We're wasting our time. We should try somewhere else. All we have is a worthless hole in the ground."

"Our original choice was made using the full extent of our knowledge," Leo reminded him. "We didn't fool ourselves into thinking it would come easily. We knew we'd have to dig hard and deep, didn't we? Or have you forgotten? Let ignorant numskulls hope for a strike in twenty-four hours, we know how to mine professionally: that was what we told ourselves."

"And look where it's landed us! Jackasses with no more brains than a turnip are finding nuggets right in the middle of town!"

"They are," agreed Sell Yost. "Look at that fellow just yesterday." A miner had pulled a chunk of gold the size of a fist from his claim, and been paraded around the streets on the shoulders of men less resentful than Chadbourne. Leo was unable to defend the Engineers' original plan with anything like enthusiasm, not when similar thoughts had been in his own mind.

"Well, then," he said, "what are you proposing?"

"I've already said: we should start again somewhere else."

"Where, in particular?"

"Just about anywhere but here."

"Throw a stone, and where it falls, dig your hole?"

"If it works for know-nothings, it should work for us. Sell thinks so too, don't you, Sell?"

Yost nodded. "In fact, Leo, we were talking with a fellow on his own who wants to go into partnership with us. He's got a claim he can't work since his partner got frostbite in his hands and went down to Leadville. He'll bring us in cheap, just so he can keep digging. You can be in on it if you want."

"No."

"Why not?"

"I'm committed to this claim. I believe in it."

Chadbourne and Yost looked at each other, then at Leo.

"The fact is," said Chadbourne, "Sell and I are going in, with or without you. We want you to buy us out, if you won't ditch the claim altogether."

"I accept," Leo said. "How much for your share?"

"We need fifty dollars each to buy into the other fellow's claim," said Yost, "and we'll need to be taking our fair share of tools. You could keep the mule, he already has two good ones."

"I don't have a hundred dollars. All I can offer is a signed IOU."

"Make it out to our new partner," said Chadbourne. "He knows you'll make good on it someday."

Zoe stepped forward. "There is no need." She counted out fifty-seven dollars in bills and coin, and included several tiny nuggets given to her as payment for her domestic duties by miners. "I have not had time to have these appraised," she said, "but if you judge them to be worth the balance, take them."

The erstwhile Engineers accepted Zoe's offering, and vacated cabin and claim within the hour. Leo sat by the stove, staring into its burning embers. He had thanked Zoe, his voice made gentle by defeat, and she had not attempted further conversation with him while she prepared the evening meal. It was Leo who finally ended the silence.

"And now," he said, "there's one thing I must do for you, in return for what you have done for me."

"What is it?"

"We should be married. With just us two and Omie here, tongues will wag."

"That isn't necessary, Leo. Why should tongues wag, when everyone has been told we're brother and sister?"

"Zoe, Zoe ... no one has believed that since the day you filed your claim in the name of Dugan. Couldn't you see what would happen the moment you did that? Has no one questioned you? They have me, and my late partners."

"No one has said a word. Oh, my, was I as foolish as that? I didn't think, simply signed my name as usual. ... No wonder every man whose cabin I swept was so interested in me. They all saw me as a fallen woman, I expect."

"No one thinks you're anything of the kind. Whatever his other faults, the common miner knows respectability when he comes across it. I daresay they've all been curious, nothing more. You haven't answered my question."

"Why do you wish to marry me?"

"For the reason stated."

"That, and nothing more?"

"And because you happen to be a fine woman. I have the greatest respect for you. I'd be a good husband, I swear. Maybe not a rich one," he added, laughing.

"You would not prefer that I was less ... different?"

"Different? How? You are as I would have you—yourself, and that's enough. Is there something lacking in me that makes you hesitate? I believe Omie is fond of me in her way, and she'll need a father, just as you need a husband, and I a wife. No, you don't love me, but you will, and I'll love you also, because there's no reason why we should not, given time. Pardon my bluntness, Zoe, but all three being in need of each other, why not accept what fate has so clearly ordained? I'm not a romantic man. This isn't a romantic proposal, but it's a realistic one." He stood and reached for his jacket. "I intend walking for an hour or so. I'd appreciate an answer when I return."

He was gone before Zoe could think what to say. Omie was watching her from the hammock she had taken as her own since the death of Lewis.

"Well?" said Zoe. "I suppose you have already seen whether or not we wed."

Omie shook her head. "I didn't see anything, Mama. Should I try?"

"Does that work, trying?"

"It happens mostly when I don't try."

"Then why waste time? Do you like Leo? Would you have him for a father?"

"He's very lonely, Mama, but tries not to show it. He wants you to say yes. You could ask him to dig up the gold elk with you if he was your husband."

"Is that reason enough?"

"I don't know, Mama, and Mama, what about Papa?"

The disappearance of Bryce Aspinall from their living room in Pueblo had hurt and infuriated Zoe so much she had seen fit to consider the man dead, to all intents and purposes. But mention of him by Omie was the feeblest of excuses for not confronting this offer of a new life, with a new husband. Why should a dead man, even if he still lived, cause her further pain? Bryce's betrayal of herself and Omie would not keep Zoe from another chance for happiness.

When Leo came through the door for his dinner, it was served to him by his wife-to-be.

It was March before the deer lick thawed sufficiently for Zoe to think of resuming work there. Leo had found a new partner to help him with his claim, but the partnership dissolved when nothing of worth came from the shaft. Now Zoe and Leo had each other and Omie and little else besides. They owed a substantial sum of money to several merchants, and had to live with the galling knowledge that Chadbourne and Yost and their partner had made a modest strike, sold out to a large commercial mining enterprise and left for lower elevations with a handsome profit. Representatives of the Rocky Mountain Mining Corporation had arrived in Glory Hole with the thaw, and begun buying up all claims that had revealed the presence of color without actually disgorging riches. Leo wished openly that his claim could be among the chosen ones; he would willingly have sold out for a song. His mood of late had become disagreeably morose, and Zoe did not ask for his help in reopening her own distant workings.

When several days of fine weather robbed Leo of any excuse for not working his claim, he enlisted the aid of Zoe, who had proved herself a steady worker after Leo's latest partner quit (Zoe provided the cash that enabled Leo to buy back his share), and they labored together for more than an hour, Leo down in the shaft, Zoe unloading the buckets the mule drew to the surface. Omie assisted her in wheeling each load to the cradle for sluicing, and lent her eyes to the task while Zoe rocked the contraption back and forth as water played over the riffle slats. It was Omie, therefore, who first saw the gold.

"Mama! Stop! There's some in there! It shines, Mama!"

Zoe sent her to fetch Leo while she plucked three nuggets the size of walnuts from the cradle. By the time Leo and Omie returned, she had washed out four more, including one as large as a peach. Leo stared, his jaw slack, then he scooped up his wife by the waist and waltzed her around the cradle while Omie clapped her hands and laughed.

The Rocky Mountain Mining Corporation paid Leo ninety thousand dollars for his claim, and when the deal had been made, and the ink allowed to dry on the bill of sale, Zoe took her husband aside and suggested a stroll up the side of the valley so they might overlook Glory Hole in its entirety before leaving for the warmer world of California, this being Leo's stated intention. She led him up to the deer lick, and bade him jump down into the hole she had made there. Leo did so, laughing at her unusual request.

"Dig," Zoe told him.

"I'm done with digging," he told her.

"No you're not. Dig with the toe of your boot."

He did, and soon thereafter was on hands and knees, unable to accept the riches crammed into so confined a space. The nuggets went down and down, a tightly packed funnel of yellow that actually began to widen, the deeper he dug.

"Your claim was empty. Its gold came from this place," said Zoe, "and I make no apology for having done what I did. Any man who has worked as hard as you for so long deserves to reap a reward of some kind, even from the great and greedy Rocky Mountain Mining Corporation. Now then, husband, are you truly done with digging?"

Literally up to his ankles in gold, co-owner by marriage of a claim that clearly would yield millions, Leo could only shake his head and admit his wife was his superior in every way.

23

Newspapers reaching Fort Mobley were distributed among those troopers who could read, before being cut into squares for use in the latrine. The news would be old by then, since the papers had to come by supply wagon from Albuquerque, a journey of ten days or more, and then the officers monopolized them for at least another week before releasing them to the lower ranks.

Drew found early on that he was the company's most capable reader, and his services were in demand when newspapers were distributed among the barracks. He would read them from the first page to the last, before an audience starved of information concerning the outside world. He found his listeners curiously uninterested in such items as the assassination of James Garfield, twentieth president of the United States; they preferred more entertaining fare, the report from Socorro, for example, that a woman had killed her husband with an ax one night, then run through the town howling like a wolf. Her explanation for the murder rested on the premise that she was not herself on account of the full moon, and so was not responsible for what she did to her spouse, whom she had loved dearly. The sheriff was informed by neighbors, however, that the couple often quarreled over the husband's excessive drinking and infidelities, and no one had ever heard the accused baying or otherwise acting peculiar at the time of the full moon, so it was generally held that the murderess was simply trying to pull the wool over the eyes of the law. The correspondent opined that the blatant lying and poor acting ability of the woman would prove prejudicial to her case when it came to court.

"She done it deliberate," said Osgood, who was considered by some to be the wisest man in the barracks. "She said it just to get put in the monkey house instead of getting stretched like she deserves." There were murmurings of agreement from several of the bunks, but it was difficult to tell from which, the only lighted lamp being above the newspaper reader, John Bones. Osgood continued: "A smarter woman now, she would've never said that about the moon. She would've said something about how she seen him come in through the window real late, and figured he was an Injun, so she took the ax to him. Maybe no one would've believed her, but they sure would've respected her brains a lot more, and maybe let her off on account of it. She never thunk it through like she should've, so now she'll get stretched for sure, even if she's a woman."

"That's right," said Fannin, Osgood's best friend and second shadow. It was said of Fannin that if Osgood ever stopped walking too suddenly, Fannin's nose would be jammed permanently up Osgood's ass, not that either party would have found this position unnatural or inconvenient. "That's what she should've done, told about the Injun, not the moon."

Drew found it sad that the level of learning at Fort Mobley was so low he had been elevated to a position of considerable status solely because he could read without a pause and explain the many complex terms that baffled his listeners. He quickly became aware that he had unwittingly supplanted Osgood as the company's most learned and erudite individual, and regretted that this should have happened, since Osgood's expression made it clear he considered Drew his enemy. It had only come about because Osgood, during one of his readings, had stumbled over the pronunciation of the word "intimidate," and Drew, without even looking over his shoulder, had deduced from the article's context what the awkward word was, and his speaking of it aloud had stunned everyone. Soon after, his star had risen higher when he assisted one of the men in the writing of a letter to his sweetheart. The writer knew his girl would never believe the flowery sentences had sprung from himself, but

POWER IN THE BLOOD

he sent it anyway, because it was a damn fine poetical piece of art.

"Too late now," continued Fannin. "She should've had Ossie for her lawyer to tell her what to do, but that won't happen, so she'll drop for sure."

Osgood nodded in acknowledgment of the truth in Fannin's words, but he was aware that there was less than the usual level of enthusiasm in the room for his pronouncements, despite Fannin's efforts on his behalf. More and more, lately, the men wanted to hear what Bones thought of the items he read to them, and Osgood was experiencing the pangs of rejection. Until the arrival of Bones, his had been the voice that relayed and interpreted the news, often with a fair amount of improvisation, since Osgood's grasp of spelling and vocabulary was limited.

"Think she'll get away with it, Bones?" asked Taynton, a lanky New Englander.

"She'd have a chance if they let women on juries; then it wouldn't matter if they believed her or not. If she killed her husband for running around with other women and drinking too much, they'd find her not guilty, because some time or other most women want to do exactly the same to their own man. Someday they'll put women on juries, and that's what'll happen to husband-killers."

"That's stupid," Osgood said, cramming as much scorn as he could muster into his words. "Think a judge'd let some bunch of women let a murderer go free? It won't happen, not in this life."

"It could," Drew countered. "I once heard of a case where the accused was a spittoon emptier, just the lowest dog in town, and he killed a man worth plenty of money, because that man spat on him intentionally when he was trying to take the spittoon away for emptying at the same moment the rich man felt the need to expectorate. The low dog came up with the spittoon in his hands and whanged the rich man so hard on the head he died on the spot. Outright murder, committed in front of dozens of witnesses, but they couldn't find a jury that would convict him, because every poor man wants to kill a rich man sometime, to balance the universal order of things, what you might call natural redress of fiscal imbalance, or just the plain old poor man's revenge."

"Sounds about right," agreed Taynton, who despised Osgood and Fannin for their weaselly ways and high opinion of themselves. He didn't believe a word of Bones's story, but that wasn't the point. The tale of the spittoon emptier and the rich man had set everyone in the room thinking, whereas Osgood's words generally fell like blankets over his audience, unconsciously freeing them from any obligation to ponder the news, since Osgood had already instructed them on what it all meant. Bones was a queer duck, as out of place in the army as a teacher in a stokehole. Taynton decided he would be Bones's friend from then on, just to poke a stick in Osgood's eye.

Drew applied himself to the newspaper again. "Here's something that concerns us," he said. "Listen: 'On Wednesday last, while being transferred from the jail at Magdalena to the jurisdiction of federal marshals, the notorious Apache fiends Panther Stalking and Kills With a Smile managed to slip free of their bonds and make good an escape which Marshals Willis Beecher and Lee Hoyt had called "impossible." While placed under guard in the center of town and surrounded by several score of citizens eager for a glimpse of the murderous duo, both Indians suddenly threw down their handcuffs, which apparently had been opened on the sly, and sprang onto horses nearby. Several shots were fired, the marshals' aim being hampered by the presence of so many innocents, and in a trice the two Apache desperadoes were gone without blood being spilt. The stolen horses were located within the hour by a heavily armed posse, but no trace at all was found to indicate in which direction the wily murderers chose to vanish.'"

"Shoot," said someone. "They oughtn't to have gotten away that easy."

Drew continued: "'These slayers in the night have proved once again they are too slippery for such forces as the federal law authorities are capable of mustering against them, and it is to be hoped that the oft-heard rumors concerning an all-out hunt by the army will at last be made real. Nothing less than a fully equipped company must be despatched to track down these red hellions and rid the southwest territories of their presence once and for all. It is reliably calculated they have tortured and killed fifty-one persons, including seventeen women and nine children, since their bloody reign of terror began last year. It is beyond understanding why they have been able to evade capture—and wriggle free again when finally caught—for this length of time. Outraged white folk and even Mexicans are demanding action that will bring surcease to this shocking episode which, if not stopped, may well inspire Apaches of lesser nerve to rise up in numbers to do even more harm than their kind already has. This editor calls upon the government to do what it must, or be answerable for the bloodbath that will surely follow.'"

"Won't happen," Osgood assured the barracks. "We're so under-manned we can't even do drill every day like we're supposed to. This outfit couldn't find them two redskins if we looked for a year."

For once, Drew was inclined to agree with Osgood. His arrival at Fort Mobley nine days before had been a shock. The "fort" was without fortifications of any kind, lacking even a row of stones to mark the perimeter. There were a dozen adobe buildings scattered about a dusty parade ground, a flagless flagpole and a view in all directions that could be described as either magnificent or hell on earth, depending upon the inclination of the viewer. On his arrival, Drew had tended to the former description, but now he understood the average trooper's firm declaration of the latter. The mountains surrounding Fort Mobley held heat like a crucible, making life in the bottom of the desert bowl around the fort the equivalent, Drew thought, of one of Dante's hellish circles.

A roster of living things at the fort included two officers, one offi-cer's wife, one noncommissioned officer, one cook, thirty-eight troop-ers, forty-one mules, two dogs, one cat, a rooster and seven chick-ens. The scorpions and flies were beyond counting. Drew regretted having held true to his promise to Judge Craven; the judge could have had no idea army life could be as pointless and soul-destroying as duty at Fort Mobley clearly was. There hung in the tortured air of the place a kind of silent shrieking, a cry from the collective heart of every human posted there. Its name in the barracks, Drew learned, was Fort Hellhole. The temperature often climbed to one hundred eighteen degrees Fahrenheit in the afternoon, and the adobe dwellings retained much of this heat through the night, mak-ing each building an oven of baked clay, slowly roasting the unfor-tunates within. The night air was considerably cooler, but it was forbidden to sleep outside the barracks, in case of Indian attack. Men risked death by marauder and punishment by officers anyway, simply to find relief from the heat in a few hours of oblivion. Fort Stanton, where Drew had enlisted and received his training over the winter months, was a paradise, a whitewashed monument to the saving graces of civilization; by comparison, Fort Mobley sat like the ruins from a forgotten age.

Taynton formed the habit of cultivating Drew's company over the breakfast table. The same miserable fare was made available in

variations on a culinary theme, and served up for all three meals.
Salted beef was the staple, bread dried to a bricklike consistency
the dessert, and coarse coffee rendered the communal throat moist
enough to pass it down for queasy digestion. Sharing his opinion of
the food was an easy way to approach the newcomer. Others had
made a casual effort to pry into Bones's life before he'd come to
Hellhole, but had been rebuffed with just enough friendliness to
prevent bad feeling. Taynton wanted to find out what others could
not. He had an innate curiosity concerning mankind, and saw in
Bones a suitable target for investigation. Slowly at first, then with
more determination, he began to assemble a notion of who John
Bones might be.

"There's men here," he said, "that murdered and ran, and
changed their names when they signed up. Me, I think it makes
sense. Anyone does wrong, they should be put in the army and punished for it."

Drew accepted the overture without responding. Taynton took his
silence for encouragement, and continued. "See Corwin over there?
Did his own sister back in Chicago."

"Killed her?"

"No, *did* her. Put it to her, you know."

"Why would he tell you a thing like that?"

"Most of these fellers, they're ashamed of what they did, but not
Corwin, he brags on it, says she was the best piece of tail he ever
had. A man that talks about his own sister like that, he's the lowest
kind of scum, in my opinion."

"Have you shared your opinion with Corwin?"

"No, that'd just get my head stove in, and Corwin, he'd still be the
same kind of scum, so why bother."

"That's practical. Who are the murderers?"

"Well, there's Benton, the one with the walleye. He's known to
have killed a man in New York City, someone he owed money to,
they say."

Drew was aware of Taynton's probing, but had little fear that he
might be found out. He had grown a short beard before enlisting,
and had seen a poster with his former unshaven self on it directly
outside the recruiting office. The beard was ample disguise, and he
appreciated the fact that it made his boyish features at least five
years older.

"Did you kill anyone, Taynton?"

"Me, no, I'd like to sometime, though. There's some men need killing, I reckon. Captain Mayles, for one, and maybe old Shrike for two."

Mayles had been in command of the fort since his superior officer died suddenly of a burst appendix. Word of the incident had been dispatched to the outside world, but had not brought any response. Dispatches from Mobley often tended to vanish into the shimmering desert air. The arrival of Drew was in response, it was assumed, to a request for several dozen men, made five months earlier. Mayles himself seemed to relish the power that was thrust upon him, and had begun to swagger when he walked, a pose that did not suit his girth. No one understood how it was that Mayles and his wife were able to maintain their corpulence when everyone else grew thin on their poor rations. Mayles seldom spoke with anyone but Lieutenant Dobson, and Dobson was not about to ask. It was rumored that Dobson was waiting for Mayles to contract some fatal affliction, whereupon he could assume control of the fort, and of Mayles's wife, who was often seen tipping Dobson the glad eye from deep within the folds of her sunbonnet. Despite her unattractive physical appearance, it was clear why Dora Mayles had won Dobson's heart: she was the only female in a hundred miles.

Conveying an occasional order from the officers to the men was the task of Sergeant Shrike, a dour individual unfit for the work, since his presence aroused in the ranks not a jot of fear or respect. Shrike was known to have given orders that were coolly ignored, and during one momentous confrontation he had screeched an order over and over again at the top of his voice, earning for himself the sobriquet Shriek. The men obeyed him if an officer was nearby, but at no other time. Shrike had a small room to himself, and spent a great deal of time inside it. Some said he prayed alone, others swore he was hatching plots against the troop for their humiliating indifference to his rank, and others said he was either playing with himself to pass the time behind his closed door, or else sleeping.

Taynton was convinced there was a mystery to Bones that time and an easy manner would penetrate. Bones had not rejected him as a companion, and seemed to listen with attention when Taynton spoke. He had given nothing away, though, and Taynton was beginning to wonder if he was merely being tolerated by Bones, rather than cultivated. It was a mildly frustrating exercise, getting behind the mask of the new trooper, but Taynton persevered, because there was nothing else of interest to do.

While they curried their mules in the stables' blistering shade one morning, Taynton informed Drew there was trouble brewing.

"What kind?" Drew asked.

"The worst kind—woman trouble."

This could only mean Captain Mayles's wife.

"What about it?"

"What about it? Bones, in this man's army, you don't mess with the post commander's missus, even if she wants you to. It can't be got away with, not in a place small as this. Dobson got seen last night peeking in her window, and the captain caught him red-handed. Wilson saw the whole thing, had the shitbox door open and could see clear across to the captain's house with the moonlight and all, and heard every word too. Dobson got called a poltroon. You know what that is, Bones?"

"I believe it's someone who sniffs the soiled undergarments of females."

"Is that right? Dobson won't have liked that one little bit, especially coming from the captain. Those two never have hit it off. I expect it was because of the wife going all fluttery-eyed when Dobson came here last year. Everyone saw it, and now finally the captain sees it too. I bet there'll be a court-martial."

"Because he peeked in her window?"

"Sure, why else is he in the guardhouse right this minute—because he likes to be?"

Nothing of this had been discussed at breakfast, so Dobson's arrest must have been recent. "Taynton, how do you know so much about what happens around here before anyone else does?"

"I keep my eyes open and my nose to the wind. It was Wilson again. Him and Rafferty got the job to put Dobson in there, captain's orders."

"They can't hold a court-martial without a court. Mayles and Dobson are the only officers here."

"I know it, and that's why Dobson'll likely stay where he's at till there's more officers arrive, or it rains yellow roses at midnight, whichever one comes first."

"Taynton, why are you here—I mean, in the army? I'm genuinely curious to know the answer."

"Well, I'll tell you, if you'll tell me the selfsame thing."

"You first."

"I run off from my wife. She was a mean woman, Bones. I mean to tell you that woman could skin a man alive at a considerable distance, just with her eyes alone, that's how powerful of a woman she was, but her biggest crime, as I see it, and I was her husband, her biggest crime was to whale the tar out'n me whenever she's drunk. Now, most men I wouldn't tell that to, Bones, but I like you, and I can see you're a notch or two above the average specimen around these parts, so now I'd appreciate an answer just as honest from you, if you don't mind."

"I got the daughter of the governor of Texas pregnant. He would've let us marry, just to hush up the scandal, but I ran, because I wasn't in love with the girl. She was a redhead, Taynton, and a conjure woman one time in New Orleans told me a redheaded woman would be the death of me."

"Why, that's practically the same story. Women, that's what brung us both here."

"It was indeed."

"You know, that kind of makes us like brothers, don't you think?"

"Kind of. Would Mayles really leave Dobson in the guardhouse forever?"

"I expect, unless there's an Indian attack. He'd get let out then. Dobson's a crack shot. We had target practice about three, four months back, and Dobson hit the bull's-eye dead center both times. That's all the bullets the captain let us have apiece. We're way down on supplies."

When they were finished grooming their mules, Drew and Taynton wandered over to the adobe block near the cookhouse that Dobson was confined in. Wilson and Rafferty were lounging nearby. Drew approached a small barred window beside the flimsy door.

"What you want?" demanded Rafferty.

"Speak to the lieutenant," said Taynton.

"Ain't allowed," Wilson informed them.

"Mayles said," added Rafferty.

"Lieutenant," Drew called, "can you hear me?"

"I hear you," came a voice from the shadowed cell. "Who is that?"

"Bones."

"'Bones, sir.'"

"Bones, sir. Just wondered if you were all right in there, Lieutenant."

"My physical comfort doesn't concern me, Bones, but I want word of this illegal action to be passed on to the appropriate officers at Fort Stanton."

"I'd be happy to do that for you, sir. I'll leave today if you give me a direct order."

"Consider it given."

"You quit talkin' to him," warned Wilson.

"He's talking to me," said Drew, and Wilson looked to Rafferty for advice. Rafferty shrugged, so Wilson allowed the conversation to continue, but he frowned mightily to make his disapproval known.

"Get yourself mounted and deliver the facts, Bones," ordered Dobson.

"Might have trouble there," said Taynton. "Nobody leaves the post unless Captain Mayles says he can."

"I'll take the responsibility, Bones. Draw your supplies and get going. We have an unbalanced officer in charge here, be sure and tell them that."

"Wait a minute now," said Rafferty. "He goes and leaves, the captain, he'll want to know who give him the order, and we'll have to tell him it was you, Lieutenant, and then we'll be in there with you because we let someone speak to you."

"You two will accompany Bones to Fort Stanton."

"Can I go too, Lieutenant?" asked Taynton.

"Yes. All of you draw the necessary supplies and leave, and try not to attract attention."

The troopers looked at each other. Anything that moved in the general area of Fort Mobley attracted attention, since inactivity was the norm. There were doubts, too, concerning the questionable nature of Dobson's authority. Mayles's orders would be flouted if they did what the lieutenant wanted. If Dobson had been popular, or even considered less of a fool than Mayles, their allegiance would not have been so reluctant, but Dobson was no friend of the common man.

"Well?" said Taynton.

Wilson shook his head. "I don't know ..."

"There's women at Fort Stanton," hinted Taynton.

Rafferty and Wilson appeared equally indecisive. Taynton looked to Drew for enthusiasm. "He gave us the order," Drew said. "We can do it."

"Not unless we let you," Wilson reminded him.

"We'd all get court-martialed," Rafferty stated.

Taynton made sounds of disgust, but the guards seemed to have made up their minds. They signaled this by standing straighter and glaring at the troopers who had caused temptation to be dangled before them by approaching the guardhouse. Taynton and Drew began a casual meandering away from the area. "You men!" came the voice of Lieutenant Dobson. "Where are you going! You have your orders ...!"

When they were a short distance off, Taynton said, "Why don't we bust Dobson out of there and let him saddle his own mule and go tell them at Stanton what happened."

Drew considered it. "Better get him out tonight. Mayles might go ahead and have him shot tomorrow."

Both men asked themselves, through the afternoon and evening, why it was that they were prepared to assist a man neither of them liked, and the answer, arrived at mutually, was the simple need to see what would happen. Even more than Drew, Taynton desired action of some kind; a year at Fort Mobley, in which time he had not had the opportunity to kill a single Indian, had frustrated his appetite for an event of some kind, an adventure or experience he could remember for the rest of his life. Studying the character of his fellow troopers, even the interesting ones like Bones, was beginning to pall as a hobby.

The sole topic of conversation before taps was the plight of Dobson. Sheckley, who had delivered meals to the prisoner, said the lieutenant appeared to be in good spirits; certainly everyone on the post had heard the off-key hymns rising like crooked smoke above the adobe guardhouse. The state of Captain Mayles's mental health was also debated, the consensus being that the man was certifiably insane, not for having jailed Dobson over the window-peeking incident, but for caring at all that anyone would want to steal his grimly unattractive wife from him in the first place. "Hell," said one trooper, "I was him, I would've give 'em the two best mules and hoped they run off together." Dora Mayles had been seen behind the curtains of the captain's house, staring across the parade ground at the tiny box enclosing her brave cavalier. "Bet she wisht she could put old Mayles in there instead, and bake the starch out'n him."

Drew and Taynton kept out of the discussion until Osgood asked why they had gone over to talk with Dobson at all.

"We thought he might need cheering up," Drew said.

"Not that it's any of your business," added Taynton.

"It's everyone's business when troopers start chumming with officers. Just curious to know what you see in him."

"We see someone in a hole, Osgood. When you see something like that, you go ask if there's anything they need, officer or not. Even if it was you in there, I'd go ask if you needed anything."

"It's still sucking around the wrong man," put in Fannin. "That Dobson, he give me guard duty seven nights running last December, including Christmas Day, the snake, and all because I didn't clean his room perfect one time."

Others joined in with a list of Dobson's unjust punishments. No one seemed concerned for the man's welfare. Fort Mobley was without any shred of camaraderie among the ranks or loyalty to the officers. There was not any sense of conquering and holding hostile lands for the white race, nor any patriotic respect for the flags of nation and unit that sometimes hung like neglected laundry from the parade ground pole and sometimes did not. His training had not prepared Drew for this. He despised the place, as did everyone else, but with a sense of his own superiority over the commonplace grumblings and idleness of the rest. He and Taynton seemed to be the only ones with any kind of spirit, and perhaps Dobson too, even if his personality was odious and his professional qualities largely absent; it had taken spirit of some kind to sneak a glimpse of the captain's wife in a state of semi-undress.

In the barracks, surrounded by a stifling effluvium of the day's trapped heat, Drew and Taynton found it easier than most to remain sleepless. They rose a little before midnight and crept outside. Quietly passing by the few troopers who risked censure by spending the night outdoors, they watched for signs of light or movement across the empty parade ground. The guardhouse squatted in moonlight like a square rock. Dobson had ceased his hymn singing at sundown. "Now," whispered Taynton, and they hurried across the open space, their socks raising small puffs of dust. Drew grasped the window bars and lifted himself up to hiss, "Dobson ... Lieutenant, sir ... Wake up ... "

There was no sound or movement within the cell. Drew could see little but darkness beyond the bars. "Lieutenant Dobson ...! Hey! Wake up, sir ...!"

"Hush it down," Taynton pleaded.

"He's not there."

"Huh?"

"I think I see a hole in the far wall."

Drew dropped down and they skirted the guardhouse. The hole

was at ground level, big enough to allow a thin man like Dobson through. Chunks of dry adobe were scattered around.

"Be darned if he didn't kick his way out. Think he's got himself mounted by now?"

"Let's check the stables," Drew said. His opinion of Dobson had been raised by the audacity of the escape.

A lamp was lit and a count made of the mules. Two were gone. "Took a spare," said Taynton. "Smart feller. Probably walked them a fair distance off so's not to wake anyone up."

"Well, our hearts were in the right place. He had more initiative than we thought."

"Be hell to pay come morning."

"Guaranteed."

Taynton's prediction was given a personal slant at the dawn roll call, when Captain Mayles demanded information on the prisoner's jailbreak. Osgood hesitated only a moment before declaring, "It was Bones and Taynton, sir. Fannin and me saw them both creeping around with no boots on over in the stable."

Mayles seemed to quiver from top to bottom. His waxed mustaches twitched perceptibly, and his coloring darkened.

"Bones! Taynton! Step forward!"

As they did so, Taynton murmured to Osgood from the side of his mouth, "You're a dead man."

"To my office!" snapped Mayles, turning on his heels.

Drew and Taynton followed him there, and stood before the worm-eaten desk of their commander, whose agitation was so great he could not sit, but had to pace back and forth between the dusty yellow squares of his two windows.

"Are you responsible for this? Speak only the truth!"

"Captain, me and Bones were in the stable, all right, but only because we heard something in there. We thought it might be a cougar."

"A cougar? Were you armed?"

"Well, nossir, we weren't. It was just in back of my mind, about there being a cougar—the mules would've been kicking their stalls down—but we sure heard something."

"We investigated, sir. It was our duty."

"And you found?"

"Nothing, sir."

"No missing mules?"

"The lieutenant must still have been around, sir," said Taynton. "There were no animals missing. It was probably the lieutenant we heard, and when we left, that's when he took them and snuck off."

"Doubtless. Send Osgood and the other fellow he mentioned to me, then wait outside."

"Yessir."

Following the captain's interview with Osgood and Fannin, Drew and Taynton were sent back inside. "I'm told you two were talking with the prisoner yesterday."

"We passed an innocent moment or two outside the guardhouse, sir. We were talking with Rafferty and Wilson."

"No word passed between the prisoner and yourselves?"

"Well, he did start talking through the window, sir. It would've seemed like impoliteness not to answer."

Mayles studied them both for a moment, then ordered Rafferty and Wilson brought before him.

Within an hour of reveille, Captain Mayles had made his decision. Joint responsibility for the breakout was assigned to the two guards and their partners in conversation. They were to draw supplies and set off after Lieutenant Dobson without delay. The rest of the troop had scouted around the fort and found fresh tracks leading south by east, toward Fort Stanton. The four would be accompanied—just in case they had somehow connived at the escape—by Osgood and Fannin. Sergeant Shrike would be in charge of the pursuit.

As Drew led his mule from the stable to the supply room for hardtack and ammunition, Dora Mayles slid from behind the company latrine and thrust something soft into his hand. "For the lieutenant," she breathed, and hastily turned away. Drew looked at the fine embroidery around the silk handkerchief's edges. A heart was stitched into a corner.

The seven manhunters assembled before the captain's porch for last-minute instructions. Mayles had put on his dress uniform for the occasion. A lengthy split smiled from the left shoulder seam; the captain's wife had been neglecting her duties with thimble and thread.

"When you apprehend the escapee, you will relieve him of any weapons he may have, and escort him directly here. You will deliver him to me in good condition, or I'll know the reason why. If you should fail to catch him, you will all face the consequences. Sergeant, be on your guard."

As Shrike led his small band away from the fort, he experienced a mounting sense of futility over the enterprise. Dobson was already long gone, and his crime had been trivial. There was no need for such an expedition as this to redress so insignificant a wrong as window peeking. Shrike knew that whatever orders he issued while in pursuit of the lieutenant, the men would obey only those they considered appropriate. He fully expected half of them to desert, since that was the average rate for disappearances ever since he had been at Mobley, and he could see why men were inclined to do it. He sometimes wished he had the nerve himself to desert, but knew he never would; the army was his life, and without it he would be nothing. He anticipated trouble, though, if he should return minus half his contingent. With luck, there might be viable explanations for the reduced number—heat exhaustion, Indian attack, possibly even ambush by the lieutenant, if they ever caught up with him. These conditions would tend to exonerate him in the eyes of Mayles. Shrike had his hopes, like any man.

Of the six under the sergeant's command, only Drew and Taynton felt any excitement over being dispatched into the desert on this mission to recapture Dobson. Rafferty and Wilson were sullen, hurt that they were under suspicion regarding the lieutenant's escape, both hoping for a quick resolution to the hunt. Osgood regarded his inclusion as the price he was obliged to pay for having implicated Bones and Taynton in the Dobson affair. He was hoping for some opportunity to kill or injure Bones, should any kind of action be engaged in, but he would have to ensure that his handiwork had the appearance of being the natural consequence of battle. Fannin was terrified to be out in the wilderness with nothing but guns and fellow troopers to keep him from harm. It was some comfort to have Osgood riding alongside, but lately Fannin had been dreaming of his own death and, being a superstitious man, was inclined to surrender all notion of escaping the fate he suspected lay waiting for him under the scorching sun. If there had been more moisture in his body, Fannin would have wept.

Drew had become accustomed to mules. An admirer of horseflesh, he had felt an initial sense of personal insult at being instructed to mount so aesthetically displeasing a creature as a mule, but was won over in the end for the same reason the army favored these beasts in the southwestern region; they were tough, hardy and enduring, even under the most unforgiving of conditions, and, despite occasional contrariness of temperament, would serve a man well in circumstances that would quickly kill even the finest horse. Mules, Drew was told, were made of nails and leather and brushwood, and could sustain any mode of punishment but love. "Never love your mule," was the advice given, "or he'll make you regret it. Just tend him in the regular fashion, without extra grooming and attention and such, and he'll see you through hell and high water. Scorn your mule as he scorns you, and the both of you will survive."

Fort Mobley had been without any Indian tracker or guide since April, when Charley Kicking Horse had demonstrated his ability to withstand snakebite by deliberately allowing a rattler to strike him twice in the forearm. Charley Kicking Horse maintained that whites were liable to succumb to such bland stuff as snake venom solely on account of their pallid skins, whereas the superior blood of the native American was fully able to withstand the poison. When his arm swelled to three times its normal size, Charley laughed it off as an inconvenience, nothing more, and there was no company surgeon available in any case to suggest that his estimation of Indian blood had been unrealistically biased. When his body weakened and his heart began fluttering in an unaccustomed manner, Charley went so far as to admit that the snake had been stocked with poison of strength and quantity, and he allowed himself the solace of whiskey, in the tight embrace of which he died, still convinced he would be able to rise again as soon as the effects of the venom abated. Everyone had agreed it served him right for having compared himself with white folks, and the general level of dissatisfaction with Charley's performance was such that he was taken far from the post for burial, and even then was not provided with an actual grave. Charley's body drew buzzards for three days.

It was fortunate, given the absence of Charley Kicking Horse, that Lieutenant Dobson had made no attempt to obscure his tracks. The two sets of hoofprints headed toward Fort Stanton with such unerring directness as to indicate Dobson's possession of a compass. Sergeant Shrike assigned Wilson, who often bragged of his eyesight, to be head tracker, and Wilson acquitted himself well in a tolerably difficult task, given that the ground sometimes was so rocky the signs of Dobson's passing were often obscured for a hundred yards or more.

As the day wore on, it became apparent Dobson was not pausing to rest, thereby obliging his pursuers to do the same. Even before noon, the sun pressed against them with a fierceness that set them sagging on their mules like wilted stalks of flesh dressed in blue, and their heads rang with the silence and heat and empty reaches of nothingness around them.

The sand-colored mountains swam like islands suspended in the shimmering air, supported by inexplicable underpinnings of sky, and sagebrush rippled and swayed like seaweed to the incandescent horizon.

Sergeant Shrike did suggest that the men conserve their water, but when he heard the telltale swish and gurgle of upended canteens behind him, he neither turned nor scolded, since this would have been a waste of time and breath; if the water swillers died of thirst, at least they would be unable to desert.

Hardtack rations were eaten in the saddle, the mules given no opportunity to rest until Rafferty chose to bring his to a halt in order that he might dismount and relieve his bowels. Taking his cue from Rafferty, Osgood also stopped, and Fannin too. This brought Taynton to inquire of Sergeant Shrike if maybe they weren't pressing ahead too hard. The sergeant said they were not, but Taynton stopped anyway, as did Drew, and when he became aware of the column's breakup behind him, Wilson followed suit. Bowing to the first of the inevitable compromises he knew were coming, Shrike gave the order to halt, knowing better than to designate a time limit.

While they rested, the men spoke little. Even Drew was chastened by the sheer effort required to focus his thoughts, and was reminded of the time he spent afoot on a desert road those many years ago, through country less harsh than this, and of the unlikely friend he found at the end of that road. Yancy had hinted at time spent in the military, and warned Drew never to take that route. Drew wondered if he might now justifiably take his leave. His promise to Judge Craven had been fulfilled—he had indeed joined the army—and the judge had not specified how long he should feel obligated to remain. It was a decision becoming easier by the hour to make. Drew asked himself if Taynton should be acquainted with the drift of his thinking; surely the man had had enough of army life by now to contemplate an unofficial leavetaking. He was a man to Drew's liking, and it would be enjoyable to share the minimal risks of desertion with a friend, rather than face the task alone.

"Supposing we catch up with Dobson," said Taynton, settling beside Drew in the shade of his mule. "Then what?"

"Then we take him back."

"You feel like doing that, Bones? What did the man do but what any man would've, look at a woman undressed, and break himself out of a cell he never should've been inside of anyway. He hasn't done a damn thing that makes me want to drag him in front of Mayles for."

"What are you saying—we should somehow not find him?"

"That's one way out. This whole thing is nothing to do with us. It's a personal quarrel between officers, neither one of which is worth a pinch of muleshit, in my opinion."

"But that's the army way, Taynton, to do as they tell us, muleshit or not."

"I know it."

"So I'm asking you, is there some way to resolve this contradiction, or do we just keep on doing what the muleshit wants us to?"

"Bones, I do admire your way with the language and all, but I wish sometimes you'd come right out and say what you mean, because I'm thinking I know what you mean, only I can't be sure, see, so I can't be answering your question, not till I know for sure."

"We're a fair distance from Mobley is what I mean, and by this time tomorrow we'll be a considerable distance more, but pretty soon after that we'll be getting closer to Fort Stanton, and I don't want to go back there, my friend, because in spite of my beard, there's portraits of me hanging in that place which, although flattering, might get me returned in chains to Texas."

"I always figured there was something more to you than the eye saw. There's punishments for what you're thinking about doing too, and chains is the least of it."

"They'd have to find us first."

"Us?"

"Don't tell me you haven't thought about it. When was the last time you heard about a deserter being caught?"

"'Bout nine months back, but he deserved it, the fool. They got him in Albuquerque, drunk and telling the world what he'd done, so I never did sympathize with him getting fifteen years like they gave him."

"You and I wouldn't be so dumb."

"No, I reckon not. Where would you be thinking to head?"

"North, to Colorado."

"That's a cooler place than this here."

"Do we do it, then, or don't we?"

Taynton scratched at the dust with a stick and ran his coated tongue around his teeth, then looked at Drew.

"I guess I can trust you, and you me. I'm game to light out from this man's army, but only if we plan it out real careful. I'm not of a mind to get captured and brung back. Desertion's more of a sin than what Dobson did."

Drew extended his hand, and Taynton shook it.

"Tomorrow night's best, I figure."

"I agree."

"Then I reckon that's settled."

The afternoon saw a slowing of the pace attempted by Shrike during the cooler morning hours. Even the mules began to plod. Wilson began losing the trail more often, and for longer periods. Sergeant Shrike guessed part of this was deliberate, a way of avoiding contact with Dobson, and all that such an encounter would entail. He sympathized with such reluctance to engage their quarry, but they had been given the order to apprehend the lieutenant before he reached Fort Stanton, and it was a matter of professional pride that they should acquit themselves, if not with honor, then at least to the best of their human ability. Wilson was sabotaging Shrike's efforts to accomplish this, with his feeble pretense of being unable to find the hoofprints of Dobson's mules. There was little point in chastising him for it; Wilson was a wonderful liar, and would simply present an injured look, and Rafferty would likely defend him by suggesting that Shrike get down off his mule and attempt to find the trail himself. It was better to say nothing.

By nightfall the hunters were thoroughly disenchanted with their mission, and flung themselves down to sleep without the benefit of a fire for their meal, since that might have alerted Dobson to their presence close behind him. Dobson apparently exercised the same wisdom, since no fire could be seen ahead, in fact the surrounding country was made dark as pitch by the absence of any moon, and the darkness itself seemed threatening, its utter absence of feature, its inky impenetrability containing any and all things a frightened man cared to project into it.

Every trooper was required to stand a shift on watch, and each one in turn was made aware of how small and vulnerable was his mortal body, how immeasurably large the night around him. Wilson said to Taynton, who relieved him after midnight, "It's no place to be, this, not while there's guilt in your soul." Taynton admitted surprise at finding Wilson believed in the soul, and Wilson said in reply, "Just you be getting one yourself, and quick, before morning comes on us all like bright hellfire." It was unlike Wilson to express himself in this manner, and Taynton was amused, yet somehow disturbed. The sleepy whimperings that came from Fannin throughout Taynton's watch did nothing to lighten his mood. He calmed himself with constant remindings of his plan to escape with Bones the following night, which presumably would be as dark as the one he found himself staring into with the helplessness of a man already hurtling down a well.

For the first few hours of the second day, Shrike was optimistic. Dobson's mules continued to leave an occasionally discernible trail that Wilson, for all that he tried to lose it, could not, and the tracks themselves seemed somehow fresher, deeper than before, even though the ground itself was no softer. At midmorning the hunting party was surprised to follow the tracks in a wide circle that turned to the left before crossing its own line and continuing on. Shortly thereafter, the hoofprints traced out a circle to the right, then resumed their original direction. It was a puzzling phenomenon, and the likelihood of Dobson having become disoriented, if not downright insane, beneath the desert sun was given consideration.

"Has to be craziness," said Rafferty, "or he wouldn't be coming back on course like he is."

"Got himself a compass, sure," said Osgood.

"Then why waste time riding in circles?" Drew asked for them all.

"Craziness," repeated Rafferty, "like I said."

"He's made us waste time too, following the circles all the way around," said Taynton. "Next time he does it, we should just skip the circle and follow on from where the lines cross. He does it enough times, we'll catch up—isn't that right, Sarge?"

"Most likely correct," Shrike agreed.

They pressed on, given new interest in their mission by Dobson's peculiar behavior. At noon they encountered a pile of human waste laid squarely in the middle of the tracks, yet Dobson's bootprints were nowhere to be seen.

"He's making fun of us," said Wilson. "Knows we're here and takes the time to do a thing like this. The lieutenant's gone in the head."

"Not even wearing his boots anymore," put in Osgood.

"But there aren't any footprints either," Drew cautioned. "Something's not right about this."

"It's Dobson's head that ain't right."

"Bones is right," whined Fannin. "There's something not normal, what Dobson's doing. Let's go back. He'll die anyway before he gets to Stanton. Let's go back ..."

"Hell, no, not before we get him and see if he's raving," said Wilson. "I never saw a crazy man before."

Shrike had already moved a little ahead of the rest, as a means of persuading them to hurry along. He was curious himself to see what kind of shape Dobson had been reduced to. It was strange, though; thirty-six hours seemed a remarkably short time in which to go insane.

Dobson's shape was revealed before one o'clock. Two more circlings had been bypassed in order to lessen the distance between hunters and hunted, and as Shrike's party rounded an outcrop of yellow rock, their quarry was revealed. Dobson sat facing them, naked, his bowels in his lap. His genitals had been removed piecemeal, and deposited on top of his head like a jaunty little cap. A long section of his digestive system's tubing had been curled around his neck like a scarf. His boots had been placed over his hands, and his gauntlets covered his feet. The effect was of some horrific prankster at work. Fannin fell from his mule in a swoon of terror. Carbines were dragged from their scabbards, and eyes frantically scanned the nearest rocks for the shadow of whatever monster had played its wicked games with Dobson's corpse. Shrike attempted to formulate a command that might serve to assert his authority, but could think of nothing, and the men under his command milled around the obscene discovery without any idea what to do. The mules were disturbed by the smell of blood and ruptured organs, and some began bucking and plunging to dislodge their riders.

"Stay together!" yelled Taynton. "There's got to be more than one! Osgood, get Fannin mounted up!"

Osgood turned his mule and began riding back the way they had come. This inspired a general panic, in which Osgood's choice of direction seemed the wisest to follow. Even Shrike was compelled to race after his subordinates, and less than a minute after Dobson was found, Drew and Taynton, along with the unconscious Fannin, were alone with the lieutenant's butchered corpse. Fannin's mule had run off with the rest.

"Bones," said Taynton, "I figure the time has come. We can just go the other way and disappear, and if any of those brave sons of bitches make it back to Mobley, they'll say we were most likely killed by whoever did that to Dobson."

"And whoever did it most likely will, don't you think? And what about Fannin?"

"I never liked him anyway, the little weasel. I'm not passing up a chance to do what we planned, just on account of Fannin. Now, are you with me or not?"

"I'm with you, but I can't leave him the way he is."

Drew went to Fannin and lightly slapped his face until his eyes opened and he suddenly sat up. The first thing Fannin saw was Dobson again, and he screamed. Drew slapped him again, harder. "Hush up, Fannin, and listen. They all lit out back the way we came, even your friend Osgood. Do you want to go that way too, or come with Taynton and me? We think it's best to split up. Whoever did it to Dobson can't track us all. What's your choice?"

Fannin scrambled on hands and knees for a short distance, then wrapped both arms around his head and began a catlike mewling, his body curled into as tight a ball as was possible. Drew approached him again. "Fannin, you have to choose."

"He can't," Taynton said. "He's lost his mind, most likely can't even hear you."

"Fannin, we're leaving here. Are you coming. or not? Quit that stupid noise!"

But Fannin could not. Drew stood over him, unable to decide himself what he should do.

"Time's a-wasting, Bones. Now or never."

Drew nodded. "Fannin, we're going now. Get up."

Fannin continued to mew, hiding his face from the terrible end he now knew had been waiting for him all his life. The thing that had happened to Dobson would happen to him, he had no doubt, and whoever kept droning words into his ear was simply coming between Fannin and that end, and so had to be ignored. If all noise stopped, the end would come, and be mercifully brief. He heard further buzzings of conversation, then the shuffle of hooves, then nothing, blessed nothing. He was aware of being very hot and thirsty, but these discomforts were without meaning. He simply had to blanket his eyes with darkness and await the end. It had been a poor kind of life in any case. He hadn't even slept with a woman, or found a friend worthy of his trust, hadn't made his mark on the world in any fashion whatsoever. This was what he had been born for, this blind huddling in the company of a mutilated man. It was horrible, but Fannin knew things could have ended for him no other way. That was why he had been dreaming his dreams of death. He felt almost calm now, having accepted that the farce called life was almost done for him. He even made an effort to stop uttering the sound that had been humming in his head and throat, and succeeded, but when the silence came, he felt something replace it, something that made no sound as it came nearer. Fannin found the courage within himself to look up at the devils sent from hell to drag him down among the darkling caverns within the earth.

Drew was not proud to have abandoned a man to whatever had killed Dobson. He felt that even a crazy person he had never liked when sane deserved forcible extraction from the immediate area of danger. Then again, there were not enough mules. If he and Taynton intended reaching civilization, two mules shared among three men would have been a considerable handicap, given the heat and distance involved. He had asked Fannin to choose, and could tell himself Fannin's choice had been to ignore him, but still Drew felt guilty as he rode alongside Taynton, his carbine held ready across the saddle. It had been an unheroic retreat, and might not in fact be a retreat at all, but an advance into worse horrors. Fannin's fate became less a matter of moral concern and more a needless distraction with every mile.

They rode north at a pace calculated not to tire the mules, when both men wanted to sprout wings and lift themselves beyond the desert. They rode in silence, each holding tight to his fear, neither willing to discuss their chances. By late afternoon it was still possible to locate the approximate position of Dobson by the distant spiraling of vultures, and their tininess was comfort of a kind. Drew preferred to think that if he and Taynton were to be targets for Dobson's killer or killers, it would already have happened. It had been wise to separate themselves from the rest of the search party, which presumably had then become the focus for attack, in that they possessed more mules and guns for the taking.

"We need to be heading for high ground for the night," advised Taynton, "somewhere we can see for a little ways around us at least. I reckon we can both forget about sleep."

Such a spot was found as the westering sun painted the landscape around them a bloody red. Drew led the way up a narrow defile to an isolated shelf of rock some fifty feet across, with sheer sides falling away around almost three quarters of its perimeter. Unless they were attacked by monkeys, they could reasonably expect to defend the point of access to their redoubt.

As the sky dimmed and darkness seemed to rise from the twisted rocks like mist, Drew and Taynton took up positions that would enable them to decimate an enemy attempting to close in. The mules were hobbled away from any potential line of fire, and were noticeable only by the occasional chinking of their bridles once the light was gone completely. The moonless sky was like spangled velvet, a curtain for whatever might be approaching. It was the darkness that created fear, and Drew wished for morning before night had truly begun. It was a worry to the nerves, being obliged to squat behind the cover of a small boulder and fix one's attention on the only pathway danger might approach by, a pathway barely visible, made even less so by constant staring. Drew had to close his eyes sometimes in order to see again. The world of shadows around him was formless, depthless, a funnel of gloom hiding even his friend from him.

"Taynton ... Taynton, are you all right?"

"Don't talk," came a low murmur. "Don't even breathe loud."

Chastened, Drew concentrated on remaining quiet. He was forced to rest his eyes more often as physical tiredness and the strain of staring into darkness wearied them, and twice found himself waking from brief snatches of sleep. The second time he did this, Drew was ashamed to have betrayed Taynton's trust. He had no watch, and could not be sure what time it was. The moon had risen at last, a sullen curve low on the horizon, shedding little light. The mules stirred for a moment, then were still. Drew wanted more than anything else to hold a whispered conversation, but resisted, knowing Taynton would only hiss at him to shut up and watch the defile for signs of movement. He stayed silent, and watched, until sleep overcame his guilt and fear again.

The third time Drew awoke, traces of dawn were evident in the sky. He was appalled at his own weakness, his personal treachery in allowing his friend to shoulder all responsibility for their safety. He could never admit what he had done to Taynton. Drew stared around himself with an intensity born of remorse. It was a good thing nothing had happened in the night because of his lack of alertness. He watched sunlight begin washing the air with a limpid brightness that quickly became harsh and clear. There was no point now in remaining silent, and in any case, he needed to stand and piss.

"Taynton ...?"

There was no reply. Drew called his name several times more, his voice low, then realized Taynton had also succumbed to tiredness and strain, and fallen asleep, as Drew had. It was almost a relief to know his weakness was shared. Drew pulled himself upright from behind his boulder and emptied his bladder. His entire body ached from the chill of the retreating night and the unyielding rock that had been his bed of unease. Adjusting his galluses, Drew approached the cleft he knew Taynton was hidden in, but Taynton was not there, having presumably gone to check the mules. Yet such a move would have been seen by Drew, who had been awake for some time now.

Alarmed, Drew hurried to the spot where he had heard the mules' bridles clinking in the night, and found that place also empty of life, although Taynton was indeed there. His throat had been sliced open, and he lay on his back, both boots neatly standing on his chest, his stockinged feet pointing at the sky. There was no mutilation other than the gaping throat, which already was attracting the attention of flies. Taynton's canteen, carbine and ammunition pouch were gone, along with both mules. Drew sank to his knees and vomited the scant remnants of yesterday's food.

He could not bring himself to delay his escape by burying Taynton's body. As he had the day before, Drew abandoned moral precept in favor of flight, but this time his terror allowed no shade of guilt to intrude. He could only assume the killers had not known he was there, and were content to have murdered one man and stolen his belongings.

He walked north, through country wild and waterless, his canteen almost empty, the sweat ring around the band of his hat drying fast in the air. As the hours passed, Drew began to stumble, and several times fell. He was as sorry for himself as he could remember having been since childhood, and wished fervently for belief in any god that might deliver him from the result of his own foolishness and inferiority.

By noon, even these mental exertions were no longer indulged in, there being room inside Drew's skull for nothing but awareness of his thirst. His tongue had the texture of a rolled-up sock, filling his mouth with its swollen presence. His feet ached inside their tight cavalry boots, each toe registering its own exquisite pain at the chafing given by its fellows, and Drew felt the beginnings of a blister on his left heel. The temptation to throw down his heavy Springfield carbine was strong, but Drew fought the impulse; if he had truly been overlooked by the fiends that had stalked himself and Taynton to the rock shelf, then his gun might serve to bring down game to feed upon. His stomach now hurt with almost as much insistence as his feet, and Drew could do nothing for either but stagger on in hopes of coming across salvation.

At last, and with little resistance, he fell onto his face and remained there, telling himself he needed the rest, and would presently rise to resume his wayward march north. It was greatly comforting, this new mode of nonmovement, and Drew briefly contemplated allowing himself to sleep, if that was possible under such a furnace as the sun. He decided he would allow himself to rest until nightfall, when the cooler air would make progress less difficult. It would have been better to lie down in shade, but he knew he could not lift himself just yet; maybe later.

"I think he sleeps," said a faintly mocking voice.

"Yes, he has no strength inside him now," came another.

"Better to let him sleep forever, do you think?"

"I think we must do this for him."

Drew raised his head, then levered his chest from the ground; he could do no more than that. Two slender Indians stood nearby, their coppery skins seeming to glow in the sunlight. They wore the long breechclout and tall moccasins and untamed hair of Apaches. Both carried government-issue Springfields, and their hips were heavily laden with ammunition. Their heads were bound in ragged cloth bands, and they wore doleful smiles on their handsome faces. They did not resemble bloodthirsty savages, were more like graceful desert spirits of some kind. Drew found it hard to credit their deeds, or to accept that these apparitions would presently do to him what they had done to Dobson and Taynton.

He brought himself to his knees by concentrating mightily, and surprised himself by croaking, "Water ..."

"To drink?" said the first Apache, coming nearer. "But that would be a waste."

"Soon now you will need no water," said the other.

"Water ...," Drew repeated, if only to delay his dying.

The first Apache shook his head. "No," he said, "we can give you none."

"We do not wish to," added the second. "You do not listen."

"White people are deaf people," agreed the first.

"A man who cannot hear, what good is he?"

"Or a woman."

"Yes, a woman too. Is this one a woman?"

"That may be. It has the feebleness of a woman."

They stood over Drew, cradling their rifles, a mild gloating in their features. Drew could smell their sweat and see clearly the many small scars etched into the skin of their muscular thighs. A rifle bore suddenly appeared inches from his nose.

"Should we play with this one?"

"I think I am too tired."

"I am not tired. Be at ease, I will play with him."

"If you wish."

"Jesus ...," said Drew.

"He calls for his savior," said the Apache who was not tired.

"Jesus ...," Drew said again. "Nail ... "

"What does he say?"

"He says our names that were."

"How can he know them?"

"You, soldier, how do you know to call us by these names? They are not good names!"

"No, they are not! Now we will both play with you for a long time."

"It's me ... Bones."

"Bones?"

The Apaches looked at each other.

"John Bones ...," Drew reminded them, "at San ... San Bartolomeo ... John Bones, dammit ..."

"Is it?" asked Nail in His Feet, peering closer.

Bleeding Heart of Jesus flipped Drew's hat off with the barrel of his gun. "It is, my brother. It is him, John Bones."

"How can he be a soldier, our friend John Bones? This can not be him!"

"It is him. He has made a bad choosing."

"Give him water."

An army canteen was offered to Drew. He unscrewed the cap and sipped, as he had been taught, then lost control and gulped greedily at the warm liquid, aware as he did so that his reunion with the mission boys of long ago was not yet a success. They stared at him with looks of consternation.

"He has good fortune. We would not have seen his face in the night."

"No, it would have been a bad thing to kill our friend without knowing."

"Why are you a soldier, John Bones?"

"I made a promise to a man. He gave me my life."

"That was a bad promise," said Bleeding Heart of Jesus.

"For my life, I would do the same," said Nail in His Feet, his tone sympathetic.

"Grandfather would not like to hear those words."

"Grandfather is dead," Nail in His Feet reminded.

"I'm sorry to hear that," said Drew. He could not tell if he was still considered a friend, given the colors of his uniform and skin.

"He knew this day would come," said Bleeding Heart of Jesus. "He told us so."

"Yes, we would meet with you again, John Bones: Grandfather told us this."

"It was you who let him inside San Bartolomeo to take us away and learn the true ways."

"Grandfather said we must be your friend forever."

"Well, uh, I'm sure the old gentleman was right."

"So we will not kill you."

"No, we will not."

"Thank you."

Drew stood up, legs quaking with relief. The brothers studied him.

"You are much older."

"You boys look different too."

"And our names, they are different."

"Yes, we do not use the names you once knew us by."

"Those are our shame."

"Now I am Panther Stalking."

"And I am Kills With a Smile."

"Grandfather gave us these names."

"He gave us the learning to kill white people."

"We have killed very many of them."

"I heard about it," said Drew. Congratulations did not seem to be in order. He was unsure what attitude to strike with these swaggering acquaintances from the past.

"Now you will tell us what you have done in the time that has gone by."

While Drew provided a summary of events, Panther and Smile led him a short distance to their new mules, and allowed him to select one. He chose his own.

"That is a good one," said Smile.

"I was myself riding that one," said Panther, "but you may have it."

"Where is it you wish to go, John Bones?"

"North, to Colorado."

"So the army does not take you again?"

"Yes."

"Then we will go with you."

"But we will come back," said Smile.

"Yes," agreed Panther. "We belong here."

"We will kill every white man."

"Unless they leave," added Panther.

"Yes, we will let them leave if they wish."

"We are fair."

"We keep our word."

"See how we kept our word to Grandfather and did not kill you?"

"I'm very appreciative," Drew assured them.

"Now you will be known to everyone," said Smile. "You will be the only white man to see our faces and live."

"No," corrected Panther. "We were seen by many in the jail at Magdalena, and they are all still living."

"Then we should go back there and kill them."

"Enough talk of killing. We have our friend John Bones, just as Grandfather said. We must take him away from here, to pay back what he did for Grandfather, and for us. Without John Bones we would still have the bad names, and be Christian men."

"Do not talk of things to make my insides sick."

The brothers kept up their mild wrangling for miles. Drew had been told that Apaches never spoke unless necessary, and saw that Smile and Panther were not ideal models of the breed. He supposed this was because they had spent too many of their early years at the mission, which had corrupted their natural Apache reticence. They had learned the murderous ways of their ancestors since having been liberated from San Bartolomeo by Smart Crow Making

Mischief, but they were a hybrid type of Indian, it seemed to Drew, as he listened to their petulant jabbering, a pair of scolding jays that delighted in pecking out the eyes of lesser birds.

In time, they felt silent, and Drew found himself able to remember Taynton. Until then, he had not spared his late friend much thought. He could not complain to his rescuers over their having killed someone he liked; it would mean nothing to them, Taynton's skin being white. Drew would have to swallow the loss without a mention, or risk Panther and Smile's turning against him. Without them, he might not reach the Colorado line. Curiously, he found he could not hate the brothers for their deeds, and this also bothered him. Was mere acquaintance sufficient for forgiveness? Drew could form no opinion, and in the end stopped trying. It was better to accept the things that had happened, incorporate them into his overall view of the world as a place in which events occurred without rhyme or reason, a constant jostling of actions and resultant reactions that were guided by no higher intelligence, no cosmic adjudicator. Smile and Panther had probably killed Taynton, instead of himself, simply because he was nearer, and for no other reason, certainly not because Smart Crow had predicted they would meet again. It was baffling, the way things turned out as they did.

The journey to Colorado lasted eleven days. Drew ate wild game shot by Panther Stalking and Kills With a Smile.

"We like these army guns," said Panther.

"They kill further off than any other."

"Springfield's a powerful piece," Drew concurred.

"But we wish they would shoot more than one bullet."

"You want a repeater, steal a Winchester."

"We have three already," boasted Smile. "We have a secret place where we keep guns."

"We wish to have a cannon also. Is there one at Fort Mobley?"

Drew recalled the small howitzer in the armory, its metal dusty from lack of use.

"No, and there's no need for you to kill anyone there either. No one ever goes out on patrol for the likes of you two. Leave the fort alone."

"We have seen there is no wall there. Why is that?"

"Nothing's the way it should be at Mobley."

Sometimes the brothers described their raids and ambushes to Drew, but he would not react to their stories, knowing they did this to goad him over the deaths of his own kind.

"You do not care that we do this?" asked Panther, when Drew had said nothing after hearing a particularly gruesome description of a family being scalped and violated.

"I care," said Drew, "but these people you speak of are dead, and nothing I say to you will make them live again."

"That is so."

"If I believed I could stop you from doing more of the same, just by talking to you, I would, but I see in your faces and hear in your voices that you like to do this killing. You like to give pain."

"Yes, we like this very much. Grandfather told us it is our life, our real Apache life, to kill whites and give pain to them before they die."

"They fear pain very much," said Smile, "and many of them will go away when they are told about the pain we give."

"Some will leave," Drew said, "but most will not. There are just too damn many for all of them to be scared of you all the time. You can never win against so many."

The brothers became silent for a while, then Panther said to Drew, "There is nothing else we can do."

"We have promised Grandfather," said Smile.

"And that's why I say nothing when you tell me what you've done," Drew said. "You won't change."

"No," agreed the brothers, without the least shade of regret, and the remainder of the ride that day was without talk of any kind.

Panther and Smile took care to avoid ranches and towns as they escorted Drew north. The trio passed the outposts of white civilization in darkness, rather than risk being seen.

"I guess you'll be stopping by at some of these places on your way back," said Drew.

"Yes, we will kill some more of your people. Even their dogs will die."

"We have a way to make them not smell us."

"Yes, white dogs are sleepy fools."

"Will you tell us not to do this, John Bones?"

"I know whatever I say means nothing to you."

"Yes, but you may ask if you wish."

"We will listen to your words," Panther assured him.

"Will my words mean more than your grandfather's words?"

The brothers shook their heads.

"Then I'll save my breath," said Drew.

"You will let us kill your kind without asking us not to? Do you hate them all as you hate the army men?"

"Look, if you want me to beg you not to kill anyone, all right, I will. I don't know if it's a game with you, or if you'll listen."

"We are listening, John Bones," said Panther.

"Then I ask you not to kill anymore. Go down to Mexico and do something else with the days you have left."

"Do you beg us to do this thing?"

"Yes, I beg you."

The brothers looked at each other.

"What will you give us in return?"

"Give you? I have nothing to give."

"Will you give us one of your small fingers?"

"What?"

"Just one," said Smile. "You may keep the other."

"You'd quit the killing if I let you cut off my finger?"

"Yes, we will do this."

"Will you let us have your finger, John Bones?"

Drew stopped his mule. "Yes," he said. It was the least he could do for the memory of Taynton.

The brothers dismounted. "Get down," Drew was told, then Panther drew his knife.

"Put the blade through a fire first," Drew said.

A small pile of brushwood was gathered and kindled. Panther passed his knife back and forth in the flames, grinning at Drew.

"You have told us we like to give pain," said Smile. "We know you think we are cruel for this, so you will cut off the finger yourself."

"I don't know that I could do that," Drew said, his stomach already lurching at what was to come. He began to wish he had not struck so humanitarian a bargain with the brothers; it wasn't as if anyone would ever hear about his sacrifice and laud him for a hero.

"You must do it, John Bones. We can not hurt you, or Grandfather would be angry."

"Suit yourselves," Drew said.

He held out his hand for the knife. Panther passed it to him. Drew could feel the heat of the metal as he held the blade close and saw the Pittsburgh manufacturer's name stamped below the hilt. It was an excellent knife, honed to razor sharpness. The brothers watched as Drew set his left little finger against the pommel of his saddle and touched the blade to his skin, then raised it several inches. He would use its weight in the manner of an ax, rather than a saw, and be done with the act in seconds.

Panther and Smile were mildly impressed that Drew cut off his finger without a sound, without much more than a compression of the lips. They liked the way he thrust the knife blade into the ground to clean it, then calmly pinched the bleeding stump between his fingertips.

"There," he said, sounding angry.

Panther retrieved his knife. Smile picked up Drew's finger and examined it before tossing the scrap of flesh into the fire. Drew quickly smelled a part of himself burning, but was in no mood to appreciate the uniqueness of the situation.

Panther and Smile mounted their mules.

"Now we go a different way to you," said Smile.

"You told me you'd take me all the way to Colorado."

"And you are there. Your finger burns in Colorado."

Drew felt vaguely cheated. His hand hurt, and the pain was building by the second. "Now you'll go to Mexico," he said, "and not kill anyone there, or on the way there."

Panther shook his head. "We will do as we please. We will kill many people yet. We promise you this."

"You ... you said if I cut off my finger you wouldn't do that any-more ...!"

Smile nodded. "Yes, we said this, but we lied. Grandfather told us never to harm you, but we have told ourselves to spill blood into the earth from every white skin we can, so your blood must touch the earth, or we will not have done as we told ourselves we would. We did you no harm, and your blood has been spilled."

"This way is best," Panther said.

"Now we will never see you again."

"Good-bye, John Bones. You have lost a little part of your hand to learn a big truth."

"Yes," agreed Smile, "and you will not forget a thing learned in pain."

"What thing! What thing did I learn but that you're liars!"

Panther said, "Never take the word of any man who is not blood of your blood."

They left him there, with his mule and burning finger, in a uniform that could yet get him hanged.

24

His first reaction, when he woke up toothless, was surprise; where was the dentist, Dr. Maxwell? Clay felt his body weighing heavy as lead on the bed beneath him. Where was that bed again? He couldn't remember the hotel's name, let alone the town, but Dr. Maxwell's name was burned into his brain. Maxwell had promised painless removal of all Clay's diseased teeth at a single session of extraction, this operation to be followed by the fitting of a set of dentures to replace what nature had seen fit to take from Clay well in advance of his years.

"Your mouth, Mr. Dugan," he had been told, "is the mouth of a man nearing seventy. Do you have the habit of chewing tobacco regularly?"

"Does it smell like I do?"

"Frankly, Mr. Dugan, I doubt that I could detect the odor among the general air of oral decay you carry. They must all come out, every tooth, before the jawbones become infected. You wouldn't wish that fate on yourself, sir, believe me, for I have seen the results of indecision in cases such as this. Horrible, sir, simply horrible results that could have been avoided by prudent and timely investment in a painless process of my own devising, which I might add is far ahead of the common practices."

"Painless?"

"No more discomforting than a stubbed toe, I guarantee."

"All of them?"

"Without exception, and without delay."

"Well, go ahead and do it while I'm here."

"I require payment in advance, Mr. Dugan."

"How much?"

"One dollar per tooth."

"How many teeth in my head, Maxwell?"

"Thirty-two, including your wisdom teeth, which certainly should have come out long ago."

"They never did give me any trouble till the rest of them started paining."

"Thirty-two dollars, Mr. Dugan, in advance if you please."

Clay counted out the cash. Maxwell had no office, being a dentist of the traveling school. His work was performed in whatever hotel room he happened to be occupying, so Clay lay down on the bed with his shirt open and a rubber sheet spread beneath his upper torso "for the inevitable runoff," Maxwell explained.

"Nitrous oxide?" Clay inquired, as Maxwell made his preparations.

"Far too unpredictable. Ether's my preference."

An assortment of wicked-looking instruments was laid out alongside Clay while Maxwell hummed tunelessly to himself. Clay began to rise, but the dentist pressed him down again with a reassuring hand. "The moment of truth, Mr. Dugan. Do you submit to my process of guaranteed painlessness, or do you invite facial deformity within twelve months or less? The choice is yours."

"Go ahead, but I want plenty of that ether, you hear?"

"I never stint my patients, sir, you may be assured."

Maxwell unstoppered a small bottle and tipped a portion of the contents onto a handkerchief. The cloth was brought to Clay's face like a funeral shroud, and laid over his nose. He felt a mule kick him slowly between the eyes, then experienced a sinking that carried him down through the unyielding hotel mattress to a place of welcoming darkness where thought was neither possible nor desirable.

His gradual return to consciousness was unpleasant. Clay's mouth howled with absence of the familiar pegs; each had been replaced with a white-hot iron screw, it seemed, and Clay was upset that Dr. Maxwell's promise had been reneged upon. Between his upper and lower gums there existed a region of torment no man should have had to endure without whiskey to blur its borders, and Clay had none, or did he? He could not recall in detail the exact nature of his circumstances prior to Maxwell's application of the ether-drenched handkerchief. The operation had certainly taken place, but where was the good doctor?

Clay levered himself upright, and was appalled at the bloody mess lacing his chest and shirt. He could feel dried blood around his neck like a crackling collar, and found he could not separate his jaws for the red cement bonding them. The room was occupied only by himself. It shouldn't have been that way. Clay was beginning to feel angry, when anger was replaced by shock at what he saw on the bedside bureau. A set of dentures grinned with skeletal cheeriness at him, surrounded by thirty-two lumps of rotting human ivory, each extracted tooth nested firmly in a bed of dull scarlet tissue; evidently the parting of the ways had not been without difficulty. Clay thought for a moment he might vomit, but was able to restrain himself by remembering that he was unable to open his mouth. Anger returned, magnified many times. He hurt. He hurt a great deal, and his thirty-two dollars had been set down as a guarantee against any such physical insult. He would get the money back, and maybe extract by fist a number of Maxwell's own molars and incisors.

On his feet at last, Clay was able to stagger toward the small mirror above the washbasin and jug. What he saw there caused his bloodied jaws to separate with shock, enabling them to begin bleeding anew. The lower portion of his face had been reduced, made less, shrunken somehow despite obvious swelling along the jawline. Were the obscene false teeth leering at his bedside supposed to fill it out again? Where was that goddamn doctor! Now that his mouth could be opened, Clay stared into a maw unrecognizable as his own, and was frightened by its ugliness and the renewed gobbets of blood spilling down his stubbled chin. ... He had shaved the morning he came to Maxwell's room, hadn't he? How much time had passed while he lay unconscious?

Clay lunged unsteadily for the door and flung it open. He pawed his way along the corridor walls to the stairs, and eased himself down to the lobby, where he encountered a clerk whose face registered considerable alarm the moment Clay began lurching toward him.

"Whay yay inth thiyy!" Clay demanded.

"I ... pardon me?"

"Whay nyay inth thiyy, gonndammith!"

"What ... day, sir? Wednesday, sir ..."

"Wenschnay ...?"

"Yessir ..."

"Wher'th Noctor Mathwell?"

"Dr. Maxwell? He left yesterday, sir. He left instructions not to disturb you. ..."

"He wha ...? Hunnavabith!"

"Are you all right, sir?"

"Hrain?"

"Pardon me, sir?"

"Mathwell tae the hrain?"

"The train, yessir, he did."

"Gonndamn!"

"Can I get you anything, sir!"

"Whithkey!"

"Yessir, I'll send a boy up directly."

"Waih ... Mathwell pay?"

"Pay? For the room, sir?"

Clay nodded. The desk clerk shook his head. "He ... he said you'd take care of that, sir. ..."

"Hunnavabith!"

While he recovered from Maxwell's ministrations, Clay planned several kinds of revenge, all centered upon pain of one kind or another. He would track the dentist down with the same determination he employed to find outlaws, and when he caught up with Maxwell there would be nothing so merciful as an ultimatum and a bullet. For the deceitful dentist there would be torture, probably administered with his own tools, but Clay would not be without clemency; he would allow the doctor to give himself a stiff dose of ether first. Or maybe he wouldn't. Clay's fury was restoked when, after three days, he tried fitting the rubber gums, with their embedded porcelain teeth, into his gradually healing mouth, and found that, like some simple yet abstruse equation, two into one simply would not go.

Remembrance had returned after Clay's first bout with the whiskey bottle. He was in Pueblo, Colorado, and his pockets had been stuffed with bills of small denomination earned by the capture of one William Sneed, escapee from a federal penitentiary. His two horses were stabled at the livery down the street, and he had not even had time to find a room for himself before noticing Maxwell's flier pasted onto a wall. His teeth had been tormenting him for months, and Clay knew, to blunt the pain, that he was drinking far too much, so he asked directions and went straight to the dentist's hotel room, the room he had woken up in twenty-four hours later. Maxwell had not gone through his pockets before departing, so although Clay was without teeth, he was not without cash. The situation could have been worse.

Clay's temper began to mellow as his gums healed, and the rubber monstrosities fitted a little easier into his violated oral cavity each day. Maybe Maxwell had been a professional after all, even if his bedside manner allowed much latitude for doubt. Clay was becoming heartily sick of soup and mush by then, and yearned with the passion of a beef-eating man for steak, thick and rich and sizzling, a slice of heaven awaiting the onslaught of teeth, real or manufactured.

Ten days after Maxwell's extractions, Clay found he could cram the dentures inside his mouth and keep them there for up to an hour at a time. They occupied his head with the snugness of a pair of boot heels, and were about as useful; biting an apple was an exercise in mess and humiliation. Clay practiced eating alone until he could consume a meal without spoiling his vest.

Three weeks after his teeth had come out, Clay decided he required another correction to his former self, and visited an optician, where he was fitted with spectacles. The crisp new world he saw around himself was almost compensation enough for the bitterness he felt at looking like some bookish type. He consoled himself with the thought that he no longer looked quite so mean, which might allow him to approach his prey in disguise, so to speak, without them suspecting the true nature of his calling. Of course, the holes in his cheeks gave the lie to that notion. He was simply a peculiar-looking man, who had become even more peculiar-looking during his stay in Pueblo. The upper row of false teeth resembled tightly packed tombstones, and the lower set stood together like a phalanx of Roman shields. They were larger than his original teeth, and the added thickness of the rubber gums distorted his jaw, making his long face even longer. He didn't like the new bulkiness inside his mouth, or the constant rubbery taste against his tongue, and he didn't like the weight of the spectacles across the bridge of his nose, or the irritating wire hooks behind his ears. Clay left town a discontented man.

Traveling south, he learned of a proclamation issued by the Chicago headquarters of the Army Division of the Missouri, which effectively encompassed all of the central United States. Citizens in the area involved were encouraged to turn in army deserters for punishment. Soldiers apparently were leaving their units in record numbers, and the government could not spare the manpower to hunt them down for recapture and court-martial. A modest reward was offered for each man returned to army custody, and Clay decided he would add deserters to his list of two-legged quarry. He had no grudge against them, the way he did against lawbreakers of more serious ilk, but if a man was moron enough to join the army, he should stay there, in Clay's opinion, and so he felt there was justification in rounding up the runaways, even if the pay for doing so was not comparable with the bounty on killers and thieves.

In Walsenburg he stopped to cut the dryness in his throat with whiskey, and saw in the bar, not fifteen feet from him, a pair of boots with the unmistakable cut of the cavalry. The man inside the boots was young, and evidently not very bright, since his tight pants also were army issue, the yellow leg stripes having been removed to reveal a strip of darker blue material beneath; even the galluses holding up his pants were standard army issue. Clay couldn't credit the young man's foolishness; he had deserter written on him as surely as if he carried a sign.

The deserter was not alone, however. He drank with several other men, and the ease with which they talked among themselves and with the barman suggested they were locals. Clay reasoned that if they had grown fond of the deserter among them, they would most likely resist any attempt on Clay's part to drag the young man away for incarceration. No normal man would blame another for leaving so constricting an institution as the army. Clay himself could see their point, but the young man drinking beer along the bar represented fifty dollars, and Clay was low on funds after purchasing teeth and spectacles for himself. He would have to wait until his prey was alone; in effect, he would have to kidnap him.

Clay remained in the bar till evening, nursing just three shots of liquor, keeping his eyes down to avoid attracting attention to himself, yet maintaining a constant watch on the young deserter. At sundown a woman just out of girlhood came inside and stood near the same knot of drinkers Clay had been watching. When finally her presence was noticed, the young man went to her, followed by comments from his friends concerning the length of the woman's apron strings. The couple left, the man happier than the woman.

Clay was not pleased with this development. Were they married? He didn't wish to take a husband from his wife. Still, a deserter should know better than to mix matrimony with the military. He waited less than thirty seconds, then went outside. The couple could be seen on the sidewalk a short distance away, the man leaning on the woman, talking loudly and singing off-key. Clay followed them along the darkening street to the edge of town, and watched them enter a small frame house with a stable in the rear. He walked around the house to count the doors and windows capable of allowing a man a fast exit, then stopped beside the stableyard. A mule stood near the pole fence, and even in the dwindling light of evening, Clay could clearly make out the U.S. branded onto its rump. Clumsy efforts had been made to alter the letters to 0.8., and a broad arrowhead or rafter was included above them to complete the change. Clay found he had even less respect for the young man now that he had seen how incredibly slipshod were the means he had employed to disguise his crime. Clay bet the fool still had his service pistol stashed in a trunk somewhere, with the army holster and belt wrapped around it. Anyone that dumb, he reasoned, was just asking for time in the stockade.

Clay returned to the center of town and found the only restaurant. He ate slowly, making plans. The waiter watched him closely, with suspicion, and Clay was obliged to set his mind at ease by opening a conversation about the weather, until the waiter accepted that the stranger with a face like a bad dream was simply an ugly nonentity. Clay had coffee, paid and left.

He led his horses to the frame house, noting with satisfaction the distance between it and the nearest dwelling; if he could get the fool outside without too much squawking, he could be on his way to a town larger than Walsenburg, where the deserter could be handed over to federal authorities. The woman would probably be a problem, though. Clay didn't want to tie and gag her to ensure cooperation. He would meet the situation as it developed.

Before knocking on the door, he stepped through the stableyard fence and caught the mule by its halter, then saddled and bridled it, ready for use by the man who soon would be his prisoner. At least the young man had seen fit to dispose of his army saddle and use the regular type. Clay tied the mule to the stable door, then led his horses around to the front of the house. He hitched them to the rail, and knocked on the door.

The young man opened it. "Evening," he said, still drunk. Behind him, Clay could see the woman sulking at a table.

"Evening. Interested in selling your mule?"

"Mule? No; I like him plenty."

"I could make you a more than fair offer. I need a good mule."

"There's a horseyard in town that'll sell you one."

"Well, I was more partial to yours. How much you want for him?"

"Mister, I wouldn't sell that animal for twenty new dollars."

"How about twenty-five?"

"Take it," said the woman, approaching the door. "Let him in and don't be so rude."

"You mind your mouth," the young man advised her, but stepped aside for Clay to enter the house.

"Get you something?" the woman asked.

"Thank you, ma'am; I just now ate."

"Well, sit yourself down anyway," she said.

Clay took a chair at the table, and the young man sat opposite him. The woman busied herself by the stove, pretending not to listen.

"Bill Adams," said Clay.

"Euen Christy. Twenty-five dollars, you said."

"I did."

"That's a lot more'n he's worth, but I expect you already know that, am I right? What kind of work are you in, mister?"

"All kinds. I move around. I need a reliable mule."

"Well, that one ain't reliable at all. You wouldn't want him, I can tell you that right now."

"How about we go take a look at him."

"I already looked at him today. He's not for you."

Clay knew he had not convinced Christy. It was his scarred face that had done it. One look, and the woman was all sympathy and politeness, the man openly suspicious.

"You're the one was in the saloon today."

"I was. Interesting brand on it, your mule."

"If you say so."

Clay saw the guarded look that came into Christy's eyes.

"Rafter circle eight. I'm not familiar with that."

"Well, you wouldn't be, without you're from around here."

"Your spread, this rafter circle eight?"

"You might say. You don't want that mule, do you?"

"I'd settle for you instead, Christy. That your real name? Would that be Corporal Christy? I just don't see you ranked any higher than that."

"What ...?"

"You can come along easy if you want, or hard, if that's your preferment; I don't care."

"You don't know what you're talkin' about...."

"I do, and you do too. Get a jacket on; it's cool outside."

"To hell with you, mister."

Christy stood and moved toward a gun belt hanging on the wall. Clay stood and swung open his coat. The sawed-off shotgun on its shoulder lanyard was up and cocked in a second. Christy's mouth gaped, and his woman began to moan, "Don't hurt him, mister, don't hurt him, he never done a thing, he's all I got, mister...."

"I ain't a deserter! You got the wrong man here.... See, I got the mule off of a feller come through here one night, army feller he was, all wore out and needing help, so I give him some old clothes and a ten-dollar horse for the mule and his pants and his boots.... I'm not him, mister, ask anyone hereabouts, I lived here a year and more."

"He's not the one, not the one you want, mister, please don't hurt him...."

"How long since you did the trade?" Clay demanded.

"Eight, nine days ... He was all wore out, and with a wounded hand, so I done what the Samaritan done, mister, you can't fault me for that, I reckon."

"Put the gun down, mister," the woman begged. "He went on north of here, if you want to take out after him."

Clay felt cheated. He could not doubt the genuine terror of the couple, and his annoyance at having misjudged the circumstances made him angry. Christy and his woman were not deserving of any explanation. He told them to sit down at the table and stay there without moving while they slowly counted to one hundred. They sat immediately. Clay lowered his shotgun as he went to the door. He unhitched his horses, mounted and became a part of the night.

Pursuit of the deserter was pointless. Instead, Clay drifted west toward Alamosa. What he needed was a job. His duties back in Keyhoe had been tedious for the most part, but the money was steady. It had been Sophie who drove him away from that line of work, not the work itself. Maybe the time had come, after his wandering for more than a year, to try again in some small town, or even a big one, and put behind him his saddle tramp days. His dentures distracted him from this fresh line of thought, and he extracted them to concentrate on what he realized was nothing less than a genuine and urgent change of heart. He could live in a house again, and not be looked down upon by law-enforcement officers, who saw him as a professional bounty killer. Clay suspected they were envious, in some ways, of his free-ranging approach to the elimination of badmen, but he acknowledged that, if given the chance to stand again in the boots of a sheriff or marshal, he would view such types as himself with a less than favorable eye. It was a moral contradiction, but Clay could live with it, for the sake of regular wages and a roof to keep the sky from his shoulders.

Alamosa seemed a likely place to begin searching out a place for himself in the standard order of things. He entered the office of the town marshal and inquired if there was any opening for a deputy marshal in a town that size. The man behind the desk looked him up and down, then asked his name.

"Clay Dugan."

"Out of Kansas?"

"That's right."

The man nodded his head several times, then said, "Don't believe I could find a place for a man that kills his own blood."

Clay was taken aback by this. "You're misinformed."

"Nope."

"My boy ... my boy was suffering."

"So you're saying you did it?"

"No ... I'm saying if I did what ... what my wife says I did, it would've been the right thing to do, end his suffering.... Wouldn't any man do that for his son? Wouldn't you?"

"I'd leave it up to the Lord, is what I'd do, mister."

Clay turned and left. He stayed in Alamosa only for the time required to replenish his supplies, then aimed himself west again. The incident had shaken him. He had not expected news of Silan's death to pass beyond the boundaries of Keyhoe County, yet here was the proof it had done just that. He supposed the story had gone even further. There had often been strange glances given him in the past year, when he stated his name in order to collect reward money for his services, but he attributed these to his unusual appearance and the reviled nature of his profession. Had the looks been on account of Sophie and Silan? He supposed it would be this way wherever he went, unless he outran the story by journeying as far as California or Oregon.

But that would be cowardice, he told himself. He was not ashamed of what he had done for poor Silan (but was, he admitted, ashamed for having denied it in front of the Alamosa marshal) and could not see any life for himself that involved flight from the consequences of his act, whether by distance or by changing his name. He was Clay Dugan, and he had done what he did, and if the world made him an outcast because of it, then that was the lot he would accept. His vision of a return to the ordinary society of townsfolk had been a mirage, an insubstantial haze distorting reality, softening the facts. Clay knew now what those facts were, and he would never again deny or ignore them. If a bed of nails was to be his fate, then he would toughen his spine to accommodate it, and the world could go hang itself by its righteous neck.

Westering still toward Durango, Clay encountered an uncommon traveler. The canvas-covered wagon was not an incongruous feature in land without trails, but its smallness was emphasized by the expanse of broad grassland around it and the massiveness of the San Juan Mountains beyond. He approached out of curiosity, rather than any need for conversation, and saw a thin man dressed in black asleep on the wagon seat while his team cropped grass. Their nickerings as Clay's horses came closer woke the man, and he reached hastily for something on the seat beside him. Clay thought at first it might have been a gun, which struck him as a sensible precaution, but it was a Bible. The man clutched it to his chest like armor as Clay drew near.

"Morning," Clay said.

"Blessings be upon you," the man responded.

Clay saw lettering along the side of the wagon: A FALSE BALANCE IS ABOMINATION TO THE LORD: BUT A JUST WEIGHT IS HIS DELIGHT. PROVERBS 11:1.

He had come upon such men as this before, wilderness preachers who shunned the comforts of civilization, the better to proselytize among the more remote regions of the west. Although he had no use for religion, Clay felt such men were kindred spirits to himself, in that they pursued their calling without regard for its inconveniences and loneliness. The man looked half starved to Clay's eyes, and was probably one of the most committed of the breed, the type Clay dubbed "wild-eyed and woolly," for the deliberate neglect of their bodies in favor of their souls. For these men, spreading the gospel through inhospitable territory was not enough; they must suffer in the doing of it, for the purging of their souls. It was wasted effort, so far as Clay was concerned, but he had respect for any man who would risk himself for an ideal, no matter how foolish the quest.

"Clay Dugan," he said.

"Dugan?"

"Heard the name before?"

Clay presumed even this wanderer of mountain meadows had heard of his mercy killing back in Kansas. He doubted that a preacher would understand or condone what he had done. He was prepared to ride on in an instant if the man on the wagon began lecturing him on the folly and evil of his chosen ways.

But the preacher shook his head. "No," he said, then added, as if remembering himself only now, "Reverend Francis Wixson, sir."

Wixson's eyes were pale, the skin stretched tightly over his face. The tendons in his hands stood out like wires, and his nails were gray and broken. Clay saw an unsocked toe peeping from a hole in the preacher's left boot.

"Reverend, I'm about to make myself some grub, and it won't bother me to make double portions, if you'd be kind enough to eat with me."

"Mr. Dugan, you will find I am kindness personified."

Clay dismounted and began unpacking flour and jerked meat. Wixson climbed weakly down from his wagon and began gathering such wood as could be found among the knee-high grasses. Clay watched from the corner of his eye as the preacher stumbled excitedly about his task. He would have to make a big meal for this starving man. He would even open the can of peach preserves he had been saving.

While the sourdough was mixed and poured into a frying pan, Wixson gnawed without shame at several strips of beef. Clay envied the man his natural teeth; he could no longer tug at his own food with such determination, had instead to cut off a portion and use his porcelain molars to grind it into a digestible state before he swallowed.

"You see before you a man without means, Mr. Dugan."

"Been that way myself from time to time."

"I must rely on charity for my bread, but there are so few souls hereabouts to practice their charity upon me."

Clay heard the undertone of pride as Wixson stated his dilemma; this one was wild-eyed and woolly for sure, probably more inclined to pass through heaven's gate than resort to easier pastures for his preaching.

"It's lonely country all right."

"May I ask what takes you across it?"

"I'm looking for someone, Reverend, several someones, as a matter of fact."

"It may be that I've seen them."

Clay fetched a handful of reward fliers from his packhorse and set them down before his guest. Wixson stared at the names and faces and their lists of wrongdoing.

"Are you a federal officer, Mr. Dugan?"

"I'm an independent. Federals tend to push paper around rather than go after a man that needs going after."

"I see. You ... hunt these fellows down for the posted reward moneys?"

"That's what I do. Outlaws, they like to hole up in lonely places generally, so they can see any man that's coming, and make plans to ambush him if they figure him to be a federal."

"And how do you avoid being shot at, Mr. Dugan?"

"By not looking like a federal, and not carrying a badge."

"This is lucrative work?"

"I get by. There are more sinners on earth than there are outlaws, Reverend, but there's plenty of outlaws and not enough lawmen, so I step right into the breach and bring them to justice."

"And if they do not come willingly?"

"I hand them a slice of justice right there, twelve gauge."

"Sir, I have eaten your food, and will eat more, but I cannot do so without confessing to you that I find your area of employment vile. I apologize for my tongue."

"Say what you like, I don't mind. There's plenty think like you do, town people mostly. Folks further out, they know what it is to be a hundred miles from the law when scum like these come riding up to their door."

He swept up the fliers and returned them to his pack animal. When he returned to the fire, Clay kept his eyes on the frying pan.

Wixson waited some minutes before asking, "Do you believe in the existence of the soul, Mr. Dugan?"

"If I've got one, Reverend, it isn't hurting from the job I do."

"You misunderstand me. I ask the question from a purely speculative or philosophical point of view."

"Then I can't answer, because I don't know. Near as I can tell, no one does, not even preachers, pardon me."

"My own particular interest, Mr. Dugan, lies in proving the existence, the actual and scientifically verifiable existence, of this shadowy thing we all have heard of, and none of us seen, even though it resides in every living human, good or bad, heathen or Christian. I am engaged in a personal search for the invisible."

"Seems like a fair amount to bite off."

"My work requires more than faith alone, and I am prepared. Allow me to show you."

Wixson levered himself up from the fire and led Clay to his wagon. He threw open the canvas flap at the rear, then stepped aside to allow Clay a clear view of the apparatus within. Clay saw an arrangement of solid brass rods and levers and platforms.

"What is it?"

"A beam balance, Mr. Dugan, and an expensive one. Its original purpose was to weigh cotton bales, but I have had its mechanism refined by an instrument maker from Massachusetts to render it capable of measuring the most minute fraction of an ounce. This device is capable of registering the weight of a feather, and is unique in all the world. I have beggared myself in its perfection. It is an instrument without peer, Mr. Dugan, and is the reason you find me in dire straits."

"What exactly does it do, besides weigh feathers?"

"The two panniers receive, on one side, whatever object is to be weighed, and, on the other, the requisite brass weights of certified standard measure. I have augmented the original set, whose lowest piece was just one pound, with additional weights down to one one-hundredth of an ounce. You see there the weights arranged according to size along the walls. My vehicle is perfectly balanced. 'A false balance is abomination to the Lord: but a just weight is his delight.'"

Clay asked, "But what exactly is it that you weigh on this contraption, Reverend?"

"Please, sir, do not refer to the balance as a contraption. This is a scientific instrument, the fruit of man's best endeavor, and engaged in holy work. What work, you ask, and I reply: the work that transcends all others!"

"What work is that, Reverend?"

"I have not made myself clear. The work of proving to the misled and unconvinced and doubting Thomases of the world that there exists within each and every one of them an immortal soul, a real and actual thing of physical substance which coincides in shape and proportion with the gross body of flesh and blood we all are heir to as mortal men."

"You weigh people?"

"Dying people, Mr. Dugan, to the very breath in their lungs. In your line of work you will doubtless have heard the death rattle as that final breath is expelled, and my device is so finely balanced it registers the expiration of that breath. I know that a man has breathed his last when the weights tell me so."

"Holding a mirror to the lips is easier."

"Let me finish. Within minutes of that final breath, my balance registers yet another loss, in every case. The loss is barely perceptible, even to an instrument such as this, but there is no doubt such a lessening of weight does occur. Can you guess what causes it, Mr. Dugan?"

"Well, now, I guess that would be the soul departing the body, if what they say is true."

"You're perfectly correct. I have weighed, at the moment of release, a total of eighteen persons thus far, and in each case have noted the phenomenon. The human soul, Mr. Dugan weighs between two and three hundredths of an ounce. I cannot explain the difference in weight for each soul, but differences there surely are, and they do not conform to advanced age, the cause of death, or the gender of the deceased. It may be that with further research into the mystery, and the compiling of more extended notations of soul weights, a pattern will emerge to indicate the exact nature of God's presence in us all."

"Interesting work, Reverend."

"Indeed, but so frustrating. I am aware that what I say has a macabre ring to it, but the fact is, sir, I require more dying persons in order to establish a lengthier set of figures."

"You'd be better off in a big town."

Clay was enjoying the conversation. He had several times met persons of unsound mind, but never one so loquacious and articulate. Wixson's crackbrained theory, in combination with the unusual machine, presented a picture of lunacy so piquant it made Clay a little sad.

Wixson shook his head. "I have on a number of occasions attempted to do just that, but somehow townspeople see fit to move me on. They have no curiosity over this greatest of discoveries, no interest at all. That is the proof, if proof were needed, we live in the most godless times of all since the Flood. Which of God's creatures, even the lowliest, would not wish to know such things, were he given the mind and tongue of man? Not one! But man himself laughs at the notion of a soul possessing actual weight and substance."

"There's a considerable number of fools around, I'll grant you."

"But here you are, a hunter of men, and you understand. Does this suggest a world made topsy-turvy, Mr. Dugan?"

"It might. I'm not given to philosophy."

"Then give me your opinion on a further step I intend taking, when my financial condition improves. Are you familiar with the principles of modern photography?"

"I've got a rough idea how it works."

"It is my intention to create, possibly with the help of an expert in the photographical science, a new kind of developing plate, one that will reveal, possibly in negative outline, the very shape of the soul as it departs its prison of flesh."

"You'd link the camera somehow to the scales."

"Yes! The fractional decrease in weight will trip the lens shutter at precisely the right moment. Your grasp of the concept is gratifying, Mr. Dugan. A man of alertness like yourself would make an admirable partner in the venture."

Clay shifted uncomfortably inside his boots. "Can't help you there, Reverend. My time's pretty much cut out for me, doing what I do. A professional photographer is the man for you."

"I suppose." Wixson's face registered deep disappointment.

"Sourdough's just about done, I'd say," Clay told him, and led the madman back to the fire.

While they ate, Wixson talked of having been granted his vision of measuring the soul's weight while watching cotton bales being weighed in New Orleans. The whiteness of the boles peeping from splits in the burlap baling material had reminded him of clouds, then ghosts, and so his revelation was visited upon him, with such force it threw him to the ground. He had worked hard for a year to purchase a beam balance big enough to place a body on, then hired a skilled artisan to refine its accuracy to the impossible scale he had described. "My balance is my life now, Mr. Dugan, and in following the star I have been told to, I have found a peace of mind I never knew before. That, too, is why I prefer the open spaces of our great land. God is here in greater abundance than in the cities. Satan has created such places as repositories for the damned."

"Could be," Clay murmured.

"Are you ... currently anticipating the capture of some outlaws, Mr. Dugan?"

"There's a bad bunch in Montezuma County. Could be I'll get a couple or three."

"And are men such as you find inclined to ... resist arrest?"

"More often than not."

"And you perforce are obliged to shoot at them."

"I am."

"I wonder, Mr. Dugan, if it might not be possible that I accompany you to Montezuma County. These fellows could serve the cause of science and Christianity both before they expire, don't you think? It would be compensation of a kind, for having lived a life of violence and criminality."

"Reverend, that just isn't going to be possible. Your wagon there won't go where I need to go. I'm sorry."

"Ah, yes, the beaten trail leads to no outlaw roost."

"But I wish you luck with your work."

"And I thank you for that."

They parted company early in the afternoon. Clay watched Wixson's wagon lurch toward the east, and wondered how long such a man, burdened with such a hopeless task, could survive alone. It was none of Clay's problem, but he worried a little as he continued west toward the mountains.

He felt the chill of their peaks already. The higher regions were scattered with yellow and red, and Clay knew the avalanche of color would have spilled down into the lower valley floors by the time he crossed the ranges to Montezuma County. He supposed everything he saw around him was beautiful, whether it had been created by Wixson's God or some great natural force blindly going about its endless business of growth and decay.

Beauty was not a subject Clay dwelt upon often, and when he

did, he assigned it almost exclusively to certain horses (Sunrise had been a prime example) or women. In particular, Clay considered ideal the model for a picture he had found on the inside of a cigar box lid in some hotel room in Wyoming. He had discarded the box, having no use for it, but saved the lid, and two or three times a week would take it from his saddlebags to stare with longing at the beautiful woman depicted there. *Venus Revealed* was the title of the picture, and Clay was in love with it. This creamy creature sprawled among inviting pillows was Clay's notion of the perfect woman, from her redly painted toes to her voluminous hair. He loved her Cupid's bow of a mouth; he wanted to run his hand along the sweep of her waist and hips, and cradle the fullness of her pink-nippled breasts; he loved her deeply indented navel and plump knees, and it made him sick to know that a woman like that would never so much as look at a homely man like himself. The cigar box lady was as remote from Clay's world as the Venus of myth, and it irritated him that he hadn't the strength of will to dispose of her before his occasional glancings at the lid became daily occurrences. He knew himself for a fool, but could do nothing about it.

During the week he required to reach Durango, Clay moped with unaccustomed intensity. He had always considered himself something of a stoic, and now it seemed he was unable to put down the sense of pity he felt toward himself. It was a distressing time, and Clay yearned, atypically, for human company. Maybe it had been the demented preacher who opened this door to introspection, or the unfortunate interview with the Alamosa marshal. It was all well and good to declare himself an outcast if that was what society deemed him fit for, another thing again to be content in that role. Yet what else was there for him to do? If he could not avenge the holes in his cheeks and the memory of his soiled pants by hunting down the thousand and one siblings in crime of the Chaffey brothers, what could he do? There was no other occupation so perfectly suited to him, given his personal history, his gloomy temperament and his intolerance of wrongdoing. The very root of his character demanded that he keep on with the life he was living, whatever his deepest reservations might be.

Surrounded by towering beauty, a landscape so unspoiled he might have been journeying through some mountainous Eden, Clay could only look upon such magnificence as mockery of himself and his puny troubles. Even being aware that he had correctly proportioned himself among this landscape of gorgeous excess brought him no shred of pride, no wry acknowledgment of his own wisdom in so seeing the truth. He was who he was, and no other self could be inserted into the actuality he inhabited with such unwillingness.

Halfway to his destination, Clay awoke one night and rolled from beneath his blankets to prowl about the campfire in nothing but his grimy union suit, while he attempted to recapture a dream so disturbing it had wakened him. A young girl had appeared before him while he traveled an unknown road, a girl with a blue mark on one side of her face, like the mask of a raccoon. The mark accentuated one of her eyes, made it appear to glow with unnatural light, and the brilliance of it had swept across him like the beam from a lighthouse. "Where are you? Who are you?" the girl had asked, without once moving her lips, and Clay had been afraid to answer, since it was clear even to a hardheaded man like himself that the girl was no girl, but an imp in cunning disguise, an innocent female sent to lure him down among the darkness she had sprung from. He lifted his dream hand to ward off the light from her masked eye, and the action had been imitated by his physical body, waking him with a hammering heart to stride about the glowing coals with his shotgun cocked and ready for any other demons that might spring from the darkness inside his head.

"Well, all right!" he bellowed at shadows beyond the light. "All right, then! Here I am!"

Clay's horses stamped and snorted as he strode back and forth in a frenzy of uncoordinated movement, afraid of he knew not what. Eventually he was able to calm himself by becoming aware of the frost settling on his shoulders and the chilled earth beneath his socks. He wrapped himself in blankets again and tried to reenter the world of sleep, but the girl he had seen would not go away; she was there inside his eyelids, demanding answers to those same cryptic questions. It was not right that such a little demon visit him by night. If a succubus should come to torment him, it should come in the guise of the cigar box lady, and he would embrace it and surrender himself, but the imp had been proud of itself, testy and insistent. Clay was unable to stop his body from shaking, and could not decide if it was the cold that made him quake so, or fear of a simple dream. He wondered also if he was becoming mad, like the lost soul dragging his beam balance through the wilderness. That would be the ultimate humiliation, he decided: to be insane, yet unaware of it.

It was his aloneness that caused such episodes, he was convinced. Not the aloneness of a man passing through uninhabited country, but rather the larger solitude of the untouchable, the pariah who has no caste but himself with which to belong. The bitterness he felt welling inside him grew from knowing he was not truly alone, merely separated from those other parts of himself, the sister and brother who shared his blood, those dim and distant portions that, if united with himself, would constitute the Dugans, a tripartite entity without fear of darkness.

He wondered, for the first time in more than a year, where they could be. It was a futile exercise, he knew, but it would fill the hours that loomed like a series of walls between himself and the dawn, and so he leaned his scarred cheek against the leather pillow of his saddle and attempted to conjure from the dwindling resource of memory a portrait of the two missing Dugans. It was likely he could pass them both on the street and not recognize either one. That was the kind of irony Clay appreciated. It made him smile. His sister and brother were gone forever, hacked away from him like a gangrenous arm and leg, leaving him a kind of cripple, an awkward facsimile of a completed man. As ever, there was nothing he could do, and he surprised himself by permitting tears of unquenchable misery to slide from his eyes, across the bridge of a nose already displaying the permanent stigmata of the spectacle wearer, and down across the ragged wounds that made him heir to his fate.

In the *Durango Herald,* Clay read of the newest slaughter committed in northern New Mexico by the red fiends Panther Stalking and Kills With a Smile; two entire families had been butchered in their sleep. Unlike ordinary Apaches, the murderous brothers had no qualms about perpetrating their crimes during the hours of darkness. The territorial governor had at last placed a reward on their heads of one thousand dollars apiece. Clay toyed with the notion of going there and hunting them, then admitted he probably couldn't match the sneakiness of Indian ways, and would likely end up with his bowels in his lap, the fate, apparently, of an army officer named Dobson who had set out alone to capture the hellions south of the most recent outrages. Dobson and another man similarly treated had been buried with full military honors. Two other troopers were still missing, and believed to have met the same end. No, he would stay where he was, hunting his regular prey, since that was work he knew himself capable of executing with skill.

In Montezuma County he came to the mountain town of Killdeer, a place so remote there was not one planed length of lumber on any one of its structures. Every dwelling wore a rough coat of unstripped bark and clay chinking to keep out the weather. The forest around Killdeer was already stripped of leaves, the pines darkening, the air crisp with approaching snow. Clay tied his horses to a rail outside a store-saloon and went within to absorb alcohol and information. Killdeer had been the town a dying man told him of, wherein Clay could find an outlaw named Archie Powell, wanted in three states for robbery and murder. Archie Powell was worth four hundred dollars. The dying man (Clay's bullet had lodged in his lungs) had only fetched one hundred, but the name of Killdeer had made the effort of tracking him down worthwhile.

Clay was the only customer. While the barkeep poured him a drink, he asked, "Arch been around?"

"Say who?"

"Arch Powell."

"Don't know the feller."

"Arch and me, we rode together some while back."

"Don't know him," reiterated the barkeep, but Clay knew he was lying. While he drank, he watched the man closely, noting the casual way the barkeep did the same to him. By the time Clay ordered his third whiskey, the barkeep decided the tall man with the spectacles and scars was drunk enough to be pumped for the truth.

"Where'd you say you rode with this feller?"

"What feller?"

"Feller you said."

"Arch? Oh, up around Montana way. Had some high old times, Arch and me. He most likely told you about that time with the pig."

Archie Powell had shot a pig that blundered beneath the legs of his horse on the main street of Shelby, and when upbraided for the deed by the pig's owner, had shot the owner, then slit open the belly of the pig and thrust the carcass over the head of the deceased, in full view of several dozen witnesses.

"What'd you say your name was?"

"Ham Deidsheimer, short for Hamilton."

This was the name of Clay's hundred-dollar man, one of Powell's lesser sidekicks during his Montana days. The gang had specialized in robbing payroll shipments in the mining area around Butte, and had profited so handsomely they had not been heard from for more than a year. It was rumored that Powell was originally from Colorado, but that was not substantiated until Clay heard the name Killdeer from Ham Deidsheimer. Clay was hopeful the clue gave him an edge over the many federal officers and Pinkerton men also interested in running Powell to earth.

"He'll know," said Clay to the barkeep.

"Who'll know?"

"Arch, he'll know the name."

"No Arch around here, mister."

"Well, sure, I know that." Clay winked, and ordered another shot of liquor. He smiled conspiratorially at the man with the bottle, but was met with a face of stone.

"You tell him," suggested Clay, "you tell him I look even prettier than him nowadays, with these holes in my face. He won't have seen them yet, since we split up, all the boys. Feller in Denver run a stick through my face on account of not wanting to pay up some dollars he owed me. He come out of it worse, though. Run a bullet through his, front to back." He laughed and tossed down the drink.

Powell was a dandy and a womanizer, proud of his looks. Clay knew a description of himself and his scars, which Ham Deidsheimer had not had, would alert Powell to the deception, unless he explained them. Clay was also taller than Deidsheimer, but not by much.

"I guess I'll just take a bottle and wait," Clay said.

"Take as many as you want," advised the barkeep, "and wait for snow in hell, far as I care."

"You're a real friendly feller."

"Anyone pays for whiskey, I'm friendly."

When the bottle was set before him, Clay grabbed the barkeep's shirtfront and pulled him close. "I drink slow," he said, "but by the time my bottle's gone, I want Arch here, see, because I come a long way to see him."

He released the man and went to a corner table to drink. The barkeep went to the back room, and Clay heard a woman's voice. The woman came out and walked by his table, staring at him as she passed on her way to the door. He watched through one of the yellow-paned windows as she hurried along the street, arms hugging a shawl around herself against the cold. She returned within ten minutes, and ignored him as she passed through to the rear of the building. Clay guessed some intermediary had saddled up and was at that moment riding from Killdeer out into the mountains to alert Arch Powell.

Clay began making plans. By the time the outlaw came through the door and saw a stranger where Ham Deidsheimer was supposed to be, Clay would have a story ready, something to do with Ham passing on the Killdeer connection before dying, maybe following an attempted bank robbery with Clay. Powell would be suspicious, but Clay would spin the yarn with conviction, and be drawn nearer to Powell if all went well. If all did not, he could always shoot the man there and then, assuming Powell arrived alone, or at least without more than one henchman. Clay sometimes wished Colt or Remington would invent a shotgun with more than two barrels, or one capable of storing shells in a tube, like a repeating rifle. To pass the time, he composed a mental letter to that effect.

Through the afternoon, several customers came and went, but no one resembling Arch Powell arrived. Toward evening, two men rode up to the hitching rail and dismounted. Their indistinct figures sent a mild flutter through Clay's heart, the instinctive warning of danger. He was prepared, had surreptitiously tipped most of his drinks from the bottle into the spittoon by his ankles. He watched through the window as the two men ran their eyes over his animals. They would probably demand to examine his packs more closely, but Clay was prepared for that eventuality also; he had burned every single outlaw flier in his possession many miles back along the trail to Killdeer.

The men entered and went to the bar. Clay was only slightly disappointed to see that neither was Arch Powell. Powell was being cautious, sending his men to sniff out a trap. Clay raised his glass to them, a gesture they pretended to ignore. They drank, speaking together softly, then approached Clay's table. Clay hooked out two chairs with his boots. "Sit yourselves," he said, smiling.

The men sat down. "Thank you," said the first.

"Buy you a drink?" offered the second.

"Got plenty right here," said Clay.

"Mort says you're looking for someone."

"That the barkeep? Well, he told no lies, gentlemen. Looking for someone's my business here."

"Mort says the feller you want, he's not here."

"Is that so. Maybe you two can direct me to where he's at, and we can all share a drink."

"Depends on the name," said the second man.

"Arch Powell."

"Not his. Yours."

"Well, what I told Mort was Ham Deidsheimer."

"And what're you telling us?"

It was unclear if one or both men knew Deidsheimer by sight, so Clay smiled even more broadly and said, "Tell him Bill Adams, and I'm ready to work."

"What kind of work would that be?"

"High-risk, high-paid work, the kind me and Ham got caught up in just recent, only Ham got the risk end of things, which was real unfortunate."

"Telling us Ham's dead, mister?"

"Afraid so."

"Never heard about it, but I guess you can back up what you say."

"Well, now, newspaper stories about the incident, that'd be a foolish thing for me to carry around, don't you think? But I'll show you something better."

Clay produced from his vest a chain and a watch fob in the shape of a horseshoe. He had taken it from Ham Deidsheimer. The two men stared at it as Mort's woman began lighting the lamps. Clay saw blankness disguising puzzlement in their faces. Neither one recognized the horseshoe fob. Clay turned it over to show them Ham's name engraved on the back, and the motto *Tempis fugit*. They examined it closely, and returned it to him. Clay could tell that they had no clear idea what to do or say next, and he began to suspect the situation was not as he had thought.

"Come on, then," he was told.

The first man stood, followed by the second. Clay picked up his bottle and went with them to the door. All three mounted their horses and began riding out of Killdeer. Clay's escorts left the trail a mile from town and began threading their way in single file through the trees. Moonlight shone down on them, picking out the metal buttons sewn on the first man's hatband. Clay was alert, pretending on occasion to swig from his bottle. When the leader stopped in a small clearing, Clay knew he was about to be interrogated. The appearance of pistols in the hands of both men did not surprise him. He grinned all the wider and tipped the bottle again, wetting his lips.

"Now, do I mistake your intentions, or are you fellers about to bushwhack me?"

"Get down and shuck that coat, mister, and don't think to grab for that sawed-off."

Clay dismounted and shrugged off his long coat.

"Ease it off," he was told. Clay's shotgun was detached from its shoulder harness and laid carefully on the ground.

"All right, now, you tell us some things we might like to know. You can start off with your real name. Bill Adams, that's not it."

"You seem mighty sure about that, and you two haven't done me the courtesy of tossing a single name in my direction. That's discourteous, and I believe I'll lock my lip till you mend your ways."

The second man got down from his horse and went directly to Clay. Avoiding his partner's line of fire, he punched Clay hard in the stomach. Clay buckled, clutching himself, exaggerating the blow's effect. He was hit again, and began slowly to sag. Moving in for another punch, the second man thought Clay's clumsy lurching toward him was some kind of plea to stop, and was not prepared for the grabbing motion that plucked his gun from its holster, or the sudden smack of its cylinder alongside his jawbone. The barrel was against his windpipe before he could react, the hammer already cocked. He was between Clay and the first man, whose gun was leveled at them both. The first man hesitated. The standoff continued for several seconds while Clay recovered his breath.

"Now what?" said the first man.

"I'll have those names," Clay said, but none were offered. The man against whose throat he held a gun suddenly spun sideways, yelling, "Get him ...!"

Clay and the man on horseback fired simultaneously. Clay felt a bullet pass by his neck, and fired again before seeing the first man begin to topple from his rearing horse. Clay couldn't tell if he had hit him, or if the horse had thrown him. The second man was running. Clay's skill with a pistol being minimal, he dropped it and grabbed for the shotgun at his feet. The running man was shot in the back at a distance of just a few yards. Clay went to the first man, lying still on the ground. This one was alive, without any wound that Clay could see in the moonlight, so it was probably the fall from his horse that had stunned him.

Clay kicked him in the hip. "Get up."

The man slowly recovered his senses, aided by Clay's boot, and sat up, then vomited. "Your name," Clay said.

"Beecher ... Willis Beecher ..."

"And the other one?"

"Lee Hoyt ..."

He vomited again. Clay had heard those names before, and reviewed in his memory the hundreds of fliers he had studied in the course of his work. Beecher wiped his mouth and stood. Clay kept the shotgun trained on him as Beecher looked across at the body of Hoyt.

"Kill him?" Clay was asked.

"I expect."

"Then you're in deep trouble, Adams, or whoever you are. May as well give me your real name right now."

"What trouble?"

"The biggest kind, mister. You just killed a United States marshal."

Clay heard a roaring in his ears, and felt momentarily faint. Now he remembered where he had come across the names—in a Denver newspaper detailing the embarrassment of the two federal marshals who had allowed Panther Stalking and Kills With a Smile to escape a month or more ago in New Mexico.

"You both should have told me before," he said.

"Tell you what, mister! For all we knew, you were some partner to Archie Powell! Are you telling me now you aren't? Just who the hell are you?"

"Bill Adams. I wouldn't have shot him if I'd known."

"You're a bounty man, am I right? Looking to get Powell? You're too late, Adams. He was shot nine days back. Hoyt and me were up here trying to get the rest of Powell's bunch, hiding out hereabouts."

"The barkeep in town, he knows?"

"He's our man. Soon as you told him you're looking for Powell, he sent for us."

"I'm sorry about your partner. He never should have jumped like that."

"You bounty hunters are liable to mess up whatever you touch. You're a fool to think you can do what the law can't."

"Seems I can recall a couple of laws who let a couple of Apaches get away right from under their noses a little while back. You two get given this job to make up for that mess?"

"You keep your mouth shut about that. This mess is plenty big enough for you to worry about. Take the shells out of that sawed-off and hand it over. You're under arrest, Adams, for the murder of a federal officer."

"It was accidental, you know that."

"You'll get a chance to tell your story."

"Beecher, I don't think you'd make an impartial witness, somehow."

"That's too bad. You can do two things—kill me like you did Hoyt, and hope the barkeep doesn't pass your description on to the authorities, which he will, or you can surrender to me right now and take your chances in a court of law. I know what happened wasn't intentional, and I'll say so, you can trust me on that. Now choose."

Clay disliked Beecher intensely for the hold the man had over him, and for the way Beecher and Hoyt had set up their confrontation with him. True professionals would have disarmed Clay and then kept their distance while they asked questions of him, not put their own lives in jeopardy by moving close enough to punch him in the stomach and have one of their own pistols yanked into play. Beecher and Hoyt were responsible for Hoyt's death, not Clay, and yet Beecher's ultimatum was the only one Clay himself could think of—kill him or trust him. Clay's dislike of Beecher was not sufficient to provoke the former, yet he was reluctant to accept the latter.

Beecher stooped to retrieve his hat and fallen gun. He was wise enough to holster the .45 and allow Clay his decision without the threat of more gunfire. Still Clay said nothing. Beecher went over to Hoyt and examined the gaping hole in his body.

"Back-shot. That's bad news for you, Adams. They won't believe that was an accident if I'm not there to testify for you. You anywheres near to making up your mind, mister?"

Clay broke open his shotgun and ejected the spent and live shells, then offered the weapon to Beecher.

"That's good, Adams. That's smart."

Beecher swung the shotgun against the side of Clay's head, a blow so hard Clay's spectacles flew from his nose. "That's for Lee, you son of a bitch!" He repeated the action. "And that's for me!" Clay sank to the ground, clutching his head. A pair of handcuffs were dropped in front of him. "Get up and put these on yourself, you sorry piece of horsemeat."

By midmorning the next day, Clay had still not been allowed so much as a drink of water. Beecher had tied his ankles beneath his horse's belly, and was not about to make any effort to release his prisoner for matters of small consequence to Beecher. Clay had already been obliged to piss into his pants, and was hoping he would not feel the urge to move his bowels before they reached whatever place Beecher was taking him to. Clay's packhorse and Hoyt's animal, bearing Hoyt, trailed behind.

Beecher was talkative, confident, at ease with a man so completely cowed and under his control. "Lee Hoyt and me, I don't mind telling you, we were drug through the mud on account of those red killers down there. There was talk we'd be showed the door, then Lee got this idea to follow up on something we heard down Magdalena way about Arch Powell, and after the mess down there we needed to show ourselves in a better light, as they say, so we followed that rumor about Powell, and found out he's on his way home to Killdeer, which we told about to certain sons of bitches in high office who wanted to show us the door, and these particular sons of bitches sent some other officers to wait for old Arch, and they're the ones that got him, instead of me and Lee, like it was supposed to happen and shine that better light on us. Well, after that we weren't about to trust any son of a bitch again, so we decided we'd come up here and round up the rest of the Powell outfit ourselves, and we were set up pretty good with old Mort the barkeep willing to pocket some dollars and be on the lookout for us. We figured you'd be the first one in the net, but you had to go mess things up for us, Adams, and I don't like how you did it, nossir, I don't."

"If you were half as smart as you think you are, you'd throw in with me and get the whole bunch. You and Hoyt aren't great planners, Beecher. You want to impress your boss, you'd better set me loose so we can talk about a way to do it. We both want the same thing, to get the rest of Powell's boys under lock and key."

"You'd just as soon shoot them, Adams. That's how bounty hunters work. Alive or dead, it never did make any difference to the likes of you."

"All the same, you'd do well to consider it."

"I'm not about to consider any such thing."

"Where are we going? Killdeer's back the other way."

"Cortez. They've got a lockup there that'll hold you just fine. I take you back to Killdeer, too many people are going to know there's something going on, and I don't want to scare off the rest of Arch's boys. They were all on their way there to join up with him for another go-round on the owlhoot trail, that's the word we got down

Magdalena, and chances are they're still coming, even if Arch is dead."

"You can get them all, with me."

"No deal, Adams. I don't do business with the man that shot my partner. You can sit awhile in Cortez till someone comes for you."

"You'll never take Arch Powell's boys on your own."

"Not all at one time, I'll admit, but that won't be how they come, Adams. They'll come alone, and I can handle snakes like that all by myself. You can ..."

Clay saw the left half of Beecher's hat suddenly compress at the same instant the right half was carried away by an exiting bullet that carried with it bone and brain. Strangely, the hat remained on Beecher's head even as he fell from his saddle and hit the ground, one boot still lodged in a twisted stirrup. Clay was about to spur his horse away, then remembered his handcuffs; the key was in Beecher's pocket. He was unable to make up his mind before a lanky boy sprang from the trees and grabbed the bridle of his horse. A man carrying a Winchester then appeared and stepped over to the body of Beecher. When he turned, Clay recognized Mort.

"That feller," said Mort, "was a fool."

"I'm in agreement," said Clay.

"Fools don't live long in this world. What me and my friend need to know, mister, is if you're a fool too."

"That would depend, now, wouldn't it?"

"Depend on who the hell you are and what exactly you want around here, and you better make more sense than you done yesterday, because you sure aren't who you said. That boy there, he's kin to Ham Deidsheimer, so you just trot out the truth right now."

Clay looked down at the boy. "Son," he said, "I hate to be the one that tells you, but Ham's dead, killed by a bounty hunter, they say. I only met him but once, and that was just for a short while, and he trusted me and told me about Arch Powell and how there was a rendezvous set up for Killdeer for him and the boys from Montana to meet again. Well, I wanted to be in on that, so I came here under false pretenses, just to get heard by Arch Powell, and I judged those two federal men wrong, and almost paid for it large. I apologize to you for taking your kinsman's name. No harm or insult was intended, and that's my story to you both."

The boy said nothing. Mort stepped closer. "Mister, I don't believe a word of it, but you killed the other one, so you're no friend of the law, and you can go, but don't you be seen hereabouts again. Arch is gone, and now Ham, you say. That's two good men and two fool laws dead, and that's enough dying for now."

"Thank you. There's a key in his pants."

Clay's wrists were released, the rawhide thongs binding his boots cut.

"You remember what I told you," Mort warned.

Clay's shotgun was passed to him, and the lead rein of his pack-horse. "Get," he was ordered.

During the first hour of his freedom, Clay wondered if another shot might come from the woods either side of the trail to Cortez, but in the second hour he began to worry less. Mort and the boy would dispose of Beecher and Hoyt, and the incident would be buried along with them. Their horses would be traded to thieves who would take them across miles of territory, beyond the reach of any investigation that might or might not arise as a result of Beecher's and Hoyt's unofficial enterprise. Clay had come to the Killdeer region with a view to accomplishing exactly what the dead men had come for, and found himself leaving with nothing more valuable than his life.

PART TWO

THE
WINE
OF
VIOLENCE

25

He had hired several lawyers, but not one of them had been able to accomplish anything beyond lightening his wallet. Nevis Dunnigan should have been a famous man, but was not, and he had at last become aware of the reason— no one really cared if he was the originator of *Venus Revealed* or not. His masterly depiction of an unclothed Lovey Doll Pines had become so popular an attraction at its home in a Kansas City saloon, the owner had allowed copies to be made, many, many copies, and unauthorized copies were made from those copies, until it seemed that Lovey Doll was everywhere seen in her glorious nakedness. But the name of the artist, that precious scrawl at the lower-right-hand corner of the original canvas, was a frustrating blank, insulting by its absence the artistic temperament of Nevis, and doing him no earthly good in the world of commerce either.

The lawyers had listened to his cry for redress, and in the end been unable to help him. He doubted now that they had even believed he was in fact the artist. Lovey Doll was not only present on barroom walls across the west, she was to be found in collections of erotica, in both pasteboard and sophisticated stereopticon versions; her fleshy charms were displayed inside the lids of cigar boxes, even rendered in miniature on snuffboxes. It was outrageous that a single work should have provided the model for so many applications of Lovey Doll's likeness, when not a cent in royalties trickled down to the creator. Nevis felt that if the manufacturers of canned goods could have braved public opinion and pasted Lovey Doll across all their products, they would have, so enticing was the goddess of love. Art, the sublime stuff of Nevis's soul, had been prostituted in the service of Mammon, and no one cared about or rewarded the man whose talent had been so abused.

An occasional drunkard, Nevis had drifted west in search of justice and financial restitution without finding either. His aim had been to reach San Francisco, where the cosmopolitan air of so great a city would surely revive his spirits, but he had progressed no further than Denver. He told himself the invigorating air of a town one full mile above sea level would be an acceptable substitute for San Francisco; he would breathe alpine clouds rather than salty fog, and be spiritually refurbished as a result of such Olympian ingestions. That had been three years before, in 1881, and Nevis was still awaiting the arrival of the muse, or recognition of his talents. He made a living for himself as assistant to an inferior painter much sought after by the newly rich mining potentates of the Rockies, and was able to keep his tongue and his envy in check only by way of liberal amounts of alcohol. The hack he worked for was without even a shred of ability, in Nevis's opinion, yet the fool was becoming rich himself through the patrons he monopolized.

One night, particularly enraged by criticism from his employer for having mixed a combination of colors not precisely to his exacting standards, Nevis began sketching caricatures of the man in various positions of abuse, subjecting him to the amorous attentions of jackasses, policemen with large batons, brutish sailors and inventive eunuchs, a bevy of vengeful furies engaged on Nevis's behalf to right the wrongs perpetrated against him by the world in general and the hack in particular. He wielded his charcoals in a bar that in recent months had become his favorite retreat, and soon attracted a host of admiring critics, some of whom were able to recognize the butt of his ill humor. Nevis sold all of his sketches to pay off his bar bill, which had become a subject of dispute between himself and the proprietor. Feeling much better for having vented his spleen for actual profit, Nevis passed out on the floor.

Two days later, Nevis was unemployed. Choice selections of his barroom artistry had been forwarded to Denver's most prominent social portrait painter, and the hack was neither impressed nor amused by his apprentice's betrayal. When he learned that the sheets in his hand represented only a fraction of Nevis's work in a similar vein, his rage had been a terrible thing, and Nevis was glad to quit his position as the hack's helper. It was liberation of a kind, and he celebrated by establishing a new bar bill at the scene of his creative crime. The celebration lasted until the following afternoon, at which time Nevis collapsed from an excess of liquor. He was put to bed by the proprietor's wife, for whom, while still relatively sober, he had executed a quick portrait emphasizing what little beauty she retained at the age of fifty-one.

Nevis returned to cruel sobriety the next day, and found an unknown man by his bed. The man was handsome, middle-aged, and had about him the aroma of wealth Nevis had grown accustomed to during his former employer's dealings with the elite of Denver. Nevis told himself not to be intimidated, even under such circumstances as this.

"Good day, Mr. Dunnigan."

"Yes ..." said Nevis, aware that his response was not appropriate, aware also of the tremendous thuddings within his head.

"Are you unwell, Mr. Dunnigan?"

"No ..."

"That is good news, sir, because I have an unprecedented offer to make you."

"Offer ...?"

"An offer, Mr. Dunnigan, of work."

"Work?"

"On a scale hitherto unknown in our fair city, sir. Work of an altogether historic character. A first, as they say. Would you be interested in embracing such a project?"

"I ... I would."

"I have overstepped myself. One moment, please." His guest took from his creaseless jacket a sheet of paper and unfolded it for Nevis's inspection. "This is your artistic handiwork, sir?" The hack, in this particular instance, was being sodomized by a gleeful centaur.

"Uh ... yes."

"I realize this is merely a quick study, but I must ask you, Mr. Dunnigan, if you are acquainted with the broader canvas, the more, how shall I say, heroically proportioned type of thing."

"Sir, I am. Sir, are you familiar with a study entitled *Venus*

Revealed, which can be found in abundance throughout the drinking establishments of the land, and elsewhere?"

"Ah, yes, the delightful lady among the pillows. You are the author of that work?"

"Of the original, which was superior in every way to the copies that abound without my permission."

"An unfortunate situation, to be sure. I have heard it voiced that art is its own reward, but I'm a practical man, Mr. Dunnigan, and I expect most painters are also. That is why you may be assured that your work for me, should you accept the task, will be rewarded according to my satisfaction with the finished result. A businessman's agreement is what I require, on paper, and signed by an attorney. Are you averse to such an arrangement?"

"No indeed, sir, so long as rights to reproduction are retained by myself. Once bitten, twice shy, as the anonymous wise man said."

"Mr. Dunnigan, I cannot agree to that stipulation, nor need you, when the nature of the work is made clear."

"I listen with open ears, sir."

"It may be best if I take you directly to the site you'll be required to work in."

"Site? You mean a studio will be provided?"

"Not exactly. Can you rise, Mr. Dunnigan? I'm able to provide lunch before we view the room."

"Room?"

"Sir, just as Michelangelo was commissioned by the Pope to cover the walls and ceiling of the Sistine Chapel in Rome, so have I commissioned you for a task of similarly epic proportions. Well, it may be that I exaggerate a little."

"A church?"

"No, Mr. Dunnigan, not a church."

Her visits from the tall man were becoming less frequent now that Omie was ten. He had flown through her dreams like a black eagle, with his long flapping coat and the broad hat that threw his face into shadow so deep she could see only his eyes, bright with a will to mete out death, and the iron bar that ran between his teeth. She had wondered, during his first visitations, why he kept it there, that iron bar spearing his cheeks like some bizarre tribal ornament, but it became clear, as she saw him again and again during the hours of night, that he kept the bar in place simply because it was so very ugly; the tall man wanted the world to see his punishment, but Omie could never determine its cause. Sometimes he saw her, as she saw him, but never for very long. She knew from his ugly, penetrated face that he was scared of her, just as she was of him, and decided it must be on account of her blue mark. Both of them were being punished, and neither knew the reason why.

Omie was known to sleepwalk around the mansion that was called Elk House by its owners, and the Big House by everyone else. It stood above Glory Hole like a brooding sentinel, its massive escarpments of brick and stone as tall as castle walls, its gables and cupolas so high they caught the winds that howled across the great divide and broke them into airborne moanings and whimperings that could sometimes be heard the length of the valley on Christmas Day, when the ore crushers were silenced, the smelters left to simmer untended. Her nocturnal perambulations were known to the town, word of them taken there by servants. It was said that Omie Brannan stood or walked or even ran full tilt along the corridors in complete darkness, demanding of some invisible entity that it reveal itself. It was because of the blue mark on her face, most people agreed; any girl so blighted would naturally become a little crazy, and the problem would likely worsen as she grew older and became aware that nature had not outfitted her for matrimony, except, of course, to a fortune hunter willing to disregard her mental and physical deficiencies for the sake of laying hands on a part of the Brannan millions.

There were other disquieting rumors about the girl with the blue mark, and many of them accounted for the steady turnover in staff at Elk House. Omie's eye, despite its inky shadowing, was able to see what other eyes could not, by natural law, ever be aware of. Omie's eye saw events that had yet to occur, and Omie's mouth was bound to describe them, whether it was the imminent demise of the cook's cousin in Maryland, the gardener's unfortunate accident when a bough from one of the trees broke off in a storm and crushed his arm, or the way in which a stray dog would cause the matched palominos of her own mother's carriage to bolt along Brannan Boulevard, injuring an elderly woman who happened to be crossing in front of the team.

These and other incidents of their kind upset and mystified all who heard of them, but at least Omie's predictions, intoned in a hollow voice on some occasions, simply remarked upon in passing at others, could be relegated to the category of the spirit world's pene-trations into the realm of physical matter, in accordance with its own baffling precepts. What to make, though, of the stories con-cerning Omie's ability to cause objects of known weight and sub-stance to dance in the air like soap bubbles? These were powers beyond common understanding or acceptance. The new scientific age was under way, with its mechanical marvels and materialistic biases at full throttle; godless, perhaps, but not without consolation for the thinking man. Where did Omie fit into this modern scheme of things? Neither ectoplasmic fish nor corporeal fowl, she was a creature in between, the fleshly conduit for hidden things, nameless concepts, a creature with feet on different planes, and people were afraid of her.

Zoe had seen what Omie could do, and the ability her daughter possessed was a wondrous gift, in Zoe's opinion, certainly not any-thing to fear. She had several times witnessed Omie moving furni-ture around a room without a single piece ever touching the floor until it was positioned according to the girl's wants. Once seen, the ponderous aerial dance of sofas and tables, bureaus and chairs, was not to be forgotten. There had been only one mishap, when Zoe came upon Omie about her mysterious business for the first time, shifting an ornate vase filled with freshly cut flowers from one side of the living room to the other; Omie had lost her concentration when she knew herself to be observed, and allowed the vase to crash onto the parquet floor. Since that time, Omie would perform on demand to amuse her mother. She was not called upon to do the same for Leo Brannan.

Leo had become used to his stepdaughter's ability to foretell future events, but her defiance of gravity was quite another matter, and he forbade any such levitations in his presence, warning her that to continue these performances would strain her mental capac-ity to the point of permanent enfeeblement. He assumed the power stemmed from her brain, and Omie did not inform him otherwise. She did confide to Zoe that her technique involved a separate pair of invisible hands that extended on invisible arms from the pit of her stomach, not her head, as Leo maintained. The arms would grow to any length Omie required, and the hands were very large indeed, about the size of soup tureens, and had an indeterminate number of fingers. Zoe told her not to tell Leo. Leo could not be dis-tracted from the never-ending business of running the mines by anything of a distressing nature, or he would become morose and incommunicative. Whenever Leo withdrew into himself, as he seemed more often to do nowadays, everyone at Elk House suffered his protracted silences. It was better to keep things secret from him, so they could all live together without discord.

Her new husband had permitted Zoe to name her discovery above Glory Hole, and she had called it the Deer Lick Mine. She wanted to name the company that grew from it the Salt of the Earth Mining Company, but Leo said this was too whimsical for so serious a venture, and insisted that it be named Brannan Mining, which to Zoe's way of thinking lacked all poetry, but she did not object. He did allow her to name many of the other shafts that soon were sunk on claims adjacent to the first, to pull from the ground more and more of the gold that laced the side of the valley like a fabulous web. The Wildcat, the Sinbad, the Flatiron and the Grand Mogul: these and lesser shafts drew to the surface a grade of ore unparalleled in richness. A spur line of the Denver and Rio Grande Railroad was extended from Leadville to Glory Hole in record time, and flatcars hauled by three and four locomotives brought in massive banks of machinery needed to pulverize the naked rock and render it tractable to further stamping, until the fist-sized chunks of ore were reduced to pellet size for amalgamation with mercury to extract their veins of brilliance. More trainloads of steel arrived, and a smelting works was built, from whose controlled infernos the most precious of metals ran in molten streams. These were channeled into ingot molds, there to lie in blazing bricks that slowly cooled to the sullen bronze color of solid gold. The new and already grimy factories of Glory Hole occupied one slope, facing the other, dotted with mine shafts. In time, the town and its environs spread almost to the valley's rim, where Elk House loomed against the sky.

Leo bought out all his competitors, most notably the Rocky Mountain Mining Corporation, within a year, whether their claims were worth the money offered or not, and so came to own the valley that ran like a filthy crease among the untouched peaks. The trains arrived each day, panting and snorting along impossible ledges, toiling across trestle bridges built with the last of the native lumber to span chasms and gorges, and they unloaded from every car tons of coal from the mines of Durango, to be shoveled into the furnaces that powered Leo's steam-driven engines of wealth—the pithead cable lifts; the conveyor belts that tirelessly carried crushed ore to the stampers; the smelters that forged bricks of gold. Day and night, smoke rose from the chimneys, even on Sunday; the crucibles of wealth were maintained at white heat by men working shifts around the clock, and the ingots that rose in million-dollar stacks were taken by train out of the valley under armed escort, destined for the treasuries of the nation. The Brannans were the richest family in Colorado, and Glory Hole was their town.

If Omie was prone to chasing ghosts along the corridors of Elk House by night, then Zoe was thought to be pale and uncomfortable enough to have seen several herself. The mistress of the house was not known for her friendly ways, nor was she considered mean or cruel. She was without friends, since no other family of similar status lived closer than Denver, and her sole joy appeared to be her matched horses and her carriage, which she drove with spirit along the mountain roads. Zoe had no interest in the day to day business of maintaining so large a residence. She allowed the servants to be directed toward this task or that by a capable individual named Mrs. Scoville, for whom Zoe's lack of concern with all matters domestic was an opportunity to conduct herself in the manner of a regional tyrant. Mrs. Scoville so intimidated the staff of polishers and washers and cooks and maids, they did not even invent an unsavory sobriquet for her, out of fear she would somehow hear of it and descend upon them with her eyes of steel and chin of granite. And yet it was known, since there were witnesses, that Mrs. Scoville, the scourge of Elk House, was deathly afraid of someone half her height and only a fraction of her weight.

Omie spent much of her time upstairs, and this was the reason Mrs. Scoville spent much of her time on the ground floor. On those occasions when Omie descended to visit the garden—a series of walled terraces hugging the valley wall—Mrs. Scoville would absent herself from any part of the house in a line extending from the bottom of the staircase to the outer door leading to the garden, in order that she might avoid meeting with the tiny witch. Omie was one of Satan's little imps in ribbons and curls, and it was bad luck even to come near her, let alone cross her path or be touched by her hand, or the hem of her petticoats. Only the power Mrs. Scoville wielded among the servants kept her from packing her bags, but such courage as it took to live beneath the same black slate roof as the devil's emissary was not summoned easily.

Mrs. Scoville saw it as no more than her perfect right, a kind of compensation, to remove a portion of the budget set aside in hard cash for necessary household purchases, and hide it in a bag beneath her bed. A dollar here, five dollars there: it was all earned by having to live with her immortal soul in constant jeopardy. It was entirely possible that the imp in pink would one day startle her with an act so outrageous it would provoke a heart attack, and if that happened, Mrs. Scoville knew her soul would jump right out of her body and be seized by the invisible presence Omie was known to court and cajole and follow on flying shoes through the corridors and rooms. So she stole, and over the course of time managed to secrete in her hideaway an accumulation of dollars totaling more than nine hundred. Mrs. Scoville loved her treasure trove of rustling paper, and would often drag the leather satchel from beneath her bed, even when she had no new bills to swell its contents, and set out the notes according to their denomination, and smooth their crinkled faces. When she had two thousand dollars saved, and not before, she would quit that place of unnatural occurrences and set herself up with a respectable boardinghouse in Baltimore, the city of her birth. It was a good and handy thing that the mistress of Elk House had no interest at all in taking care of the domestic budget. Mrs. Scoville was even responsible for ordering the hay and feed Mrs. Brannan's precious nags required, and she stole from those moneys also, because not to do so would be to allow the presence of evil in the world to go uncontested. The imp's family were aware of her impishness, and yet did nothing to have her saved, so it was only right that it was their money (only a tiny smidgen of it, after all) Mrs. Scoville siphoned off into the bag beneath her bed. God surely understood. She would run a clean and Christian boardinghouse when the time came, and would allow neither drinking nor smoking on a Sunday, as proof of her thievery's good intent.

"Sorrowful" was the adjective most often applied to Zoe by those who did not know her, and these were many, since she socialized scarcely at all with the outside world. Her face bore the stamp of pride, it was true, but not pride of the haughty or arrogant kind; Zoe's pride was drawn from the need to conceal her disappointment with life. Her husband was the source of her sadness, or rather, Leo's own disappointment over Zoe's inability to give him living children caused him to look upon her with less affection than before. Three miscarriages in three years had soured his love. Where another man might have been drawn closer to his wife by their shared suffering, Leo allowed himself to blame Zoe. She had given birth to Omie without difficulty, and borne a healthy son (Zoe kept from Leo the fact that Omie was not Bryce Aspinall's child, but the product of rape), so it was difficult for him to understand why she could not do the same for him. As his patience thinned, he grew less inclined to mourn along with his wife for the latest of their partially formed progeny. Leo had given her his name, and become a father to her daughter by another man; it was little enough to ask of her that she give him a son in return. But she did not, and he took himself away from her through the day while he managed the huge mining operation that bore his name, a name and fortune he could not hand on to a male heir, and in the evening he seldom arrived home in time to eat with Zoe and Omie. His wife was often asleep in her bedroom when Leo climbed the stairs at last to his own. Avoidance, subtle yet hurtful, was his stratagem, but Leo would have denied this.

It was clear to Omie that her mother had been made sad by Leo, and she could not understand why this should be so. She tried many times to creep inside her stepfather's mind to seek out the reason, but was unable to penetrate his skull. There had been a time when she was able to read his emotions, and sometimes his actual thoughts, but that time was gone, and Omie received from Leo's head nothing more illuminating than a general aura of darkness and ill temper. Some people wore their thoughts like fantastic hats, but Leo was not that kind, not anymore.

Omie often pushed herself inside her mother's head, there to examine the colors of her mood, which generally were of a beautiful but melancholy purple. Omie would sprinkle vivid yellow everywhere in an effort to create happiness, and sometimes the purple landscape of Zoe's interior self did brighten in response, but not to the extent Omie desired. Zoe must be sad indeed to feel so purple, and those thoughts which she could receive from her mother told Omie it was Leo who was responsible for them. He was purpling Zoe by way of his deliberate neglect, and it was not something Omie would have expected of him. When Leo had married her mother, Omie knew him to be a nice man, who treated them both with courtesy and affection, but that had been when they were poor, living in the cabin Leo and his friends had built. Now that they lived in what was probably the biggest house in the world, Leo was a changed man, and life was less happy than before.

Because Omie could not bring herself to punish Leo for what he was doing to Zoe, she directed her annoyance instead toward the huge lady who lived downstairs, the big boss lady of the house who told the servants to put back in place the various articles of furniture moved by Omie during her episodes of telekinesis. Omie did this less often now, because it wasn't fair to make the servants have to undo what she had done; if she still felt the inclination to make things move, she usually restored them to their original positions before turning to other avenues of amusement. The latest of these was her stalking of Mrs. Scoville.

Most of the fun lay in knowing her prey was already afraid of her. Mrs. Scoville was the type who projected her thoughts around her like coach lanterns, simple and direct, but without much brilliance or penetration. In earlier days Omie had ignored the flashes of fear that reached her from downstairs, because she had become used to similar feelings from the various servants who came and went; but the fear that came from Mrs. Scoville was of a different nature than most; for one thing, it was much stronger, so strong it made Omie feel a little sick, as if she herself were afraid of some nighttime monster lurking beneath the bed or in the shadows of her closet. Was that how Mrs. Scoville saw her? Omie was mortified at first, and avoided the downstairs region if she possibly could manage, rather than cause another black wave of revulsion to sweep across her from below.

Now, when the Brannans were less happy than they were, and Omie wished to punish Leo for it but could not, since she still nursed a liking for him, she decided that the target for her feelings of thwarted requital should be Mrs. Scoville. It wasn't fair that Omie was considered a horrible monster by a woman who hadn't spoken so much as a word to her since the day she came to take charge of things. Omie would show her.

She began by probing the mind of her enemy for thoughts that might be of tactical use in the campaign, but the few images Omie was able to glean through wood and lathe and plaster were not very interesting, and certainly had nothing to do with her. The most powerful picture to emerge was of a bag filled with money, and the next was of a large house with Mrs. Scoville standing in the doorway as if she owned it. The two things were linked somehow, but Omie could not quite see why, so she dismissed them, and searched for more evidence of fear directed at herself. It had been some time since she had been anywhere near the woman, so her fear was slight at the moment, a kind of background noise, like the humming of bees on a summer day. Omie would fix that.

The first inkling Mrs. Scoville had that she had become the target of the imp was when she found her bed turned around. It was aligned with the corner walls as usual, but turned completely around. Mrs. Scoville's puzzlement was replaced in an instant by panic over her money bag, and she hurriedly dropped to her knees beside the reversed bed to flail beneath it with her hands. The bag was there, and a hasty tally reassured her that not a single dollar was missing. Holding a plump hand over her palpitating chest, Mrs. Scoville asked herself how this inexplicable thing might have occurred, and did not need to think for more than a few seconds to know the culprit was Omie. The imp had declared war, for reasons Mrs. Scoville could not discern, having no means of understanding the ways of the damned. She would be on her guard from that moment; Satan's minion would not drive her from the most lucrative position she had known, not before the two thousand dollars she had promised herself were siphoned off.

The staff were aware of a change in Mrs. Scoville, and discussed it among themselves only when sure they were not within her hearing. She had of late begun to look over her shoulder, as if anticipating the appearance of someone there. Who that someone might be was made obvious when Omie presented herself in the kitchen doorway one morning, while Mrs. Scoville was delivering instructions to the cook for the midday and evening meals. Mrs. Scoville suddenly broke off her brisk directive and turned around. When she saw Omie just a few yards away, the girl's mottled face staring in her direction, Mrs. Scoville gasped several times, as if her throat had closed itself off, and she took several steps backward, away from Omie, until she bumped into the cook's table, still producing the gasping sound that could clearly be heard by the several persons there, since all other activity had ceased by then. Mrs. Scoville's performance was witnessed in its entirety, and would become the latest talking point among the servants, a fact Mrs. Scoville was aware of even before Omie left the doorway and allowed air to pass again through the throat of her target. Mrs. Scoville was able to tell the cook, "Just ... do as I said ..." before sinking to the floor in a dead faint.

Omie was well pleased at the reaction she had brought about, although she missed its startling end. Tomorrow, or even as soon as that afternoon, she would do something else to make the big woman uncomfortable. Omie went to her room and lay down on the bed to think of some suitable torment, and felt a kind of breeze pass across her skin. The windows were closed, and Omie knew it was no movement of air that caused her skin to dimple into goose bumps; this had happened many times before, and she prepared herself for what was to follow by relaxing her body; it was preferable that these moments of psychic possession (she called them "dream-awakes") should come when she was alone, and in a comfortable place, but this did not often happen, so Omie was particularly glad on this occasion to allow the forces that visited her to do as they wished.

First there came a darkness, encroaching slowly from the periphery of her vision, as if the walls of her room were being blackened by soot, and when the area around her was almost completely dark, Omie felt the approach of something as unlike that darkness as noon is from midnight. It was glowing, this thing that came nearer, shining with a golden light of great beauty and restfulness. Omie expected it would be an angel, when fully revealed, but she was unable to turn her head and see. The golden light was much closer now, and she felt a sluggish excitement run through her numbed body at the prospect of seeing her first otherworldly entity, a being she felt would resemble closely the divine beings she had seen represented in illustrated Bibles and religious works of art.

To her surprise, the golden creature entering her room was no angel, was not even remotely human in appearance. It was an elk, massive and proud, and it carried atop its powerful head and neck a rack of antlers so tall they brushed the ceiling, an impossible aggregation of curved surfaces and scallopings no real elk could have supported. The antlers, all of their myriad twistings and twinings, glowed with the intensity of fire, limning the structure with a luminosity so fierce Omie expected to see it burst into flame, but like the burning bush of Moses, this crown only became brighter as she watched, and was not consumed by its own brilliance. The elk strode with purpose before her eyes, then stopped and slowly turned its great head until both eyes, shining like diamonds, directed their gaze into hers, and the elk said to Omie, "I am brought by you from beneath the earth, and am yours forever." Omie wished to speak, to acknowledge that she understood, but no words would come, and when the elk approached her, searing her eyes with its brightness, she still could not move or speak, and when the elk lay down upon her with its body, she felt the air pressed from her lungs by its weight, and the blackness surrounding it closed in around her head like a hangman's sack.

Mrs. Scoville had almost recovered herself, and was being particularly brutal with the servants to make restitution for having been seen in circumstances of embarrassing weakness. If she allowed them to think for one moment that her fainting fit meant she required assistance, or that she was in any way grateful for the inquiries after her health, they would never respect her again, so Mrs. Scoville flung a blizzard of instructions around herself like a fence of thorns, and sent all the servants on their way to carry out her orders before herself retiring to her room for a bracing mouthful or two of Dr. Cazaubon's Nostrum, a heady elixir she resorted to only under extreme duress. Dr. Cazaubon's potent remedy for almost anything soothed Mrs. Scoville to the pit of her ample stomach, and temporarily put at ease all fears for her soul. The imp had challenged her outright, and caused her considerable distress, but Mrs. Scoville was made of sturdier stuff than could be broken by such tactics. She was in fact more concerned for her potential loss of standing among the servants than she was by Omie's attack upon her.

It was not until Omie did not present herself for the lunch she customarily shared with her mother that Zoe began to wonder if Omie was well; her daughter almost never missed their midday meal together. After waiting a short while for her to appear, Zoe went to Omie's room, knocked and entered, and found Omie apparently asleep. A closer look revealed the shallowest of breathing, and Omie's face had the pallor of wax. Most disturbing of all were the staring eyes, fixed on the ceiling above her bed. Zoe spoke her name and shook her several times, but Omie's state did not change at all, and Zoe became worried. She slapped her daughter's face lightly, and when this action brought no response, Zoe emptied flowers from a vase beside the bed and threw the water directly into Omie's face, again without result.

Convinced by then that Omie had fallen into some dangerous and unnatural trance, Zoe rushed for help, first issuing instructions for her carriage and team to be made ready, then shouting for the stablehand to exercise his brawn in carrying the unconscious Omie downstairs. The stablehand was brought along to hold Omie steady while Zoe whipped her palominos along the winding road that led downhill to Glory Hole. Traffic and pedestrians in the crowded streets were obliged to move smartly aside as Zoe's carriage careened among them, her horses frothing, Zoe's whip stinging their rumps as she forced a way through the throng to reach the office of Dr. Phillip Gannett.

When Omie had been laid carefully on the sofa in his antechamber, Dr. Gannett examined her swiftly, and declared himself nonplussed. "I can't give a name to the condition, Mrs. Brannan, but her pulse is steady and her breathing regular, if weak. It seems to be some kind of narcoleptic state, but the cause is unfamiliar to me, and the cure. Have you attempted to revive her with smelling salts?"

"No."

Dr. Gannett tried this and several other remedies before achieving success with the simple application of a boiled candy to Omie's tongue. The doctor was addicted to these, and kept a supply in his desk, and the transformation wrought by the sweetness of the morsel as he touched it to the tongue protruding from Omie's pinched-open lips was immediate; she began to suck at the candy, and her eyes lost their fixated staring. She looked about herself with some puzzlement, but was reassured by the presence of her mother, and of Dr. Gannett, a familiar figure to Omie, since it was he who had attended Zoe during each of her truncated pregnancies.

"Butterscotch," said Omie.

"Yes indeed," said the doctor, "and would you care for another?"

"Yes, please. Why is Cameron here?" she asked, looking across at the room at the stablehand.

"Cameron carried you," Zoe explained.

"What for? I'm too big for carrying."

"You fell asleep and we couldn't wake you up."

"That's silly."

"Perhaps, but that is what happened."

Omie would not talk about the subject as she was driven home, nor did she want any food, and the postponed luncheon was carried away to the kitchen, where the servants devoured it, since Mrs. Scoville was nowhere in sight to insist that they save the ingredients for a later meal. It was unlike Mrs. Scoville to be absent from her duties for more than a few minutes, and the unusual nature of the morning's events was discussed at length, and a connection between them openly debated.

The topic was abruptly laid to rest when Mrs. Scoville appeared suddenly and demanded to know why so many lazy individuals were gathered in one place, the only part of their anatomies in motion their jaws. When she was told of Omie's mysterious seizure, Mrs. Scoville's cantankerous mood softened, and she requested more information than could adequately be provided, but the servants were not chastised for that, and were grateful to be sent about their business without further reprimand.

Mrs. Scoville sat to ponder the meaning of what she had learned. Could it be that the imp had become ill as a result of her insults to Mrs. Scoville? Was God on the side of the righteous, and letting her know? It did not seem impossible. Mrs. Scoville was thrilled. Just let the little demon try something like that again, shifting beds around and staring daggers at innocent folk; just let her try, and God would strike her dead. Omie had been warned, but it was in the nature of evil to ignore God's injunctions, so she would probably go ahead and earn for herself the ultimate punishment, and good riddance, thought Mrs. Scoville.

Word was passed around Elk House that evening of Omie's relapse into a mildly feverish state that held both parents to her bedside. Mrs. Scoville kept herself apprised of the latest bulletins concerning Omie's condition, and was disappointed that it did not worsen. By bedtime, after Dr. Gannett had come and gone without being able to prescribe anything for his patient beyond warmth and fluids and a close watch through the night, Mrs. Scoville had become quite testy, but did her best not to display this.

She went so far as to venture upstairs, astounding herself with her own bravery, and was gratified to sense no danger at all from the imp's end of the south wing. The Lord was lending her a tiny part of his great strength, allowing Mrs. Scoville to penetrate the enemy's lair without so much as a twinge. She was a little taken aback to find herself suddenly confronted by Leo Brannan, and managed to blurt out, "A terrible thing, sir, just terrible ..." but he merely nodded and hurried away down the corridor to his own rooms. Mrs. Scoville, convinced she had accomplished something of importance, took herself away to bed and prayed mightily to her God, thanking Him for smiting the creature ailing upstairs, and for having given his loyal and true servant hope for permanent relief from the presence of the same. As she tucked the blankets around herself, Mrs. Scoville felt more at peace with the world than she could remember ever feeling.

It was the hall clock that woke her, the mahogany grandfather standing like an upright coffin, with its sonorous chimes that seemed to reverberate throughout the house. Mrs. Scoville counted two strokes, but allowed she might have missed any that preceded them. It became important to her that she know the time of night, so she threw aside her covers and went to the mantel clock ticking quietly across the room. Three o'clock. She had missed only the first stroke after all. Satisfied, she turned away from the clock, and that is when she saw the man in the corner, and felt her heart begin a wild galloping that threatened to carry it from her chest.

He was very tall and thin, and wore a long dark coat that bore the aspect of drooping wings, raven black. His shoulders were less broad than the brim of his hat, also black, which hid from her a face she knew was horrible, even in shadow, because the face of the man was transfixed by a golden arrow that impaled both cheeks like some exquisite device of torture from the days of old. Then Mrs. Scoville knew her visitor for who he was, and her annoyance that God would allow so gross a violation of her bedroom was almost of a quality to stifle her fear, but it could not, and Mrs. Scoville's heart galloped away from the dark man in the corner, so far away it left Mrs. Scoville without anything to pump her chilled blood, and so she died, vaguely aware, as she slid to the floor for the second time in twenty-four hours, that a tremendous injustice was being perpetrated by unknown forces against which God had no recourse but to absent Himself and hide within the grandfather clock, there to issue His doleful warning of what was to follow.

News of Mrs. Scoville's passing was kept from Omie for three days, in case it should upset her and bring about a further relapse. Her recovery from whatever malady assailed her was slow in any case, and Zoe spent most of her time, day and night, beside Omie's bed. Sometimes the furniture twitched and jumped under Omie's unconscious influence, and once Zoe awakened from a shallow sleep to see a pair of softly chiming bells of silver come drifting through the room, tied together with undulating ribbon of deepest red. Zoe thought they sounded too sweet to be church bells, and so did not take their appearance for an omen of death. There were subtle fluctuations of temperature at odd times in Omie's room, and the lamps often burned with greater intensity for minutes at a time for no apparent reason. Throughout all this, Omie slept and sweated and chewed her lips, and was not truly awake even when she drank water poured from the pitcher at Zoe's elbow.

While she stood vigil, Zoe could not help but wonder if she would do the same for her husband, and if she did, would it be largely for propriety's sake, rather than a hunger to be near the one she loved during a time of danger? She preferred not to address the question too closely. Her marriage was not without material comforts, and she still had Omie, her strange elf-girl, unique in all the world. Leo had his mines.

Eleven days after her condition began, Omie awoke from it as if from a troubled sleep, and declared herself starving for pancakes and syrup. These were made and dispatched to her, and Zoe watched as Omie ate greedily. When she was finished, Omie wiped her mouth undaintily on her sleeve and said, "She's in a house that isn't there, but she thinks it is."

"Who, dear?"

"Mrs. Scoville. She's in a house full of people, but the house isn't there, she just thinks it is, and she tells them all what to do, and they pay her money."

"I see. Are you ... aware that Mrs. Scoville has died?"

"I know. She's in hell, but she thinks she's in heaven. She's so silly. It was the dark man who did it."

"Did what?"

"Killed her. He's ... I think he's the angel of death. He used to frighten me, but not anymore. He frightened her, though. She jumped right out of herself and ran away. The money's under her bed."

"The money the people in her imaginary house pay her?"

"That's not real. I mean the money she stole. It's under her bed."

"Stole from who, dear?"

"From *whom,* Mama. From us. She thought about it when she jumped out of herself and ran away. She was running away from the money as well as the dark man, but she couldn't turn around because it was too late by then, because she was dead. She ran too far, Mama."

"Shall I order you more pancakes?"

"I'd puke it all up."

"Then I won't bother. Would you like me to read to you instead?"

"Yes, please."

Later that day, Zoe found the satchel where Omie had said. She did not mention it to Leo, who came home in a foul mood over some kind of mechanical difficulty at the smelter. He had expressed relief at Omie's recovery, bolted a meal and returned to the blackened far side of the valley to oversee the repairs being carried out there.

26

The room, when finished, would be known as the Grand Concourse, and be filled with sofas and love seats, the furniture of dalliance and flirtation. It occupied virtually all of the first floor of a building at the edge of Denver; upstairs were a further two floors of bedrooms. The Grand Concourse had windows along the front, but these would be kept under permanent cover by heavy velvet drapes, the color of which would be determined by Nevis, once he had completed his artistic work on the walls. For the moment, he required the light that came streaming through onto his three vast "canvases."

His employer, the finely dressed gentleman who had appeared at his bedside, was Mr. Adair, but Mr. Adair would not say for whom he worked. Nevis Dunnigan had been hired to decorate a new brothel, but he reminded himself it would not be just any brothel; when completed, it would be the finest between Saint Louis and San Francisco, and he had been promised that his signature would never be erased from the walls. In addition to the chance for immortality and the direct appreciation of his talent by large numbers of people, Nevis was being paid handsomely for his creative endeavors.

Mr. Adair had left the proposed mural's theme open to Nevis, merely stipulating that it should be "of the most uncompromisingly sensual nature, Mr. Dunnigan, the kind of thing that makes a man

hard, you see, the moment he lays eyes on it. Minute detail, lascivi-
ous poses, much mounting of female flesh by the rampant male is
what's called for here, don't you think? Breasts and buttocks, sir,
the artist's bread and butter."

Nevis pondered his commission. He had no qualms about depicting nudity, this being the *sine qua non* of the painter, but felt he
should grant the project an air of intellectual justification by pursuing some classic theme, rather than covering the walls with anonymous and random acts of copulation. Inspiration steered him before
long to a worthy subject, and he made it known at once to Mr.
Adair.

"The Rape of the Sabine Women. Yes, yes, I like that idea, Mr.
Dunnigan. We have inherent in the theme a great deal of fornicato-
ry possibilities, yet we also have the, how shall I say it, the prestige
and artistic authenticity of ancient times to commend the thing,
make it more ..."

"Acceptable?"

"Acceptable, yes. The clientele anticipated will not be riffraff, Mr.
Dunnigan, and they will appreciate, some of them, the historical
significance of the event you intend depicting. I am most pleased.
Make a list, if you would, of all your needs: paints and brushes,
models and so on."

"Models?"

"Dear me, yes. Without the human form to work from, how can
we expect an artist such as yourself to give of his best? You shall
have as many bodies as you need, sir, and the humor of it is that
they'll all be working here in any case when the preparations are
complete. I hadn't actually considered that before. Why, a customer
might make his selection from the wall, so to speak, if the young
lady is occupied elsewhere at the time, and unavailable for inspection in the flesh. Now, that's a selling point, Mr. Dunnigan, a wonderful crowd-getter, not that we'll be catering to crowds as such, but
word of this will get around, oh, yes, and won't they flock here to
see what you've done and compare it with the goods on display!
Most pleased, Mr. Dunnigan."

Nevis quickly assembled a series of scaled-down drawings that
conveyed his intention for the room as a whole. There were fifty-
three nude studies to be made in all, thirty-seven of them female.
All the Sabine women would be nude, or draped with wisps of flimsy material so fine their nipples could be seen, and their male

assailants would be partially armored, as befitted troops of the conquering Roman army, but such armor as Nevis granted them would
largely be confined to the upper torso. "Include the male appendage
in abundance, Mr. Dunnigan," his employer had instructed, "and be
sure to enhance its dimensions somewhat, for added effect. Clubs,
Mr. Dunnigan, cocks and balls, orbs and scepters, the weaponry of
love, don't you know, every man a stud horse and every woman a
mare in submission."

Nevis was disappointed that the first of his models was a young
man. Mr. Adair apologized for this, and explained that the girls
could not be spared just yet from their more lucrative work, but
they would be forthcoming, one at a time, as Nevis required. Meantime, he could complete studies of the soldiery with the aid of the
young man. Mr. Adair made it known that male models were a
sight harder to come by than females, at least in Denver, so Nevis
would have to use the one and only willing participant thus far to
create several different poses, altering his physical characteristics a
little each time, so as to make it appear there had been many individual models.

Nevis began work, arranging his model, in breastplate and helmet, in an attitude of uncompromising threat, with sword held high
in one hand, while the other cupped an invisible breast. This left
hand was missing its little finger, but Nevis could overlook the loss
and sketch in the digit. While he worked, he asked the model for his
name.

"Ilium."

"Pardon me?"

"Jay Ilium."

"Unusual name, Mr. Ilium. You're probably aware that Ilium was
the Latin name for Troy. Have you read Homer, Mr. Ilium?"

"I have."

"Also the name of a bone in the human skeleton. Let me think ... I
was familiar with them all as a student of anatomy—an art student, I mean, not the medical kind, but we did receive a thorough
grounding in such basics, just to ensure we could draw a foot that
looked like a foot. Ilium. Not a foot bone—talus, tarsal, metatarsal.
Let me think now ... atlas, axis, coccyx, costal, humerus, radius,
ulna, carpal, metacarpal ... pelvis, ischium, ilium! Hipbone, sir."

"Bones aren't as romantic as Troy."

"We are not responsible for what we're called, Mr. Ilium. May I
call you Jay?"

"Please do."

"Nevis is the name I bear, but Dunnigan is what will appear on these walls: N. Dunnigan. Have you engaged in this line of work before, Jay Ilium?"

"Nope."

"What line do you regularly pursue, if I might ask?"

"Any line at all, so long as it pays."

"A free man, then. I am bound by my calling, for better or worse. Are you a wanderer, by any chance? Free men often are."

"I've strayed this way and that."

"Adventures?"

"Incidents," said Drew, after reflection.

"Mine have been confined to canvas. For the next month or two it will be my task to rape several dozen women, figuratively speaking. How did you happen to be chosen for my first model?"

"Your friend Mr. Adair came up to me on the street and asked if I was hungry, which I was, and he bought me a solid meal. The least I could do was listen. He's paying me a dollar an hour to stand like this, not bad wages."

"And what will you do with your hard-earned dollars at the end of the day?"

"Get another meal," Drew lied. He intended getting back his gun. Since deserting from the army three years before, he had worked as hired hand for a number of outfits, farming or cowboying, and lately had become discontented over his inability to accrue a sizable wad of cash. Drew was twenty-two years old, and he did not like his life. The only solution to such disappointment seemed to lie in the immediate gratification of his need for money, in quantity. A gun would give him the means to that end. He had owned a Colt on first arriving in Denver, but had been obliged to pawn it. He would redeem the pawn, since the gun had sentimental value, and the cost of a new gun would not be covered by the limited nature of the work he was engaged in. When it was back in its holster, he would enter a bank and rob the place. He had not yet selected which bank to make the withdrawal from, but was in no particular hurry. Drew was aware that haste is the enemy of success.

This unusual job of art modeling was special, in that it would be his last lawful employment. He had broken the law many times while working for Marion de Quille back in Texas, but avoidance of import taxes had hardly been a hanging offense. Bank holdups would be different, a whole new way of life, and Drew was cynical

enough, young as he was, to believe that not much else would give
him any kind of satisfaction. He had made his choice, and intended
making his move.

"America is dying, Mr. Ilium, Jay."

"Is that right."

"Don't be misled by the hustle and bustle of the big town. There is
spiritual decay abroad in the land. I don't refer to a general turning
away from God, no, I'm of atheistic persuasion myself, but I have
seen a steady whittling away at our moral armature, the skeletal
values, so to say, of society. There are few idealists left. Everything
must be done for the sake of the dollar, and for no other reason. Art
and beauty have no intrinsic worth unless they be of a type worth
marketing to an uncultured populace, and that, sir, is a tragedy. I
myself would prefer to decorate a house of flesh than to paint portraits of rich men and their jeweled wives. No such toadying for me.
This enterprise we both are engaged in, each in his fashion, is more
honest than that, I truly believe."

"Could be you're right."

Nevis sketched on, thinking of Lovey Doll Pines and the many
other women who had rejected him for his poverty, while Drew
stood with raised sword, thinking of his gun.

Business was bad for Noble Burgin; the Arcadian Players had not
succeeded in winning either the hearts or the attention of their
audience during their latest engagement at Behan's Theater and
Saloon. Noble had always been leery of alcohol's close proximity to
any stage upon which he took his troupe, and Behan's had proven
once again that the mixing of drink and drama resulted in poor performances on the boards and wounded dignity backstage.

The clientele at Behan's simply did not appreciate a good play.
The Arcadians should have been engaged for an extended run at
one of Denver's finest theaters, a place of chandeliers and silk bro-
cade curtains and plush carpeting, not the sawdust-floored
imbiber's barn they currently graced. Noble was doubly upset
because the play they were presenting was from his own pen, and
he considered it his finest offering to date, far and away the best of
his dramas. *A Heart Divided* had a wonderful story line, in Noble's
opinion; Flora, the winsome heroine, had inherited a goodly sum of
money from her ailing father, for whom she had cared at great loss
of liberty for herself. Now that she was freed from her father's

sickbed, and had been rewarded for her sacrifice, Flora wished to meet with and marry a nice young man, to begin a life together. She had rejected several suitors whom she considered immodest or unscrupulous, and finally had met, quite by accident, a chaste fellow, pure of heart yet crushingly poor, a doctor who worked among the slum dwellers of New York. This character, Desmond Trueblood, was the perfect match for Flora, but he seemed not to notice her at all, even when she joined him in his work among the poor. Desmond was intensely concerned for the life of little Dorothy Daniels, an orphaned waif of the streets, dying slowly of consumption. Dorothy was not unhappy with her lot, knowing as she did that Jesus was waiting to sweep her up to his home in the sky. Dorothy, on her deathbed in the final scene, exhorted Flora and Desmond to wed, and bring into the world a child to replace herself. They vowed they would, and Dorothy died knowing she had accomplished some good in the world.

The deathbed speech had caused Noble to weep even as he penned it, and the troupe all agreed it was his finest work, but the clods at Behan's had merely hooted with laughter and thrown articles of trash at the stage. Behan himself had told Noble the play would end its run early, that very night in fact, and the curtain had come down on his masterpiece for the last time. Noble found it necessary, after calming the Arcadians, to absent himself from their company in order that he might get drunk. There was no other remedy for such outright humiliation and disappointment. Five years had passed since the name of Noble Burgin and his Arcadian Players brought smiles to the faces of theater managers on either coast, and tears to the eyes of all who saw the heartrending plays he brought forth from his soul. Life had been good then, but life now was not good. Something in Noble had become lost, some creative tool worn down by overuse, its edge blunted by repetition, perhaps.

Ensconced in a bar, Noble attempted to pin down the flaw that rendered all his offerings these last five years unacceptable to the public. He could not see why the plays had failed, since they employed all the devices that had worked so brilliantly in his earlier works. Could that in itself be the root cause of the problem? he asked himself. Was he merely repeating, or attempting to repeat, what had gone before? But he genuinely admired such stuff. What other kind of drama could he possibly attempt? He knew he was no Shakespeare, but success should still have been his.

He drank brandy, a great deal of it, and eventually tired of attempting to analyze his predicament. He would simply get drunk and forget his worries for an evening. He did not worry about his wife and leading lady, Hortense, since she was in the hands of the Arcadians at their lowly hotel several blocks away. Hortense did not approve of his drinking bouts, and would sometimes flirt with younger men to punish him. Noble made a point of hiring only those actors who he knew with certainty were not attracted to women, as a measure against Hortense's betraying him outright. She had performed well as Flora, even though the makeup could not conceal that her years were considerably in advance of her character's, and the rest of the cast had been similarly excellent in their roles, especially Marcie, who was young and slender enough to play Dorothy convincingly. Noble had lately been experiencing feelings of great tenderness toward Marcie, and felt compelled, on occasion, to place an arm around her shoulders. Hortense had caught him doing this the week before, and warned him never to do any such thing again, or she would leave him and take up with a successful man, any successful man in any field. It had been a hurtful moment, and Noble promised himself never again to do what he had done with Marcie while Hortense was anywhere near.

A newspaper abandoned by a fellow drinker at the next table caught Noble's eye, and he reached across to grab it before anyone else should think to. The headlines bored him, since they addressed political issues, a field Noble considered beneath his attention, but on page three he noticed an intriguing banner: RED SAVAGES MEET GRISLY END. He read the article, concerning the capture and deaths of two renegade Apaches named Panther Stalking and Kills With a Smile, and recalled having been aware of the depredations and mayhem these two had created for years in the southwestern territories. Trapped in a box canyon, their ammunition exhausted, the brothers had been attempting to smash their own skulls in with rocks when finally apprehended by an army unit that had been tracking them for weeks. Taken to Socorro and incarcerated in jail, the redskins had outwitted their captors, and thwarted the long-postponed expectations of the authorities to administer a stiff dose of hempen justice, by ignoring their chains and biting each other's jugular veins open in the night, an act of such bizarre single-mindedness it took Noble's breath away. He read on, and was apprised of their former names, Nail in His Feet and Bleeding

Heart of Jesus, and of the peculiar fashion in which their grandfather and a mysterious youth had stolen the brothers away from a Spanish mission after murdering the priests. Returned to their heathenish way of life, they had reverted quickly to type and begun a bloodthirsty reign that lasted for years, only to end in an appropriately bloody way on the floor of a jail cell.

Noble felt something stirring inside himself, a familiar sensation he identified, despite his drunkenness, as the flexing of the creative muscle, the insistent prodding of the muse, and he heeded its message. Could anything be less like his former works? No innocent damsels here; no virtuous heroes or happy endings. Blood. More blood than the Scottish play. *Brothers in Blood*. That was good, but *Red Hellions* was even better. He wouldn't even need to think up a story; it was right there before him in the newspaper, complete from first act to last, although he would need to invent characters and scenes to flesh out the basic plot. But what a plot! Barbaric. Cruel. Indigenous! This was a story wrested from the uncivilized heart of America, a true story, a tragedy steeped in redness. To write and stage such an epic would be an unprecedented flouting of conventional theater's rules. Did he have the courage within himself to do such a thing? He must! The play already was springing ready-formed from his brain. It would be a new beginning, for himself and the Arcadians, and for *Thespis Americanus*! New theatrical worlds awaited conquest, and Noble Burgin would be in the vanguard, a bold innovator, working against the grain, leaving behind the shopworn candy apples of yesterday's proscenium! He fell from his chair and struck his temple against the floor, was assisted to his feet, bleeding slightly, and aimed himself at the door. Destiny had called his name, and Noble would not hesitate now.

It had begun with the puppy. His mother gave it to Tatum on his tenth birthday, an adorable ball of fur that delighted in biting fingertips. He liked to play with it, but not for very long; its habit of playfully biting him annoyed Tatum in the end, and he hit the puppy to make it stop. The pup was confused, then approached him again, biting as before, and Tatum snapped its neck to teach it a lesson. He smuggled the tiny corpse from the house beneath his jacket, and flung it into a stream, then sat watching the waters flow, trying to understand what it was that he had done. Two things were clear to Tatum: it was easy to kill things, and it was possible to do so without feeling bad about it. He really didn't care that the puppy his mother had saved her money for was dead. It seemed to Tatum that spending money on something that was so easily killed and disposed of had been an awful waste. His mother was a fool.

When he was twelve, Tatum found that riding piggyback on one of his friends in the schoolyard produced a wonderful sensation in his groin. His penis hardened in an inexplicable way, so he urged his friend to run faster, and the jerkings of a backbone against Tatum's crotch aroused him further, pleasing him so much he demanded of his friend that he keep running and running, even when he grew tired. The friend stopped and flung Tatum off, aware that the piggyback ride had been more than just that, and Tatum smacked him hard across the face to punish him for having denied further enjoyment. The friend had cried, and Tatum despised him for that. He usually despised his friends after a very short time, without quite knowing why, but at least in this instance he had a definite reason.

Tatum found he could reproduce the effects of the piggyback ride by rubbing himself against the side of his mattress, and he kept this up until a terrible thing happened: his belly exploded and leaked a peculiar kind of fishy-smelling glue all over the front of his nightshirt. Tatum felt that death was near, but was glad to die while in a state of physical contentment that he could not explain.

Further experimentation along these lines led Tatum at last to the basic act of masturbation, but he found that however many times he might cause himself to spurt the belly glue, it was never so enjoyable as when he had ridden on the back of his erstwhile friend; in fact he could not produce the glue half so readily if he did not imagine himself again being carried around the schoolyard, high and hard.

Boys his own age soon learned to avoid Tatum; he was always trying to make them play piggyback, and they began to make fun of him, calling him piggy-wiggy. They would not allow him to play leapfrog with them, because Tatum had developed the habit of landing on top of the boys he was supposed to be vaulting over, which spoiled everyone's enjoyment. In time he was made an outcast for his seemingly irreconcilable needs to be physically close to the other boys and to punish them with his fists when they would not play piggyback or leapfrog the way he wanted.

Before Tatum was fourteen, the school informed his mother his attendance there was no longer required, and on inquiring the reason for this surprising statement, Mrs. Tatum was told that her son had been caught engaging in unnatural acts with a much younger boy, who had also been dismissed from further schooling, even though it was clear Tatum had been the event's instigator. Mrs. Tatum could not even broach the subject when she arrived home, and wished as she had never wished before that her husband had not died when their son was just one year old. She had struggled since then to provide him with love and a roof over his head and clothing he need not be ashamed of, but she could not talk with him of the things she had been told. It was easier to move away from Ohio and join her spinster sister Lydia in Denver, taking Tatum with her to begin again, far from the scene of such unpalatable and unbelievable allegations.

When he was eighteen, Tatum knew what he liked, but he knew also that proclaiming his likes would earn him nothing but scorn and very possibly a beating. He looked into the eyes of every young man who crossed his path, seeking out the ones like himself, and when he found them, he was kind to them, and generous with his money, until they balked at his suggestions for additional pleasures of an unusual nature. When they refused, he would hit them with the stout dog-headed cane he carried, until they begged for a chance to perform the service he had requested, a service that left them with rope burns around their necks, and more than the usual anal bruising.

Tatum became known in the gathering places of the sexually dispossessed, and stories of his excesses led some to cultivate his company, although few remained his friend for long. He was a handsome, smooth-skinned young man, with facial hair so fine it required shaving no more than once a week. He dressed well and took pains to present a neat appearance at all times. He did no work, allowed his mother to support him, and wondered if he would always live thus.

In 1884, when he was twenty-one, he posed nude for an artist who was covering the walls of a large room with life-sized depictions of whorish abandon, most of it without much interest for Tatum, since it involved the penetration of women, although he was somewhat smitten by the image of a young soldier cupping his victim's breast while brandishing a sword as he took her from behind. The juxtapositioning of the weapon and the act appealed to Tatum, and he asked the artist, a florid-faced drinker running to seed, who the handsome model might be.

"That one," said Nevis Dunnigan, "was a mystery. Had a finger missing, but an excellent study: no twitching, perfectly composed. Would you mind not wobbling your helmet that way, my good fellow? It distracts me something awful."

"Is that him again over there, with the spear?"

"The same, and again to your left, with the young lady's face hiding his member. He wouldn't stay for more posing than that. Pity. You'll let me use you for several more studies, won't you?"

"What was his name?"

"Ilium, he said, but I didn't believe it. There were secrets in his eyes, buried deep. It's hard to find young fellows willing to pose. I prefer fellows—as a painter, I mean—with all their planes and angles. Michelangelo was that way too. Ever notice how his women look like men with tits? Well, they do say he was homely, so maybe he never knew a woman the way a man should."

Tatum had never heard of Michelangelo, but was content to let the painter drone on while he worked, for the opportunity it gave him to stare at the naked soldier on the wall. Tatum had stayed on with his aunt Lydia following the death of his mother, and held the woman in a permanent state of dread. She did not dare to question his comings and goings, or inquire who the young men entering his room might be. The one occasion when she did so had resulted in a beating around her varicose-veined legs, and the pain of it had been so excruciating and lasted so long she never again queried his least movement or choice of company. Tatum was silently provided with meals at any hour of the day or night, and Lydia could not refuse him a portion of the money she had saved over a lifetime of toil. He took, he spent, and not once did he thank her, but his aunt said nothing, valuing a life without physical pain over a life with pride.

Leaving Nevis Dunnigan's "studio," as the artist referred to it, Tatum wandered up one street and down another until evening, then paid for a meal with the few dollars he had earned by posing. Curiosity rather than any urgent need for money had caused him to apply for the work when he saw a small advertisement placed in a newspaper. It had been an interesting experience in its way, but he was not willing to pose again. He might have reconsidered, had the other model been returning, but Dunnigan had told him the young man with the missing finger had come and gone, his artistic purpose served.

Finished with his meal, Tatum again took to the streets, strolling aimlessly in the dark until he found himself far from his usual haunts. He had wandered almost to the edge of town, and was somewhere near the railroad tracks; he could hear boxcars being shunted and coupled in the dark, and smell the acrid odor of coal smoke, and was just about to turn and retrace his steps toward brighter lights when he heard a low coughing from some brush nearby.

Investigating, he found a tramp asleep in a shallow ditch. The tramp was filthy, ragged, and coughing in his sleep. Tatum was offended by such shabbiness, such disregard for the sartorial arts; he himself spent a considerable amount of his aunt's money on clothing of the latest cut, and delighted in the figure he presented, from his narrow-brimmed hat to his elastic-sided boots and dog-headed cane. The tramp was an insult to man, to the world at large, with his unshaven cheeks and busted-out boots, and Tatum conceived a great dislike of and contempt for him as he stood above the quietly coughing figure.

The cane was raised as if lifted by another arm, some invisible appendage not connected to Tatum. He felt the arm lift his cane, felt it bring the golden dog down hard upon the flimsy hat, felt the cranium give way with surprising ease, and he heard the coughing stop. He thought at first it had been no more difficult to kill the tramp than break an egg, but then the fellow's eyes opened and he began to shout, so Tatum was forced to silence him with repeated blows, laid on by his own arm now, and laid on with a will, until the head and face below him became an indistinct smear of blood and bone.

When he was convinced the job had been completed, Tatum hurried away, sweat running down his sides. He calmed himself as the scene was left behind, then became a little hysterical, laughing at the tramp's pathetic efforts to defend himself, never more than a spasmodic clutching at the air. Really, it had been a fine thing he did, ridding the city of so degenerate a specimen of rude humanity. Arriving home, Tatum was annoyed to find embedded in the wood of his cane a human tooth.

Work on the new play kept Noble isolated from the players, and from his wife. Hortense had never seen him so consumed by a project; he would not discuss the nature of the piece, wouldn't even hint at the plot. He did go so far as to let her know there was no role in it for herself, a fact that stunned Hortense; Noble's plays had always included a plum part for her.

She asked, "Is there a role for Marcie?" and Noble told her no. "For any female?" she asked, and this time Noble paused before answering.

"No, but so far they haven't begun their murderous rampage. I suppose I could include you and Marcie later on, when some rancher's wife and daughter are being slaughtered. Yes, you could plead for your lives and they would laugh at you before cutting your throats."

"Noble! What beastliness are you creating? Ranchers? No one wishes to see a play about ranchers. Where would the interest lie? And slaughter? Cows, Noble?"

"Not cows, my dear—humans, yourself and Marcie among others. There will be several dozen in all. I'll have to devise a way of splashing blood around that won't create too much mess, or stain the costumes permanently."

"What on earth are you talking about?"

"Hortense, I am revolutionizing the theater. This play will become a cornerstone of the new American drama. This is something rooted in reality, actual occurrences so recent they have been included in the newspapers."

"Newspapers?"

Hortense was aghast. She had never read any part of a newspaper except for theatrical reviews, and even then she only consented to scan those articles that concerned plays she herself was appearing in. The rest of the newspaper was for common people, not artists like herself and Noble.

"You must explain yourself this instant," she said. "I fear for your sanity, with this talk of ranchers and blood."

"My dear, this play is not about ranchers. Such ranchers as will appear are incidental to the main thrust of the plot, which basically is about two Indian brothers."

"Indians! Noble, how can you even think to dabble in such low stuff ...?"

"Not just any Indians—Panther Stalking and Kills With a Smile! Raised in the church, then stolen away and taught to kill without mercy in the way of their kind."

"What! What! Noble, you are demented...."

"It was their grandfather who did it. I haven't been able to find out his name, so I'll call him Flaming Arrow, and there's another fascinating character, the one who let Flaming Arrow into the mission to steal his grandsons away. I'm calling him Augustus Chillington, and he won't be aware of the consequences of what he did until later, when he learns what the brothers have become. His own family is killed by them, you see. He'll swear vengeance and track the redskins down single-handed and bring them to justice, to set right the unconscious wrong he perpetrated in the first place. It's a wonderful story, Hortense. I have some doubts about the ending, though. In actual fact the brothers bit open each other's necks and bled to death.... Hortense?"

Noble's wife slid gently to the floor.

26

He entered the bank in a highly nervous state, then could not find his voice, even though his gun was already out and aimed at the teller. Drew felt himself freeze, and wondered if was too late to back out before matters went any further.

"Yessir, yessir ...," said the teller, understanding that the silent man with the gun was a robber. Drew felt his heart sink as cash was scooped from the drawers for him; the robbery had begun, and there could be no going back now. He forced himself to thrust a canvas bag under the teller's bars, and the money was clumsily stuffed inside.

There were no other customers in the bank, and just the one teller. Drew could hear someone moving around and coughing in an office to the rear, oblivious to the theft occurring mere yards away. Drew felt he had chosen wisely for his initial foray into crime; the bank was in a small mountain town west of Denver. He did not expect the haul to be large, but he did anticipate easy pickings and no interference from lawmen; he had established before entering the bank that the town had no marshal, just a part-time constable currently laid up in his home with a bad case of gout. The teller was being cooperative, and the manager, if that was who the cougher was, remained in his office. Everything was proceeding as it should, and Drew began to feel his throat loosen as the prospects for success grew.

"Hurry," he said.

"Yessir, that's all there is, I'm sorry."

The bag was returned to him, disappointingly flat, but it could be that the bills were of large denomination.

"About how much is this?" Drew asked.

"Oh, around three hundred, I guess."

"Well, thank you."

"Thank you, sir."

"I wouldn't really have shot you."

"Yessir."

"I just need the money."

"Yessir."

"Good-bye."

"Good-bye, sir."

Drew walked out of the bank, then turned around and went back in. The teller had not moved. The same dry cough came from the office.

"I forgot to tell you not to make a fuss, and don't come after me with a gun, because then I'd have to shoot back."

"Yessir."

"I'm a good shot. You'd get hit."

"Yessir."

"Well, so long."

Drew mounted his horse and began riding slowly out of town. He turned in the saddle once to reassure himself that the teller had done as he asked, and was relieved to see that the sidewalk in front of the bank was clear, in fact the whole street was tranquil, virtually unpopulated. It had been easier than expected. Next time he wouldn't freeze up. He might restrict himself to the smaller towns until he was more comfortable with the role of robber, though, just to be sure nothing went wrong.

Drew felt his horse lurch beneath him before the sound of the shot reached his ears, and the sound was unmistakably that of a buffalo gun. His horse was sinking beneath him, simply collapsing onto its buckled legs, and Drew had to jump clear before it fell on its side. He could see no wound, but blood was gouting from its mouth. Looking back, Drew could see someone standing outside the bank, reloading what looked like a Sharps fifty-caliber. It was not the teller, so it must have been the cougher. The bullet had entered his horse's anus and plowed straight through into its chest; the next bullet would be for him.

He began to run, ducking and weaving to present a difficult target. A horse was tethered outside a store further along the street, but before Drew could reach it the buffalo gun boomed again, and that horse also sank to its knees, shot through the belly. It began to scream, and the sound unnerved Drew so much he dropped his canvas bag. There were people on the street now. Drew could hear the man in front of the bank yelling about the robbery, and see his arm pointing. People were looking at him. He felt sick to his stomach. There had to be another horse that he could steal and ride away from such embarrassment. It seemed like the right time to yank out his pistol to prevent anyone from thinking he could be stopped, but this act also went astray when Drew fumbled his grip and dropped the Colt. He had the presence of mind to pick it up before dashing into an alley.

There seemed little else to do than leave the town on foot, his access to any available horses having been removed now that the citizenry were alerted to the presence of a robber among them. If he could reach the cover of the trees he had a chance to escape, but the trees had been thinned considerably during construction of the town, so real cover lay more than a quarter mile away. Drew's high-heeled boots were not made for running, and he had covered less than half the distance when he heard hoofbeats behind him. Turning, he saw two men on horseback, both armed. He would have to shoot them or be captured, and if he shot at them they would shoot back, and most likely kill him right there, since they outgunned him.

Drew aimed his pistol, but could not pull the trigger. The men separated to present two targets, both still beyond accurate pistol range. They reined in, and one put a rifle to his shoulder. Drew decided surrender was his only choice, and dropped his gun to raise both hands in the air. The rifleman seemed not to be interested in capturing him alive, and sent a bullet beneath his armpit. The second man was shouting at the first to stop firing. Drew didn't know what to do in the face of such ungallant behavior. While the men argued, the second riding to rejoin the first, still shouting, another bullet was aimed at Drew, this time penetrating the hem of his jacket. Angry now, he picked up his gun and emptied all six shots at the man with the rifle. To Drew's consternation, the man toppled from his horse and lay on the ground. The horse danced sideways, then was still. The second man had turned and was riding back toward the town, a fact that stunned Drew; the fallen rifle could have been snatched up and fired again before Drew had time to reload, but the rider clearly was no longer in any mood to apprehend him. Drew ran to the horse, took hold of its reins and picked up the rifle. The man on the ground was not dead; one of Drew's bullets had struck him in the stomach, and he lay groaning with the pain of it, his eyes unfocused. Drew mounted the horse and rode away, teeth chattering with fear and shock.

After nightfall, many miles from his bungled first attempt at robbery, Drew knew he would have to either approach his new line of work with a completely different attitude or give it up. In future, he must enter his chosen bank with expectations of encountering real trouble when he left, and of being obliged to open fire without hesitation, should that be necessary. He toyed briefly with the notion of abandoning all efforts of a criminal nature, then rejected it; to give in after just one try would have been cowardly. He thought of the man whose horse and rifle he had stolen, and felt a twinge of guilt for having given him the kind of wound that almost always resulted in death, but he reminded himself that the man had shot at him after Drew raised his hands in surrender, so the absence of that man would not leave the world a poorer place. Drew was lost under the full moon, headed in no particular direction, so long as it was away from the scene of the day's events. He was without money, had been separated from his only change of clothing, left behind in the saddlebags on his dead horse, and had just seven bullets remaining in the loops of his gun belt, but Drew faced the distant morning with a renewed sense of certainty. He had begun badly, but was determined to become an expert, the best bank robber since Jesse James.

His aunt was nearly penniless, but had kept the news from Tatum for as long as she could, fearing his temper when he learned he could no longer take money from her. She had given and given to her dead sister's boy, until there remained little to give, unless she sold her house, the thing she valued most. No, she must not surrender that, no matter how much he bullied her. Without her house, she would have nowhere to live, nor any reason to keep on living. She would resist such a forlorn end, even if this meant looking the devil squarely in the eye.

Her moment of defiance came just one day after her resolution.

Tatum approached her for money, having last seen her four days earlier, under identical circumstances. She told him no. Tatum required several seconds to digest this. He cocked his head a little to one side, like an intelligent dog, and asked that she repeat what he thought she had just said.

"I cannot give you any more money."

"And why is that, dearest Aunt?"

"I have no more to give. I am poor. I have nothing."

"You have some very nice furniture. Sell some of it."

"No."

"No?"

"Never. I will give you nothing more, not a cent."

"I see. I guess you'll also want me to be moving out from under your roof, is that it?"

She had not dared to broach so dangerous a topic in the same breath she had refused him money, but since he himself had raised the question, she would not shy away from it.

"Yes ..."

"Yes? You want me gone?"

Lydia could not speak, could only nod. Tatum studied her face and saw the terror there. He wished to break his cane across her shoulders, but did not; beating a woman of his aunt's character would bring the police into his life, create too many difficulties for him, and so he made himself smile at Lydia instead of beating her; surprisingly, her fear-whitened features blanched further at the sight of this unusual expression on his face, and Tatum saw himself, briefly, as did his aunt—a creature without any emotion other than general disdain and occasional rage, an entity upon whose lips a smile was as insincere as the welcoming face of a whore. Lydia hated and feared him, but Tatum would spare her, even though she had done what few ever dared to do; she had denied him his wants, face-to-face, and she had won. Amused by his own sense of magnanimity, he leaned closer to her and said, "Pack my things, Aunt. I'll return for them later."

"Yes ...," she said, and sent thanks to God when Tatum turned away from her and left the house without having laid so much as a finger on her person. She felt ill, took herself to the kitchen and vomited copiously into a bucket.

For Tatum, his dismissal from Lydia's home came at an opportune time. He recently had met a young man who shared his tastes in flesh and his newly acquired yen to gamble. This friend, the son of a wealthy banker, would allow Tatum to share his rooms at one of Denver's finest hotels, because Tatum was the dominant partner, and could bend Jared Morrow to accommodate any whim that suited him. Tatum already owed Jared more than a thousand dollars for having covered his gambling debts, but was confident the test of friendship could be extended further.

Entering Jared's rooms, Tatum found his friend in an unreceptive mood. Jared was in no position to help him, since his father had rescinded Jared's line of credit and refused to pay off Jared's own debts, until such time as Jared reformed himself, stopped flaunting himself among bad company and dedicated himself to a position in his father's bank. Until these requirements were met, Jared was utterly without funds, and in the circles among which he moved, a lack of money meant public humiliation. Jared was disinclined to set foot outside the door, circumstances being as they were.

Tatum offered comfort after his own fashion, by taking Jared to bed for soothing talk and a bracing round of boodling, as Tatum referred to their sexual act. In the wake of their exertions, Tatum was struck by the perfect solution to Jared's difficulties, and his own.

"Do you love him at all, your father?"

"No, I can't say I do."

"Like him?"

"No, never. He always called me a mother's boy."

"Would you be made miserable if he was to die?"

"I'd be the happiest fellow in Denver, Tatie, and one of the richest besides."

"Then what say we do the old man in, you and me?"

"Do him in?"

"Put him away. Under Mother Nature's blanket of earth. Understand?"

"Yes, but ... no, I couldn't do that, not kill him."

"Are you sure? Think of what you stand to gain if father dear goes to a better place before his rightful time."

"No, Tatie, I won't even think of it. I just couldn't."

"Even though you hate him?"

"I didn't say I hate him. I said I've never liked him. There's a difference. He's my father after all."

"He's not mine."

"Meaning?"

"If you can't bring yourself to be my partner, I'll do it by myself. I'll do it for you."

"I believe you're serious."

"Will you keep your mouth shut if I do it?"

"Oh, Tatie, this is ridiculous. You couldn't kill anyone."

"No? Are you sure?"

Jared watched his lover's face, and saw a disturbing stoniness there. Once, while drunk, Tatum had hinted of a murder he committed some time ago, but he had not provided details, so Jared had not believed him, and had forgotten the incident until Tatum's eyes, inches from his own, now gave him cause for belief.

"You wouldn't," he breathed, giving his words the teasing quality of a dare.

"I would," said Tatum, without any hint of levity, and Jared realized he had stepped into waters that might possibly rise to swallow him. He admired Tatum for his commanding ways in bed, for the semiplayful force with which he made Jared submit to him in ways that gave pleasure to them both. Tatum was a special person, not someone to be taken lightly. He meant what he said, and he was waiting for Jared's reply.

"How would you do it? I wouldn't want there to be any unnecessary suffering."

"Quickly, I'd do it quickly and be gone. No one would ever know who did it. Everyone would suspect you, since you're the one who'll inherit everything he has, but you can be among swarms of people the whole day or evening or whenever I choose to do it, so they won't be able to accuse you of a damn thing."

"And your reward for such risk taking would be?"

"A large settlement of cash, and your undying love."

Jared laughed. "I might be able to guarantee the first, but Tatie, you're so fickle I doubt that you'll want me forever. Let's order food and forget about this nonsense."

Tatum took him by the throat. "Grow up, Jared. Look around and see the world as it truly is, my friend. If I don't get rid of him, you'll have nothing, and you'll have it soon. Order food now, and it will arrive. Tomorrow it may not. They know here who pays your bills. He only needs to close the spigot, and you're through, finished. Be a man for once, sweetness, and make the decision you have to make."

Tatum released him. "Well?"

"I ... You hurt me, you shit ..."

"Tell me to do it."

"It doesn't have to be decided now ..."

"Tell me to do it."

"Will you kindly stop! I won't tell you any such thing! You have no right to bully me this way ..."

Tatum slapped him across the face. Jared hit back and they began to wrestle back and forth across the bed. Tatum quickly asserted himself as victor by pinning Jared beneath him in a position they often assumed while engaged in sexual penetration, in fact both felt themselves aroused by the tussle, and Tatum entered his friend while entreating him to give Tatum what he needed—a direct order to "deal with the situation now, before word gets around that he's reining you in. Do it. Tell me. Tell me ...!"

Jared finally granted his consent to the pact in a rush of gratification that left him breathless. Tatum stroked his damp hair and kissed his ear.

"This will be for the best," he whispered, "for everyone."

Before leaving Jared the following day, Tatum had equipped himself with knowledge of Walter Morrow's habits of movement and relaxation, and with a small nickel-plated Remington revolver Jared had purchased but never fired.

He liked to think of himself as a man of few vices, so Walter Morrow chose to view his evening snifter of brandy as an elegant ritual, rather than a habit. Walter found brandy wonderfully soothing, and he paid well for the finest. Ambrosia, he called it, and kept a supply at the home of his mistress, so the evening ritual could be performed there as well. His mistress was not permitted to visit him at his mansion, but Walter felt that the house he provided for her was compensation enough for the lady's having to exist in the shade, as it were, of his reputation for propriety and rectitude. He would not even have required a mistress, he often reminded himself, if his wife had not died.

The brandy ritual was best enjoyed in solitude, so Walter preferred to indulge himself at home, surrounded by the silence only opulent living can guarantee. His study was eighty yards from the street, and the clattering of coaches was muffled by a high wall, a wide lawn and French windows. He served himself a generous measure and sat in his most comfortable armchair before the fireplace. Sometimes, after the first few mouthfuls, he grew introspective, even melancholy, and sometimes, as he did tonight, he became bitter. The cause for this was no mystery to Walter; his son had disappointed him—again.

Jared had been a delightful child, but as he grew older, there remained a strong element of the faintly girlish qualities Walter had found endearing in a seven-year-old but far less appealing in a boy of fifteen. He had tried everything to make Jared manly, including physical training and lessons in horsemanship and hunting by way of an ex-army sergeant, but all of that had come to nothing. Jared walked in a hesitant, tiptoed manner that infuriated Walter whenever he witnessed it. Heavier boots had not solved the problem, nor had a parental whipping. The whipping had been an especially grievous error on Walter's part; his wife had never forgiven him for treating her poor dear boy so, and until the time of his wife's death, Walter left Jared alone, to become whatever it was that he seemed bent on becoming; certainly it was not a banker.

Once a widower, Walter attempted to reassert himself as the moral custodian of his son, now twenty, but found he had assumed this duty too late. Jared was a confirmed pantywaist by then, a caricature of masculinity gone awry, a pouting, preening little vixen of a creature whom Walter suspected of actually applying a light blush to his cheeks with rouge. It was a tremendous blow to a father's heart, seeing the product of love between man and wife evolve into the brightly poisonous bloom Jared had become.

That was when Walter sought comfort in the arms of a woman, as a kind of affirmation that he was truly a man, and in no way responsible for the blood coursing in the veins of his son. For some time he was distracted from the thorn he carried, but his mistress, although a beautiful and compliant woman, was not in love with him, and Walter began to suspect she was in fact using him, as lovely women have always used rich men of middle age. Suspicious of his mistress, distressed over the wayward tendencies of Jared, Walter immersed himself in the thousand and one details of a banking man's life in an effort to distract himself, but thoughts of his boy were hard to escape. He decided there must be one last effort on his part to bring Jared back into the fold of normalcy, to prepare him for his ultimate responsibilities as heir to a fortune and, in time, as a husband and father. If he failed to accomplish this, Walter would disown Jared completely, and might even contemplate remarriage and the conception of new, untainted progeny. All or nothing, Walter intoned to himself several times a day, while waiting for some kind of response from Jared, who had been informed by Walter's attorneys that he longer had access to any line of credit connected with his father. Time would tell if the boy was prepared to see reason.

Walter did that night what he had never done before—he poured himself a second brandy, equal in size to the first, and began drinking it without even bothering to savor its bouquet. He recognized that he was upset, but forgave himself the indulgence his mood required. What good man should have to tolerate the kinds of disappointment Walter was obliged to endure? His wealth was unable to dislodge the misery clutching at his soul. Lovey Doll was faithful to him, he was sure, but no mistress could be trusted entirely. If she was prepared to share her bed with Walter, to whom she was not married, then might she not perform the same service to some other man who happened to take her eye? A mistress was by definition a woman without morals, and Walter was obliged to be on his guard.

She had come to him by way of a shipping magnate in San Francisco, whose paramour she had been for almost a year. The poor fellow found himself dying of cancer, and had requested of Walter that he take Lovey Doll Pines with him to Denver, far from the wrath of his family, who suspected she would hire an army of lawyers to gouge a chunk of the magnate's millions for herself. The dying man had similar suspicions, but retained enough affection for Lovey Doll to ensure that she was passed along into the hands of a righteous man with enough capital to smooth her feathers. He had known Walter Morrow professionally for several years, and had formed the notion that here was the likeliest benefactor Lovey Doll could latch onto.

The arrangement was made at the dying man's bedside, without the presence of Lovey Doll, and news of it was brought to her by messenger. She had thought it over for twenty-four hours, then accompanied Walter across the deserts and mountains of the west in his private railroad car, treating him en route to a variety of sexual displays his wife and Walter had never been cognizant of. He was captivated, and his sense of rejuvenated maleness had lasted until Walter noticed for the first time how utterly empty were Lovey Doll's eyes when he chanced to gaze into them in search of warmth, of passion, of simple friendliness. No woman with eyes such as hers could possibly hold Walter in the high regard Walter considered his by right. Someday she would have to go, but not yet, not while she still aroused in him the need for her body. She belonged to him. He could wait.

Other matters concerned him that evening, matters of conse- quence in the business world. Walter belonged to an organization centered in Denver, with unofficial branches in Cheyenne and Kansas City, whose purpose it was to control and profit by the vari- ous markets in the west. Their aims were achieved through back- room manipulations by unscrupulous negotiators, or by threatening anyone who stood in the way of their aspirations in some field, be it ranching or farming or mining. Outright spying was part of the organization's stock-in-trade, and bribery was its principal weapon. When this failed, as it sometimes did, coercion was applied. Anyone foolish enough to ignore this was disposed of, in such a way as to resemble an accident or act of God, but it was understood, by those in the know, that the death of the fool had been sanctioned by the mysterious organization called Big Circle.

The members of Big Circle were rich men, so rich they no longer saw themselves as connected by any but the thinnest of societal strings to men of ordinary means and achievements. Most of the Big Circle fraternity had made their money themselves; there were few who inherited wealth, like the rich men of the east, and they were proud to be the authors of their own fiscal importance. They liked to imagine themselves working fellows who had worked hard- er than most, and in some cases this was true, but more often than not they had been lucky, or more vicious in their business practices than most men cared to be, and that was what rendered them eligi- ble for membership. Once accepted, whatever their origins or the source of their wealth, Big Circle men were lost to the common herd by way of their very inclusion; the air of Olympus has never been for mortals.

The latest man under consideration for membership, did he but know it, was an individual of tremendous fortune, acknowledged to be the richest man in Colorado. Leo Brannan, it was confidently stated, was the richest man in the western half of the nation, and likely to be the richest man in America by the turn of the century, if his fabulous mines maintained their current phenomenal output. There had been hesitation for a year or more, among some of Big Circle's more influential members, regarding the inclusion of Brannan among their ranks. He was rumored to be a queer duck, reclusive by inclination, not given to moving among others of his ilk. Brannan virtually owned a valley high among the peaks of the Rocky Mountains, and he seldom ventured outside his fiefdom. He smelted his own gold, rather than ship it by rail to the furnaces of other companies, and bought coal from the mines around Durango only because the stuff did not exist in his own part of the state.

He was his own man in every way, and while the members of Big Circle lauded the fellow for his fantastic earnings which had sprung from an unlikely claim located halfway up a mountainside, they were a trifle suspicious of Brannan's exclusivity, the way he ran his little empire. He could not be ignored, dominating the gold market as he did, but it was a matter of opinion whether he should be drafted into Big Circle to become one of their own. He might well refuse, if the stories about his independence were true, and then where would the members be? It was unthinkable that someone should refuse their offer, but the one man capable of doing just that was Leo Brannan. They would not be able to coerce him, or intimidate him, rich as he was.

It was the custom of Big Circle to be sure of every move it made, a process that required the casting of votes in a democratic manner, and Leo Brannan's name had twice been put up for membership, only to be voted down by one or two of the members in longest standing, who tended to be more cautious than the rest by virtue of their wider experience. Wait and see, was their advice, and since inclusion as a member of Big Circle could be brought about only when the membership was in complete accord regarding the suitability of the latest name offered, Leo was rejected. Eventually newer members insisted that Leo be the next to be offered a seat among them. The nay-sayers produced evidence that Brannan was not right for inclusion, despite his success. There were stories, they said, of strange goings-on at Brannan's mansion overlooking Glory Hole, peculiar happenings laid upon the unlikely shoulders of his stepdaughter, who, it was rumored, had powers that would have earned her a place at the stake in an earlier century. There was something not quite right about the man and his family and the way he ran his business; Brannan was not Big Circle material, not yet.

A secret meeting was convened, and an emissary brought to Walter the decision arrived at by this smaller circle within Big Circle: Walter Morrow had been selected as unofficial ambassador to

approach Leo Brannan with a view to offering him membership. If
he refused, no more would be said, and those members who did not
advocate his acceptance would be none the wiser. If, on the other
hand, he accepted the offer, those supporting him would make sure
he became a member of the new splinter group within Big Circle.
With Colorado's richest man admitted into the inner sanctum of the
initiated, the smaller circle would, in time, engulf the larger circle
and emerge as its new voice.

It was an assignment that made Walter proud, a sign his star
was rising within Big Circle. He had been selected for this clandestine task, he was told, because he radiated an earnestness of manner that was not to be found among most members. It would be a
tricky assignment, but Walter had invested in him the confidence of
the secret enclave. If he brought Brannan home, figuratively speaking, his status within the fold would be considerably enhanced.
There were changes afoot, and he was not too old to be included
among those orchestrating the revision. The excitement he felt over
the task ahead was almost sufficient to erase from his thoughts the
subjects of Lovey Doll Pines and Jared. Walter would leave for
Glory Hole the day after next, and he felt that Columbus could not
have been more excited at the prospect of what lay before him.

The muted shattering of glass somewhere nearby intruded upon
Walter's thoughts in a manner not sufficiently alarming to cause
him concern; he assumed one of the servants had dropped something, and was in such an expansive frame of mind he could not be
bothered investigating so trivial an offense. He planned the speech
he would make to Leo Brannan, emphasizing the benefits to be
enjoyed as a member of the clandestine offspring hiding within Big
Circle. It was a speech that might possibly change his life, and he
wished to perfect its tone well in advance of the encounter.

He did not hear the study door open, nor see the slender young
man who slid through like a shadow. The soft click of the lock did
alert Walter, and he turned from the fire just as the intruder
approached. He wondered at first if this was some new servant
hired without his knowledge, and was angry that the fellow had
entered without having been summoned, and without knocking.

"What the devil do you mean by this!"

"Mr. Morrow?"

"Who are you?"

"I have a message from Jared. I thought it best, sir, to deliver it
in private."

"Who let you in! This is outrageous ..."

"Jared's over there," said the young man, nodding toward the far side of the room. When Walter turned, Tatum took the pistol from his pocket, held it close to Walter's temple and fired one shot. Walter died instantly, still searching the area near the bookshelves for evidence that his son was there.

Tatum placed the pistol near Walter's right hand, then walked quickly to the French windows. He unlocked one, extracted the key and stepped outside, locked the window behind himself and ran for the high wall around Walter Morrow's mansion. He was over the top and strolling along the street beyond while servants were still knocking at the study door.

28

Clay caught up with Dr. Maxwell in 1884, in southern Arizona, where the dentist was on trial for having administered so large a dose of nitrous oxide to his patient the recipient did not awaken. That the deceased had been a girl of only eleven years did not bode well for Maxwell, nor did the fact that he had attempted to depart town by way of his hotel room's window, leaving the girl's mother in a separate room from that in which the surgery for extraction took place. It was only because the mother finally lost patience and entered the second room to make sure her daughter was not suffering any pain that the alarm was raised. Maxwell was found under a wooden sidewalk, blubbering with fear.

His trial was immediate, and had just begun when Clay Dugan entered town. Finding the saloon empty, Clay inquired the reason for such unusual abstinence in a sizable town like Dry Wash. A quick summary of events from the bartender sent Clay down the street to the courthouse, where he stood at the back of the courtroom along with dozens of others, every available seat having been taken. Testimony from the mother was crisp and uncluttered, her final statement being that a hanging was too good for such a snake; she suggested he be made to inhale a sufficient amount of his own poison to send him to perdition, and there was much shouted agreement. The judge admitted such punishment made sense, but let it be known that death by gassing was beyond the law, and would not be considered by the court should the accused be found guilty.

"Any further witnesses?" asked the judge.

Clay pushed forward through the crowd, made bold by two fast whiskeys and a need to see Maxwell's face when he came closer. "Your Honor, I believe I can contribute something here," he said, and was beckoned forward. Sworn in, he gave his name, and stated the facts pertaining to his own unsatisfactory usage of Dr. Maxwell's professional services. He was asked by the defense to produce evidence that he had ever had dental treatment, from Maxwell or anyone else, and Clay responded by emptying his mouth of the rubberized plates that had smiled at him when he awoke after Maxwell's less than complete ministrations in Pueblo. The courtroom was swept by laughter, which Maxwell's lawyer attempted to quieten by insisting that there was no proof the dentures on display had been manufactured by his client, and just who, he asked, was the witness anyway? Once the laughter had died away, the judge requested that Clay tell a little something about himself, just for the record.

"I'm a bounty hunter," Clay stated, and the last ripples of mirth among the crowd were silenced.

"I hunt down men who broke the law and got away. They don't get away from me. It's big country out here, and plenty can get clear of the law and what the law demands of them for what they did, namely punishment, but I get them. Scum like that," he said, pointing to Maxwell, "they keep on doing what they do until someone stops them. That's what I do. It isn't pretty work, but someone has to round them up. Bounty hunter, that's a nasty thing to be, most people think, but I don't think so. I do what I do, the same as criminals and degenerates do what they do, only I do my job better, so I'm whittling them down, slow but sure. I make no apologies, ladies and gentlemen. I am the man I am."

Someone at the rear of the courtroom began clapping, and the sound became contagious. The judge allowed it to continue for a minute or so before banging his gavel and calling for order in the court. When it came, he said, "Mr. Dugan, I believe I speak for most of us here when I say that your line of work is necessary but unappreciated. Most justices of my acquaintance, they won't touch the hand that deals sudden death to criminals if they don't come along easy, but I'm not so sure that men such as yourself aren't an essential ingredient in the service of the law hereabouts, unpretty though it may be, as you said. Mr. Dugan, I'd be proud to shake your hand, sir."

There was much cheering and general approbation as Clay stepped forward to take the judge's hand in his. Maxwell's lawyer sat down, shaking his head in disapproval, and Dr. Maxwell was seen to smile a ghostly smile, as if having seen the end to his trial and determined its outcome. When the clamor had subsided, Maxwell stood and demanded the opportunity to present his side of things, and the judge allowed it.

"Townspeople of Dry Wash," Maxwell began, "you think nothing of your teeth, except when they cause you pain, and such is the attitude of all Americans. Who is there to grant you relief from your oral ailments? Only professors of dentistry such as myself, good citizens, and where would you be without us, I ask. The oral science is not exact, I admit, and there remain many advances to come, among them a means of ascertaining precise dosages of painkiller for the patient. That day has not yet arrived. I am a sailor in uncharted waters, an explorer among the cavities of America, and yet I am victimized for having been found less than perfect. Is this the fault of myself, some flaw in my character, or is the tragedy that has brought us all here today the result of an infant branch of learning o'erreaching itself, perhaps, in pursuit of succor and easement among the suffering of the nation? A life has been lost, but am I solely to blame? Where is the evidence of malice aforethought? Good people, there is none. I am myself a victim in this matter, an emissary among you, a pilgrim of pain, doing what little I can to ward off dental hurt and loss.

"Nature, it has been said, is red in tooth and claw, but those same teeth may also be brown, men and women of Dry Wash, and that is the color of decay, from which there is no retreat, only the choice of extraction, which as you know is a painful process, made less so by the stringent application of scientific gases that render the sufferer oblivious to the wrenching and yanking which must accompany the removal of the decayed article. Yes, I play my part in the scheme of things, but it is a part imperfectly written, therefore imperfectly executed—I should say, imperfectly performed—and so I ask of you that you bear witness to my imperfection as a man, one of God's suffering creatures, and see reflected in me a part of yourselves, for who among us is without sin ... not that I have committed any such crime as sin, but ... we are none of us expert in our field, I maintain, else every farmer would create a crop of grain without equal, and every rancher be the proud owner of herds beyond numbering. So it is with the oral arts, ladies and gentlemen, and I throw myself upon your charity and mercy and good sense in this matter, which I was in no wise responsible for at all but am myself a victim of as heretofore stated ... and I thank you for your indulgence in this matter, good and wise citizens of Dry Wash."

Maxwell waited for some kind of response, but none came.

"Final arguments, if you please," said the judge.

These did not take long. Maxwell's lawyer was less eloquent than his client; the prosecutor borrowed heavily and without apology from Clay's speech about catching up with criminals. There was little tension in the courtroom when the jurors retired, since everyone knew what the verdict would be; there were an uncle and a second cousin of the dead girl on the jury, and the uncle, who ran the general store, held notes of credit against at least seven of the other ten jurors. But most important, everyone knew the dentist had done wrong; it was there in his thin face and weaselly mannerisms, and the way he had run like a coward from the scene of his tragic misdeed. The town would have its revenge, and community spirit would be revitalized as a result.

While a verdict was awaited, a process most people calculated would take no more than ten to fifteen minutes, Judge Poudre invited Clay into his tiny chambers at the rear of the courtroom for a quick snort, to celebrate their mutual yet exclusive approaches to the solving of society's ills.

"Mr. Dugan, sir, I'm a blunt man, so I'll ask you in a blunt manner if you're a successful manhunter."

"I make a living."

"And is it your intention to continue in this profession indefinitely?"

"One of these days I'll quit."

"What if a better offer should come along, some job requiring skills at tough law enforcement but without all the traveling around that goes with your current line of employment?"

"I guess I'd ask just what kind of job that might be, Judge. Something local?"

"Right here, sir. Dry Wash needs a town marshal of large caliber, because frankly, Mr. Dugan, we've seen marshals come and go, and a goodly number of them left in a box. There's a rough element hereabouts that needs curbing before they get out of hand. A case like today's, why, that's easy pickings, when the feller lets himself get caught underneath a sidewalk, but there's others that'll shoot if you try to arrest them, and that's why we need a marshal who can shoot back. Do I have your interest, Mr. Dugan?"

"You do, sir. Does this job come with a wage a man wouldn't be ashamed to bring home to his wife, if he had one?"

"Sir, it does, and if a feller happens not to have either a home or a wife, I'm sure both can be found in our fair town. I don't mean to push you, Mr. Dugan, but I'm blunt, as I said. Another shot for you?"

He poured whiskey into Clay's glass.

When a verdict of guilty was returned, and a sentence of death by hanging imposed, Maxwell slumped in his chair and began to sob as the air in the courtroom filled with shouts and whistling. Maxwell was marched away to the cells in the rear of the building, and the room began to empty, when Judge Poudre smacked his gavel down hard.

"Hold on just one minute there, you people! Get back and pay attention, if you please. You in back there, turn yourselves around right now, thank you kindly. I have an important announcement to make here, and now's the time to make it, with just about everyone who can cast a vote present and accounted for in one place."

When the crowd had resettled, he continued. "Mr. Dugan here has impressed me as a man of the world who can handle the various kinds of dangerous situation that do arise in the line of duty. I'm referring to the job of town marshal, which lately was vacated by shootout in regards to the lamented B. D. Clitheroe. Mr. Dugan has said to me that if we pay him well we can pin B.D.'s badge on him, assuming you people want him for the job. He gets my endorsement here and now. Anyone have anything to say about it before we put this matter to an official vote?"

There were murmurings for a moment, then a voice asked, "Mister, how many men you killed?"

"Twelve or thirteen," said Clay, "all bad."

There were no further questions.

"Those in favor," said the judge, "raise your hands."

Clay was surprised at the response.

"Those against, if any?"

Not a single hand was raised. Judge Poudre turned to Clay. "I believe you just now got yourself one tough job."

He was officially made marshal that afternoon. As the badge was pinned to his chest, Clay experienced a sentimental twinge, and had to remind himself that no one witnessing the ceremony in Judge Poudre's chambers would be so warm toward him if they knew of his past effort at law enforcement in Kansas, and the manner in which it had ended. His name apparently had not spread as far west as Arizona, and the job he wanted most had been handed to him like a birthday gift. It brought a momentary lump to his throat, and an urge to look over his shoulder. He had been accepted instantly by the citizens of Dry Wash, and he would not let them down.

"Thank you," was all he could say when invited to give an acceptance speech. "Thank you all. ..."

His first official act as marshal was to visit the cells and inquire of the only occupant if he was being treated well.

"Well enough," Maxwell admitted. "So you're the boss here now. It was me that got you the job. They wouldn't have been so fired up if you didn't help put me where I am. Ironic, isn't it."

"It's a peculiar world sometimes."

"I, who take away pain and decay, will die two days from now, while you, who specialize in death, have been given a county-paid job for as long as you want it. There's more than irony here."

"Maybe. I'm no philosopher. You never should've left me like that, Maxwell, with blood running down my neck. If it had've gone back down my throat I'd likely have choked. I don't believe you're evil, but you're a menace to folks. How much of your stuff did you give that little girl anyway?"

"The standard amount for someone of her years. I tried to explain that some people, maybe one in a million, have an allergic reaction to chemicals. It's impossible to say who, until it's too late. I was by no means careless."

"But you ran out on her, just like you did me. Did you think I was a goner too?"

"I simply had a train to catch."

"Well, now you've got another kind of schedule to keep."

"Thank you so much for reminding me."

"Pleasure's all mine. Care to place your order now?"

"Order?"

"Last meal. I'm a believer in tradition."

Maxwell pursed his lips in thought. "Pork chops."

"I'll see if we can't rustle some up. Need a Bible or anything?"

"I have never believed a word of it."

"Me neither."

Maxwell and Clay held a number of stimulating conversations over the next forty-eight hours, and Clay began to regret the need to stretch the dentist's neck; this was one of the most intelligent men he had met. He could do nothing, of course, since he had contributed to Maxwell's conviction, and that conviction had been in part responsible for Clay's new job, as Maxwell himself had pointed out. The dentist exonerated Clay for what was to come, understanding the position of his ex-patient with a breadth of forgiveness Clay found nothing less than remarkable.

"I've decided to approach my death from an experimental point of view, Dugan."

"How so?"

"In the morning, I'll find out one way or the other if there is indeed an afterlife."

"I thought you didn't believe in the Bible."

"That book has nothing to do with it. Civilizations that preceded Christianity, and those without its dubious benefits, all agree that after this thing we call life, there is existence of another kind. It will be most interesting to discover what shape it assumes, if there be such a place."

"I'm kind of curious myself about what there might or might not be once a man dies. I met with a feller one time, he believed he could prove the soul leaves the body just after death. He had a special beam balance that could measure the difference before and after, he said. I don't think that's likely, though, do you?"

"I couldn't venture an opinion without examining the device beforehand."

"Guess not. Well, can I get you anything for tonight? Your pork chops are all set by for breakfast."

"I ... well, I hesitate to ask this of you, Dugan, but since you're clearly not a churchgoing man, I'll speak my mind. I believe I have a right to do that, as one of the condemned."

"You surely do. Spit it out."

"Is there any chance you might arrange the presence of a young lady of attractive appearance to share my last hours with me? Dry Wash is a big enough town to have at least one house of ill repute, is it not? I do so like young ladies, Dugan, and frankly, it's been quite some time since I enjoyed the feel of female flesh. Do I shock you?"

"No. I'll see what I can do."

Clay went to the house of Judge Poudre and consulted with him in the drawing room, once the judge's wife had departed, leaving behind coffee and brandy.

"I appreciate the man's request," said the judge, when Clay had explained the purpose of his visit. "I can give you a name, but you better be sure and not let any of this reach anyone's ears but mine. Tell the girl you'll go hard on her too, if she breathes a word."

"I don't like to threaten women."

"With whores it's different. She'll do it and stay quiet, if I'm any judge. ... Ha ha! Hear that, Clay? Any judge! Well, she's a smart girl, smarter than most whores, so I guess you'll just need to ask her nice, that's all. Go on down to Willow Street, second to last house on the left, got a fair-sized chinaberry tree in front. Madge is her name. Lives with her old crippled-up mama. Madge looks after her pretty good, so even the women hereabouts that know what she does don't get too snippy about her. Go see Madge, and put the bill onto something like feed for your horses, or ammunition, or some such."

"Thank you."

Clay strolled to the address given and knocked on the door, thankful that the house was separated from its nearest neighbors by a broad front yard and moonless darkness. The door opened, and he was beckoned inside without hesitation.

"Good evening, Marshal Dugan."

She closed the door and invited him to take a seat in the tiny parlor. Madge was in her mid-thirties, dark-haired and round of face and form. Clay was ill at ease to be confronting a whore under such unusual circumstances. He tended to include whores alongside others of the criminal class.

"Miss, uh, Madge, I have a request from someone that requires your, uh, company."

"You may call me Miss Clifton if it makes you uncomfortable to address me by name, Marshal."

"Thank you. Uh, Miss Clifton, there's a man in jail right now, you probably heard, and tomorrow he'll be hanged by the neck. Well, he wants some ... female company tonight, if that'd be all right with you. There's no obligation on your part, understand, but I did tell him I'd find out if there's an agreeable party to do what he wants."

"I would be most happy to accommodate the gentleman, Marshal. I was not present at the trial. Is he a young man, or old?"

"He'd be about twenty-nine, thirty, maybe younger."

"I see. Please allow me a moment to inform my mother I'll be gone for some time."

"Yes, ma'am."

Madge returned to the parlor after just a few minutes, a shawl around her shoulders. "If you depart now, Marshal, I'll follow along presently."

"Yes, ma'am."

He stood and reached for his hat.

"I really would prefer Madge."

"Madge ..."

"And may I call you Clay when we're face-to-face, Marshal, or would that be considered too familiar?"

"That's ... fine."

"Should I enter the jail through the courthouse door or through the marshal's office door? They are all connected, are they not?"

"Connected, that's right ... Better use the marshal's door."

Clay hurried out of Madge's home and returned to the jail to inform Maxwell of his good fortune.

"Is she attractive, Dugan? It's important."

"She's a nice-looking lady."

"Would you consider making the two-backed beast with her yourself, is what I'm asking."

"I don't go with whores, Maxwell."

"But if she were not?"

"I'd consider it, yes."

"Good. You'll leave us our privacy, I hope."

"I'll do that."

He heard the front door open and close, and went out to the office, where Madge Clifton was shedding her shawl. Clay jerked his thumb to indicate the route she should take to reach her client, and she nodded, smiling, and went through to the cells. Clay shut and locked the door behind her. He should have searched her first for weapons, but it was too late by then. If Madge was part of an elaborate plot to spring Maxwell from jail, then Clay would just have to be on the alert for whatever happened.

He took a seat behind his desk, a nicer desk than he had had in Keyhoe, and waited for whatever might follow. He had not thought to ask how long Madge was required to stay. Maxwell might want her to remain till dawn, which would be riskier than if she did her business with him and then went home again. The whole thing could be transacted within a half hour at most, by Clay's calculation. He busied himself cleaning his shotgun, and the assortment of rifles and small arms that came with the job. He guessed he would stick with his tried and true sawed-off, but the other weapons were in need of cleaning anyway. Clay took his work seriously.

While he cleaned and polished, he heard Maxwell moaning on the far side of the door to the cells, and saw his own hand shake as it hesitated over the barrel of a .45. Clay made himself continue his work as the sounds became more anguished before ceasing. Clay was glad of the silence, and began cleaning all the guns a second time. Then the sounds began again, and he flung down his rags and oils to jam his hat down on his head and leave the office for the streets of Dry Wash, which were quieter at that late hour than his office.

Maxwell's noise had reminded him of the things he used to do with Sophie, his wife. Clay had not touched a woman since riding away from Keyhoe; he regarded it as part of his punishment for having killed his boy, no matter how well-reasoned the motives for that singular act. Punishment was called for, in a moral universe, and Clay was willing to submit, and had done so for all those years. Now the ecstasy of a man who would die come morning had upset his notion of what his life should be. Silan had departed the world four years before, and Clay had been celibate for that long. Maxwell had spoiled everything with his shameless caterwauling. Now Clay had to begin all over again. It was no help to him whatsoever that Madge Clifton was a nice woman whom he would like to talk with some more, and inquire after the health of her mother. No, he admitted with an inward curse, he wanted to discuss more than that with her. He wanted to ask her if she would let down her hair and pop her corset hooks and place her breasts in his hands. That was what he wanted from Madge Clifton, and Clay was mortified that the monkish existence he had followed for so long should have collapsed around him so quickly, with so little encouragement.

It had been the simple act of talking with her. If he had done no more than pass her in the street, Clay knew he would not have become so enraptured by her. It was the talking, and what he could not understand was, she was a whore. How could he have allowed himself to become so upset and foolish and lovesick over a woman who allowed men to paw her for cash. He pictured them pawing her, and was obliged to lean against a wall to recover his balance. They should not do that, those nameless, faceless men. She should not allow it. Clay should not allow it. There should be no whores in the world, no whores and no whoremongers. It was not fit behavior for humans of good intent.... They should all stop!

He shifted himself from the wall and entered the nearest bar. Greeted by the bartender, he said simply, "Bottle." Given what he wanted, he found a corner in which to drink. Seating himself, Clay realized he had left his sawed-off behind on his desk. He had never done that before. What was the matter with him? He poured himself a drink and tossed it down. He had better not do anything wrong in Dry Wash, better mind his business and do his job and not set foot off the path of righteousness, or all the devils from his past would come riding down from the sky to mock him in front of the entire community, tear his clothes from his body and cover him with scorn, and he would be powerless, unable to drive them off, those devils swarming around him. He drank again, shaking like a man with fever, felt the whiskey coiling down into his guts like a hot snake, and wanted for a moment to vomit over the table, turn himself inside out like a glove soiled from within by sweat. He was an impostor, but the people of Dry Wash had accepted him as some kind of savior. They must never know anything, or he would be driven out, banished again to the deserts and the mountains and the endless blue emptiness pressing down upon it all. He could not do that, had no wish to be wandering again. Two days in this town, wearing a cheap tin badge, and he was caught up once more in the business of working steadily for wages. There was nothing wrong with that, he told himself, but all thoughts of Madge Clifton would have to be erased from his mind. She was a person who lived in the same town, nothing more. A whore. He would learn to despise her. It would be easy.

He drank again, and again, until half the bottle was gone, before becoming aware that the clientele were staring at him. If he wished to avoid a reputation as a drinking man, he had to stop. Clay stood and walked in a straight line to the bar. He handed the bartender his bottle and said, "Put my name on that." Clay was aware of every eye as he left. The night outside was like a welcoming blanket.

By the time he returned to the office he was staggering. He had left the door unlocked, an assortment of oiled weaponry on the desk for anyone to steal. He was ashamed to have done that. He was not himself. Tomorrow he would be the person he was supposed to be, and everything would be all right.

"Marshal Dugan?"

He turned to the cell room door. A face was looking at him from the small barred window there.

"You have locked me in here, Marshal."

"Oh ... Miss Clifton ... I'm sorry as hell. I didn't mean to ... Wait now, where's the keys ...?"

"They're on the peg over there."

"Peg ... Yes, ma'am."

He fetched them and fumbled to insert the correct key, then yanked the door open to let her out.

"I didn't mean to, I really didn't, just walked out and left you there without thinking."

"No harm done. Dr. Maxwell is asleep."

"Well, fine ... fine. I expect you'll need payment."

"Not right this minute, Mr. Dugan. You may bring me the money at any time. I trust you."

"That's ... how much?"

"Dr. Maxwell is a condemned man. I couldn't accept more than five dollars. I only request that because I have a sick mother to tend, Mr. Dugan. She needs medicine. It sounds like a very sad plot in some play, don't you think?"

"I wouldn't know, ma'am."

"Please call me Madge. Good night."

"Night. Will you be needing someone to walk you home?"

"I know the way, thank you."

"Just asking."

"Thank you anyway."

She left, winding the shawl around herself. It was a green shawl, with many tassels, a fine and wonderful shawl. Clay wished he could have given it to her for a present, but she already had it. He was thinking like a fool, an idiot, and behaving like one too. It had to stop. He stepped through to the cells and watched Maxwell sleeping on his bunk. How could the man do that when he had only a few more hours to live? Clay felt he understood nothing about life, or death either. He had killed many men, yet had no idea where he had sent them, or how they had felt as the thing called living was taken from them and became the thing called dying, then the thing called death. He knew nothing. Dismayed by his own ignorance, Clay dragged himself upstairs to the quarters he was obliged to occupy whenever there was someone in the cells, then dragged himself downstairs again in his long johns to lock the front door. He would never go back to claim the other half of that bottle in the saloon. Lurching toward his bed, he pictured Madge Clifton drinking wine. Clay had never drunk wine, nor known anyone who had.

Maxwell was prepared for the hanging. Clay could not help but admire the man's calm demeanor as he ate his pork chops with a side dish of hashed browns. He wanted to ask Maxwell many things, among them his opinion of the woman with whom he had shared part of his final night of life, but that subject would not have been proper, even between men. He paced the office and fretted about things, and shouted at the preacher who came to comfort the prisoner, then apologized.

"Sorry, Reverend, but he's an atheist, he told me so himself. Excuse me for being rude like that. This is the first time I've had to be responsible for hanging a man."

"That is Mr. Quick's concern, Marshal, not yours. I should like to speak with Mr. Maxwell anyway, if you please."

"Dr. Maxwell, not mister. He's a genuine dentist."

"And a Christian beneath his atheistic pose, I'm sure."

"Oh, you are? Step right on through, Reverend." They went to the cells. "Dr. Maxwell? Got a man here insists you want to see him this morning."

Clay lingered by the door to listen while Maxwell informed the preacher he was a lowly toad, a pimple on the buttock of a creature called superstition, a purveyor of knowledge without foundation in fact, and an unoriginal thinker masquerading as the conscience of the community.

"Told you," said Clay as the preacher departed.

"Allow no one else in here, please," Maxwell said.

"All right."

"Incidentally, how have your false teeth served you, Dugan? I ask out of professional curiosity."

"They're fine, once you get used to them. It took a while."

"I'm gratified. What time is it?"

"Coming up to eight forty-nine."

"I have one hour and eleven minutes left to me. Dugan, please leave me alone for the time remaining."

"I'll do it, and no one else gets near you either."

"Thank you for your thoughtfulness."

"You won't go and kill yourself in there, will you?"

"I couldn't deny the populace their pleasure. I'm mindful of your position here now, Dugan. You want this to go smoothly, don't you?"

"I'd appreciate it, frankly."

"Then I won't spoil things for you. Go away now."

Clay closed the door. Inexplicably, he felt like weeping. There was something wrong inside his head, but he didn't know what.

Another visitor arrived at the jail. This was Mr. Quick, mentioned in passing by the preacher, and Mr. Quick explained to Clay that while most folk considered it a heinous task, dispatching the wicked to their just reward, Mr. Quick saw things differently. "It's an opportunity," he said, "to send these fellers that's done wrong to the other side, where they'll get judgment a damn sight more powerful than they got here. God Almighty, that's the gentleman I'll be sending this one to, just like the rest it's been my privilege to send to the great beyond. God'll give them what's rightfully or wrongfully theirs, mark my word on it, and that's why I'm content to do the work I do, see, because it's all a part of the divine plan for apportionment of punishment among the wicked in this world and the next. I play my part, and play it with pride, because if it weren't me as did it, then some fool that don't know how to would come along and not be aware of just exactly what it is he's doing and mess up the job, and that'd be a shame, is my way of looking at it."

Clay could think of no suitable comment.

Maxwell was brought forth at the appointed hour. Dry Wash being located in arid country, it did not have any trees of sufficient height or strength to serve as a gallows. The permanent gallows built under Mr. Quick's supervision had been destroyed by fire almost six months before, deliberately doused with kerosene and set alight by the widow of the last man to be hanged there, and the county treasury had not yet advanced any cash to replace it. Mr. Quick was not about to be cheated of his holy work, and so contrived a device utilizing the hay bale hoisting beam that projected from the loft of Monoghan's livery stable. "Nice and high off the ground, so his boots won't touch the dust," Mr. Quick explained to Clay, "and the livery owner only wants a dollar for the use of it."

The dentist was taken up to the loft and told he must launch himself into the air, to plummet twenty-five feet or so before the noose around his neck should bring him up short and snap or dislocate his vertebrae, causing instantaneous death. He was assured of this by Mr. Quick. "It's a darn sight better than getting hoisted slow and being strangulated gradual," said the hangman, and Maxwell nodded to indicate his understanding of what was required.

He stood in the large square opening through which hay was lifted into the loft, and addressed the crowd below, many of whom had left their outlying farms well before dawn to witness the hanging. "People," he said, his voice carrying well from that elevation, "I do not deserve this fate, but I am resigned to it. You must have blood in requital for blood. I do see this, and yet I hate you. Yes, I hate you, and I place my curse upon you, every man and woman and child gathered here. You will all suffer terribly from dental decay from this day on, and your newborn children will have the fangs of wolves and will eat the hearts of their elders. Aah, I see you squirm in discomfort at my words, even though I do not myself believe in them. Only a fool gives credence to curses, and that, citizens of Sillytown, is the measure of your intellect. My last words will be to Marshal Dugan. Marshal?"

Clay stepped forward, made nervous by his proximity to the edge of the opening high up in the livery stable's wall. He could sense the anger of the crowd milling below. "Closer," Maxwell told him, and Clay placed his head beside the mouth of the dentist. "Marry her," whispered Maxwell. "She's too fine to be what she is. You'll see it in her eyes, if you have the courage to look."

Having said these words, he flung himself out from the opening, and just three seconds later met the limits of Mr. Quick's hemp. Mr. Quick had apparently miscalculated either the distance of drop or the differing strength of individual bodies, for Maxwell's head separated from his neck with an audible crack. His body continued to plummet earthward with barely a pause, to raise a cloud of dust there, while his head, with wildly staring eyes, was catapulted, by a twanging of the suddenly unburdened noose, high into the air, then came down in a leisurely arc to bounce among the spectators, whose screaming rose to twine about Clay's ears.

Mr. Quick was on hands and knees at the opening's edge, aghast at the mayhem wrought below by his bungling. "It shouldn't have ..." he said, time after time, as if repetition would wind back the moment and allow for a second chance at success. Clay watched the head that suddenly was at the center of a widening circle of fleeing people. He could swear Maxwell was looking up at him, staring directly into his eyes, the opened mouth repeating its final message.

"All right then," whispered Clay, "I will. See if I don't."

29

The highest echelon of Big Circle preferred that suicide be listed as the official cause of death in the case of Walter Morrow. Big Circle requested of the police commissioner that the one thing supporting a theory of murder—the missing key to one of the French windows—be ignored. The commissioner was not reluctant to accommodate the anonymous request, since it came with an envelope containing one thousand dollars. Big Circle wanted to investigate the death of one of its own.

Initial suspicion fell on the well-coiffed head of Jared, since he was the immediate heir to Morrow's millions, but he did seem an unlikely murderer. Jared's sexual proclivities were known to several members of Big Circle, but they had never embarrassed Walter by mentioning the subject in his presence. Inquiries made by Melvin Hodge, a private detective employed on occasion by Big Circle, proved Jared had been at a notorious haunt of homosexuals on the far side of Denver on the night of the murder. Suggestions that Jared might have hired someone to perform the killing on his behalf were considered farfetched, yet there seemed to be no other motive for Walter's death. Not a single article was missing from the study except for the window key. Hodge was instructed by a gentleman he knew simply as "Mr. Jones" to pursue the case and discover the identity of the killer, however long it might take.

Hodge began shadowing Jared Morrow. Jared had been exhibiting signs of great distress since the death of his father, but Hodge did not necessarily believe the young man's emotion was genuine. One night, while standing near the entrance to Jared's hotel suite (Hodge had bribed the hotel's own detective to allow him onto the premises for extended periods), Hodge witnessed the arrival of a smooth-faced fellow with a waistline Hodge could have spanned with his two meaty hands. The hotel detective informed Hodge the visitor was called Tatum, and seemed to be a favorite of young Mr. Morrow's. Hodge waited all night for Tatum to emerge, then followed him to a restaurant where both ate ham and eggs and bacon, then continued on to what presumably was Tatum's home, a room in a cheap hotel near the railroad station. Hodge slipped the desk clerk five dollars for the number of Tatum's room and information concerning his comings and goings. He then made arrangements with the clerk to revisit the hotel at night, when Tatum was in the habit of rising from his bed to gamble and otherwise entertain himself until the hours just before dawn.

Hodge waited that evening until he saw Tatum leave the hotel, then picked up a key from the desk clerk and climbed the stairs to Tatum's room. He found it bare of any but the most meager possessions, although Tatum did appear to be something of a dandy in matters of dress. Hodge searched thoroughly, and was appalled to come across some illustrated volumes of an erotic nature that shocked him greatly, since the couples depicted in contorted embraces of one kind or another were exclusively male. Hodge knew Jared Morrow was a man-fancier, and Tatum was just too smooth of skin to be a genuine male, so Hodge was not surprised to find such stuff; what did distress him was the arousal he felt within himself as he studied the pictures. Hodge was a married man with two children, and his reaction to the volume was inexplicable.

He hurriedly replaced the book as he had found it, and tried to rally his professional instincts to continue with the job at hand. He went carefully through every drawer, examined the underside of the mattress, and found nothing to indicate Tatum might have killed Walter Morrow for Jared. There was no gun, not so much as a pocket knife to indicate that Tatum bore the least propensity for violence.

Becoming a little despondent by then, Hodge sat on a chair and allowed his gaze to drift without particular purpose around Tatum's lowly room. He had found nothing. It was likely Tatum was no more than Jared's boyfriend. Mr. Jones would not be pleased that Hodge could unearth no clue at all to the mystery. Mr. Jones was himself a mystery to Hodge. He had used Hodge's services several times, but never discussed his own identity or revealed his precise connection with the individuals Hodge was hired to investigate. Hodge suspected that Mr. Jones was working for someone higher up the ladder of wealth that grew out of Denver like a stairway to heaven. There were too many rich people controlling too much money, in Hodge's opinion, but he had never breached professional etiquette by asking Mr. Jones to explain himself or the office in which they met. It might have been a lawyer's office, or a businessman's; there was no name on the door, just a silent bookkeeper in an outer room scratching at his accounts, or pretending to.

It would not pay to be overly curious; Mr. Jones paid well, and always in crisp new notes. It would have helped, though, to know for whom he was working. Hodge would have liked to be aware of some link between himself and the powerful of the city, even if he had a lingering disapproval for such wealthy types, being himself the son of a shoemaker. He reminded himself that the persons Mr. Jones represented were unlikely to hire him again if he did not produce results, but he could not think for the moment where those results might be found. Could the mistress somehow be involved? There had been no binding contract between herself and her benefactor to cover the possibility of his death and her sudden removal from a position of comfort, according to Mr. Jones, but Hodge felt that maybe he should dig further in that direction anyway. He had certainly drawn a blank with regard to the son's fay friend.

He heard voices outside in the corridor, and went to the partially opened transom to eavesdrop, but quickly ascertained it was a foolish argument between a drunken man and woman, of no interest or use to Hodge. He had raised his face toward the transom while listening, and as the voices receded around a corner, Hodge noticed a streak of comparative cleanliness along the transom's lower edge, as if fingers had reached up there a time or two and inadvertently brushed aside a portion of the accumulated grime. He reached up there himself, and felt his fingertips encounter a small metallic object. He lifted it down, and felt his heart begin to accelerate. It was a key, with an ornately scrolled hasp. Hodge knew it would fit perfectly the central French window of Walter Morrow's study.

* * *

He still had not collected payment from Jared, but the excuse seemed reasonable; it was too soon following his father's death for Jared to have been granted control of the Morrow estate. "A few weeks more," Tatum was told. He kept a close eye on Jared meantime, to make sure he kept his mouth shut when liquored. Tatum made the point several times that Jared was equally culpable under the law as an accessory to the act. "It was a conspiracy, my dear, and don't you forget it." He kept other young men away from Jared, would-be pickpockets who saw him as an easy mark for loans and handouts. Tatum wanted Jared to keep a tight rein on the mountain of cash heading his way, so Tatum alone could advise him on its investment and disbursement. That much money spelled considerable power for whoever controlled it, and Jared was a weakling, uninterested in the actual practice of business. Tatum would guide him, although he himself had no clear idea how fiscal worth was propagated. They would learn together, and Jared would do as Tatum told him.

One evening about a week following the Morrow suicide (Tatum was especially pleased the police had no inkling it had been murder), as Tatum strolled along a quiet street, a coach rolled to a stop alongside him, and an elderly gentleman addressed him through the window. "Sir, do you know anything of medicine? My grandson here seems to have fainted."

"I'm no doctor, but I'll look at him."

The coach door was opened, and Tatum stepped inside past the gentleman's knees. The blinds were drawn, and he could see no grandson, but there were two burly men, and these grabbed him by the shoulders and hauled Tatum inside as if he weighed nothing at all. Before he could protest, a cloth drenched in ether was pressed over his mouth. Tatum heard the door close behind him, and felt the coach lurch into motion. He wondered, before lapsing into unconsciousness, if it was the police or Jared who had arranged his kidnapping.

"Mr. Tatum? Can you hear me, Mr. Tatum?"

He responded blearily. The room was unfamiliar, a farmhouse by all appearances. The three who had taken him into their coach were facing him. Tatum became aware of the ropes around his wrists and ankles, and the hardness of the chair beneath him. The only lamp burning was behind the elderly gentleman's head. Tatum could see no one with any clarity. He knew then it was not the police.

"Mr. Tatum, I wish to know who paid you to kill Walter Morrow."

"I didn't kill him. He killed himself."

"A key was found in your room. I don't need to tell you what key."

Tatum felt something slip inside himself. He never should have kept the little memento. That had been the act of a fool. The key should have been buried along with the gun. They had him, and they knew they had him. He could deny it, but the two who had grabbed him in the coach would be happy to beat him insensible. An immediate confession, however, would not ingratiate him to them either. He would have to conduct himself with care.

"Who are you?" he asked.

"That does not concern you. Why did you do it? At whose behest?"

"No one's. I'm an anarchist. All robber barons should die."

The gentleman chuckled. "Come now, Mr. Tatum, you are no more an anarchist than my cat. For whom did you do it?"

"Why should I tell you anything."

"John, show Mr. Tatum the wire cutters with which you will remove his fingers one by one until he becomes cooperative."

A long-handled device was dangled before Tatum's face. He could smell the earth clinging to its cutting edges, and the smell suddenly made him feel sick.

"Jared," he said. "Jared told me to."

"Thank you, Mr. Tatum. What was to be your reward for services rendered?"

"Some money."

"The sum?"

"No specific sum."

"Really? You murdered a man without first making a watertight deal? How very unprofessional."

"I guess that's because I'm an amateur."

"Yes, that would explain the key. What do you think will happen to you now?"

"That depends on who you are. You aren't the police."

"Oh, no, not the police."

He chuckled again, and the two larger men joined in. Tatum felt his face burning with humiliation. He had not resisted at all; the wire cutters were too real, too ugly to defy with courage. He was a worm, a coward, a betrayer. Jared himself would have caved in no less quickly. Tatum felt he might vomit at any moment.

"Tell me, Mr. Tatum, just to satisfy my curiosity: did you feel the slightest twinge of conscience as you sent your bullet into the head of a man you never met before?"

"No," said Tatum, in an attempt to recover his pride.

"Not in the least?"

"Not a jot."

"Dear me, but you seem somehow to be missing an essential part of the thing which makes us human, Mr. Tatum."

"Your opinion doesn't interest me, old man."

"I do regret that. Now then, what should be the manner of your death, do you think?"

"I should choke on your cock, you old humbug shit fuck."

"I regret I am not attracted to such acts. John, do you think Mr. Tatum should lose his own cock for such impoliteness?"

John stepped forward again with the wire cutters, and jabbed roughly at Tatum's groin. Tatum could not accept that they would actually perform such torture on him, and John did seem to be conducting himself in a halfhearted manner that suggested a reluctance to continue.

"Enough," said the elderly gentleman. "We are all civilized men here; even you, Mr. Tatum. Would a bullet in the head be more to your liking? I see poetic justice in such an end."

"A bullet is fine."

"John, shoot Mr. Tatum in the right temple."

The cutters were dropped, their place in John's hand taken by a revolver. Tatum felt the muzzle's hardness against his scalp. The hammer was cocked. Tatum's mouth became tinglingly dry, and he accepted that he was about to die. Curiously, he had no regret; this way was preferable to bleeding from a stumped cock. He supposed he should be grateful. The hammer fell. Tatum jumped as high as his bonds and the chair would allow. When he realized a trick had been played on him, he felt like weeping. Now he could anticipate nothing, control nothing, even the expression on his features. He realized also that the warmth he now felt in his pants was piss, and his shame was complete. They were laughing softly at his degradation.

"Mr. Tatum, did your life flash before your eyes as they say it does at such a moment?"

"No ... "

"A merciful thing. I'm sure a life such as yours is not worthy of review. Are you ready now for the true event?"

"Get it done ... "

"John, proceed."

The gun was placed again to Tatum's head, the hammer cocked, the trigger pulled. Again the chamber was empty. Tatum felt rage building in himself.

"Don't you know how to load a pistol, you moron!"

John hit Tatum across the collarbone with the gun barrel, and the second man stepped forward to punch him hard in the side of the head, so hard the chair tipped over.

"That will do. Set him upright."

The chair was put on its feet. Tatum's head and breast roared with pain, and vomit burst from him, to splash across his knees.

"Mr. Tatum, I'll strike a bargain with you. The terms may not be to your liking. Then again, to a creature unusual as yourself, they might."

"What ... what bargain?"

Tatum hired the surrey himself, and escorted Jared down to the street to climb aboard. He whisked a sheet from the picnic basket placed carefully behind the seat, and said, "I know a fellow who needs cheering up in the great outdoors."

"Tatie, you're more thoughtful sometimes than I give you credit for."

"I agree. I'll take the reins; you just relax and enjoy the ride, as the king said to the page boy."

"Tatie, really."

Tatum drove them into the mountains, along little known trails, and eventually announced that they had arrived. Their destination was high enough to see Denver below, and the plains beyond. Jared pronounced himself well content with the place, and ravenously hungry. Tatum spread a blanket and unpacked the basket. While they ate, he teased Jared over his hangdog behavior of late.

"Tatie, I can't help it. My papa has died, you know."

"No need to bring up unpleasantness, Jarie. What's done is done, and will forever stay done. You have a life of your own now, not some feeble arrangement that gave you what you wanted only by kind permission of your great and wonderful papa. Am I correct?"

"Yes, but ... I don't know. I just feel so guilty over all this. He could have treated me much worse."

"And much better too. Spilled milk, Jarie—it never tastes as good as champagne. Present your glass, sir."

When they were done with eating and drinking, they lay beside each other, smoking cigars while they watched eagles soar above them. It was unusual for either man to be silent for so long when in each other's company.

"Jarie, do you want to?"

"Want to what?"

"Be mine, in the way you like to be mine?"

"I might be persuaded."

"I had hoped to hear that, sweet. What a happy fellow you can make me sometimes."

"My pleasure, Tatie."

"I'm sure, and mine too."

Jared laughed as Tatum took his thigh in a tight grip.

When they were done with each other, Tatum asked, "Was that a fine end to the day?"

"The day isn't over yet."

"True, but the best part is behind us. Does that make you sad at all?"

"I feel too content to be sad. You do that to me, Tatie, when you're in the mood. You should be that way more often."

"I'll make it my duty to be so. But do you agree the best has come and gone for this particular afternoon?"

"If you insist, yes, I guess it has."

"And you are content?"

"I am."

"That makes me happy too, my friend."

"Good."

"Did you ever see so big a bird?"

"Where?"

"Directly above us. What a wingspan!"

Jared tipped back his head and squinted into the sunlight. Tatum drew from his boot a six inch ice pick and drove it deftly into Jared's throat, at such an angle as to penetrate the brain. Jared's body stiffened convulsively, as it had just minutes before under Tatum's thrusting, then was still. Tatum left the ice pick there; very little blood seeped out around the wooden handle.

Tatum picked up his friend and took him back among the trees. The hole he had prepared the day before was as he had left it, a shovel still jammed into the mound of fresh earth. He flung the body into its waiting grave and began covering it, humming one of Jared's favorite tunes as he did so. When the task was completed,

the mound patted down and strewn with leaves, Tatum packed up
the picnic dishes and climbed into the surrey for a return to town.

The dismay she had felt at Walter's death was one thing, but to
learn that his son had now disappeared without any trace set Lovey
Doll's mind to wondering. That the two things were linked was
obvious. The newspaper reports were lurid in their imaginings,
with a different plot laid out for each day that Jared refused to
show himself. Lovey Doll had never met the boy, but had formed the
opinion that Walter was disappointed in him somehow. Could the
source of the disappointment have been a suspicion that young
Jared coveted his father's riches, and was not inclined to wait and
receive them in the fullness of time? Hints to that effect had been
published, but the disappearance of Jared Morrow well in advance
of his legal acceptance of Walter's wealth had sent the rumormon-
gers scurrying in twelve different directions for a motive or scenario
that would explain the facts as they were known; certainly no one
in Denver now accepted the notion that Walter had committed suicide. Lovey Doll had said as much herself when interviewed by the
police detectives, and when they returned to question her regarding
the vanishment of Jared, she told them it was not her job to solve
such mysterious goings-on, and would they mind very much wiping
their muddy boots before entering a clean house in future.

The question Lovey Doll truly wanted answered concerned her
financial position now that Walter was gone. He had bought the
house outright, but never told her if the deed was in her name or
his. If the former, she was secure for the moment, but would eventually have to find work; if the latter, she was in trouble. Lovey Doll
had never known permanent security in her life, and so was
inclined to expect the worst.

Her expectations were confirmed when Tatum came to call. Lovey
Doll was impressed by the elegant appearance of the slim young
man at her door, and allowed him in when he presented a card stating that he was an employee of Walter's bank, an institution Lovey
Doll understood from the newspapers was in a state of limbo, pend-
ing an outcome to the search for Jared Morrow. She seated Tatum
in the parlor and asked sweetly what brought him to her home.

"A coach brought me"—he smiled—"and it isn't your home."

Lovey Doll knew then that Walter had not provided for her the
way a man of honor would have. Like all the other rich men she had

encountered, he had been a skinflint at heart, and she crushed her memory of him, until now laced with mild pleasantness, into the black chest of her past, never to be scrutinized again. Her immediate attention was required by the young man, who continued smiling as he studied her reaction. Lovey Doll smiled also as she asked for proof that what her guest had suggested was true.

"I should like to see some kind of court order stating that the house is not mine."

"It isn't. Take my word."

"I will not take your word."

"You'll begin packing your personal things at once."

"Indeed I will not."

"When you're done packing, I'll take you to the station. You can have a ticket to anywhere you like, for nothing."

"I have no intention of doing any of that."

Tatum slid a throwing knife from beneath his silk vest and threw it at the wall. It punctured the heart of an oil portrait of Lovey Doll that Walter had commissioned from Denver's finest portrait artist. Tatum produced two more of the wicked little knives and flung them into her canvas nipples. Lovey Doll continued to smile.

"Am I to be impressed by this?"

"You're to pack. Begin now."

A fourth blade flew from Tatum's hand to bury its point in the back of Lovey Doll's chair, an inch or so from her ear. She ceased smiling. The young man of the knives would not be denied. She saw in him now a different aspect, one that had eluded her at first, hidden as it was behind his fine clothing and smooth good looks. He was not human in quite the same way as most. Lovey Doll recognized the quality, possessing it to some degree herself, but in Tatum the absence of emotion or sympathy was in concentrated form, a kind of shell surrounding him, shielding him from ordinary folk and the workings of their hearts. Nothing could penetrate such armor. Tatum was a sleek beast of the jungles, a panther, perhaps, with a taste for blood. Lovey Doll felt herself become a little frightened. She saw also that it would serve no purpose to flirt with him; he was not a man for women. She had met several of his kind, but never one like Tatum. He was uniquely awful, and she resigned herself to his will.

Standing, she asked him, "Where is Jared?" The question had come from her mind without bidding, simply popped from her mouth as she rose. She was not sure why she had asked it.

"Jared is running to save his guilty hide, madam. You'll read about it in the evening papers, or maybe you won't, since you'll be on a train by then. A letter has been found, a confession to the murder of his father. He'll likely end up in Patagonia. It's none of your concern in any case."

Lovey Doll packed what she could in the time available, but she owned so many dresses it was impossible to carry them all. Tatum assured her the rest would be packed and forwarded to her, care of whichever destination she chose. Lovey Doll did not believe him, and came close to weeping at the loss of her finery. She made sure every piece of jewelry was included in her trunk. Tatum brought in a large man he addressed as John, and had the chest taken downstairs to the coach. John drove them to the station and lifted Lovey Doll's chest down from the roof.

"Where do you wish to go?" asked Tatum.

"I'm surprised you haven't decided for me."

"I will, if you like. Choose now."

"Glory Hole."

"You won't like it there. Glory Hole only has one rich man, and he likes his wife."

"Glory Hole," she repeated, and Tatum nodded to John, who approached the ticket counter.

"I dislike you very much," Lovey Doll said.

"Do you now."

"I do, and it is my sincere hope you die with your boots off, a slow death from tuberculosis, or syphilis."

"When I die, whore, my boots will be on, and I'll take with me the lucky fool who killed me."

Tatum escorted Lovey Doll Pines to her car and sat with her until the train began to move. His last act before jumping from the car was to hiss in her ear, "Spread your legs wide as you please, but keep your mouth shut."

His wife informed Melvin Hodge that a message had been delivered while he was out of the house. Mrs. Hodge understood little of her husband's profession, and had sometimes been given sealed notes such as this before. Hodge took it to the kitchen gaslight, tore open the envelope and read the message within, then touched it to the naked flame for incineration. Before his fingers could be burned, he tossed the remaining corner of the sheet into the enamelled sink, where it hissed for a moment. Hodge went to the hall for his coat. "Business," he said, opening the front door. "I may be back late." When he was gone, Mrs. Hodge inspected the scrap of moist paper in her sink. All it bore was the initial of the sender: "J."

When Hodge arrived at the place designated in the note, he found a coach there. A large man sat in the driver's seat, and another sat inside, beckoning him forward. When Hodge entered the coach it began to move. The man inside would answer no questions, and Hodge sat back to await what he expected would be some clandestine meeting with Mr. Jones. He knew it would concern the reports in the evening newspapers of a confession signed by Jared Morrow. Hodge could not see how the confession, if true, jibed with what he had found in Tatum's room. Something peculiar was afoot, and doubtless Jones wished to explain it.

The coach traveled for some time, leaving the city behind. It came at last to a farmhouse with dimly lighted windows, and Hodge was escorted across the yard. Near the barn, a slim figure stepped from the shadows into Hodge's path. "You ...," said Hodge, very much surprised to see Tatum before him.

"Me," Tatum said. "I presume you want to know about that key you snooped for in my room."

"I do, yes. Where is Mr. Jones?"

"Don't be in a rush. Take time to admire nature, why don't you." Tatum lifted his eyes. "Did you ever see stars like that before?" he asked. "They look like diamonds, don't you think?"

Hodge looked up.

"Now then, Mr. Tatum, you understand what it is we require of you."

Tatum was in the office of Mr. Jones. He understood it was not a true office, nor was Jones the name of the man staring at him over a broad expanse of mahogany desktop.

"You want me to keep on doing what I've done for you twice now."

"But only on my instruction. If you attempt anything like it for your own ends, word will reach me, and you will regret it. Any attempt to fathom the purpose of your assignments will be frowned upon. Your task is the very last line of resort. I do not issue such orders for my own amusement, Mr. Tatum. You are part of an organization dedicated to its own agenda. We wish no harm to anyone who does not stand in the way of that agenda."

"Have you someone in mind who does not meet that description?"

"You are here today only to be given advice by myself. This is the advice. Find yourself a modest dwelling place. Do not attract attention to yourself in any way. Live within your means. You will be well paid for future work carried out according to instructions. Naturally you will inform no one of our arrangement with you, not one word to one soul. Have I made myself perfectly clear?"

"As the proverbial bell."

"There is a flippancy about you I do not approve of. You would do well to get rid of it. That is all for today, Mr. Tatum. Good-bye."

"Good day, Mr. Jones."

When Tatum was gone, Mr. Jones took a small file from his desk drawer and began shaping his nails. Mr. Jones was allied with the more conservative element within Big Circle. These men had known of their opposition's plans for sending Walter Morrow to Glory Hole for the purpose of issuing an invitation to Leo Brannan. The conservatives had decided to allow this act of rebellion to proceed, rather than reveal their knowledge of it beforehand. The death of Morrow had been a shock to them all, and suspicion had focused on several of the members more adamantly opposed to the scheme, but Hodge had found out the truth for them, and been placed in the unfortunate noose of circumstance. Big Circle had need of an individual such as Tatum; their previous assassin had choked on a chicken bone a month before. But if Big Circle wished to retain the services of Tatum, then the one man who knew him to be guilty of Morrow's murder had to be silenced. Bribery would not have worked with so decent a man as Hodge. His death, along with that of young Morrow, had been a test that Tatum had passed with ease. He was the perfect killer, utterly without remorse. He was now a part of Big Circle, even if he would never hear the name or know for whom he carried out his killings. His first two murders for them, without any financial reward for Tatum, had been a matter of expediency, as so much of Big Circle's work was.

Tatum spent the rest of the day searching out a new cane for himself. His dog-headed cane was old and chipped. He found what he wanted in the afternoon, and settled for a price higher than he would have liked, but the cane was a beauty, with a lion's-head handle and a slender blade concealed inside.

29

"B oys, we see before us a pathetic study for sure."

Drew had grown used to the gawking and comments. His cell was no more than a cage of flat iron bars adjacent to the sidewalk, and generally used for the confinement of drunks. This day the cell contained a would-be bank robber.

"My, my, he looks dangerous, don't he?"

Drew had tried again to rob and run, but this time met with even less success than on his first attempt. On leaving the bank he had tripped over a legless cripple, entering the building on a small wheeled platform. It was the cripple who commandeered Drew's pistol and held him at gunpoint until others arrived to aim a variety of weapons at his blushing face.

From the sidewalk outside the bank to the open cell beside the general store was only a few yards. He had been behind bars now for several hours, and almost everyone in that small town had already come to stare and taunt. The latest arrivals were three in number, but only one seemed interested in talking to Drew.

"Been a bank robber long?" The interested party leered. He was bearded, and wore a feather in his hatband.

"Long enough to watch where I'm going next time."

"Next time! Hear that, boys? He figures there'll be a next time."

Leaning closer to Drew's face, he said, "It's the next life you ought to be considering. A life of crime in this one, that's not for you, not if you can't do it right."

"Thanks for the advice, now poke your ugly head up a mule's ass and let me get some peace."

"Oh, my, a banty rooster. Crows loud for someone in a cage, don't he."

"Sure does," agreed one of the men either side of the bearded man. Drew turned away from them. The bearded man said, "Think you'll wind up in hell, banty boy?"

"Might be worth it," said Drew, "just to get away from your voice."

"I'm insulted, yessir, I sure am. Look at me, boys—can't you see the insult writ large on my brow?"

"Sure can."

"Looks to me like our banty wants to just put his fool head under his wing and maybe cry a little."

"Lay a egg, maybe," suggested the third man.

"Roosters don't lay no eggs," said the first. "Then again, maybe I was wrong about this one. Just a little old hen, that's what he is. Better watch out there, hen. Mister rooster comes along, he'll trample you good."

Drew ignored them until he could hear their boots receding along the sidewalk. When he turned to the street again, a small girl was staring at him.

"Afternoon," Drew said.

"Did you rob the bank?"

"Almost."

"Why?"

Drew considered the question, but could think of no answer adequate for himself or the child. He had been a fool, but could not even explain that part to himself.

"Little girl, I don't know. You go away now, all right?"

"No."

"Why not?"

"Ma says I got to come see you."

"Why?"

"For a lesson. She say don't come close to him, the bank robber man."

"You go home and tell your ma you saw me, and ask could she kindly get me a loaded gun down here right away."

The girl nodded and wandered off down the street. Drew felt the need to urinate, but his cell was completely exposed on three sides, the fourth being the brick wall of the store. He could turn his back to the street and piss against that, but was disinclined to foul his own nest.

"Hey!" he called to nobody in particular. "Hey!"

The storekeeper came out, wiping his hands on an apron.

"What you want?"

"I have to piss."

"Hold your water, robber man."

The storekeeper went back inside his premises, and another man, whom Drew recognized as the town constable who had arrested him, appeared.

"What you want?"

"Didn't he tell you? I need to take a piss."

"Too bad for you."

"At least get me a bucket or something."

"Got no bucket."

"Well, then, a bottle, just something I can piss in, for Christ's sake."

"Thou shall not be taking the Lord's name in vain."

"I'm not; I just need to piss."

"Too bad for you."

"Mister, were you elected to your office? How could that happen, if you don't mind my asking."

The constable looked at Drew, trying to determine if he had been insulted. Unable to reach a conclusion, he went back inside the store. Drew's bladder produced sensations of urgency he could not ignore. He unbuttoned his pants and pissed, then had to sit on the iron bench beside his own reeking froth. No one had come by while he relieved himself, but the incident did nothing to cheer him. It might very well have been his last act of free choice. He had been promised, or threatened with, a quick trial and speedy execution.

The same three men were approaching along the street, mounted this time, trailing several saddled horses behind them. Drew decided they were cowboys. The bearded man addressed him. "Hey, banty boy, where's that town policeman at, you know?"

"Inside the store," said Drew.

The man dismounted and entered the store, returning less than a minute later with the constable. The constable had a long-barreled

Colt to the side of his head. "Open it up," he was told. The keys in his hand shook as the cell door was unlocked.

"Banty boy," said the man with the gun, "if you step outside now, you belong to me, understand?"

"Sounds fine," said Drew, and pushed past the quaking constable. He would have liked to trip the man and push his face into the pissed-on earth floor, but time would not allow such self-indulgence. He sprang onto the nearest riderless horse and took the reins from the man who led it. The bearded man seemed in no hurry to depart. Several townspeople had gathered to watch.

"Lodi, we got to go."

"I'm coming."

The bearded man hit the constable's head with his gun barrel and watched him fall slowly to the sidewalk, then he walked into the street and mounted his horse. Drew wanted to ride out at a gallop, but the leader of his three abductors had a brazen confidence that kept them all at a trot. Drew waited for bullets to come flying at them from store doorways, but none did.

When rescuers and rescued were beyond sight of the town, the leader beckoned Drew forward to ride alongside him.

"What's your name, boy?"

"John Bones."

"You want to learn how banks are robbed the right way?"

"Might come in handy."

"It better, or I don't have any use for you, or your lip. You belong to me, remember?"

"I recall it."

"Don't be forgetting. We lost a man three days ago up around Silver Plume. You're his replacement, but things better pan out right between us—understand, Bones?"

"Mister, I'm grateful to be out of there, and willing to learn what I didn't know before."

"That's good. I like you, boy. Call me Lodi. That's Nate Haggin and Clarence Dustey back there, and we work like a team. I believe you'll fit right in."

Drew was not so sure, but smiled anyway.

It had been seven months since her husband touched her. It was more than a reluctance on Leo's part to visit her bedroom; it seemed he did not wish to touch her at all. He would not kiss her cheek or take her hand. He seldom spoke to Zoe, even over the rare meal they shared. She had never been overwhelmingly in love with her husband, but his neglect of her now stung Zoe more than she cared to admit.

Early in their marriage he had mounted her often, then less frequently as the years passed, and finally not at all. She drew the conclusion that his attentions to her had been solely for the purpose of impregnating her with a son for himself. As miscarriage followed miscarriage, he had apparently given up hope of ever getting the one thing he lacked. While the act itself had given Zoe neither pleasure nor pain, its absence from her life created a void deeper than she had anticipated.

Leo's withdrawal from her company left Zoe without any meaningful role to play at Elk House. If Omie had chosen to ignore her, Zoe felt her life would have been without purpose. As it was, Omie was more secretive now than she had ever been. Zoe assumed this was a result of her daughter's recent illness, and did not resent the hours she had to spend in ignorance of Omie's whereabouts or thoughts. The closeness between them had lessened, but Zoe would not cling to Omie any more than she would to Leo; her pride would not permit it.

During this time of isolation, Zoe's daydreaming turned to the brothers she barely remembered. If only they could have been there to comfort her, Zoe's lot would have been tolerable. But they were not, nor would they ever be, she told herself. It was a fool's wish, and Zoe knew herself to be no fool. Her moments of weakness, as she called them, were becoming more frequent, and she scolded herself for indulging in such sentiment. It was necessary to remind herself that she was the wife of Colorado's wealthiest man. That someone in her position should feel miserable was ridiculous, and so she would not allow such thoughts into her mind.

The thoughts and misgivings came anyway, and sometimes Zoe found herself in tears over nothing. She distracted herself with needlework, but abandoned that avenue of escape when she looked hard at the picture taking shape inside her hoop and discerned a gravestone hidden in the pastoral scene there. She had not intended any such thing, and the fact that her fingers had conspired to place it there, stitched into undeniable place, upset her for an entire day.

A rich man's wife. The actuality was far removed from the popular conception of so privileged a creature. Zoe saw no one but the domestic staff and her own daughter from one Christmas to the next, not that she demanded or desired to meet with anyone other than Leo. It had long since occurred to Zoe that she was not equipped for social intercourse; certainly she had no wish to sweep like some storybook princess into chandeliered halls to dine with the nation's elite; any such scenario embarrassed her even to think of. Her life at Elk House would have been sufficient, circumscribed though it was, if only her husband cared for her. He did not even have to love her with any great passion, just care for her and make known in simple ways his affection. That would have been enough.

She wondered if all women felt as she did, and became aware, not for the first time, that women and their ways were largely unknown to her. Zoe had moved among men, for better or worse, and had no clear notion of the best way to approach other females, even the maids, with anything like confidence or basic understanding of their femaleness. She was herself a sexless entity, she sometimes felt, despite having given birth twice, been the wife of two men and the victim of a third. Looking at her reflection in a mirror did nothing to alleviate Zoe's growing sense of unreality. The remarkable business of Omie's ability to foresee the future and move articles of furniture without effort was no more dreamlike than the face Zoe saw staring back at her from an elegant frame of gilt. I have no idea who I am, she mouthed at her mirror image, and the image responded with a forlorn smirk that boded no improvement in matters.

The town had developed as Omie said it would, in advancing waves of ugliness that crept up the valley walls, the smokestacks of Leo's empire spewing darkness into the air. The rumble of the crushers and stampers, the humming of the massive pithead wheels, the constant clash of couplings from the railyard: these sounds and the subtle undertone of human activity day and night kept Zoe isolated inside Elk House, where most of the cacophony from far below her windows was filtered by distance and glass and stone. But the isolation itself became more than Zoe could bear, and one morning she made a firm decision: she would demand of Leo a vacation, if not for the family, then at least for herself and Omie. It was not some glittering metropolis she wished to escape to, but a place such as Glory Hole once had been, with none but the most rudimentary evidence of man's presence. It was natural silence, the whispering of trees and the sounds of bird song she required; that and the company of her child. With these simple things it might be possible to regain some sense of wholeness.

She would not delay another minute, now that her mind was made up, but would demonstrate her newfound strength by doing what she had never done before; she would not wait for Leo to arrive home, but would go directly to him, down below in the grime of Glory Hole. She was under instruction from Leo never to bother him with anything but matters of great consequence during his long hours away from Elk House, but Zoe was in no mood to obey such dicta.

She placed a hat upon her head and walked out the front door without bothering to call for her carriage and team. The task would be accomplished on foot. Zoe felt such an approach had merit, but could not decide, as she headed down the lengthy driveway, if she was a humble beggar asking favors of the king, or a barefoot prophet come to demand changes in the land before fate should bring down the mighty. Both roles played themselves out as she descended. The very stones of the driveway became less clean, the pinkness of the crushed rock turning to gray. The trees, already leafless in October, revealed their smoke-blackened bark, and the air itself became not only more difficult to breathe but less clear. It was a peculiarity of the valley that temperature inversions would hold much of its airborne filth close to the ground rather than allowing it to disperse, and so it was that morning as Zoe walked down to confront her husband. Before long she was obliged to hold a handkerchief across her lower face, and hold her skirts clear of soot covering the ground.

The driveway became a road leading directly to Glory Hole's main street, but as she drew closer, Zoe chose a side road instead, and asked herself as she veered from the usual route if she was doing this to postpone her confrontation with Leo. She was sure that was not the case; she simply wished to go another way, owing to the novelty of her being on foot. It would allow her to pass through more of the residential area of the town than she had ever seen before. It was unorthodox behavior, but such seemed to be the only kind Zoe was capable of that morning, and she struck out into the unknown with a confidence that had been missing from her step for a long time.

Down past the miners' shacks she went, and was stared at from the doorways and windows by wives with careworn faces and eyes that became flinty when they recognized her for who she was. Her presence among them, face covered as if seeking anonymity, was some kind of perverse insult. They could not understand why the wife of Leo Brannan would choose to walk the muddy rows between their shacks, averting her eyes guiltily from the unpainted boards, the lines of gray laundry slung across alleyways and the faces that looked her way. Poorly clad children ceased their games and stared at the woman from the Big House as she passed them by, a being from another world.

Zoe felt the eyes of the women on her, felt herself riddled by their antipathy and contempt. She had not intended drawing attention to herself by coming this way, had not expected so many people to be outside their dwellings on so chilly a day, but they were, in knots of conversation here and there that broke off into silence at her approach. They were dowdy women, their shawls hugged tightly about them, their hair untidily pinned or hidden beneath shapeless hats, their boots thick-soled, without grace. Some smoked pipes, a sight Zoe thought bizarre, and one woman had a chicken perched like a parrot on her shoulder. Altogether, they were citizens of another country, and Zoe felt open hatred emanating from them in waves. She wanted to take the handkerchief from her mouth and tell the women she had suffered also, in her way, and been envious of others who seemed to own the best of everything. She was not so very different from them; chance alone had elevated her above their smoke-wreathed shacks and muddy streets. They should not blame her for not being down there, one of them, a miner's wife waiting for her grimy man to return exhausted at the end of the day. Each of these women probably saw more of her husband than did Zoe, but she could not tell them that, or any of her other stifled musings, and be believed. She must simply walk on until the last row was passed, the last stares put behind her.

Once she stumbled, dragging the hem of her skirts in the muck, and after that she did not bother to keep them high, but walked with a peculiar, stiff-legged gait further down the slope that would bring her to the soot-encrusted heart of Glory Hole. This place of high windowless walls enclosed machinery of such vast proportion it dwarfed the human attendants scurrying among pistons and pulleys and hammers that seemed big enough to crack the world beneath their relentless pounding. Zoe glanced inside various doorways as she passed, witnessing the controlled pulverization of ores, the hellish light and heat and roaring inside the smelters, and the whining, humming wheels drawing miles of steel cable up from the bowels of the mine and sending it down again.

She felt sick, made ill by everything that surrounded her, and her brain seemed to spin with the towering wheels and their blurring of mighty spokes and the rush of air their spinning displaced. She came closer, drawn by the siren song of these mighty wheels, and the thrumming of the massive cable drum spinning on its axis, and the snorting, piping, panting of the steam engines driving the mechanical dervish. The cable house was filled with stray wisps and blasts of vapor that swirled in the eddies and vortices and blew by Zoe's face like playful phantoms. She felt the floor beneath her shivering like the skin of a gigantic beast made nervous by her feet upon its back, and she felt the pounding of its faraway heart, and took the oily exhalations from its lungs into her own, and choked on the underground moisture and smell of human sweat it bore. She felt herself drifting sideways, closer to the hypnotic spinning and humming and breathing, heard distant voices raised in alarm but lost in steam, then felt the beast swipe her with its steely paw.

His office had not known many visitors, even at the height of his company's production, and Leo was reluctant to admit the man who presented himself that day. He had been expecting an emissary from Denver for some time, following a series of letters alerting him to a wish on the part of certain unnamed gentlemen of influence in that city to include his name among their ranks. Leo had formed the opinion he was being asked to join some kind of exclusive rich man's club, and the notion held little appeal. He was proud to be the richest of all men in the state, but had no need of self-styled kingmakers and fellow millionaires around him to reinforce his own sense of importance.

The man's name was Rowland Price, and the written message he sent through to Leo by way of Mr. Jenks, Leo's personal secretary, was an exercise in polite beseechment that cunningly flattered and cajoled, and yet warned of hidden consequences for the nation if the bearer was not granted an audience. Intrigued despite himself, Leo read it through twice, then told Jenks to allow the fellow in.

The visitor was young, not much older than Leo, and he seemed both genuinely pleased to be in the presence of a legendary figure and at the same time very sure of himself. Leo invited him to be seated, uncertain if he had done the right thing by allowing him where few others had been.

"Mr. Brannan," Price began, "I am indebted to you for this meeting. I know you're the busiest of men."

"No one is in my debt until I give him something, Mr. Price. What may I do for you?"

"Sir, I represent a body of like-minded men who are concerned for the future of Colorado and the surrounding states and territories. We are businessmen who often are at odds with government policies which we deem to be bad for business. We believe, to a man, in unrestricted growth, be it in whichever field of endeavor. Restrictions and ordinances and laws of containment are what we abhor, but of course, we do not openly protest such things. We prefer instead to move in special ways behind the scenes, as it were, to achieve our ends. We believe that we, as practical men, know what is best, or at least better, for the country than most elected representatives in Washington. We have a separate agenda, based on the known superiority of our beliefs, as these are applied to the actual working world."

"You're a Republican, Mr. Price."

"Indeed I am not, sir, nor are my colleagues."

"You are, then, a secret society."

"That would not be the nomenclature of our choice, sir. We seek only to implement our agenda with the least public knowledge of such that we possibly can."

"But you do so with secretiveness, do you not?"

"That is so, but the expression 'secret society' has about it a medieval ring, some arcane gathering of persons in robes and armor. We are nothing like that, I assure you."

"What is it that you want of me, Mr. Price."

"Sir, you will have received several letters of late from us, requesting this interview."

"I have indeed."

"But you did not reply, and it was arranged that one of our number should talk with you in person to lay out a certain proposal we earnestly ask you to consider. That individual was murdered, Mr. Brannan, before he could do so. You will have read the recent newspaper reports of Walter Morrow's death?"

"Ah, yes. At first it was suicide, then it became patricide, as I recall."

"There was initial confusion. In any case, I am Mr. Morrow's replacement, so to say."

Leo listened attentively as Rowland Price described in circumloquacious fashion the workings of the organization he represented but would not name. It was an outline shrouded in fog, shot through with moral contradiction, an edifice of cold moonbeams whose sole purpose lay in serving only those responsible for its construction.

"Mr. Brannan, I'll be direct; there are some among us who believe that future development of the country will require different strategies than have been used to date, a more modern approach to suit these modern times we live in. Others disagree, and the result has been a measure of factional conflict within the organization. Needless to say, I represent the Praetorians, as we term ourselves. Mr. Brannan it's our sincere hope you will join with us in the shaping of a new and more prosperous America. Half the land in the west belongs to foreigners, English lords and the like, and we in the organization see changing that as yet another plank in our platform of overall reform."

"Your secret society interests me greatly, Mr. Price."

Price smiled crookedly. "Were we to achieve political power, Mr. Brannan, we would need be secretive no longer."

"Politics? I understood you were all businessmen."

"Politics and business, sir, have always been linked together like rose and brier."

"Politics presumably represented by the brier."

"I know you speak in jest, but there are many who would agree. Politics has become fouled by business interests in the east, and every man in Congress is to be had for a song."

"And what should be the role of your organization?"

"Sir, we are committed to the patrician ideal. We look to ancient Rome for our model. The country must be run by men out of the ordinary, who understand the levers of power, yet are beyond the reach of bribery, since they already have all they need in the way of earthly riches."

"Mr. Price, you are referring to an aristocracy."

"Sir, I am."

"Have you not studied the lesson of the French Revolution, Mr. Price? Aristocrats tend to lose their ideals, after which they lose their heads."

"Those Frenchies, sir, were made decadent through generations of idleness. That is not the American way, nor could it ever be. Our patrician class, as we refer to it, would be tireless in pursuit of the best possible means to lift up every man in the country by his boot-straps. It cannot happen while Washington is at the beck and call of certain individuals for whom the democratic principles of government are a convenient cover for purest self-interest. We, on the other hand, would make no secret of our aims."

"Is this to be done under the banner of the Democratic party, Mr. Price? You have already said you aren't a Republican."

"Neither banner will do, Mr. Brannan, and we have arrived at the crux of my mission. We foresee the legitimate and overdue need in America for a third political party."

"To be called?"

"We have in mind—what else?—the Praetorian party."

"And you would aim yourself at Washington, like the other parties."

"Unlike the other parties. Like a clean prairie wind, Mr. Brannan, sweeping the common chaff before it. Something new, something without peer, a party that will care for the workingman without exploiting him, a party that will allow wealth, even excessive wealth, because we know that the rich man who follows our creed will not neglect the workers who created that wealth for him. We are not Socialists. There exists in the natural world all manner of inequality. Nowhere do we see absolute uniformity of strength or intelligence, of aptitude and ability. Equality for all persons is a facile dream, but with a new kind of man behind the helm of the ship of state, Mr. Brannan, a new society will emerge, not necessarily Utopian, but without the poverty and squalor we see so much of, especially in our great cities. America could become the model for a new kind of world, given the opportunity to demonstrate how it can be done, and for that we require the right leadership, the man who is right for so unique and far-reaching a quest."

Leo watched Price's face. There was a light sheen of sweat on his brow and upper lip, a flush to his skin, and his voice had become more animated than before. The man truly believed in and was moved by his own words, and Leo admitted the speech had been worth listening to, but it was politics still, however prettied up by talk of ideals and newness, and politics was a field that had never held the least interest for Leo. He assumed that the fledgling Praetorian party required a cash donation from the likes of himself in order to begin its earthshaking work. He supposed he could donate several thousand for their cause; they could do no more harm to the country than the hacks and thieves currently jostling for supremacy in Washington.

"A third alternative, eh, Mr. Price? I think I approve. You say there are those within your own existing group who do not?"

"A bunch of diehard traditionalists, sir. There is under way a mass defection to our side. If your name should be associated with our cause, there would certainly be a landslide, and after that, little to stop us beginning our crusade. I say crusade, Mr. Brannan, and I do not exaggerate. It will be nothing less than the moral awakening of our nation, the true flowering of the spirit of independence and opportunity America was founded upon."

"Strong words. Mr. Price, powerful sentiments. Am I correct in my assumption that your cause has need of funds?"

"We have sufficient for the time being, sir. As I said, we all are fortunate. The thing we require is your consent to be the leader such a movement requires."

"I beg your pardon? Leader?"

"Sir, I see I have not made my case clear. We wish you to represent us."

"I, Mr. Price?"

"You, Mr. Brannan. You are one of the most famous men in America, famous not only for your wealth but for the way in which you avoid, with scrupulous modesty, the appearance or practice of flaunting that selfsame wealth. A pauper will not begrudge a rich man his riches if it was earned by legitimate means, and the pauper will respect that man if he presents himself as a frugal and honest person, for whom demonstrable excess is anathema. Sir, you are that man. You are perfect for the role that destiny and my colleagues are at this moment preparing."

Leo went to the window and looked out at his town, the little of it he could see beneath the swirling grayness.

"Do you know anything of air movements, Mr. Price?"

"Air movements, sir?"

"We have a considerable problem at various times of the year. The air will not allow smoke from the chimneys to rise and be borne away. I have thought of blasting away part of the western slope to allow the prevailing westerlies access to our valley, but it is a project that requires engineering skills I doubt that any man has yet developed, despite our modern times."

"The impossible can become the possible, given the will and the means."

"You will not be distracted, will you, Mr. Price?"

"No, sir, I will not."

Leo could see a man running along the street, but could see no reason for his haste; he was not chasing anyone, nor being chased. The running man disappeared below Leo's window ledge. Leo was always slightly surprised when an individual stood out for some reason, however inconsequential the moment, because that individual worked for Leo. He could not look at anyone in Glory Hole without unconsciously acknowledging that the person worked for him in some capacity or other, or else was supported by the wage Leo paid to someone else. It was all his, a tiny kingdom in the clouds, and he was, he supposed, content to have it remain thus, for Glory Hole and for himself. Yet here was a complete stranger, with visionary talk of a new America, offering a wholly different kind of crown to Leo, almost begging him to take it. Price was not a crackpot. Leo had heard rumors of a secretive network at large in the west, and now had learned it did exist, and was in the process of dividing itself in two, the conservatives and the so-called Praetorians, and those same revolutionaries who were causing the division wanted him, Leo Brannan, to be their figurehead, their spokesman, the face and name that would launch them from whatever clandestine warrens they presently inhabited into the light of day. They wanted him to be President of the United States. He was not prepared for so radical a notion, nor could he put it from him with any certainty. He admitted he was momentarily helpless, unable to think calmly and cogently about the thunderbolt that had been delivered to his office by the intense young man seated in front of his desk.

Jenks knocked and entered the room. Jenks had always waited for an instruction to enter before doing so, but Leo was in no mood to chastise him, discomforted as he was by the decision he was being asked to make.

"Sir ... there has been an accident."

"Accident?"

"A bad accident, I'm told ... Your wife, sir, your wife is involved.... At the pithead, some kind of accident with the machinery ..."

Those on the main street of Glory Hole witnessed an unusual event that morning; they saw Leo Brannan running as if all the demons of hell were in pursuit. He ran to the Deer Lick and found

Dr. Gannett already in attendance. An alert worker had applied a tourniquet to Zoe's upper arm, above the mangled elbow. The floor around her was slick and red with her blood.

Leo heard babbled words of his wife's strange drift toward the cable gears despite shouted warnings, and the inexplicable insertion of her arm into the toothed wheels despite the safety rail there. Another voice told Leo his wife was seen to slip, and her arm had been thrust out to right herself, but had missed the rail and been plunged into the gears before anyone could shut the engine down. It had happened in an instant, and Zoe Brannan's right arm resembled something that might have fallen from a butcher's cart and been gnawed at by dogs. Leo turned away to vomit, while the doctor proceeded to remove the destroyed portion of Zoe's arm during her convenient state of unconsciousness.

Omie's face was the first thing Zoe recognized. She was in her bed, propped up by pillows, and Omie stood like a sentinel beside the covers, staring at her mother. Zoe wondered how she had come to be in bed at that hour—wan sunlight came through the windows—and why she felt that her right side was being squeezed in a vise. Looking down, she saw the cocoon of bandages around her shoulder and arm. The arm itself felt terribly painful, the fingers of her hand clenching and unclenching like a wounded starfish. Then Zoe saw that she had no right hand, and no right arm, and a scream that could not be uttered rose to plug her throat. Now she recalled entering the cable house, approaching the machinery there, and being struck so hard in her right side she had been lifted from the floor. The thing that struck her had done this—taken her arm off above the elbow and left a stump behind.

Her head sank back onto the pillows. She could not bear to think of what her arm would look like when the swathes of cotton were removed. A one-armed woman; could anything be more revolting than such an asymmetric creature? What might pass for a war loss on a man would simply look ugly and incongruous on a woman. Zoe wished the machine had killed her. The grief she felt over her discovery was like a humming in her brain, a desperate noise seeking escape, but there was none. A one-armed woman. She would never leave the room again, never allow anyone to see her deformity. She would kill herself, she decided, and erase the entire incident, along with a life no longer worth living.

"I didn't see it," said Omie, her voice made tiny by guilt.

Zoe could not even look at her. She wanted Omie to go away and stop staring at her. Zoe wanted to be alone so she could fling herself from the window on the north side of her room; the drop was at least forty feet onto solid rock; she would leap out headfirst to ensure her death. It would be done the moment Omie went away.

"I didn't see it happen, Mama, I'm sorry.... If I had've seen it, I would've told you not to go ... but I didn't see it. My eye didn't work."

For just a few seconds Zoe was tempted to accept that her loss was Omie's fault. What good was a clairvoyant daughter if she could not be relied upon to steer her own mother away from such a disaster? Omie was weeping, her mouth twisted. Zoe looked at her; she had never seen Omie so miserable.

"It wasn't you.... It had nothing to do with you. It just ... happened. Stop crying, please. It isn't your fault, Omie. Now, please ... seeing tears just makes my arm hurt more."

"How ... how can it hurt, Mama?"

"I don't know. I can still feel it, though. I met a man once, a long time ago when I was your age, and he had just one arm, and he said he could feel his arm still, and his fingers...."

Omie watched her mother's face crease with sorrow as her voice died away, then a sob unlike any Omie had ever heard came bursting from Zoe, a huge sob, followed by a string of little sobbings, then her mother began to moan and cry in earnest, and roll her body from side to side, all the while crying tears so heavy they flooded down her cheeks like rain, and her moans became a wailing that made the hair on Omie's neck stand straight up. Mama is in hell, Omie thought, and became frightened by the intensity of Zoe's anguish. It came rushing from her in waves of horror and self-loathing that Omie could sense without truly understanding; where was the anger her mother should be feeling toward her for not having foreseen the accident? Could she truly have meant it when she said Omie was not to blame? The waves from Zoe were huge and dark, many voices and fears rolled together, and they rocked Omie on her heels as they swept by her like the wind from massive beating wings.

A nurse finally entered the room, having heard the horrendous wailing from the far end of the passageway, and told Omie to get out. Omie did so, and was followed all the way to her room by the rolling waves of grief and desolation and one other thing, a thing Omie would never have thought could come from her mother, but it was unmistakably there—a picture of the window in Mama's room, and Mama throwing herself down onto the rocks below that window. Omie fell to the floor in shock, then picked herself up and raced back to Zoe's door, but the nurse had locked it, and Zoe's pitiful howling was lessening even as Omie tugged at the doorknob, and eventually gave out with a single racking sob, a smaller sob than the one that had begun everything. When all was quiet, Omie walked away. She would come back later and tell Mama not to go near the window. This time her eye was working.

Zoe learned of the presence in Elk House of a stranger by way of the nurse. The nurse did not know the gentleman's name, but allowed that he was very dignified for a man so young. Zoe gave instructions that the gentleman was not to be allowed anywhere near her, and her husband was to stay away also. Leo had been at her bedside twice that Zoe could recall, and both times he had been unable to do anything but stand there, shaking his head, saying, "My dear ... my dear ..." until Zoe told him to go away. She did not want him looking at her bandaged stump, and she did not want to look at him. She found she hated him, for no particular reason, and it would be best for them both if he stayed away. The nurse neither agreed to deliver such a message nor said outright that she would not. She busied herself with the sheets, and hoped that Dr. Gannett would arrive soon to administer more laudanum to his patient. The nurse had no medical training, and could do little more than fetch and empty chamber pots and keep the patient's room tidy.

When Omie visited, Zoe asked her for information on the stranger. Leo had never invited anyone to stay at the house before; he usually entertained those few men with whom he had business dealings at the Stag Hotel in town.

"His name is Rowland," said Omie, "and he's from Denver. He likes Papa very much, but I don't care for him."

"Why not? What is his reason for being here?"

"He says he came to pay his respects to Papa, and that's what Papa says too."

"Can you learn any more?"

Omie knew what that meant, but she had already lanced Rowland's head several times with her special eye, and the results had been a puzzlement. "There are lots of men with no faces, Mama."

"No faces?"

"Well, I can't see them, not clearly. They wear nice clothes, and they meet in a big room with dark wood all around the walls and smoke cigars and talk a lot."

It meant nothing to Zoe beyond suggesting some kind of business meeting. She was no longer interested in Mr. Rowland Price.

"Can you still feel the fingers, Mama?"

"Yes, but not all the time, and they won't do what I tell them to; isn't that peculiar? Well, perhaps not, since they aren't even there, Why should something that isn't there do what I want?"

Omie smiled. Mama was making a joke, although not a very funny one, so she must be getting better.

"Have you been getting out of bed?"

"Once or twice."

Zoe watched Omie's face. She had been warned by Omie to stay clear of the windows; Omie would not say why. Zoe knew she could never do now what she had fully intended doing in those first awful hours when she became aware of her condition. Omie was the true nurse, not the woman appointed by Dr. Gannett; that bustling individual could not stop gushing about the doctor's wonderful and awe-inspiring abilities as a man of medicine. Zoe suspected the nurse was in love with her employer, and even suspected the good doctor might be using her in his bed. Thoughts of that kind had become repugnant to Zoe. She did not wish to be touched by any man again. Her missing arm was like a returned hymen, a barrier to intimacy. This would be her lot from that time on, a shotgun marriage to her lessened self, with shame the bridesmaid.

She wondered how she might fill the hours and days and years ahead of her, spent as they would be within the walls of her room. If she was not going to kill herself, there would have to be some manner of distraction from her torment. Dr. Gannett's laudanum was fairly efficacious as a solvent for her pain, even more effective as a means of loosening the strings around her mind. Sometimes she would daydream for hours after a stiff dose of the green liquid, her thoughts unspooling like ribbons hurled into an abyss, and her mood would veer from its habitual self-pity, allowing Zoe to roam the pastures of yesterday with Mr. Duckfeet and Mr. Pigeontoes, Nettie Dugan's names for Clay and Drew. She pictured them both as boys, even as they ran alongside herself, a grown woman with two good arms, and as the drug relinquished its hold, Zoe would cry softly for what was gone forever.

* * *

When Rowland Price at last departed for Denver, Leo was left unde-
cided over the proposition that had been offered to him. To enter
politics, when his business required all of his attention, did not
seem wise, yet he found he could not dismiss the vision Price had
conjured for his consideration; to be the leader of the first new political entity in the land for more than a century was not a role to
refuse without first carefully weighing the disadvantages against
the satisfaction that would be his if the gamble should pay off and
he be made the nation's president.

The opportunities for remaking America were enticing. He would
be able to tackle all the old problems the modern age had not allevi-
ated: the poverty and ignorance, the social injustices that prolifer-
ated now more than ever, as the wealthy became more so, and the
poor made do with the little they had. It was a challenge only a special man could hope to meet and overcome. The nation's ills were
like the mountains Leo stared at from his windows, massive, seemingly immovable, so entrenched in their current form they defied
conquest. Yet Leo had heard of a design for a mining process that
someday would eat entire mountains for their hidden minerals, literally raze them with vast machines as yet undeveloped, and crush
them into submission between mechanical jaws that would dwarf
his own crushers and stampers. Might not the problems no man
had yet found a solution to yield under similar farsightedness and
scientific application?

It would require a man such as himself to make the new social
order work for everyone. Price had said a pure man, a person of
moral integrity and proven ability to organize the complex strands
required in business, was the only viable type to manage the long-
overdue transition from the America of yesterday to the America of
tomorrow. The twentieth century was fast approaching; as the old
century thudded shut like a stone sealing a tomb, a new doorway
filled with light must open, and the Praetorian party, with Leo at
its forefront, was the only possible keeper of the keys.

He knew that such dreams of power and influence were also a
distraction for himself from the nightmare of Zoe's tragedy. The
horrific accident had changed his wife utterly, and the least part of
it was the actual loss of her arm; she would not see him when he
came to her, nor eat with him in the dining room, no matter how
early he came home. She would not even leave her bedroom, and
permitted only Omie to see her. Once the stitches had been removed

from the stump by Dr. Gannett, the doctor and the nurse he had hired on behalf of the Brannans were dismissed by Zoe. She wanted no one near her but her daughter. It was Omie who fetched and carried her mother's meals and emptied her chamber pot and changed her bedding, a little blue-faced servant who performed her chores seemingly without complaint, and read to Zoe from storybooks, and comforted her. Omie had become a doting parent, and Zoe a capricious child. Leo knew it was not healthy for such a reversal to take place, but he could not think how else to cope with the aftermath of Zoe's misfortune other than by allowing it to continue.

Would a man of integrity, as Price insisted Leo was, let his wife become what Zoe had become, simply because that was the easiest option? Should he dismiss all thoughts of accepting the political challenge until such time as Zoe was herself again, or was it ethically permissible to launch himself into newer, deeper waters while she had already withdrawn herself from himself and his interests? What difference could it make to Zoe if her husband became involved in a venture that would doubtless take him far from Glory Hole on many occasions, even before a successful electoral bid should take him away to the east for four solid years. Perhaps by that time Zoe would be recovered, and in a position to accompany him to Washington. The imponderables of Leo's dilemma sat like vultures on either shoulder. He would have to decide for himself, and do so quickly; Price had left him in no doubt that although his name was at the head of a list of suitable candidates for the position of party leader, the list itself was proof that his refusal would not stop the Praetorians from proceeding under the leadership of a lesser light. He wished sometimes he were a drinking man.

"Papa has gone away to Denver."

"For what purpose?"

"He said it was business, Mama, but I saw Mr. Price in his thoughts."

"It may be that Mr. Price is in the mining business."

"No, he doesn't know anything about mines, I looked."

"What did you see?"

"The same men, Mama, with big cigars. Their faces were clearer than the last time, but I didn't know any of them."

"Then we shan't worry about them. I'm sure Papa has his reasons for going."

"Why won't you talk to him?"

"I do not wish to."

"But why?"

"I'm ugly now."

"No, Mama, you're not."

"I am, and I have no wish to be seen by anyone but you."

Omie knew her mother was telling the truth; inside Zoe's mind was a picture of herself, grossly distorted, with the missing arm even shorter than it really was, while her other limbs were gigantic appendages that made her resemble a lopsided octopus. Omie did not bother to contradict with mere words what Zoe saw; the repellent image was far too strong to be broken by argument, especially from someone as young as herself. She was more or less resigned to being Zoe's servant forever, having attempted on several occasions to peer into the future for a glimpse of less tragic times ahead. Despite her best efforts, no pictures came to her, and again she began to doubt the efficacy of her special eye. If she should ever lose it permanently, as her mother had lost an arm, would she react in a similar fashion, cutting herself off from almost everyone? It disturbed Omie to imagine herself and Mama together in the bedroom, looking after each other like a pair of invalids.

"We might be here till we die, Mama."

"I shall. You won't."

"Why won't I?"

"Because you will leave this place and marry some man and bring up his children, those that survive, and your life will be what it should."

This did not sound any more acceptable to Omie than the bleak future she had pictured for herself and Zoe.

"I don't want to get married."

"And why not?"

"The husbands run away after a while."

Zoe gave a laugh that was more akin to a bark, making Omie jump. "Perhaps you're right. Stay a virgin, and be true to yourself alone."

"Were you married to my real papa?"

"No. He was a brute, a farmer. He raped me. Do you know what rape is?"

"No," said Omie, but was immediately struck between the eyes by Zoe's recollection of the event, a memory so painful still, and so inexplicable in its leering violence, that Omie's breath was taken from her for a moment or two. She began to cry, and seeing the tears, Zoe hated herself for having deliberately caused them by uttering a truth that was best kept hidden, if such things could be hidden from Omie's eye.

"I'm sorry. I shouldn't have told you. I had no right. The point is, Omie, it doesn't matter in the least who put you inside me. You don't resemble him at all, not even to look at. You are not his daughter. You are mine, and mine alone. That's the thing to remember. I apologize, my darling. I think ... I think I wanted you to see how awful a place the world can be. That is part of growing up, seeing the world as it truly is. Sometimes it is ugly, but that isn't my fault or your fault or even the fault of people like the man who raped me. I don't know whose fault it is. No one does, but we have religion for those who insist on an answer."

"Did he make my face the wrong color, the man?"

"Certainly not. That is just bad luck ... like my arm. We're not responsible for every unfortunate thing that befalls us, Omie, but we must recognize those things for which we are. Listen to me: I sound like a sage."

"That's a plant, Mama."

"Another kind of sage. Really, I know nothing, nothing at all that's worth ten cents. Isn't that terrible?"

"I suppose."

Omie inspected her shoes, then asked, "Mama, did you ever know a man that's tall, with holes in his face for a spike or an arrow to go through, and a big hat?"

"Gracious, no. I would have remembered a man like that. Why do you ask?"

"I see him sometimes, and sometimes he sees me too, but I don't know why. I thought he might be my real papa...."

"Absolutely not. He was a fairly short man, as I recall, and even if he was not at all handsome, he certainly didn't have holes in his face, apart from his nostrils and mouth."

"I haven't seen him for a long time now."

"He may have been nothing but a dream."

"I don't think so, Mama."

31

When Madge Clifton's mother began to die, there was little sympathy in the neighborhood for either woman. The presence of Madge had been tolerated without enthusiasm for a number of years, and it was hoped by the female population of Dry Wash that with the passing of her invalid mother to a better world, Madge would consider moving on also. If Madge chose not to do so, she would be encouraged by means as yet undefined. There had been sympathy for her, even if she was a whore, for as long as she tended her ailing mother, but communal tolerance was nearing its limit.

But Mrs. Clifton, eighty-one years old and incapable of meaningful speech or movement, lingered for a week, then another week, ingesting only a little soup and sips of water. It was considered miraculous that she clung so tightly to a life that must have been sheer misery for years, but cling she did, well into a third week. The women were becoming impatient with such delay to their plans for encouraging Madge to leave, and kept a close watch on the Clifton home for drawn shades in the daytime, or the appearance of Madge with a black shawl around her, anything to indicate that the time for implementing their plan had arrived.

It was during Mrs. Clifton's third week of lingering at death's door that an unusual figure came to Dry Wash. Within twenty minutes of his arrival, he drew up his wagon outside Madge's door, knocked and introduced himself. "Ma'am, I am Reverend Francis Wixson, and I ask you for just a short moment of your time, pursuant to a request that may advance the cause of science and religion both, with your cooperation. They tell me at the store you have a parent in close proximity to her maker, and I beg your indulgence."

Madge scandalized the town in a new and different manner when it became known she had allowed Reverend Wixson to park his wagon behind the house, then moved her dying mother into it. This apparent callousness and licentiousness (it was assumed the reverend had betrayed his cloth and would move into the house with Madge) was reason enough for a party of women to approach Clay Dugan with a view to having him arrest Madge and the preacher both for outright moral corruption.

"Ladies," he told them, "you know Madge's occupation. I guess she has the right to take a man inside her own house if she wants."

"But her mother is dying, Marshal. She's gone and put the old lady outside in the feller's wagon, and don't be telling us she's got the right to do that."

"Well, that does seem like an unusual thing to do...."

"You get down there and make her throw that feller out and bring her mother back inside. It's a disgrace to the community when a woman like her thinks she can get away with murder, and that's what it'll be, Marshal, if that old lady dies out there in the wagon while Madge Clifton's inside tucked up warm with a customer, and I don't believe for one minute he's a real preacher. What man of God would have dealings with a whore, I ask you? You get down there and put things right like it's your job to do."

Clay suppressed a sigh and did as he was told, but he insisted that the women allow him to do his duty without all of them trailing down to Willow Street on his heels. They agreed, and let him approach Madge's house without an escort.

When he knocked, Madge let him in immediately.

"Good afternoon, Marshal."

"Afternoon, Miss Clifton."

When he saw the rawboned figure at the kitchen table, Clay stared. "Don't I know you?"

"I believe so. The name was Dugan, was it not?"

"Was and still is. I forgot yours. Waxman?"

"Wixson. Reverend Francis Wixson. My calling remains the same, but I see yours has changed."

Clay saw Wixson's eye on the badge he wore on his vest.

"People here know about my previous occupation," he said.

"Oh, I intended no insult, Mr. Dugan. It was an innocent remark, I assure you."

"Please sit down, Marshal," Madge invited.

Clay sat and placed his hat on his knee. Madge plucked it off and placed it on a hatrack. Clay was irritated by that, but said nothing. He hadn't wanted to come to Madge Clifton's house at all, and had been nowhere near it since the hanging of Maxwell the dentist. The temptation to do so had been there in his mind, but he had resisted until now, because he knew it would do him no good at all to get mixed up with a woman like Madge, not while he was supposed to represent law and order. He thought about her often, though, and lifted his hat to her in passing on the street. No one could have guessed he wanted her so badly he often could not sleep without first pouring himself several stiff shots of whiskey. But he suspected Madge knew, with the cunning instinct of the whore for a potential customer. She said and did nothing to relay her secret knowledge of him, but it was there in her eyes whenever they exchanged the briefest of looks in public. I know you want me, her eyes said, and someday you'll come knocking at my door. And today he had, but only because a bunch of outraged women had obliged him to. He knew why Wixson was there.

"Your mother, Miss Clifton ... she's in the wagon for weighing when the time comes?"

"That's correct. I'm sure Mama would want to take part in an experiment like this. She was always very curious about things until her mind went."

"Well, I have to explain this to folks. Can you guarantee she's comfortable and warm? If I can tell them that, they'll likely be less upset."

"She is indeed, Marshal," said Wixson, "and I invite you to inspect the wagon for yourself."

Clay accompanied Madge and Wixson to the backyard and climbed into the wagon. Mrs. Clifton was laid out on a mattress on one of the beam balance's pans, the other being occupied by a selection of metal weights, large and small. The central needle indicated a perfect balance between the two. The woman's eyes were open, and she gazed at the wagon's canvas roof with a rapt expression that suggested to Clay she was out of her head.

"Mrs. Clifton, are you happy with this arrangement here? Are you comfortable, ma'am?"

She offered no reply, seemed in fact unaware that he squatted beside her. She was covered by a heavy quilted comforter, and her breathing was easy. Clay could find no fault with the setup, and stepped back outside.

"All right, Marshal?" asked Wixson.

"I suppose. You really expect to weigh her at the exact moment she passes on, and have the difference register?"

"When her soul departs the physical body, yes."

"Been finding many takers these past years?"

"Quite a number. My portfolio of statistics is swelling, and in a few years more I expect to be in a position to publish my results."

"Is that right. Miss Clifton, is there any kind of financial arrangement involved here, I mean, is the reverend paying you for the right to weigh your mother's soul?"

"No, Marshal. Should he?"

"I don't know. You ever pay anyone before, Reverend?"

"Indeed no, not once. There are very few individuals who are prepared to submit their loved one into my care, unfortunately, but those that do, do so with a will. They wish to contribute to mankind's understanding of the unknown, you see, and that is a privilege beyond price."

"I'll go ahead and tell people you're not doing anything wrong here. Any idea how long this'll take?"

"Miss Clifton informs me her mother is tenacious of life, and in any case I'm no doctor. It may happen at any moment, or not for days. We'll remain here with Mrs. Clifton regardless, to provide her with comfort until the end, whenever that may be."

Clay took his hat and left. He had felt extremely uncomfortable in Madge's house. The bedroom door had been open, and he had seen in passing the bed she made her living by. Most of her customers, Clay had learned, approached the house from the rear, to avoid being seen. He had lately mounted a watch over the open space behind Madge's house to see just who arrived, and how often. He had done this for two nights, and seen only one man knock and enter through the back door. It had been too dark to identify him. If that was the regular number, it was a wonder Madge was able to survive. Clay himself kept his distance during those two nights, unwilling to risk being seen and associated with Madge's clientele.

The same delegation of women arrived at his office shortly after his return, and were far from satisfied with Clay's explanation of Wixson's apparatus. There were gasps of incredulity as Clay expressed his own satisfaction with the situation.

"It isn't Christian, Marshal! It shouldn't be let alone, a foolish business like that. They should be made to quit right now, before the old lady passes on in the back of a wagon when she's got a perfectly good bed to lay herself down in and die natural-like."

"Ladies, there's nothing illegal about what Miss Clifton and the reverend have agreed to between them. Mrs. Clifton is just fine where she is, believe me."

"Marshal, why are you protecting that woman?"

"I'm not protecting anyone, ma'am; I just don't see any criminal activity taking place in her backyard."

"See anything else taking place in Madge's backyard?" asked another woman. "Heard you were seen snooping around there last week in the dark."

"That's an outright lie, ma'am. Whoever told you that is mistaken."

"Well, which is it—a mistake or a lie?"

"Either or both," said Clay. "Now I want my office cleared. Good day to you, ladies, and a pleasant evening."

He herded them out the door like a gaggle of hissing geese, and closed it behind him. So he'd been seen. He shouldn't have gone anywhere near the place, even as far from Madge's back door as he had stationed himself. Maybe it was the man he'd seen who passed the sighting on. If the women talked loud enough, it might blacken his reputation, and Clay didn't want that. He liked his job and its steady wages, and would no more have risked losing it than shot off his toes. The women were still outside his window, peering in at him. Clay hated them for the self-righteous interfering busybodies they were. He wondered how many of their husbands had visited Madge, and found the thought upset him even more.

Word of a scientific experiment conducted in the name of God could not be kept quiet for long. By the end of the day a small crowd had gathered around the leaning picket fence enclosing Madge's backyard. A lamp burned inside the wagon, and the silhouettes of Madge and Wixson could be seen on the dirty canvas. It was noted that they placed themselves at opposite ends of the wagon. Clay went down to Willow Street himself to see how matters were progressing, and passed through the gathering until he came to the wagon's tailgate.

"Mind if I join you?"

"Please do, Marshal."

Clay sat beside Wixson. "How is she?"

"Failing, I believe. Miss Clifton says her mother's breathing has never sounded like this."

Clay listened; the woman's breath was barely there, but it came and went with such rapidity her nostrils appeared to quiver. He looked at Madge, who smiled back. Clay looked away. He didn't know why he wanted her; she was not especially attractive. It must have been hearing her with Maxwell in the cell the night before the hanging, but even that reason made no sense to Clay; in fact it was humiliating to think he had been snared by such unabashedly crude sounds. He wanted someday to marry again with a good woman, and have children by her to replace poor Silan, but Madge could never be that woman, not if Clay intended remaining in Dry Wash.

His presence appeared to grant the project a sudden legitimacy; soon the watching crowd ignored Madge's fence and gathered closely around the wagon, expressing awe at the singular appearance of the contraption upon which Mrs. Clifton lay like an unprotesting human sacrifice. Someone asked Wixson to explain his theory, and he stood upon the tailgate to deliver a lecture on the work of a lifetime.

"Here is the message," he said, pointing along the sides of his wagon. "'A false balance is abomination to the Lord: but a just weight is His delight.' This is no casual reference to honest shopkeeping, my friends, but an exhortation to seek actual proof of the soul's existence within us. In the days of old, that was not possible, since mankind lacked the precision instruments of modern science, but now at last we may take up the Lord's work, and seek to prove beyond even the scorn of such doubting Thomases as there might be among you that the soul is indeed there, a thing of such fragile substance it makes the finest gossamer web among twigs and grass on a spring morning seem a veritable tangle of fisherman's net, so great is the contrast. The soul, good people, is of such rarefied stuff it cannot bear the touch of air upon it, but must hide inside us all until the moment of its release, at which time its natural lightness takes it up among the fluffy clouds, and beyond, to its rightful home in the heavenly abode. My task—nay, my pledge to my maker—is this: that I shall make evident what the book of books has stated, and carry the proof of it before the court of public opinion in this and any other country so disposed to see and acknowledge the holy truth!"

There was scattered applause. Wixson accepted a variety of unsophisticated questions concerning his scientific technique for establishing the weight of the soul, then held up his hands to indicate he would accept no more.

"My friends, I have work to do. I ask that you be as quiet as you can in the presence of your neighbor Mrs. Clifton. We all should pass from this life to the next without unnecessary hubbub and conbobulation, so I ask you please to refrain from conversation while you remain in the area. I thank you."

He made a stiff bow and resumed his seat.

"Pretty good speech," said Clay.

"A receptive audience brings out the best in any man with a message worth hearing."

Clay wondered what his own message to mankind might be. He thought about it for several minutes, then gave up; nothing of an original nature entered his head, certainly nothing of such importance as Wixson's quest for the soul. Clay had labeled him a madman at their first meeting, but now was not so sure. Clay had a soul himself, if everyone else did, but he had never felt it stirring inside him. Maybe the soul just lay quiet until the time of death, then uncoiled like a snake from hibernation and began its undulations toward heaven, as Wixson said. Then again, maybe not.

He stole another look at Madge, who seemed to be dozing. If he took her to another town they might be able to marry without anyone knowing of her past, but that would mean looking for a new job, so it wouldn't work. He couldn't marry her in Dry Wash, where everyone knew what she was. It annoyed him that such prejudice should thwart his plans. He saw for the first time that they were indeed plans, not vague longings or misplaced sexual yearning; he wanted to marry Madge Clifton and live with her. But he couldn't.

Two days after the backyard vigil began, a reporter arrived from Tucson to cover the story that already had spread beyond Dry Wash. Wixson was more than prepared to speak his mind, never before having been accorded any interest or credence by the newspapers. The reporter took copious notes from interviews with all concerned, including Clay, who stated that although he was not convinced there was merit to Wixson's theory, he was not opposed to the experiment, given that all parties were agreeable and no money was changing hands. The reporter asked many questions of Madge, as daughter of the woman on the scales, and Clay overheard Madge give her profession as seamstress. Madge knew he had overheard, and when the reporter excused himself to conduct interviews among the crowd that had become a fixture around the Clifton place, she went to him and said, "I darn socks very well, as a matter of fact. Do you have any holes in your socks, Clay?"

Her use of his name unnerved him. He could not decide if he should resent it or begin calling her Madge.

"I darn 'em myself," he responded. "I got in the habit, living the way I did."

She gave him a look he could not define, then went to sit beside her mother, who was at last beginning to resemble a body without a soul, even if her lungs still took in their shallow sips of air. Mrs. Clifton had eaten nothing in five days, and it was considered a medical miracle that she persisted in living. A joke in local circulation had it that the old lady would give up the ghost and consent to have it weighed by its absence only when she was sure a good man had come along to make her erring daughter into an equally good woman, which meant she was going to live forever, probably, because no man would be fool enough to marry a whore; no good man anyway.

When Clay heard the joke from Judge Poudre he found he couldn't laugh, and the judge resented that, since he was accustomed to people laughing at his jokes. The judge had begun forming reservations about Clay of late, ever since hearing rumors of his hanging around Madge Clifton's back door. Judge Poudre had visited the Willow Street house himself a number of years back, when his wife had been especially mean to him for several months because he would not countenance the purchase of new furniture for their home, and he had not been impressed by Madge's skills as a courtesan. The judge had been considered something of a rake as a youth, and so thought himself an expert in matters of love. There was more to Clay Dugan than met the eye, Judge Poudre decided, and wondered when some of it might be revealed.

Although supervising the bizarre experiment formed no part of

Clay's duties, he began spending more and more time in or around the wagon. He would not go inside Madge's house, but considered the wagon, where he usually shared a hard bench with Wixson during the vigil, to be neutral territory, therefore no threat to his reputation. He made a point of telling several people of his encounter with Wixson years before, hoping to convince them he and the preacher were old acquaintances, thereby explaining his extended visits.

Some of his listeners believed him, but Judge Poudre did not. The judge had personal knowledge of a young man in another town who had almost driven himself crazy over some kind of unrequited love for a whore whose services he didn't even avail himself of. In the end the boy's nervous system had collapsed, and he was not seen in public again, except for occasional glimpses of him behind the windows of his mother's house. It was a fact that the whore in question used to walk past the house every Wednesday just before sundown, to taunt the boy, it was supposed, until the mother one evening ran out and shot her with her dead husband's old Civil War revolver. Judge Poudre himself had tried the case, and the mother had been found not guilty by reason of extenuating circumstances, namely the destruction of her son and the murdered party's wanton provocation. It had been a tragic case, and the judge saw elements of the same thing beginning to form under his nose in Dry Wash, even if Clay was a grown man. Further developments would bear watching.

At last it appeared that the dying woman might succumb. Her breathing ceased on several occasions, only to resume again a minute or so later, but the incidents were becoming more common, the gaps between them lessening. Bets on the exact hour and minute of her passing were made among the crowd that swelled to unusual proportions as word spread through the town. Wixson's theory was finally about to be proven or disproven, and the reporter from Tucson was again on hand to record the result.

Clay hurried over to Willow Street and was allowed his usual seat of privilege near the soon-to-be-departed. Wixson had lately adjusted his scales, since Mrs. Clifton had lost much of her meat during the extended waiting period, and he had to be sure, for scientific purposes, that his instrument was perfectly balanced before the spirit should depart.

The town doctor was standing by, his expression disdainful; he was a rationalist, even though he attended church regularly, and he fully expected to witness nothing more dramatic than the overdue expiration of a body unnaturally reluctant to depart the land of the living. He monitored the dying woman's heartbeat every few minutes, at Wixson's insistence, and pronounced it a little fainter, a shade more fluttery, each time, until at twelve minutes past seven in the evening he calmly pronounced her dead.

There was general excitation among the onlookers at this news, until Wixson begged them to be silent and still for the next minute or so. His mood conveyed itself to the crowd, and an absolute hush was observed. The canvas sides of his wagon had been raised two hours earlier to facilitate the public's view of the long needle mounted in the center of Wixson's beam balance, aligned precisely with a vertical notch in the brass plate behind it to indicate zero, or perfect balance. Seconds passed, and every eye maintained a watch on the needle. And the needle moved—a tiny fraction of a degree, but it moved—and there came from the crowd a soft rushing of indrawn breath, then a woman screamed that she could see the soul of Mrs. Clifton rising like chimney smoke from the wagon, and no sooner had she declared it than others saw it too. There was general pandemonium as those wishing for a similarly uplifting experience rushed at the scales, clambering inside the wagon to be closer to the source of the phantom, which even now was said to be hovering mere feet above the wagon's exposed hoops as if to display itself and dispel once and for all the doubts of the witnesses, before drifting to its appointed abode in the starry realm above.

Wixson was begging the intruders to depart before his experiment's results were ruined beyond recovery by their stomping and jostling. There were joyous wailings from many women in the crowd, who declared themselves true believers for having seen with their own eyes the ghostly evidence of a soul's departure heavenward, exactly as had been predicted, and there were howls from others, who had seen nothing, nothing at all, not even the needle's hesitant trembling, and they wished that the spectacle had been something they had paid for the privilege of witnessing, so they might ask for their money back.

Clay had to appropriate a bystander's pistol and fire two shots in the air to calm these hysterical reactions. Madge was still seated beside her mother. Clay couldn't tell if she had seen the soul or not, but he wanted things to calm down for her sake. He hadn't seen a damn thing himself, and was somewhat angry as a result, even though the absence of visible phenomena confirmed his own bias toward a material explanation for the world and its workings.

He laid a hand on Madge's shoulder, and she looked up at him. "I'm all right," she said, and Clay withdrew the hand immediately. He turned to the crowd and called for order. "Just settle down there, all of you!" There was a lessening of the general excitement, and Wixson took over from Clay.

"I invite each of you to come forward and examine the position of the indicator needle—one at a time!—and verify for yourselves that it has moved a fraction from the vertical, and remains there, absolute material proof that the deceased weighs less now than she did in the moments preceding her demise. When sufficient numbers of you have ascertained this to be the fact of the matter, I shall remove the least of my weights from the balancing pan and restore perfect equilibrium to the scales, further proving that what I say is true. You, madam, may be the first to scrutinize the needle."

A woman was boosted into the wagon. She squinted at the needle from a distance of less than a foot, and declared herself uncertain that there was in fact a declination. "Put your glasses on, Maude!" her husband called, and the woman flushed, then took from her bodice a pair of spectacles. Once these were perched on her nose she repeated her inspection, and found the needle "a tiny wee bit off-center, seems like." She was assisted down from the tailgate, and another onlooker invited to witness the needle's new position. Madge fetched an old chair from the house to aid those who followed in stepping into and out of the wagon, then she stood to one side with Clay until more than a dozen townsfolk verified that the needle had indeed performed as Wixson's theory anticipated.

"Now," said Wixson, "further proof, if proof were needed, that the deceased weighs less than the pan of weights counterbalanced against her. I pluck from the pile you see before you the tiniest weight of all, one one-hundredth of an ounce." He produced a pair of tweezers and removed from the weights assembled in the pan a tiny bell of metal. "Now I remove another of the same weight, adding up to one fiftieth of an ounce.... You see! The needle returns to dead center! Proof, ladies and gentlemen, of God's gift which he giveth to all, and taketh back at the end of our allotted span! Come one, come all, and see for yourselves the needle's new alignment. Step up, Marshal Dugan, and be the first."

Clay hesitated, then examined the needle. It appeared to be resting opposite the notch indicating perfect balance, but if he moved his head a fraction to the right or left, the needle no longer seemed to be centered so exactly, and he was no longer sure if his head had been correctly placed to begin with. The distance between the needle and the brass plate, about half an inch, invited variations in reading the degree to which the needle had moved. "Looks to be on the center line all right," he mumbled, and stepped down to make way for the next examiner.

"Is it?" asked Madge. She had not taken a close look at the needle since the doctor pronounced her mother dead.

Clay shrugged. "Pretty close," he said.

A dozen or more people inspected the beam balance, including the doctor, who declared himself unconvinced by the entire experiment. His statement was greeted by muted booing, which upset the doctor. "This is bogus science," he said, "and bogus religion too!"

"Retract that statement!" demanded Wixson.

"I will not, sir! You are a charlatan and a hoaxter! Let us see beneath your set of scales and determine for ourselves if there is not some device hidden away which might tip your needle."

"I will do no such thing! My instrument is delicate despite its size and weight, and I will permit no tipping over whatsoever."

"Because you fear for what might be found, I say!"

The crowd began to enjoy the shouting match, yelling support for one man or the other, sometimes both.

"Very well, then," said Wixson, "you may examine the underside of the instrument, but you will do so by removing floorboards from beneath the wagon. I repeat, there will be no tipping over or lifting of the instrument."

"I accept your offer," said the doctor. "Let us satisfy ourselves on this matter now. Is there anyone present with the tools necessary for a job such as this?"

"I can get something that'll rip planks off right quick," offered the blacksmith.

"Please proceed, sir, and thank you."

"Ripping? There will be no ripping of my vehicle! If there is to be removal of a certain number of floorboards, then it will be done with care!"

"Are you reneging on your offer, sir!" challenged the doctor.

"I am not, sir, nor will I allow damage to my wagon solely to satisfy your needs!"

Amid the bickering, Mrs. Clifton sat up.

"Johnny, fetch the cider," she croaked, and lay down again.

"Alive ...!" screamed a woman, then swooned, and the wagon was mobbed again.

Clay had returned the pistol he borrowed to restore order the first time, and could see no one else wearing one. His voice alone was not enough to prevent what followed. The body of Mrs. Clifton was lifted from the scales and passed through many hands to the safety of the back porch, then the wagon itself was overturned. The heavy beam balance came crashing down in Madge's yard. Wixson's wailings of protest hung above the rampagers like a circling bird as his precious instrument was dismantled to its component parts by wrenching and kicking. The underside of the platform it had stood upon was closely scrutinized for evidence of mechanical fakery. It was smooth and featureless, but this did nothing to alleviate the crowd's vengeful mood. They had been made fools of by allowing themselves to agree in public with Wixson that the needle had moved, then become centered again when the tiny counterweights were removed. None of that was possible if the dead woman was not dead at all, so there had to have been tricks of some sort to convince people they were seeing what Wixson wanted them to see.

Wixson was not alone in facing their collective ire; the doctor had blundered by declaring Mrs. Clifton dead, when clearly she was not, and his hat was knocked from his head and trampled upon to let him know that he, too, was a faker and a cheat. Wixson's punishment was more severe: not only were his beam balance and wagon overturned, his face and body suffered a degree of battery that would leave him bruised and swollen for days afterward.

Clay knew he was abandoning his duty by following the body to the porch. Criminal assault and destruction of property were taking place behind his back, but Clay preferred to let happen what might, rather than attempt to quell what he saw as righteous anger. Madge was with her mother, and Clay wished to be near Madge. It became apparent, even as Mrs. Clifton was laid down on the split-cane chaise, that she had succumbed once more. There was no pulse, no breath to mist a mirror hastily fetched by Madge, and the old woman's face was made a sickly yellow by the lamps held above her. Still, no one was prepared to pronounce her dead a second time, and Madge maintained a steady fanning of her mother's brow, just in case.

"Who's Johnny?" asked Clay.

"My little brother that died," Madge said. "He used to fetch Mama's jug."

Clay was standing closer to Madge than anyone else. Madge was still a whore, and no one was prepared to risk charges of unwanted intimate contact with her, even by accident. Several of her regular customers were on the porch, watching the pandemonium in the yard, but their wives were there also, so they kept their backs to her.

"You'd better make them quit," Madge told Clay.

He marched into the yard and smacked together the two nearest male heads, then repeated the action a little further into the melee, only to have his cheek scratched by a woman who resented his picking on her husband so. Clay saw the doctor fleeing the scene with his crushed hat, and looked around for Wixson. The reverend was hunched over his disassembled scales, sobbing without tears, and Clay felt sorry enough for him to make sure nobody else came within punching or kicking distance. "Better leave it and get indoors," he advised, but Wixson appeared not to hear him. He passed his hands across the brass plates and rods and chains of his beautiful device and continued to sob.

The reporter from Tucson approached, his face lit up by enthusiasm; he had never before been present at so unlikely a series of events, and his editor would be filled with praise for the story; his earlier report on the vigil beside the slowly expiring Mrs. Clifton had been of sufficient interest to his editor that it was forwarded to other newspapers by wire for inclusion on their pages.

"Marshal Dugan, sir, could I have a quote from you regarding what happened here this evening?"

"You can say I think the line between life and death is as blurred as ever, and likely supposed to be that way."

"Will any of this affect your churchgoing habits, sir?"

"I don't believe so."

"Thank you. Is she dead yet, can anyone tell?"

"Looks dead to me, but she did before, so don't go quoting me on that. Maybe you better forget that other thing I said too. I don't want to be quoted about anything."

"As you wish, Marshal."

The reporter went to Madge and began asking questions. Clay wandered around the yard, keeping an eye on what remained of the crowd. Most had left or were in the process of leaving, some of them

shamefaced about their behavior, some not. Even the gathering
near the porch was thinning. Soon the only persons remaining in
the vicinity were Madge and her mother (lying still as a log), the
reporter and Wixson and Clay.

Madge went into the house and returned with a tray bearing bottles of beer and glasses, and an impromptu wake began, despite the
lack of any official declaration of death for the woman on the split-
cane chaise. The evening was fine and warm, with just a hint of
breeze bringing the smell of the desert to town, and the chinaberry
tree in the front yard could be heard softly stirring. Clay forced a
beer on Wixson, and the reverend drained it in four or five lengthy
gulpings. Clay handed him another. "You can put it back together
with some help," he said. "Something built as solid as that, you
can't wreck it just by tipping it over."

Wixson nodded but would not talk, so Clay drifted back to the
porch, where the reporter was entertaining Madge with a story he
had recently written concerning an incident in Tucson. "I know for a
fact, ma'am, how hard it can be to determine a precise state of, uh,
deceasement. There was a fellow tried to hang himself down our
way just a short while back, and he just couldn't seem to get it
right. He tried three times in as many weeks, and bungled the job
each time, and the strange thing is, when people cut him down, he'd
tell them, 'I did it again, I did it again.' I can see why he'd say something like that the second and third times, but not the first, unless
he did it to himself other times before he came to public attention.
Smelled of drink, they say, and had some letters on him from a
woman in Rhode Island, Miss Sally Quick."

"You say Quick?" Clay asked.

"That's right."

"This feller that can't hang himself right, is he little and pock-
marked, losing hair on the top of his head?"

"That's the one, Marshal. You know him?"

"Used to handle hangings in this town till just recent, didn't he,
Madge?"

"Mr. Quick disgraced himself a short while back," said Madge.
"He attempted to hang a certain man, and pulled his head clean
off." Madge provided more details of the Maxwell hanging, and the
reporter took notes. "Mr. Quick took to drinking after that, I heard,
and disappeared. Is he being cared for by someone?"

"No, ma'am; he's in jail for trying to hang himself all the time.

There's talk he'll be sent to an asylum if he doesn't mend his ways. Does he have family out this way that could take care of him?"

"Lived with just a cat, I heard," said Clay.

"That's a shame. Well, at least I'm able to clear up the mystery, thanks to you folks. Marshal, I'm told you used to be a bounty man. Care to share with my readership a few of your exploits?"

"No."

"I believe I could arrange with my editor for monetary compensation if the stories were the right kind, filled with action and derring-do, you know the kind of thing."

"Not interested."

"Earp and Hickock, they weren't famous men till they found their way into the newspapers, Marshal."

"I wouldn't care to be famous."

"Not even a little bit?"

Clay walked off to see if Wixson needed another beer. He was still crouched among the pieces of his beam balance, and would not respond to attempts at conversation. Clay swigged beer and kept his back toward the porch. The reporter had annoyed him. He didn't like anyone who tried to dig up his past and shine a light on it. He listened as the reporter said good night to Madge, and ignored the man when the same words were offered to him. Clay kept staring into the darkness beyond the yard until he could no longer hear the reporter's retreating footsteps, then turned around.

"Help me get her inside, would you, Clay?" Madge asked.

Clay picked up the body of Mrs. Clifton and carried it through to the old lady's bedroom. He set her down carefully, then retreated with Madge, closing the door behind them.

"I'll send the doctor around again come morning."

"Thank you."

"Even he should be able to tell for sure if she's gone by then."

"I feel she is."

"Well, I guess we learned tonight you can't be sure."

"What shall we do with Reverend Wixson?"

"Leave him to cry for a while. He brought it on himself, telling folks his contraption could tell the difference between the living and the dead. Last time I met him he was intending to rig up a special camera to take pictures of the soul coming out. Guess he couldn't afford it. He's a fool if he keeps on the way he is."

"We all are fools at some time or other."

"Could be."

"Would you care to sit down in the parlor? I have some more beer."

"No, thank you. I need to be doing what they pay me for."

"I doubt that the town will burst into flames tonight. People have already let off steam."

"Most likely they have."

"Then you may put your feet up."

Clay was becoming uncomfortable. The temptation to linger inside Madge's house was strong. They were alone, assuming her mother was truly dead this time, and Clay knew that putting his boots up would result in them being drawn off his feet, purely for the added comfort, and once his boots were off his pants would follow, and the neighbors were probably watching to see if he left or stayed. It would be more than his job could sustain. He was probably going to draw fire in any case for his casual handling of the riot in Madge's backyard. Tracking wanted men had been a lonely and uncomfortable life, and not even very rewarding financially in the long run, but it had been simple, and he could fill each day and hour with conduct of his own choosing.

He stood up. "I'll take Wixson along with me and give him a clean cell for the night."

"As you wish."

Her face and voice gave nothing away. He moved awkwardly toward the door, nodded and left. Crossing the yard to the overturned wagon, he kicked up clouds of dust and swore at himself and the town and the fool who had caused everything to collapse around him tonight.

"Reverend? Get up. You're coming with me."

Wixson made no move to comply, did not even turn his head. Clay grabbed him by the collar and hauled him to his feet. "You can put it back together tomorrow. Right now you need to come with me." He assisted Wixson for several steps by keeping him upright, then the man found his own legs and began walking. Clay released his collar, and they fell into reluctant step with each other.

"This is the end ...," Wixson intoned.

"Is that so."

"They believed me, and then ... they turned against me."

"Can't blame them for that. When she sat up like she did it ruined your pitch, all right."

"Pitch? I have no 'pitch.' I have a message from the Lord, and on this night it was trampled beneath the feet of the ignorant. They do not deserve the opportunity for learning that I offer...."

"Maybe you should be a regular preacher again. That's what they like: sermons on Sundays, and to hell with science."

"They deserve nothing...."

"Maybe so. You won't get an argument from me."

Wixson lapsed into silence, and accepted Clay's offer of a cell without comment.

In the morning he drank coffee without a word of thanks, then left. Clay had intended to assist him in getting the wagon back onto its wheels, but Wixson's mood irritated him. It came as a surprise to learn, later in the day, that the preacher had sold his team and wagon to the livery stable, and his beam balance to the blacksmith. He had purchased a saddle horse and packhorse and left town. Now Clay had no reason to go over to Madge's house, and he blamed Wixson for having moved too fast without consulting him first; Clay would have changed his mind about helping with the wagon before the day was out, just for an excuse to return to Willow Street. Now he could not, and he was irritated all over again because of it.

For several weeks his life was without incident. He stayed away from Madge, arrested drunks and settled minor barroom disputes by his presence alone. The riot over Wixson's religious gadgetry had not harmed his reputation, nor that of the town. Copies of the Tucson newspaper reached Dry Wash, and its citizens were pleased to find themselves portrayed as commonsense types with a sharp eye for snake oil. The humorous account of "Wixson's folly" and the subsequent act of communal vengeance was like something out of a book, it was said, by those in town who happened to have read a book.

Copies of the article were passed around until tattered, then preserved in family Bibles for future generations to enjoy. Clay was less than pleased to find himself rendered in dark tones, a journalist's notion of a tough and forbidding lawman who was opposed to the farcical goings-on before they even began, and who ran the perpetrator out of town with the same ruthlessness with which he had in days gone by hunted down outlaws. He could not recognize himself, but no one seemed to mind that their law officer had been misrepresented; the important thing for Dry Wash was that its name had found its way into print, and there was talk of setting up a local news sheet to cover future stories, although two such ventures had already failed in the recent past. In short, Dry Wash was filled with pride and self-congratulation.

Clay felt none of this, and despised those who did, thereby placing himself silently at odds with the community that he served. It was nothing new for Clay to feel that way, but he hated to walk down the street and be obliged to respond with smiles to the cheery greetings that came his way from people for whom he had no real affection or respect. Nothing that they felt so good about had actually happened, at least not the way it had been depicted in the Tucson paper. They had swallowed whole a misrepresentation of themselves because it was more flattering than reality. They had been dupes, then angry dupes, that was all, and Clay had done nothing to stop any of it. If he could see the truth, why could no one else? It angered him, and made him drink. He would have liked to throttle the reporter who had concocted so amusing a fantasy, or else make him retract the entire story and rewrite it the way it actually happened.

There was one individual in town who would have understood the way he felt, but he had promised himself never again to venture anywhere near her house unless it be on official business. He had even gone so far as to cross the street rather than confront Madge for the blandest exchange of greetings. Madge Clifton would have agreed with him that the incident in her backyard and its aftermath were a sour joke on the town, and they could have laughed together over the prevalence of fools in the region. But he couldn't talk to her, let alone share a beer and privacy. So he drank alone in his cramped room above the office, or in the saloons at a corner table, which amounted to the same thing. The things that were inside him were obliged to stay there, like it or not.

Three weeks after the burial of her mother, Madge entered Clay's office. Clay had attended the funeral out of respect, but had stayed at the rear of the graveside gathering, and hurried away without expressing his commiserations face-to-face with Madge. When he saw her coming through the doorway, his heart gave a guilty lurch before settling into a steady gallop that carried it nowhere at all.

"Good afternoon, Marshal."

"Miss Clifton. What can I do for you?"

"I have asked myself that question. May I sit?"

"Help yourself. I mean ... please do."

Once seated, she cocked her head and looked at his face. Clay generally did not like people staring at him; he knew he was ugly, and their stares seemed intrusive and downright rude. He never revealed this, since it would have granted the starers a kind of power over him. But with Madge it was different; she was staring not at the holes in his face but into the eyes behind his spectacles, as if awaiting some kind of revelation there. Clay tolerated the stare because it gave him the opportunity to stare right back, and he found that Madge looked better than he remembered. He guessed she had lost some weight beneath her jaw; in fact she seemed to have slimmed down all over. Clay had heard that this was a fairly common sign of unhappiness and distress, and he supposed it was due to the loss of her mother, even though from Clay's perspective such a loss would have represented a tremendous relief from familial obligation; but maybe it was different with women.

"I'm leaving," Madge said at last.

"Leaving?"

"This town and this territory."

"Why?"

"Why not? Why should I stay here? Mama has left me a little money I had no idea she owned, and the house has been put up for sale. You might make an offer on it yourself. You can't possibly be comfortable upstairs here. See the agent down the street if you're interested. I'll accept a reasonable sum."

"But why not stay?"

"Because for me there is nothing here to which I am attached, Mr. Dugan, sir. I'm not a popular figure around town, not during the hours of daylight. We have no need to speak in riddles. I'm a soiled dove, as they say, and no longer young. The road from here isn't a pretty one. I intend remaking my life before it's too late, and to do that I must go away. Far away. I believe I'll try California. They say the climate in the northern half is mild. Not San Francisco, no, nothing so grand. A small town, not dissimilar to this in size, but with a touch more ... how to put it ... a touch more *savoir faire*. I don't ask for much, just the opportunity to begin again. Mama has given me that. You stare at me. Have you nothing to say?"

"I ... well, this is ... a surprise, uh, Madge."

"Life is filled with them, they say. This surely isn't your first."

"When are you leaving?"

"I've purchased a ticket on the stage line for tomorrow morning. I'm quite excited at the prospect of new horizons. A much-traveled man like yourself must know how that feels."

"I guess so."

"You guess so. Indeed. To begin again, elsewhere—that is a worthwhile dream, don't you agree?"

"I do, yes...."

"Where no one may look askance at you, because they know nothing of you, and must accept what they see."

"Yes."

"I'm not making my plans known to many, just the house agent and yourself."

"I hope things work out for you in California, Madge."

"And I hope things work out here for you." She stood and offered her hand. "Good-bye."

Clay stood and clumsily took her hand in his. She smiled at him, then turned and left. Clay collapsed slowly back into his chair, surprised at his own sense of devastation at the news. She was leaving. He was not. Her purpose in telling him had been obvious; she wished him to throw in his hand with hers, and start over. They both were misfits, suited for each other on that basis alone. Away from Dry Wash there would be no clucking tongues if they should marry, no disapproval showered on them as they walked down a public street together. She was a whore, but a decent woman regardless. He could love her, and she him. He had only to surrender his badge and buy a ticket on the stage line, as she had done. He did not even have to leave with her, so long as there was an understanding between them that he would follow along as soon as possible. He could ride away from Dry Wash on horseback if he chose, and journey to California by any route he wanted, if only he could be sure that a life with Madge was the thing he needed most in all the world. He simply had to decide. She had presented him with a choice, exerted no pressure at all, and walked out like a lady, leaving Clay with turmoil in his heart and black desperation in his head.

He walked a lot for the rest of that day, unable to sit in the office while thoughts rampaged through his mind, thoughts in favor of accepting Madge's implicit offer, and thoughts against. She was a whore, an ex-whore; who knew what diseases lurked beneath her skirts. She appeared healthy, but that was no proof she would not infect him with a slow poison for which no real cure existed. Clay recalled Captain Switchback, the pitiful syphilitic from Keyhoe, and shuddered. No, he could not risk such a fate. And yet he knew he would be able to talk with Madge Clifton and understand her, and she him, until they died. She wanted him, and knew he wanted her. It was up to Clay.

He walked and walked, and ignored all greetings directed at him on the street. Should he go directly to Madge's house and declare himself hers, or wait for darkness? Should he slip a note under her door, or simply loiter in the neighborhood like a smitten schoolboy. It was infuriating that he could not make up his mind. He was sure of nothing but the risks involved. To go with Madge, or not. He need do nothing but avoid the stage line's depot the following day in order to absent himself from Madge's future. He need not see her or talk to her. She had made it easy for him by letting him know in advance of her proposed movements. She could be his; he could be hers, in a new place where they might be together as husband and wife, if he cared to bite the bullet and fall in with her offer.

But he could not. Hour upon hour he paced the streets of Dry Wash, and could not make up his mind. As evening fell he avoided the area around Willow Street and concentrated his attention on the usual haunts a marshal was supposed to patrol. Duty first, he reminded himself, and believed not a syllable of it. He was cheating fate, walking backward, ignoring the obvious, and denying all of it. Clay drank in every saloon his routine patrolling brought him into, and as the night wore on, became drunk, too drunk to think, and he took a bottle with him when he retired to his narrow bachelor bunk to celebrate with more whiskey the lonely freedom of the celibate. He poured liquor inside himself like never before in his life, knowing while he did so that he was a coward and a fool who did not even deserve the opportunity for change that had been proffered by a woman who, although she was a whore, almost certainly was stronger and smarter than he. No man with Madge's qualities would have allowed himself to become the stinking, blubbering thing Clay Dugan was reduced to, before alcoholic oblivion swept him up in its mighty wing to plummet between the stars until well after dawn.

Clay knew, when he awoke, that the time of the stage's departure was long past. He had successfully avoided any real confrontation with the option Madge had opened for him. She was already gone,

with no hint from him regarding his intentions, no verbal commitment to hold inside her for comfort on the long road to California.
He had let her down, and could not forgive himself. It was obvious
even to such a lowly fool as himself that the opportunity, once lost,
could never be regained. He had made his choice by not choosing—
the coward's route of last resort—and in doing so had sacrificed a
portion of himself, offered up to nameless gods a piece of the man
he had been just hours before, and become less of a man for it. He
could not face himself in the mirror over his basin and jug, nor
examine his shadowy self in store windows. He was a non-man, a
slinking, furtive yellowbelly who drank shame from the air and did
not choke.

It was noticed around Dry Wash that following the departure of
Madge Clifton the marshal became morose, and his condition worsened by the day, if not the hour. He smelled of liquor, day or night,
and did not change his clothing at all. He would ignore greetings
directed at him, and walk away from anyone attempting to engage
him in conversation. Clay Dugan had become a shambling, drunken
wreck of a man, and it only confirmed what many people had begun
to suspect before Madge left town—that she and Clay had been
more than just whore and customer. Clay Dugan must have been in
love with her! It was an unlikely pairing, but the only thing that
accounted for his pathetic behavior of late. He was becoming a joke
among the community.

Judge Poudre held himself partially responsible for the situation,
since it was he who had suggested that Clay be elected as town
marshal, and he who sent him to Madge's house in the first place to
hire her for Maxwell's last night of love. The judge went to Clay's
office to confront him.

"Dugan, you're making yourself look bad. What the hell do you
mean by conducting yourself this way? What happened to you? You
look like a worn out mongrel someone ought to shoot. Do you have
anything at all to say to me, Dugan?"

"Not right now."

Judge Poudre stabbed a finger at him. "You've got just twenty-
four hours to pull yourself into shape and start acting like a law
officer ought to, or I'm calling a special town meeting to have you
fired, you hear me?"

"I hear you."

"You can begin by getting over to the bathhouse and soaking for an hour or so, and have your clothes taken care of, why don't you. One more thing—she was only a whore."

Clay wanted to launch himself across the desk and choke Judge Poudre until he coughed up an apology, but he found he couldn't move. It was partly advanced inebriation, and partly shock at having his secret heartache stepped on so brutally. Did everyone know? When the judge left, Clay took off his badge and tossed it onto the desk, but the gesture lacked drama since he was alone. He repinned the badge to his vest, and began thinking hard. He had made a fool of himself, but it was not too late to reform and present a professional front to the public again. He would do that, beginning immediately. Losing a woman was no excuse for losing a job. He would make himself clean, as the judge had ordered. It was difficult to accept that he had fallen so low, but the truth was plain; if he did not turn himself around and recover the respect of the citizens, he would lose the job they had elected him to, and become a drifter again.

Clay Dugan was seen on the streets next day with a freshly shaven face, a completely new outfit of clothes, and a rock-steady gait as he marched up one street and down another, essentially parading his remade self before the public for their approval. He tipped his hat to every female and responded heartily to all greetings cast in his direction. Even his spectacles seemed to glint and gleam with renewed civic purpose. He was once again in control of himself.

Clay was fairly sure he had passed muster with the citizens, but to convince himself he was truly over his infatuation with Madge Clifton, he strode down to the stage-line depot to walk over the ground she had last stood upon before departing. He had avoided the place until now, and a casual stroll in the area would set the seal on his overnight rehabilitation. When that task was done with, he would ride around the town on horseback, looking as imposing and businesslike as possible, just to make sure everyone understood that he was a reformed character, ready once again to take charge of the law. His horse was at that moment being saddled and made ready for him, so sure was Clay that his plans for the day would roll along on oiled wheels.

The morning stage had already pulled in as Clay approached the depot, and passengers were disembarking to slap the dust from themselves and stretch their backs while luggage was being passed down from the roof rack and the boot. Clay paused to watch the scene.

One passenger in particular caught his eye, a woman in a dark skirt and broad hat. She seemed familiar, although her back was to him, and for one delirious moment Clay imagined that Madge had returned. She seemed taller than Madge, and her hair was darker, under the gray trail dust powdering the bun beneath her hat. Clay shook his head. It wasn't Madge at all. He was being a fool all over again. Yet the woman did seem to have about her something that made him think she was known to him.

When she turned, he saw that he was right. It was Sophie Stunce, who became Sophie Dugan, his wife and the mother of their child; Sophie who had shot Clay's wonderful horse, Sunrise; Sophie who was his wife still, for all Clay knew. And she had seen him too.

They stared at each other without expression. Clay saw her through a haze that was more than mere dust; she was the past come to haunt him after all this time, and his head was filled with a strange humming as he stared. Sophie, his wife, had found him, had come hundreds of miles to see him again. She must have read about himself and Dry Wash in the newspapers, in the story of Wixson's soul-weighing device. It had been a good story, if distorted, and must have found its way even to Kansas, because here was Sophie, standing still as a tree, clutching a little tote bag at her waist.

Clay felt a curious mixture of guilt and longing overcome him. She had sought him out for reconciliation, he knew, for a resumption of their marriage now that time had healed the grievous wrong she imagined he had committed against her. Sophie had seen the light and decided that forgiveness was wiser than hatred, and had come to deliver that message to her husband. Clay felt light-headed, almost faint, and he made himself take a hesitant step or two toward his wife, a smile struggling to shape itself on his face.

Sophie moved toward him, and her hands began to loosen the drawstring around her bag. Clay stopped. Sophie drew a pistol from the bag and lifted it to aim at his heart. Clay made himself jump sideways, his body made sluggish by the unreality of what was happening. The first shot whined past his ear, and the second passed through the armpit of his new jacket. By then his hazy, dreamlike state of mind had become sharpened by the need for flight. He had no gun, and could not have brought himself to use one in his own defense anyway, not against his wife, even if she was determined to kill him. A crazy woman, he told himself, and ducked from the path of a third bullet by flinging himself into an alley beside the depot. His legs found strength and began propelling him to the safety of the next street, where the livery stable was. The instruction to have his horse saddled up had been given less than ten minutes before; would the boy have had time to carry it out?

Another shot passed him as Clay flung himself around the corner, out of the alley, and began sprinting along the sidewalk toward the livery stable, his feet hurting in their new high-heeled boots. And there was his horse, tethered to the hitching rail outside the livery's big double doors. He knew, as he mounted, that any man who ran from his wife in full view of the public was finished, a laughingstock, even if the wife was armed and angry.

Clay dug in his heels and rode hard for the office, where he paused only as long as it took to snatch up his sawed-off and a few dollars in cash, then he ran down the side stairs three at a time and mounted again. Clay rode through an alley to another street, then kicked his horse into a gallop. He was clear of Dry Wash minutes later.

32

The sensation of feeling the world drop away beneath him always brought a smile to Slade's face. As his stomach pressed up against his lungs the smile broadened. No one ever saw the smile, since the elevator cage's descent was undertaken in complete darkness. Vertical distance from the top of the shaft to its bottom was seventeen hundred feet. Slade was packed into the cage shoulder-to-shoulder with a dozen or so miners, the gate was slammed; the abrupt descent began, and that was when Slade always smiled. He wondered why he felt the need to do so, and decided it was the sense of dizziness inside his head as he and his coworkers plummeted down the shaft. He had heard drinkers describe a similar sensation that overtook them gradually as they drank, but Slade felt no need for alcohol. If the pleasantness could be given to his head for nothing once each day, that was preferable to spending cash on whiskey and sharing the company of drunken men he preferred not to know. Standing among them during the cage's controlled falling was bad enough, but the dizziness made that bearable.

The descent was filled with noise as guide wheels at each corner of the cage spun and hummed along rails holding it away from the shaft's rock walls. As each of the mine's working levels was passed, a wan golden light burst briefly upon the descending cage, and was gone again. The temperature began to rise. Newcomers to the mine were told the shaft was so deep it encroached upon the cavernous and brimstone-filled regions of hell. At the surface, snow was falling, but in the shaft each man felt himself begin to sweat as the cage rumbled and rattled deeper still. The air itself began to change, becoming thicker, laced with a sickly humidity ripe with the smell of oil and nitroglycerin fumes, and the more pungent odor of mule and human excrement. It was a sinking from brightness to darkness, from a world of sun to a stygian hole pricked by carbide lamps and candlelight

The cage neared the bottom of the shaft and began to slow through a series of jerkings, eventually coming to a halt at the lowest level. The gate was opened and the cage emptied quickly, each man knowing his task and the place appointed for it. The tunnel they walked through begat a maze of similar tunnels branching in all directions. The Grand Mogul mine was one of the most complex in Glory Hole, and currently extended eleven miles along forty-seven individual tunnels on seven different levels. Narrow-gauge ore-cart rails ran through the tunnels, and alongside these ran the compressed-air hoses that powered each tunnel face's mechanical drill.

Slade worked with Shoupe and McCaulay, these being the only two men capable of enduring the silences Slade was known to maintain for days at a time. He had been thought mute by some until he spoke, and his unwillingness to hold even the simplest conversation with anyone made him an unpopular figure. Shoupe and McCaulay were nontalkers also, and it was arranged by the pit boss that the three of them should become a team. The arrangement had withstood their mutual silences for almost a month now, and their output equaled that of any four-man team.

The foul-smelling pipeway through rock these three tramped, pushing an empty ore cart before them, was recorded on the mining director's chart seventeen hundred feet above them as Southwest Seven Nine, indicating its direction, tunnel number and level. It was currently one hundred twenty-nine feet long, but the blasting set off at the end of the preceding shift should have lengthened it by another three or four feet. The first task of Slade, Shoupe and McCaulay was to clear away the rubble of ore the blast had left behind.

They began without consultation, each man an expert at the lifting of jagged chunks big as their chest, heavy as a small man, and they quickly loaded most of it into the cart. While Shoupe went to fetch a mule, McCaulay and Slade began setting up the thick metal column that would support the mechanical drill for its next assault on the new rock face exposed at the tunnel's end. The column was jacked and wedged between floor and ceiling, then kicked several times to ensure that it was solid. The universal joint was coupled to it midway, and the two-hundred-twenty-pound drill lifted by both men to fit into its receiving slot. By the time Shoupe returned with a mule, the air hoses had been coupled and tightened. The mule, blinded by a lifetime spent in darkness, was hitched to the ore cart. The last chunks of ore were stacked on top of the load, and the mule was led away, straining against its harness.

Every shift began in this fashion, with a clearing away of the preceding shift's displaced rock. Blasting was always carried out at the end of a shift, since the dust and explosive vapors made air in the vicinity unfit to breathe for some time afterward. For the miners, though, their true work began when the task of hauling away the rubble had been completed; that was when they could begin preparing the rock face for their own blast; that was when the drill's control valves were opened and it came alive.

Slade's delight was to manipulate the machine they called the widow-maker. Its power and noise and the startling ease with which it rammed holes through solid rock had impressed him the moment he first saw one in operation. He loved the powerful vibrations it sent through his body when the piston and drill bit began their crazed hammering. All three men had their ears plugged with cotton against the deafening sound as its jarring, Gatling-gun delivery of power drove the drill into rock like a toothpick into cheese, its staccato hammering like some colossal woodpecker of the netherworld. Slade felt his body thrumming in a kind of ecstasy. The drill was a part of him, linked by an umbilical of air hoses to the distant steam-driven compressor. He was the machine's guiding eye, its brain, the thing that determined where it should enter virgin rock, at what angle and to what depth, and Slade became even more a part of the drill as he was forced to close his eyes against the fine particles spitting from the hole he bored. Blinded by his own device, he leaned against the trembling heart of it, felt its concussions set his teeth clicking, and willed the turning bit to bite deeper still, penetrating an endless, depthless wall set in place at the beginning of time.

Shoupe and McCaulay were content to allow Slade exclusive use of the widow-maker. McCaulay had once attempted, out of a sense of fair-mindedness, to relieve Slade from the task of guiding it, and had been pushed away. The lesson was not lost on Shoupe; Slade had some kind of perverse need to feel the drill's awesome hammering run through his body, and since his partners were not similarly addicted to vibration, Slade commandeered the machine for the duration of its usage each shift, without complaint and without competition. Like the silence each man practiced, the arrangement was part of what allowed them to operate together as a team. Shoupe and McCaulay were sufficiently cognizant of the Grand Mogul's operation as a whole to understand that the three of them were in a sense unique; Slade reserved that sense for himself alone. If he served on the only three-man team beneath Glory Hole, it was because he did not like to be crowded, and the exclusive trio was made possible solely in order to please him, in acknowledgment of his superiority.

The rock face required on average five to seven holes to accommodate dynamite. Slade drilled them all, stopping only to change the drill steels, as each one in turn wore out its cutting tip. The dulled steels were taken away for reforging, a new one was inserted into the drill, and the process resumed. When the final hole was completed, the widow maker was uncoupled from its supporting column and transported back along the tunnel, out of harm's way, and the supporting column followed it. By then, enough time had passed for the men to sit and eat the lunch each had brought with him in a tin pail.

Slade ate at a distance from his partners, who sometimes profaned the silence with a word or two expressing approval of the food their wives had packed for them. Slade preferred nothing more intrusive than the distant sounds from other tunnels where men performed identical tasks. The echoing of faraway drills seemed almost to relax him as he ate. Having no wife, he ate a meal prepared for fifty-cents by a woman whose husband had perished in the mines; she made sandwiches for scores of bachelor miners, and eked out a living not much reduced from the time her husband had brought home a wage. Slade always found his fifty cent sandwich enjoyable. It was generally roast beef, thickly built and well worth the money. He had eaten roast beef sandwiches every day on another job, work he had done somewhere else, aboveground work among trees, but he could not remember the details of it. Certainly there had been no thunderous machines involved, so he doubted that he had liked it as much as mining. He could not quite recall how he had become a miner, but that was not a matter of any importance, since it was the-day to-day operation of the drill that mattered, not the route whereby Slade had found his calling.

While he ate, he thought of something overheard as he passed a knot of children the previous evening, miners' brats playing in the snow; they had spoken of giants beneath the earth, slumbering titans on beds of stone, their dreamless sleep centuries old, and they had spoken of the shattering of that sleep by intruding hard-rock miners, and the consequences thereof. Slade pondered his options if he should drill through into the chamber of a giant. If the creature attacked him, he would aim his widow-maker at its heart, impale it as a harpooner kills his whale. It would be a fine thing to kill a giant. Slade had never killed anyone that he could remember, but a giant would be a fine thing to kill. If he could not kill it, the giant would have proved itself superior to Slade, and it would not be shameful to die at the hands of so great a being. He would be content if he killed the giant, or the giant killed him. It made no real difference either way. Slade hardly thought of death at all, even if dying suddenly was commonplace in the mines. No pocket of explosive gas would kill him, no weakened timber supports come down on his head, no thousands of tons of rock collapse and crush him. It would take a giant, and Slade was glad to have overheard the children talking; now he knew what kind of death might possibly await him in the Grand Mogul.

When he had finished eating, Slade went a short distance back along the tunnel to relieve his bowels. All the tunnels stank of shit, but he was not offended by it anymore. The smell of the mine was simply a price he had to pay for the privilege of working there and sinking the long steel tooth of the widow-maker deep into rock that might give way at any moment to reveal the sleeping giants. Being a hard-rock miner was the best life there could be, and Slade was living it. The occasional headaches that came to plague him were nothing to do with the mine; he remembered that the pain between his temples had always been a part of him, long before he came to Glory Hole from whichever place he had been before. It was not good, though, when he woke up some mornings and could not remember who he was, or where, or even that he was a miner. He would have to lie very still and concentrate for a while, and it would all come back to him before breakfast, which he ate in the food shack run by the woman who sold him his lunch every day. She was a nice woman and always gave him a big sandwich. He sometimes could see why men married women, but Slade didn't want to, not when he could get the sandwiches and breakfasts whenever he wanted, for a very reasonable cost. He was married to the widow-maker, even if it spat rock dust at him and shook his bones to pieces and was slowly deafening him. His life was complete as it was. He wouldn't want to change anything, except maybe the headaches and the forgetting.

Slade attended to his anus with the greasy paper his lunch had been wrapped in, and returned to the face, where his partners had already resumed work. Shoupe was a master at inserting and tamping red paperbound sticks of dynamite into the holes Slade had drilled, each stick with a fulminate-of-mercury blasting cap inserted into the end. It was painstaking work, and he would not be rushed. Shoupe checked every stick before insertion, unwrapping a section of each to be sure the nitroglycerin had not separated out from the inert stabilizing compound and begun to lace the outside of the stick with dangerously sensitive crystals, as sometimes happened in winter. He worked slowly and methodically, and when he was satisfied, he stepped aside for the wick man.

McCaulay's talent lay in being able to estimate exactly how long the black powder fuses he attached to the blasting caps needed to be. He arranged them in a precise pattern and twined their ends together to ensure that they not only would be lit simultaneously but would detonate at precisely the same instant. He, too, would not be hurried through his specialty, and Slade found his attention drifting. Shoupe had carried away the last of the dulled steels for transportation back to the surface for blacksmithing, and had not returned, in all likelihood had stopped somewhere en route to relieve himself.

Watching McCaulay as he worked with lengths of fuse, Slade experienced one of his very rare moments of insight into the existence of other humans. He usually looked on his fellow men with the same lack of empathy with which he might have viewed a herd of cattle; he accepted that they existed, but did not believe they resembled him, at least not in anything but physical form. McCaulay, Slade saw with a sudden burst of acumen, was a man;

he ate and slept and performed his work in much the same fashion as Slade, and very likely had thoughts about the world, as did Slade. McCaulay might even have secret difficulties, like Slade. But that was too much to accept. If McCaulay had troubles, they could not have been like Slade's. It almost scared Slade to think of another man, mere yards away, who might be anything like himself, deep down inside, where he knew the real man lived. No one, Slade reasoned, could be the same as himself in the deep inside part, because if it were so, then Slade would not be who he had always thought himself to be. If there was someone else like him in the world, Slade would be made smaller because of that man.

It was not something Slade could accept as being likely or desirable. In his own subversive way, McCaulay was a threat. Slade had not been aware of it until then, and his discovery placed McCaulay in a new light. He would have to be watched carefully, or else he might attempt somehow to remove Slade from existence and take his place without anyone knowing the difference. Now Slade was worried. He could not recall ever having had such thoughts before, so they must be important. He reviewed quickly the points of his revelation, and reached the same conclusion, but this time was more certain he was correct, even if the thing he had realized was terrible to contemplate: McCaulay was planning to *replace* him while they were alone. With Shoupe away, it could be done, and when Shoupe returned he would find just one man there at the rock face, and he would be told that Slade was gone, just plain gone from the mine without explanation, and Shoupe would accept what McCaulay told him, because they were friends.

The full extent of McCaulay's deviousness was fast becoming apparent. Slade was outraged that someone should even think of doing such a thing, let alone be planning it in detail, as McCaulay clearly was. The man's back was kept turned to Slade to shield his guilt. McCaulay knew that if he allowed Slade a good long look into his eyes, the plan would fail, so he was pretending to concentrate on his fuses with more than his usual intensity. Shoupe was still gone. Slade could not recall now just how long a time it had been since Shoupe shouldered the steels and walked away into the darkness. Was there some kind of collusion between the two? It was possible. They had talked in low tones while eating their lunches, the words they exchanged garbled by the echo that persisted in so restricted an area as a mine face. Sometimes it was possible to hear things at a distance more clearly than a conversation taking place just around a bend in the tunnel. They had known that, and not objected when Slade went away on his own to eat. He should have sneaked back and listened to them, but he hadn't known at the time what they were planning for him.

Suddenly he hated them both. He would allow no one to replace him, least of all two fools like Shoupe and McCaulay. They had underestimated Slade if they thought replacing him would be easy. He was ready for them now, and could not be taken by surprise. Slade could not remember how long he had worked alongside the two traitors, but it was long enough for him to feel angry that they had turned against him this way. It was betrayal of the lowest order, and it would not succeed.

A detonation from another mine face distracted him. It was followed quickly by another. The shift was ending, the teams finally done with preparation, lighting their fuses and retiring with the cry "Fire in the hole!" Slade hadn't heard the familiar warning before either blast. Could that be linked somehow with the plot to replace him? Could all the miners in the Grand Mogul be part of the plan? Another detonation shook the rock wall he leaned against. "Pretty near done," McCaulay said over his shoulder. Slade didn't believe him. There was something going on he was not supposed to be aware of, but he was. With sudden insight, he realized he did not know the meaning of the name Grand Mogul. Could it mean some kind of big plan? Had they been preparing it for him even before he came to Glory Hole and began working under the earth? Slade saw no reason to doubt it. They had seen him coming, and made arrangements, and those arrangements were about to be implemented. The explosions in other tunnels were intended to make him believe the usual routine was being followed, but Slade was too smart to be fooled by any of it. He should have known that sooner or later he would be hunted like this. They would not be content to kill him, not someone like himself; they wanted to replace him with McCaulay, so they could all feel comfortable again. They had probably been causing the headaches too, and the moments of forgetfulness ... and he saw that even the nice woman who made his sandwiches was part of the plan, because it was she who fed him, and the food had been poisoned with bad things to make him hurt, make him forget, but not strong enough to kill him, so now they were preparing something else, something more powerful to bring about his death ... no, something worse than that: they wanted him gone completely, swallowed up into the body of McCaulay like a fly inside a toad. Well, he wouldn't let it happen. He knew he was able to withstand anything they cared to throw at him, be it poisoned sandwiches or this planned aloneness with McCaulay. He was ready and, in a strange way, glad to have learned of the plan to wipe him from existence. It was exciting to know that he was under siege by inferior men. He would show them, and show them good.

The rock beneath Slade's shoulder quivered as another blast, in one of the nearer tunnels, sent shook waves through the ground. The miners responsible would be gathered at the cage, readying themselves for the long ride to the upper world, where the sun was gone beyond the western slope of the valley filled by Glory Hole, and the snow continued to fall. They did not want him to see any of that again, but they would fail, because they understood nothing. Now there was more vibration feeding itself into him, not from any dynamite explosion but from the rock itself, and Slade knew the next part of the plan had been made to occur. He did not know what shape it would assume, but he was ready.

The tunnel itself began to speak, a throat choked of air, made hoarse by sudden constriction, the words reduced to crackings and splinterings and a rumbling from the heart of the mine that set the hairs on Slade's head quivering. The tunnel was collapsing, pushing air and sound toward him. He caught the briefest glimpse of light from Shoupe's returning lamp before the ceiling descended in chunks the size of wagons and crushed it. Shoupe's scream, lasting only a second, could barely be heard above the groaning of timbers and thudding of displaced rock. A cloud of stinking dust was blasted into Slade's eyes. He stepped backward to the rock face and stumbled over McCaulay. Both men were on the ground when the final descent of rock from the tunnel ceiling fell just yards away, and the noise began to subside.

Slade couldn't breathe; the air was filled with dust, McCaulay's lamp a blur even at arm's length, and the sounds of coughing that came from beneath it were muffled, as if heard from the far side of a wall. Slade's own lungs burned with the particles he had inhaled, and his eyelids squeezed shut again. He covered his face with both hands and attempted to breathe slowly through his nose, but could not get enough air into himself; he was obliged to gasp and suck through his opened mouth, which produced a fit of coughing to equal McCaulay's.

The men huddled where they had fallen, pressed against the rock face Slade had drilled for Shoupe to load with dynamite and McCaulay to prime. There were more distant rumblings, then silence. They continued to cough until the dust began to settle.

"Was that Shoupe I heard?" McCaulay asked.

Slade nodded, tasting the airborne grime that filled his mouth and coated his teeth.

"Jesus God a'mighty, we're dead men sure.... Oh Jesus God a'mighty we are ... "

Slade found McCaulay's words insincere. The cave-in was staged in order to confine the two men in a closed-off space, to let McCaulay replace Slade by whatever method had been agreed upon. Slade would have to be on guard for the least indication that violence was about to be used against him. The cave-in had been impressively staged, but he was not fooled.

"Too many fires in the hole ..., " sobbed McCaulay. "It shouldn't all be set off around the same time like they tell us to.... Now we're in here till they find us.... "

Slade had never heard so many words spill from McCaulay at one time. McCaulay was pretending to be frightened, but again, Slade could see through the ruse. He didn't believe that Shoupe was dead either; it was another piece of deception. He wondered how long it would be before McCaulay began the process of replacing him. Slade's one fear was that he would fall asleep and allow it to happen then. He would have to remain awake whenever McCaulay was, and sleep when he slept. There was the danger that McCaulay would waken first, but every sound within the irregular cell they occupied was magnified; McCaulay would have to be silent as a cat to make any move toward a sleeping man without waking him, and Slade had always had the ability to come awake instantly. He would prepare for that possibility by napping with his clasp knife opened and ready, but hidden from sight.

"Too many fellers doin' it at the same time," McCaulay repeated. "They should do it different, space 'em out more. By God, think if I hadda lit ours and then we never had time to get out. Shoupe, his missus had a baby.... They won't ever see him again in this life. You seen him get buried under it all?"

Slade nodded. McCaulay's make-believe sorrow was interesting to watch. Slade could hardly credit his luck at having realized what was being plotted just minutes before the performance began. Without his foreknowledge of the plan, it might well have succeeded, but it never would now. He despised McCaulay for his part in it, and for the shallow insincerity of his tears. McCaulay's face was hidden by his hands. Slade wished he hadn't already eaten his sandwich; he was hungry again. Then he remembered that the woman who made it for him was also trying to replace him with McCaulay. There might even have been something in the roast beef to make him think the cave-in had occurred, when in fact it hadn't. Slade had heard of drunkards seeing things that weren't actually there, and for all he knew, it was possible to put the same stuff contained in drink into a sandwich. He leaned over and touched a massive chunk of fallen rock. It felt very real, but there existed the possibility that it was not. Slade would have to act as if he thought it was, just to fool McCaulay.

"They'll be diggin', start right to it directly, they will. Shoupe, though, poor feller. There's likely others. Might not just be ours that fell. Might be tunnels aplenty need diggin' out, you think?"

Slade shrugged. He was inside only one tunnel, so it would have made no sense for the plotters to cause others to fall. McCaulay was trying to sound like a worried man, that was all, and doing a poor job of it.

"What you got to be smilin' at, hey?"

Slade frowned. He didn't like to be spoken to in that tone of voice, even if the rudeness was just a sham. He said nothing, did nothing, waiting to see if McCaulay might apologize, but the man turned away and began extracting his carefully laid fuses from the blasting caps beside them.

"Wouldn't do to have these here go up in our faces now, would it, with the fellers diggin' for us. Don't want 'em to find us all of a mess now, do we, hey? Hey?"

Slade shook his head. The last of the caps was defused, then McCaulay began the task of easing each cap from the dynamite sticks, in case it should detonate through an accidental bump or further shifting of the rock. When all had been disarmed, he lay back and took several deep breaths, the skin of his face running with sweat.

"Best be turnin' off our lights, I'm thinkin', save 'em for later. No tellin' how long a job it'll be, the diggin'."

Both carbide lamps were turned off, and the darkness became
absolute. Slade felt that without light, the thing called darkness
extended beyond the confines of the tunnel's end; it reached as far
as Slade cared to extend it, further even than the natural darkness
of night that must by now have fallen far above them in the world.
The darkness that had swept across his eyeballs when the lamps
were shut down was of a velvety richness, a darkness without
depth. It seemed to Slade's suddenly blinded eyes like water into
which ink had been poured, or air so choked with chimney soot it
became something else, some other, impenetrable substance that
probably could be found nowhere but down where he saw it, an
underground dark of blackness beyond all known shades.

"Be able to hear 'em comin', most likely. Hear 'em diggin' even
when they're far off still. Then we'll know. Could be a day or two,
even so. Too bad for us we et our lunch already. Be starvin' hungry
by the time they fetches us out, the both of us. Got anythin' left in
your water flask? Near empty, mine. Can hear drippin', though.
Always some water in a mine. Hear it, just a little ways off? That'll
see us through all right. Ought to put our flasks under it to catch
what's there. Waste not, see? I'll do that now, I will."

The shocking brilliance when McCaulay turned on his lamp
again caused Slade to turn his head away. When the light passing
through his eyelids had lessened, he opened them, and saw
McCaulay scrambling over the nearest chunks in search of the dripping he had heard. Slade made no move to assist him; if McCaulay
wanted to play at acting concerned, Slade would let him. With
McCaulay out of sight, Slade drank the last from his metal water
flask and restoppered it. He would have drunk what was left in
McCaulay's but he had taken it with him. It would have been interesting to see the look on McCaulay's face when he came back to find
his flask empty. The thought of that made Slade smile. It would
irritate McCaulay if a lot of pranks like that were played on him.
Instead of Slade becoming more and more fearful of the danger they
were in, which would make him easier to replace when the time
came, he would do just the opposite, and cause McCaulay every
kind of upset he could think of. It would pass the time, and keep
him alive.

"Found it! Just a trickle, but it'll do for us. Pass your flask over."

Slade moved cautiously toward the light of McCaulay's lamp, suspecting a trick, but McCaulay lay on his back beneath an overhang

of rock created by the cave-in, completely vulnerable to attack. His arms were stretched into darkness, despite his lamp. "It's back here, hell of a squeeze.... Flask's under the drip now. We'll fill yours when this'n gets full."

Slade handed his flask over, then resumed his position by the rock wall. McCaulay followed, and both turned off their lamps. "Take a couple hours maybe, to fill all the way up. We can wait, I reckon." McCaulay laughed briefly.

Soon McCaulay slept. Slade waited for the sound of his slowed breathing before allowing himself to relax. The air was hot enough to permit his removing his shirt to make a cushion. Slade folded this and tucked it beneath himself, then placed both forearms across his knees and bowed his forehead to rest on them. He was calm, although he had been unable to figure out how the replacement of himself by McCaulay was supposed to occur. It could not be anything too difficult, because McCaulay was not a smart man. Maybe it was Shoupe who had been elected as replacement, but the tunnel had collapsed a minute too soon. No, it was McCaulay, because it had been while he watched the man working with his fuses that Slade first became aware of the plan to replace him. It was the actual business of replacement he could not understand, in fact he had already forgotten how it was that he realized in the first place that replacement, not simple murder, was the object. He had been positive about it at the time, though, so he would not change his mind now on account of a little haziness. Replacement, that was their game. What had they planned to do with his body? Was it to be swallowed somehow by the mine? There were plenty of played-out tunnels and corridors where no one went except to shit. They might place him far along one of those, then seal it up. No one would notice the stink of a rotting man along with all the other bad stenches down there. He would make McCaulay tell him all the details before he died. McCaulay would have to die so Slade could survive. There was no doubt in his mind about that. Slade considered doing it while McCaulay slept. It would have been easy, even in total darkness, thanks to McCaulay's plugged sinuses; the man gave himself away with every whistling intake of breath.

Slade considered sleep, but decided against it. He could hear no sound from outside the collapsed tunnel, no thump of pick against rock, no hammering of drills reaching for the trapped men, and the absence of these sounds told him there would be no rescue until

McCaulay somehow informed those on the outside that Slade had successfully been replaced. It was irritating to understand so very little of what was afoot, but Slade reasoned that time would reveal everything. Others had tried to fool him before, and had paid the price. He could recall neither the men nor the circumstances, but was sure he had survived whatever it had been that they arranged to bring him to his knees, or he would not have been alive still; he would have been replaced long before. He had bested them then, and he would do so again. It would be smart to sleep while McCaulay did, he thought, or he would fall asleep later, when McCaulay was awake. McCaulay was no match for him in any case, but it would be prudent to match his periods of wakefulness with those of his partner. Having decided that sleep was wise, Slade released himself into a deeper darkness.

He knew it was a dream when he felt himself rising through the ground. Afraid at first, he held his panic in check, then found he enjoyed the slight rasping sensation as he passed through solid rock during his ascent. The dream body was moving slowly, steadily upward. Slade had never experienced a dream like it before, or at least had no memory of anything so strange. He seemed to rise forever, but eventually his head passed into open air, and his shoulders and torso followed, although they seemed to stretch themselves like a wad of molasses to do so. A moment later he was free of the earth, drifting upward still. Falling snowflakes passed him by, but he felt no chill against his naked skin. He continued to rise, and on looking down to see if maybe he had left some kind of hole in the ground behind, saw that he was some distance above a town. Like a bird, he thought. The novelty of flight pleased him greatly, and Slade found that he could cause himself to move left or right simply by desiring to do so. He made himself stop in midair, not wishing to rise too high above the town, which he now recognized as Glory Hole. It looked much different from above, but the various chimney stacks aligned his sense of direction, and he drifted slowly to a position above the Grand Mogul.

There was a great deal of commotion beneath him, a chaotic assemblage of horses and men and vehicles of one kind or another, all illuminated by torches that danced like blazing flowers below. Then he remembered the cave-in. He had escaped somehow, but McCaulay was still down there, buried deep in the ground. How had it happened? Slade felt sad for McCaulay, even if he knew the man intended replacing him before too long. If McCaulay could come up into the air and float like a bird on the wind as Slade was doing, he might abandon his plan, because the feeling of being high above the earth produced in Slade a sensation of exquisite pleasure. He had never felt so serene, so content. It no longer seemed like a dream, although he knew it could be nothing else. It would be a shame when the dream ended, he thought, and he had to waken.

Something was near, some unknown thing. Slade felt its presence, and turned to confront it. The thing was formed like a young girl, but he believed it was a false form; the true nature of the thing was in its face, which was half covered by an ugly shadow. The thing was staring at him with much concentration, coming closer to examine his face, and as it moved through the air, the hem of its nightdress stretched out behind it like a swatch of fine muslin, and Slade knew himself to be in the presence of a ghost. If the shadow-faced girl was a ghost, and she flew in the air as Slade did, could it be that he, too, was a spirit, like her? Had McCaulay gone ahead and murdered him while he slept? Had he truly allowed that to happen?

He had to know, and no sooner was the wish to see his real body expressed than he found himself hurtling toward the ground, passing through it with a mild tearing sensation along his sides, then he could see the tiny space beneath the ground where he squatted with head and arms on knees, with McCaulay sleeping still beside him. Slade rushed into himself, a feeling akin to inserting his body sideways through a crack between window and windowsill, and he burst out again from the body he had reinhabited, taking the body with him as he rose in utter darkness to step forward and strike his boots against rock.

The sound of it, and the reawakened awareness of confinement it brought, drove Slade to a state of rage. He punched at the black winding shroud around himself, skinned his knuckles against rock and howled. To his right, McCaulay rose up in confusion to add his own voice, a querulous, fearful shouting that brought Slade's fists and boots down on him before he was fully upright, and feeling them, McCaulay began to scream, unsure if the thing attacking him was Slade, or some demon of the darkness that had also given Slade cause to bellow and howl. McCaulay dropped to the tunnel floor and began casting about frantically for his lamp, but his confusion sent him in the wrong direction, and the whimpering that came from him gave Slade a target he could not miss despite their mutual blindness. He kicked and pounded the body crouched at his feet, infuriated by the sounds it made, unmanly sounds that Slade associated with beaten dogs, and so he beat the creature groveling in pain and bewilderment beneath him, until it absorbed the blows without any further protest.

Exhausted, Slade collapsed beside McCaulay, blood thudding like a drumbeat through his head. He held the skinned hand that had begun the rampage, cradled it and moaned in sympathy for its hurt. McCaulay was responsible for the fix both men were in, Slade knew that much, but he could not remember why. McCaulay had done something with the dynamite to cause the cave-in, and he had no right to be shouting and getting under Slade's feet like that, sounding like a fool dog. Slade would have kicked him some more if he had the strength, just to teach him a lesson about tangling with a man like himself. The pain in his hand was losing its excruciating edge, becoming a dull throb that could fuel only a sense of misery. Slade felt as sorry for himself as he felt angry with McCaulay. Something had happened in his sleep, something very strange and important, but he could not recall even a tiny part of it. That, too, was McCaulay's fault; the man's whining had woken Slade from a dream beyond dreams, and ruined it. Slade was sure he had never dreamed before in his life, although he had heard other men talk of dreams, and now that he had at last experienced one, it had been cut short by the fool lying close by in the dark.

Now he wanted light. He must have light, or he would become fearful of the dark. Where was his lamp? Slade crawled about on hands and knees until the familiar contours of his lamp were felt beneath his bloodied hand. He hugged it to his breast like a lost friend, then pulled matches from his pocket and struck one alight. The flaring before his unprotected eyes was like the sun, and the match burned itself out against his fingertips before Slade could open his eyes again. He struck a second match, keeping his head turned away, and lit the lamp. When he was able to see by its beam, he looked at his hand. It did not look as bad as it felt, and Slade's spirits rose a little. McCaulay was groaning, partially conscious, and the sound was an interruption, another insult from the weakling who had caused everything to go wrong. Slade suspected there were others involved, but could not bring their names, or the precise nature of their wrongdoing, to mind. He had slept too deeply, he suspected, and some of the thoughts inside his head had trickled out like liquid from an overturned bottle, and dribbled away into the dark. The things he had thought before falling asleep were hiding now behind the massive boulders choking the tunnel. Slade imagined that displaced thoughts such as those that had escaped him were supple things, rather like worms or centipedes, which accounted for their ability to wriggle out through his ears while he slept, and scuttle away. They would be heading for the tunnel's far end, where it joined the main tunnel, which led to the lifting cages. The thoughts would want to rise up and be warmed by sunshine, if it was daylight again, and not stay behind under the ground with Slade. He wondered how many of his thoughts had been lost to him that way over the years.

McCaulay groaned again, and his left hand stirred. This caused Slade to become angry again, but in a more controlled manner than before; it was the presence of light that enabled him to do what he did next without losing his temper. Slade searched among the lesser rocks that had descended from the tunnel roof along with the massive chunks that held him prisoner, and found one to his liking. He took this to McCaulay and applied it with considerable force to the side of his head. McCaulay shuddered several times as the rock was raised and smashed down again. Eventually he was still. Now there would be no more interruptions while Slade thought.

The lamp was turned off as a precaution against waste. He could not judge how long it might take for the tunnel to be cleared. He would have plenty of time to jam McCaulay's head under a rock, to make it appear he had been a victim of the cave-in. That did not concern him for the present. The darkness was welcome after so much light, so much chaos. If Slade had been cut off by himself in the first place, McCaulay would not have paid the price for his interruption and panic. Slade felt it necessary to absolve himself again of any wrongdoing. He wished to concentrate on the darkness and, if possible, go back to sleep and reinsert himself into the dream that McCaulay had ruined.

To facilitate his return, Slade arranged himself as before, and waited for sleep to come, but his apprehension over whether the dream would be waiting for him prevented any rest. He squirmed about to make himself more comfortable, but that increased his awareness of himself. Slade wanted himself to go away and leave the other Slade there, the one that could enter dreams, but his physical body would not allow it. He was very hungry. His empty stomach would prevent him from achieving sleep. The dream was held at bay for want of food. Slade used his lamp again to locate McCaulay's lunch pail, and found it empty of everything but the tantalizing odor of roast beef. Slade thought he should be suspicious of roast beef, but could not remember why. Today his memory was worse than usual. He knew he had forgotten several important things since beginning the shift. Maybe the forgotten things were waiting for him inside the dream. Believing this might be so made him more vexed than before over his body's resistance to sleep. If he filled his belly with water it might allow him to forget the hunger gnawing at him, and allow the dream's return. McCaulay had shown him where the flask was placed to catch water dripping from the wall, but Slade was not sure now where that was, even though it could only have been within several yards of him. He would have to locate it by sound. The droplets had produced a hollow echo as they entered the flask and splashed inside; he clearly remembered it, but now that he was listening for that same sound, it was not there. Had the dripping stopped? If it had, he was in trouble; a man could last a lot longer without food than he could without water.

Slade began to search for the seep, yanking McCaulay's body clear of the fallen rocks. It had been deeper inside the tunnel, he was sure, and low to the ground. He wormed his way among the jumbled blockage, pausing often to listen for the telltale dripping. He found he could smell the water, but he could not hear it, and the frustrating closeness of it caused his thirst to escalate. Now the water was paramount in his thoughts, the one thing he must have, and his inability to find it in so small an area made him angry all over again. Then he heard it, the faintest of drippings. The sound came from behind a rock he had examined several times, and he felt a fool for not having discovered the source earlier. With far greater difficulty than McCaulay, who had been a skinny man, Slade wormed his way beneath and around the rock. There stood the flask, filled to its narrow neck with water. The distance from the top of the flask to the tiny rock ledge from which the drips descended was less than an inch, too brief a descent to create anything but the least sounds of impact. The flask was overflowing down its sides, and had already formed a small puddle around its base. Slade's own flask stood nearby, waiting to be placed beneath the niggardly spigot.

He grabbed the full flask and drank greedily, lying on his side. The water entered his chest and coursed down through Slade like cool quicksilver. He had never drunk anything so fine as the hard mineral-tasting water exuded by the broken walls of his prison. He drank until the flask was half empty, then placed his own beneath the dripping rock. The droplets fell inside and landed with a hearty splash, the sweetest sound he had ever heard. Slade wormed his way back to the tunnel face and set the first flask down nearby before turning out his lamp. His gulpings had produced a stomachache, and he doubted that he would be able to sleep again for a little while.

Waiting, he felt a strange contentment, and attempted to find the reason for it. He could only conclude that it was pleasant to be alone, even in such dangerous circumstances. The body of his partner counted for nothing. He would arrange McCaulay's crushed head under a rock the next time he went for water. Sooner or later men would break through the rocky barrier separating him from them, and they would ask how McCaulay died. Slade listened for the sounds of digging; there were none. He slept.

The sounds were there when he awoke, a distant rattle of drills. It seemed somehow to have nothing to do with Slade. He felt disappointment, but could not think why, until he remembered having gone to sleep in hope of finding a dream. The dream had not come, or he had forgotten about it. Slade thought the day might come when he woke up to find he could not remember his own name. When that happened he would be lost to himself forever. The notion made him sad. He began to cry, an event so unusual, within Slade's limited recollection of his own actions, he was shocked. What was happening to him? It seemed the cave-in had brought about some kind of collapse within Slade. He could not understand himself any longer, could not recall why he had killed McCaulay, wanted only to sleep again, sleep for a long time, like a hibernating bear, and when the long sleep was done, he could emerge into sunlight and begin a new life.

Thirsty again, he drank the last of the water from the flask, turned on his lamp and crawled past McCaulay to replace it with the other, now brimming, then crawled back. He drank again, and turned the lamp off. Darkness, being infinite, was preferable to light that did nothing but reveal the tininess of his world. Darkness was a comfort, a blanket of night. Seated with his back against unyielding rock, Slade felt himself become smaller as the darkness became larger, until he was no more than a speck surrounded by blackness beyond knowing, beyond comprehension. He was a drifting mote, nameless and alone, and he was content to be so. It was a dream, he decided, a dream of darkness, maybe the very dream he had longed for. He knew he should expect some kind of surprise within the dream, some startling thing such as he had encountered the last time, but the nature of it was open to question, since all clear recollection of it was gone. Maybe a new thing would reveal itself this time. He would not know the difference anyway. Drifting through a void was a pleasant enough experience to bring him happiness, but he did hope he would not wake up and be returned to himself before his purpose in the void was revealed.

The time that passed was not time that could be measured by clocks. Time in the darkness was fluid, moving along with Slade as he drifted, although he could not be sure anymore that he did drift, since there was nothing against which to compare his position. He was unsure how long he had been in that place; it might have been days, or weeks. Calculation was impossible, given the nature of the dream, and he did not worry himself over it.

Something in the darkness became less dark, some great mass ahead of him—an endless plain of stone, its edges lost in distance. Slade was above the plain, slowly descending toward it, but as he came closer it seemed to him that the plain was not horizontal, nor was it a plain; the thing was a wall, a colossal structure of squared stones, and he was approaching it at right angles. He could not see its top; he could not see its bottom or sides. The wall was infinite, separating completely the region of darkness Slade inhabited from whatever lay behind it. Watching it as he drifted closer, Slade became afraid. No wall such as this had a right to exist; its scale was too vast, it was too massive, and now that he had some object against which to measure himself and his aerial progress, Slade knew fear. He did not understand how he could be suspended in the air like a hummingbird, and he knew no human hands could have built the thing ahead.

He wanted to travel in some other direction, away from the wall, but it drew him onward, and as he came closer Slade saw how very large the stones were, each one perfectly square and smooth, dun gray in color, like granite under moonlight. Hovering inches from the wall, he reached for the stone to touch it, and the block he attempted to touch was suddenly not there anymore. He could see through the wall to the far side, a place equally black and impenetrable. But there was something different, a series of rustlings and whisperings from beyond the hole, unidentifiable sounds that made him more afraid than before. Invisible entities there were beckoning him forward, inviting him to pass through the hole and join them, but Slade would not, and demanded that they show themselves first. There was smothered laughter at his request, and snickering so confident, so disdainful of him that Slade, who had always thought of himself as fearless, accepted without shame the terror he felt. The beings who would not reveal themselves laughed louder and told him he was a coward. Slade's mood altered abruptly; he knew he could not allow them to call him any such thing, and flung himself through the hole to fight with them.

As his head and shoulders passed into the place beyond the wall, he was grabbed by many invisible hands, cold hands with clawlike nails. He felt the nearness of the things and smelled the fetid breath they blew past his face as they laughed again, exultant to have him among them. He felt many small teeth fasten upon his limbs and bite down hard into his flesh, but no matter how hard he kicked and struggled, more hands took hold of every part of him, and more teeth sank into his flesh, and Slade screamed for release, screamed louder than he had thought possible, and the laughter became different, a mechanical yammering that seemed to come from far away even as the things pressed themselves more tightly against him.

He flexed himself in a paroxysm of loathing, and flung his body across space until his feet tripped on McCaulay and he was brought down, the side of his face grazing against rock as he fell. The screams continued pouring from his mouth, a torrent of sound he could not shut off for fear of allowing the things that had held him to regain their hold. He stopped screaming only long enough to fill his lungs, then screamed again. Their laughter could still be heard, even though he no longer felt their hands upon him, a muffled staccato that turned from laughter to the familiar sound of air drills. He made himself stop. There were no invisible creatures clutching at him, mocking him. He was in the tunnel, and the darkness around him was the safe darkness of rock, the air smelling of his own sweat and the mortifying flesh of McCaulay, who had died during the cave-in and lay rotting beside him now, his body the very breath of decay.

He must have been trapped for days already. His stomach knotted and writhed its empty tubes like mating serpents, and his throat burned for water. He searched for the lamps, his own or McCaulay's, and could not find them, and knocked over his water flask in the process, then could not find it despite the soft gurglings as it emptied itself. His hand eventually touched moisture, and he righted the flask, still containing a third or so of its contents, and drank it all down. It was not enough, not nearly enough. He had to find the other flask, the one being filled under the seep. He had only two matches left. If he could not find the lamps by their briefly flaring light, he would have to search in darkness. He attempted to light the first match; its tip flew off after a brief sputter. The second match would not ignite at all. Slade took several deep breaths and began his work.

He bumped many parts of himself against rock as he wriggled in search of the filled flask. He screamed and he cried, and when it still could not be found despite his efforts, he came near to blacking out from sheer rage. His frustration was cruel, unjust, against the natural order of things. He was sure he had found the place where the flask stood, had felt the rock around it wet from the overflow, but the flask was gone, and so was the steady dripping that had been there since the cave-in. Someone had taken them away. It was done to torment him, make him suffer more than he had already, and to punish him for being superior to other men. The water thief had probably enjoyed listening to Slade crawl around and shout and cry. It was humiliating. It was unfair.

It had to be McCaulay; there was no one else. But the man was dead, actually dead, his body giving off the aroma of a trash heap in midsummer. Yet the water was gone. If he could just find a lamp and make sure he had been looking in the right place, he could begin asking how it was possible. He began a methodical search for his own lamp or McCaulay's. Light would solve the problem of his thirst. There was no mystery really, just disorientation. He must have been looking in the wrong place for the seep. No other explanation made sense. Unless it was Shoupe.

Slade stopped to consider this possibility. He was positive he had seen the distant figure of Shoupe fall and be crushed by the descending ceiling of the tunnel, but it was by no means certain that he had been killed. It may have been that from Shoupe's line of sight Slade appeared to be the one caught beneath the tons of falling rock. It had happened too quickly; there had been too much dust, too little light. Now he could be sure of nothing. Shoupe was alive and lurking in the darkness, listening closely, keeping quiet, and stealing water.

Slade had to smile. Shoupe would not have expected him to work out what was wrong so fast. Slade had only to pretend he still did not understand the situation, and Shoupe would reveal himself in some way. The water had been stolen while Slade was asleep, that much was clear. Reminded of his dream, Slade felt a momentary fear dimple his skin. The dream was gone, and had left no part of itself in Slade's memory other than the terror that had wakened hlm. He dismissed the dream, whatever it had been; now he had something else to consider.

Shoupe must have found a way through the rubble to the rock face at the end of the tunnel, a route Slade had overlooked. He would need a lamp to find it, and once he did, he would set a trap for the thief. He felt like a man who has become aware of a large and cunning rat in his cabin. Strategy was called for. Slade didn't doubt that he could arrive at a plan that would work, because Slade, the planner, was smarter than Shoupe, the rat.

Moving about in the dark, his hand encountered what was unmistakably a lamp. Slade hugged it, then reminded himself he had no matches with which to light it. This thought was followed by a realization that McCaulay must have matches in his pants, since he was the one responsible for lighting the fuses at the end of each shift. Slade searched until he located McCaulay's body, then rummaged in the pockets until he found a small tin box which, when shaken, gave out a comforting rattle of matches.

Slade lit the lamp and began a thorough inspection of the collapsed section of the tunnel. Somewhere among the shadowy recesses there was a passageway to Shoupe's lair. Slade looked for a long time without finding the entrance, and his lamp began to grow dim. He returned to the rock face, found the other lamp, lit it and continued his search. Every possible route of access back into the jumbled rock and rubble was probed, but nothing that would accommodate the body of a man was found. Slade's thirst was by then a constant torment. His throat had dried so much it hurt him to breathe, and his head was filled with pain from dehydration. Eventually the second lamp began to wane. Slade felt he must have spent the best part of a day, or a night, searching for Shoupe's secret hole. His time, and the carbide lamps, had been wasted.

He stumbled back toward the rock face, his spirits and physical strength considerably depleted, and saw beneath his feet a patch of dampness. Shining his enfeebled beam on it, he saw that the moisture extended to the hidden place where the water flask had been placed for refilling before Shoupe had stolen it. Reaching behind, Slade found the flask had been returned. It was overflowing, creating the dampness. But he had looked there, and found nothing but a little moisture. Or had he looked somewhere else, and placed his hand on ground wetted by his own piss? He could not remember pissing, but assumed that he must have. Now he understood. The first search had been conducted in darkness, and after finding the lamps, he had not bothered to examine the flask's logical location again, until now. His discovery suggested to Slade that Shoupe was not alive after all. The entire search had been a fool's mission. He had simply been looking for the flask where it was not, and had never been, and his explanation for its absence had prompted him to waste both lamps in looking for a dead man's doorway. Shoupe was dead, buried by rock thirty or forty yards back into the tunnel, as dead as McCaulay. Slade's body slumped. He drank from the flask like a man celebrating his own stupidity. Even the welcome coolness of water flooding through him could not soothe his shame.

He felt defeated, truly beaten for the first time since the cave-in occurred. Slade dragged himself to the rock face. He set his flask down, found the empty flask and took it to the seep for refilling, then went back to the rock face and turned his guttering lamp out. The sound of the drills was louder now, he thought, or maybe it was not. He simply could not care for the moment. His misery was complete. Sleep began to invade his body. Slade did not want to sleep, recalling the way he had awoken from his nightmare the time, but he had made himself tired by his fool's search.

It was a shame McCaulay had died so early; if his death had been more recent, Slade could have eaten his flesh to satisfy the serpents of hunger coiling and uncoiling inside him. He did not know how long it had been since McCaulay died, but the man's meat had certainly gone bad in the heat. Or maybe it hadn't. Now Slade found himself unable to stop thinking of McCaulay as a food source. He was weak with hunger; if nothing could be fed to the serpents soon, he might die. The stink surrounding him might be from his own filthy body, his own deposits of excrement further down the tunnel, and the badness that came with air that could not circulate properly. McCaulay might not be as rotten as Slade had assumed. He put the thought from him, but it kept returning.

Slade stirred himself and moved toward the place where he knew the body lay. Finding it, he touched its flesh. When searching for McCaulay's matches he had touched nothing but cloth. The body was neither hot nor cold. Slade assumed the sensible thing to do was take a chunk from the fleshiest part. He unbuckled McCaulay's belt and pulled down the greasy pants. Examining the buttocks, he found that the body had emptied its bowels. That would account for much of the stench. He passed on down the left leg to the calf, and pinched the meat there. Slade took out his clasp knife.

Before he could bring himself to cut into McCaulay's leg, Slade made himself pause to form a plan. He knew he was justified in using the dead man this way, but others might not agree. If he did not use McCaulay to sustain his strength now, before the flesh became inedible, he would have wasted the opportunity to keep himself alive. Slade was not about to die because of what other men might think, but he was not so foolish as to take another's flesh into his stomach without first pausing to consider ways in which he might avoid the consequences when his act was found out.

Deception seemed the best tactic. He would hide the body before his rescuers broke through, and deny that McCaulay was ever with him when the tunnel collapsed. He would suggest that they search for him back where Shoupe was crushed. That was what he would do. He took a fold of the calf and sliced beneath it. They would believe him. The knife was sharp, and cut easily. It was not his fault McCaulay had died. The strip came free. There were many small rocks to conceal the body. He placed one end of the strip in his mouth, gagged, then chewed. They would believe him, because he was Slade.

He dreamed often of the universal wall, always approaching it in the same way, feeling himself compelled to touch it, passing through the hole that always appeared, in answer to taunting from the invisible demons populating the other side. He would awaken with their fingers and teeth upon him, and when he was able to calm himself, Slade used his own fingers and teeth to keep himself alive. He ate only as much as his stomach required to appease the serpents. Much of the flesh had been stripped from the legs and back of McCaulay. Slade drank from his flasks and replaced them

beneath the water seep, finding his way easily in the darkness by
sheer habit, the repetition of his simple routine. The drills came
nearer, their chattering punctuated now and then by single-stick
explosions of dynamite as the more massive chunks of rock were
broken down.

He reminded himself often, knowing his memory was plagued by
holes, to be sure and cover the remains of his larder before the final
breakthrough came. Slade was less confident now of convincing
anyone of anything. He could not concentrate on any particular
thought for more than a moment before it flew away into the dark
and left him wondering what it was that had lately been on his
mind. He could not recall with any accuracy his bunk in the unmarried miners' dormitory, or the face of the woman who sold him his
meals. Shoupe and McCaulay were the same bearded, grimy face
partially hidden by a hatbrim. He had never heard them talk often
enough to retain an impression of their voices, or anyone else's
voice. Sometimes he spoke with himself to be reminded of his own
voice, but these one-sided conversations were forgotten immediately. Slade was aware that other miners tacked small photographs or
tintypes to the wall beside their bunk, pictures of wives or sweet-
hearts far away, or else they ripped from magazines portraits of
plump actresses and illustrations of young women advertising gir-
dles and corsets. Slade's wall had always been empty, as empty as
the wall he visited now in dreams. If he had ever had a picture to
gaze at in former times, he could not remember. It was an injustice
that the simple passage of time—sometimes mere minutes were
enough—should rob him of another tiny piece of himself.

He was fast becoming a stranger inside his own skin, and he
knew it was the darkness that accelerated his condition. In darkness a man might turn inward to review his life, summon images
from the past and relive moments of happiness, but if a man had
little or no memory of himself, the darkness mocked him, reflecting
with its boundless emptiness the hollow space inside the man.
Slade cried a great deal as the drills and dynamite ate their way
toward him. There was almost nothing left of him to be found. As
the body of McCaulay was stripped of flesh, so the mind of Slade
was flayed of recollection, layer by layer, until there remained only
his name, and the instruction to himself concerning the man he ate.

Then the drills were accompanied by voices, and Slade was more
scared by the muffled words seeping through to him than he was by

the shapeless creatures tormenting him in dreams. Soon they would be there, where he huddled in filth and stench and darkness, with their lights and faces and words. He was terrified over the coming confrontation. He must not let them see his fear, and he must not let them see the dead man. With the last of his matches, Slade coaxed a feeble glow from the carbide lamps and scuttled hastily about, collecting rocks suitable for stacking atop a corpse. He buried his clasp knife also, and used the last of his strength to tip over a large rock, shielding the makeshift grave from view. The lamps gave off their last light and expired, and he waited then in the darkness that now was less friendly, shattered and shaken as it was by the din of sledgehammers and shouting.

He began to quake, as if the air suddenly had turned cold, and he could not stop. His flesh vibrated on his bones, his teeth clattered uncontrollably, and he voided his bowels of a hot slime. He could not keep from moaning low and long; every breath he took into himself he let escape as a moan or sigh, and his hands clasped at each other with a grip so weak with fear his fingers slid constantly from their fellows in an unconscious washing motion he was unable to stop.

At last rubble began cascading nearby, and he saw a beam of light brighter than the sun come lancing through into his chamber. Slade vomited and turned his eyes from the carbide flame, and dared not look into the furthest corner, at the stones piled there, for fear they did not hide his secret as well as he hoped.

"I see him!" yelled a voice, but Slade could no more understand it than he could have a foreign tongue. The voice called more words back into the tunnel, and more rubble was loosened. Slade faced the streaming light through latticed fingers, and rose clumsily to meet the figure that came sliding down into his hole.

"Me ..., " he said, as the figure stood and approached him. "There's only me ... Nobody else, just me ... "

The bathhouse was honored to wash him clean. He was given new clothing and boots and a new hat, all finer than he was accustomed to. He ate like a king, but would drink only water, and would say of his ordeal only that he remembered nothing, nothing at all after the timbers broke and the tunnel came crashing in from above. He learned he had been trapped sixteen days and nights. Newspaper reporters asked if faith in God had saved him, and Slade nodded.

He was four hours out of the ground, and life was good until a well-dressed man disturbed his meal at Molly's Eating House by sitting at the table without asking permission. Slade disliked him for that, and took his time answering the question, "Would you care to meet your employer? He certainly would like to meet you."

Slade was fairly certain he had never been inside so fine a carriage before. It carried him up the eastern slope of Glory Hole and deposited him outside the mahogany doors of Elk House. The well-dressed man escorted him into the presence of Leo Brannan, of whom Slade knew precisely nothing. He certainly was not an impressive fellow to look at, and he appeared even more ill at ease than his guest.

"Please sit down, Mr. Slade. A man in your position must not feel quite able to stand for long. Please, sit."

Slade listened while Leo Brannan offered his congratulations over the timely rescue and the remarkable fortitude displayed by one of his men. "I have in mind a small ceremony, Mr. Slade, scheduled for tomorrow if you feel able to manage it, that will celebrate, or consolidate if you will, the joy every person in Glory Hole feels at your liberation from darkness and despair. The town square would be an appropriate venue, I think, don't you, Price?"

"A perfect setting," agreed the well-dressed man.

"Do you feel yourself capable of attending, so short a time after your ordeal, Mr. Slade?"

Slade nodded. He had noticed at last that the man talking to him had one blue eye and one brown eye, a combination Slade thought fascinating. Leo Brannan reached into his jacket and produced a hundred dollar bill. This was passed to Price, who passed it to Slade. "You are indeed a stout fellow, and it's my wish that you take this small offering to use as you please. There can of course be no true compensation for your suffering, but this may go some small way toward easing your return to the world."

Slade fingered the note. He had never seen one before.

"Maybe you'd like to thank Mr. Brannan," hinted Price.

"Thank you."

"Good day to you, Mr. Slade, and also good luck, although you probably have no need of that commodity at the moment."

Slade pocketed the money and stood. He let Price open the door for him. Slade began walking down the wood-paneled hall, retracing his steps toward the front door, keeping Price a step or so behind, just to let him know he didn't care for him. He wondered, as he walked, what he should do with the one hundred dollars. Turning a corner into the main corridor, he saw an extraordinarily large vase of delicate blue color, almost as tall as a man. Standing beside it was a young girl whose face bore a large stain, her left eye lost in a half-mask of blue much deeper than that of the vase.

Rowland Price did nothing to stop Slade's descent onto the plush carpeting, but stared at the man as he lay twitching on his back. Price had himself found young Miss Brannan's face a shock on first arriving at Elk House to act as personal secretary to Leo Brannan and liaison between him and the Praetorians, but he thought a reaction such as Slade's was excessive.

The fit ended as quickly as it had begun, and Price assisted the man to his feet. "Mr. Slade, are you quite sure you're ready for Mr. Brannan's proposal? I know I could persuade him to postpone the celebration a day or two."

Slade shrugged him off and looked around. Price saw that Omie was gone, as if she never had been there. He had been warned in Denver that the girl was strange, and was under instruction to assess any potential embarrassment to her stepfather once Brannan entered public life as leader of the Praetorians.

Slade began walking again, this time with less swagger. Price assumed the fall was a result of not having slept since being freed from the mine. The man was remarkably tough, but there was something behind his eyes Price disliked, some other entity besides that of a brave miner.

On the drive back down to Glory Hole, Price suggested to Slade that he take himself to bed and recover fully for the next day's gala occasion. Slade ignored him. Price thought it ironic that such a boorish individual was about to receive public approbation as a hero.

"I'm told they haven't yet found your other partner, Slade. They found Shoupe on the way through. Where was McCaulay, do you know?"

"With Shoupe."

"That whole area has been explored, all the rubble taken out, but no McCaulay. They're continuing to search. Mr. Brannan has promised both the widows a company funeral for their men, so he'll be found."

"I want to walk."

"Pardon me?"

"Let me out."

"You prefer to walk?"

"Stop and let me out."

"You need to stretch your legs, is that it?"

Price hammered on the carriage roof. A small door behind the driver's box opened. "Yessir?"

"Stop here, please."

When Slade stepped down, Price closed the door and said, "I know where you live. The carriage will be sent for you a little before noon tomorrow."

Slade nodded, then watched the carriage continue descending the road to town. When it passed around a curve he began leaping down the mountainside as fast as the slope and his diminished strength would allow, his new boots kicking up dirt and cinders from the denuded earth. At the bottom he waited by the railroad tracks for a short while until one of the three daily coal trains passed by, returning its empty cars to Durango. He hid behind low brush as the locomotive steamed by, then ran alongside the train until he could grab hold and swing himself aboard one of the cars. Knowing he might be seen riding on the platform, Slade climbed inside the open clanking steel box. His new clothing was instantly blackened by coal dust.

He had known from the moment he saw the girl in Brannan's big house that they would find the body of McCaulay. She was connected somehow with his time buried in the mine, he could not remember why, but her face with its inky blot around the left eye saw through him, Slade could tell. He had to get away while he could, before they dug up McCaulay, or the girl spoke to someone in the big house, and they came to capture him and hang him. He could not allow that to happen. He had done nothing wrong. They could search for him all they wanted, but they wouldn't find him, now that he was moving again. It had ended that way before, with Slade being carried away to safety from the scene of some tragedy he had not caused, an accident of some kind for which he would be blamed anyway. It was not fair that he was not permitted to remember the details. He could think of no good reason for such punishment. Slade felt the car's vibration running through his flesh like the aftershock of an underground explosion. "Fire in the hole ...," he whispered.

Slade knew the empty cars were taken to Leadville, but from there he was uncertain of their direction. It made little difference, really, so long as he was able to keep heading away from the Grand Mogul mine and what had happened there. The air was cold but his new coat was warm. He would ride the car as far as circumstance allowed, then disappear with his hundred dollars into another state, another life.

33

During the first month Drew rode with Lodi, no one was killed. The gang successfully robbed two banks and one stage. Shots had been fired, but none found their mark. Wealthier by more than seven thousand dollars, Lodi decided they should rest up in a place he knew, a cabin deep in the mountains, inaccessible to anyone unfamiliar with its hidden approaches.

Drew admired the man who had rescued him from jail, but did not like him. Lodi was not a man who encouraged friendship from his followers so much as he required loyalty, unquestioning and unstinted. Drew managed to act the role of grateful acolyte without undue strain on his pride, but he could not warm to Lodi as he did to Clarence Dustey. Nate Haggin was not without friendliness, when Drew had been accepted as a functioning member of the gang, but Clarence, a compulsive talker once his confidence was won, found in Drew a listener with endless patience and little criticism.

Drew learned from Clarence more than any man had a right to know about another, including intimate descriptions of Clarence's three marriages to women unaware of each other's existence. He had a wife in Montana, another in Utah and a third in Grand Junction, Colorado. His fourth wife he did not count, since she had been seventy-eight when he married her in Missouri as a favor to a friend who wanted his mother worn to death in the marital bed so the friend might inherit her reputed wealth, some of which was supposed to come Clarence's way once he had sent Minnie Rourke to her reward in heaven. He had entered upon matrimony in that instance, he assured Drew, not only for the benefit of himself and his friend, but for the sake of the widow Rourke, a decent old soul who should have been granted surcease from earthly toil by way of cupid's arrow, but had taken that arrow in her teeth instead, and worn Clarence's manufactured passion to a nub. Clarence had fled Missouri when his wrinkled wife began demanding more attention after dark than Clarence was accustomed to paying women a third Minnie's age. "She was a hellion between the sheets, more'n a woman that old had a right to be, you ask me about it. Could be she was a witch even, I don't know, but I never went back to find out, not this boy. I lost a good friend on account of that woman."

"How do you support the other three, Clarence?"

"Well, I don't, not regular, but they're all good workers themselves, so the kids don't starve."

"How many?"

"Be eight of 'em when Mae drops around next July. She's the one in Utah. Lodi says I can go see her pretty soon, take her some cash if I got any left by then."

"You won't spend any up here, Clarence."

"No, but here to Utah's a fair stretch, with temptation along the way. By God, I just better be good if she's gonna get some. I never hit any one of 'em, but I tipped my hat to temptation a considerable number of times in between getting hitched. That's where the money goes, boy."

"How does Lodi spend his?"

"I never asked. He's a sinner, same as me, and Nate too, but not near so much. I believe Lodi, he'd put it in a bank if he could just find one that's robber-proof. That ain't his name, by the way. He's from Lodi, Wisconsin, he told me one time, but that's all he told. Where you from, Bones?"

"New York State."

"I never went further east than Saint Louis, myself. Nate, I believe he's been to New York, only he don't talk about it, or anything else much. This outfit never did have anyone in it that's willing to talk."

Drew's share of the robbery proceeds came to less than a thousand dollars, since he was considered an apprentice. He was tempted, while they lazed around the cabin waiting for time to pass, to saddle up and ride away before harm came to himself or anyone who might get in Lodi's way during the course of a holdup. This idea seldom lasted longer than five minutes. Working with a gang had not been his plan, but his efforts alone had brought such poor results, he was not driven to leave his teachers until he had learned more of their technique. When he had a substantial bankroll of his own he would quit, without asking Lodi first. Lodi had reminded Drew several times of his debt, and seemed the kind of individual who would not be inclined to accept nonpayment; a dangerous man to cross, was Drew's cautious assessment, and he planned to take his leave of Lodi only if he should chance upon an opportunity to do so without risk.

The weather forced Lodi's men into closer fraternity than any of them, with the exception of Clarence, had any liking for. A blizzard late in February kept them snowed in for several days, their only opportunity for relief from the cabin's smoky air the occasional trip to a latrine hole nearby, or to ensure that their horses were safe in the stable.

When the skies cleared, Drew was ordered to fetch oats and supplies from White Cloud, a town about nine miles away. Nate Haggin would accompany him, and they would take another two horses to serve as pack animals. Drew understood that Nate was to be his partner on the trip, rather than Clarence, because Nate was capable of shooting him should he attempt to absent himself indefinitely. He was not permitted to take any money other than the amount necessary for their purchases. No warning was given, nor needed, to let Drew know he was still serving a term of probation in Lodi's eyes.

On the ride to town Nate kept his horse a few paces behind Drew's, even when the trail was wide enough to permit riding side by side. The insinuation was so clear it began to irritate Drew.

"How long does it take before Lodi trusts a man?"

"Depends on the man. A year, maybe, for some. Lodi's a careful feller is all. He's got his own way of doing things, and you better do it like he says or be answerable for it, so I'm doing like he said. Don't take no offense."

"How many years have you been riding with him?"

"Three. Men that rode longer with Lodi are all dead now. Lodi, he's never been winged, even. Got a charm from a nigger woman tied around his ankle, keeps him from harm, they say. I expect every man's got to die, but Lodi don't intend for it to happen any-time soon."

In White Cloud, Drew purchased all the necessary supplies while Nate busied himself in the saloon. Drew joined him there after loading the horses and hitching them outside. Another snowstorm was advancing on the town, darkening the sky as Drew entered, and the lamps over the bar caused the glasses lined up there to twinkle and shine in a way that made him instantly thirsty, eager to linger and make conversation, even with so untalkative a man as Nate Haggin.

Nate had a bottle before him at a corner table, a quarter of its contents already gone. Drew pulled out a chair and sat. "More snow coming," he said, noting that Nate had been companionable enough to provide a second glass.

"Figures," said Nate. "I ain't gonna pour it for you."

Drew tipped whiskey into his glass and drank it down.

"You get everything?"

"I did, and there's money left over."

"We'll lose it here, then."

"You want to try for home while there's light?"

"No, and it ain't what I'd call home. They won't be expecting us back till tomorrow anyway."

"Then I'll go put the horses in the livery stable."

"After you drunk another drink you can do that. You the kind that's got to be taking care of business right this exact minute, Bones?"

"I believe I am. Does that cause you pain?"

"I see enough of it, it might."

Drew poured himself another drink, aware of a draft against his back as the door was opened and closed. He turned briefly to exam-ine the man who entered, then tossed his drink down. Nate said, "Don't go turning your head again, Bones, but the feller that just come in with the long mustaches is someone I seen before one time, and he's trouble for you and me."

"Why so?"

"On account of he's a deputy marshal or detective or some such. I seen him a year or two back, poking around after us when we done the bank in Monte Vista. He's the one. Name's Torrence. He's a Pinkerton, I remember now."

"Think he's watching out for us?"

"Naw, most likely come around here to make sure his granny got her liquor supply all right. Listen, fool, he's gone over to the stove to get warm, and he's pertending not to look this way, but now and then he does, so it's him all right, and I figure he knows me for who I am, only he don't know you. Shame you went and sat down here like you done, Bones. You coulda stalked him like he's doing to me. Well, he's seen us together now, so you're in this thing deep as me. This feller, he's a mean one, I heard, so you and me together, we're gonna have to kill him dead before too long, see."

"Why not just leave and lose him in the dark?"

"Because with snow coming on like you said, he'd track us easy, dark or not. Better get used to the notion there'll be blood before we make it back to the others, you hear me? You got the stomach for what we need to do, Bones?"

"Surely."

"Surely, shit. You better not fade out on me now. He's here to get my hide and yours too now, so don't be letting him, is all I'm saying. You do what I tell you and we'll take them supplies back like we planned, and the Pinkertons, they'll have to recruit theirselves another detective man, because this one here won't be around by sunrise."

"How do you want to play it?"

"Like we don't know who he is, and we're just a couple of nobodies that come in for a drink and now we're leaving. The bottle's paid for. In a minute or so we'll take it outside and get mounted, and I'll act like I'm a little drunk, see, just to make him rest easy, I hope, and we start riding and wait till we come to a place we can get the drop on him, because that shiteater, he'll be following behind like a baby duck after its mama. You got that, Bones?"

"I've got it."

"Take another drink, then take the bottle. I got to use the jakes. Be with you soon."

When Nate rose and walked to the rear of the barroom, Drew watched him pass by the stove, and noted the man with the long mustaches, whose face turned slightly as Nate passed him by. Drew was already looking into the bottom of his glass by the time the Pinkerton man sneaked a glance back at him. He corked the bottle and slipped it into his coat pocket, then rose and headed for the door.

Outside, he unhitched all four horses and readied Nate's beside him for a fast mount-up. He was sufficiently drunk, despite the brevity of his stay inside the saloon, to wonder without alarm if blood would indeed be spilled as Nate predicted. The storm had covered White Cloud with darkness in advance of the hour, and flakes of snow already were drifting down through the air. The town's single street was made beautiful by silently drifting whiteness, and Drew experienced a momentary lapse of concentration as he watched individual flakes swirl past his nose. It seemed most unlikely that from this moment of calm repose there might spring a confrontation resulting in blood. He did not doubt that Nate had correctly identified the Pinkerton man, but to kill him somewhere along the trail struck Drew as an infringement upon a naturally peaceful setting. He wanted no part in it, and hoped enough snow might fall to prevent Torrence from following them. The means by which detectives were able to track down outlaws were interesting to Drew. He admired men capable of such intense dedication to the law, even if they threatened him personally with their expertise. He hoped, if Torrence fell into their hands, to question him about his profession. Better still would be ignorance, because a Pinkerton in the hands of Nate was sure to be a dead man soon. Drew felt again the compulsion to cut himself adrift from Lodi by abandoning Nate, but also the obligation of outlawry to defend his fellow robber; allegiance was a powerful force, applied by circumstance to the unlikeliest of partners. He was in deep, as Nate had said, and there was no means of escape for Drew that would have sat comfortably on his shoulders. Being a little drunk helped, but not by much.

The saloon door slammed open, then shut. Nate swung into the saddle and they began ambling along the street.

"Don't turn around," Nate said. "You do that and he sees it, he'll know he's been suspicioned."

"I know."

"You don't know nothing. These Pinkertons, they always do this, wait around in a town they figure we'll show up in sometime. Lodi run with Arch Powell up in Montana, and when the gang busted up, there was bounty hunters and detectives combing three states for them. A couple U.S. marshals even went down Killdeer way to flush him out, only Arch happened to be dead already, and they got to be the same way theirselves before too long. Lodi laughed about

that when he heard. This feller, now, he'll have the same thing happen to him, and it's a lesson in how not to be a fool."

Drew turned to see if the man with the long mustaches had left
the saloon. They were at the edge of town by then, and heavier
snow was spilling from the sky. The man was not on the sidewalk yet.

"I told you not to turn around."

"He didn't see. He's not there. You could be wrong about him."

"Nope."

In less than a minute the saloon could not be seen any longer, cut
off by the last building in White Cloud and the thickening snowfall.

"He'll be along," Nate said.

"Then what?"

"Then we kill him, what else? You up to that, Bones? Ever killed
a man before?"

"Wounded one in the gut. I guess he died."

"Well, this time you can do it right and be sure."

Drew hoped Torrence had been wise enough to stay in White
Cloud. He had no wish to shoot a Pinkerton, even if the man was
trailing them with a mind to killing or arresting them. There was
not enough snow to cover their tracks unless Torrence delayed following them by at least an hour, an unlikely event.

When Drew and Nate had ridden for a while, Nate said, "Far
enough from town now, they won't hear nothing. Get down and go
back to the last bend. Wait for him there and get him good, you
hear? I'll be expecting to see the feller dead on the ground. Take
this." Nate threw him his Winchester.

Drew dismounted and retraced his trail to the bend, then positioned himself behind some trees. This was a test he would have to
pass if he wanted to remain with Lodi on Lodi's terms, and those
terms would not permit allowing a Pinkerton to go free when he
was so close to the hideout. He thought about shooting Nate
instead, but that seemed equally odious, even if Nate was sure to
have killed men during his outlaw years. The only chance for Drew
to escape moral compromise was if Torrence had not followed them.

That possibility was expunged several minutes later, when Drew
heard the approach of hooves, a single horse walking slowly. He saw
it coming through the snow, its rider leaning low in the saddle to
assure himself he was still on the double set of tracks he had followed from White Cloud. He passed within three yards of Drew

without noticing, then was further up the trail toward Nate, who would not hesitate to shoot him down if Drew failed.

"Hold it there!"

The horse shied a little and the rider came upright in the saddle as he turned. Drew had the rifle trained on his chest in case there should be a gun in the rider's hand, but there was not. The horse danced nervously as Drew came closer. "Get down," he told the rider.

"Why would I want to?"

"Get down or get shot down."

The man dismounted.

"Now lead your horse up ahead. Keep your hands wide apart where I can see them."

"I don't have any money. You're wasting your time."

"Turn around and start walking."

Nate was waiting beside the trail with the horses.

"Bones, I told you to shoot him, not deliver him."

"We need to be sure who he is first."

"You never even took his gun, you jackass. Torrence, dump that belt now."

"The name isn't Torrence, mister."

"Unbuckle it right now."

Torrence dropped his gun belt.

"Now step away. Pick it up, Bones."

Drew collected the belt. Nate edged his horse closer.

"It's you, Torrence. You done the wrong thing, following us. You'd be dead right now if Bones had've done what I said."

"We need to be sure," Drew repeated.

"You think so, huh? Well, all right. Take the rifle out'n his saddle, then both of you get mounted. We'll take a little ride and maybe dig out more truth than you can handle, Bones, but if that's what you want, we'll do it that way."

"You men are mistaking me for someone else. I'm Bob Weeks, from Sioux City."

"No you ain't; now do like I say."

Some time later, the riders heard two shots from the direction of the cabin, then a third. Nate asked Torrence, "You got a partner working with you?"

"I don't have any partner, and I'm not who you think I am, my friend."

"Go on ahead," Nate told Drew. "Scout things out and be careful you don't get seen. Could be there's more like this one around."

Drew understood that the job had been given to him because Nate considered him an unreliable guard over Torrence. He went on up the trail another half mile and came in sight of the cabin. Far from finding Clarence and Lodi pinned down inside by Pinkertons, he saw them by the corral with a lantern apiece, inspecting the ground. Drew rode up and asked why the shots had been fired.

"Mountain lion," said Clarence. "The horses started screaming, and I come out to see why. Seen him for just a moment, a big one. Take a look at these tracks here—you ever see a print the size of that?"

"Where's Nate?" asked Lodi.

"Back a little ways. There's a man with him Nate says is a Pinkerton."

"Go get the both of them here now."

Drew fetched Nate and Torrence. The supplies were unloaded and the horses quickly rubbed down by Drew while Clarence stood guard with a rifle.

"Lions, they can be tricky," said Clarence. "Now he knows there's a bunch of horses here, he'll come back. That feller really a detective?"

"I don't know. Nate thinks so."

"They won't let him out of that cabin breathing, you can bet on it."

Drew dumped feed into the trough and began walking to the cabin with a sack of flour. Clarence said, "Come out and spell me soon, all right? It's cold out here."

Torrence was on the floor as Drew entered, Nate standing above him with a chunk of firewood in his hands. Lodi was smoking his pipe, a pistol on the table before him. Nate kicked Torrence in the ribs to stir him, but the downed man simply grunted in response.

"You hit him too hard," Lodi admonished. "You won't get a thing out of him like that."

"It's Torrence," Nate said. "I know it. I told you about him when we were still up around Butte that time."

"I recall it, but I never did set eyes on the man myself. Unless he breaks, it's your word against his."

"Oh, he'll say what he needs to, never you mind. I ain't about to let one of his kind lie his way out of here."

"Did you go through his pockets yet?" Drew asked, setting down the flour. "He might have proof of who he is."

"Pinkertons carry everything they need to fool you," Lodi said, "so whatever's in his pockets don't mean a damn thing. Get the rest of the supplies in, then stay out and watch the corral."

Drew sent Clarence inside and cradled the rifle, huddled in a corner of the stable. Torrence would die, probably after being severely beaten. It would have been a mercy to shoot him as Nate had told him to. Now the man would suffer before death came to release him. Nate would almost certainly insist that Drew be the one to finish him off with a bullet, if he did not die quickly enough when they were done with questioning him. Drew could saddle up a horse now and lead it away from the cabin while the other three were occupied with Torrence. The snow was coming down heavier than before, and would hide his tracks if he could just get far enough away before they discovered he was gone.

It might work, but it would not help Torrence. Drew found himself resenting the man for having blundered into the situation that was going to end only when he was dead. He had thought Pinkertons were smarter than that. He told himself it was not his fault. He knew he was not about to ride away; he had almost a thousand dollars inside the cabin, and Torrence would soon be a dead man in any case. Drew tried to ignore the weak scream that came to him across the wind-whipped corral. The horses munched their fresh oats, already unmindful of the lion. Drew wished he could be so placid, so uncaring.

When Nate came out to watch for the lion, Drew went inside.

Torrence was alive but unconscious. "Well," said Lodi, "he's a Pinkerton, all right. Talked up nice and loud when Nate got done persuading him. You should have done what Nate said, Bones, and spared the man some pain."

"I was just thinking that myself."

"Were you now. Then I guess that makes it all right with you if you're the one that does what has to be done."

"He looks like he's pretty near dead already."

"Nowhere near it. I've seen more dead men than you'll ever see, and he's got life in him yet, just a little busted up is all. He'll be useful to us just like he is."

"Useful?"

"There's two problems we've got right now, Bones. One's him, and the other's that lion out there looking to rip open a horse or two. A man with brains, he'd take those two problems and put them together, and you know what, Bones? He doesn't get a double problem, he gets both of them taken care of. You following me yet?"

"No."

"Then I'll keep it simple. Take him outside, not too far off, and stake him down, then wait for the lion. It'll smell the blood that's on him and come for fresh meat. When it does, you shoot it."

"Bait?"

"That's it, Bones. Get yourself set up in a tree perch is my advice, less chance the lion'll smell you too."

Drew looked over at Clarence, plaiting a rawhide quirt on his bunk. Clarence would not look up.

"Looks like you don't approve," said Lodi.

"I don't."

"Makes no difference. I tell you to do it, you do it. I'm not agreeable like Nate is when someone don't do what I said. I always get my way, Bones, I'm lucky like that. Take him out now while there's no fight left in him. Take rope for him so he don't run off, and some for you to tie yourself onto a tree. Better go high, Bones. Lions can jump pretty good. Clarence, go help him get set up."

After Torrence had been laid on the snow in a clearing some hundred yards from the cabin, Drew sent Clarence back for a chair and blanket to keep the unconscious man from freezing on the ground. When Clarence came back he said Lodi had laughed, but allowed the extra comforts anyway. They set Torrence on the chair and swathed him in the thick blanket.

"This ain't my notion of a good idea," Clarence said.

"Mine neither. I can't climb a pine tree. You see anything around here but pines? That part won't work."

"Lodi said to climb a tree."

"Not around here. I'll just hide myself."

"Lion might smell you out."

"That he might."

"Well, you do what you think is gonna work, but I won't be the one that says to Lodi you wouldn't get in a tree."

"Then don't. Let Lodi come outside and find out."

"He won't do that. He's got Nate in the corral still. Lodi don't like to be out where it's cold."

"Then he won't ever know, will he? Go on back, Clarence."

"It ain't my kind of a good idea to put a man out for lion bait."

"It won't come. Lions are smart animals."

"I wouldn't know about that," Clarence said, and turned to go back to the cabin.

Drew listened until the crunching of his footsteps had faded, then stationed himself beneath the low boughs of a nearby tree. He turned out his lamp and watched his own breath form clouds in front of his face. Similar clouds formed around Torrence's slumped shoulders and were carried away on the wind, whisked to invisibility within seconds. The snow had stopped abruptly while Torrence was being roped onto the chair. Drew could see him clearly through a network of pine needles, a figure barely recognizable as human. Drew had seen the blood clotting in his hair as they took him from the cabin; Nate had struck Torrence's head with force many times. In a way it was better that he remained unaware of his new circumstances.

Drew had no faith at all in Lodi's plan, and suspected Lodi had no faith in it either. Torrence and Drew were both being punished, one for being a Pinkerton, the other for being weak. The worst that could happen was being obliged to spend the entire night outside, freezing his feet and trying to stay awake in case of the lion's improbable return. Torrence would very likely freeze before dawn, inactive as he was, but there was little Drew felt he could do to avoid that, apart from providing the blanket. Freezing might prove a merciful release from whatever Lodi had in mind if the lion did not take the bait offered to it. Drew surmised death by freezing must be akin to falling asleep and never waking up, a civilized way to pass on, and one that Drew would have preferred himself over hanging, for instance.

He stamped his feet to keep the blood moving through his toes and to scare away the lion, should it be in the vicinity. Sometimes he asked Torrence if he was all right, but there was never any reply beyond the breath drifting from beneath his hat. Drew became miserable. He had chosen the wrong path, fallen in with bad company, and could see no practical way of escaping with his skin intact.

He had never seen a mountain lion, but had heard stories of their attacking children. Drew could not be sure the lion would prefer easy meat in a chair over something more to its natural taste, like horses. He would keep it away from Torrence if it came anywhere near. Of course, if the lion had no chance to kill the Pinkerton, Lodi would give the job to Drew. There was no escaping the dilemma. The best thing would be for Torrence to die of exposure, and yet Drew had gone and provided a blanket for him. It was becoming more difficult to think about. Cold was seeping beneath his skin, creeping through the flesh, invading his bones. He wanted to be anywhere but where he was, doing anything but watching over a man set up for lion bait. He felt sleepy despite his discomfort, less concerned for himself or Torrence, and he felt a warm flush of shame prickle his face and neck.

Drew stepped out from beneath the tree and approached the bound man on the chair. "Torrence? Hey, Torrence." Breath still came from his mouth, but the wisps were less powerful than before, the pauses between them longer. Torrence was dying, succumbing to the cold, the best of all possible deaths, under the circumstances. Drew shook him several times without eliciting any response. He stood there, hating himself, helpless.

The scream came to his ears like a steam whistle, beginning low and rising in pitch to a crescendo that suddenly was cut off completely. Drew turned to face the direction it had come from. It was not the scream of a horse, so it had to have been the lion, and it was over toward the cabin. The scream returned, and this time he knew it was human. Drew began to run. Whoever was screaming had stopped, and the silence was replaced by a deep coughing that became a snarl. Drew stopped, then began running again. He heard shouting from the cabin and the corral, but the lion was closer than that, much closer, coughing and snarling again, and the nearer he came to it, the more Drew felt his scalp crawl.

The lion lay on top of someone half hidden in a snowbank, its back to Drew. It turned and sprang into a defensive stance as it heard him, and the lips pulled away from its teeth so fast the upper portion of its head appeared to gather itself in a series of creases back between its flattened ears. A hissing and rumbling came from its throat, and its long tail lashed snow from the body behind it. Drew raised his rifle, sighted and fired. The lion sprang straight up into the air, then fell across its victim, howling and thrashing. Drew levered another round into the chamber and fired again. The lion reared back and collapsed.

Voices were approaching from the cabin. Drew came closer to the lion and nudged it with the rifle barrel. He saw the man beneath its body was Clarence, and Clarence was still alive despite the blood spilled around him on the snow.

"Get him ...?" he asked.

"I got him."

"Come down hard on me.... That's a big cat.... "

A faint whisper of breath came from Clarence's mouth, then stopped. His eyes remained open, but Drew knew he was dead. Nate and Lodi entered the clearing. Drew noticed for the first time the coffeepot and cup near Clarence; the man had died while bringing warmth to Drew. Lodi held his lamp near to Clarence.

"Gone," he said.

"I told him not to come out with no damn coffee," said Nate. "It had to go and get Clarence instead of the goddamn Pinkerton.... By God, that feller won't live if Clarence ain't."

Nate headed in the direction of the chair and Torrence. Drew wondered if there was any way to stop him, and decided there was not.

Lodi was admiring the lion. "Damn, that's a big one. Skinny, though—see the ribs on it? Looks like you got him clean through the chest, then again in the side, both good hits. Clarence never did listen to good advice."

"Kids."

"Say what?"

"He had kids, and a wife. Three wives."

"Well, that's the end of Clarence."

Nate's .45 boomed among the trees.

"And that's the end of Torrence. Don't look so down-in-the-mouth, Bones. You didn't ask for no coffee. It just happened that way."

Both stared at the dead man and the lion until Nate returned. "You fellers know how to skin a cat?" Nate asked.

"Not me," said Lodi.

"They're good eating if it's done right. You know how, Bones?"

"No."

"You don't know how to kill a man as needs killing either, do you?"

"Any man I decide needs killing, I can kill."

"You say."

"I don't want to hear argument," Lodi told them. "Get packed up. I want to be gone from here before sunrise. If there's one Pinkerton been sniffing around, there'll be others."

"What about Clarence?" Drew asked.

"We don't have time for burying. The ground's like rock anyway, clear through April."

"And Torrence?"

"He's comfy enough," said Nate."Got himself a chair."

"They'll both be taken care of by varmints. Get going."

Riding away from the cabin by the light of dawn, Drew knew a part of himself had been left behind in the woods, a part he should have fought harder to hold on to. The thing left behind was just a sliver of a larger thing inside him, a reservoir of sorts, containing his elemental human soul, which Drew supposed had been created with a full measure of goodness inside it. This soul reservoir was probably of finite proportions, Drew reasoned, and he had lost a spoonful of it forever.

"Don't be long-in-the-face, Bones," Lodi told him. "All of us have got more money now. That's what happens when a man dies. That's his legacy to his friends. Clarence wouldn't want to see you looking so miserable, boy."

"He's a sorry-looking son of a bitch anyway," Nate said.

Drew ignored him. He knew he would kill Nate someday, and he had no doubt at all that he could do so without losing another piece of the best part of himself.

34

Lovey Doll recognized as one of her virtues the ability to concentrate with single-minded purpose on a subject of her choosing. Since rich men were the only subject of any real interest to her, Lovey Doll spent many hours considering their ways. As a species, rich men were becoming less available for her consumption than had once been the case. Lovey Doll knew the mirror did not lie. It was time to get for herself a rich man who would take care of her in perpetuity, even in the event of his death. To ensure that the mortality of the male would not inconvenience her plans for a life of luxurious ease, Lovey Doll would have to marry. She had never been married, despite sharing the lives and fortunes of a number of wealthy men, so the prospect had the added appeal of novelty.

Being that she had moved her things to Glory Hole, the man in question would have to be Leo Brannan, the richest man in the nation's western half, it was said. That he had a wife already was seen by Lovey Doll as no great obstacle in her path to winning him. Lovey Doll, although not a religious woman, believed God might possibly have blessed her enterprise when it became known that the wife had lost an arm in a freakish accident, and had thereafter taken to her room like a mad recluse. No normal man could tolerate such behavior for long, Lovey Doll was sure, and when the time came for him to stray in search of more pleasant pastures, she would be prepared. The fact that Brannan's only child was a girl, ugly and a little crazy, it was said, made Lovey Doll's plans even more viable. All rich men required an heir, a boy to pass their wealth on to, and Lovey Doll was even prepared to give birth, if that was required, though the thought of herself swelling out like a barrel was repugnant. The winning of Leo Brannan from his wife, marriage and impregnation: it would all have to be accomplished without delay, before her mirror told Lovey Doll she was no longer the fairest of them all, and before the money she had raised by selling her jewelry was gone.

A close study of her target proved difficult. The man had little interest in public appearances, and on the one occasion she caught a glimpse of him outside the mining office, having waited for more than two hours, she was surprised to see how modestly dressed he was, and how very unremarkable he seemed, if his mismatched eyes of blue and brown were overlooked; an ordinary fellow, still quite young despite the early symptoms of a potbelly and baldness. He certainly did not look like anyone capable of resisting her. Lovey Doll went home with the warm glow inside that came from certainty, a conviction that if she made her first move soon, it would pay off quickly and handsomely.

Lovey Doll had changed her name before arriving in Glory Hole, deeming it prudent to be known from that time on as Imogen Starr. She lived in a modest boardinghouse run by a Mrs. Garfinkle, the wife of one of Brannan's lower echelon of bookkeepers. The size of her room, and the plain fare served at mealtimes, were a daily reminder to Lovey Doll of how very far she had fallen since being obliged to leave Denver. The circuitous journey itself—south to Pueblo, west to Salida, then north again to Leadville and the Glory Hole spur—had taken a day and a night, even though the town lay less than a hundred miles from her starting point as the crow flies, and Lovey Doll had taken it as an omen of difficult times ahead. Now that she had Leo Brannan in her sights, Glory Hole's inaccessibility was simply another personal challenge. After they were married, she would tell Leo he ought to build a direct line from Glory Hole to Denver, no matter what the cost or technical problems involved in laying track over the great divide might be. It would be her first act of influence upon him, and they would visit Denver frequently to savor its brighter lights, its faster pace and flashier style. She might even have Leo build her a mansion in Denver so they might live there for most of the year. That would be delightful, thought Lovey Doll, and she did not seriously doubt that all of it would happen the way she wanted.

By surreptitious inquiry of Mrs. Garfinkle and her dreary little husband, Lovey Doll learned that Leo had of late begun making the lengthy, three-cornered trip to Denver by rail every other week or so, always in the company of a young man named Rowland Price. The private Brannan car made the trip less arduous for Leo than for the common traveler on that route, but it was not clear just why Denver had become such a magnet for the man. He had been in the habit of visiting the Denver Mining Exchange no more than twice a year until recently, and had not even owned a private railroad car until the advent of the mysterious Mr. Price.

There was speculation throughout the town, and presumably in Denver too, over the back and forth journeyings of western America's richest son, but Mr. Garfinkle confessed himself ignorant of their meaning. "I guess I'd be the last to know," he said, and Lovey Doll silently agreed. She believed Mr. Garfinkle admired her person very much, but was too afraid of his wife to do more than glance in Lovey Doll's direction, even when addressing her in conversation at the dinner table. The other guests at Mrs. Garfinkle's were equally nonplussed, but surmised that whatever it was that took their patron away from the valley for days at a time, it was bound to make him more millions, and that could only be good for everyone in Glory Hole.

Lovey Doll's stratagem for causing her path to cross that of Leo was arrived at after considerable thought. It had the boldness and simplicity of a classic maneuver, and while not in any way original, would almost certainly prove effective when used upon a man as unworldly as Leo Brannan, for all his wealth, apparently was. The one unknown factor was Price, who seemed to have become closer to Leo than his own shadow; Lovey Doll would cope with his presence somehow.

The car had been a worthwhile, if extravagant, investment. Painted a deep maroon, with gilt curlicues around the windows, it presented a splendid sight. The interior was velvet plush, the studded leather armchairs commodious, the sleeping quarters palatial by any standard. At one end of the car was a small kitchen, amply stocked with fresh food and old liquor, more than Leo alone, or Leo and Rowland Price together, could possibly have consumed on the ride to Denver and back. The modern toilet apparatus, with its hand-carved mahogany seat and porcelain pedestal, was the last word in comfort. Leo, still not trustful of the menacingly sloshing cistern poised above the user, referred to it as his throne of Damocles.

En route to Denver again with Price, Leo pondered his new and secretive way of life. He was aware of Glory Hole's conjecturings regarding the frequent trips, and had no plans to satisfy anyone's curiosity. The scenario laid out for him by the Praetorians was a long-term venture, with public declaration at least five years distant, or whenever the newborn cabal within Big Circle was assured it could successfully take control of its parent. He was being groomed for the role of a lifetime, and his visits to Denver, being newsworthy because of his fame, were explained to reporters as business meetings at the Mining Exchange.

Such meetings did take place, but there were other, more important gatherings for Leo to attend. Surprisingly, the members of Big Circle who previously had blackballed the admission of Leo Brannan into their ranks had relented quite suddenly, and issued the most cordial of invitations. Price had been suspicious of the offer at first, then advised Leo to accept. "After all, to be a Praetorian, you must first be *persona grata* with Big Circle. Now you may talk to every man inside the larger group, and not alert them to the stirrings within their own organization. It's the perfect cover, a Trojan horse that places you inside the citadel years in advance of our own plans! You'll be within the circle that's within the circle, Leo, and only the initiated will know."

Access to Leo whenever he visited Denver was strictly controlled by Price. After departing from the smoky chambers of the Mining Exchange, he was escorted to the plush sanctums of Big Circle, where he saw several of the same faces he had seen at his previous engagement, and from there he would be taken to another place, wherein several of the individuals he had so recently been talking with also appeared. Leo was obliged to learn who was an important figure in Colorado's mining elite, who a part of Big Circle, and who a Praetorian. Some men were all three, and the juggling of their separate identities was not an easy task for Leo. The secret of his being the newest Praetorian was entrusted to a very few. He was whisked from his hotel room via back stairways and closed car-

riages to their various meetings, and these were never held in the
same place twice.

Leo found he took to the atmosphere of mystery and subterfuge
with an enthusiasm that was almost boyish, and was heedful never
to reveal this aspect of his participation, even to Rowland Price,
who accompanied him everywhere. Price was well liked by all members of Big Circle, and so was considered by the Praetorians to be
the ideal companion for their leader-in-waiting. For Leo, the excitement of being feted and flattered had come too late in life to turn
his head. He considered himself a practical man, a pragmatist, and
no fool to be manipulated by scheming inferiors. He accepted the
Praetorians for the idealists they clearly were, and was committed
to their cause. Still, he would have cooperated with none of it had
the pursuit of a clandestine goal proved less invigorating. Leo
required the stimulus more often, now that he had become accustomed to it, and so would travel to Denver on the least pretext, not
just to satisfy the faith held in him by others, but to get away from
Elk House and Zoe.

It had not been his fault she had lost her arm, but his wife's
behavior suggested it had. Leo no longer pretended to understand
the workings of Zoe's mind. Her thoughts were as hidden from him
as her daughter's. They were strange birds of distinctly esoteric
feather, and he felt uncomfortable in their presence nowadays. His
own secret life paralleled that of his wife and stepdaughter, and Elk
House contained two separate worlds as a result. He supposed he
had never truly understood Zoe. It was she who had caused his elevation to the upper strata of the very wealthy with her belief in
Omie's vision of a golden stag beneath the ground, yet Zoe had not
once reminded him of it, nor mentioned her audacious salting of the
worthless mine she had bought for him from his partners. She gave
the impression of being above such tawdry stuff as the accumulation of riches, and her silence on the subject of Leo's fortune and its
peculiar beginnings had of late begun to irritate him. Zoe's removal
of herself and Omie from his life was a kind of insult, Leo thought,
a standing away, as if the business he practiced was far below the
realm occupied by the pair of incomprehensible females he once had
shared a humble cabin and life with.

Everything had changed, and the changes had begun long before
Zoe lost her arm. Leo doubted that what had been left behind would
ever return, and compensated himself for the loss (he had genuine-

ly been fond of them both) by concentrating even more intensely on those things of the material world which they rejected. Leo was a comparatively young man still, with physical needs that were no longer met by his legal bedmate. The absence of carnal love in his life was something Leo had not dared to dwell upon at length, preferring to lose himself in his usual work as owner of the nation's most successful string of gold mines, and more recently as the undisclosed agent of political reform awaiting his chance to walk upon an even larger stage. Satisfaction of the flesh was not essential to the business of living, even if its denial did produce innumerable sleepless nights.

As he watched some of the most beautiful land in the west roll by his window, Leo felt a little sorry for himself. It seemed that a man could never have all that a man required, but must sacrifice a measure of something or other in order to maintain whatever it was that pleased him most. Leo was not ready to accept that wealth was the thing that pleased him most, but it was certainly the only commodity he possessed in abundance. If there was a moral lesson to be drawn from his life, he could neither approve of nor acquiesce in the meanness of its parameters. He was not a happy man, and so was ideally positioned to embrace salvation in the appealing form of Lovey Doll Pines.

It was Price who first made him aware. Leo had been lost in thought as he stared at the mountainside ravines, when Price approached him. "We have a stowaway," he said.

"Pardon?"

"A woman on the front platform. She must have climbed over the rail from the last passenger car. She says she won't go away until you speak with her."

"Remarkable. Is she a lunatic?"

"Not in my opinion."

"What does she want to speak with me about?"

"She wouldn't say. She was most polite."

"Then I suppose I'll have to see her before she tries to climb back and falls under the wheels."

"I'll open her purse first, if you don't mind."

"What for?"

"To be sure she isn't carrying a pistol."

"Good God, Rowland, have you been reading dime novels? Why on earth would she wish to shoot me?"

"Who knows? A grudge of some kind, real or imagined."

"But you say she appears sane."

"Attractive too, but that's beside the point. If you want to see her, I'll have to search her purse."

"Then do so, and don't keep the lady waiting."

Lovey Doll was presented to Leo several minutes later. He thought her a most presentable woman, smartly dressed, with a charming smudge of soot on her blushing cheek.

"Good day to you, ma'am."

"And to yourself, Mr. Brannan. I apologize for the dramatic intrusion, but really, how else does a nobody such as myself find a way into your presence?"

"How indeed. Please sit down. Price, be so kind as to fetch our guest a cup of coffee, would you?"

Lovey Doll arranged herself in one of the leather armchairs. Leo took a silk handkerchief from his breast pocket and offered it to her. "Pardon me, but you have a trace of smokestack on your left cheek."

She took the handkerchief and dabbed at her face.

"I am Miss Imogen Starr, Mr. Brannan, and I have a bone to pick with you."

"What manner of bone might that be, Miss Starr?"

Lovey Doll took from her purse a newspaper clipping, and handed it to Leo. He scanned it briefly, recognizing it as a story from the previous week concerning the discovery in New Mexico of a mutilated corpse, its innards strewn around for the buzzards to eat. "Yes, a shocking business, to be sure, but why bring it to my attention, Miss Starr?"

"Because the party responsible for the outrage is without a doubt the same fiend who came from your Grand Mogul mine so very recently with blood upon his hands."

"Oh, well now, I don't quite see how we can make such a bold assumption as that, Miss Starr. The fellow who was trapped, Slade, might be anywhere at all. He could have reached New York by now if he chose. It makes small sense to commit further outrages such as this New Mexican incident, when all he needs to do is lay low."

"A man of sound mind would do exactly that, Mr. Brannan, but it is my belief this Slade person is mad, an animal in the guise of a man. This is his work, I know it, and since he escaped from your mine, don't you think it would be a responsible act on your part to declare a connection between Slade and the latest outrage, before he quenches his thirst for blood again? Another such attack and the newspapers will certainly draw the conclusion I have shared with you. You must get there ahead of the press, Mr. Brannan, by personally posting a reward for the criminal. Your name alone would stimulate great interest in the affair, and in all likelihood lead to a quick arrest and hanging for the brute. Pardon my forwardness, but you do see the merit of my argument, do you not?"

"Oh, indeed yes. After he disappeared there were stories about his peculiarity of temperament, nothing very far from the ordinary, but in retrospect it may be that he was in actual fact a maniac of some kind. The accepted notion was that he ... did what he did solely out of self-preservation, quite disgusting, of course, but understandable under the circumstances. And now you have opened my eyes, Miss Starr, to the fellow's true nature. This may indeed be his handiwork, and you may very well be correct in assuming there will be other instances before too long."

Price returned and set down a silver coffee tray.

"Rowland, have you heard what Miss Starr has to say?"

"The latter portion, yes. Milk, Miss Starr?"

"Thank you."

"And what do you think?"

"I believe Miss Starr has introduced an original slant on a tragedy most of us have been trying to forget."

"Are you agreeing that she's right?"

"The point to consider is, if Miss Starr's theory is sound, her suggestion is masterly. A reward for the capture or death of Slade would reflect well upon the company that inadvertently spawned him."

"You're not suggesting that we created the fellow."

"Not at all, but we can certainly take the lead in eradicating him, can we not?"

Leo recalled the almost jocular tone some newspapers had adopted when it was revealed that he had presented the cannibal with one hundred dollars which undoubtedly was used to facilitate Slade's escape from Glory Hole. Justice would be served if Miss Starr's plan was adopted, and every newspaper reader would be made aware of it, thereby expunging any lingering sense of guilt or responsibility Brannan Mining might be perceived as having to account for.

"Miss Starr, I believe you fell onto the platform of my car direct from heaven."

"Oh, no, Mr. Brannan." Lovey Doll laughed. "I am an earthly creature to be sure."

Price assumed Miss Starr would be set down at Leadville and provided with a ticket back to Glory Hole, but Leo seemed quite taken with her company, and chatted in a most cordial fashion with her all the way south to Salida, where once again she was not asked to leave. Price said nothing then, nor when night began to darken the mountains and the car lamps were lit. The chef prepared a dinner for three, at which Leo consumed more wine than usual and laughed aloud at Miss Starr's many quips and comments. As the hour drew late, Price suggested that their guest might prefer to retire in comfort to the sleeping quarters he was prepared to vacate for her sake, and Miss Starr agreed with many thanks. Price tossed uncomfortably in an armchair until dawn, and was in a less than ebullient mood as breakfast for three was served while the train steamed north along the Front Range, through Colorado Springs to Denver.

Price began to worry once he became aware, when the train reached its destination, that Leo intended seeing more of Miss Starr. Taking Leo to one side, he said, "Are you sure this is wise?"

"Wise? To buy her dinner? Shame on you, Rowland. The lady has brought us a wonderful idea, at considerable risk to herself. Would you have me send her away with nothing more substantial than a thank you for her pains?"

"Miss Starr certainly deserves our gratitude, but Leo, you don't entertain thoughts of seeing any more of her after tonight, do you?"

"Certainly not. I believe you see yourself as my chaperon sometimes."

"Please select a restaurant with dim lighting. I suggest a private booth. If word of this perfectly innocent dinner engagement was to be passed around, it would do you no good at all."

"I'm aware of that, and can assure you no harm will come to anyone. You worry too much."

"Leo, a man in the public eye can worry too little, but never too much."

"I shall have it engraved in stone."

Price's concern increased over the next two days. Leo escorted Imogen Starr to the theater, and after that to another dinner, this time at a restaurant far more popular among Denver's elite than the shadowy place where he had dined her on the first evening. He

bought her several dresses of expensive cut, insisting that her own
had been ruined by exposure to flying particles of soot on the platform of his car. He bought hats to match the dresses, and purses to
match the hats, then shoes to match the rest of Imogen's ensemble.
She was a delight to lavish money upon, he said with a smile, and
Price felt a chill invade his stomach; Leo was not behaving as he
ought to do.

When details of the plan to list a reward of five thousand dollars
for the apprehension of the man-eater Slade were made public, Leo
attended the declaration with Imogen in tow, and scandal was
avoided only by Price's insistence that she view the proceedings
from his side, rather than Leo's. Imogen obeyed, but Price had
glimpsed a tiny spark of angry fire in her eyes as she sat beside
him. The look she directed at Leo while he made the announcement
to a carefully assembled group of reporters was bright with admiration of the worst kind; Price knew Leo had a smitten woman on his
hands. Matters proceeded to worsen when Leo informed Price that
Miss Starr would be returning to Glory Hole in Leo's private car.
That was bad enough, but the revelation that Rowland would not
accompany them came as a shock.

"Leo, this is madness. ... I confess I find myself disturbed by this
course of action."

"I'm aware of your concern, but my mind is made up. The chef
will also take another train. We'll serve ourselves dinner and enjoy
each other's company like civilized people. I must have some
moments of personal privacy, Rowland, like any man."

"As you wish."

Price decided the matter should not be raised with the Praetorians yet; Leo might well burn the foolishness out of himself on the
ride back to Glory Hole, and there the incident could rest, no danger to the man or the political movement Leo had thus far devoted
much of his personal time toward. Price was aware of the many
marital infidelities transpiring among the wealthy of Denver; the
perpetrators were seldom if ever hauled before the court of public
opinion to explain themselves, and the betrayed marriages
remained marriages, despite the hollowing of their foundations. He
supposed something of this nature was bound to occur sooner or
later, given that Leo's wife was not a normal woman. Zoe Brannan's
peculiarities and disfigurement would not in any way keep Leo

from the highest public office; in fact, as a tragic figure kept well behind the scenes she might well assist him by way of her reclusiveness. But Imogen Starr was another proposition entirely. Price could see in her the lineaments of ambition, a yen for importance that Leo unwittingly was feeding, with his dinners and clothing and evenings at the theater. Price had been impressed by the quickness of her mind, but now saw her differently. If Imogen Starr was digging for gold the easy way, he would find her out and reveal to Leo the true face of his paramour. No woman was worth the ruination of a career about to be elevated to a broader plane. Rowland Price promised himself, and Leo, that he would never allow such a thing to happen. Meantime, he would by careful inquiry seek out information on the lady in question.

Afterward, Leo would be able to plot the course of his decline from the moment when he made his impulsive decision to journey with no one but Imogen Starr for a day and a night on the long, boxed route to Glory Hole. That had been the beginning, not Price's announcement that a woman had climbed onto the private car's platform and was demanding to see him. At the outset, however, as he and Imogen watched Denver recede from the rear platform of his car, he felt nothing but anticipation of the most agreeable kind racing in his blood. Special champagnes had been loaded aboard, and a supper of cold meats, fresh fruit and sherbet prepared in advance.

Leo could not be sure to what extent Imogen knew what was to follow; she exhibited at first a charmingly coy reluctance to accompany him on the return trip, then had agreed, her cheeks aflame. He decided she was probably as unfamiliar with the ways of the opposite sex as himself; Leo had had carnal relations with only two women before marrying Zoe, neither one for any extended period. Imogen struck him as less than virginal—no female as attractive as she was could possibly have escaped the predatory attentions of men—but she conveyed a modicum of bashfulness that appealed to him very much. He wanted her, and was fairly certain she could be had, if he only made love to her in a way calculated not to shock or disturb her obvious regard for him as a famous man. The meal and champagne would lower her resistance, he was sure, and bolster his own slight nervousness at the same time. All would proceed as he wished it to, and Leo crammed intrusive thoughts of Zoe into the furthest corner of his mind, the better to pursue what he regarded as something owed him by virtue of his station and his tremendous forbearance in the face of coldness heaped upon him like snow by his wife.

Lovey Doll could scarcely believe the ease with which her scheme was bearing fruit of the most satisfying kind. Leo Brannan was as guileless as a schoolboy, as proud to have her on his arm as any other fool eager for her flesh. She was disappointed to find in so famous a personage the standard reaction to her beauty. He had presented no challenge at all, and now, as the silver rails behind them were made invisible by darkness, Lovey Doll prepared herself for the performance of a lifetime. The direction her remaining years would take depended on what was to follow, and she was determined, as only a single-minded individual can be, to guide the evening according to her own agenda, even though Leo Brannan might assume matters were proceeding according to his. He was already nervous, she could tell, seeing the light sweat that sprang to his forehead beneath the receding hair. She knew also, as if she had seen it revealed in a crystal ball, that when the sun rose tomorrow over the shining mountains, the man beside her would belong to Lovey Doll Pines, body and soul and fortune too.

35

Since her illness, the invisible hands that once had sprung from Omie's midriff to grasp and move the furniture of Elk House had not manifested themselves once. Omie had tried on several occasions to make them come forth, wishing to reassure herself that, like old and familiar toys, the giant hands were still available for her amusement and distraction; but they were not. It must have been the illness that killed them off, Omie concluded, all the heat from her fever somehow burning the hands and their equally invisible arms away to nothing. She had not missed them at first, her attention having been caught up by her mother's sad condition. Zoe had lost a real arm and hand, obliging Omie to see her own loss as trivial by comparison.

Now that Zoe was no longer so sad, Omie wished she had her unique furniture movers back again. She summoned them by willpower, but they did not respond. It had been a long time, too, since she had been granted a glimpse of the future, and Omie felt for the first time that perhaps she was becoming an ordinary person. This possibility was not welcome. While forgoing the hands and visions would not in itself have distressed her overmuch, Omie felt that their passing from her should have been compensated by another kind of removal, the lifting from her face of the deep-blue birthmark. With that still in place, she could never hope to be anything but what she was—an ugly girl. She spent hours doing what she had not done before, examining herself minutely in her mirror, bringing her skin so close to the glass she could see its pores and the faintest of blemishes. Clearly, no trade-off was being prepared for her; the things that made her different appeared to be waning, while the thing that made her hideous was in no way diminished. It was not fair, but then, Mama had not been granted anything at all replace her lost arm; in fact she had lost her husband as well, or so it seemed to Omie.

The man she had learned to call Papa was seldom seen at home anymore. Mama had said Leo now had another house in town, a smaller house, nearer to the mines, so he had no need of Elk House. Omie sneaked into Leo's room one day and saw that his closets and drawers were half empty. He still came up the winding road from Glory Hole every ten days or so, to get things he required, but on the last such occasion he had not even bothered to seek out Omie for so much as a casual greeting, let alone the kiss on her cheek she had been accustomed to in times past. It was true that Omie had hidden herself in her room during that latest visit by Leo, but that did not excuse his not attempting to find her. Papa didn't care for her anymore, and it was obvious to Omie that the reason for it was his wish to avoid having to kiss that ugly blue cheek ever again. She assumed he no longer spoke to or looked at Mama for the same reason—an unwillingness to see her stump. While Omie could understand the retraction of Papa's love from their lives, she could not bring herself to forgive it. Leo was doing something he ought not to have done. It was not Omie's fault she was cursed with the blue mark, nor Zoe's for having lost her arm. Leo should have been able to see that, but apparently he chose not to. It was bitter medicine for herself and Mama to swallow.

One evening, Omie asked Zoe if her analysis of recent events was correct, and when Zoe said no, Omie demanded to know what other reason there could be for the withdrawal of Papa from their house.

Zoe put down her book. Omie's face was flushed with emotion; even the birthmark was darker than usual. It was time, Zoe decided, to tell Omie the little that she knew. The truth had come to her less than a week before, by way of the mail. The letter bore no return address, and was written with an awkward hand, unused to composition or the pen. The few lines contained references to an "absent husband" and his "dalliances" with a "scarlet hussy woman" by the name of Imogen Starr. Zoe had the very next day after receipt of the letter gone down to Glory Hole and knocked on the door of Leo's town house. The maid who answered had refused to allow her in, although the effort required to withstand Zoe's sudden rage had been considerable. The door having been shut in her face, Zoe retreated to the far side of the street and waited. Within minutes a figure appeared in an upper-story window, and Zoe knew the letter was truthful. The woman in the window was lovely, even at a distance, and it was clear why Leo had left instructions with the maid never to allow his wife inside. Against such beauty Zoe felt helpless. Even had she still possessed both arms, she could not have held Leo back from the woman displayed above her. Perhaps it was coincidence, but Imogen Starr had looked out the window at her rival while wearing a dress that revealed not only her creamy shoulders but the full extent of her shapely arms. Zoe had stood on the sidewalk, mesmerized by her own dismay, until her rival reached up and drew shut the curtains.

Omie's sullen face demanded to be told, and Zoe did exactly that. When she was done, having encapsulated her betrayal in a few crisp sentences, she saw Omie's expression soften with what Zoe recognized, surprisingly, as relief.

"Oh," said Omie. "I thought it was the blue mark."

"That's a foolish thought."

"Does Mr. Price live there with Papa and the lady?"

"I don't know, but I doubt it."

"He was always here when Papa was. Why wouldn't he be there too?"

"Because Mr. Price is a business partner, or acquaintance, or some such, not a ... friend, as this woman appears to be."

"So we're not Papa's friends anymore?"

"Not for the moment. We may be again, at some later date. That is how these matters are sometimes resolved."

"How long will it take, Mama?"

"That I cannot say. It may not happen at all. I tell you this because I hate to lie."

"I know. Mama, can't we go away from here until he comes home again?"

"Away?"

"To somewhere else, and when we come back he might be here again."

"Where would you like to go?"

Omie thought hard for a moment, then ran to the globe that stood in the corner of the library and dragged it back to Zoe.

"There," she said, stabbing a finger at the largest landmass she saw, and the furthest from America.

"That's China, Omie. There is a great deal of disease and suffering there. I shouldn't care to see it, so choose again."

"I want to go on a sailing ship somewhere."

"There are steamships now, that go much faster."

"I want it to be one with big white sails, or I won't go anywhere."

"You still have not decided where it is we're to go."

Zoe found herself lifted from the leaden mood that had settled over her since she'd sighted Imogen Starr in the window of Leo's love nest. Could Omie's simple plan have been all she needed to shake off sorrow? Zoe was not averse to it, and with every passing minute was absorbing more of Omie's intensity over the proposal. She had never been on the ocean, had never even seen it, and was as ignorant of foreign ports as her daughter.

"There," said Omie, pointing again. Zoe looked closer.

"Zanzibar. I believe the weather is appallingly hot there, my darling."

"Well, then, you pick where, Mama, only make sure it's over the sea."

"Very well."

She stared at the globe. It began to spin, although no one was touching it. "Are you doing that?" Zoe asked.

"Yes ... I haven't done anything like it for such a long time. I wasn't even trying to, Mama ..."

"Slow it down so I can see all the countries."

The globe lurched to a clumsy stop and rocked a little on its polished wooden stand.

"I've always wanted to see England. Would that please you? The climate there is mild, and the people speak the same language as us."

"It isn't very far, though."

"If you wanted to, we could go further, and see Europe."

"Yes! Oh, Mama, when can we leave? Can we go tomorrow?"

"Not so soon as that, but as fast as we can. First we must go by train to New York, then book passage on a steamer for England."

"No, a sailing ship!"

"Very well, a sailing ship if we can find one."

"We can stay away till Papa misses us and says to come home."

"Europe is further away than you might think. We would be gone for at least a year, or even longer."

"I don't care."

Zoe realized that she did not care either.

The departure of mother and daughter from Glory Hole was sudden. Leo Brannan heard of it from his coachman, who had taken Zoe and Omie to the station. Paying his first call to Elk House in two weeks, Leo found a letter on the mantel shelf of his room, explaining in vague terms the itinerary the runaways intended following. Zoe made it clear she expected letters of credit to be made available for her to pick up in New York City prior to embarking for Liverpool. She allowed Leo a year or more in which to come to his senses. If he did not, she wrote, there would be an unseemly public dissolution of the marriage. Annoyed at the brusqueness of her tone, and the utterly unapologetic manner in which she had absented herself and Omie from his life, Leo tore the letter to pieces and flung it into the fireplace. He wondered, as he descended from Elk House, what Rowland Price and the Praetorians would have to say about it.

Traveling the broad valley between Leadville and Buena Vista, Zoe was aware of the staring directed at herself and Omie. She could not be sure if the passengers had recognized them as the wife and stepdaughter of Leo Brannan, and were confused to see such illustrious folk riding in a common car, or if they were simply unable to detach their eyes from the unusual sight of a one-armed woman and a blue-faced girl. Either way, it was an annoyance, but she revealed nothing of her feelings, preferring to stare right back at the starers until their gaze faltered and was turned away for several minutes, when curiosity brought about its return. Zoe had worn a heavy veil to guard against recognition, and saw now that it had been a waste of time.

In time, Zoe tired of matching looks with her neighbors, and sought distraction elsewhere. Omie seemed content to watch the country rolling by, but she had the advantage of the window seat. Zoe's attention was drawn to the young man several seats away who had passed his eyes across them just once, then looked away, whether from politeness or sympathy she could not tell. The young man had recently shaved off his beard, the nose and cheeks being sunburned, the upper lip and chin pale. He appeared to be concentrating mightily on something in his thoughts, and his features changed subtly from moment to moment as he cogitated, granting him the look of a thinker. Zoe was convinced, simply by watching him, that the young man was both intelligent and troubled. She liked his face and form very much, and was reminded that her husband liked nothing about hers.

Closing her eyes, Zoe asked herself again if she was being bold or cowardly. If she had been asked for the truth at gunpoint, she would have admitted that her love for Leo had never been strong. It was not so much the loss of him that upset her, but his loss to a woman of such physical attraction. Zoe's anger over Imogen Starr's beauty was far more intense than her annoyance with Leo for having first neglected herself and Omie to concentrate on his shady doings with Rowland Price, and then abandoned them completely for the woman who paraded behind Zoe's eyelids like a lovely ghost come to haunt her waking hours. She must hope that Leo would tire eventually of so exotic a companion and assume the duties of husband and stepfather in time for their return from Europe. If his lust was not played out by then, Zoe was fully prepared to divorce him and begin her life over again, as she had done before. With mysterious Omie by her side, she would not lack for the necessary strength.

The handsome young man was watching her as Zoe's eyes opened, but his gaze was not intrusive. He smiled at her briefly, then looked out the window, his brow knitting as before. Zoe wished she could have sat beside him and talked of the things that caused him such an appearance of worry. Of course, she would do no such thing. Zoe allowed her eyes to close again. She was tired, having slept very little the night before their departure, and was looking forward to the arrival of night, so she might catch a little sleep in her seat. By morning they would be in Denver, where they would transfer to the Union Pacific line and continue east.

She opened her eyes again, fearful of nodding off and falling from her seat. The young man was gone. She looked around for him despite herself, but he was no longer in the car. The train was slowing down, but Zoe knew they were not yet anywhere near Buena Vista. Other passengers were becoming aware of the slowdown, and were craning their necks to see why.

"Mama, there are men on horses by the track."

Now there was an undercurrent of murmured alarm inside the car as the brakes were applied and the train slid to a gradual stop. "The men are coming, Mama." Zoe could see them herself, a half-dozen riders, all armed, their faces hidden by bandannas. "Robbers!" screeched a woman further down the car, and fainted dead away. The riders had dismounted and were boarding the train, two per car.

Zoe was in the lead car, immediately behind the baggage car attached to the tender and locomotive. One man stepped up onto the platform and came inside, but when he walked through the door from the platform, he was accompanied by another—the young man Zoe had so much admired. She thought at first he might have been a hostage to ensure the cooperation of the other passengers, but there was a pistol in his hand, and she felt a blow of disappointment to realize that it had been none other than he who had gone forward, probably over the roof of the baggage car, to point his weapon at the engineers and bring the train to a halt.

"Beg pardon, ladies and gents," he said, "but we have to cause you a little delay this fine morning. I thank you in advance for your good sense in not reaching for concealed weapons, or otherwise risking life and limb. Reach instead, if you please, for valuables and cash, and when these have been collected to our satisfaction, we'll be on our way. You first, sir, with that fine watch."

The second man stood watch at the end of the car while his young partner worked his way along the aisle, cajoling jewelry and wallets from stone-faced passengers. Zoe was angry with herself for having misinterpreted his character so foolishly. When the young man smiled at her and proffered his hat, already brimming with loot, she glared frostily at him and said, "I have nothing of worth."

"Oh, ma'am, that can't be so. Think harder and I'll bet you can recall a little something to surrender."

"She won't," said Omie, and the young man was seen by others to become hesitant, presumably because he was unused to being defied in the course of a robbery by two such unusual females as these.

"Ma'am, come on now, I don't have time to waste."

"Your life is a waste," Zoe told him.

"The ring, ma'am, it looks like gold from here."

"Oh, you wish to steal my wedding band from me? That must certainly be easier than working for a living."

"Ma'am, please ..."

"Here, take it if you must."

She thrust her left arm at him. The young man stared at the ring. Every other passenger who had lost rings had twisted them from their own fingers, but a one-armed woman obviously could not.

"Well?" Zoe challenged him.

Omie was staring at the Colt aimed at her mother, and nearby passengers observed that its muzzle began tilting upward in a series of tiny jerks. The young man was watching it himself, as if unable to understand why his own gun in his own hand should be doing such an unusual thing. Making a small sound of exasperation, he holstered his weapon and reached for Zoe's ring.

"Shame," muttered a woman nearby, and the young man stopped. It was then that Zoe noticed that the little finger was missing from his left hand.

"Get the hell moving, why don't you," said the man at the end of the car. "We ain't got all day, goddammit."

Drew backed away from his sister and niece with a smile and said, "Excuse me, ladies, I wasn't thinking."

He moved on to the next seat, and Zoe dropped her arm. Her heart was thudding in an alarming fashion, and she wished she could have hit the handsome young man with a cane or an umbrella for having disillusioned her with his fine and friendly eyes and beardless face. So great was her agitation, she was not aware when he left through the platform door at the far end of the car, and his companion turned and exited through the door he had guarded.

"They're getting on their horses, Mama."

Zoe looked through the window. Similar assaults on the other cars had been concluded, it seemed, and the robber gang was assembling to ride off with their takings. She searched for the young man, and thought she caught a glimpse of him behind a tall man with a feather in his hat, then the riders turned as one and set spurs to their horses, and were swallowed by dust as they rode for the western slope of the valley.

When Zoe and Omie reached New York they began looking through the newspapers for reports of the train robbery they had lived through, but found no mention of it. The Denver papers had included it in their evening editions before Zoe and Omie boarded a Union Pacific train and departed for the east. Apparently the story held little interest for New Yorkers, or else was already stale news, having occurred four days earlier. Instead, she found the front pages filled with news of the reward Leo had posted for the capture of the cannibal known only as Slade.

There were rehashed accounts of the Grand Mogul's collapse and the eventual discovery of a miner's gnawed remains. The hunt for Slade had been extended to most of the western states and territories, and there was talk of extending it nationwide, given the munificence of Leo Brannan's reward. There were many illustrations of Slade, each of them depicting, with variations, a brute of a fellow with wildly flying hair and beard and a deranged look about the eyes; in one of the city's less literate journals the picture actually suggested the man had fangs of a wolflike nature projecting over his lower lip. The reports simply confirmed for Zoe the great distance that had opened between herself and Leo in recent months. She had been given no prior inkling of his plans to boost the search for what the newspapers called the Colorado Cannibal.

Omie found the coverage fascinating. "Will they find him, do you think, Mama?"

"I couldn't say, and frankly, Omie, I would prefer not to be reminded of anything we have left behind us."

"He looks like the wild man from Borneo."

"And will probably be pickled and put on display if they capture him, like a freak of nature."

"Can we go see him if they do?"

"Omie, please! Now turn to the back pages for the shipping lists."

After considerable searching, they determined that the schooner *Acropolis* was scheduled to depart for England in two days' time. Zoe asked if Omie was still determined to go by sail rather than steam. "Yes," said Omie.

"Have you ... seen that we will arrive safely?"

"No, Mama; I haven't seen anything lately. I don't know if I can anymore."

"Well, no matter. I'm sure the *Acropolis* is a sturdy vessel. We'll book our passage first thing tomorrow."

"Will there be pirates when we cross the ocean?"

"No, there will not. I daresay there are more train robbers in the country nowadays than there are pirates in the whole world. The most we will lose on our crossing will be our supper. Steamships are far more stable, Omie. Won't you change your mind?"

"I want to see the sails flapping. Can't I?"

"Very well, but don't lay the blame at my door if you become ill."

"Can we see all the lights tonight? There are so many!"

Omie had spent much of the time since dusk at the window of their hotel room, amazed by the gas and electrical lighting of New York.

"After dinner, yes, we'll take a stroll."

Their walk around lower Manhattan was a delight. Zoe, as a girl in Schenectady, had never been near the big city, and its towering buildings were like something from a fairy tale, its bustling crowds like some eastern bazaar, and the brilliant lighting in the streets a scientific marvel. They paused outside a theater marquee studded with what appeared to be hundreds of lights, a frame of electric radiance around a sign declaring: NOBLE BURGIN'S GREATEST THEATRI-CAL OFFERING—THE NATION'S MOST POWERFUL DRAMA—SEE IT HERE UNDER EXCLUSIVE PRESENTATION—"RED HELLIONS" OR "BROTHERS IN BLOOD"—A TRUE STORY OF OUR TIMES—YOU WILL BE SHOCKED OR YOUR MONEY WILL BE REFUNDED.

"Mama, I haven't ever seen a play, have you?"

"No."

"May we see this one? It must be ever so thrilling."

"It sounds ghastly," said Zoe, recalling reports of its debut in Denver, to scorching notices that did nothing but persuade the public to witness for themselves the outrageous bloodletting on stage that had so irked the critics. She bought two tickets anyway, and they went inside.

Despite all the success *Red Hellions* had brought to himself and the Arcadian Players, especially since its transferal to New York, Noble Burgin was restless. The play had been penned almost a year ago, and his literary urges were again hounding him for release. As he applied makeup to his face for the evening performance, Noble could not help but wonder where he might possibly venture next, dramatically speaking. The very nature of the current success precluded any return to his former fare. He had established a bold precedent with his volatile mixture of mayhem and savagery, and was obliged to follow through, his current theatrical manager had advised, with another play of the same ilk. But where was the story to come from? The deadly redskins had been handed to Noble by way of the press, and his muse had seen instantly that it was the stuff of literary notoriety. His muse had not, however, seen fit to provide anything further, and Noble's enjoyment of his newfound riches was diminished as a result. He knew this to be the proof that he was indeed a true artist, less concerned with profit than with authoring a drama to last down through the ages, as the best of the Greeks had done. Noble yearned to be placed alongside the geniuses of ancient times, but knew it was not possible until he wrote another masterpiece, the equal of *Red Hellions*.

There had been comments concerning his portrayal of Augustus Chillington, the youth who had unwittingly released Panther Stalking and Kills With a Smile upon the southwest. The critics were unkind in their condemnation of a middle-aged man (Noble blanched at this) acting the role of someone thirty years his junior. Noble thought it outrageous that attention should be drawn to the extent of his waistline and the contour of his jaw, when Art was the thing being offered for consideration, not youthfulness. What callow actor of Augustus's age could possibly handle the delicacy of emotion that Noble conveyed, as realization that his childhood companions had become deadly killers of white settlers brought Augustus to a feverish resolve, and he swore on bended knee over the family Bible to avenge every unmerciful killing. No, it was a job for an experienced thespian, not some smooth-cheeked newcomer, and Noble was not about to allow any wet-behind-the-ears usurper to steal his thunder away, even if Hortense and Marcie had both been henpecking him over the issue. "You are becoming a laughingstock," his wife had said, and Marcie had been even more cruel. "When you rescue me from the burning stake," she had said, referring to the climactic scene, wherein Augustus saved his bride-to-be from a fiery fate before dispatching the redskins with his pistol, "kindly do not squeeze me so hard against your belly, or the audience will not be able to see me. And your breath, Noble, has deteriorated of late."

Noble was aware that Marcie, who in times gone by had permitted him various liberties about her comely person, no longer allowed such intimacy in shadowed corners and behind locked doors. She had made it known that she had eyes for Monty, the strapping stagehand who dreamed of becoming an actor himself someday, "The perfect type," Marcie had hinted, "to play Augustus—beneath your masterly direction, Noble, of course." The same suggestion had been made by Hortense, who saw Monty as a means of reclaiming her husband's affections.

It was all becoming too much, Noble thought. He might consider surrendering the role, he admitted, if only he had some other project to occupy his attention. The writing of another play would fill this requirement admirably, but the necessary inspiration had not shone down upon him. He had tried many times to cudgel a suitable drama from his brain, but nothing came of it but a sense of frustration. Where was the story that would deliver him from his travails!

Noble's mood suddenly brightened. He set down his paints and rushed to the door of his dressing room. "Johnny!" he called. "Johnny, my lad, where are you!" A boy of fifteen answered his call and came at a run. Johnny was the theater's general factotum, its fetch-and-carry boy, and he was in awe of Noble Burgin. "Yessir, Mr. Burgin, sir?"

"Johnny, put wings upon your feet and bring to me without delay the evening editions." He handed the boy ten cents. "You may keep the change if you return within five minutes. Now fly like the wind!"

"Yessir!"

Johnny returned, red of face and three cents wealthier, before Noble had time to apply a complete layer of makeup to his cheeks, an act he was obliged nowadays to perform in order to hide the lattice of burst capillaries there. "Thank you, my boy, and may the proscenium never descend upon your shapely head. Go now."

Johnny vacated the dressing room, rubbing his pennies, and Noble set out the newspapers for his perusal while he worked at erasing thirty years from his face. Very few of those years were painted away before he saw the story he had been searching for. It leapt at him from the pages as if set down in print for himself alone, the perfect vehicle for his talents and those of the Arcadians. A cannibal story! It was a breathtakingly daring concept, but he knew, as he scanned the gist of each paragraph, that only this monstrous event in distant Colorado (scene of Noble's recent resurgence to fame—an omen, perhaps?) could overreach *Red Hellions* and bring even vaster audiences flocking to the marquee bearing his name. *The Man-eater! or Horror in a Gold Mine.* It was a stroke of genius to have summoned Johnny when he did! He would give the boy another dime tomorrow, just for bringing him the salvation he needed. Dame Fortune was smiling on Noble again, and he could think of no one more deserving.

He applied himself to preparations for the evening role, his mind humming with character and plot. He would play Slade himself, naturally, and no one would laugh at him, since the fellow's age was stated in the newspapers to be around fifty. He hoped the real cannibal was not caught, since he was already shaping a scene wherein Slade confessed his crime to God at some forsaken place in the wilderness. Noble would have liked to play the role of God also, but since that was impossible, and because he wanted no other actor in the troupe to have a role the equal of his own, he would represent God as a burning bush or some such thing, an interesting challenge in stage effects. Virtually the entire play would take place beneath the earth, a daring idea in itself, and would be in the form of a grand soliloquy every bit as moving as Hamlet's, and considerably longer, as Slade bemoaned his fate and debated with himself the morality of staying alive by feasting on the flesh of another man. It would be a play unlike any written or performed before. Noble would be hailed at last as one of the immortals, and rightly so. Then let Marcie comment on his belly, the little snip.

36

Being a drunk in Denver eventually became unacceptable to Nevis Dunnigan, so he rode a freight train to Glory Hole with every intention of becoming a drunk there. He owned no paints or brushes, these having been pawned along with his easel, so the move was accomplished with little inconvenience beyond his exposure to the elements en route. Nevis asked himself, as he rode beneath a boxcar, how it was that someone with as much talent as himself had become what he was, but no clear answer presented itself. He supposed it was fate, and found comfort in so romantically impervious a force. Because his failure as an artist was not his own fault, Nevis could continue drinking without substantial guilt or self-loathing. He liked to do nothing so much as he liked to drink, and since fate had been unkind to him, Nevis would treat himself to the thing he liked most, whenever and however he could get hold of it. The trip to Glory Hole was a two bottle ride, and he dropped from beneath the train in Leo Brannan's marshaling yards partially deaf in both ears from the continual grinding of steel upon steel, and bone dry.

He had no firm recollection of why he had chosen Glory Hole, but since he was there, Nevis decided he would make the best of his choice, and discover where the watering holes were located. A town the size of Glory Hole must have plenty, he told himself, and Nevis was not wrong. He asked for and received several free drinks in saloons along Brannan Boulevard, enough to revive him after his ordeal by rail, and he found a meal of sorts in the trash bins behind several of the restaurants in between the saloons.

Life was good, he felt, and Nevis had no regrets over his decision to relocate himself. By late afternoon he was actively searching for a barrel or packing crate in which to curl himself for sleep. No appropriate receptacle being encountered by sundown, which came early in a town jammed in a cleft between towering valley walls, Nevis compromised by wedging his body into a narrow space between a brick wall at the rear of a large building, and the lesser structure of wood nestling alongside. It was a tight fit, even for a man as thin as Nevis, but he did manage to squeeze himself in and sit down on a box that lay there. Fate had denied him greatness as an artist, but fate did provide boxes on which to sit when no more comfortable bed could be found. Nevis was proud of the mellowing within himself, which allowed him to see the world in such good-natured philosophical terms. He was almost asleep when Nightsoil Smith found him.

"Hey there."

Nevis opened his eyes. So little light remained in the sky that he could see nothing more than a bulky silhouette blocking the narrow space between buildings.

"Hey there," the silhouette said again.

"Good evening to you," Nevis responded.

"Need a place?"

"I do."

"Haul yourself out of there and come on with me."

Nevis trusted the cheeriness in the man's voice; it had a boister-ous edge that most likely came from alcohol, and Nevis knew from experience that drinkers were often a sharing breed. Sure enough, no sooner had he extricated himself from his hideaway than the fel-low produced a bottle and offered it without a word. Nevis drank deeply, then thanked him.

"No charge," said his new friend, and put out his hand. "Smith," he said.

"Dunnigan."

"I got a place that's warm, even got a little woman inside of it."

"You have all the elements of happiness, Smith."

"That I do. Come on."

Nevis followed him through a series of narrow alleyways to a shack built against the side of a stable. From the moment he had accepted the bottle from Smith, Nevis had been aware of an unpleasant odor clinging to the man, and as they drew near the shack, he learned the reason for it.

"See that wagon there?" said Smith, pointing through the stable's open door. "That's mine, every plank and nail. Got another'n behind it too."

Nevis could see a large metal tank of some kind behind the driver's seat.

"Are you a hauler, Smith?"

"Oh, I am that, yessir."

"And what is it, might I ask, that you haul?"

"Shit."

"Ah, yes—shit."

"Nightsoil Smith, I'm called. Haul away the shit from everyone's can—well, not everyone, but plenty. I make a living, good living at it." He passed the bottle again and they shared its dregs before approaching the shack. "Winnie, that's my woman, she can go get her own dang drink."

Passing through the doorway, Nevis found the odor unabated within, and decided to breathe through his mouth until such time as Smith's hospitality ceased and he could leave. The shack's interior was furnished with what appeared to be cast-off tables and chairs and cabinets, and the woman in domestic reign appeared herself to be one of society's castoffs. Although young, she had about her face the lines and shadows of middle age, and she did not look kindly upon the guest.

"Who's this?"

"Donovan," Smith told her.

"Dunnigan," Nevis corrected.

"What's he want?"

"You just wipe that look off of your face and be polite when I bring a friend home, you hear?"

Winnie turned away from them both and left the room, slamming a door behind her.

"She gets that way," Smith explained. "Don't mind her."

"No offense taken," Nevis assured him.

"There'll be grub; just sit yourself down."

Smith joined Winnie in what Nevis presumed was the bedroom. A pot simmered on the corner stove, tantalizing his nostrils. Nevis thought it might be stew, but the smell was difficult to identify, overwhelmed as it was by septic waftings from the stable. His garbage pickings of the afternoon had not fully satisfied the man within, and Nevis became impatient for supper; it was all very well for a stranger to invite him home after sharing a drink, but he saw no reason to place a man within sniffing distance of food and not dish up a bowlful immediately.

He approached the stove; definitely stew. Smith and Winnie were arguing behind the door, and rather than wait for a possible throwing-out if the woman won, Nevis picked up a greasy ladle and began scooping stew into his mouth. It burned his tongue and gums with exquisite fire, and he made small whimpering sounds of pleasure as taste overcame pain and his body begged for more. He managed to ingest several scoopings before the argument ceased and he was obliged to replace the ladle as he had found it. Nevis had time to wipe his chin before his hosts returned.

"Smells good," said Smith, rubbing his hands together.

Winnie began smacking bowls onto the table, and the men sat down to await her serving, Smith tipping Nevis a broad wink to let him know all was well. Soon all three were noisily eating. Smith ordered bread to go with the stew, and Winnie fetched it without a word. She had not spoken at all since leaving the bedroom.

"Come to Glory Hole for a reason?" Smith asked.

"My health," said Nevis. "I heard the mountain air takes years off a fellow's life, and I do so yearn to be a child again."

Smith stared at him for several seconds, then howled and slapped the table. "Hear that, Winnie? Hear what he said? A child again!"

Winnie glared at Nevis and bit into her bread.

"Men are children anyway," she said.

"Oh, you just need a drink," Smith chided. "Hell, I reckon we children do too, don't we, Donovan?"

"Dunnigan. Call me Nevis, please."

"Nevis? Well, all right, if you want me to."

Smith went outside with a promise to return momentarily.

"He hides it," said Winnie. "He thinks I don't know where, but I do."

"I see."

"You don't see a thing. What kind of work do you do?"

"I used to be a painter, as a matter of fact."

"Well, this place never saw a lick. Want to paint it? He can pay you, even if he looks like he couldn't. He saves it up and hides it away, every cent."

"Not that kind; a picture painter. An artist." He groaned, reminded of his former self. It was strange, he thought, that he should want to impress the drab thing across the table.

"Oh, that kind. You can paint my picture, then."

"I don't have my materials anymore; I'm sorry."

Winnie got up and fetched a stub of pencil and a creased sheet of paper with a jumble of scribbled figures on one side. She turned it over and presented both to Nevis.

"Show me."

"Very well. Sit, please."

Smith came inside with a bottle and sat down to uncork it before noticing the event taking place at the table.

"What's this?"

"He's an artist, he says, so he can just prove it."

"Artist?"

"I'll draw you too, if you like, Smith."

"Draw a picture of me? Hell, no one ever done that before. Had a camera picture one time, but I lost it."

"Cameras are machines. I am an artist. This pencil is not at all suitable."

"It's all we got."

Nevis completed the sketch and showed it to Winnie. The change that came over her features was startling, and for a moment Nevis saw how very young she was.

"He really is ...! Look!"

She thrust the paper at Smith, who took his time staring at it. "Looks like you, all right," he admitted.

"It's exactly how I am!"

Nevis had softened the lines bordering her lips and erased the dark shadows beneath Winnie's eyes in his rendering, as a form of politeness toward her; he had even worked a slight wave into her hair, and avoided any suggestion of a poor complexion. Winnie took the portrait back and looked at it again, mesmerized by Nevis's flattering version of herself. "You really are," she breathed.

"Thank you. Are there glasses?"

"I'll get them," said Winnie, and drifted away from the table, still admiring her sketch.

"You got her to smiling," admired Smith. "That's good, she's a whole different woman when she smiles. Don't happen often enough. Most of the time it's spitting and meanness, like a bobcat, but she can be a loving woman when she wants."

"Oh, you hush," said Winnie, returning with three cloudy glasses, but her voice was mild.

They began to drink, Winnie taking in as much as the men. Nevis was pressed for his story, and told them of his artistry's finest flowering.

"Only a brothel, if you'll excuse the word at your table, Miss Winnie, but a place of class and refinement, probably the finest in Denver; I can't be sure, not being a man to patronize such establishments. A work of epic proportions it was, with a multitude of studies from nature, as we artists express it; fifty-three, if my memory serves me, and that does not include the animals."

"There's animals in the picture too?"

"Yes ... dogs and cats here and there, you know, and a donkey eating hay; perfectly innocent behavior."

"But why didn't it make you famous?" Winnie asked.

"A sporting house is no gallery. Success such as I found in that venture—and they paid me well, I admit—does not bring further reward in the broader field of artistic endeavor. No, there were no commissions as a result of my efforts there, sad to say, and the money was all too soon gone where money was made to go."

"That's a shame," declared Winnie, fairly drunk by then.

"It is indeed, but I bear no malice. Fate, you see, has conspired against me, and in the face of such daunting opposition, I have bowed my careworn head before the inevitable."

"So you didn't come here to make pictures?" Smith asked.

"I came here for no reason at all, my friend, and I expect no reason to sustain me while I am here."

Smith beamed widely, revealing large green teeth. "I can give you a job, regular work, alongside of me. I need a man, I do. It's no favor; it's real work for real wages."

"He's a painter, not a shit collector."

"Well, I know that, stupid, but he needs a job just like anyone else does, to be paying his way till he paints a picture again, see."

"It's not his line, is it, Nevis?"

"I have no line anymore."

"Then you can get a new one, which is what I'm offering, dammit.

Are the both of you not seeing straight here? Work is work, that's the truth of it, and if you don't do something to get paid for, why then, you're just a scarecrow without a home, and that's no good, nossir, not for someone that ain't crippled and can't do nothing anyhow, which Nevis ain't a cripple, are you, Nevis?"

"There are many pathways to failure," said Nevis grandly.

"That's what I mean, see; you need a job."

The conversation pursued an elliptical course, with much shouting and not a little laughter. When the bottle finally was emptied, all three felt they were the oldest of friends, and the last secret between them was placed on the table alongside the bottle when Winnie left to relieve herself. "Used to be a whore down Leadville way," confided Smith, "but she's got a good nature if you stay on the right side of her. I'd be a lonely man, I reckon, without my Winnie, and I don't care who knows."

"A charming companion," agreed Nevis. "You're a lucky fellow, Smith."

"That I am, and so're you." Smith winked.

"To be sure."

"No, you are, same as me. She likes you. We're lucky, the both of us, see. I let her, so don't you be worried."

Failing to understand, Nevis smiled and nodded, and saluted Winnie on her return. "Hail, Winifred, queen among women, morning bloom of femalekind ... and pretty besides!"

Her face became flushed beneath its coating of grime as Winnie gave him a curious smile and took herself into the bedroom, closing the door behind her.

Smith winked again. "Give her a minute. Bottle's gone anyway. Need to piss?"

"I believe I do, yes."

They went out together and pissed twin streams beneath a full moon. "Over there," said Smith, pointing to the outhouse. "For shitting, if you need to."

"Not at the moment."

"Just so's you know where. That one, that's always the first to get emptied when I do my rounds. Start at home, I do, and work all around town and come back, that's after I dump the honey, a course."

"Naturally. A man shouldn't bring his work home with him, now should he."

Smith chuckled pleasantly. "You're a funny feller, you are. We can work together, and you can stay here with us, I know she won't make no fuss. She likes you, see, so there's the extra thing to make you jump at the chance, all right?"

"All right."

"Good. She'll be ready now."

"Ready?"

"For us, you know?"

Nevis began to feel there was something in the relationship spelled out by Smith that had not been explained fully enough, but he was too drunk to attempt making sense of it. He followed his new employer inside the shack and through to the bedroom before becoming aware of his blunder.

"Excuse me, Smith ... Winnie. ... Uh, where shall I sleep—would you mind showing me?"

Smith shook his head, laughing softly, and began shedding his clothes. "No need to be shy," he said. "We're all of us God's creatures that he made, as my granny said."

"She wasn't thinking about what you're thinking about, though," said Winnie, her face barely visible above the comforter of the room's only bed.

"That she wasn't," Smith agreed, "but then, she was an old lady, with her thinkings behind her."

Winnie giggled and flung the covers aside for him to get beneath. Nevis caught a glimpse of her nakedness, and Smith's, and did not know what to do.

"Get them duds off and turn out the lamp, why don't you, Nevis."

"I ... uh ..., is this my bed too?"

"Ain't no other, is there, Win?"

"No other at all. Don't be all night over there."

Nevis began unbuttoning his shirt, aware of the inner quaking he wished would go away. At the age of twenty-nine, he was about to lose his virginity to an ex-whore, in the close presence of a shitcan emptier. It was not the tableau of romantic conquest he had once been in the habit of picturing for himself, but in the harsher light of waning expectations, the faces and opportunity turned toward him were the finest there could be.

Working with Nightsoil Smith drove Nevis deeper into the arms of his new companions, since their odor became his, and he was made unwelcome in the usual haunts of drinkers. Offended by the reaction to his aroma, Nevis drew away from society and found company enough with Smith and Winnie. They brought their liquor from a store with a window through which Smith could be seen from within; bottles were brought outside and cash quickly changed hands. "They give me a good price too," bragged Smith, "because of two reasons, which the first one is I'm a regular customer which they like, and the second reason is I said I'd come right inside the store if I ain't happy with the charge, see, so they keep me sweet the way I like, and they'll do the same for you on account of you're my partner now."

Nights in Winnie's double bed were drunken, orgiastic and remarkably amiable, given the conflicting temperaments of the participants. Nevis grew to realize, as the weeks passed, that he had become a happy man. It was such an unlikely sensation that he treated it as a man would a basket of fragile eggs, anxious for its preservation while anticipating its end. One evening he went so far as to declare that the man and woman who had saved him from celibacy and a life without hope were the finest human beings he could ever have wished to encounter in this or any other life. Three-fourths of the way through a bottle, all three broke down and cried.

"We love you, Nevis," sobbed Winnie.

"And I love you," he bawled, "both of you."

Winnie allowed the men simultaneous access to her body shortly after this declaration, as a means of cementing the bond each held dear.

Nightsoil Smith's work as driver and loader of a honey cart did not occupy all of his working day, especially after he had Nevis to assist him in the retrieval and emptying of shitcans from the back alleys of Glory Hole. "This line of work ain't gonna last forever," he advised his partner. "Leo Brannan, he says he's gonna put that newfangled plummery in every house and building in town, and that'll be the end of the honey cart."

"Plumbing, it's called."

"Once the plummery's inside everyplace, it's the end of the line for you and me, doing what we do, so it's a good thing there's the other line."

"Plumbing. Yes, a good thing."

With Smith's second wagon they would drive as far up the valley as the road allowed, then unhitch the mules and strike a path almost straight up, to an overhanging ledge of rock on the western slope. In the shadow of the ledge was a wall of ice that did not melt away all year, although it became a little smaller during the brief months of summer. The ledge provided Nightsoil Smith with his secondary occupation, as supplier of ice for the fancier restaurants of Glory Hole, and even, he had heard, the table of Leo Brannan himself, by way of a third party. "What we do here is we get connected to the richest man west of the Mississippi—ain't that something?"

"Indeed, but I've heard of a new process by which they are able to manufacture ice on demand."

"Huh? It ain't possible! Cold air, that's how ice gets made."

"It has something to do with salt, I believe."

"Salt! Who the hell wants salty ice! That's for Eskimos! You must've heard wrong about that."

"I hope so."

They hacked at the ice wall and wrapped the chunks in several layers of burlap before loading them onto the heavily blanketed mules for transportation to the wagon, then went back for more. When the wagon was filled, usually after four or five trips to the wall, the mules were rehitched and they returned along the road to town, where Smith delivered his cold cargo to three separate customers in the food business, and came away with enough dollars to make their efforts worthwhile.

"Smith," asked Nevis (even now he had not been made privy to the man's first name), "why doesn't anyone else go up and take the ice that's there for the taking? It doesn't belong to anyone, yet you and I can sell it for cash profit."

"Same reason we make money hauling turds, my friend: it's not the kind of work your regular feller wants to do, which is good news for us, I figure."

The domestic idyll Nevis imagined he had fallen into was broken on occasion by outbursts of inexplicable hysteria from Winnie, who sometimes gained liquor from sources other than Smith during the day while her men were working. An excess of drink would tip some finely balanced scale in her mind and reduce Winnie to a screaming shrew who drove Smith and Nevis from the shack with her abuse. She would call them the filthiest, vilest names, and Smith would respond in kind for a while, then admit defeat. Nevis witnessed these exchanges with mortification, but attempted to intercede only once, at which time Winnie threw a chair at his head and called him a no-dick fool, which Nevis thought unnecessarily hurtful and quite wrong in any case. He and Smith would beat a fast retreat on these occasions, with the evening bottle safely secreted beneath a protective armpit, and share their usual measure, and Winnie's too, in a place far from the stable and shack. "I sometimes wonder," Smith confided, "if she don't, you know, sell herself when we ain't there, and get the stuff thataway."

"Oh, I doubt it. I think Winnie is devoted to us both, in her own inimitable fashion."

"What's that mean?"

"It means, my friend, that she is an unusual creature, with unusual needs, some of which may not be met by our good selves, sad to say."

"Nevis, you can talk like a preacher when you want to, but at least I know what kind of lies a preacher's spouting."

"All I imply is, the lady, for all her wondrous virtues and elastic compliance, is her own woman, just as we, Smith old fellow, are our own men, and there are mysteries within each of us that the others will never divine, no matter how hard the effort to do so. Accept her as she is, and the morning that follows her bad temper will see Winnie welcome us back with open arms."

"Well, she always did get like this every now and then, even before you come along, so I guess that's just the way she is."

"Exactly so. You have a grasp of the obvious that most men would offer a limb for, Smith."

"You don't mean that." The shitcan hauler blushed.

"Oh, but I do. I'm a happy man, you see, and happy men speak their mind without hesitation."

"Is that right."

"You may be sure it is."

37

Leo was inclined to view Zoe's departure for Europe as desertion. She was his wife, and he had not given her permission to go anywhere. It was an insult, but he financed the grand tour Zoe and Omie were embarking upon because it left him free to pursue his dalliance with Imogen without fear of domestic upset. He was tempted to move Imogen into Elk House, purely for the convenience of having her near, but Rowland Price dissuaded him with a reminder that when Zoe returned there would be a tremendous fight if she found her very home had been invaded by the other woman. Leo demurred, but blamed Zoe anyway for the necessity of his continued visits to the house he had bought for Imogen.

News had reached Leo from his home state of California that the cannibal Slade was wanted there also, on a charge of double murder at a lumber camp in Mendocino County. This additional crime, when released to the press, sent the nation into another frenzy over Slade. Many people claimed to have seen him, especially in the southwest, where two more acts of a bestial nature had been committed against ranchers in remote areas, murders considered too gruesome to be detailed in print; "Extensive mutilation of the abdomen, chest and cranial cavity in both instances," was the fullest description published of Slade's newest outrages. Leo added another two thousand dollars to his reward for Slade's capture, and called for greater vigilance among the law officers and civilian populations of New Mexico and Arizona territories, which appeared to hold a fascination for the madman criminal. For all his derangement, Slade was credited with great cunning in having evaded capture so far, despite the hue and cry raised in his wake. Leo hoped for a quick return on his investment, but could not help admiring the way in which the creature seemed able to melt away into the desert country without a trace. His picture was everywhere, but Slade himself seemed invisible.

It was during one of his increasingly rare visits to his own home that Leo learned from the servants that a man had called at the front gate several times, demanding to see Zoe Brannan. He had been told on each occasion that she was away, and on the latest attempt to see her had been given the further information that she was overseas, and was not expected back for a year or more. It had been almost a week now since the man paid that final call. Leo was made curious by news of these visits, but had forgotten about it by the time he left Elk House with several more changes of clothing.

He was reminded of the stranger several days later, when Jenks, his secretary, announced that a certain person was in the waiting room outside his office, insisting that he meet with Leo face-to-face. "He refuses to give his name, sir," said Jenks. "I've tried several times to get it from him. Shall I have him escorted to the door?"

"If he won't state his name like an honest man should, then yes, have him thrown out."

"Yes, sir," Jenks said, and left to give the necessary order to the burly fellows Price insisted be posted near Leo's person at all times, wherever his location.

Jenks returned to Leo's office a few minutes later.

"Sir, he says ... he says he's the husband of your wife."

"I beg your pardon?"

"The husband of your wife, sir. He says he has tried several times to see her, but has learned she is not in the country, so he insists upon seeing you instead. He appears to be quite serious. Shall I have him thrown out?"

"No, send him in. Has anyone else heard what he said?"

"No, sir, only myself."

"Keep it that way, Jenks. I don't want this sort of nonsense getting around, even if the fellow's a simpleton."

"Yes, sir."

Leo felt a strange humming in his head. He knew that his life was about to change. The claim was outrageous, but he half believed it even before the fellow set foot inside his office. The door opened and closed, and there he stood, a man without any stamp of uniqueness whatever, an anonymous individual wearing anonymous clothing much in need of repair.

"Your name," demanded Leo.

"Bryce Aspinall."

"What do you mean by saying you're the husband of my wife? That's a patent lie. What is it you want?"

"She's my wife, not yours. We were never divorced, you see, so she's still legally mine."

"A lie. She told me her husband was dead."

"Then it's her that lied."

"You claim to be Omie's father, I suppose."

"No, that was some other man. She already had Omie when I married her."

"Where did this alleged marriage take place?"

"Pueblo. These are notarized copies of the certificate."

Aspinall handed several sheets to Leo. They appeared authentic, but could have been forgeries. He would assign to Price the task of verifying their content.

"You're saying that my wife is a bigamist, sir."

"She's not your wife," Aspinall said again, "she's mine. You have the papers there. The minister who married us is still living, and will confirm what I say, if the papers don't convince you."

"Why would Zoe lie to me?"

"To be married again, to a rich man this time."

Leo realized Aspinall was unaware that he had not been rich when he and Zoe married. He wondered how little the man knew about other matters pertaining to the ceremony between himself and Zoe.

"What precisely do you hope to gain from bringing this story to me?"

"A small piece of what you and her have got."

"You mean this is an appeal for money?

"Yes, it hurts me to say. I'm not a proud man anymore, Mr. Brannan. My hands are crippling up with rheumatism, so I can't do the work I trained to do."

"What work is that?"

"Stonemason. I need a pension of some kind. I don't ask for thousands, just a regular payment to keep myself in the common comforts. It's not too much to ask. I wouldn't have bothered you if Zoe was still here to look after this."

"I see. May I ask what it was that caused you to be separated?"

"We just ... drifted away; her from me, me from her. It was after our boy died. We did have a son, and with him gone ... That's how it is sometimes, Mr. Brannan. Marriages aren't made in heaven like they say. It just worked out that way, and she never did want to admit she knew me after that, is my guess."

"Where are you staying at present, Mr. Aspinall?"

"The Great Divide."

Leo knew the place, a cheap hotel several blocks away.

"This has been a considerable surprise to me, of course. I don't see why I shouldn't help you, in the absence of my wife ... of Zoe, but first I should like to consult with my attorney; you can see why, I'm sure."

"It's only natural, sir. I want you to be aware that my motive is not mercenary, even if money is the reason for my approaching you this way. I ask only for a reasonable pension."

"And I'm sure the matter can be resolved to our mutual satisfaction. Be assured, I shall be in touch."

"Thank you." Aspinall began moving toward the door. "I heard you were a solid gentleman, and I see now it's true."

"Good day to you."

When his visitor was gone, Leo sent Jenks to fetch Rowland Price from the barbershop he had departed for just minutes prior to the first announcement of Aspinall's arrival. When Price hurried into the office, one sideburn trimmed and the other still bushy, Leo told him what had occurred, and handed him the papers Aspinall had left.

Examining them, Price was appalled. "This is a disaster. ... Would your wife truly have done such a thing?"

"My wife is a peculiar woman in many ways, Rowland. If this fellow disappointed her as a husband, I can picture her consigning his memory to some cellar of the mind, the better to get on with her life. The fact that Omie is not his could only have made Zoe's choice easier. I want you to go immediately to Pueblo and verify this certificate. Find out everything you can about the marriage. In the meantime, I'll have a small amount of money delivered to him at the Great Divide to keep him quiet."

"Is that wise, Leo? It might encourage him to demand more. He seems content to ask for very little at the moment."

"The risk is mine, Rowland. Leave as soon as you can, please."

Alone again, Leo went to his window and looked across Glory Hole. The view was relatively unimpaired, the sky clear for once. Glory Hole belonged to him only because he had married the woman who made the original strike high up on the valley wall. That strike had become the Deer Lick mine, still the most productive and trouble-free of them all. The claim on that precious land was in the name of one Zoe Dugan, Leo recalled. The claim might be invalid, since Zoe had in fact been Zoe Aspinall at the time, if his visitor's story was true. If the claim was not invalid, and Zoe had legally owned the Deer Lick, then all the subsequent expansion, all those other mines tapping into the same mother lode, might also be hers, since every additional claim had been financed by profit from the Deer Lick.

Leo's mind began to race with potential repercussions. He had never before questioned the chain of finance and ownership; now its genesis was critical. If Rowland came back from Pueblo with a report confirming the worst, there was a labyrinth of legal documents to sort through; decisions would have to be made. Behind the dreadful tangle of possibilities loomed one all-important question, frightening in its implications, a question terrible to contemplate: after all Leo's efforts in establishing the town and the mines as the center of gold production in America, did Glory Hole actually belong to Zoe?

Price returned after four days to deliver bad news. Reluctant to broach such an explosive topic in his office, Leo received him at Elk House, and listened with a sinking heart.

"The fellow carved his own tombstone, Leo, then simply walked away, and Omie ... well, Omie predicted everything, according to the newspaper files. There was quite a hullabaloo, then your wife left town with her."

"Rowland, we need no longer refer to Zoe as my wife."

Price had confirmed the legitimacy of the marriage certificate, and sought out pictures of Bryce Aspinall that had appeared in the *Chieftain.* The man was who and what he said he was.

"Have you decided what to do about this?" Price asked.

"Not yet."

"If you were of a mind to divorce Zoe because of ... recent developments, you could have the marriage declared null and void on the basis of her bigamy."

"The problem does not lie with my love or lack of it for Zoe, Rowland. The problem has to do with the nature of property rights. Ownership, Rowland, is the problem. I have been engaged in research of my own in your absence, and the results may startle you."

"Should I pour myself a drink and be seated?"

"Pour for us both. What I have to tell you has gone no further than Jenks and my attorney. They have plowed through documents and lawbooks by the cartload, and they have found no way around the predicament."

"What predicament?"

"I am not the owner of Brannan Mining. She is."

"This has to be some kind of mistake.... It's impossible! Brannan Mining not owned by Leo Brannan?"

"Believe it, Rowland. The mining claim regulations are a Gordian knot only a lawyer could disentangle, and it has been done. Ownership of the company is in this instance directly linked to ownership of the original claim. The Deer Lick was the rock upon which everything else was built, and the Deer Lick is Zoe's, even though she registered her claim under the name of Zoe Dugan. It is allowable under Colorado law for a deserted woman to assume her maiden name if she so chooses. If I were her legally wedded spouse, half of what she owns would be mine by law, but she is not my wife, and so I have nothing. My life and work, Rowland, have been a house of cards, because of Zoe's lie."

"But it was the sale of your claim along the creek, the one you dug with your partners, that enabled you to begin the work of buying up other claims."

"I netted ninety thousand for it from the Rocky Mountain Mining Corporation, which you may not have heard of, since the company has been defunct for a number of years. The cash was used to develop the Deer Lick, and it was the Deer Lick that earned enough to buy almost the entire valley. Zoe salted that claim by the creek, incidentally."

"She salted it?"

"With gold taken from the Deer Lick. She was a brazen minx, I have to admit. That story, Rowland, is between ourselves."

"You're sure there are no unexplored avenues to press your case for ownership?"

"None that my attorney has found, and the man is an expert. He chided me for negligence in matters pertaining to these very questions, but I said to him, as I say to you, that my business is mining, not legalities. My former attorney died less than a year ago, you may recall. He clearly was not so astute as my current expert. In any case, neither man knew the all-important fact upon which everything else hinges—Zoe was never my wife, and I have never been her husband. All that I worked for is hers, and do you know, Rowland, I believe the woman has no actual notion of it. I swear she has never shown the least interest in the company, never asked a single question with regard to ownership of Brannan Mining, never made any attempt to impose herself on the running of things. She doesn't know what she has, I'm sure of it."

"Then you'd best not even mention the word divorce when she returns. Leo, Imogen Starr must go. You risk everything by upsetting Zoe further with this ... dalliance. Give her up, for the sake of the business and your stake in what the Praetorians have in mind for you. Chances are, Zoe will never learn what we now know. ... I have it! In Denver recently a man and his wife married again after forty years of marriage, just to reaffirm their love, for sentiment's sake, I suppose. When Zoe comes back you must humble yourself and apologize for straying with another woman, then propose marriage all over again. This second ceremony will be legal ..." Price's face fell. "Oh ... we still have Mr. Aspinall to contend with. Pardon my enthusiasm for a useless suggestion."

"Drink up, friend, and let us place our heads together. If there exists no legal process to wrest back what I created, then we must consider an alternate route, no?"

"By all means. I intend no offense to the lady, but she is not responsible for Brannan Mining having become what it is, whatever her role in the early days."

"I agree, but Mr. Aspinall may not agree. It was Zoe he wanted to talk to, not myself. When she returns he may well approach her again, and tell all."

"Then he must be prevented."

"And how is that to be accomplished, pray tell?"

"He must be ... taken away from here before Zoe returns, or before he gets drunk and opens his mouth to interested parties. This is not a stable person, Leo. What kind of man would carve his own tombstone, for heaven's sake? He has to be silenced as soon as possible."

"A hefty bribe, you mean?"

"He may still talk. He should be silenced permanently, Leo; it's the only way to ensure none of this gets loose to ruin you. With Aspinall dead, you could proceed with the remarriage, and Zoe would be none the wiser for what happened behind her back."

"Are you a student of Machiavelli, Rowland?"

"You know as well as I that only death will make Aspinall hold his peace. Even if Zoe someday finds out how powerful her position really is, and for some reason wanted a divorce, at least you'll retain half the company, as her legal husband."

"You're suggesting we murder the man?"

"Not us; someone more suited to such work. There are such professionals, Leo."

"An assassin? This is too absurd."

"Is it? Do you want to lose it all? Do you? Zoe need never learn this husband of hers returned from the shadows. What is he but a wastrel who deserted a woman and child he accepted legal responsibility for by way of marriage? This is no heroic figure, no one to be admired or even pitied. The man is a wretch, Leo, a tramp begging for a handout from the very woman he wronged! What loss to humanity is there in his removal?"

"You're serious."

"As you should be. You know the plans we have for you. They hinge upon your fame. Do you wish to become even more renowned as the man who lost everything because he never knew his wife was a bigamist, and when he finally learned of it took no steps to protect his interests? Excuse my strong words, but listen to me, Leo—we have no use for a man who has become a joke among the common people. You stand to lose far more than Brannan Mining by allowing Aspinall to live. Are you listening to me?"

Leo set down his drink. "Yes," he said. "Nothing you have said has not already occurred to me. Perhaps I'm a coward, Rowland, but I wanted to hear the selfsame plan from your lips before I could admit to forming it myself. I've thought of nothing else for the last twenty-four hours. What kind of man does that make me, do you think?"

"A man who has fought hard for what he wanted, too hard to allow it all to slide away from under him now. Posterity will never judge you by the disappearance of a fellow nobody knew. Greater things are at stake here than your own pride, your own conscience. Have these thoughts made themselves known to you also?"

"They have."

"And what was their resolution, may I ask?"

Leo pushed his glass forward. "Kindly pour me another."

"There is a man," said Price, on his way to the liquor cabinet.

"A man? Yes?"

"A man who is not unknown to me, although I am unknown to him."

"Please, no riddles."

"He works for Big Circle, and has performed certain services on demand, without blinking an eye. I believe I could lure him away for work unconnected with his masters."

"A killer."

"Oh, yes, quite the best there is. I'm sure I could hire his expertise without anyone else being in the know. I like the idea of using Big Circle's own man to protect you, their eventual nemesis."

"Rowland, your love of irony is beside the point. Do nothing to compromise the secrecy of the Praetorians, I beg you."

"This will be a transaction of a purely commercial nature. The fellow likes to live well, and Big Circle simply doesn't ask him to dispose of enough enemies to keep him in the style he prefers. He'll be our man for the right price, and keep his mouth shut too, in case we ever need him again."

"Then perhaps you should travel some more, Rowland, and engage his services on our behalf. But tell me nothing of it, do you understand?"

"Aspinall is still at the Great Divide?"

"He is. I have sent him enough cash anonymously to cover his bills for several weeks."

"It shouldn't take that long."

Tatum had seldom paused to admire the natural beauty of the mountains, but even he could not help but be impressed by the sheer scale of the landscape he passed through on his way to Glory Hole. The precipitous ledges hugging their steel rails close were a wondrous platform from which to view a world of vastness. Rivers plunging beneath trestle bridges were like spools of silver thread unwinding, and the sky spread alongside his window beckoned like a siren, urging him to plunge into it and fly. Everything was too big, too far away. He saw eagles soaring at impossible heights; he saw waterfalls so tall and slender half their volume blew away on the breeze before reaching the rocks below. For Tatum, mountains were a pleasant backdrop to his life in Denver, not something to be ventured among for pleasure. Business, of course, was another matter.

The money had arrived in an envelope addressed to him care of the hotel. Bryce counted it and was pleased at Leo Brannan's generosity. He had no idea if the three hundred dollars was Brannan's idea of a monthly stipend or had been offered as a temporary stopgap, while a regular payment was organized. Bryce had not mentioned actual amounts of cash in Brannan's presence, trusting that a gentleman of his caliber would judge what was fair, and make the necessary arrangements. In the meantime, Bryce could buy new clothing and eat better than an unemployed stonemason had a right to expect.

The pain in his hands was bothersome, especially at the altitude of Glory Hole. He kept them warm inside thick woolen mittens, and cursed the affliction that had brought an end to his career. Bryce had been proud of his ability, and after leaving Pueblo had begun a new business from scratch in Ohio. Memories of his dead son intruded less and less upon his thoughts, and his business prospered. He sometimes felt a guilty twinge over having left Zoe and Omie behind, but the girl was not his daughter, and he suspected Zoe had never truly loved him. Bryce was shy of women, and had never remarried. He worked hard and well, and was content to be what he was, until the rheumatism began twisting his fingers. His mother had suffered from the same condition, and he was not surprised to witness its increasing hold on his own body. He calculated he had maybe two more good years left as a stonecutter; his life beyond that was not something he cared to think about.

When he read in the newspapers a report on Leo Brannan's reward for the capture of Slade, the Colorado Cannibal, Bryce saw included in the piece a short history of the man's rise to prominence, included in which were the names of his wife and daughter. Bryce knew then that he need not worry about providing for himself again. He was pleased that Zoe had prospered, and doubly pleased to think that she might share a little of her wealth with him. The consequences for Zoe if she did not were too great for refusal. Bryce packed a bag and entrained for Glory Hole.

It had been a disappointment to learn that she was away on a sea voyage, but Bryce had come too far to be put off, and so he visited the office of Leo Brannan himself, knowing there was the risk of Brannan's becoming so infuriated at Zoe's duplicity he would have nothing further to do with her, but even there, Brannan might reward the fellow who brought him news of his own bogus marriage. Bryce had been well pleased with the results so far; it seemed that Brannan preferred to whitewash Zoe's crime rather than throw her out. The gamble had proved worthwhile, and soon, he hoped, would begin paying off on a regular basis.

In the evening, after a generous meal, Bryce began what had become his ritual stroll along Brannan Boulevard. Glory Hole was a town that slept little, and although he was disinclined to take part in the revelry available in saloons and the company of low women, Bryce did like to observe the human traffic as he passed it by. On this night he was a little less cheerful than he had been since meeting with Brannan; that had been ten days ago, and there had been only the one envelope of cash so far. Ten days were time enough for a man like that to pass along the necessary orders for Bryce's stipend. If nothing came for him tomorrow, he would go again to Brannan's office and insist that the matter be taken care of forthwith. Bryce supposed that rich men liked to act according to their own agenda, but he would have none of that. His hands were hurting him rather more than usual, and he wanted to be able to leave Glory Hole before the end of the week, all arrangements in place.

A young woman in a simple hat and shawl tripped directly in front of Bryce and fell awkwardly to her knees. He stopped and assisted her to her feet, asking if she was all right, and when the young woman said she believed her ankle was sprained, Bryce did not know what to do.

"May I lean on your arm for a little way?" she asked.

"I suppose," said Bryce, and stiffly held out his arm. The touch of female fingers, even through several layers of cloth, sent a jolt through his entire body. Bryce had not touched or been touched by a woman since leaving Zoe. A familiar warmth invaded his groin, and he tried to ignore it. The situation was ludicrous; a mere hand on his sleeve and he was close to swooning with physical desire.

"Thank you so much for being kind," she said, hobbling daintily alongside him. "Some fellows would have walked right on and not cared if a girl was hurt."

Her voice was sweetly husky, and it sent a shiver of delight across Bryce's skin. Glancing sideways as they passed a street lamp, he saw that she was respectable in appearance, certainly not a whore. Her face was without any trace of makeup, and when she turned toward him at that same moment he noticed how brightly her eyes seemed to sparkle. She was an enchanting creature, and Bryce could barely credit his good fortune in having been the one she had stumbled in front of. Already his face was becoming flushed with his habitual shyness, but he would not surrender to it, not this time, when fate had delivered to him so appealing a bloom to smell.

"Wh ... what's your name?"

"Cassie. What's yours?"

"Bryce."

"Am I taking you out of your way, Mr. Bryce?"

"No, that's my first name. Bryce Aspinall. No, I wasn't going anywhere special."

"Just in a footloose mood."

"... Yes."

"I feel that way myself sometimes, but now you might say my silly old foot's really come loose."

She laughed, and Bryce laughed with her. She was charming and lively and had a merry wit. He was instantly smitten, recognized it, and was not inclined to resist the feeling. It could be that Cassie was a lonely soul, much as he was, and if so, they might make a life together, if only he could spin their accidental nearness into something more substantial. With any luck, she would invite him inside her house for a cup of coffee as a reward for his gallantry. He hoped she wouldn't be repulsed by his hands when she saw them. He would keep the mittens on until she had learned by spending time with him, talking with him, that he was a kindly, sensitive type of fellow, not the usual braggart or drinker a nice girl like Cassie would cross the street to avoid. She would see the man inside the man, and become aware of his potential as a husband, despite his infirmity. He would tell her the money that came each month was an inheritance or some such. If Leo Brannan didn't provide enough for two to live on, Bryce would have harsh words to say on that subject.

An opportunity to make his life over again had been presented out of the blue, and he would do his damnedest to ensure that it did not escape him. Bryce acknowledged that he was contemplating the very thing Zoe had done in marrying again without divorcing first, but he told himself it couldn't be any kind of sin, not when two people as pleasant and misunderstood as himself and Cassie were the parties concerned. He was in love with her, and they had barely exchanged a few dozen words. He could feel no pain at all in his hands, and his heart was light. There was a future ahead for him after all.

"Mr. Aspinall, would you mind taking me all the way to my door? It really isn't far at all, and my ankle does hurt so. Would you mind?"

"I don't mind. You shouldn't walk on a bad ankle."

"You're a gentleman."

"Call me Bryce, why don't you."

"Well, I shall, if it pleases you, and you must call me Cassie. I know this will sound very silly, Bryce, but I almost feel as if we'd known each other for some time already. Does it sound silly? You must tell me if it does."

"It doesn't sound silly at all. That's what happens sometimes, they say, when two people that don't know each other kind of ... bump into each other. It happens that way sometimes."

"Do you suppose it has happened this time, Mr. Bryce Aspinall?"

She was looking deeply into his eyes, smiling at him, but the effect was of friendliness, not flirtation, and he descended several notches deeper into infatuation.

"I ... don't know. I had the same feeling myself just now ... about you."

"You did? Oh, my, but that must mean something, mustn't it? Would you say it means something ... something nice?"

"I guess it would ... I mean, I guess it does."

"Down here, Mr. Aspinall. It isn't far now."

They turned into an alleyway, and a cat darted between Bryce's feet, causing him to execute a clumsy dance of avoidance.

"Oh, goodness, don't you go turning your ankle too."

"I won't. You could call me Bryce if you want."

"I will, I really will. I'm just a little nervous. Will you take China tea with myself and my mama, Bryce? She doesn't have much company apart from me. I know she'd like to meet a nice gentleman like yourself. Will you?"

"All right."

"Almost there. Drat this ankle. Wait just a moment while I fix something."

She disengaged herself from his arm and reached beneath her skirts. Bryce was mildly shocked, but supposed Cassie was having trouble with her stocking hose.

"Do excuse me." She smiled, and Bryce smiled in return to allay any embarrassment she might be feeling. "Oh, dear, would you mind turning away for just the teensiest moment, Bryce? I have a little difficulty here."

He turned his back to her. She had invited him into her house. He would meet with Cassie's mother and drink tea with them both. He had better prepare a story to explain his presence in Glory Hole, so when he asked to come back again and visit he would be welcome. A new life, that's what the sweet girl behind him represented, and Bryce found himself brimming with anticipation. When the stiletto blade entered beneath his shoulder blade he barely felt it, and when its full length was rammed through sheets of muscle and into his heart he could not understand the sudden discomfort he felt, a sensation that blossomed into horrible pain. He staggered for several steps, then sank abruptly to his knees, clawing behind himself for the unknown thing that had entered him and caused the pain that kept him from breathing. He hoped Cassie had not been hit by whatever it was that had done this to him, and concern for her enabled him to gasp her name.

"I'm here, Bryce," she said, and stepped around in front of him. Bryce was appalled to see that she carried the front of her skirts at waist height, like a saloon dancer. A scabbard or sheath of some kind was attached to a garter around her lovely thigh, and he could see the whitely billowing froth of her undergarments too. Why was she doing this, and why was she unaware of his pain? Had he been struck by a heart attack? The pain was worsening, and still he could not breathe. "Cassie ...," he gasped again, and in response she yanked down her pantaloons to reveal a penis. Bryce felt the life ebbing from him, and collapsed onto the ground, still unable to understand what had happened. The pain became excruciating as the stiletto's long triangular blade was extracted from his back and wiped clean on his new jacket, and then Bryce died.

Tatum looked around to ensure that there was no one in sight, then lifted his skirts and squatted to piss in Bryce's face. Finished, he stood and arranged himself, making sure that the weapon was tightly encased in its hideaway, then walked swiftly to the street again, and became part of the human stream flowing there.

The murder was not a great sensation, even in Glory Hole; news of another attack by Slade in southern Colorado eclipsed press interest in the stabbing of an unknown man. Slade had dissected his latest victims, a woman and a boy, in a particularly repulsive fashion before opening their skulls, as if searching for something there. Leo decided that if there was another killing by the cannibal (reportedly he had eaten no part of his victims since escaping from Glory Hole), he would increase the reward even further. He spent more time reading about Slade than he did about Aspinall, and when Rowland Price entered the room, neither man mentioned the business that had been so swiftly taken care of.

At Imogen's house that evening, Leo found himself unable to perform even the simplest act of love, and when asked if there was something troubling him, replied only that production figures at both the Flatiron and the Sinbad mines had dipped slightly. Imogen patted his hand and told him things would surely improve, and Leo appreciated her concern. Zoe would have glared at him and said, "You mean you'll make a thousand dollars less today than yesterday? How awful for you." Imogen was a superior class of woman in many ways, a thoughtful person, never sarcastic. It would be a wrenching moment when he was obliged to remove her from his life prior to Zoe's homecoming, but no woman, even a sweet and considerate creature such as Imogen Starr, was worth losing Brannan Mining over. Leo had decided to adopt Rowland's plan for a remarriage to Zoe, a reconsecration of their vows to reawaken the love that had dimmed between them. Leo could not help but imagine Zoe's reply to such an offer: "You wish us to repeat our original mistake? What kind of businessman invests good money on top of bad?" It galled him to recall the tone her voice had taken since the accident. Zoe was an embittered and cheerless woman, but he would have to persuade her that the ceremony was necessary, without arousing in her any suspicion of an ulterior motive. It should not prove so difficult, he told himself, since Zoe was genuinely uninterested in every aspect of the mines. Her ignorance was his best weapon, in fact his only one, unless he decided to arrange for Zoe what Price had arranged for Aspinall. He thrust the thought from him, ashamed to have allowed it into his mind even for a second. His head began to throb. Leo had not felt well all day.

"Is there nothing I can do, my dear?" asked Imogen.

"Nothing, no. I believe I'll return home. I am not the best company tonight, I regret."

"There's no need for that. I shall make a bed for myself in the spare room."

"Please don't trouble yourself. Good night, Imogen."

Lovey Doll escorted him to the door and blew a kiss at his departing back. Alone, she allowed her expression to drop and harden to its habitual look of glacial contempt. The worm was out of sorts tonight, all because of some stupid list of numbers, a feeble excuse for misery, in Lovey Doll's opinion. She took herself into the living room and poured for herself a generous measure of brandy. She knew she should not drink, since it coarsened the skin and expanded the waistline, but sometimes Leo Brannan and his whining was enough to make her overcome caution.

It was high time she broached the subject of divorce from his one-armed shrew. Imogen Starr deserved to take Zoe's place, Lovey Doll would hint, and after a few extra touches to the performances and acts she knew pleased him, Leo would begin accepting her suggestions as worth his consideration. Soon he would no more think of taking the shrew back into his home and bed than he would a side of beef. The man was stubborn, in a childish way, peevish and irritable more often than not of late, but Lovey Doll was confident her influence was increasing with every visit Leo Brannan made to her door.

CHAPTER

38

Even before the *Acropolis* reached Bermuda there was concern among the passengers over the appearance of a man on the forward deck at night, a tall man in a long dark coat, his skull-like face half hidden by a wide hat. The truly disturbing aspect of the entity, who matched the description of no one aboard, were the holes in his cheeks. When she heard of the tall man, Zoe went to her cabin, where Omie lay on her bunk, still as a corpse.

"What can you tell me of the man everyone has seen?"

"I don't know what man you mean."

"Yes you do. You described him to me once, back home. Why is he here?"

"I don't know," said Omie, rolling her face and body away from her mother's eyes.

"You do know. You have brought him here; don't tell me you haven't. Now look at me and explain yourself. Look at me when I say!"

Omie reluctantly faced her, and admitted she knew the man was there, even if she had not actually laid eyes on him herself, being in her bunk asleep at the time of his visitations. She could not say with any certainty why it was that he had chosen to visit with her again after so long an absence from her dreams, and Omie tearfully exonerated herself from any scheme intended deliberately to frighten or alarm the other passengers.

"He just does what he wants, Mama; I can't stop him. He doesn't even know himself why he's here. He looks lost and lonely when I see him, and sometimes he can't see me at all. I think ... I think he's drunk, Mama."

"Drunk? A dream man drunk? How could that be?"

"I don't know. The night before last he saw me, and I told him to go away and behave himself, but he only laughed and said who did I think I was to give him orders. Then he asked me who I was, and where we both were. He said he never saw the ocean before. I think he was scared of it, being so big and wide the way it is. He's a very sad man, Mama, only he won't tell me why."

"Can't you make him go away?"

"I told him to, but he won't. He said no one else would have him."

"What on earth does that mean?"

Omie shrugged, her blotched face miserable. Zoe felt a pang of love, and put an arm around her daughter. "I know you've done nothing wrong. If the man comes wherever you are, that's not a bad thing. He must be lonely, as you say, and sad people must be helped, if possible. Say nothing to anyone about him, though."

"Well, of course not, Mama; they'd throw me over the side, and you too."

"Captain Crandall is a very nice gentleman, and would permit no such thing."

"They'd commit mutiny, all the crew and the other passengers, and make us walk the plank."

"Indeed they would not. Now cease and desist with such nonsense, before I become angry with you and the dark man both."

She released Omie and stood up, supporting herself against the vessel's leisurely pitch and roll by grasping the bunk post.

"There's a storm coming, Mama."

"Will it be terrible and frightening?"

"No, but Doolin will get killed."

Doolin was a crew member much admired by the passengers for his ability to perform acrobatics for their amusement in the rigging, against the mock protests of Captain Crandall, who knew better than to stop anything that put his guests, as he referred to the passenger list, in a playful mood. Doolin was the ship's monkey, Crandall said several times at the dinner table, and could only understand human English once in a long while, so everyone was stuck with his careless caperings against the shrouds and the sky.

"How will it happen?" asked Zoe.

"He'll fall."

"Is there no way to prevent this from happening?"

"No, Mama, but he'll be happy after he dies."

"How can you know that?"

"I just do."

Zoe recalled Omie's description of the life led by their housekeeper, Mrs. Scoville, after she died and had gone to hell. "She deserved to," stated Omie. "She was horrible."

"Were you peeking into my mind just now?"

"I didn't mean to. I can do that again without even trying. I couldn't do it for ever so long, not since I was sick with the fever, but I can now, Mama, a little bit, and see things that are going to happen, like the storm coming and Doolin falling. Does it mean I'm getting better after all this time?"

"I don't know what it means, but you mustn't discuss it with anyone but me."

"I know, Mama."

The dark man did not make an appearance that night. Captain Crandall had assigned extra men on watch to look out for the mysterious stowaway, even though every part of the ship had already been searched and found empty of anyone not on the passenger list. He had not seen the dark man himself, but several of the crew swore they had witnessed events similar to those described by the passengers, usually a fleeting glimpse of the fellow,—"a string-bean shadow man," as one crew member put it, "with a face like death."

The dark man's failure to reveal himself was of little relief to the captain, who by midmorning was more concerned over the falling barometer than about phantoms. He also had knowledge of stirrings in the fo'c'sle, where several of the men had begun spreading stories about the little Brannan girl with the unfortunate blue face mark. Doolin, his unofficial spy among the crew, had informed him there was a plan brewing to insist that the girl and her mother be put ashore in Bermuda; they were fearful of crossing the North Atlantic with the blue-faced girl aboard. Pressed for reasons why they should feel as they did, one of the men had told Doolin, "She's got the mark of a witch, that one, little as she be." Another man swore he had seen the girl promenading amidships with the dark

man, "and not either one with their feet a-touchin' the timbers, so
help me!"

Captain Crandall was in no mood for supernatural tales and
moon talk on his ship, not with a storm coming down hard on them
from the south. As the barometer plunged before his eyes, he
ordered all unnecessary sail furled, and all passengers below decks.
The *Acropolis* was battened down and made ready for the wall of
darkness approaching like runaway cliffs. The captain had seen
worse storms racing toward him, and had weathered them all with
a minimum of inconvenience or damage, but as he watched the latest of them looming along the southern horizon, and felt the ship
heel hard to port as the first of its wind reached out, he experienced
something a man as stoic and professionally unruffled as himself
seldom felt: the captain became aware of a sensation he could
describe only as dread creeping from the region of his solar plexus;
it came stealthily up his spinal column like a magically sprouting
vine, and wrapped his brain with its tendrils. Sweat sprang from
every pore in his skin, and he fought for breath as the dreadful vine
sent creepers down into his chest to surround his heart and lungs.
It was not the storm his vessel was headed into that provoked the
fear inside him, but some presence aboard. Was it the dark man? he
asked himself. He did not believe in omens and portents or forces
that could not be measured with compass and sextant, but Captain
Crandall could not deny he was sailing into uncharted waters, no
matter that he knew the precise location by latitude and longitude
of himself and his ship.

Now the wind was gusting fiercely, snapping the sails, coating
Crandall's lips with the taste of spume, whipping the words he
attempted to pass to the helmsman soundlessly away. He was
unsure if he had actually spoken or not, and commanded his lips to
move, but they remained as before, rimed with salt spray, numbed
by the same dread that held him now in an invisible vise, rooted to
the poop deck like a mast. It was no storm to fear, no wind beyond
coping, but he felt a clawing at his breast as the creeper planted in
him grew thorns to rake his heart, rake it till the blood must gush
from its bag. He thought briefly of his two wives, the one in Manch-
ester and the one on Rhode Island, and could not be sure which one
he loved best. It had always irritated him that he, a man of decision, had never been able to place one above the other when at sea,
although he was generally happiest with whichever wife happened

to be the one he was with. I am a fool and a weakling, he told himself, and the thorns tore him open.

The helmsman became aware that all was not well with the captain when no orders came to bring the ship closer to the wind. Captain Crandall stood beside him, deathly white, his eyes fixed on some distant thing, and then he came crashing to the deck like a fallen tree. The helmsman stared, then began bawling for the first mate.

Omie had taken to her bunk when the ship began to be buffeted by high winds. Zoe thought at first she might be seasick, but Omie simply lay there, grasping the edges of her bunk to keep from rolling out onto the cabin floor. Zoe preferred to sit on a chair bolted to the floor; lying down only made her nauseous, and she had no wish to thicken the close air inside their cabin with the reek of vomit. She attempted to divert herself from the pitching and tossing with thoughts of home, but home was a concept that had become increasingly abstract. Home was a town where Leo had his hussy woman; home was a huge house without a husband in it; home was a place she had been attempting to find ever since departing Schenectady as a girl. Home, the last real home she could think of, had been the waterless tenement in which Nettie Dugan had died. Home had died with her, and all the years since then had been a search for another. Whatever the town, whatever the man whose ring she wore, the home she had thought was hers had been taken from her. The one constant was Omie, who belonged with Zoe as Zoe had always hoped someday to belong in a home. She wondered, watching her daughter stare at the planking of the bunk above her, if Omie regarded home as the place, wherever it happened to be, wherein they shared each other's life. It was a sparsely appointed home, to be sure, but perhaps the only one that could not be taken away by anything less than death. Zoe held on to the chair with her only hand, waiting for time and the storm to pass.

After a night of rough weather, the *Acropolis* was left wallowing in the choppy seas remaining in the storm's wake. News of Captain Crandall's death was given to the passengers by Doolin, who did not pass on the newest fo'c'sle rumblings over Omie Brannan. After a makeshift breakfast, everyone aboard gathered at the starboard rail for the captain's sea burial. His body was wrapped in sailmaker's canvas and weighted with five yards of chain. There being no man of God among them, the mate elected to read a few verses from the captain's own Bible, and when he was done, the mate nodded to Doolin and another crewman to tip forward the plank on which Captain Crandall's body lay. They heaved up the shipside end, but the captain remained where he was. The plank was raised to an angle of fifty degrees without shifting its burden more than a few inches toward the seaward end, and there was whispered comment among the crew.

One sailor said aloud, pointing to Omie, "He won't be going while she's there to watch, by God."

His words created louder whisperings, and the mate was obliged to order silence. The plank was tipped higher, almost vertical now, and the captain's body sagged within its canvas shroud, but did not slide off into the deep.

"Get her below!" called the same sailor, and Zoe took Omie by the hand to march with her across to the port side. She would not take her below, since that would have been a victory of sorts for whatever foolish suspicions the crew clearly held; nor would she allow Omie to remain where the sailor could point and shout at her; the port side rail was a compromise, but going to it improved Omie's standing not at all, since no sooner did mother and daughter turn away than the splinter snagging the canvas broke off, and the dead man slipped from the plank with a rush and plummeted into a rolling trough of blue-green that swallowed him instantly.

Ocean foam had barely passed over Captain Crandall when the sailor clenched his fist and shook it at the departing woman and child. "See there! When the devil turns his back on good folk, they can go about their business!" The mate again ordered the man to be quiet, but he could not ignore the buzz of excited talk passing among the passengers, most of whom were watching Zoe and Omie to see what they would do. The mate ordered his crew to their stations, then suggested to the passengers that they likewise remove themselves. All the while, as the gathering behind them slowly dispersed, Zoe and Omie stood by the port rail, looking at the sea and sky.

The mate approached them, somewhat abashed. "My apologies, ma'am. Some of these fellows, they don't know much, but that doesn't stop them."

"It was none of your doing. How far are we from our next port of call?"

"Bermuda in two days, ma'am."

"We will disembark there and allow you to continue without us.

Please tell the crew. Tell them also that I carry a pistol with me at all times," lied Zoe. "If any man touches my daughter or attempts in any way whatsoever to intimidate her, I will shoot him dead."

"Ma'am, I'll tell them. They're not educated, most of them, and they believe what they see and hear."

"They will see and hear us depart in Bermuda."

"Yes, ma'am."

When the mate left them, Zoe said to Omie, "Why wasn't it Doolin, the way you said?"

"I don't know how I got it mixed up, Mama."

"I suggest that in future you consider your words carefully before uttering any prognostications. You did the same thing once with regard to your father."

"Which father?"

"Leo. You said a man with one blue eye and one brown eye—that could only mean him—was robbing us, but the money stolen from our room had nothing to do with him. Do you remember that, back in Leadville, before we came with him to Glory Hole?"

"No. I'm sorry if I was wrong. I didn't mean to be."

"Let us try to put all this behind us and enjoy ourselves. Look! A flying fish! Did you see it?"

"I've seen lots. Mama, when we get to the place he said, will we turn around?"

"Why should we do that? We're only partway across the ocean to where we're going. We just need to get on another ship. This time, if you don't mind, we'll take a steamer, with lots more people on board to lose ourselves among."

"I ... I don't want to."

"There is nothing wrong with steamships, Omie."

"No, I mean I don't want to go over the ocean anymore."

"Oh, Omie, we mustn't quit now, just because some ignorant sailors have been rude to us."

"I don't want to, Mama ..."

Omie suddenly vomited over herself.

The two days inbound to Bermuda were spent with Omie tossing restlessly on her bunk, sometimes awake, sometimes not, and often somewhere in between. The passengers were quick to ascribe blame for Omie's condition on the crewman who had shouted at her during the sea burial, but no one actually went to the Brannans' cabin to express sympathy; there was something not altogether right about the girl, and her mother was equally alarming, with her rigid expression of contempt for everything and everyone, and her pinned-up right sleeve. They were a peculiar duo, and befriending them for the short time remaining till landfall at Bermuda might have prejudiced the crew against anyone attempting to do so. The longest part of the voyage lay ahead, and it would be better, everyone silently concluded, to let the Brannans keep their own company until the ship was rid of them.

Isolated though Omie was, her influence continued to instill fear and ill will toward her among the crew. The dark man was seen again, his long coat hanging straight down even in the strongest breeze, and one seaman on the dog watch swore he witnessed a ghostly train pass by in the darkness, its cowcatcher plowing through the waves, smokestack spitting purple fire, and another swore a band of phantom horsemen had followed the ship for almost half a league before riding their glowing steeds beneath the waves.

Zoe and Omie took meals in their cabin, and did not go on deck until dusk. When the *Acropolis* dropped its anchor, they were packed and ready to disembark. The crew had rolled dice to see who would row them ashore, and that task was accomplished in silence by the losers. Standing on the harbor wall, surrounded by their luggage, Zoe wanted to weep at the injustice of it, but did not, for Omie's sake. Omie had been unnaturally quiet for the last two days, and Zoe thought it wisest to leave her alone, rather than engage her in conversation filled with false brightness. Watching the dinghy being rowed back to the ship, Zoe wished she could draw a lightning bolt down from the sky to wipe out everyone aboard who had condemned them.

Omie tugged at her sleeve. "Mama, can we go home from here, please?"

"Yes. Home."

They found passage on the *Tiger Shark,* bound for Charleston, and began their return voyage to America. The dark man was seen only twice; there were no ghost trains or phantom riders; no one aboard died or thought overmuch about the girl with the blue mark on her face, or her one-armed mother. Zoe and Omie never learned that two days after weighing anchor to continue eastward, the *Acropolis* ran into more rough weather, and Doolin fell from the mainmast to split his skull open on the deck below.

39

From the high western slope of the valley they could see the cabin with ease. It was a broad valley, the one sign of human habitation an isolated oblong of weather-worn logs and crumbling sod. A corral beside the cabin held seven horses. Clay and his new partner could not approach the place during daylight, the area around it being open as it was, nothing but high plains grasses turning brown in the summer heat. If they wanted the men inside, it would have to be a night raid.

Aemon Jennings was still not sure about Dugan. The man had a reputation for keeping a cool head in a tight corner, but there had been evidence since they teamed up together that Clay's bottle had assumed an equal role in the partnership. Jennings was keeping a close watch on his partner while they hid out among the trees above the valley. Both men had worked the most distant reaches of Wyoming before, but never for such prey as occupied the cabin below.

Wiley and Casper Bentine had set out to establish themselves as the natural inheritors of the James brothers' mantle of celebrated outlawry, but quickly proved themselves lacking in Frank and Jesse's cunning and skill in the planning and execution of criminal acts. The money on the Bentines' heads was solely on account of the mayhem they had caused during their clumsy attempts at fame.

For a sum just short of four hundred dollars, the brothers had killed eight people during a single robbery in Thermopolis. The reward posted for them within days of the fiasco (Wiley and Casper had obligingly left their names at the scene, for the convenience of newspaper reporters) was double that amount.

Aemon Jennings received a tip from a cousin of the Bentines that they were hiding out in an old cabin a friend of their father's had built up in the Wind River Range near the great divide. Jennings had been told the brothers were heavily armed, committed to their freedom and their goal of becoming living legends. Two such fools would likely be hard to take alone, and so Jennings hired Clay Dugan to assist him. Dugan would take one fourth of the reward money, and Jennings's informant another fourth, leaving a worthwhile profit for Aemon.

He and Clay set out for the Wind River Range, confident they could take care of the Bentines inside of two weeks, but halfway there, it became clear that Clay was a drinker. He carried several bottles in his saddlebags, and a reserve supply on his packhorse. He was not ungenerous, offering Aemon a swig every time he took one for himself, but was turned down each time. Aemon hoped enough of these blunt refusals would let Clay know sobriety was what his partner required of him, but Clay had chosen to ignore the hints, and drunk on, until Aemon told him, "Either those bottles go, Dugan, or you do. I need a man that can think fast and shoot straight when the time comes, hear me?"

"I hear you," Clay said, and immediately dismounted to remove all the whiskey from both his horses. He placed the bottles under a log at the side of a stream, saying he would pick them up on their way back, following the death or capture of the Bentines. Aemon Jennings found the arrangement fair; he could not have cared less what Clay did once the business he was hired for had been taken care of. They rode on together, the subtle air of discord between them smoothed somewhat by the quickness of Clay's decision.

The next two nights were difficult for both men. Clay woke from sleep several times, disturbed by dreams of sailing ships, he said, but Aemon could tell there was more to the dreams than that. He ascribed his partner's restless nights to the sudden removal of alcohol from his life, and was reasonably sure the situation would be in hand by the time the Bentines' cabin in the high lonesome was found.

Locating the right valley required several days. An observation post had been established among the trees above the cabin, and Aemon shared his binoculars with Clay, maintaining a constant watch on the place until they were sure the brothers were inside. A third man, short and completely bald, presumably the cabin's permanent occupant, was with them. There were no dogs to catch wind of the watchers should they come closer, but the great expanse of open ground presented a problem only darkness could solve. They decided to wait one more day, to ensure that the moon would be at its dimmest before an approach was made.

While they waited, Jennings became aware of another unexpected condition of Clay's; the man suffered from kidney stones, and the passage of these from the kidney to the bladder was almost as excruciating to behold as to experience. Clay would double over and clutch at his abdomen, his face turning white with pain as the stones eased their way through tubes less broad than they, and far smoother.

"That why you had the liquor?" asked Aemon.

"Partly ..." Clay gasped, made honest by agony. He had begun the steady drinking shortly after being run out of Dry Wash by his vengeful wife. That incident had been too much to bear without whiskey, and he had adopted the habit of drinking a little and often ever since, even though the original smarting of his public humiliation had worn off. The dreams he had known for years, the ones inhabited by the blue-faced girl, were another reason to embrace the bottle, since Clay assumed he was going crazy be degrees. The kidney stones were just another kind of torment directed at him by fate, Clay felt, to balance his mind's anguish with something for his physical self to endure.

A doctor in Grand Junction had told him there was no cure that guaranteed banishment from the jagged lumps that eventually scraped their way through Clay's penis and were pissed out into the world, but he did have a suggestion for relieving the urethra's final agony. Clay bought a glass eyedropper with a rubber bulb at its wide end, and a bottle of mineral oil. As each stone passed from his bladder to the root of his manhood and began its ultimate descent, Clay filled the eyedropper with oil and injected a measure of the slimy stuff through the eye of his penis; thus lubricated, the urethra allowed its transient stone easier passage, even if this meant Clay's underclothing became greasy and soiled from the overflow.

The doctor had advised inserting a clean handkerchief around the region of the crotch each day to absorb much of this, but since leaving for the mountains to hunt down the Bentine brothers, Clay had found little opportunity to wash his laundry.

It was an embarrassment to squirt the oil into himself during close proximity to Jennings, but there was no other way to assist the small crystalline lumps out. Clay's sense of who and what he was had altered in no small way since Sophie's attempted shooting of him. He felt some essential part of his inner self eroding, becoming less with every day that passed, and imagined sometimes that his courage, his stoicism, the things that had allowed him to live in the world without being crushed, were leaking away, leaving him forever, perhaps in the very stones that caused him such suffering. The prickly, brownish fragments might have been his soul breaking apart, jettisoning its rough edges prior to complete disintegration. Maybe Reverend Wixson had been right about the existence of a tangible soul within the physical body of every man, but it was no ghostly thing of trailing robes and spectral luminosity. The soul, as Clay saw it, was probably as ugly as anything that could be seen pickled in a jar of formaldehyde in a doctor's office, a soft and lumpy organ of negligible size and nondescript appearance, most likely a pinkish white when healthy, made hard and brittle and brown when under attack. Clay had neglected his soul, and the inevitable had occurred; his soul was deserting him in tiny, excruciating chunks.

Aemon Jennings was beginning to doubt his own wisdom in selecting Dugan as a partner. The man clearly had deteriorated since the founding of his reputation among the bounty hunting brethren some years before. Aemon had sympathy for him over the kidney stones, and was able to condone a measure of liquor to ease the pain of such things, but his misgivings ran deeper than that; Clay Dugan's eyes were no longer those of a man in charge of his destiny. Aemon had met Clay twice before in the Rocky Mountain region, and exchanged professional courtesies. He had not liked him, but Dugan's obvious aura of menace had produced respect; now that aura was gone, replaced by a haunted look behind the eyes. The man was breaking up inside somehow, harboring demons within himself, allowing them to eat him alive. The dreams that woke Clay several times each night were an annoyance to Aemon, disturbing his own sleep as they did, at a time when he and his partner both had to maintain vigilance in their watch over the cabin. None of it could be helped now; he would simply have to trust Dugan to do what had to be done, in a timely and efficacious manner, or both of them might wind up as dead men.

Clay had his back turned while he squirted more oil into himself. Aemon shook his head and viewed the cabin again through his binoculars. Wiley Bentine was strolling toward the outhouse, unhitching the galluses from his shoulders. Casper was smoking a pipe by the door, while the bald man busied himself feeding the horses. One more night and one more day of watching, and then the moonless dark would let them sneak up on the cabin to catch the Bentines and their hairless friend asleep. Aemon hoped the extra time would also give Dugan a chance to recover from his troubles.

It was near dusk when the four riders came. Clay saw them first, and beckoned for Aemon to join him at the lookout point. Together they watched the horsemen approach from the south, and saw the Bentines appear in their doorway with drawn guns, only to put them aside at their host's request as the riders came nearer. Shouted words of welcome came drifting through the purple evening air. The lead horseman, who wore a feather in his hatband, raised a hand to the bald man who had made the Bentines lower their guns, and all four dismounted. The man with the feathered hat embraced the bald man, and their laughter came on a shift in the breeze, the easy laughter of friends.

"Complicates the situation," said Clay.

"It does," agreed Jennings. "Those fellers aren't horse traders, not if they know the bald one so well."

"Make out that tall one with the feather's face at all?"

"Not in this light," Aemon said, squinting through the binoculars. "Him and Baldy are talking like long-lost brothers. I don't think the rest of them know him ... no, one of them does, but not the other two. Looks like no one knows the Bentines at all. They're hanging back in the doorway there like a couple of wallflowers."

"Could be they'll be gone by tomorrow night."

"Don't fool yourself. The party just got started, I'm thinking. Come daylight we can maybe figure out who they are. Anyone knows Baldy that way, and him knowing the Bentines, they've just got to be bad, the whole bunch. Dugan, we might just be looking at a couple thousand dollars or more worth of outlaws down there, booted and breathing."

"Seven to two is long odds."

"Not if you went across the valley and we could catch them in a crossfire come morning."

"I'm not good with a rifle."

"I don't intend letting men worth cash money slide out of here without you and me taking as many as we can, Dugan."

"If I can get close, they're mine. A rifle, though, that won't do it. My eyes aren't made for distance shooting, Jennings, and that's a fact, so build yourself another plan."

"Well, then, since the easy way doesn't suit you, I guess we'll just have to wait and see what happens. Maybe some of them won't stay around too long."

Clay said nothing. Jennings was beginning to irritate him. Clay had ditched his entire supply of whiskey to please the man, and because it made good sense to sober himself up for the job ahead, but his sacrifice seemed to have lowered him even further in Jennings's eyes, if that was possible, and there was no sympathy at all over his belly stones. "Had an uncle one time with the same problem," Jennings had said, "but it never killed him. He just went about his business and kind of squeezed his mouth tight, you know. Tough old bird, that uncle."

"Maybe his stones were small," said Clay, but he could see Aemon Jennings was not impressed by such an argument. This would be the first and last time Clay ever hired himself out to another man in the same line of work as himself. He was made to operate alone, and would always do so in future. A partnership that grated was not something that would likely produce the kind of results both men wanted.

"There they go, unsaddling. Guess he made them good and welcome, all right. These fellers are no-goods, Dugan, I can smell the bad on them, even from here."

It had been a long hard ride up from Colorado. Lodi had insisted on a change of state following the train robbery outside Buena Vista, and Drew was not inclined to contradict him. One of the men who had taken part in that raid was dead simply because he had wanted his cut of the proceeds before Lodi was inclined to allow a split-up, and after that quick death, another man had sneaked away into the night rather than face a possible dose of the same if he opened his mouth. Both had been amateurs, but the sixth man in their party,

Levon, had proved himself able to take orders. Drew liked him a little, but thought that his preference for Levon was amplified by his dislike of Nate Haggin and Lodi. Levon was not so entertaining an individual as Clarence Dustey had been, but was amiable enough. They rode together for most of the way, with Nate and Lodi up ahead, and had bunched up only as they approached the cabin in the Wind River Range. Lodi said it housed a firm friend of his from the old days in Montana, when he had ridden with Arch Powell on mining-payroll robberies.

Horace Neet was the name of Lodi's friend. Drew had never before seen a man so bald, there was not a single hair to be found on his head. Horace wouldn't wear a hat to cover his cranial nakedness except when he went outside in the hours of daylight, to prevent sunburn. As he prepared a meal for the new arrivals, he told them how he came to be so bald. Lodi already knew the story, but saw that Horace was distracting everyone else's attention with the tale so his old friend had a chance to run his nose over the Bentines. Lodi didn't like what he saw. The brothers were listening to Horace with resentment on their faces, and Lodi knew they resented the bald man's sudden talkativeness now that others had come to share the cabin. Horace hadn't told them the story because he didn't like them, and Lodi had always valued Horace's horse sense when it came to judging men. Horace only had to introduce them, and Lodi recalled the recent news concerning Wiley and Casper's bloodbath in Thermopolis. He knew they would want to join up with him, but Lodi didn't want fools on his team.

"It was a barber that done it," Horace was saying, "and I'm the idiot that asked him to. I never knew ahead of time what was gonna happen to me on account of that barber, nossir, but I have to share the blame. See, I always let my old lady trim my hair up till then, but it's our wedding anniversary and I figured, go get yourself a real close shave and a trim down at the barbershop, just for the wife, which is what I did, but soon as he laid that razor on my face I had the feeling there was something wrong, had kind of a tickling feeling to it, you know, and when he was done with scraping me my face was sore as a kicked behind, only I didn't know why it would've felt that way so I never said a word about it, and then he starts to cutting my hair, which let me tell you was thick as a blackberry vine back then, and I paid the man and went on home, only this itch came a-crawling up off of my face from the shave and started to travel across my head, a real peculiar feeling, and I had the wife wash my hair to get rid of it, which it done for a day or so, but then it's back, and by then there's this rash all over my face and creeping up into my hair as well.

"I went back to that barbershop and watched him through the window, and that son of a bitch, you know what he did? He never boiled the goddamn razor is what, the dirty dog, so now I knew what it was that's afflicting me, and I marched in there and whomped that barber till he can't stand up straight. He lost the customer that was there too, when I told why I was so mad. Well, that gave me satisfaction, but it never helped my hair. It commenced to come out in handfuls, just falling down like someone sheared it off, and I had to grow a beard at the same time on account of the rash that's still on my face, and inside of a week or so I'm bald as a bullet above the ears and hairy below, a turnaround, as you might say, and it's a shame, because this was a real handsome face before it got covered with a beard, but you know, I couldn't stand to shave it ever again and be bald all over from the neck up, nossir. So, boys, you better be sure when you go to a barber he's clean and does what he's supposed to with that razor."

Horace dished up ham and beans, and Lodi contributed two bottles of whiskey to the meal. The Bentine brothers had by that time announced themselves responsible for the robbery in Thermopolis.

"Never heard of it," said Lodi, turning away.

"Our daddy built this here cabin," said Wiley, "but then he sold it when the blizzard wiped out his herd."

"He lost near 'bout everything," Casper stated to an unresponsive audience. Taking their cue from Lodi, Drew and Nate and Levon were disinclined to make conversation with two such unprofessional murderers as the Bentines.

"And Horace here got it off of that feller later on," Wiley continued, "which Horace is a second cousin to our daddy, so we never minded him being here, and he never minded us laying low for a little while now—ain't that so, Horace?"

"I never minded anything in my life but a dirty razor."

Horace was not partial to his original guests, and resented their presence, especially now that a genuine friend from the past had arrived with a bunch of boys that looked true blue. It was a relief to have real company, but Horace was aware that Lodi's tolerance of morons was notoriously low, and his reaction to such types speedy and final. Horace was embarrassed that Wiley had insisted on pointing out the distant family tie between the brothers and himself.

"You fellers," said Casper, meaning Lodi and his men, "you mean to pull off something up this way?"

"No."

"Wiley and me, we'd help you out."

"Well, you and Wiley can take it easy, because like I said, we don't have any plans. Want me to say it again just so's you can remember?"

"No need to talk like that," warned Wiley.

He had taken a dislike to Lodi as soon as Horace told him who it was riding toward the cabin. Lodi had the kind of reputation Wiley and Casper wanted for themselves. The brothers had felt crowded out even before the newcomers entered the cabin. It was already plain that Lodi considered them nobodies, and Wiley in particular took exception to that. It occurred to him, as he glared in Lodi's direction, then away again as Lodi's eyes bored through him, that to be the one who killed such a famous outlaw would boost him instantly into the stellar region of universal recognition, himself and Casper both. Of course, they would have to kill the other three as well, and maybe Horace Neet besides, but all that extra killing would be just what was required to make all men fear them. They would be the deadliest brothers in America since Panther Stalking and Kills With a Smile, and be in more newspapers than Slade, the Colorado Cannibal. Wiley decided he would talk to Casper about it the first chance he got.

A casual bonhomie began filling the cabin as the first bottle was emptied and the second begun. Wiley thought it might be smart to make Lodi believe he admired him, and so demanded details of his various robberies. Lodi preferred not to talk with Wiley, and after refusing several times to "discuss the past," simply turned his back on the man and opened a conversation with Horace that centered on nothing but the past. Watching the exchange, Drew saw Wiley's features harden. A look passed between the brothers that Drew likened to a visual pact, or mutual understanding, and he knew trouble was looming.

"Hey," said Wiley, leaning forward in his chair. "How come you want to talk to him about that old stuff, and you won't talk to me about it?"

Lodi finished speaking with Horace and slowly turned. "Pretty near your bedtime now, wouldn't you say?" he drawled.

Wiley shifted in his chair, but placed a smile on his face. Casper was watching everyone else in the room but his brother and Lodi. Drew saw Nate's hand stray toward his gun.

"Gentlemen," said Drew, "the reason Lodi doesn't want to discuss his career is because he's promised exclusive rights to his biographer. I'm sure you'll respect his predicament and not bother the man anymore."

The Bentines stared at Drew as if he had uttered phrases in Arabic. Nate and Levon were also puzzled, but kept their eyes on the Bentines and their hands near their guns. Lodi began to laugh, and Horace joined in. The rest followed, one at a time.

The merriment was bogus but convenient, since it obviated the need for gunplay to resolve the offenses committed by both sides. It was a postponement, Drew concluded, of the inevitable. The Bentines were trash, far below the kind of man Lodi took into his company, and Wiley seemed bent on scraping up alongside Lodi in a manner calculated to produce fire before too long.

It was no surprise to Drew that the brothers chose to visit the outhouse together not long after, and he leaned over to Levon and said, "Trouble coming from those two pretty soon." Levon nodded and said to Nate Haggin, "They might come back at full cock, those boys." Overhearing this, Lodi said, "Those dimwits? They went out together to plan a double jack-off, that's all." He laughed, and Nate and Horace laughed with him. Drew decided he and Levon were less drunk than the rest, therefore obliged to keep a sharper eye on things on behalf of everyone else. He would not have placed it beyond the ability of Wiley and Casper Bentine to sneak around and open fire through the opened windows while their targets laughed and drank.

"I feel like I've got a bull's-eye pinned on me," he said.

"Me too," Levon agreed. "Care to take the air?"

They left through a window that faced away from the outhouse. "Hey, you boys circus acrobats, or what?" yelled Horace. Drew and Levon cut through the corral without disturbing the horses and peered around the cabin corner. The brothers were talking together a short distance away, their voices low. The moon gave so little light they appeared to be one man. They fell silent, and Drew heard urine splashing onto the ground.

Levon whispered, "They're just pissin'."

"You go back in if you want," murmured Drew. "I don't trust either one."

"They just come out to piss is all."

"Go back, then. I'm waiting for them."

"Who's over there?" called Wiley. "Hey, who's that hiding! Come on out!"

Drew pushed Levon back into the shadows before stepping clear of the cabin wall. "Only me, boys, don't panic."

"What the hell you mean, hiding away back there?"

The brothers were buttoning their pants as Drew approached them.

"Hiding? Making water, same as you both."

"Never seen you come out the door," said Casper.

"Must've been concentrating too hard." Drew smiled. "Got the same difficulty myself. Have to handle my rod careful, or it'll drop and break my toe."

Casper began to giggle. "Break your toe ..." he said.

"You ain't so funny," Wiley told Drew.

"Well, you didn't pay to hear me, so that's all right."

"You ain't so funny," Wiley said again, then slapped his brother lightly on the shoulder. "You sound like a fool."

Casper became silent. All three peered at each other in the darkness. "Well," said Drew, "if we're all done watering the garden, there's more whiskey waiting."

He turned and began walking back to the cabin. After a few paces he heard Wiley and Casper fall in behind. Opening the door, he saw Levon seated on his chair. The back window had been closed. Drew accepted the bottle from Horace and took a sip before passing it to the Bentines as they came through the door. "Your good health, gents."

Wiley drank without comment and handed the bottle to Casper. Lodi was shuffling cards. "Who's in for poker?" he asked. Drew and Horace abstained; the rest gathered around the rickety table, and it quickly became obvious the Bentines were poor players, the only difference between them being that Casper accepted his losses with a rueful shake of the head, while his brother grew progressively more angry.

"You boys wouldn't be teaming up against us now, would you?" he suggested, veiling the insult with a tight smile.

"Nope," Nate assured him. "You just play lousy cards."

"We won plenty other times before," Casper insisted.

"Must've been playing against your granny," said Levon.

"No; she's dead," Casper told him. "It was fellers we played against, and we won, didn't we, Wiley?"

Wiley ignored him, concentrating on his cards. When Lodi scooped up the wagers minutes later, Wiley jumped to his feet. "Fuck ...!" he yelled, addressing the room at large. Everyone but Casper waited to see if he would try to draw his gun. Drew's hand was already on his own.

"Bentine," said Lodi, "I've seen more men die over the green cloth than I ever saw die any other way, and those deaths were avoidable, if only those men had've kept a cool head and learned how to play their cards right and take their losses like gentlemen. That isn't too much to ask, to keep on living in this world of ours, now is it?"

Wiley sat down. "You just better not do it again," he warned.

"Win, you mean?"

"You know what I mean."

"Something eating you tonight, Bentine?"

"I don't like to see cheats take my hard-earned money."

"Oh, you mean the money you two got from Thermopolis. I heard you shot a bunch of people to get it, and the money wasn't enough to justify the bloodshed, or did I hear wrong?"

"It was a riskier job than that train you took."

"You know, Bentine, I really don't agree with you, but I'm prepared to steer the conversation away from the place you took it, and keep on playing like I never heard any of the crap you seem to think is talk worth listening to. I'm even prepared to forget that you called me and my friends cheats, which normally I wouldn't do, but I can see in this case I'm dealing with a goddamn moron, so the rules are relaxed."

This time Wiley drew his pistol as he rose, and the first shot went wild, passing within an inch of Lodi's cheekbone. Lodi had time to yank his own pistol out and shoot Wiley square in the stomach. By then Casper was on his feet, and his first shot, aimed at Nate, who had also risen, missed and caught Horace Neet in the side of the head. Nate fired at Casper, hitting him in the ribs, and Casper fired again, almost hitting Levon, who was having trouble releasing the hammer tie on his holster. Lodi put a second bullet into Wiley, who staggered backward. Gunsmoke swirled around the lamp overhead. Casper was on the floor, holding his side, as Wiley collapsed a few feet away, already dying. Horace was still in his chair by the wall, eyes open, brain tissue covering his left shoulder. Drew's ears were ringing from the shots exchanged, and his hand was frozen on his gun butt.

"Damn thing ..." muttered Levon, freeing his gun too late. The survivors looked at each other, at the two dead men and at Casper, writhing in pain now from his splintered rib cage and the shards of bullet lodged inside him.

"Finish him," Lodi told Nate.

Nate shook his head. "Did that the last time, with that Pinkerton. Bones, this'n belongs to you. Shouldn't be too hard, even for a candy-ass. Feller's in real pain, Bones. You fix it for him."

Lodi seemed to accept the situation, and watched Drew slowly take out his pistol. No one had seen Drew kill a man, whole or injured. He aimed at Casper's head and pulled the trigger. Casper jerked once and was still.

"There now," said Nate. "Easier than poking your first woman—am I right, Bones?"

Drew said nothing, but admitted to himself that the thing he had done was simplicity itself; one second Casper Bentine had been in torment, the next second gone from the body that caused him pain. Drew felt neither good nor bad about the shooting. He hadn't liked either of the Bentines, and they were not men to cry over; still, it did seem that he should have felt more than he did.

"That's Horace gone," said Lodi, holstering his gun. "He was a game feller, not even very old. It was his baldy head made him look older than he was. Well, we need to get them all outside. I'm not sleeping next to dead men."

Above the cabin, Clay and Aemon Jennings had been awakened from sleep by the gunfire. They scrambled to their watching post and peered down through the darkness, but could see nothing but a tiny square of lamplit window below.

"Got to be a falling-out of some kind," Jennings said. "It'll be the new ones caused it. Everything was peaceful till they showed up."

"Bentines most likely gunned them down for no good reason. They're the type to do that."

"Could be no one got hurt. I saw a fight in Tucumcari, seven men, and all of them near about emptied their guns at each other, and just one got winged. He wasn't even hurt very bad, but he died later from infection."

The cabin door opened, and in the oblong of light two men appeared, carrying a third. "There goes your no-harm-done idea," said Clay.

A second and a third body were brought outside, but the darkness made it unclear exactly where they were set down.

"Three gone out of seven," said Aemon. "That's better odds for us. Care to sneak down and find out which three?"

"I'll let you do that."

"They won't put them under the ground till sunup. I'd sure like to know which ones were hit."

"Go right ahead."

"You don't have much confidence for a bounty man, Dugan. There's no dog going to sniff you out."

"Or you."

"That's correct, but you're the one that was hired by me, not the other way around, so you can get yourself down there and snoop around for something that'll maybe help us out tomorrow, or we cancel the partnership right now, that's the way I feel about it."

"I wouldn't want the partnership to lose out, Jennings, I like you too much to let that happen."

"Fine, so you get down there and poke around."

It took Clay almost fifteen minutes to reach the cabin. The little moonlight available was hidden by cloud, and he had to grope around in the dark for a further ten minutes before locating the bodies over by the stable. The men who had carried them there had not used a lamp, and the bodies were not laid out neatly; one was at least five yards from the other two. Clay ran his fingers over their features, trying to find some clue to their identities, but the only corpse he was sure of was the one with the smooth pate.

Since he was already so close to the cabin, and because he was frustrated by not knowing who the second and third dead men were, Clay decided to extend his risk by peeking through the window to see who had lived through the gunfight and who had not. He was within ten feet of the yellow square set in the cabin's side wall when he heard the door open and close at the front. He scrambled for the deeper darkness beyond the wan beam of light streaming from the windowpanes, and had barely found it before two sets of boots came around the corner. Clay sent a prayer of thanks to the god of unbelievers when he saw they had again come outside without a lamp, presumably because the cabin was so poorly appointed there was only one on the premises, the one that shone so feebly through the window. He saw two dim figures pass through its wan beam and stop in the vicinity of the bodies.

"It ain't right, to my way of thinking," said a voice.

"It's a question of practicality," said another. "You get that one."

Clay heard sounds of effort, and realized the corpses were being robbed of their boots. He had noticed during his own examination that their gun belts were already gone.

"Where's the other one?" asked the first voice.

"Over there somewhere."

Clay listened to the footfalls passing back and forth.

"Dark as a whale belly out here," grumbled the first voice. "You find him yet, Bones?"

"Maybe he got up and walked away."

"That ain't even funny."

"Levon, when a man that can't see two feet in front of his face can't make a joke, he may as well quit being human."

"Just find him, that's all. I don't like this. ... Shit!"

"Find him?"

"He's here. I swear this ain't the place we dropped him."

"Like I said, he got up and walked around awhile."

"Quit that joke. All right, I got the boots off of him."

"Did his toes twitch, Levon?'

"No, they never. Quit it, I said."

The figures passed back through the window light, and Clay's ears followed their footsteps around to the door. It opened and closed, and he began moving toward the window again. When he had positioned himself directly beneath it, he began slowly to rise, bathing his hat, then his forehead, in its light.

The first thing he saw were the boots, three pairs on the table. Two men had their backs to him and a third was drinking from an upended bottle; the fourth man was nowhere to be seen. Clay waited for the two with their backs toward him to reveal their faces. The drinker lowered the bottle and wiped his lips; that one at least was not a Bentine. The fourth man passed in front of the window, a young man in a blue shirt, and he sat down at the table to clean his gun. The other two still had not turned. Clay heard rumblings of conversation, but could understand none of it. He felt a small sensation in his belly and knew the latest stone had passed from his bladder into the tubes leading to his penis. He had pissed out a broken fraction of stone earlier that day, and so was not surprised that the main body of the thing had at last moved. He hoped it wouldn't scratch and sting on its way through the way the last big chunk had, despite the oil Clay had squirted into his urethra. Kidney stones were something to be handled while taking one's ease in a cane chair, with a plentiful supply of drink nearby, Clay thought, not while peering through a window into a cabin full of killers.

The one with the bottle was pointing at him, yelling. Clay ducked and ran, avoiding the window's light. He moved as fast as he could away from the cabin until he heard the door open, then fell to the ground and lay still, knowing that this time they would all come out looking for him, and they would bring along the lamp. He hoped the place where he lay was lower than the earth around it, but couldn't risk lifting his head to find out; if it was, he was probably safe, considering the ground he'd covered with his long legs before the door opened behind him. If it wasn't, he could consider himself dead.

Four voices passed across him from different directions as they fanned out to search for the face at the window. Two voices expressed doubt that there had been such a face, considering how drunk the one who saw it was, but another voice (Clay recognized it as belonging to one of the boot removers) insisted there had been "a skellington face lookin' in at everyone! Like death, he was, so help me!" A fourth voice (the other boot remover) said, "Levon, I don't believe old man death has a face, and if he did, it'd probably be more like a good-looking woman's, to tempt you close so he could catch hold of you. Something like you described, that'd make a man run like a rabbit to get away. Death'd be smarter than that, if he existed, which he doesn't."

"I did too see him!"

"I can't see a goddamn thing," said one of the first voices.

Too much darkness, thought Clay, and not enough lamps. He just might get away after all. The voices thereafter merged together around the lamp bearer and moved back around to the side of the cabin where Clay had looked through the window. "They're still here," he heard someone say, "and all dead, so it wasn't them either. You better quit sucking that bottle, boy."

"I seen him, I did," insisted a disgruntled Levon.

"Well, he's gone now. Most likely he'll come back and haunt your dreams, at least till you sober up."

"I seen something."

"Then you go look for it, only we're keeping the lamp, Levon. You want to go looking for death in the dark, huh?"

"We can look for his tracks tomorrow," said Levon.

"Should be easy. They'll be split-hoofed and kind of burned into the ground."

The laughter silenced Levon completely, and Clay soon after heard the cabin door close. He stayed where he was, in case one or more men had stayed outside to trick him into betraying his position by movement, but when time passed without the least sound reaching him, he slowly lifted his head. The cabin squatted in darkness, a darker block with light flowing from the window at one side. They all were too drunk to take seriously the claim that a face had been watching them. Death indeed. Clay knew he was ugly, but that was a goddamned insult.

He stood up and made his way back up to the watching post in the trees, stumbling and banging his knee badly once he was among the rocks there.

"Hold it," said Aemon Jennings's voice.

"It's me," Clay told him, "old man death."

"Dugan? What the hell are you saying?"

"Nothing. The bald one's dead, and I'm pretty sure the other two are the Bentines. The others almost got hold of me, but they're drunk."

"Saw them come out and look. You were lucky, Dugan."

"Always have been," said Clay, untruthfully.

They planned more reconnaissance for the following day, and took turns at keeping watch until the sun rose, in case the four unknown men below should suddenly leave. Clay offered to take the first watch, since his abdomen was clutching at him, making sleep impossible. He was still on watch well after sunrise, moaning softly to himself, when there was movement below.

"Jennings, wake up. Looks like a burial party."

Clay trained the binoculars on the men. "Well, that makes it definite. The ones on their feet are the same four that rode up last night. The Bentines are getting ripe over by the stable. Someone did our job for us, looks like."

A grave was dug at some distance from the cabin, the body of the bald man lowered into it and covered. No words were said over the grave when the job was completed. The four men saddled all the horses in the corral and rode away with them toward the west. When they had disappeared from view, Clay and Jennings rode down to the cabin, where Wiley and Casper lay under the open sky like forgotten packages.

"Dugan, your luck runneth over and rubbed off on me too. If we can get these two back to Thermopolis before their faces fall off we're due some cash money. Get the pack animals down here."

Clay did it, and performed most of the tying down necessary to keep the Bentines from kissing dirt on their way to Thermopolis. He had tied quite a number of dead outlaws to packhorses in his time, and knew how to do it the right way. Jennings knew how also, but was Clay's employer, for all his talk of partnership, and so allowed Clay to complete the task unaided. Clay had to pause often and wait for the pain inside him to pass.

"Them stones again?" asked Jennings.

"I double up this way out of boredom, mostly."

"You're an unusual fellow, Dugan. Care to work with me some more? We could be riding a lucky streak."

"I believe I'll pass."

"Thought you'd say that. You're too proud, Dugan, for a man in your position."

"What position's that?"

"Word is you're pretty much all washed up. Liquor, they say, and I've seen it for myself, but you could still be useful to me, Dugan. It's likely the last serious offer you'll get, from me or anyone else."

"That's your opinion."

"You should listen to opinions sometimes, you might learn something."

"Jennings, I already learned as much from you as I care to, so take it and push it as far up your ass as you can, which should be about as far up as your lips."

Jennings laughed, and Clay hated him for the confidence he heard in the laughter. "Dugan, you're not long for this kind of life, my friend. I was you, I'd look for some other line of employment— hotel detective, maybe, something where they won't expect too much."

"I told you already what to do with those opinions."

Clay tugged at the final knots; the Bentines were secure. He asked himself if he despised Aemon Jennings enough to kill the man in a fair gunfight, and decided he did not. They would split the money as agreed, Clay receiving only half of what Jennings would collect, even though Clay had done most of the work and taken all of the risks, despite his pain. He would never work for another man again. It was going to be an expensive lesson, but he wouldn't need to learn it twice.

CHAPTER

40

The telegram was blunt: TRIP
CANCELED ARRIVING HOME SOON ZOE. Leo panicked on receipt of it.
What had happened to make Zoe change her mind; how soon was
soon; and what would he do with Imogen Starr now that his wife
was homeward bound? Rowland Price's plan for Leo to remarry Zoe
in a ceremony masked by sentiment was clearly a necessity, but Leo
had anticipated another year of physical enjoyment from his mistress before being obliged to take that necessary step.

He would have to tell Imogen immediately, to ensure that Zoe
caught no whiff of her once she returned. His wife (his soon-to-be-
legitimate wife) had to be kept sweet and pliant and in deepest
ignorance, or he would lose everything. Price was shown the telegram, and instructed to hire a minister to marry Leo and Zoe all
over again. The ceremony would take place at Elk House, Zoe's
atheism being no secret, and there would be flowers, entire rooms
filled with flowers, to make the occasion memorable. Having taken
care of those arrangements, Leo was faced with a far more difficult
task. He dispatched Jenks to the bank, then visited Imogen at her
home.

Lovey Doll was aware the instant he set foot over the threshold
that Leo was in the grip of considerable agitation. She smiled win-
ningly as he surrendered his coat, and asked, "My darling, is anything wrong?"

"No, no ... certainly not. I should like a drink, if you please, Imogen."

He fidgeted on the sofa while she prepared a whiskey and lemon, and drank the glass down in one gulp when she brought it to him. Lovey Doll suspected it was not the first drink Leo had taken that day, and the sun had barely passed behind the valley rim.

"Leo, you can't hide trouble from a woman who loves you. What is it, my dear?"

"I ... received a telegram today. My wife is ... on her way home."

"Oh, but I thought she was to tour Europe with your daughter."

"I thought so too, but there has been a change of plans, I'm afraid. Imogen ... "

"Yes, Leo?"

"You realize this places me in the most awkward position, do you not? With my wife returning so abruptly, I must ... we must ... Imogen, you must leave Glory Hole!"

"Leave, my precious? And go where?"

"Here, this will take you to any destination of your choosing." Leo took from his jacket an envelope and thrust it at Lovey Doll, who viewed it with a perfect facsimile of consternation on her face.

"What is it, Leo?"

"Ten thousand dollars. With this you can go anywhere, start over again in any way you desire."

"I desire only one thing, Leo, and that is you."

"I regret, I truly regret, Imogen my dear, that it cannot be."

"Cannot?"

"Must not. She is my wife. I have strayed from the straight and narrow path, and must retrace my steps to righteousness. I blame you not at all. The mistake was my own, and that is why I have given you this." He waved the envelope at her impatiently. "Take it, please."

"Leo, you've come to me with dreadful news, and on the very day I was so looking forward to giving you news of my own, but news of an altogether different nature. The happiest of news, Leo."

"Happy news?"

"I carry our child inside me."

"Child ...?"

"Yours and mine. Our own darling baby."

"But ... no, Imogen. No, no, *no!*"

"Leo, my love, isn't this what you wanted of me? I'm confused, Leo...."

"I cannot acknowledge this thing. I have told you what you must do, Imogen. The money—take it, please—will allow you to have this … child in perfect comfort and safety, at some distant location. Imogen, I'll arrange for a further ten thousand, since this … news of yours is so unexpected and … and inconvenient for us both. Fifteen thousand! There, I can do no more."

"But Leo, our baby will be a boy."

"A boy? How can you possibly know such a thing?"

"I … feel it. Call this feeling a mother's instinct, Leo, but I do know. I'm carrying your son. Will you give him up so easily, out of … sheer expedience? You have no other son, Leo. I can give to you what your wife cannot. Had you considered that for even a moment, you would never have hurt me in this … *cruel* fashion. I am to be the mother of your son," she insisted, tears welling in her blue eyes, "and all you wish for me to do is fly to some far-off place so your wife, who does not love you and by your own admission can give you no more living children … so your *wife* can come home to the castle, the *palace* you provided for her, but which she cannot fill with love or sons. Oh, Leo … how can a man of your integrity do such a thing!"

"Imogen, my dearest darling …"

The envelope fell from Leo's fingers. Lovey Doll's face was covered by her hands while she thought frantically, summoning all her skills as an actress. The instantaneous pregnancy had been an inspired piece of work, but she must now concentrate on building Leo's guilt, and his hopes for an heir. For all Lovey Doll knew, she could not conceive; she had abandoned douching her vagina from the moment she began sleeping with Leo, but there was not the slightest indication that his seed had found lodgment inside her. Such an event was not impossible at some future time, but Lovey Doll had need of Leo's offspring at that very moment, to sway him, to persuade him from the folly of accepting the one-armed shrew back into his home before the year they both had anticipated had elapsed. Given the full twelve months, Lovey Doll was positive she could become pregnant, or else find a newborn male child somehow and convince Leo it was his. But this sudden return of the shrew had left her plan in tatters. It could not be abandoned now, not when the man was hers, body and soul. Some other fear was at work within him, she could tell, some secret terror that had to do with his wife, but Lovey Doll could not tell what it might be. With time, she could, and time was the thing she would insist he give her. Twenty-five thousand dollars was nothing, a single feather on the great bird of fortune, and she would not allow herself to be sold so cheaply, just because the man of her choice was a weakling and a fool.

She placed a hand against her forehead and swooned to the carpet. Leo was on his feet instantly. "Imogen! Oh, my dearest ... " He scooped her clumsily into his arms and held her tightly, swamping her nose with his whiskey breath.

"Imogen, Imogen ... "

She opened her eyes, allowing them to roll a little in their shapely sockets. "Oh, Leo ... I felt him stirring within me.... Our son, Leo, tiny as he is ... he made himself known to me.... to us!"

"My darling ..."

"I ... I feel quite faint, Leo ... "

"Rest yourself, Imogen. Here, take the sofa...."

He wrestled her onto the sateen cushions and sank down at her knees, suddenly filled with reverence for her exalted state. His offer of extra cash if she would go away to bear the child elsewhere had been truly shameful, and he hoped Imogen would forgive him. There was to be a son after all! He had all but given up hope for such an event by way of Zoe, and now here was Imogen, with the most wonderful news he could imagine—an heir for the Brannan empire! Provided, of course, that Leo retained the lion's share of the company, following his remarriage to Zoe. Provided Zoe never learned of his other child, his son, and took steps to ensure that the boy would not gain what would be denied her own daughter. Zoe and Omie, what nuisances they were. If only they could have sailed away for the world's far side and never been heard of again, the nasty business concerning Bryce Aspinall need never have arisen, and the boy growing inside his darling Imogen would come into being as his rightful son, his blood heir without a doubt, the natural recipient of power and wealth that had been years in the making.

Leo was already scrambling among names of masculine gender for his boy—David, Benjamin, perhaps even another Leo! Leo Brannan junior. Leo Brannan the second. It had a dynastic ring to it that Leo found irresistible. But there was Zoe, there was Omie.... The problem was insoluble, it seemed, and he was cast into despair by its serpentine coilings, the tenacious grip of the actual over the possible, the hold of past over future, misery over happiness. Zoe was causing Leo great pain, and the faithless creature was not even his legally wedded wife! It was intolerable! Zoe had betrayed him, yet it was she who stood to reap the richest harvest of golden dollars from the situation. Where was justice? Where were order and reason and the natural rightness of things for a man who had done no wrong and the woman who loved him enough to bear him a son? The world was indeed a topsy-turvy place, godless, without moral equilibrium of any kind, if Zoe, who had knowingly posed as a widow in order to snare him, was allowed to claim the prize that was not rightfully hers. It would be a triumph for the forces of darkness and deceit, and it must not be allowed to happen.

Rowland Price's personal investigation into the background of Imogen Starr had borne no fruit of any kind. His contacts in Colorado Springs were unable to place the name into conjunction with any person known to them, yet Colorado Springs was the place Imogen had come from, by her own admission to Leo, who had casually passed the information on to Rowland. The conclusion to be drawn from such anonymity and lack of verifiable public record was not a pleasant one: Leo apparently had found himself another liar. Rowland decided he would say nothing for the moment, and await the results of deeper inquiry. The first liar was already providing sufficient headaches for now. It was disturbing enough that Zoe was returning almost as quickly as she had departed, allowing Leo no real opportunity to burn out his lust for liar number two; the difficulties ahead had been exacerbated by the startling news that Imogen was expecting a child. Rowland had demanded the name of the doctor who told her this, but Leo was opposed to such acts of unsubstantiated suspicion; if Imogen said she was pregnant, then she was, but even Leo could not convey total conviction when speaking of the mother-to-be's certainty of her baby's sex. "It isn't possible for her to know, Leo, it just isn't," Rowland said, but Leo insisted women were creatures of instinct, and her prediction would very likely prove to be true. Rowland saw he was arguing with a man not only smitten still by Cupid's dart but desirous of having at last the one thing he had until now lacked—a son and heir. There was no reasoning with him over Imogen and her progeny-in-the-making, so Rowland decided to pursue other alternatives in an effort to open Leo's eyes before any of this came to the attention of the Praetorians.

"A man cannot have two women, Leo, and succeed in public life, unless he is a Frenchman."

"I'm an American, Rowland."

"And you're obliged, therefore, to choose."

"Between them? Rowland, are you not the one who suggested I remarry Zoe at the earliest opportunity?"

"I was, and since that time we have learned of a supposed child. Your child, Leo, if Miss Starr is correct."

"It does complicate matters enormously.... But what are you suggesting now?"

"Zoe is not your wife. Even without the presence of Bryce Aspinall to verify it, we have the church records from Pueblo stating she was married to the fellow. She will be unable to produce papers of divorce, and will have no legal ground to stand on if you choose to divorce her."

"Divorce? Rowland, may I remind you that if Zoe is not my wife, then I am a poor man indeed, in a very literal sense. If she is not mine, neither is Brannan Mining."

"You and I know that, Leo, and your attorney and his staff know it, but Zoe Aspinall does not, and I see no reason why news of it should ever reach her. You've said yourself that she never concerns herself with legal niceties and the intricacies of ownership. To be crude, Leo, the lady seemed only ever interested in yourself."

"Women have no head for such matters, it's true, but supposing she did ask questions of an embarrassing nature with regard to the company—then what?"

"You make such questionings unnecessary, Leo, by offering her a generous settlement to remove herself from any claims upon you and yours."

"How generous?"

"Offer her a million dollars to sign a document stating that she tricked you into a false marriage and has no claim against you as a result of that trickery. She may not be happy to admit she lied, but a settlement of such proportions will cheer her up in no time. Why would she be dissatisfied with it? She'll take the money and be grateful you don't bring suit against her for bigamy."

"But a million dollars ... "

"Cheap, my friend, dirt cheap. You have your company, and you're free to marry Miss Starr, if that is your choice. It's the perfect solution for everyone."

"I'm thinking, Rowland ... I'm thinking it might have been better to leave Mr. Aspinall alone, kept him on the payroll, so to speak, to confront her with her own past, you see.... "

"All very well to see that now, Leo, but hindsight offers clearer skies than the daily fog we plow through. We have hit a reef, and Mr. Aspinall's end is neither here nor there. Do you wish to remarry Zoe, or take the other lady for your wife?"

"I have made my feelings known to you."

"And so there can be but one path to follow, yes?"

"Yes ... "

She sent a telegram from Denver, giving the time of her arrival home, and a carriage was waiting for herself and Omie at the Glory Hole station. They were taken directly to Elk House, where Leo nervously awaited their arrival. He had wanted to avoid any confrontation so soon, but Rowland advised against it. "Be there when she arrives. Tell her what you know. Take the wind from her sails without pause, without mercy. Postpone nothing." And when Zoe came through the front doors of their home, Leo was there, working himself into a cold rage, the better to accuse her of her crimes.

"Leo, home at this early hour?" asked Zoe, breezing past him on her way to the staircase.

"Some things must take precedence over business, my dear."

"How remarkable that we should agree on something."

He followed her up the stairs. She had not even allowed him a kiss in passing. Leo was finding it easy to be annoyed with her. He became aware of Omie's belated entrance only when he was halfway to the first floor, and gave her a stiff wave, which was not returned with nearly enough speed or enthusiasm to placate him; it would be better when Omie was gone, along with her mother; the girl had always made him uneasy with her uncanny ways, her blue face and its staring eyes.

"We must talk, Zoe. We must talk immediately."

"Of course."

She entered her room. Leo hesitated at the doorway, then followed her inside. "Why have you returned so soon?"

"Seasickness. We both suffered most abominably. Sea voyages are no longer under consideration for either of us."

"But ... why not a trip by land?"

"To where—Mexico? Canada?"

"Oh, anywhere at all in our own country. The railroads nowadays ... such wonderful scenery, so easily admired from a comfortable seat ... I do believe it will be a thing of future times, Zoe—travel for the sake of scenery alone."

"You may be right." Zoe unpinned her hat and set it down on the dresser. "Is she still here? In town, I mean."

"Here ...?"

"Your mistress, Leo."

"I ... well, yes. Yes, she is here, and here she'll stay!"

The sudden change of tone in his voice made Zoe look up at him. Leo's face was flushed with anger.

"I did inform you, Leo, that you must make a decision before my return. I admit I've come home earlier than expected, but my conditions remain as stated."

"Oh, do they, do they indeed. Well, let me tell you ... *wife,* that conditions hereabouts have changed, oh, yes! Nothing is the same anymore. There have been fundamental changes since your departure, indeed there have!"

"Will you share these changes with me, Leo? You seem upset. Has the market for gold plummeted overnight?"

"The market for gold is steady, and will continue that way. The market for truth and fidelity, however, has crashed, and the market for honesty within the state of matrimony has likewise come tumbling down, at least in this house, my dear, my *darling*...."

"You're referring to your mistress, Leo?"

"I am referring to Zoe Aspinall, who pretended to be Zoe Dugan, who attempted to become Zoe Brannan, but is not! That is the woman to whom I refer!"

Zoe's expression of casual contempt faltered. She attempted to replace it with a scornful mask, but knew it made no impression on the red-faced man before her. How had he found out?

"Well?" he bellowed. "What do you have to say for yourself! Do you have the gall to deny what I say? Do you? I have the proof! I have it on paper, Miss Bigamist, Miss Treachery and Deceit, Miss Make-a-fool-of-me ...! Do you wish to speak?"

"Leo ... I had no plan, no wish to be unkind...."

"But you were! You were unkind! Why did you say nothing of this man! Why did you let me believe myself your husband! Good God, woman, supposing we had managed to have children between us! Bastards! You said nothing! *Nothing!*"

"It was ... it had no meaning for me. He was gone. He was no longer real. I thought ... I thought it might upset you to learn of him...."

"And it has, it has upset me to learn of him. It has upset me far more than it would have had you mentioned him before we undertook certain sacred vows, Mrs. Aspinall."

"Leo, I ... I meant you no harm by it, truly.... "

"And no harm will come to me, or to you, or to Omie, because no word, no word at all, of this disgrace to us all, will be made public, do you hear? I will not have my name, and yours, and, more importantly, Omie's, dragged though the filth that public knowledge would smear upon us all if any inkling of this ... this *humiliation* became known to the world. I wish to spare us all any such thing, especially Omie, who is blameless. Are you listening to me?"

"Yes ... "

"My attorney has drawn up a paper releasing one million dollars for your personal use in any fashion you desire—one million dollars, Zoe, simply to absolve yourself of any connection to myself and my business holdings. My attorney has tried several times to dissuade me from this course of action, since I owe you nothing at all, but that has never been my way. I wish for you and Omie to be taken care of, and have insisted that your payment of severance be not one dollar less. You and Omie will quit this house and say nothing to anyone concerning the reasons why. The contract is clear, the terms fair. I would not have gone this far, Zoe, if I thought you truly had loved me, but your actions have made it plain you did not. No woman of integrity would ever have deceived a man so. You have had your own trials, and I admit you have suffered, but that is no excuse. You wronged me with unforgivable duplicity and mendacity and ... you made me believe you loved me when you did not!"

The papers were produced from his jacket like a rabbit from the silk hat of a magician. They landed with a rustle and a swoosh in front of Zoe, page upon page of close-written absolution, denial and renouncement. She could barely read the words. He had found out, after all this time, and now she was without armor, defenseless before buried truths that had been unearthed and flung into her face. Zoe had entered Elk House like a returning queen, and within minutes had been reduced to some kind of conniving kitchen maid, a worthless slut whose futile aim it had been to bring down a worthy man by lies and deceit. She truly felt he had reason to hate her, given the secret she had kept from him for so many years. She was found out. She was undone. A pen and inkwell were fetched from her writing desk. She scanned the clause Leo's finger pointed out to her, the one concerning immediate payment of one million dollars to herself if she would acknowledge her lie. One million dollars, compensation of regal proportion, and who was she to say it was not enough, she who had knowingly married one man while married to another. Leo was unshakable in his wrath, immovable in his certainty that what was done could be made over with the scratching of a steel nib on fine paper prepared for that purpose. He was, she supposed, being generous. There was, she supposed, nothing else she could do, other than sign the sheets spread before her, sign them in the name of herself, but a self she found it difficult to recognize after so long.

"Be sure and write Zoe Aspinall," Leo said, his voice gentler now that it was obvious he had bested her, flattened her with the heavy truths of yesterday.

One million dollars. She signed.

41

When he saw the man-shaped shadow, almost hidden beneath the ledge, Nevis asked himself if liquor was responsible. He had been hacking at the ice for less than ten minutes, at some distance from Nightsoil Smith, further down the ice slope. The area immediately beneath the ledge's overhang was particularly cold to work in, and Smith had declared himself unable to cope with it, his chest being what it was that day, so Nevis Dunnigan worked his way up toward the thickest ice in the ledge's deepest shade, and began to hack at it with his pick, unresentful at having been obliged by Smith's wheezing chest to perform the hardest work on his own.

The shadow of the man within the ice was indistinct, unrecognizable at first as human, but as he hacked a little deeper, and began to concentrate on the shape revealing itself slowly to the pick, Nevis convinced himself the thing was a man. It was impossible to tell how deeply it lay, the ice distorting depth as it did, but Nevis thought he could dig out his find with some assistance from his friend, and so called Smith up to his perch beneath the ledge.

When Smith at last joined him, red of face and short of breath, Nevis pointed with significance at the ice before him. "What?" said Smith, put out by his exertions.

"Look harder," Nevis advised, smiling.

"I am. Ice. Tomorrow I'll show you some shit."

He began to move away, and Nevis caught his shoulder. "Look again. Trust me, there's something there, my friend."

"All right, there's something there, but what is it?"

"It's a man, can't you see? There's the head, there the feet, and in between, the body and legs, for heaven's sake! You can't see him?"

"Is he ... kind of curled up?"

"He is indeed. My congratulations to you. Shall we dig him out?"

"He won't be alive."

"I know that, but my curiosity demands that I see his face. The fellow might have been there for hundreds of years, possibly thousands!"

"Aww, not that long," said Smith, for whom the nation's founding fathers were as remote as the Old Testament's prophets.

"Help me dig him out. He may have some article on his person to indicate how many years have passed since he felt the sun."

"Think he's a white man? He looks awful dark to me."

It required an hour's labor simply to bring the shadow man's features closer to air and light, his body being wedged into as tight a space beneath the ledge as it was, but at the end of that time it was proven that the thing was truly human, although its race was still in question.

"Long hair," said Smith. "It's an Injun."

"The fur trappers of yesteryear were hairy fellows also, I believe."

"But they had beards, and this one don't."

"But it may be a woman, you see. Let's dig on."

"We don't have hardly any ice yet for the wagon, and you want to waste more time digging out an Injun? What for?"

"Simple curiosity, or respect for the dead, perhaps. If you don't care to assist me, I'll do it by myself."

"Don't be taking that tone with me now, or I'll let you, and you'll be here till sundown chipping it out."

They stayed until sundown anyway, both men working faster as the air around them descended the Fahrenheit scale and caused their flesh to shiver. The figure trapped in ice was awkward to reach by pickax, and the best part of the daylight hours were used up before a block containing the complete article was hacked free of the slope. Released from its larger prison, the block immediately escaped the clutches of Nevis and Smith and began sliding down toward the patiently waiting mules.

"Noooo ...," breathed Nevis, as the shining sarcophagus accelerated toward the rocks below. It broadsided into a large boulder and
shattered into many pieces, some of which flew upward to catch the
last rays of sunlight spilling over the valley's western rim, then
these shards descended with the rest around the small dark figure
slithering still to the very bottom of the ice slope. It arrived quite
close to the mules, which greeted its arrival with the same aplomb
with which they had accepted the small explosion preceding it.

Smith reached it first, and had drawn his conclusions by the time
Nevis joined him. "Injun, definite."

"How can you be so sure?"

"See that on the foot? What's that if it ain't a moccasin?"

Nevis squinted in the failing light. He had seen ceremonial moccasins before, exquisitely beaded things, quite beautiful to look at.
The things wrapped around the feet of their find were graceless
bags of animal hide bound clumsily about the ankle. The legs themselves were remarkably ugly, shrunken to a sticklike thinness
inside pants of the same material that clothed its feet. Ice still
clung to the upper torso, making further examination impossible.

"Let's get the crittur back to town and take a real close look."

"This is a man, Smith, therefore deserving of our respect."

"Well, I do respect him, but my goddamn hands are froze from
being up here all goddamn day, and we wasted every minute of it
for not even a nickel's worth of ice!"

"Our haul today is more important than that."

"Does he look like he carries a wallet?"

"In a scientific age, science pays the piper, Smith."

"What's that mean?"

"It means our shrunken fellow here may be worth more than you
and I could make in a year of chipping ice and hauling dung."

Smith shook his head. He expected they would even have to pay
for the little man's funeral, once they took him down to Glory Hole.

Winnie objected to the presence of the thing immediately. It was
dead, and it was clearly an Indian. The remainder of the ice had
fallen from its upper body during the descent to town, its deerhide
vest and the feathers in its braids revealed. "It's an object of scientific value, Winnie," Nevis told her, and was told in return to put it
out in the stable. "It stinks!" she said. Nevis could not see how this
might be of consequence in so odoriferous a household as Smith's,
but his partner sided with Winnie, and the Indian was removed to

the stable, where its closer proximity to the honey wagon rendered all objectionable odors redundant. Nevis thought his friends were exaggerating; how could something as deeply frozen as the corpse possibly begin to smell so soon after its release from the ice?

Over dinner he proposed that their unique find be made available to a paying audience, after the fashion of P. T. Barnum's various freaks and curiosities. "There's money to be had from such displays," he told them, but Smith and Winnie were unconvinced.

"It's just a dead old Injun, not like a famous king or something that folks'd want to see," protested Smith.

"And it's ugly," added Winnie. "You can see the ribs poking through, practically, and he's got no lips."

The face of the frozen man was indeed startling, its tendon-tough rictus giving it the appearance of a skull tightly encased in old leather. The teeth, seemingly in excellent condition, leered unpleasantly below the empty nasal passage. Its eyes, like poorly molded marbles, were set crookedly beneath lids distorted by cold and time. It was, Nevis had to admit, an object without aesthetic appeal, but this was the very characteristic that would, he insisted, bring paying customers to the glass case containing such a curiosity.

"What glass case?"

"Use your imagination! We'll order one built, a special airtight case to keep him fresh and presentable without losing his ugliness. I only wish he had two heads or a third leg to make him even more repellent, but you can't expect to have everything."

Smith said, "I seen a two-headed baby in a bottle one time. It made me cry, it did, seeing something like that."

"You big baby," said Winnie, not without affection.

"I was only seven," Smith defended himself.

"Are we united in this enterprise or not?" Nevis demanded.

"I guess it's worth a shot," Smith conceded. "We lost a day's work over it, so maybe we should try and get it back."

"Just as long as you take it away from here," Winnie said, "and don't expect me to be touching it at all."

"Your tiny hands will not be soiled," Nevis assured her, then stood and put on his hat. "No time to lose now," he said. "I'm off to alert the newspaper fellows. Our discovery will doubtless be front-page news in tomorrow's edition."

The office of the *Glory Hole Sentinel,* owned by Leo Brannan himself, as were most other enterprises in town, was a brisk walk away, on Brannan Boulevard. Nevis found the place lighted and filled with activity despite the hour's lateness. He asked to see the editor, and was informed the editor was at home, dining.

"But he should be here to receive important news," protested Nevis.

"What news is that?" asked the printing crew's boss.

Nevis told him about the Indian in the ice.

"A dead Injun? That all? I grant you it's good news when another one dies, but that don't make it something to put in the paper."

The printing boss wanted Nevis to leave; the man stank of shit. "You the feller that runs the honey wagon with Smith?"

"I am, but we found the object while engaged in our other line of work, namely ice collecting."

"That's right, I heard you did that too. Well, there's an item you and Smith'll be real interested in reading come tomorrow, let me tell you."

"Item, sir?"

"Come on along back here and I'll show you."

Nevis followed the printing boss to the clanking presses. A freshly printed sheet was taken from a pile and thrust at him. "There, read that there, halfway down."

Nevis saw the bold headline: NEW IMPROVEMENTS FOR GLORY HOLE. The article sent a chill crawling across his skin. Leo Brannan intended bringing the town up-to-date by building an electrical generating plant, which, as well as providing brighter lights for the community, would also power a small ice-making factory. Brannan was not content to stop there, but had committed himself to installing modern plumbing in every home and building, all at his own expense. The projects were to begin just as soon as the plans were finalized.

"Why ...?" asked Nevis.

"Why? So folks can read the news without getting bad eyes from it, and have a real cold beer, and not have to smell your wagon rolling around town. It's progress, see."

"But it will put Smith and myself out of work...."

"Well, what kind of work is it anyway, huh? You can get yourselves better jobs, can't you, huh? Can't stop progress. Brannan, he knows that. Had a bug up his ass about progress ever since his old lady left town again, permanent this time, they say. He's got to have progress here, and no mistake. It's a rich man's distraction, that's how I see it, to keep his mind off of how she went away like she did.

Mind you, what man wants a wife with just one arm, when he's got a piece like he's got stashed on Bowman Street. I had a piece like that, I'd tell my wife to go someplace else too."

"May I ... may I keep this?"

"Sure you can; no charge. Listen, just you go bury that dead Injun before the law finds out. Dead men have to be buried, that's the rules in this town, mister."

Nevis hurried back to Smith and Winnie with the news sheet, and their faces blanched as he read to them the obituary of their twin professions. "A double blow," he said, laying the paper down. "If it was only an ice factory he intended building, or just the modern plumbing ... but both! This is the end for us, Smith."

"The shitty bastard!" Winnie raged. "Why's he have to do that to us! Why doesn't he give his money to poor folk if he wants to get rid of it! Shitty rich man ...!"

"We never done nothing to him. Hell, he don't even have poop pots in his house, got that plummery instead, up on the hill and at that fancy lady's place that he keeps. Fancy plummery, and now he wants everyone to have it, so's we can't do the work anymore. Why would he do that to us?"

"Brannan isn't doing it to us. He very likely doesn't even know we exist. He simply wants to give his town the latest and best. It's an unfortunate coincidence that the very improvements he wishes to make will force us to seek other employment."

"Not me," Smith said. "This is what I do, and it's a good living. What's he want to spend money making ice for, when we can get it for free just up the valley?"

"For us, it's free, but we charge anyone who takes it from us. That is the free enterprise system upon which our nation is built. We're obliged to change our ways to accommodate a changing world. I abandoned art for the same reason, my friend. No one wanted it, so I ceased to create it. The lessons of change are harsh, but we all must learn them in the end."

"Quitter," Winnie sneered.

"Realist," countered Nevis.

"Weakling," she said.

Nevis was hurt. He could see that Winnie had been drinking for the better part of the day while he and Smith labored to release their Indian from the ice, but drunkenness alone could not excuse such insults.

"I'm a pragmatist, Winnie. Life has fashioned me that way. You may hate Brannan for the thing he intends doing, but he'll do it anyway, without ever knowing you hated him for it. That is the gulf that yawns between rich and poor."

"We ain't poor," Smith said. "We make a good living, doing what we do. You ever starve for a meal or a drink since we teamed up? It's a good living, and the son of a bitch wants to wipe it out for us."

"Progress, Smith ... "

"Shit on it! And shit on Brannan too! Maybe he owns the town, but he don't own me!"

"Me neither!" declared Winnie.

Nevis was fast becoming upset at the way in which his friends seemed to have assumed he was taking Leo Brannan's side, when he was not. He knew Winnie and Smith were unsophisticated individuals, but couldn't they see how inevitable it was that their lowly work would someday be made redundant by progress, which seemed to have become the nation's watchword of late?

"Nor I," said Nevis, but the mildness of his voice seemed only to infuriate the other two. He saw now that both had been drinking heavily during his absence, and resented their selfishness. Nevis had walked all the way to the newspaper office to make some money for them, and yet here they were, siding against him as if he had somehow been responsible for the disastrous news he returned with. It was not fair that someone of his intelligence and integrity be accused so, and he took a drink from the bottle on the table and told them so.

"Who are you to talk?" Winnie said. "You didn't work for a living till you came here."

"I told you, I was an artist...."

"That ain't work," said Smith, "not real work anyway."

"It certainly is! Do you imagine Rembrandt painted his portraits without monetary compensation? Are you truly so ignorant? Art is the most honorable work known to man, with the possible exception of doctoring the poor and needy!"

"Then go back to it, why don't you!"

"Winnie, please ... This bad news has upset us all ..."

"She's right," Smith declared. "I don't often say so, but she's right. If you had've belonged here, you never would've been this way about Brannan, not caring what he's gonna do to us. For you, it ain't really real, is what I'm saying, even after I brung you in and set you down and give you a drink and a job and a woman besides."

"You never gave me to him," Winnie protested. "I made up my own mind about that." Turning to Nevis, she said. "And I regret it now, if that's the way you feel."

"Stop it! Stop it, both of you! What have I done ...?"

"It's that Injun," stated Smith. "I never wanted to mess with it, but you had to go and dig it out and bring it down here, and now look what happened because of it. It's a bad-luck dead-man Injun, is what it is, and if you had've done like I wanted and left it where it was, we never would've been in the trouble we're in, and that's a fact."

"No, no, Smith, the nows would have reached us sooner or later anyway. You're not being logical, not sensible about this. The Indian has nothing to do with Brannan's plans, in fact it may be the very thing that allows us to weather the approaching storm. The thing is worth money, as I explained before. If we act quickly to preserve it, the Indian will serve us well. Finding him was not bad luck, but the very best of good luck, don't you see?"

He had their grudging attention, and continued with a passion. "People are interested in the unusual, the bizarre, the ugly and the horrific, and will pay to experience these things at second hand. Look at this, for example." He snatched up the news sheet again and pointed to the leading article: SLADE STRIKES AGAIN! FIEND STILL AT LARGE! "The whole southwestern region is petrified by the presence of this cannibal, but the rest of the country spends money reading about their terror. Man is a creature fascinated by the awful, the ghastly, the lurking horrors of the world. We have such a horror, and it cost us the sweat of one working day. Must I make my point all over again? Must I?"

Smith and Winnie exchanged sullen looks. Smith's expression relented first, and he held out his hand for the bottle Nevis held. "You sure about this Injun?"

"As sure as any man in this vale of tears can be of anything."

"Well, all right, then." Smith drank deeply by way of acceptance.

Nevis looked at Winnie. "Will you believe I've done no wrong, and want only to help us all?"

Winnie said, "I suppose," and reached for the bottle.

"Thing is," said Smith, surrendering it, "we don't have us a glass case that's airtight. I never even heard of such a thing. That Injun, he's already ripe, I say."

"Then we'll pickle him until the case is made."

"Pickle?"

"Exactly. Preservation is not in itself a difficult task. The problem is to preserve the object one is desirous of preserving without hiding it away from view inside a pickling barrel, and that is where the airtight case comes into its own. Until we have it, though, we must resort to dunking our frigid friend in vinegar brine, like so much herring. It should only be a temporary measure, until the case is built. Do we have the financial wherewithal to order such a specialized piece of work, Smith?"

"I reckon."

Nevis smote his forehead. "And we shall enlist the aid of Mr. Leo Brannan in making our find known to the scientific community and the world at large!"

"I don't want him having nothing to do with it," said Smith, and Winnie agreed.

"But the man is perfectly suited to our ends," Nevis enthused. "What was Slade before Leo Brannan placed a reward upon his head? An unspeakable wretch who ate of his fellow man's flesh in a collapsed mine, a disgusting specimen of humanity to be sure, but of little note in the sweep of history. However, once our illustrious magnate made known to the public his personal desire that Slade be found and punished, the talk has been of nothing else. The man-eater has become a walking plague, a shadow over the land, the subject on every lip, and Leo Brannan could do the same with our Indian, I don't doubt."

"But why would he want to?" asked Winnie.

"Because ... " Nevis faltered. He could think of no compelling reason. The fact that the Indian had been discovered above Glory Hole might pique Brannan's interest, and any man committed to modern plumbing and ice production would surely be willing to invest in a scientific curiosity such as theirs, even if this meant nothing more than informing the world of its existence. Nevis doubted that remorse over throwing two men out of work would play any role in Brannan's thinking.

"Who knows why a man such as he might or might not help us, but my friends, he won't accept or reject our proposal until we ask."

"That'll be your job, then," said Smith. "You got the words that'll make him sit up and listen, I guess."

"Thank you, Smith. I am in complete agreement. I will, however, require a new suit of clothing, plus extensive bathhouse time. You, as custodian of the purse strings, will have to supply the cash for these necessary items."

"Me?"

"I can't appear before the wealthiest man in the west as I am. I must appear urbane, confident and sweet-smelling before I enter the sanctum of the great man."

"Why don't you pay for that stuff? I pay you wages, don't I? Use 'em for the stuff, why can't you?"

"Smith, you don't pay me anywhere near as much as you pay yourself. If this plan is to stand any chance for success, you must part with fifty dollars for my own requirements, and considerably more, I should think, for the glass case. Nothing spent, nothing won, I fear."

Smith took back the bottle and drained it.

Seeking out the personal interest of Leo Brannan, and receiving it, were two different matters. Freshly scrubbed, shaved, coiffed and attired, Nevis presented himself first at the offices of Brannan Mining, but was shown the door when he explained his business. He then walked all the way up the valley to Elk House in an attempt to confront the owner there, but could get no further than the front doors, having been issued no personal invitation to visit.

Undeterred, Nevis strode back to town in the gathering gloom of evening, his new shoes pinching quite painfully by that time, and concocted on the downward journey yet another gambit, his most audacious. If Leo Brannan would not see him, prevented as he was from knowing Nevis's need because of the intervening employees at his doorways and portals, then Nevis would have to approach the man by way of someone even closer than his servants. He would take the risky step of consulting with the man's mistress. He knew her house on Bowman Street as did most of the town, and had heard the rumors that placed her in a less salubrious location at an earlier moment in her life at Glory Hole—a common boardinghouse close to the railroad tracks. It was the humble origins of the mistress that inspired Nevis with faith in his plan; such a female would not be arrogant or dismissive of his entreaties. He was filled with self-assurance as he lifted the lion-headed knocker on Imogen Starr's door.

It had been a dreadful day. Her breakfast had been unacceptably burned, and her green parrot, a recent gift from Leo, had somehow slipped free of its perch chain and flown through the nearest open window. Leo would be furious when he found out. Lovey Doll had not liked the bird, not trusting its beady little eyes and wickedly curved beak, and it had revealed previous tuition in its filthy vocabulary, something she was sure Leo had been unaware of when he purchased it for her. Anyway, it was gone, and after its abrupt leavetaking, Lovey Doll had shouted at the maid who left the window open, and at the maid whose responsibility it was to take care of the parrot's needs; the lazy girl had not even noticed the parrot's leg ring was not secure, and so was responsible for its loss. Lovey Doll doubted that a Brazilian parrot would last long in the rarer atmosphere of Colorado. Perhaps she should order another from whichever exotic store in Denver had provided the first,and hope that Leo did not notice the difference.

Leo had of late been quite testy in his dealings with her. The one-armed wife had packed her bags and left, dragging her odious daughter with her, but this had not improved Leo's temper at all; he was brusque, demanding, not at all his usual self. The parrot had been a gift by way of apologizing for certain intemperate remarks he had passed recently, remarks concerning the flatness of Lovey Doll's belly. She had taken to gorging on food since that day, in hopes of plumping herself out to an agreeable width and depth, but still Leo grumbled about his need for a son "or else." Surprisingly, he had not forced her to visit a doctor for official confirmation of the lie, an oversight for which Lovey Doll was grateful. She could not hope to fool him forever, though, and since conception seemed beyond her body's abilities, she was fearful for the future, when Leo found out he had been deceived. Any man who sent away his wife because she was barren and his mistress was not would surely be very angry to learn his mistress was a liar. It was the daily postponement of his learning the truth that gave Lovey Doll headaches of terrible proportion, and prevented her from gaining the flesh she required to further the deception for a month or two more. She was in such a state of nerves she could not keep food inside herself, but vomited it up within a half hour of eating, or else lost precious weight through the embarrassing affliction of running bowels.

She was in no mood, therefore, to answer her own doorbell when it became obvious the maids she had shouted at earlier had gone into hiding somewhere inside the house, and could not hear the visitor announcing himself on her step. Lovey Doll's face, as she opened the oak door, was not conducive to unwarranted conversation.

The fellow there had a vaguely familiar air about him that confused her momentarily. It was intolerable that she should be expected to answer her own door, without knowing who her visitor was in advance. "Yes?" she snapped. The man was staring with an impudence she considered worth reporting to Leo, so he could have the fellow run out of town for his lack of manners. "What is it?" she asked in exasperation.

"Lovey Doll?"

The words transfixed her with fear. How did he know? Who was he, this red-nosed stranger?

"No," she said. "You're mistaken."

"Lovey Doll ... It's you, it's really you."

"Please depart this instant."

"It's me, Nevis!"

"Nevis?"

"Nevis Dunnigan! I painted your picture, Lovey Doll. You don't mean to say you've forgotten posing for *Venus Revealed*. Lovey Doll, I never thought ... oh my goodness ... to see you again."

"Nevis Dunnigan ... "

"Yes! Yes! May I come in?"

"Nevis ... Yes, you may."

She stepped aside and let him pass into her life again.

"Do you work here?" he asked, looking around at the richly appointed hallway.

"I ... no, this is my house."

"Yours? But ... how fortuitous, Lovey Doll! How wonderful you look!"

"We'll sit in the parlor."

She led him to a comfortable settee, her mind whirling. If Nevis Dunnigan breathed a word about her former identity, all her plans would be washed away in an instant. Leo Brannan would never marry a woman who had posed in the nude for a painter, and deceived him over her very name. Nevis's reappearance in her life had come at the very worst moment she could conceive of. He looked awful, despite his new suit of cheap material and his over-scented pomade, like a tramp made over by good works and a few dollars, yet still a tramp beneath it all. His nose was a large strawberry, his cheeks heavily veined by the unmistakable drinker's web.

She had not known him for long, back in Kansas City, but even if she had, his appearance had changed so very greatly over the years, she would never have recognized him without his own introduction.

"So, Nevis, how have things been with you?"

"Oh, excellent. You find me in the pink, as they say."

"You are still a painter?"

"No, not anymore. They stole my work, the picture of you, and never compensated me with a single cent."

"Compensated?"

"Imitations of my work became commonplace. Surely you knew your picture, or at least a copy of it, was in every saloon in the country."

"No, I did not," said Lovey Doll, appalled.

"And on cigar boxes too, and a host of other commercial canvases, so to speak. But you look utterly unchanged, Lovey Doll, from the days when I made that first immortal study."

"Please, don't call me by that name, I beg you. My real name is ... Imogen Starr, and I have reverted to its use. Lovey Doll is so ... theatrical, don't you think?"

"I confess I always thought it suited you to perfection, but if you insist ... Imogen." He glanced around himself at the polished parquet flooring and ornate wallpaper. "So you are ... Leo Brannan's special friend?"

"I am."

"I thought I had the right house, then when you appeared in the doorway I felt I must surely have made a mistake, but no, it was truly you, and you're the very one I came to see, in your capacity as Mr. Brannan's ... confidante. Such an amazing coincidence. This is the work of invisible hands, to be sure. Are you a believer in fate, Lovey Doll ... I mean, Imogen?"

"I scarce know what I believe anymore. What is it you want, Nevis?"

"Oh, yes, I had quite forgotten. Put simply, I have a business proposal for Mr. Brannan to ... shall we say, endorse? He does not have to contribute money toward the venture, merely discuss it at length in his newspaper, and make sure other newspapers become interested."

"Interested in what?"

Nevis told her, in considerable detail.

"You pickled the thing ...?" asked Lovey Doll, aghast.

"He crouches inside a rain barrel even as we speak."

"Nevis, this is foolishness."

"Not at all. 'The Sleeping Savage,' we shall call him. He may be hundreds of years old, you know. His ghoulish appeal for the masses is strong. Why, P. T. Barnum has interested himself in lesser displays, and they certainly made money. It isn't the kind of thing a lady of refinement such as yourself would care for, of course, but purely as a philanthropist, would Mr. Brannan care to assist us, do you think?"

"I shall ask him for you. In the meantime, I wish to contribute a small sum toward the construction of your glass case. Please wait here."

Lovey Doll fetched fifty dollars from her bedroom and returned to Nevis. "Here, take it with my very best wishes for your plan."

"Thank you indeed, Lovey ... Imogen. And you'll raise the subject with Mr. Brannan?"

"Of course I shall, but you must not come here again, Nevis, not ever. Mr. Brannan is a jealous fellow, and won't allow any man to cross the threshold but himself. I shan't mention to him that you actually came inside, since that would make him disinclined to include mention of your Indian in his newspaper. I shall tell him instead that I have heard of the thing, and recommend that he take notice of it. There must be no connection whatsoever between you and myself, do you understand?"

"Perfectly, and I thank you again. You are, as ever, an enchanting woman, and I have fallen under your spell once more. Your slightest wish is my stern command."

"Very good, Nevis, and now I must hasten your departure, before Mr. Brannan arrives, you understand."

"I am gone from your doorway already."

He stood with her, and took hold of her hand. Before Lovey Doll could snatch it back, he had pressed it to his lips, then released it. "Ahh," he breathed, "if only fate had conspired otherwise ... "

"Indeed, and now you must go. Immediately, Nevis."

She took his arm and began marching him toward the door. Nevis appeared close to tears as he stumbled alongside her.

"My feet are walking where they have seldom trod these many years since we parted—on the thinnest of air, my dear Lovey Doll, a dance of contentment at having chanced upon you again in this unlikely fashion.... "

"Yes, yes, a happy occasion for us both, Nevis." She pushed him gently out into the night. "Now remember, don't come here anymore, not even once, do you hear?"

"As you command, O queen."

"Well, just remember it. Good night, Nevis."

The door was closed in his face. Nevis stared at it in a daze for a moment, then turned and walked to the gate, and then along the street. He was in ecstasy. Lovey Doll Pines had come back into his life! He felt quite drunk, even if he hadn't had a sip all day; it was the wine of remembrance and sentiment coursing through his veins, he supposed, and such sweet wine it was, lightly bubbling, intoxicating him with wispy yearnings that he had smothered years before. She really was the only woman for him in all the world, the female supreme, a queen incarnate. Beside Lovey Doll, Winnie was a drab harlot, coarsened by use. It disturbed him a little that Lovey Doll was a kept woman, but at least the man keeping her in such style was an important fellow, not some brute who would not appreciate her wonderful qualities. He understood now why Leo Brannan had sent his one-armed wife away; she could never have been compared to Lovey Doll, no matter how fine. And Lovey Doll had been most pleased to see him, he could tell. Even for people who had risen to inhabit the upper reaches of society, life could be a lonely place, Nevis was sure. She had needed to see a face from the past, just as he had, and the encounter had enlivened her features so prettily. Nevis himself felt handsome for the first time in a long while, and it did not stem from his new clothing and the two hours he had spent in the bathhouse. It was the inner man who glowed so brightly, aflame with the radiance of reawakened love.

His mood was ended abruptly by the sudden swooping onto his hat of a bird. The hat fell down, the bird screeched once like a soul in torment and was gone again, a long-tailed bird that even by the somber gleam of street gaslighting was a brilliant green. Nevis would have preferred a visitation from the bluebird of happiness, but was content to have been attacked by something green and unusual. He picked up his hat and continued homeward.

The news he brought to them this time was greeted by Smith and Winnie with subdued enthusiasm. Nevis thought their lack of outright joy was caused by fear of a new beginning for themselves; then again, they had not rediscovered the love of their lives, as he had done, so their awkward smiles were bound to suffer by comparison with his own.

"She really said she'd talk to him?"

"She gave her word as a woman of honor," assured Nevis.

"What's so honorable about being a rich man's whore?" Winnie asked, and Nevis bridled.

"She is not a whore! How dare you! Lovey ... Miss Starr is a decent woman who happens to have fallen in ... in love with a man who happens to be married. And he isn't even married anymore, it seems. I don't wish to hear any further comments about the lady. Didn't she give us fifty dollars? How dare you call her names ... you, of all people!"

This remark caused Winnie's mouth to open in surprise.

"Here now," said Smith, "don't you be calling no one names yourself."

"I cannot stand a hypocrite," Nevis announced, and walked stiffly outside. He was furious with Winnie, and thought of leaving his friends if they did not grant their benefactress the respect Nevis deemed appropriate. He went to the stable and stared for some time at the barrel containing their sleeping savage. It was an unremarkable tomb for so exotic a corpse, but thanks to Lovey Doll's largess, it would be a temporary resting place. Nevis knew Smith would not spend hard cash on a glass case if the extra money and the promise of a word in Brannan's ear had not come home with him. The project would succeed now because of the happy circumstances surrounding it. Nevis was so entranced by Lovey Doll he could not even resent her status as a wealthy man's mistress. It was enough to know that she had prospered in the world, even as he had sunk to the gutter. It was fortunate for Nevis that they had met while he was well dressed and clean; it would have been mortifying had she recognized him while he rode the honey wagon. The reunion had worked out perfectly, considering the pitfalls that might have made it a nightmare. Nevis found it hard to concentrate on the barrel and its contents, so taken was his mind by visions of Lovey Doll Pines.

The remainder of the evening was strained. Nevis drank with his friends, but did not enjoy the liquor or their company, even when the talk was of their proposed investment in the savage. He chose to sleep on the floor rather than share the bed as usual, but could find no rest, so stirred was he by meeting again with the subject of *Venus Revealed*. He pretended to be asleep when Winnie rose from the bed and silently passed him by on her way to the door.

When Winnie was done in the outhouse, she paused in the yard.

Her life in the last few days had been turned upside down. The finding of the Indian had been a harbinger of some kind, the prelude to a sequence of events that upset her a little more as each new thing revealed itself. Leo Brannan's proposed ice factory and newfangled shitters for the whole town seemed calculated to lay her men low, and Nevis' proposal for a sideshow with their savage had struck her as lunacy. Winnie had been obliged to change her mind when Nevis came home with cash and promises, but there had been something about his face and manner that made her suspicious. If she had not known better, Winnie would have sworn by her womanly instincts that Nevis was in love, and she knew it could not be with herself.

Winnie's notion of love had undergone a transformation since her girlhood, a reduction of expectation from the severely limited to the nonexistent. From the time of her deflowering by an uncle, through the various mishandlings by boys and men until she decided to utilize their need for her body by joining Vanda Gentles's brothel in Galveston, to her days at Gods of the Dance in Leadville, and on to her life with Smith, then with Smith and Nevis, Winnie had expected no love, and received none. Smith and Nevis both made her happy from time to time, but it was never love, nor could she reasonably demand it of them. A mutual warmth was the best any of them could provide for each other, and Winnie was able to content herself with that for most of the time.

The look on Nevis's face that evening, though, had been remarkable. Winnie had seen it only once before, when one of Vanda's girls had fallen in love with a customer, truly believing he loved her also. The customer had visited regularly, then never returned. The girl had killed herself. Nevis had that same look of sublime expectation, and Winnie was disturbed by it. His quick defense of Brannan's whore had been remarkably vociferous, furthering Winnie's suspicions, but then had come a sense of reality: why would a pathetic creature like Nevis imagine himself in love with a woman like Imogen Starr? Winnie had seen her once on the street, and she was indeed a beautiful woman; it was unthinkable that some kind of spark had passed between elegant Imogen and hapless favor-seeker Nevis. Winnie realized she would have been jealous, had such an unlikely thing occurred. But it had not. Nevis was merely excited over the prospect of a successful launching of the Sleeping Savage; there was no more to his exuberant mood than that.

Looking up, Winnie could see the lights of Elk House far above Glory Hole. Zoe Dugan, who once had danced with love-starved men in Leadville Taffy's place, just as Winnie had, lived there, or had until recently. When Winnie first came to Glory Hole from Leadville, Elk House was already completed, the Brannans in occupancy. It had been some time before Winnie, attempting to change her life by working as a hotel maid, heard that Leo Brannan's wife was called Zoe, and she had a daughter with a blue birthmark on her face. That could only have been Zoe Dugan and little Omie. Winnie had been consumed by envy for days. Such impossible good fortune as Zoe had found might have come Winnie's way if only she had done as Zoe did, and left Gods of the Dance for legitimate work. Zoe's new life was so utterly different from the one she had shared with Winnie that it was not possible to approach her; Winnie would have felt ashamed somehow. And so she stayed in the town below the mansion of her friend, and told no one of their former lives. Even when Zoe lost an arm, Winnie had been unable to muster the nerve to visit and offer her commiseration; it had been too long by then.

That was when Winnie began to drink in earnest. She drank herself out of work, and sold herself for more liquor, and drank even more to erase her shame over having fallen again into the life of a whore. Then Smith had introduced himself and offered her another kind of life. There would be no marriage, he told her, because men don't marry whores that they know for sure are whores, but he would treat her well, he said, and never beat her if she would cook for him and occupy his bed to the exclusion of all others. Winnie had thought about it for several seconds, then agreed. It was not much of an offer, but it was the only one she had ever received. Smith had not lied; he was tender in his own clumsy fashion, and once she became used to the smell of him, she was not unhappy. Smith sometimes broke his own rules by bringing home friends with whom he wished to share Winnie, but these friends always passed out of their lives after a few weeks or months, and the basic pairing of herself and Smith was undisturbed. But then had come Nevis Dunnigan, a forlorn-looking fellow both of them had taken pity on, and the equation had been irrevocably altered. Now they were three, and Winnie wanted no part of Nevis to be yearning for some other woman, even one as unattainable as Leo Brannan's fancy-dressed whore on Bowman Street.

Zoe was gone from the big house above the valley, sent away, it was rumored, because her husband could not bear to look upon her stump of an arm, or stand the presence of the blue-faced daughter who could make strange things happen; but most of all, he had found a comely woman with whom he was infatuated. Winnie knew this was the real reason for her old friend's dismissal from paradise. She supposed there was a kind of justice to Zoe's fall, since she had no right to such riches anyway, not being born to them. Winnie did not gloat over Zoe's fate, or feel especially sorry for her, since she had, for a few years anyway, tasted the luxury of good food and fine clothing and a house big as a castle. No, Winnie could not weep for her, or bring herself even now to tell anyone of her own connection to the one-armed woman whose star had burned too brightly for too short a time. She did wonder where Zoe might have gone, but she did not wonder for very long, and returned to the warmth of her bed, where Smith lay gently rumbling, like a hibernating bear.

"Nevis," she called softly, knowing he was only pretending to sleep over in the corner. "Nevis, you stop this nonsense and get into bed right now, before you catch a chill. Do you hear me, Nevis?"

He came quickly enough, and she warmed him with herself.

Her many recent transitions were mounting up, causing Omie some confusion. They had been at Elk House, then on a train that was robbed, then in the biggest city in the world, then on the ocean, then on more trains back to Colorado and Elk House, and scarcely had they arrived than they were out the door again, with all their baggage. It was interesting, in a way, all the hustle and bustle that had accompanied their quickstep wandering, but this last move away from Elk House—for the last time, Mama said—was not interesting at all, unless a body happened to find misery interesting.

Mama had not explained their latest journeying, other than to say she could not live with Papa another minute, nor he with her, and Papa had a new lady to talk to now anyway, the lady in Glory Hole, whose house Papa had been going to all those times he had not come home.

"Will the lady come and live at our house now, Mama?"

"I expect she will, one way or another."

"But she isn't married to Papa; you are."

"Not for very much longer. He has arranged for something called an annulment. That means the marriage between us will be ... as if it never had been."

"Just because of the other lady?"

"That and other things. Please, I don't wish to discuss it further."

Omie stared out the window beside her. They were on yet another train, this one taking them south to Durango. Zoe had said they would stay there for a time, while she thought about where they should go to spend the rest of their lives. Such an important decision could not be rushed. Omie hoped it would be somewhere with mountains as high as Colorado's, but was not hopeful that this wish would be granted. It seemed likely that Mama would want to go as far from the scene of her disgrace as money could take them. Omie wondered if a flat desert was to be their final destination, or the grasslands of Nebraska. They might go back to New York City, which would be a very good choice, in Omie's opinion; she remembered with delight all the electric brilliance of that place, and the wonderfully bloody play they had seen about the awful Indian brothers who killed and killed until they were themselves killed. Mama had said the play was trash, but Omie liked it very much.

"Can we go to New York, Mama?"

"Perhaps. I must think about so many things."

Omie looked into her mother's mind and saw there a swirling cloud of grayish purple, its folding surfaces forming faces upon faces: her old papa, Bryce; her new papa who was no longer her papa; a very beautiful lady Omie had never seen before, with lovely arms that seemed to multiply as she watched, like the statue of an ancient Hindu goddess Omie had seen in a museum in New York before they boarded the ship; and there were two other faces present also, although these were indistinct: Omie could barely tell they were boys, so vague were their outlines, but their voices were sharp enough; they called each other Mr. Duckfeet and Mr. Pigeontoes, and laughed, then were driven away by the three grown-up faces again. Omie noticed that Papa Leo's face was uglier than she remembered it, with a mean expression and thunderous words rolling backward from his mouth. She extracted her eye from Zoe's thoughts and resumed her dreams of seeing New York again.

The house Zoe rented on the edge of Durango was small and neat, with just enough room for herself and Omie. Omie called it Elk Baby House, but Zoe didn't like that, so Omie learned simply to call it home-for-now. She did not attend school, but went for long walks with Zoe in the hills around the town. Mother and daughter talked little on these lengthy rambles, and once, when Omie sneaked inside Zoe's skull for just a moment, she saw there a more temperate arrangement of form and color than before. The cloudy faces were gone, replaced by an interior landscape best described as featureless. Zoe looked hard at her when she did this, and Omie retreated quickly. "Leave me alone," Zoe said, and Omie blushed.

They had followed this casual regimen for less than three weeks, when a caller knocked on their door. Zoe found herself facing a man who introduced himself as the local postmaster, who then asked, "Your name Dugan, by any chance, missus?"

"Yes."

"Letter here for you," he said, producing it from his coat. "Come by way of general delivery a couple weeks ago, but there's no one in this town I know of has got that name, then my sister's husband says her cousin rented this place out just recent to a party called Dugan, and I figured maybe you're the one."

Zoe knew the name had been fixed in the renter's mind because of her missing arm and Omie's blue birthmark.

"First name, ma'am, if you please? Got to be sure now."

"Zoe."

"Strange how things work out sometimes, don't you think?" he said, handing her the letter.

"Yes, very strange. Thank you."

"Might be best to check at the post office every now and then, ma'am, in case there's more."

"I will. Thank you again."

Zoe recognized the handwriting, although she did not know the writer; it was the same hand that had penned the letter informing her of the existence of Imogen Starr. How had her mysterious informant known she was in Durango? Zoe opened the envelope and read, in the same awkward scrawl: *You have been cheated. Go back and get a lawyer, a smart one, then have him get you the green book from your husband the cheat. You went away too soon and too easy. He is laughing at you now you are gone. A friend.*

Zoe read the letter over again, trying to understand. How could Leo have cheated her, and what on earth was the green book? The envelope was postmarked Glory Hole. She felt faint. Her anonymous friend had been right the first time; could he be right again? She had felt shame (for having deceived Leo, and even more for having been found out) and humiliation (for having meekly signed away her marriage without protest) and the all-encompassing wave of despair that comes with having lost everything, and being responsible for the loss. Now these emotions of failure were supplanted, as she leaned against the doorway, by another; Zoe felt the cold hand of suspicion clutch at her, and close behind came anger, and hard on its jagged heels came the need for unspecified vengeance, all from the reading of a few lines inked on cheap paper. Someone was watching over her, some faceless earthbound angel, wingless, but with eyes and ears close to Leo.

"Who was at the door, Mama?"

"A post office man."

"With a letter? Who sent it?"

"I ... don't know. Please don't ask me questions just now. Why not go outside and play."

Omie pursed her lips sulkily, then went out to the backyard, where there was a rope swing suspended from a large cottonwood tree. Omie soon had its wooden seat swinging back and forth in dangerously high arcs, although she herself did not set foot off the porch.

Zoe forced herself to be calm. If Leo had cheated her, she could not think of what, apart from a lifelong commitment to her. Should he have given her more than a million dollars? Did it matter that he did not? Who could possibly need more than that huge amount? It lay in a Denver bank, transferred from Leo's account, and she could take all of it at any time and do with it as she wished. How could she have been cheated? Why had the writer taken the trouble to upset her this way? She found she could not dismiss the message as some kind of troublemaking; the first letter had helped her see what had been hidden from her, and it was unlikely the same individual would now attempt to steer her astray. Should she do something, hire a lawyer as suggested? Or should she take what she had and sever herself completely from any further connection to Leo and Glory Hole?

She went to the back window and watched the swing heaving itself to and fro, unoccupied, while Omie scowled at it from the porch. There were no other houses nearby, no neighbors to witness the scene and carry word of it to the population of Durango, but how long would their isolation last? Sooner or later Omie would commit an outrageous act of some kind in public view; and even if she did not, the news that the house had been rented by the ex-wife and daughter of Leo Brannan must eventually catch up with them. There would be no peace for Zoe and Omie in Colorado, possibly no

peace anywhere, unless they went abroad. Perhaps she should ask
Omie if she would like to live in Australia, which Zoe had heard
was warm and dry. But that would involve a lengthy sea voyage,
and the short trip to Bermuda had soured Zoe on that mode of
transportation. Perhaps they should move to Canada, even if the
winters there were longer and harsher. Or even Mexico, despite its
lack of civilized comforts. She really could not make up her mind,
the letter had upset her so. The swing was slowing as Omie became
bored with it.

And then it came to Zoe, the certainty that Leo was indeed stealing what was hers. Before she even met the man, on her first
evening in Leadville, Zoe had been told by Omie that a man with
one blue eye and one brown eye was stealing from them. The money
they had hidden in their hotel room was gone, but Leo Brannan had
not taken it; Omie's vision and the theft of that money were coincidental but unrelated; Omie had seen further into the future than
she herself had realized, and been a witness to events only now
unfolding. Zoe should have guessed the truth much earlier, when
evidence for the fickle nature of Omie's prognostications began
revealing itself, but that would have tainted her relations with Leo
long before these were soured of their own volition, in accordance
with whatever forces shaped the affairs of men. Omie tapped into
these forces rarely, often without true understanding of their capri-
ciousness, the way in which they let slip their natural veils for a
hasty glimpse of incidents out of time, out of context. Omie had
unwittingly seen the Leo who one distant day would become what
he was in her fleeting impression of him—a thief.

The swing had stopped. Zoe knew what she must do.

The afternoon was warm, so while they waited for the train, Drew
lay down and tipped his hat over his face to doze. The rest of the
gang were some distance from him, talking among themselves, and
he found it easy to ignore anything but the dark interior of his Stet-
son. The train was still forty minutes away, carrying in its express
car a fortune in wages for the miners of Glory Hole.

No one had ever robbed a Brannan payroll before, and that was
enough for Lodi; this was the robbery that would put his name on
the front pages of newspapers nationwide; "history-making" was his
term for the job, and he was made confident by its very dangers.
Drew had often heard Lodi say he had a "nose" for the success or

failure of a plan, and Lodi made a point of telling Nate and Levon and himself that his nose had declared the Brannan robbery a winner in advance, with plenty of cash for everyone, more cash than they would ever see again if they robbed trains till they were ninety.

While he dozed, Drew became aware of a faint humming. Something was close to his face, producing the sound. When he looked, he saw it was a hummingbird, tiny and beautiful, its body a blaze of pink and blue, the wings mere blurrings alongside. Its beak was aimed directly between Drew's eyes as it hovered there, the fantastic beating of its invisible wings cooling his brow with the small wind they created. It was the loveliest thing Drew could recall ever having seen, and he was amazed at its tameness; the hummingbird was less than four inches from him, the tiny thunder of its wings louder than the droning of a bumblebee.

Watching its stationary flight, Drew became aware of another strange thing—his hat was still over his face. How was it possible that the bird was so close to him? How could he see it at all, since it could not have flown inside his hat, the band of which fitted snugly along his jaw and across his brow. Yet it was there, fanning him like a diminutive slave, peering into his eyes with its own, and Drew suddenly was afraid. Something that could not happen was happening, and that contradicted Drew's notion of an ordered world. The hummingbird inside his hat was alarming, a delicate intruder that should not have been there. Drew sought understanding of the event by assuming it was a dream, yet he was conscious in a very physical way of the warm earth beneath him and the sun on his hands; he felt the hole in the heel of his left sock and the mild discomfort of his gun belt pressing into the small of his back; he could hear the rest of the gang murmuring nearby, and still the hummingbird thrummed its impossible monotone inches from his nose. Drew tried to move, to stir his body and throw off the hat covering his face, but found he could not. The hummingbird had paralyzed him somehow with its siren song, made him helpless, a giant held down by wires of wind. Now the vibration of its wings seemed to resonate inside his skull, causing the very bone to quiver, and Drew was close to panicking, when his body suddenly lurched upward from the ground in a single convulsive paroxysm, a spasm that carried him several inches into the air and let him down hard on the bullets girdling his hips.

Hands now freed by his galvanic release snatched the hat from his face, and there was no hummingbird there at all. He looked and looked inside it, convinced so real an object must have been present to affect him as it had, but there was no hummingbird. He heard the sound of laughter, and saw the gang watching him.

"Get yourself stung there, Bones?" asked Levon.

"There was a hummingbird ...," Drew said.

"A what?"

"A hummingbird ... inside my hat."

"Oh, a hummingbird. I hate to get hummingbirds inside my hat, I really do. They shit in your hair, the little bastards."

Nate cackled softly. Even Lodi was smiling. Drew felt like a fool. He jammed the hat onto his head, embarrassed to have told them about the hummingbird. It had been a dream after all, the most realistic he had ever experienced.

"When's that goddamn train coming?" he said.

"Be along in ten minutes or so," Lodi told him. "Plenty of time yet for you to catch that hummingbird, Bones."

Drew turned from them and checked the load in his Colt, his face burning.

"Here she comes," drawled Levon.

A smudge of whitish smoke rose into the air like distant dragon's breath.

Leo's reluctance to marry again so soon after the annulment was reason enough for Rowland Price to be grateful. He still had not found out a single verifiable fact concerning the lovely Imogen Starr, and was convinced by then the woman had invented the name. It was too charming, too appropriate for someone such as herself, to be true. But short of his arranging to have the truth beaten from her, Rowland's hands were tied. Leo was still infatuated, and would allow no discussion whatsoever of his personal life. The departure of Zoe and Omie had been accomplished with a minimum of fuss, the false wife completely cowed by the confrontation with her mendacity, and Leo was disinclined to tempt fate by allowing any further delving into the private past of the woman he currently slept beside. What had worked in exposing Zoe might work equally well in disclosing a side to Imogen that Leo preferred not to know of; that was how Rowland saw the situation. Leo Brannan had revealed himself, during the course of the marital crisis, to be a man much like any other, but Rowland's commitment to the agenda of the Praetorians was unswerving; Leo Brannan was the man of the future hour, and his reputation was Rowland's responsibility, however onerous or disappointing on a personal level that task might prove to be. He still did not trust Imogen, and would not allow himself to do so until a small white-haired woman should come to him, declare herself Imogen's grandmother, and quote chapter and verse to Rowland concerning her granddaughter's many virtues and complete absence of vice. Even then he would be wary.

The summons to Leo's office was delivered by Jenks. When Rowland arrived he found Leo pacing the floor in his customary circles, his lengthening brow creased by concern. Rowland took a chair without waiting for an invitation, so firm was the bond between them now.

"On my desk," said Leo, without ceasing to pace. "A letter from her."

"Her?"

"Zoe. Read it aloud, please."

Rowland picked up the sheet. "'Dear Leo, unless you can explain to me by return mail the significance of the green book and your attempt to cheat me of what is rightfully mine, there will be legal repercussions such as you have never known. I mean what I say. Explain yourself with speed and honesty. Regards, Zoe.'"

Leo flung himself into his overstuffed chair and spun it to the left and right in consternation. "How does she know ...?" he asked himself. "How could she possibly be aware ...?"

"Of what? Green book? What might that be?"

"It isn't a book, it's a file, a perfectly ordinary folder, which happens to be green."

"And the perfectly ordinary folder contains?"

"The agreement I made with her. The papers she signed."

"Nothing else?"

"The report prepared by my attorney on the exact nature of Zoe's legal ownership of Brannan Mining. The file is rather thick, which makes it resemble a book, I suppose, but how in hell's name can she possibly know about it? Someone is spying for her, Rowland, and I want to find out who it is before she's given more shells to fire against me, by God!"

"This is dangerous ground the lady has stepped upon. Her knowledge must be scant, or she would state what she knows, rather than challenging you to provide it. Whatever clues her spy is feeding her, they can only be scraps, Leo, cryptic bits and pieces."

"Even so, I want it stopped!"

"Of course. You regard your attorney as being above suspicion?"

"Absolutely. He candidly admits that his role in the deception of Zoe is a criminal offense. He's the last person who would betray me."

"And his staff?"

"My own people, but unknown to me personally."

"And there is where you'll find your spy, I don't doubt."

"Find him for me, Rowland, and when you have him, don't let the fellow know we're onto him. I wish to anticipate every move in Zoe's game."

"Leo, the game should never have begun. Zoe should have taken her million and retired to a life of ease. The fact that she has not, and chooses instead to provoke you with threats, suggests to me that the game must be ended immediately. You know the stakes, Leo."

"I do, and am determined to win any battle she cares to mount against me."

"Leo, there is no time here for open warfare. Zoe has elected to burrow back into your life by subterfuge. You must stop her by different means. I can arrange it, without further effort on your part. You understand, of course, that we are discussing the endgame."

"The endgame."

"One move, out of the blue, and it will be over and done with. Finished."

"I understand you."

"Then shall I proceed?"

"Immediately. Find the one responsible for telling her about the green file. I won't have traitors in my business."

"And the endgame?"

Leo spun his chair around to face the window. Rowland studied the back of his head; Leo was becoming very bald there. The silence between them lengthened.

Eventually Leo said, "I suppose you must proceed."

Rowland left the room, quietly closing the door.

She was proud of herself for demanding an answer from Leo. It would be interesting to see if he responded with protestations of innocence, or threats and bluster. He was a weak man in many ways, and would very likely try the first means before the second. In either case, Zoe would resist his efforts to silence or placate her. It was not so much the money at stake (she assumed that was the only commodity he could cheat her of) as the principle of justice. Zoe did not know yet how strong were her grounds for accusing him, since her correspondent had failed to provide specific information. In the beginning, at least, it would be a game of bluff. She felt confident of outbluffing Leo, a man with so little strength of character he had allowed his life to be diverted by nothing more than a pretty face and a shapely pair of arms. He was despicable, really, and it would be a fine thing to bring him down several pegs.

She told Omie nothing of these developments, but of course Omie was aware, in her own sly fashion, of the tension emanating from her mother, and its familiar source.

"You hate Papa very much now, don't you?"

"Stop calling him Papa. He was no more your papa than the other one. Both have betrayed us. Call him Leo if you must mention him at all."

"You hate Leo more now than you did before."

"And if I do, I have my reasons. Please keep your nose out of my thoughts, or I shall become angry with you."

"You already are," grumbled Omie. "You're angry with everyone about everything. You're all black and swirly inside."

"Then don't look, do you hear me?"

"Yes." Omie pouted, and went away to throw twigs at squirrels, her most recent pastime. The squirrels would become most agitated when the twigs hit them without visible means of movement, and Omie took a grumpy delight in watching them scramble frantically about in the cottonwood tree, trying to see what it was that threw twigs at them with such malicious accuracy.

Zoe called every other day at the post office to see if any further mail from her informant had arrived. It had been twelve days since she sent her ultimatum to Leo, but he had not responded so far. Zoe often pictured two envelopes waiting for her in the general delivery pigeonhole behind the postmaster's counter—one from Leo and one from her informant—but came away each time with nothing more than a cheery greeting from the man who had set her quest in motion by taking the trouble to hand-deliver a letter.

As the days passed, frustrating Zoe with their mild weather and uneventful hours, she began losing interest in the matter, surprising herself by the lack of concern she now felt. She became convinced her gradual dismissal of the indefinable outrage committed against her by Leo was of no real consequence; again, she told herself that discovering the man was a cheat was in itself not such a great surprise, and if he had stolen from her a fortune of some kind, what did it matter: she had more than enough for herself and Omie; demanding more from him might be tantamount to lowering herself into the same moral quagmire he obviously inhabited. Revenge was not a notion that Zoe, a gentle woman by inclination, could goad herself with indefinitely. Perhaps it was just as well, she told herself, that no letters arrived to stir up her feelings all over again. It was time to think instead of a permanent home somewhere, a place in which to begin anew with the one person in all the world Zoe knew she could trust.

Her trip to the post office had become routine, a pleasant walk of a half hour or so from the house on the edge of town to the main street, either by way of a narrow foot trail alongside a creek, or by the more direct route of a road leading across a small bridge to another, wider road that aimed itself at Durango's heart. Zoe found she enjoyed the leisurely, secluded stroll along the creek more and more, and decided that whatever shape her new life took, it would include the simple enjoyment of long walks. She had learned to ignore the occasional glances at her missing arm, but Omie, during the earliest walks into town with her mother, had learned to hate the stares directed at her birthmark. She refused to accompany Zoe now, and was not ordered to. Zoe would help her become strong later on, when their current life in limbo was ended, their new life together begun.

Entering the post office, she smiled at the postmaster.

"Good afternoon, Mr. Beasely."

"Oh, Mrs. Dugan. I wasn't expecting you till tomorrow."

"The day is too fine to waste indoors."

"Yes, ma'am, and I'd be out there myself if I could. Got a letter for you, Mrs. Dugan."

"You have?"

"Only thing is, it isn't here anymore."

"Not here? I don't understand."

"Well, the lady took it with her. Said she was looking for you, so I gave her the address and letter both, to save you the walk tomorrow, you see."

"What lady, Mr. Beasely?"

"Well, now, she said she was a friend of yours as had been sending you letters, only you never wrote back, some story like that. Nice lady, seems like. You didn't see her on the road?"

"I came into town by the foot path. She didn't give you her name?"

"No, ma'am, and I couldn't exactly ask her for it, not and be polite too."

"No, of course not. Thank you, Mr. Beasely."

Zoe turned toward the door.

"Like as not she'll be out there waiting when you get back, Mrs. Dugan."

"Yes, I'm sure. Good day."

Zoe found herself hurrying on the homeward walk. Could it be her mysterious letter-writer? But why would she say to Mr. Beasely that Zoe had not written back, when there had never been any return address? Perhaps that had been to allay his interest. Zoe had never thought the information might be from a woman; the handwriting was distinctly unfeminine, for one thing, and she could imagine no way in which a woman might gain access to Leo's secrets, unless that woman was his mistress, and the letters certainly had not come from Imogen Starr. Zoe's feet flew along the path by the creek. She wanted, with the anxious anticipation of a child nearing a Christmas tree, to see who her visitor was.

From a distance of several hundred yards she could make out the woman's surrey by the yard gate, and the woman herself, wearing a brown dress, on the front porch with Omie. Approaching, she saw the name of a Durango livery stable on the surrey's side; her guest had come by train, then hired a vehicle to reach her; that would be the expected thing if she had come from Glory Hole. Hurrying across the yard to the porch, Zoe realized something was very wrong with the picture she saw there. The woman, young and pretty, was pressed against the clapboard walls of the house, as if backing away from a ferocious dog, but the only figure facing her was Omie, and now that she was closer still, Zoe saw that her daughter's face was a mask of intense concentration, the lips pressed into a line, her eyes narrowed to slits.

"Good afternoon," Zoe said, breathless and a little confused. "I came back as fast as I could ... Omie, is something wrong?"

"Make her stop!" hissed the woman, speaking with apparent difficulty. The color in her cheeks was heightened, and her eyes bulged slightly as they glared in Omie's direction. "Make her stop it!"

"Stop what? Omie, are you doing something you oughtn't to?"

"Mama, it's a man," intoned Omie, her voice low, depleted by the effort required to keep their visitor pinned against the wall with her invisible arms.

"A man? What on earth do you mean? Stop it this instant." To the woman she said, "I'm so sorry, Miss. Are you from Glory Hole? Omie, I said stop it!"

"It's a man, Mama ... and there's a knife under her dress she keeps thinking about. He wants to kill us, Mama."

"What nonsense ... Miss? Are you who I believe you to be?"

"Make her stop!" the young woman said again, her voice deepened this time by the extra force Omie was exerting out of sheer frustration at Zoe's unwillingness to believe what she was told.

"Mama, it's a man with a knife under his dress, it really is. Look and see!"

"This is so silly, Omie.... Stop it this instant!"

Omie grew white in the face, and the young woman's skirts flew up around her head, petticoats and all, and there, strapped to her lacy bloomers, was a long leather sheath with a slender haft protruding from it.

"Oh ...," said Zoe. The sight before her was too fantastic for immediate assimilation. This was not her informant after all, but someone bent on doing harm to herself and Omie.

"Who are you! Who sent you here! How dare you ...!"

Omie let the skirts fall, but made a further point by skewing the wig on Tatum's head sideways, giving him a faintly ridiculous look. Zoe was aghast at the deception. Only one person could want her silenced. "Did my husband send you? Did he?"

Tatum was frightened by the invisible force exerted against him by the girl. His waist was in the grip of what felt like enormous hands, and he was at a loss to extricate himself. He wanted only to peel his body from the wall and kill the woman he had been sent to kill. There had been no instructions regarding the girl, but Tatum wanted to kill her also, because she had humiliated him and because he was afraid of whatever power she was employing against him. He had tried a half-dozen times since setting foot onto the porch to be free of the hands he could not see. There had not even been enough time to cajole the girl into allowing him inside to wait for her mother; barely had their eyes met than she slammed him against the wall, then kept him there for at least twenty minutes until the woman returned. He had no idea how to proceed; no one had warned him of Omie's gifts, and he was vulnerable now to her whims.

"Keep him there," Zoe ordered, and went inside. She reappeared moments later with a Smith & Wesson bought in Georgetown when she and Omie had disembarked from the *Tiger Shark*. The pistol was intended to protect them both from harm at the hands of people made afraid and vengeful by Omie's unusual abilities, and the time for its first use had arrived. Omie was weakening; Zoe could tell by the sweat beginning to darken the armpits of her dress. "I have him now," she said, aiming the pistol at Tatum's chest. Omie sank onto the porch step and breathed heavily.

This new arrangement encouraged Tatum; the girl was obviously weakened by excessive use of the hypnotism or whatever it had been she used against him, and the mother did not have the look of someone prepared to pull a trigger. The impossible hands were gone from his waist. The first thing he did, giving himself time to think of a stratagem for escape, was slowly to lift his hands and adjust his wig and little flowered hat. "Is she all right?" he asked, moderating his voice to express sympathy.

"Who has sent you here? Answer me!"

"I have no idea what you mean, ma'am," he purred, "nor any notion on what your little girl said about me."

"Why do you carry a knife there?"

"For protection, ma'am, just as you carry a pistol. A woman can never be too careful, the world being as it is."

"He's a man, Mama," moaned Omie. "Don't believe him...."

"I don't," said Zoe, and saw the face before her harden subtly. She was afraid of the androgynous creature with the wicked blade strapped against his thigh, afraid of the cold darkness behind his eyes. He had come to murder them both, as Omie said, and Zoe could not think what to do with him now that she had him at gunpoint. She could not simply shoot him, although that was probably the safest option.

"I had no idea Leo hated me so," she told him.

"Leo?" said Tatum, lifting an eyebrow.

"My husband, Leo Brannan. I suppose you'll deny he sent you. How can you do such work? What kind of ghoul are you?"

Tatum shrugged with casual nonchalance. The pistol had begun to weigh heavily in the woman's grip, and she lacked another hand to support it; soon it would begin to waver, and he would be able to pounce, providing the girl had not recovered by then. She was still slumped against a porch pillar, breathing heavily, paying little attention to him. He had only to take the pistol from the woman, and his first target would be the girl, before she hypnotized him again; without her daughter, the woman would be easy meat. He would kill her slowly, painfully, as compensation for having bungled the job at first.

"Woll? Did he send you? I won't be intimidated by him. I won't!"

Tatum let her talk; the more time passed, the heavier the pistol would become. He was intrigued to hear the name of Leo Brannan; he had been told nothing but to look around Durango for a one-armed woman called Zoe Dugan. Locating the target had been easier than anticipated; batting his eyes at the postmaster had charmed the fool into offering an address and a letter besides. He hadn't bothered to open it yet, but he would, after he had taken care of the work he was paid to perform. The letter might even be worth an extra few hundred dollars to Price; Tatum could always threaten to take it to Mr. Jones instead, if Price demurred. Tatum sensed there was some kind of uneasy competition between the men, and that was why Price asked him to perform work on the side, extracting as a condition his promise never to breathe a word of his free-lance activities to Jones. Yes, Leo Brannan's name could well be the perfect tool for blackmail, and the letter as well. Tatum knew he was regaining his sense of control, taken from him without warning by the girl. It was coming back now, calming him; he had always had the ability to think clearly when he knew he was in control of a situation. The gun barrel pointed at him was beginning to droop, but he kept his eyes from it, not wishing to draw the attention of Zoe Dugan to her faulty aim.

"Mama, there's a letter.... He put it in his purse."

Tatum was taken by surprise again. He hadn't mentioned the letter to the girl. The postmaster must have mentioned it to the mother, but how could the girl have known, and be reminding her about it? He felt irritation over the inexplicable begin to agitate him again.

"In his purse, Mama. It's important, he thinks."

"I don't have any letter."

"You most certainly do," said Zoe. "It belongs to me, so kindly hand it over."

"Oh, yes, the letter they gave me at the post office. Yes, ma'am, I certainly do have that letter with me. I forgot about it, what with one thing and another...." He gave a little laugh intended to disarm the woman as he began opening the purse. Tatum wished he had a derringer hidden inside, but he did not, so confident was he of his ability with the stiletto. "I have it here somewhere ... ah, yes."

He pulled out the crumpled envelope and offered it to her, hoping she was sufficiently dazed by events to dither over how best to accept it, since her only hand was occupied by a gun. One small hesitation, a look of indecision in the eyes, and Tatum would know the time had come to pounce.

"Drop it," ordered Zoe.

"Ma'am?"

"I have only the one arm, in case you hadn't noticed."

"Oh, excuse me."

Tatum allowed the envelope to fall between them onto the porch boards. If she stooped to pick it up, if she so much as looked down at it, he would have her.

"Move sideways."

"Pardon me?" asked Tatum, disappointed by Zoe's cleverness. He should have been warned of that, as well as the girl's hypnotic ability. He would shoot the girl in both eyes, so as not to give her another chance at pinning him down with nothing more than her gaze.

"Move away from the letter, or I'll have to shoot you."

Tatum shuffled sideways, moving clumsily to convey the idea that he was somehow hampered by the unaccustomed dress; in fact he felt less encumbered in women's clothing than in men's, and often wore dresses when alone, just to hear and feel them swish through the air when he twirled and kicked and twirled again before the many mirrors in his bedroom.

"Turn around and face the wall."

"Ma'am, I've tried to explain to you that I was given the letter to deliver, and that's why I'm here...."

"Stop lying! I am not a fool! Now turn around, you ... you monster!"

Tatum sighed and turned himself awkwardly around. The woman was taking fewer chances than most would have taken; he would need to resort to stealth. He could hear the girl stand up again and come closer to her mother. That was bad; he wanted her at several arms' lengths from him when the moment came to strike. She was picking up the letter now, although the woman hadn't told her to, almost as if she could read thoughts.

"It's addressed to you, Mama, by general delivery."

"Put it in your pocket, then go and pack our bags. Are you well enough to do that by yourself?"

"Yes. What will we do with the man?"

"I don't know. It may depend on him. Go on now, and don't bother to fold things neatly, just fling them in the bags and bring everything outside."

Tatum caught a glimpse of the girl as she went through the front door. That was good; he knew he could get the drop on the woman much more easily while they were alone. She was shifting position, moving a little further from him. Bad.

"Lift your dress and remove the knife."

"Ma'am, it's my only protection...."

"Stop this nonsense! You're a man, a ... a killer for hire! I despise you. Take it out very slowly, and drop it at your feet."

Tatum lifted his dress and extracted the stiletto from its sheath. The weapon was his pride; he much preferred it to noisy guns. He had read of the Borgia assassins, Italy's dagger men of stealth and cunning, and chosen to emulate their skills, rather than those of his own society's dime-novel pistoleros.

"Drop your knife."

Tatum sneered to himself. The woman didn't know the difference between a knife and a stiletto. He wished he had his brace of throwing knives strapped along his ribs; he could have spun and sunk one into her throat before she had a chance to gun him down; but he had left them all behind, like a fool, thinking a woman less of a challenge than a man. He had learned a lesson on this assignment, and would never again underestimate any one of his targets. The stiletto clattered to the boards between his dainty button boots, and Zoe was startled to see that the blade, unlike that of an ordinary dagger, had three sides.

"Move away from it."

Tatum did as he was told. He had just remembered another weapon, not one he had trained himself to use, but one that would serve him well in an emergency.

"What is your name?" Zoe asked him.

"Julia, ma'am."

"Stop that! I wish to know your name, and how much my husband has paid you to do this!"

"No one has paid me to do anything, ma'am," said Tatum. He had employed his female voice throughout, except when the girl had him held against the wall, when it had been difficult to talk at all. He didn't know why he continued playing a role that clearly had been seen through; probably because to abandon it would have been an indication of defeat, he decided.

"Tell him that I will not be cowed. Tell him I will have what's mine, regardless."

Tatum was encouraged by these words. If he was expected to tell Leo Brannan something, it meant he was not about to be killed, and a woman who had no intention of killing the man she held at gunpoint was already halfway to reversing their positions. She was not so clever after all, he concluded.

"Do you hear me?"

"Yes, ma'am, I hear you, only I don't understand any of this, I really don't, ma'am."

"And tell him to send someone of intelligence to negotiate in good faith, not some operetta buffoon."

Tatum knew then that his usual delights would have to be augmented for this woman. She had insulted him openly, and would pay with a slower death than any he had heretofore orchestrated. The slowest death he had conducted at the behest of Mr. Jones had been a rancher in northern New Mexico who refused to join his spread to that belonging to his neighbor, presumably an associate of Mr. Jones. Tatum never concerned himself with the details of why a murder had to be committed, and often did not adhere to the sparse instructions given to him before such an undertaking. He had been encouraged of late to indulge his fancy for protracted death, especially in that region, by the convenient presence of Slade, the Colorado Cannibal. Tatum knew his torture of the rancher had been considered the work of that elusive man-beast, and had been glad of it, even if Mr. Jones was not fooled and had censured him for embellishing an otherwise straightforward murder.

"Ma'am, I just don't know what any of this means. You won't hurt me, will you?"

Zoe made a sound of frustration and disgust, another good sign. The party whose head was cool was the party who generally survived any kind of showdown, in Tatum's experience. His own head felt as cool as it did when he snorted cocaine into his nasal passages. Tatum had given up liquor when he discovered the white dust; nothing compared to its glacial thundering in his veins. Cocaine took him to distant mountaintops, where he breathed the chill atmosphere of ultimate aloneness and satisfaction. He often snorted the dust, and obliged his partners to share the experience before making brutal love to them. Nothing so enhanced his self-aware performances as stud-bugger *extraordinaire*. The heavenly powder was both opiate and stimulant, and Tatum accorded it the reverence other men gave to money.

Omie reappeared on the porch. "Everything, Mama? The big trunk too?"

"No, leave that. Just the small bags. Hurry!"

Omie went back inside the house. Tatum thought about how best to employ his alternative weapon. Zoe Dugan was still too far away.

"I won't be so easy to find next time. You tell him that."

"Tell who, ma'am?"

"Don't talk to me in that idiotic fashion! Talk like the man that you are!" Zoe took several breaths to calm herself. "Tell him he has disappointed me. I thought him above such practices. Tell him he has become a lesser man than the one I knew. The one I thought I knew. Can you remember that?"

"I don't know what to say, ma'am. I believe I'm too confused to remember anything...."

"Stop it!"

He was stoking her agitation with professional aplomb. Another few degrees of anger and she would be incapable of good judgment and split-second reaction. Tatum was backing his prey into the corner Zoe had elected to occupy, a kind of slaughtering pen his intended victims always built around themselves without being aware that they did so. Tatum was fascinated by the responses of people to imminent danger; so very few of them actually believed they would come to harm. He could not understand why they made this assumption, but was glad their minds worked so contrarily, since it gave him the advantage every time. Tatum saw death everywhere, and was always prepared for it, day or night, like a creature of the jungle. Even as he killed them, his targets expressed disbelief in their eyes, and he scorned them for their naive weakness, their pathetic belief in physical immortality. They deserved to die solely on account of that, in his opinion.

Time was passing. He had to turn around and kill the woman

while her daughter with the dangerous eyes was inside. Tatum asked, "May I remove my hat and wig?" He used his male voice.

"You may. I should like to see how you look."

Tatum lifted both arms and unpinned the hat from the wig, then dropped both behind him, knowing Zoe's eyes would follow whatever moved. During her few seconds of distraction, he palmed the hatpin.

"There," he said. "I'll have to turn if you want to see my face, ma'am."

"Then do so, very slowly."

Tatum shuffled himself around to face Zoe.

"What is your name?"

"David Mulrooney."

"Have you done this many times before?"

"Never. I have considerable debt. Your husband offered me the work for ten thousand dollars. He didn't say you were his wife. He said your name was Dugan. If I had known ... He said you were blackmailing him, but gave me no details. He said you were ... excuse me, ma'am, but he said you were an ex-whore who gave nothing but trouble to the world. I suppose that was to make everything more acceptable to me. I failed, of course, and now that I have, I'm glad. You aren't what he described at all, I can see. Ma'am, I don't know what grudge your husband may hold against you, but I want no part in erasing it. I've been deceived by him, as I imagine you have been. I humbly beg your pardon."

His tone was haltingly sincere. Zoe began to wonder if she had been wrong to treat him with such caution.

"They told me to bring a gun," he said, "but I couldn't shoot someone. I bought the other thing instead, like a fool who doesn't know what's best. What kind of killer arms himself with a pigsticker, ma'am, I ask you? It was all doomed to fail, even if your little girl hadn't been so clever as to see through this ... this *ridiculous* disguise. I feel so humiliated.... Ma'am, I urge you to hide yourself away from him, because as soon as he learns how badly I've bungled the task, he'll dispatch someone who knows what he's doing, someone who won't be so clumsy as myself."

"I shall certainly do that, Mr. Mulrooney, and you may tell him so yourself."

"Oh, no, ma'am, I don't dare face him now, not after failing. He'd have me punished, I just know he would. No, ma'am, I can't go back there...."

"I have sympathy for you, but very little. You have allowed yourself to be drawn into this horrible situation, and you must get yourself out."

"Yes, ma'am ... but ..." He fell to his knees and held his clenched hands out toward her. "Ma'am, if you could just let me have ten dollars for a train ticket and, ... and take me with you to the station, ma'am, so I can get on a train and try to hide from him ... oh, ma'am, please ..."

His face was twisted with the effort of imploring. He shuffled several feet toward Zoe on his knees, sobbing now, the tears squeezing from his eyes. "Please, ma'am, I'm begging you...."

"You must look after yourself, Mr. Mulrooney. I have my daughter to take care of. You're a grown man, and must take the responsibility."

"Yes, ma'am, I suppose ...," he blubbered, then said, "May I get up, ma'am, please?"

"Of course you may."

The gun had dragged her hand down so far now it was aimed at the area around her feet; a small woman like her, Tatum thought, should have got herself a smaller-caliber weapon, not a heavy .45. He levered himself clumsily up from his knees, seeming to tangle himself in the folds of his dress, but when he was halfway upright, and his legs were bent to spring, the hatpin appeared in his hand, and he lunged upward at Zoe. The pin penetrated her upper arm as she tried to lift the pistol, and Zoe cried out. Tatum was drawing back the pin again to strike at her chest, his other hand clutching at the pistol barrel to keep it aimed away from himself. The hatpin was already moving forward again, and Zoe's stumped arm was thrashing uselessly inside its tucked sleeve in an effort to ward off the blow that appeared certain to find its mark and be driven deep.

Then he was gone, knocked sideways clean off the porch, removed so suddenly from proximity to her that the pin had fallen from his fingers and struck the boards while he was still flying through the air. Omie was rushing past Zoe, her hair literally standing on end with the effort of moving a full-grown man across the yard against his will. His boots struck the ground, and he fell, but was picked up immediately and dragged as if being hauled on wires across to the water pump, and delivered so hard against the iron stand that the sound of his head meeting metal was clearly heard. Blood began to run from his temple. His body slumped into an untidy heap where he lay, and his mouth fell open, slackened by unconsciousness.

Omie ran to him, her head entirely hidden from behind by the writhing and beribboned tentacles of her rage. Zoe was reminded of Medusa, and the man Omie had attacked did seem to have been turned to stone, so still did he lie beside the pump. Omie picked up the gun that lay halfway across the yard, dragged from Zoe's hand as Tatum was flung away from her. It was far too large for Omie's hands, but she raised it and aimed the barrel.

"Omie! No!"

She turned to look at her mother, and the waving tangle of her hair began to subside. The gun fell with a thud into the dust. Omie's expression suddenly was blank, the look of a sleepwalker awakened in an unfamiliar room.

"Omie ... come here."

She came with awkward steps, frowning slightly, and Zoe went to her with open arms. She held her daughter tightly, then asked, "Is everything ready?" Omie nodded slowly.

Zoe picked up the gun. They loaded their baggage into the surrey. Tatum lay as before. Zoe chided herself for having relaxed her guard enough to allow his attempt with the hatpin. She would never again be so foolish. Leo wanted her dead, but Zoe was equally determined to remain alive.

Tatum's surrey was returned to the livery stable in Durango. Zoe told the proprietor that her "sister who came to visit" was too tired after her journey to accompany them. Their baggage had already been unloaded at the station, and they waited there for nineteen long minutes before catching the first train that came.

Zoe watched through the open window until they had drawn completely away from the platform, to be sure that the killer sent by Leo did not make a last-moment appearance and board the train, but he did not. She closed the window and sat beside Omie. They had the seat to themselves, and the seat opposite was vacant.

"Mama, I heard him say Papa ... I mean, Leo ... sent him to hurt us. Did he?"

"Yes."

"He really wants to hurt us?"

"Yes."

"But what did we *do?*"

"We have done nothing to hurt him."

"Then *why*, Mama ...?"

"I don't know why."

"I feel sick ..."

"Place your head between your knees. Go on, Omie, no one is watching. Now breathe slowly and steadily, and try not to think of what has happened."

Omie lifted her head. "I don't like that. Mama, may I go to sleep now? I feel so tired...."

"Yes, you may, my darling. I'll stay right here while you do, so nothing bad will happen."

Omie succumbed almost immediately, and lay against her mother's side with all her young weight. The train had gone many miles before Zoe thought to read the letter that had been delivered by so macabre a messenger. She plucked it carefully from the front pocket of Omie's pinafore. The envelope was addressed in the now familiar scrawl, and contained nothing but a clipping from the *Glory Hole Sentinel*.

Murder of a disturbing kind was committed in the town last night, by persons as yet unknown. The victim, new to these environs, was declared by Sheriff Simms to be Bryce Aspinall, registered at the Great Divide Hotel and not one to discuss his business among us. The victim was found before dawn along Welsh Lane by an inebriant, who sobered himself and raised the alarm. The wound to Aspinall's back was deep enough to reach the heart, and likely caused his instantaneous demise. The wound was unusual in that it was inflicted by a blade of triangular configuration. Any citizen having knowledge relating to this grisly event is asked to step forward.

Zoe crumpled the clipping into a ball, and sat gazing at the passing scenery. The place in her upper arm where the hatpin had jabbed her was extremely painful.

43

I have your spies, Leo."

Rowland Price wore an expression of satisfaction.

"Spies? More than one?"

"Does the name Garfinkle strike a chord with you?"

"It does not."

"He works for your attorney."

"Aha! Who paid the fellow to do it?"

"No one, he says. He simply doesn't like you, nor does his wife. She was his compatriot in crime."

"Someone must have paid him. What connection is there between these Garfinkles and my ex-wife?"

"No connection at all that I can see, but there is a connection between them and your mistress."

"I beg your pardon?"

"Miss Starr used to board with the Garfinkles. Mrs. Garfinkle runs a respectable house on Mason Street. Miss Starr lived there until you bought the place for her on Bowman."

"I don't understand."

"Mr. Garfinkle insists they did what they did because you're a despicable fellow for having rid yourself of your crippled wife and stepdaughter. The Garfinkles maintain extremely high standards of human behavior, and are somewhat judgmental. I suspect Mrs.

Garfinkle did not approve of your taking Miss Starr out of her house to be installed elsewhere as your paramour. Women tend to view that kind of arrangement with less favor than men."

"Indeed they do."

"I assume she passed on her ill will to Mr. Garfinkle, who was already indisposed toward you over the nature of the work your attorney assigned him. He knows the details of the green file, Leo, so he was in a position to inform Zoe that your generous settlement was not so generous after all. He says he gave her no details, merely hints and clues to pursue."

"You believe him?"

"I didn't, and put Sheriff Simms and a burly deputy to work on him, but Mr. Garfinkle did not change his story. I believe him now. This was no organized plot against you. We have two rather naive idealists who have poked and prodded to no great effect, no lasting hurt. The little they told Zoe will do her no good at all, even if she attempts to win a case against you in court. The green file has been destroyed, and the Garfinkles are both in Simms's custody."

"On what charge?"

"Murder. They're jointly responsible, you see, for the slaying of one Bryce Aspinall."

"This will never do, Rowland."

"Hear me out. Bryce was lured to their home by Mrs. Garfinkle, who posed as a woman of ill repute, with the intention of lifting his extensive bankroll. Husband and wife both took part in the fatal stabbing. Bryce was done away with in the cellar, where blood-stains have been placed by yours truly—sheep's blood, as a matter of fact—then he was taken to the alleyway and dumped. The distance between these two points is conveniently short. Do you admire my creativity so far?"

"Go on."

"The money—Bryce's money, provided by yourself—has been found in the Garfinkles' attic. The murder weapon was an unusual one, a stiletto, and this also has been found in the attic by Sheriff Simms, after I showed him where to look."

"How did you get hold of it?"

"Our assassin provided it on my request. He failed to locate your ex-wife in Durango, unfortunately. She fled the day before he arrived, probably warned off by the Garfinkles. I suspect the lady will run far and lie low."

"That isn't good enough, Rowland."

"Our man of the blade will follow, be assured of that. He'll find her, no matter how long it may take, but the Garfinkle incident will be closed within twenty-four hours."

"How so?"

"They'll be stricken, shall we say, with an extreme case of guilty conscience. There'll be no public outcry. The *Sentinel* will editorialize on the subject of the devious criminal mind and its capacity to manifest itself even in seemingly decent types such as the Garfinkles. There'll be no link to you, nothing to excite the public imagination or the secretive fellows of Big Circle, nor the Praetorians. You needn't fear any repercussion, Leo, I guarantee it."

"I need to be very sure about that."

"And you may be."

When Price had left him, Leo began striding about the room. The Garfinkles were the least of his problems. He had ordered by indirect means the murder of his ex-wife, a woman he once had loved. How was it possible that he could do this, and yet feel nothing other than a consuming worry that the job would not be taken care of in time? Had he become a monster? Leo felt much as he always had; he certainly did not feel evil or deranged. It was simply a question of business taking precedence over emotion and sentiment, he supposed, and the consequences could not be helped. He had given Zoe a fortune, but she was not satisfied with that, and so he had taken other measures to protect himself. It was not his fault.

He was beset by other difficulties also. A payroll train had been robbed, reportedly by the outlaw known as Lodi, the entire shipment of cash made off with, and not a robber had so much as been wounded. There had been no word of Slade's capture, despite the length of time since his escape and the growing numbers of violated bodies being found in remote parts of the southwest. And then there was Imogen. She wanted marriage, and was becoming quite insistent, referring to herself as "a kept woman" and adopting a mournful expression whenever he told her she must wait until certain problems to do with Brannan Mining had been taken care of. She had also been badgering him about a dead Indian some fools had pickled in a rain barrel with a view to exhibiting the corpse beneath a glass case, like some fairy tale princess. The very idea repulsed him, and he had told Imogen so. "I will not involve myself with sideshows. Kindly refrain from mentioning this monstrosity to me again."

Imogen had wept prettily, obliging him to beg for love later in the evening. "All you need to do," she had said, following a brief but satisfying act, "is say in your newspaper you believe the thing is an Indian from ancient times, not one that died last week." Her imploring tone eventually won him over, and he had instructed the *Sentinel*'s editor to arrange a story on the so-called Sleeping Savage. Imogen had proven herself suitably grateful by allowing Leo a certain liberty she was not often inclined to participate in. Still there remained his other vexations. The life of a rich man was indeed no bed of roses.

Tatum had never enjoyed time spent in Mr. Jones' office. He suspected Mr. Jones was a smarter man than he appeared, with more powerful friends than he would ever admit to knowing. Each of the assignments given to him by Mr. Jones had been carefully laid out, with much detail concerning the target, unlike the work given to him by Rowland Price, which always included an instruction not to mention anything of it to Jones. Tatum felt he could keep secrets as well as any man, and the extra cash came in very handy for gambling and clothing and cocaine.

"You have a nasty bruise there, Mr. Tatum."

Tatum's temple was swollen and scabbed from his contact with the water pump. He had attempted to hide it by rearranging his long hair, but the wound was still visible.

"I fell."

"Where did you fall?"

"In my room."

"You have a room in Durango, Mr. Tatum?"

"What does that mean?"

Mr. Jones formed a steeple with his fingertips and leaned back in the leather chair behind his desk.

"It means, Mr. Tatum, that you have been accepting work from a certain party who is not myself. That is in direct contradiction to your agreement with me."

"If someone's been telling you stories ..."

"Someone has, and I believe the stories, Mr. Tatum. You have reneged upon your contract with me, and I am extremely disappointed to learn of it. Please explain yourself."

Tatum took several breaths. "I needed the money."

"And Mr. Price paid you well."

"He did."

Tatum knew he must not lie to Mr. Jones. If Mr. Jones already knew it was Price who had given him the secret assignments, he probably knew everything else.

"Kindly give me all the particulars."

Tatum talked without pause for ten minutes. Rather than tell the lie he had given Price to explain their escape, he even confessed that the woman and girl had bested him in Durango. When he was done, Tatum waited for comment, but Mr. Jones simply stared at him for a long time.

"Do I still work for you?" Tatum asked.

"Most certainly you work for me, Mr. Tatum. You will never work for anyone else. The day you leave my employment will be the day of your death. Now I anticipate your next question—you wish to know what reply to give Rowland Price when next he comes to you with work suited to your talents, do you not."

"Yes."

"You will accept the work, and tell me all about it. You will continue to search for Mrs. Dugan, by the way, and report to me with the results, as well as to Mr. Price. When you find her you may fulfill the terms of your contract with Price, since that is only good business, but you will under no circumstances do any harm to the girl. Instead, you will bring her to me, safe and sound, with not a hair on her head out of place, is that clear?"

"Clear enough."

"You seem somewhat unhappy about this arrangement. Are you afraid of this unusual girl with her unusual powers, Mr. Tatum? Say so now if you are, and I'll arrange for someone else to perform the work."

"No."

"You have disappointed me once, as I said. I do hate to be disappointed twice by the same individual, Mr. Tatum. It undermines my faith in humanity, you see."

"You won't be disappointed again, Mr. Jones, not by me."

"Good-bye, Mr. Tatum."

Alone, Mr. Jones mulled over these new developments. He had been aware for some time that there existed within Big Circle the nucleus of a splinter group called, with dizzying conceit, the Praetorians. He knew also that Rowland Price was high among the leadership of this group, and he knew their ultimate agenda. Political power of the kind allegedly gained through the ballot box held no

appeal for Mr. Jones and the upper echelon of Big Circle. These
men preferred to get what they required from the world by subterfuge, or by force, if that became necessary. They had no need of
armies or elected representatives, understanding as they did that
one man often will hold the key to a doorway of opportunity. That
same man, if unwilling to open that doorway for the betterment of
Big Circle, was easily removed in most cases. Tatum was necessary
for such actions, and Mr. Jones had no intention of replacing him as
punishment for the extra work he had performed, all unknowingly,
for the Praetorians.

The arrogance of the group growing inside Big Circle like a cancer was an irritant to Mr. Jones. He was not impressed with their
plans to form a political party, since there already existed one party
too many in the nation, in Mr. Jones's opinion, and he was even less
impressed by the clumsiness of their machinations toward a
takeover of Big Circle to further their ends. The Praetorians would
never succeed in this, because they were not in possession of a complete list of the members of Big Circle. Such a list, names written
on a sheet of paper, did not even exist, so important was it to maintain secrecy within the organization. Only five men other than Mr.
Jones knew the list, and kept it safely inside their heads. These
individuals termed themselves The Six. Not only were the Praetorians unaware of the existence and identities of The Six, they
remained in ignorance of the fact that fully half their own number
were traitors, reporting directly to himself, most of these spies
unaware even of each other. The Praetorian organization was as
riddled by foolishness and duplicity and hubris as a Swiss cheese
was riddled by holes, yet its leaders congratulated themselves on
their cunning and the farsightedness of their vision. It all made Mr.
Jones shake his head.

Of particular interest to him was the role lately undertaken by
Leo Brannan as a member of the Praetorians. Mr. Jones had been
one of the old guard of Big Circle consistently to blackball Brannan's admission to their ranks, and had relented only when it
became clear Brannan had been recruited into the Praetorians by
Price. The decision to bring him into the broader fold of Big Circle,
primarily to keep a closer watch on him, was made in secret session
by The Six. Mr. Jones had worried that the coincidence in timing
might cause suspicion among the Praetorians, but such was their
confidence that they thought nothing of it, other than to congratu-

late themselves on now being able to allow Brannan free circulation among members of the larger organization they were committed to undermining. Mr. Jones's low opinion of Price and his cohorts had sunk even lower.

It was gratifying to learn that Leo Brannan was indeed a man of lesser moral stuff than many had once thought. Mr. Jones was fascinated by the ease with which the trollop who had been Walter Morrow's whore had, since being escorted out of Denver by none other than Tatum, insinuated herself into the bed of Brannan, employing no other deceit than a simple change of name. The whore was clearly more talented in the practice of duplicity than was her new protector; even Rowland Price remained unaware that the two women were one and the same whore, despite his clumsy investigation (still proceeding) into her past. Price and his Praetorians were amateurs, and when the time came to winnow Big Circle of its useless but proliferating chaff, all would be revealed, so that the Praetorians might appreciate the enormity of their many shortcomings before punishment was meted out.

Brannan's treatment of his wife was abominable, even if the woman had been inattentive to his needs following her dreadful accident. The stepdaughter also had been much maligned, given the unfortunate combination of physical ugliness and her rumored penchant for conversing with spirits. This last attribute intrigued Mr. Jones, who had lately lost his wife to cancer of the stomach. He had loved her very much, and wished to speak with her via the etheric plane, if that was possible. He had visited the parlors of so-called mediums in Denver and Chicago, but been greatly dissatisfied by their bogus performances and general flimflammery. He was taken by the notion that if he had the opportunity to meet with young Omie Dugan he might be granted the interview with his beloved Dorie he so longed for. Mr. Jones was a materialist by inclination, but was not about to sever any possible ties with the one person he had ever loved by ignoring the supernatural out of stubborn intellectual conviction. He hoped Tatum would locate Omie and bring her to him. If she was able to perform as a conduit between the living and the dead, he would reward her, possibly by taking her into his home; but if the rumors were untrue, if her powers were negligible or fraudulent, he would hand her back to Tatum for disposal.

Brannan himself was a fool, in the estimation of Mr. Jones. Clandestine investigation into his affairs had revealed that it was his

wife who was responsible for the bulk of his wealth; Brannan was
an astute businessman, and his vast holdings were managed with
the necessary firmness and resolve such an empire demanded, but
the fact remained that if his wife had not staked a claim to the original Deer Lick mine, Glory Hole would never have been his alone.
Mr. Jones did not dismiss Brannan as merely lucky, but he did condemn the man for not having acknowledged the essential part
played by his wife in his rise to riches. Brannan was not required to
build statues in her honor, or to place her in his boardroom, nothing
so ridiculous as that; but he should have kept her as his wife. If he
insisted on supporting a mistress also, that could have been overlooked, but to have dismissed Zoe Dugan as he did because he preferred the thighs of Walter Morrow's ex-whore was an indication of
moral enfeeblement, of the poorest judgment, especially since he
was supposedly being groomed for high office by the Praetorians.
The idea of Leo Brannan as President of the United States was
ludicrous, of course, and the Praetorian bubble would be burst long
before any such eventuality could even begin to see the light of day.

Zoe Dugan was being hunted down because Brannan wanted her
gone completely from his life. Further investigations into Brannan
Mining were called for, to provide a reason for so unnecessary a
vendetta. Mr. Jones already suspected the woman was legally entitled to far more than the million dollars Brannan had bestowed. It
would be interesting to see if his suspicions were correct. The personal fate of Mrs. Dugan was of no concern to Mr. Jones, but the
fate of her daughter was tremendously important.

He took from the drawer beside him a picture of his wife as she
had been in the early years of their marriage, and looked upon it
with a terrible yearning.

The cell was below street level, like a medieval dungeon, and was
without any kind of window. A crude iron bunk was bolted to one of
the three brick walls, and a shamefully inadequate bucket stood in
the corner. A gaslight burned day and night in the narrow corridor
beyond the fourth, barred wall. Even though she had been provided
with adequate blankets, Mrs. Garfinkle found herself shivering
often.

She and her husband had been arrested without warning by
Sheriff Simms and brought directly to the jail. She had not seen Mr.
Garfinkle since then. It was plain that their attempt at subverting

Leo Brannan had been found out. Mrs. Garfinkle had been happy to let the sheriff know exactly what she and Mr. Garfinkle had done, and took pains to demonstrate her pride in having defied so great and powerful a man. She could not be sure, but she thought they had been held incommunicado for at least a day and a half. People would be wondering about their fate, asking questions and demanding to see them in person. Leo Brannan was trying to intimidate them, that was all, and his foolish game soon would come to an end, when he realized the truth could not be kept locked away forever. She quite looked forward to telling folks what she and Mr. Garfinkle had done, and if it ever came to court, why then, she would speak her piece about his shameful conduct even louder, and let the world know what manner of man Leo Brannan was.

It had begun with Imogen Starr. Mrs. Garfinkle had not taken to her at all while she was a boarder at her house, and had seen the way in which she sized up every male in the place, including Mr. Garfinkle, and found each of them wanting. Mrs. Garfinkle had seen right away that Imogen Starr was a smoothly polite gold digger looking to stake a claim, and not the kind to be satisfied with just anything. It had been a shock, but no surprise, when she abruptly moved her things out without a word, and was not heard of until the story began circulating around Glory Hole of Leo Brannan's beautiful mistress. Mrs. Garfinkle had known, even before the name of Imogen Starr was linked to the rumor, that it was she. Mrs. Garfinkle had conceived an outright dislike for the man at that moment, and shared her feelings with Mr. Garfinkle, always a man of moral rectitude and stern example, and Mr. Garfinkle had agreed that it was a disgrace.

Mrs. Garfinkle had penned a letter to Brannan's wife, using her left hand to disguise her naturally flowing calligraphy, for which she had won prizes at school. Mailing the result, she had experienced a flush of righteousness; Zoe Brannan deserved to know the worst, in order that she be able to fight against it. The result was a hastily arranged departure by the wife and unfortunate daughter in an easterly direction, the word being that both were bound for the grand tour of old Europe. This was not the reaction Mrs. Garfinkle had anticipated, but she supposed it was all that Zoe could have done, considering her husband's status as one of the nation's wealthiest men.

There matters might have rested, had not her husband brought

home news of a troubling nature several weeks later. As head clerk
to Brannan's attorney, Mr. Garfinkle was privy to many documents
of a highly secretive nature, and he had lately been involved in
work of a decidedly immoral bent. Learning of it from his unhappy
lips, Mrs. Garfinkle declared they must fight against such forces as
Brannan had at his disposal, by informing Zoe that what was hers
by obscure legal right was being stolen away through devious
means.

The Garfinkles reasoned that they were unable to do anything
about such perfidious conduct, given that Zoe was beyond communication across the ocean, but then had come the astounding news
that she and Omie had returned. Mrs. Garfinkle suggested to her
husband that she send another letter, giving hints of the plot, but
before such a letter could be penned, Zoe had taken her daughter
and again departed Glory Hole, this time for parts unknown. Mr.
Garfinkle had access to certain financial documents which stated
that Zoe had been awarded one million dollars, to be deposited for
her personal use in a Denver bank. The first installment had been
withdrawn through a bank in Durango a few days later, and Mr.
Garfinkle brought this news of Zoe's new location home to his wife.

Knowing a bank would reveal nothing of its clientele, Mrs.
Garfinkle had written the letter as planned, and mailed it to
Durango care of general delivery, hoping it would find the woman
so grievously wronged, even if that woman had more money than
the Garfinkles might earn in a hundred years. She had addressed it
to Zoe Dugan, on the assumption that a proud woman would have
reverted to her former name, even if she had called herself Brannan
for the purpose of making the bank withdrawal.

Mr. Garfinkle had shortly thereafter perceived himself to be
under suspicion at the office, since his employer had found him
studying the latest addendum to the so-called green file, this being
the simple addition of a newspaper clipping, already yellowed by
the passage of weeks since its printing, which concerned the murder of a transient named Bryce Aspinall. This same name had
appeared in the green file's opening sheets, wherein it was stated
that this man had been, and still was, the husband of Zoe. Learning
this caused the Garfinkles great soul-searching. They were opposed
to bigamy, but far more adamantly opposed to cold-blooded murder
for monetary gain. Zoe might have been a sinner, but she was more
sinned against. A search through old newspapers in their basement

had given the Garfinkles exactly what they needed to alert Zoe, a woman they now saw as an errant daughter in need of parental advice. Scarcely had the clipping been mailed to Durango, however, than Simms and his hulking deputy had come to take them away.

She hoped Mr. Garfinkle was not suffering unduly; he was plagued by a weak stomach, and required special meals only his wife could provide. Mrs. Garfinkle was filled with pride. She and Mr. Garfinkle were little people, unimportant people, yet they had spoiled the selfish plans of a man richer than many a king, and there was little or nothing that Brannan could do to silence them, should he attempt to stifle news of what they had done. She truly was not intimidated, and hoped Mr. Garfinkle was similarly emboldened in the face of such blatant bullying as had been practiced against her by Simms, who clearly was one of Brannan's minions.

Her only regrets were the disgusting toilet arrangements and the fact that she was separated from her husband by several thicknesses of brick. She had imagined quite some time ago now that she heard his voice crying out at a distance, through the intervening walls, but was able to convince herself that she had imagined the sound.

All that was required of her was fortitude and the courage to submit for a time to inhuman conditions. Mrs. Garfinkle had heard about jails and the many kinds of hell in evidence there, but thus far her term of imprisonment had not been unduly harsh. She was determined to maintain a brave face, eat the dreadful fare provided by the deputy, and use the bucket as little as possible; this should be the first place fitted with Brannan's much-vaunted flushing commodes, she decided.

When the deputy unlocked her door, she was a little surprised to note that he carried no tray of food. Mrs. Garfinkle was quite hungry by then, having had her last tray removed a long time ago, it seemed; the deputy was always reluctant to tell her how long she had been held.

"Good afternoon," she said. "Or is it morning, or night?"

"Makes no difference," said the deputy.

"I suppose not." Mrs. Garfinkle smiled, deeming agreeableness the appropriate response to so primitive a creature as this one. He was very large and stupid, the type of man she could best describe as "limited" if she wished to be kind. His name was Bob, but he had told her no more than that.

Bob went to the bed and began stripping off the sheets.

"Thank you," Mrs. Garfinkle said. "They were becoming a little gamy. I really must insist that you place at my disposal a washbowl and jug of clean water, plus soap and a towel. You may get them from my home if these things are not available here."

"Makes no difference," said Bob, now shaking out the sheets.

"May I ask what it is you're doing?" inquired Mrs. Garfinkle

"Gotta get 'em straightened out," said Bob, doing just that. He began twisting the sheets into a rope. Sheriff Simms had promised him two hundred dollars and a whore for taking care of the man, and three hundred dollars and two whores for taking care of the woman, that being a more odious task. The man had already been visited. Bob had initial misgivings over the woman, being that a nice lady like the one in the cell seemed an unlikely murderer, but the sheriff had shown him the peculiar-looking dagger and the money he had found in their home. That was all the evidence required, the sheriff had said. Bob still could not quite figure out what Garfinkle had been talking about when he finally beat some information out of him, but the sheriff seemed to, and Bob was not about to question his judgment.

But there was a problem, Simms had told him; the Garfinkles were Jews, and you couldn't trust them not to be sprung from jail by other Jews, who were a fanatical bunch and very clever when it came to protecting their own, probably part of some deal they made with the devil. Simms said that folks would be so incensed if the Garfinkles got away that they'd likely storm the courthouse and haul the sheriff and deputy into the street and lynch them, so it was Bob's duty to take care of the Garfinkles before that happened. Real justice would be served, and Bob would save the town the cost of a trial besides.

Mr. Garfinkle had struggled a lot for such a little fellow, and Bob had been obliged to string him up on a sheet rope while in a state of unconsciousness brought about by Bob's large and merciless fists. He hoped the woman would be more cooperative, since beating a woman was not something he cared to do unless it was strictly necessary. He began shaping a crude noose.

"What are you doing?"

"Nothin' as makes a difference."

"But ... what exactly are you doing with my sheets?"

"You just hush now."

"I will not. Stop that!"

Mrs. Garfinkle had divined the purpose of the object taking shape in the deputy's hands. "I won't be scared off by that kind of nonsense, you know.... Don't think you can fluster me with such silliness."

"All right," said Bob, testing the strength of his creation between both hands. It would hold. He moved in her direction, holding the noose.

"What are you doing? Go away...."

"You never should've done it to him."

"Done what? What are you saying? Done it to whom?"

"That feller. Feller you brung home to do that to."

"What ... what fellow? Please, I don't understand what it is you're saying...."

"Should've let him alone, missus."

"Get away.... Get out of here this instant!"

Bob felt bad, doing what he was about to do, but justice had to be served. If he didn't do it, someone else would have to, and that would be a cowardly thing for Bob to do, make someone else kill a woman that needed killing, so he closed his ears and hardened his heart and went ahead. The woman backed herself into the corner, then stumbled over her own shit bucket, and while she looked down in distress at the mess emptied onto the floor, Bob pounced.

Once he had the noose around her neck the rest was easy, and when he was certain she had died, he tied the end of the sheet rope around the upper bars of the cell, making sure her toes couldn't touch the floor. He wondered, as he arranged Mrs. Garfinkle there, if the whores made available to him would be pretty ones.

44

He wondered now if his heart was truly set for more of the same work. Hauling in the usually dead bodies of outlaws for cash payment seemed futile somehow, a low grade of employment, and yet he was suited for no other. Clay was beginning to doubt all those aspects of himself which in former times had been the source of his strength, his conviction. There were bad people galore, and those bad people had to be caught and locked away, if not killed outright, before they did more mischief than they already had done. No one made bad people do what they did; they chose to do it, and so Clay had chosen to stop them from doing it, and had met with a measure of success in his field.

But now the certainty was gone. There were too many bad people, more than he could ever hope to round up in a lifetime of seeking them out. If he stopped, if he found a new kind of work, the world would continue to spin as before, with bad people preying on good people, as if he had never stalked any of them down and killed them, as if no one had. Badness was a permanent part of the landscape, he had decided, and Clay's acceptance that this was so came as a disheartening surprise. He had always pictured bad men being weeded one by one from a garden, until that garden became free of weeds, but now he knew the weeds would always spring up anew behind his back to mock his efforts. There was no perfect garden to be had, nor had there ever been one. And he was no gardener, although he had pulled weeds for years now, with a steady rage at their proliferation underfoot.

In the absence of any other line of work he could realistically engage in, Clay made a decision to revive his enthusiasm for bounty hunting by pursuing the one man everyone in the nation agreed was so bad he deserved a category of badness all his own. Clay would go after Slade.

A long time ago he had considered collecting the bounty on Panther Stalking and Kills With a Smile, but had not followed through. He had regretted that decision after the Apache brothers finally were caught, and had committed mutual suicide in their jail cell. If he had been the one to capture them, preferably dead, his reputation as dispenser of justice would have been without peer. There could not have been a more rewarding memory to take with him into old age than knowing he was the one who had ended a terrible reign of blood lust. And now, in that same region of the country, another ghoul was taking the lives of innocent people, opening their bodies and strewing their insides around for the flies and buzzards to feast on. Slade was barely human, so heinous were his acts; at least the brothers had been Apaches, their killings to be expected, but Slade was a white man. Capturing him would be worth more than the killing of a hundred ordinary bad men. As the one who rid the world of Slade, Clay could hold his head up high, and also collect the reward offered by mining magnate Leo Brannan, currently standing at ten thousand dollars. With money like that, he could retire while still young, and have the leisure to find another direction for his life. Capturing Slade would set the capstone on a career too often blighted by feelings of shame, of being some kind of pariah, even if the work he did was necessary. Everyone would applaud him without reserve for having taken the shadow of Slade away. Of course, he would have to collect his reward and disappear pronto, or Sophie would read of his fame and come hurrying in his direction with her thirst for vengeance and her gun.

Dreaming of success was one thing, earning it another. Clay took himself and his horses by train to Santa Fe, and began his search from there. He had no formal plan; there were no clues to Slade's habits, apart from a clear preference for rugged desert country where he could hide with impunity. There were no traitorous companions prepared to sell Slade out, no gang members to trail toward some hidden redoubt. Slade came and went with the desert wind, descending on his prey like a demon from the air, leaving no tracks that could be followed, even by expert trackers with Indian blood. Among the Indian population a cult was growing around the cannibal. Slade, it was said, was not a white man after all, but the vengeful spirit of all Indians who had suffered defeat and death at the hands of whites. The Indians ascribed to Slade supernatural powers of the most outrageous kind: the ability to turn himself into a coyote or an eagle; the ability to see from afar, even by night; the ability to sense the presence of danger, and fly away to evade capture. Slade had to date killed and eviscerated no Indians at all, and so the belief persisted and grew that he was killing whites on behalf of red men, and his exploits were carefully monitored, and his legendary status grew.

For Clay, the means to be employed in capturing the man-eater would have to be unorthodox, since the territories Slade hovered over like a cloud were becoming filled with bounty hunters and glory seekers of every ilk, all determined to be the one who found and destroyed the monster. If Clay was to succeed where legions of the like-minded had thus far failed, he would have to do what others had not done. He did not know what this unconventional method might be, since his own procedures were in no way unique. He would have to think of something.

The first order of Clay's plan was to isolate himself, in order that he might be visited by inspiration. He stocked up on water and supplies, including several bottles of mineral oil to inject up his suffering penis, and left Santa Fe in the dead of night, to shake off any lesser hunter who might be tempted to follow along, with notions of sharing the prize. Clay wanted to capture Slade unassisted; one bad man captured by one good man—that was how the story should end.

He rode into the wilderness with a new and urgent need within himself; this quest for Slade would exonerate Clay of all his sins. He was unclear over the precise nature of these sins, but he had of late felt unclean in some indefinable way, as if the smell of every man he brought in for federal reimbursement had wiped off on his hands, his face, the clothes he wore, smothering him with the reek of death, down to the very roots of his hair. When he caught Slade he would become sweet-smelling, in a figurative sense, and the past would be wafted away on lavender breezes, wiping him clean of all wrongdoing, creating him all over again, in a newer, more acceptable image. He would be reborn, without recourse to religion, a state of being well worth this final burst of dedicated manhunting. His nose was to the feral winds that would bring to him the stench of evil, Slade's unmistakable scent. He knew, without knowing how or why he knew, that where all others had failed, he would win through and emerge triumphant, Slade's body slung over a pack-horse like so many before.

The days were hot, the nights cold, and even as his supplies ran low, Clay did not cease to believe in the destiny he wished upon himself. Somewhere in the arid void of mountains and canyons there dwelt a demon, a beast in human guise, and like some knight come riding into the lair of a dragon, Clay would strike down the thing that haunted and terrorized and preyed upon the innocent. He would do it for the dead who could not return, and for the living who would not join the dead until their appointed time; but above all, he would do it for the purification of his own soul, if he had one.

But search as he might, there came to him no mystic glimpse of Slade's location, no smattering of Slade's intent, not the slightest inkling of where or when he might strike, not even any sense that Slade was alive and cognizant of the threat bearing down upon him with two thin horses and a dwindling supply of coffee. Clay's faith began to waver. Where was the sign that would bring himself and Slade together as they should be, good man and bad man; where was the fullness of purpose in which he had begun his search?

Hope and expectation were running from him now like flour from a ruptured sack. Every sunrise swept across his eyes, the oldest of light, revealing nothing, for nothing was there. Skies without rain, land without succor, and in every sun-blasted arroyo, across every empty mesa, came whisperings of the greater emptiness beyond. He found deserted farms, entire adobe villages abandoned in advance of Slade's inevitable coming. The territory was emptying itself of people, it seemed, and as he wandered, Clay saw no distant riders he could not identify at a glance—hunters like himself, swirling motes in the vastness of red earth and rock, searching for the one who would not leave. He took what he needed from pantries left to desert mice, raised precious water from wells undrawn, and ignored when he chanced upon them, lined up before the scabrous mirrors in dusty-floored cantinas and saloons, the remnants of liquor he once would have drained.

His circlings through and round about the emptiness were weak-

ening him. He felt flesh falling from his bones, blood seeping from
his veins, boiling out through skin turned to leather. He was becoming a husk, blown this way and that by the turgid air, but somewhere inside Clay his great desire for one last kill rattled like a
dried pea, and would not go away. The rattling pea drove him on.
His packhorse died, and Clay rode on. His saddle horse fell, and
Clay drove the suffering from it with a shotgun shell, and walked
on with his gun and empty canteen and rattling pea, until finally
he came to a place, another place of nothing, and fell down himself,
and at last the pea was silent. This is my time of dying, thought
Clay, and I never did see the son of a bitch.

He closed his eyes against the afternoon light, but it was too
bright still, so he dragged himself to shade beneath a rock ledge,
and arranged his body for a comfortable leave-taking. His head was
filled with a steady swishing sound, insistent but not distracting.
Clay stared across the barren ground he had covered, watched it
dance and shimmer before his eyes in languid waves of heat, saw
the dust funnels raise themselves and scuttle nervously across the
earth before falling apart in the air and drifting downward again.
He had come a long, long way to be in that place, and the trip had
not been worth it, because he had failed. Life itself was ebbing
within him, and had already ebbed too far for caring. Soon he would
depart from there, like everyone else, leave it all to the rattlesnakes
and Slade, who must have been a man of smoke and dust to survive
so long without being seen.

Clay's kidneys gave him no peace, even so close to the end, but
insisted on pushing another stone down through his belly's side, its
passage eased not at all by the absence of water in his tubes. To die
unfulfilled was harsh enough, but to die with the pain of a kidney
stone prodding at him was downright cruel. The stone would get
maybe halfway down, then stop, because Clay would be dead by
then, and that would be his revenge against the stone, to strand it
partway to its destination, never allow it to plunge into the warm
lagoon of his bladder or ride his yellow foaming rapids out into the
light. The stone might one day be found among his bones, nestled
there like a croquet ball among a tangle of hoops, and the man who
discovered the stone would carry it away to place upon his mantel
shelf and tell his wife how lucky he had been to find it there.

Now it was dusk. Purple shadows came slowly down from the
rock escarpment behind him to steal along the ground, silently

bleeding its purple darkness back into the sky. Clay hurt. He hurt everywhere, but mainly in the left side of his belly and between his eyes. The pain was keeping him alive, drawing him back when he attempted to escape its clawing, and he would willingly have cried in sympathy with himself and his suffering if only his body could have summoned the moisture.

Darkness at last. He felt his skin cracking in the cooler air. The pain was easing a little, as if realizing its own pointlessness. With luck, he might be able to slip away quietly, without provoking another attack. He could have hastened the process, of course, by placing the barrels of his sawed-off into his mouth and pulling both triggers, but that end held no appeal. Clay admitted he had lost out in his last game, strewn his cards carelessly instead of holding them close against his chest. It had all been a sorry waste, he told himself, this life he had used up too soon. There was nothing at all to show for it, no children to bear his name, nobody to weep over his body and trim the wild grasses from his marker down through the years. At his birth there had been a woman; at his death there would be no one.

Cold was creeping inside him. Soon he could go, and in the morning the empty shell that had been Clay Dugan would be made warm again by sunlight, and the mornings and afternoons to follow would turn him to dust fit only for blowing away. His arms and legs already were immovable, and his head could barely turn on his neck. Sometimes his eyes opened, and when they did he saw herds unlike any he had seen before. Creatures tall as ostriches ran like the wind, their striped backs and tails undulating smoothly. Lizard heads outthrust, they dashed among impossibly tall trees, scampering lightly through the shadows, phantom runners beneath a larger moon than Clay ever knew. The forest of his dreaming rang with mysterious trumpetings and forlorn cries, whether animal or human Clay could not be sure. He thought he might already have died and been taken to some darkling world for his sins among humanity, and his crimes against himself. The forest was a lonely place, and Clay was glad to see it fade away as the sun came up.

He should have been gone by then. It really was too bad. Now he'd have to endure more heat, more agony from his kidney stone, and be that much longer in the dying. Even death was not going to do Clay any favors.

The girl was easily recognized because of her blue-sided face, even if Clay had never seen her before in daylight, nor at any time when he had not been dreaming. He was not dreaming this time; his body hurt him too much. The girl was truly there, and yet she was not. She cast no shadow, and the light she was illuminated by was not from the same direction as the sun. Clay knew then that he either was mad or else finally had died, and was being greeted on the other side by this familiar ghost. He nodded at her.

"Are you sick?" she asked, her voice hollow, as if she spoke into a tin can.

"Dying, I guess," said Clay. He could not remember talking to the girl before. In his dreams they simply shared the same time and space, and were sometimes able to shout at each other without receiving any reply. She seemed like a well-mannered girl, and he was glad of the company.

"Over there," she said, pointing. "There's some water over there, just a little way off."

"Water?"

"Not very much, though."

Clay stared in the direction she had pointed, along the escarpment. It looked like more of the same dreary desert to him, and he turned back to tell the girl so, but found himself alone.

"Little girl ...? Little girl ...!"

She was gone, and he was crushed by her absence. He had been looking forward to asking her if he was mad or dead, and now that wouldn't happen. Worse, he was confronted with a choice—to see if there really was water where she had indicated, or ignore the episode as some kind of mirage, like the forest he had seen in the night. He could die where he was, in considerable discomfort, or give himself more pain on top of what he already had, in hopes of finding the water and surviving. To trust a dream spirit, or not.

Clay thought he would be unable to rise, and once having accomplished this, believed he could not possibly start walking, and when he had gone a quarter mile or so, was shocked to find himself still upright. He stayed close to the escarpment, glad of its shade, and only occasionally fell over the rocks that time and weather had spawned and tumbled from the sheer cliff beside him. The water, when he found it, was seeping into a shallow pool no more than two feet across. Clay dropped to his knees and began drinking.

He literally drank the pool dry over the course of an hour or so, and had to wait for it to refill itself. He saw the tiny rippling of liquid as it entered the natural cup from below, and restrained himself until it had acquired a depth sufficient for him to scoop up water in his hands again. He drank now to free the stone and flush it through into his bladder. Clay was determined not to leave the tiny soak until the stone had completed its journey. He crawled into deeper shade as the sun came around to strike him, and ventured out only to sip some more from what he called the girlpool. She had saved him, and he decided she must be his guardian angel, despite her unusual, distinctly unheavenly appearance.

The stone began to shift again, scraping its way down through passages that now ran with water like spring freshets, and by early evening it had entered Clay's overflowing bladder. The pain died away within minutes. Sometime between dusk and dawn it would begin its second tight squeeze, along his penis. Clay still had his bottle of mineral oil and eyedropper; he would no more have parted from it than he would from his canteen or sawed-off.

When dusk came he stood and took his filled canteen from the girlpool, and began walking. Lubricated again, his body worked as it always had, supplying a steady loping gait that caused his head to bob up and down slightly as he proceeded across the desert floor beneath a three-quarter moon. His stone was held in abeyance, and his head was no longer troubled by humming or pounding. Clay's mood was almost jaunty. He was alive, in good health, considering, and his mood was one of determination again, not the wan acceptance of, if not actual beckoning for death that had overcome him the night before. He was alive, and he would live for as long as the water in his canteen lasted, and a little bit longer besides. And even then, if the water should give out, he would find more, because he had a guardian angel. Clay was beginning to doubt the underpinnings of his atheism. If guardian angels were real, might not the regular kind also be flitting about in abundance, presumably invisible to human eyes, especially those of a doubter like himself? And if there were angels, did that oblige God to climb onto a throne somewhere? Would there be judgment after death, a siphoning of good souls heavenward, a deluge of sinners sent cascading down to hell? The whole thing troubled him; he did not know if he was a good man after all, or just a man less bad than the worst of them. If his life was truly a test, he should definitely begin setting it in order. If he walked out of the desert alive (which he would, with the assistance of his blue-faced friend), he must begin anew. There must be an end to manhunting, a seeking-out of less bloody work. He had no idea what form this new work would take, since killing or apprehending bad men was all he knew, but he would find something. His life had been spared for a reason, a purpose of some kind, and he would not ignore so explicit an imperative.

When he first saw it, the ranch appeared deserted in the moonlight, another home abandoned in fear of Slade. The place was small, one adobe house with a stable and corral. No dogs barked, no lamps burned. The deep window wells were black with emptiness. Clay could hear a windmill somewhere, slowly creaking, but could not see it. The ranch was tucked away into a shallow draw, the windmill presumably somewhere more open to the air; he would find it tomorrow, and hope it was still pumping water into a cattle pond. His first need was for food.

The door yielded to his touch, the latch rising with a faint squeal. He smelled cold stove ashes as he searched for a lamp and for food. He found neither, but continued blundering through the darkness of the house, opening shutters to allow moonlight inside. They had taken everything edible, those frightened people, but left their few articles of hand-hewn furniture, too heavy for their wagon, maybe, thought Clay. Although the place was poor, it was a shame to leave such stuff as they had owned behind them as they had. Fear made men act in haste, he concluded, and lay down on an actual bed for the first time in over a month. Its straw-tick mattress caused him to moan with pleasure as he sank into its rustling embrace, and sleep came rushing over him despite his hunger and his blistered heels. The last sound Clay was aware of, as he fell into the welcome darkness of oblivion, was the windmill cranking out its one fractured, rusting note time and again, a metronome for the damned.

Daylight woke him. Clay felt much refreshed but ravenously hungry, and so began searching the house in earnest, now that he could see his way from room to room. The former occupants had left a lot more than his first inspection had revealed, in fact it seemed that they had done no more than take their food and run, and not very long ago either. There was little dust on the floor and other horizontal surfaces; clothing of the many-times-patched kind hung on pegs; there were three chickens in the yard. Why hadn't they taken their chickens along? What had scared them so badly that they fled in a panic, leaving behind most of what they owned? Even fear of Slade could not account for it.

Clay found some tortilla flour and set about building a fire in the stove. The kitchen utensils were hanging on the wall. He baked himself several tasteless rounds and crammed them into his stomach. There was a coffeepot, but no coffee. Now he was beginning to feel a vague disquiet, a sense that something was not right with the house. It held an air of menace not fully explained by the presumed circumstances of its abandonment. The feeling gnawed at him, unsettling the glaze of physical contentment granted by a good night's rest and a full belly. Some enigmatic displacement of the ordinary was impinging on him, brushing his awareness with a feather's touch, unsettling him for reasons beyond his understanding.

He began looking again, hoping that a more thorough search would reveal to his eyes what the deepest part of his brain was attempting to assimilate, so that he might be warned. Panic, the thing he had self-righteously assigned to the owners of the house, began to prick at Clay. He was fretting over the inexplicable, worrying himself about what had or might have happened there. That something bad had left its imprint upon the walls and air within the house he no longer doubted. He asked his guardian angel to appear and explain everything to him, but she remained where angels tread. He was whimpering now, like a frightened dog, anxious yet fearful to know why it was he felt as he did.

The stable, he told himself, and went there in full expectation of answers, but there were none; in fact his confusion was deepened by the discovery there of a wagon. Why had the owners fled on foot? The hidden windmill continued its ceaseless creaking. No animals, but their dung was fresh, no more than a day old. Clay was becoming frantic, shaming himself with the noises that came unbidden from his throat. He could not control his thoughts, which formed no particular notion or picture, but were flooded with an unspecified dread. What was there in the house, or around it, to make him feel that way?

The windmill. It had been calling him since his arrival. He would attend to it now, having exhausted every place else. Clay went outside and followed its dismal creakings, found a pathway to higher ground and came through a thicket of scrub to stand before the source of the endless grinding and clanking. The windmill was large, a more expensive model than Clay had expected for such a lowly spread; the owners must have scrimped and saved to pay for the tall metal tower and the twelve-foot span of vanes. One of the owners was spread-eagled across those vanes, wrists and ankles bound by wire, the body's nakedness so smeared with blood it was impossible to guess its gender. Turning and turning upon its gutted axis, the featureless body had emptied its intestines onto the small utility platform beneath. At the base of the tower was another adult, and a boy, both naked, opened and emptied. The boy's skull was smashed open, the adult's head removed completely. Flies formed a small and noisome cloud about their gaping wounds and the truncated neck. Coming closer, Clay saw that the adult on the ground was male, the one turning in circles above him female. He knelt and vomited the tortillas that had required so much effort to make, and the one word his mind was capable of formulating could not even pass his lips: Slade.

When he was able, Clay pulled the man and boy aside, then climbed the windmill tower to release the woman. Starting up the rungs, he wondered why it was that no buzzards circled overhead. Could they have been scared off by the slowly spinning vanes, or was there in the region about the house and windmill some smell of evil too brutal, too unfamiliar to allow creatures near. It was an unrealistic notion, he supposed, but there were indeed no buzzards. Reaching the platform, he found both her breasts there, neatly arranged side by side. He pulled the brake and brought the spinning vanes to a stop, then unbound the wires holding her, keeping his mouth closed and his eyes squinted against the humming cloud of flies, but they crawled up his nostrils anyway. She was a small woman, less than five feet, and the natural crease between her legs had been opened all the way to her breastbone. Clay began to cry. He could barely untwist the lengths of wire. When the woman was free, her body fell from the vanes into his arms, almost taking him over the platform edge.

He had to sling her over his shoulder to descend, and when he reached the ground, his clothing was covered in gore. He tore shirt and pants from himself and ran toward the house, to be away from the sight of the slaughtered family and the sound of the flies. Naked, he rolled in dust to smother the stench of death adhering to his skin, then ran three times around the corral, howling. Clay fell to the ground by the front porch, panting, asking himself if he could go on and do what must be done. The deep gashes on the bodies contained no maggots yet, despite the flies; Slade could not be much more than a day's ride or walk away. He could be caught at last, and by the one man fit to catch him. Clay would not stop to bury the bodies; there was no time. When Slade was dead, there would be time to return and put his last victims under the earth.

The shirt and overalls hanging in the house were a poor fit, but Clay could not bear to put on his own clothing again. He gathered up all the tortilla flour in a sack, took several canteens up to the windmill, where he kept his eyes averted from the bodies, and filled them from the tank. Then he was ready to follow the trail of the monster.

But there was no trail, no wagon tracks or hoofprints, no trickling droplets of blood in the dust to indicate the route Slade had taken. While he pondered, Clay felt the stone begin to descend his urethra, and fetched his bottle of oil and eyedropper to facilitate its passage. Striding restlessly back and forth along the shaded porch, pausing to inject oil into himself, Clay felt his rage and determination begin to ebb. Vengeance was all very fine, but it could not be had if Slade had vanished as he was rumored to do after every atrocity. Clay required some indication, however small, to set him in the right direction, but despite a second examination of the ground, there was none to be found.

He was administering a final dose of oil (the stone was nearly through) when he saw the girl again. Clay froze, immobilized by embarrassment. She was staring at him without any expression on her mournful face, at least twenty yards distant, along the draw to the west of the house. Clay wished she had shown up earlier or later, anytime but that moment. He felt himself blushing, but would not remove the eyedropper from his penis at the crucial last stage of relief. She would just have to see, and he would just have to be seen. He looked down at his hands, ashamed and annoyed. A guardian angel should not be so thoughtless as to manifest itself at such a time. When he looked up, he saw her pointing along the draw, and was about to ask her if that was where Slade had gone, when she abruptly vanished, simply faded from sight, her arm still outstretched.

"All right, then!" Clay called after her, and the stone came oozing into his hand on a sluggish wave of oil. He took it for a good sign.

The draw opened out a short distance from the ranch house, entering a broad red valley that meandered east and west. Clay saw no hoofprints still, not even a boot mark in the dust. Might his guardian angel girl have misdirected him out of impish spite? He still could not quite accept the presence of so unnatural a figure in his life, even if he had been glimpsing her for years. He decided to seek her advice outright, as a test of her good faith.

"Which way?" he asked the air before his nose. The angel did not appear to inform him, so Clay asked the question again, and again was left without the direction he required. It was confirmation of his doubt concerning the girl. Might she not be some fairy or spirit that had sprung directly from his own head into actuality, the product of a mind slowly becoming crazed? Clay was no expert judge of sanity, but it did seem inevitable that a madman would in all likelihood consider himself completely sane, and accept his own version of the world as the correct one. Had that happened to him? It was a disturbing thought, and it did nothing to assist him in making a choice—east or west.

He headed west for no discernible reason, sure that the valley to the east would have proven equally unrewarding: no tracks, no sign at all that Slade had ever passed by. Was Slade also some unnatural being, truly a demon, as some of the newspapers would have it? That might explain the absence of a trail to follow, and the fiend's ability to evade capture even when so many were after him for Leo Brannan's reward and the gratitude of a nation. The killer had wings, maybe, that carried him from place to place, enabling him to descend like a hawk from the skies onto the very backs of his victims. Clay had seen pictures of winged demons from hell, and he had no wish to tangle with one, not even armed with his sawed-off. He wondered, as he admitted his fear, if he was becoming a coward as well as a madman, and was not encouraged by this new train of thought.

The valley became redder as afternoon turned to evening. Clay drank sparingly from his canteens, and wished he had more than tortilla flour to eat. He placed dabs of it onto his tongue and mixed it with saliva to form a kind of paste he called spit dough, and it eased his hunger pangs without convincing him he had eaten. The angel did not appear, and Clay became fairly sure he had been imagining her all this time, which was reassuring in the sense that he could not be altogether mad if he acknowledged a symptom of his madness, but was distressing in that it indicated he had followed the direction along the draw that had been given to him by an entity that was not there, which in turn suggested he was following nothing to nowhere. None of the conflicting awarenesses within him gave Clay the strength he needed, not only to find and capture Slade, but to survive in the place where he now found himself. He had water enough for two days, if he rationed the quenching of his thirst. In that time he hoped to discover if he was indeed mad. He wished, before dying, to be cognizant of his own state of mind. To die while in a state of delusion would be a terrible thing, and a man's entire life and accomplishments would be thrown into a new and unfavorable light in consequence of such a revelation. Clay desperately wanted his life to have been worthwhile. He had killed a sufficient number of awful individuals, and needed to be sure that his actions, although rewarded with human coin, had pleased some higher authority, whose definition came hard to an atheist. It had all been for something, the advancement of moral good in the world, had it not? He couldn't say, and his footsteps slowed as the hopelessness of ever understanding the least thing about himself and his place in the vast scheme of things drove itself like a nail into his skull.

Slade was nowhere near. The one thing Clay could finally be sure of was that. He had bungled his chance for immortality, walked away from fame because a blue-faced girl in his head had misdirected him, probably as a means of alerting him to his own seriously impaired brain. There was no guardian angel and there was no Slade; these things had nothing whatsoever to do with Clay Dugan, no matter how hard he might try to link himself with them. He was a fool in the wilderness, and sometime soon he would be a dead fool, buzzard food, the meanest end a man could imagine for himself. It was too bad. Clay genuinely felt his existence should have counted for more than that. Of course, his wishes might be nothing more than the yearnings of a little man, a frightened man, one who finally had seen himself in the mirror of ultimate truth and was unable to accept the pitiful figure shivering there.

Clay sat abruptly in the reddish dust of the valley floor. What was the point of going on, when he hadn't the least indication that he was accomplishing anything worthwhile, not just wandering without purpose toward an untimely and insignificant end? He wanted to cry. He had cried already that day, when confronted with the wanton ugliness of Slade's latest marauding. It was not right that he could not find the tears now for himself. Did he deserve less than the nameless family left slaughtered behind him? He would not budge from that spot until answers were given to him, or arrived at via the workings of his own mind. Clay wanted to know what it was that had brought him to this unique time and place, his ass inside a dead man's pants, set down in the dust of a nameless valley filled with orange light from a setting sun. He had a right to some answers. The fact that he was there, defeated and in full knowledge of his defeat, gave him the right to answers.

In the absence of these, he decided to sleep. The air was still warm, and would remain so for at least another half hour. He lay down and managed to close his eyes for several minutes, but could not rest. Sitting up, he saw a momentary flash several miles away. It lasted less than a second, possibly the result of the lowering sun reflecting off metal or glass. Clay knew it was Slade. It might also have been a chunk of quartz, or an abandoned bottle. But he knew it was not. It was Slade.

Something like a terrible hunger began filling Clay. He felt it rising from the pit of his stomach, an unstoppable need, devouring him. The only thing that could ever cause the feeling to ease would be the sight of Slade lying dead at his feet, and Clay knew also that it would happen. He had been guided there and made to sit in exactly that place, and made to open his eyes at the precise moment the telltale flash was sent to him. All his doubts had been for nothing. Slade was being delivered into his hands in order that the earth might rest easy again. Clay felt himself the agent of those same higher forces he so recently had pondered over. Now he would do what it was they required of him. Charged with purpose, his blistered feet forgotten, Clay began to walk hard and fast toward the darkening land ahead.

Finding Slade was more difficult than he hoped. The man lit no fire, so Clay was obliged to sneak around in the moonlight, watching every step he took to ensure that he made no noise; his prey might be nearer than he thought. The moon hung low and heavy, softly glowing, illuminating the desert with a silvery-blue light. Clay could see as well as hear tiny rodents scuttling across the ground, and once was able to detect a rattlesnake with his eyes before it shook its tail at his approach. He could make out individual twigs on the waist-high brush, the exact lineaments of every rock he passed by, the location of the planet Venus and the silhouette of nearby mountains against the stars, but he could not see Slade.

He stopped and thought what he might do now, given the hopelessness of stumbling across the killer by good luck. Slade was silent. Had he heard Clay moving around, and hidden himself? Could he be stalking Clay, at the same time Clay was stalking him? Clay spun around, ready to fend off the hairy creature that might have been rushing at him, knife in hand, eyes burning with the inner fires of madness. There was nothing. His heartbeat had accelerated over nothing more dangerous than his own imagination. Where was the blue-faced girl when he needed her silently pointing finger most?

Then he heard the voice, a male voice, speaking softly. It came from his left, and Clay began walking carefully in that direction, his breathing suddenly tight with expectation, the blood thundering through him so strongly it seemed he must alert Slade to his presence with its roaring. Now the voice was louder, sometimes pausing, sometimes breaking into a tuneless humming for several minutes before resuming its one-sided conversation.

And there was the speaker, seated in a clearing, addressing himself to some object in his hands. Moonlight reflecting from spectacles on the thing told Clay it was a human head. He had no doubt that sunlight glancing from those same lenses had been what he saw in the late afternoon, nor did he doubt that the head belonged to the man left with his wife and boy at the windmill. Slade wore a hat, and did not appear to be a large man, to Clay's surprise. He listened to the words dribbling from Slade's mouth in a childish singsong, but could not make them out. Made bold by his luck, Clay cocked both hammers on his shotgun and stepped forward.

The small man cradling the head in his hands looked up and became silent. Clay waited for a sudden move, any indication that Slade did not intend to surrender peacefully, but there was not the least suggestion in the figure seated before him that he considered himself in any way threatened by the sudden presence of a stranger with an aimed gun.

The silence became too much for Clay. "Put it down," he croaked, then cleared his throat and said, with greater sternness, "Put it down, the head, put it down right now."

The head was placed on the ground.

"Take off your hat," Clay ordered, and was obeyed.

The face bathed in moonlight was familiar to him, despite bearing no resemblance whatever to the depictions of Slade every newspaper had provided.

"Wixson ... "

"Dugan? Is that Dugan ...?"

"Where'd you get that head, Wixson ...? What the hell are you doing here anyway?"

"Dugan ... what a small world."

"I said, where'd you get that head?"

"This head?" Reverend Wixson picked it up again.

"That head."

"From off somebody's neck, Dugan, where else would I get it, do you think?"

"Where is he? Are you a team?"

"Team? To whom do you refer, Dugan?"

"Him! Slade! Where is he?"

"Could this be the man?" asked Wixson, proffering the head. Clay felt confusion invading him, causing his arms to shake. He lowered the shotgun.

"Wixson, are you saying you're the one ...?"

"What one?"

"The one ... the one that's been cutting people up around here. Are you him?"

"I have my work, Dugan. You, of all people, should know that."

"What work? What are you saying?"

"To find the soul. A mechanical device was not the way, I saw that very clearly after what happened in ... wherever it was. No more weights and balances, I told myself. The thing is, Dugan, it requires another approach entirely."

"You cut them open to ... look for their souls?"

"It may be in the heart, or it may be in the head. Or it may be in a place no one has ever suspected. I have to examine every part of the deceased."

"But you killed them, you crazy man! You killed them yourself!"

"And it was necessary. An interior search has to be conducted while the blood is still warm, the heart still beating, sometimes. That's the best moment, in my experience. The soul is small and fleet, a tiny twinkling star, and it migrates from place to place within the body, I suspect, when death is near, attempting to revive the physical being. When that cannot be done, why then, it leaves, and although I don't hope to snare an actual soul, I know I can observe its departure."

Clay understood at last that everyone was wrong. There was no Slade, or if there was, he had died or disappeared since being

released from Brannan's mine. The atrocities blamed on Slade were
the work of Wixson. No one had ever seen the face of the murderer
and lived. The labeling of Slade as the one responsible had been a
mistake, an assumption unsupported by factual evidence. It had
been Wixson all along. He had fooled them all, and was probably
not even aware of the furor he had created with his bloody delvings
for the soul.

"How many has it been so far, Wixson? Do you keep count?"

"No; why would I do that? It doesn't matter how many. However
many it takes, that will be how many it takes. The work is too
important for counting and tallying. You can see that, can't you,
Dugan?"

"I see ... a crazy man, that's what I see."

Wixson smiled forgivingly. "Then you aren't the man I thought
you were."

"You're sure as hell not the man I thought *you* were. Did you
know there's ten thousand dollars reward for you, and they're calling you by the name of Slade?"

"The one you're looking for?"

"You're the one. It's a mix-up. I'll straighten it out all right. Jesus,
Wixson, I had you figured for a fool, but not ... for any of this that
you've been doing. Did God tell you to do it?"

"God has told me nothing, not outright. I have used logic to see
the waste of time the balance had become. The people of ... what
was that place again?"

"Dry Wash," said Clay, reminding himself painfully of Madge
Clifton and all that had not happened between them.

"That's the town. They did me a service, opened my eyes, so to
say. They made me think out the whole thing, Dugan. I owe them
my thanks."

"I'll be sure and pass it on. You hear what I said about the money,
Wixson?"

"You imagine someone will give you thousands of dollars for me?"

"I don't imagine anything—I know."

"The work is worth far more. It's a priceless endeavor, something
you could share with me. You're a stronger man than me, Dugan.
Sometimes I ... I have to struggle with them. The Lord gives me
strength when I need it, but I fear my body is becoming worn out.
Sometimes I faint dead away for no reason. This is harsh country,
but the desert places are where a man finds his maker, Dugan."

"Could be right. You're about to make me rich, Wixson."

"You don't know anything."

"I know that much."

"The people who have helped me, the ones who gave up their bodies for me, they all have a place in heaven."

"Then you won't be seeing them again. I'd say you're hellbound for sure when they drop you on a rope."

"That can never happen, not to me. I have a special dispensation from the Lord. He watches over me, even in my most painful hour."

Clay shook his head pityingly. "You're gone from this world, and you haven't even left it yet. What made you crazy, Wixson—too much Bible studying?"

Wixson's smile mirrored Clay's. "You are one of the minions sent to deter me," he said, sounding vaguely disappointed.

"What kind of minion would that be?"

"Satan's own. I should have guessed it when you crossed my path a second time, and now you're here for a third. Evil moves in threes, did you know? But of course you do."

Wixson stood. Clay lifted the sawed-off with a lazy slowness. Wixson dusted himself off. His clothing was ragged, his boots in need of repair, so badly worn he had them wrapped in filthy strips of cloth to hold the upper to the sole. Clay guessed it was the rags that had obscured what few tracks Wixson left behind him. He had achieved stealth by accident. The irony of it was depressing.

"You're a sorry figure for the Lord's right hand," Clay said.

"And you are exactly right for what you are, Dugan, if that's your true name."

"I guess you'd have one of those long, foreign-sounding angelic names, doing the holy work you're engaged in."

Wixson smiled more broadly and took a hatchet from his belt. Clay chided himself for not having made him surrender what weapons he had earlier.

"All right, now, you can just drop that."

Wixson began walking toward Clay, smiling still.

"He has given me many names, but only one purpose, and he watches from on high to protect me for that purpose."

"He won't stop a load of double-aught, so hold it right there and drop the ax."

Wixson advanced with a smile, like a man greeting a long-lost friend. The hatchet was not even lifted yet to strike. The foolhardiness of it frightened Clay more than the blade; anyone that careless of his life was capable of the unexpected, and that could be what Wixson was counting on. Clay could call the bluff of any normal man without a qualm, but Wixson wore the blithe face of unreason, and Clay was scared.

"I'm telling you straight—you put it down and quit walking or you're a dead man."

"My name is my own, for me and him who made me to know."

Clay was backing away, unwilling to kill a man for whom he had no horse on which to carry the body away.

"Quit it now, Wixson. I don't want to be the one that kills you.... "

"Liar," sighed Wixson, sounding tired, "liar from Satan. You can't help lying, I know.... "

Clay fired both barrels. Wixson was flung back several yards before collapsing. Clay listened to the reverberation of the double blast. It seemed to travel outward from the gun like ripples on the surface of a pond, line after curving line leaving his hands, stretching wider, wider, bowed strings already traveling at distances of a hundred miles, two hundred, expanding outward from him forever, a circle of sound that would one day reach the edge of all things and be swallowed, by which time Clay would himself be dust.

The empty shotgun fell at his feet. He felt nothing in his heart to equal the trembling in his hands. Wixson lay dead, his innards bared like those of his victims. Clay wondered if the preacher's soul had departed intact, or was drifting in shreds on the night breeze. If Wixson's soul were weighed, as Wixson had attempted to do with the souls of others, it would be found wanting. In Wixson's soul a deficit would be found, the missing portion made note of. Did incomplete souls wander the earth? Clay asked himself, knowing that the answer, if one existed, would never be given.

He stared at the sky for some time, then reloaded his gun and lay down to sleep. There was a deep satisfaction creeping into him, now that the twitching had left his hands. He had killed the man everyone mistakenly called Slade. It would be interesting to see the reaction when he informed the nation of its error. The story would be plastered across every newspaper's front page. He would be a famous man. Even Sophie wouldn't dare try shooting at him again. And there was the money, those ten thousand beautiful dollars, an impossible sum, but his for the taking, because he had earned it by squashing the nastiest bug in existence. His life would never be the same again. It would be heaven on earth. And he would ... *he would use his fame to seek out Zoe and Drew!* Clay sat upright, excited by the brilliance of the idea. Everyone from one side of the country to the other would be eager to read about the man who had killed Slade, even if Slade was only pathetic little Wixson, and when it became known that he sought a brother and a sister lost to him so long ago, every reader would ask himself if he knew the man or woman Clay Dugan called his kin.

It would be a whole new story for the newspapers to follow, this search for the Dugan siblings. They would be found, sooner or later, and then his life would be complete. Clay lay back on the desert floor and hugged himself. Everything would be wonderful, better than a flawed man like himself deserved to have, but he would grab hold of all the wonderfulness with both hands anyway, because not to do so would be the act of a fool, and Nettie Dugan had raised no fools. He lay awake another hour or more, congratulating himself on accomplishing what he had, alone and unassisted. He wouldn't tell the newspapers about his guardian angel; they would look at him askance, and he could not blame them for that; he was not sure the blue-faced girl was not something that had slipped into his brain out of sheer exhaustion. The subject was best left in limbo.

The morning was well advanced before Clay awoke. He sat up and looked at the crumpled body of Wixson, wondering for several seconds what it was. When he remembered, he recaptured all the attendant planning and happy expectation that had been his before he fell asleep the night before. The one problem facing him was transportation of Wixson's body to the nearest town. He would need to take the spectacled head too, as confirmation of his story. The revelation that Wixson was the notorious Slade would require proof. Clay had no idea where the nearest town might be, nor how he might find the strength to carry Wixson's body to it. His ebullient mood began to dissipate in the light of these insoluble practicalities. Without Wixson and the head he had no proof of anything, and proof was the very thing his dreams of greatness and contentment rested upon.

Disturbed now, he began searching among Wixson's few possessions to find extra food that might make the task ahead easier. He found nothing in the battered canvas sack at the edge of the clearing but a Bible. Clay leafed through it in annoyance. It was a book that had seen better days, its cover slightly scorched, as if it had fallen briefly into a fire. He flipped through the thousand and more pages in idle irritation, and arrived at the flyleaf in front. There, penned in a careful hand, were the usual entries of births and deaths recorded for posterity in a family Bible. Clay browsed among the fading lines for mention of the name Wixson, but it was not there. Had he stolen the Bible from one of his victims? The name that cropped up again and again was Kindred. The latest owner of the book, according to the notations, was one Morgan Kindred. This man and his wife, Sylvie, were apparently childless, having conceived nothing but a string of five stillborns, their names set down in the Bible according to custom. But then, Clay read, they had adopted a boy by the name of Drew Dugan. Clay read that line several times. The adoption had taken place in May of 1869, the month Clay and Zoe and Drew had been placed aboard the orphan train and sent west to find new families.

He set the Bible down, then picked it up again. The coincidence was too fantastic, but there it was, in brown ink: Drew Dugan. Was Wixson actually Morgan Kindred? Had Clay's brother been raised by the man whom Clay shot the night before? It couldn't be so! And yet it might. The last notation on the flyleaf, after mention of Drew's adoption into the family, was a cryptic entry reading: *We leave for the Desert Place. The Lord will Provide.* Hadn't Wixson mentioned something about a desert place moments before Clay shot him? Clay was sure he had.

He began searching through the Bible again, this time reading several of the notations in pencil along the borders and margins. None of the comments beside underlined passages made much sense to Clay, since he had never studied religious matters, but the hand that wrote the notations was the same hand that had written on the flyleaf. Clay dug into the canvas bag again, looking for a pencil, and found one, a stub less than two inches long. He scrawled a few curlicues alongside the penciled notations to compare the color of the lead, and it looked like a reasonable match to him. But the writer would have used many pencils over the years, so this test meant nothing. And yet Clay was convinced Wixson was Kindred, a man who had gone, presumably with his wife and adopted son, to a desert place. What had happened there? He read again the notations, ignoring the cramps of hunger in his belly. The story of Abraham and Isaac was heavily underscored, and beside it was written: *Drew.* Had Wixson/Kindred intended killing Drew as a sacrifice to God? It was not impossible, given the despicable acts of murder to follow later on. But had it actually happened? Clay was forced to acknowledge that it probably had. If Wixson, unmuscular though he had been, was able to kill so many, what chance would a boy have stood? Drew had most likely been gone from the world a long, long time, but fate had provided him with vengeance in the form of his older brother, who slew the man who had taken Drew away. Now it wouldn't matter if Clay became famous and asked the newspaper readers of the nation to find his brother. Drew was gone. Clay wondered if Zoe might not have met with misfortune also, and his mood admitted the possibility.

He felt sick. He could never share any of this with anyone. Brannan could keep his ten thousand dollars; Clay had no means of transporting the body of Wixson back to civilization in any case, and his story would be laughed at. Clay's greatest stalk and kill, with its personal revelations, had occurred in a vacuum. Wixson/Kindred's death under the stars had no meaning now for anyone but Clay. He would never tell a soul, would mourn for Drew in silence, alone. It was meant to be this way, Clay could see that much, even if he could not understand how it had happened in so neat a fashion, the retribution visited upon the wicked by his hand. It was all beyond him. He would most likely die himself soon, if he failed to find a way out of the wilderness, and that would compound the abstruse secret he had uncovered. It was fitting.

He stood up, the Bible in one hand, his sawed-off in the other, and began walking.

45

There having been not the least sign of public suspicion over the dual suicides of the Garfinkles while in official custody, Rowland Price was free to pursue other interests, and so became intrigued by the Sleeping Savage. He knew Leo was not at all concerned about the success of the venture proposed to him by Imogen, but the Indian in the rain barrel had triggered inside Rowland a kind of fascination. The thing, once laid out in its gleaming new sarcophagus of glass, which had come all the way from Chicago, was dreadful to behold, but its very ugliness was the lure that, according to its co-owner, Nevis Dunnigan, would bring crowds flocking around it, eager to pay fifty cents apiece for a glimpse of hideous antiquity. Rowland did not doubt he was right.

Dunnigan had himself become an object of interest to Rowland, who had twice seen him leaving Imogen's house on Bowman Street with the air of a man well pleased. Suspecting Leo's mistress might be betraying him, Rowland began cultivating the company of Dunnigan in order to ascertain the truth of the matter. Nevis did have a legitimate reason to visit Imogen, in that she was the unofficial sponsor of the Sleeping Savage, and yet, Rowland told himself, there was more to the relationship than mere business. Dunnigan had the look of a man smitten by love; Imogen the look of a woman who knows it. The discovery of secret trystings between Nevis and

Imogen would have served Rowland's interests well. He wanted Leo to rid himself of the lady before he entered public life. Imogen was far too lovely to be the consort of a politician, or even (Rowland shuddered at this) his wife.

And so he went often to the store wherein Nevis was establishing his display. The windows were covered by sheets to deny the curious a free look at the Indian on his bed of velvet, but Rowland was always welcomed there. He had yet to meet Nevis's partner, and could not understand the man's reluctance to participate in the setting up of their joint enterprise. "Smith is too shy by half for this kind of thing," Nevis told him.

There was about Dunnigan an odor Rowland could not define, a miasmic quality lurking beneath the bouquet-laden pomade he doused his hair with. The odor was unpleasant, vaguely redolent of the outhouse. Rowland formed the improbable opinion that Nevis had yet to master the basic art of wiping his ass properly, but overcame his mild disgust for the sake of digging out the facts hovering between Nevis and Imogen like a wisp of cloud, or an unacceptable stink.

"How soon before the public may see your sleeping beauty, Nevis?"

"A day or two more. I feel the curtains behind the dais should have a deeper fold to them, a more richly luxuriant appearance. That would enhance the crystal casket's visual qualities greatly, don't you think?"

"Oh, absolutely. You seem to have the requisite eye for such detail, Nevis. Have you engaged in this line of business before?"

"In a sense," said Nevis, his eyes suddenly wary.

Rowland noted the reaction and pressed further. "May I ask for greater detail? The time, the place, the nature of the enterprise? Your work does so impress me."

"Denver," Nevis mumbled, and went to occupy himself with a fussy rearranging of the plush green drapes. Rowland felt that progress of a kind had been made, but not enough. He followed Nevis and asked, "Is that where you met Miss Starr?"

"Lovey Doll? No, that was Kansas City...."

Nevis realized his mistake and began turning crimson from the neck up. He had been nipping at a bottle in secret all morning, and the liquor had found its way to his tongue. Rowland pretended not to notice the furious blushing of unintended betrayal. Lovey Doll;

he was sure he had heard that name before. He had the scent now of what had been bothering him about the unlikely pairing of these two—Imogen Starr (or Lovey Doll, if the name was not merely a personal endearment Dunnigan had attached to the woman) and the blushing entrepreneur who had again turned his back to hide a guilty conscience. Rowland smelled blood. His target was not Nevis, who happened simply to be the unwitting bait; the trap he wished to set was for Imogen, whose names, he now suspected, might be legion.

Nevis went that night to Lovey Doll's house, and told her outright he had inadvertently let slip her real name. Rowland Price, he said, was sniffing around him for some reason unconnected with the Savage. "I know an insincere face when I see one, and that fellow has the closest thing to a mask I've ever seen. I don't like him, Lovey Doll. He says he knows you and Mr. Brannan, but he doesn't act as a true friend would."

Lovey Doll listened to his anguished gushing, and wished Nevis Dunnigan far away, in China perhaps, where he could do her no further harm. Nevis was too guileless for the constant practice of deception, and although this faculty made him a charming companion and true friend, as he would express it, such open-mouthed foolishness could not be allowed to continue. Nevis must leave town forthwith, before Rowland Price, whom Lovey Doll was aware had never liked or trusted her, dug deeper into the fallow fields of Nevis's past, where just one gorgeous flower bloomed—herself. If Price ever learned of her previous life, he would run to Leo with the news, and all her plans for ultimate wealth and the security only Leo could provide would come crashing down like painted scenery. Nevis would never knowingly disappoint her, but he already had.

"Nevis, you alarm yourself over small things that mean nothing, truly they don't. You should concern yourself less with my needs than your own. I have been thinking. Would it not make better sense for you to begin showing your Indian in Denver, rather than Glory Hole, or even better, Chicago or New York, or San Francisco if the mood takes you. Anywhere but here, Nevis."

"But ... this is where we found him, Smith and I. This is where he should be seen, as close to the site of his demise as possible. You didn't mention these places before."

"And that is because I have no head for such things, dear friend, but Mr. Brannan has, to be sure, and it was only yesterday he said to me what a pity it was that you were not taking your specimen to a more expansive venue for commercial gain than here."

"He did?"

"His exact words were, if I recall correctly, 'Those fellows have a unique offering, but they offer it to the wrong crowd, in the wrong place.' Yes, I believe that's what he said."

"But ... we have a solid deal with the owner of a vacant store. The Savage is already installed, the fliers already posted on walls hither and yon. Mr. Brannan's own newspaper has whipped public anticipation to a fever pitch ... This is all too late, I fear."

"Oh, how unfortunate." Lovey Doll smiled. "Well, then, you must make the best of it, I suppose."

She could see how crestfallen Nevis had become. It was amazing how very seriously men took her comments. Lovey Doll sometimes imagined that if a man came to her and called her a liar and a lazy know-nothing whore, she would follow him anywhere. But such an occurrence was unlikely; men were fools, one and all, and Nevis was surely one of the biggest.

"I do hope I have not upset you."

"No, no ... Perhaps you're right about finding a broader venue, but ... but here we are, and here we'll stay, at least for the time being."

Lovey Doll knew Nevis would do what he said, and that would not be good for her. He must be made to go away before any further scraps of personal history escaped his lips and found their way into the receptive ears of Rowland Price.

She found two likely men lounging outside a store, both with the look of poverty about them. "You fellows there," she said from the window of her carriage. "Do you wish to earn some easy money?"

"I reckon that's the best kind," said one, sauntering closer.

"Get in. Is your friend interested also?"

"He is if he knows what's good for him, ma'am."

She explained their work in detail. They were to begin after midnight, and make no noise. The stolen Indian would be carried by them through certain alleys to a place where a wagon hired with Lovey Doll's cash stood waiting. The men were to drive their cargo to a remote place, and there bury it. They would receive fifty dollars each for their thievery, and would be hunted to the ends of the earth and punished severely if they disclosed any part of the arrangement. The men were agreeable, and received ten dollars apiece to seal their commitment.

"How come you want this done, ma'am?" asked one.

"I believe it is indecent to present a dead body for public display," she said, "even if it is a redskin. There must be no encouragement for this type of circus in a Christian world."

"That's right, ma'am, that sure is right. We'll take care of it for you, don't you worry."

"Gentlemen, you are the ones who will have cause for worry if you don't do exactly what I have told you to do. I do hope I have made my intentions clear."

"Yes, ma'am. We get the rest of what's owed us tomorrow night, same place as the wagon'll be tonight."

"Be careful, do."

Nevis came rushing to her early next morning, as Lovey Doll anticipated he would.

"It's gone ... gone completely!"

"What is gone, Nevis?"

"My Sleeping Savage is gone! Someone has taken him from me! Why would anyone do such a thing? What could the purpose be? If they attempt to show him elsewhere, I'll have them arrested for fraud and theft and ... Oh, Lovey Doll, whatever shall I do now?"

"My goodness, I have no idea at all what steps you might take, Nevis. How shocking this is."

"They took him in the dead of night, broke open the back door and opened the case ... He'll spoil in the air, I know he will. He has to be kept in an airtight case. He'll be ruined!"

"You must ask yourself, Nevis, who would do such a thing."

"Why would *anyone* want to? It makes no sense. The Savage can't be exhibited elsewhere, not after Mr. Brannan made its existence known here. No one would dare!"

"Then perhaps it was taken out of spite. Who has become your enemy of late?"

"Enemy? I have no enemies."

"Were you not telling me just yesterday of a certain individual you have no trust in?"

"Price? But ... he's a friend of Mr. Brannan's."

"Not so much a friend, I gather, as a business associate."

"He has no reason, though...."

"None that you know of. Mr. Price is a dark horse, and not to be trusted."

Lovey Doll had not intended to implicate Rowland Price in the disappearance of the Savage, but it occurred to her, observing Nevis's agitation, that the threat to her plans for marriage to Leo was not so much from Nevis, who had let slip her true name to Price, as Price himself. Price was the one attempting to sabotage her dream. She suspected he was not so foolish as to attempt dissuading Leo openly; instead, he would find proof of Imogen Starr's past and confront Leo with that, making the point that the richest man in the west would risk his fine name by marrying a woman with an alias. If Nevis could only be persuaded to see Price as his enemy, her own precarious position might be considerably strengthened.

Lovey Doll went to a drawer and took from it a small pistol. She offered it to Nevis with the advice, "Be prepared for anything, my good friend. When someone like that begins his work against you, it may end with outright threats against your person. He has the eyes of a man-killer. Take it."

Nevis accepted the pistol with a hesitant hand. Lovey Doll's description of Price did not jibe with his own impression of the man—ingratiating yet distant; a sly fox, not a bloodthirsty wolf. He put the gun inside his jacket anyway, so as not to offend Lovey Doll, who had his best interests in mind.

Lovey Doll lowered her eyes and said, "Mr. Price has offended me also, Nevis."

"He has? In what way?"

"He has ... made suggestions to me which are impolite, to say the least."

"Mr. Brannan's own friend? But you must tell him, Lovey Doll, so he knows what kind of snake the fellow is."

In love with her though he was, Nevis could accept the cold fact of Lovey Doll's involvement with a rich and powerful man, but the outrageous conduct of Price was another matter entirely. How dare he soil the delicate ear of Lovey Doll with such impropriety, the swine! If Price had been there in the room, Nevis didn't doubt he would have drawn the pistol and forced an apology from him, right there in front of the woman Price had offended. Lovey Doll would reward him for defending her with a hug at the very least, and the thought of that hug sent Nevis's pulse, already galloping with anger, into a frenzy.

"Nevis, you have gone so pale. Is something wrong?"

"No, I ... I must sit down."

He collapsed onto an ottoman and placed a hand across his chest, breath whistling between his teeth. Lovey Doll thought for a moment or two that he might die then and there, ridding her of her problem's lesser half, but the color began returning to Nevis's face as she watched, and Lovey Doll was obliged to arrange a look of relief across her features.

"A drink, if you please ...," gasped Nevis.

"A drink?"

"Any kind will do."

She fetched him a generous brandy. Nevis disposed of it in two swallows, then raised a beseeching eyebrow along with the empty glass. She poured him another, and he was more inclined this time to drink like a civilized man. His nose began to redden visibly, as if suffused with fresh life. Lovey Doll thought him quite pathetic. If only he would go away, looking for his disgusting Indian, and become lost. She returned the grateful smile he gave her, and wondered just how far she might be able to goad him toward putting a bullet or two into Rowland Price.

Nightsoil Smith was greatly upset. With their Sleeping Savage gone, and the dissolution of their ice and shitcan monopolies about to be replaced by modern methods of production and disposal, he and Dunnigan would be out of business in less than a year, by Smith's calculation.

"She says it was this Price feller?"

"Imogen has no idea who perpetrated the theft."

"But you said she said it was him, most likely, and he's been sniffing around the Indian, you said. What'd he do that for if he never intended to steal it?"

"I don't know," admitted Nevis, "but it hardly constitutes proof."

"He did it, I bet," said Winnie.

All three had resorted strongly to the bottle following news of their disaster. The mood in Smith's shack was somber, all the optimism of recent weeks gone. Nevis felt responsible somehow. At least they still had the glass case, unharmed and complete, although what use it could serve now was debatable. Winnie was the least perturbed; she had thought the scheme foolish to begin with, and the loss of the Indian seemed no more than what was called for to bring her men to their senses. They should have been thinking about real work to replace the jobs that soon would be lost, not setting themselves up as amateur Barnums with their pickled redskin. She knew better than to say so; they would see the error of their ways soon enough, and do what they should already have done.

"Where would he take it, do you think?" asked Smith.

"We don't know that he did take it," Nevis reminded him.

"But who else would?"

"I haven't the least notion, but that doesn't necessarily mean Price is implicated."

"You don't want to believe it because he works for the feller that's keeping your lady friend."

"She is not my lady friend! What a ridiculous thing to say. You're drunk, Smith."

"I am not. You're always visiting with her. Who is she really? Did you know her before?"

"Never in my life! Lovey Doll and I were complete strangers before I approached her regarding the Savage ... Oh ... I meant Miss Starr, that is ..."

Smith and Winnie looked at each other, then at Nevis, whose face was becoming mottled by confusion.

"Lovey Doll?" Winnie leered. "Did you say Lovey Doll?"

"He did," said Smith, "I heard him. Now I want to hear some more, and I don't want no lies about never knowing the fine lady before, all right?"

Nevis squirmed with discomfort. He had done it again, for the second time in as many days. Price might have been polite enough to overlook the name, even if his ears had pricked, but Smith and Winnie were a different proposition.

"I ... may have misled you, but for perfectly acceptable reasons," he said, a sickly smile on his face.

Lovey Doll made her suggestion again, this time with some asperity. Leo had of late been distracted by problems he would not discuss with her, and had been running a mild fever that seemed to have weakened his constitution somewhat. The time to be firm had arrived, and Lovey Doll would not be put off any longer.

"Are you attempting to humiliate me, Leo?"

"Whatever do you mean? I would never do such a thing."

She sat close to him and assumed a sorrowful expression.

"Humiliation is my lot, nonetheless."

"I find myself unable to understand you, Imogen. Please speak plainly. I feel dreadful tonight."

"If you cannot understand, Leo, it's because you don't wish to. You know very well the topic to which I refer. The topic, Leo my love, is holy matrimony, and there is none closer to a woman's heart, yet you insist on ignoring my needs, while fulfilling your own. How very like a man that is. I'm dismayed and disappointed to find that you are, perhaps, without integrity in this matter. There! I have said it aloud! Whip me if you will for speaking my mind!"

"I ... whip you? Nonsense!" blustered Leo, for whom the idea was suddenly very appealing. Ashamed of himself, he said, "I could never hurt you, my dear, not for the world, but you must cease these accusations, indeed you must! What have I done to be so deserving of your scorn?"

Lovey Doll became contrite, and suggested meekly that Leo might consider making her happier than any woman on earth by the simple expedient of proposing marriage to her, especially since she was carrying their child, their son.

Leo had a ready answer. "I am not yet legally separated from my wife," he stated. His attorney was arranging matters, but not very quickly; Leo was reasonably confident that Rowland's assassin-for-hire would locate Zoe faster than any legal document of separation.

"But why, Leo?"

"These things take time, my dearest one. The mills of jurisprudence grind exceeding slow, you see."

"But when you have your annulment, what will happen then?"

"Then? I suppose ... I intend to make you my wife. Yes, that will certainly be my intention. We'll be married when I am free of ... her. There now, does that make you happy, Imogen? You have my promise, my word on it, and I see no reason why the question should be raised again until that time, by God, do you hear?"

"Yes, Leo. Leo?"

"Well?"

"You have made me the luckiest woman in creation."

"Just so."

"Leo?"

"Yes? Yes?"

"Might I have some token of your intent?"

"A ring, you mean? That might not be seemly, under the circumstances. Would you like a necklace or tiara?"

"You have been so generous already, my darling, but Leo, there is something that has been thrust into my thoughts lately. I hesitate to make this suggestion, because I'm not yet your wife, but the house, Leo, it concerns the house."

"This house?"

"Your house. Elk House, Leo."

"What of it? Naturally you'll take up residence there, when things have been formalized. A wedding ceremony with all the trimmings—how does that sound to you?"

"Wonderful, my love, but the purchase I had in mind is of a kind that will require considerable time for preparation in advance of that wonderful day. I should so like to see it there when I arrive at Elk House as your bride, Leo."

"Find what?"

"A statue, dearest, for the front yard."

"Statue? What kind of statue? A fountain, you mean?"

"A stag."

"A stag ...," said Leo, his concentration failing. His fever was becoming worse, much worse. It was the various worries he currently faced that were causing his gradual debilitation, he was sure. It had been a mistake to visit Imogen that night, feeling as he did. He had already proposed marriage, in a roundabout kind of way, and he had intended no such drastic step when he raised the knocker on her door. His mind was becoming unhinged, incapable of fully understanding the words that reached it. Now Imogen was talking of a statue, but all he could think of was whipping her naked buttocks to a fine pinkness.

"I have a model here. Wait one moment and I'll fetch it."

"Model ..." said Leo softly.

Lovey Doll was gone from the room for less than a minute, returning with a statuette in her hands. She set it down before Leo, and he dragged his attention from the beguiling images quivering in his brain to take note of what it was. The thing stood ten inches or so high, and was made of heavy brass, a proud stag with its head lifted, the tremendous rack of antlers tipped back almost to its spine. It was a fine piece, and Leo stared at it for some time.

"Just like that," said Lovey Doll, "but large as life."

"Ah, yes ... certainly."

"You'll get it for me?" Lovey Doll beamed.

"To be sure."

"Oh, Leo, how generous you are! Did I tell you the other thing?"

"Other thing?"

"Its metallic structure, I suppose one would call it."

"No, you didn't tell me."

"It should be of gold, solid gold, Leo, to be the symbol of your mining business. Your first mine was named after a deer, was it not, and from that mine has come more gold than from any other in the entire nation. A gold deer, Leo. It would be so perfect for Elk House."

"Deer are not elk, and elk are not deer."

He wanted very much to lift her skirts and bend her over like a naughty child, and lay on with a whip until she begged him to stop, at which point he would be ready to mount her.

"A gold elk, then," she said, "as big as a real one, a big bull elk, Leo, of solid gold taken from your own mine. Wouldn't that be the most thrilling statue in the world?"

"Yes indeed, and you shall have it, my dear, but you must first allow me to be your big bull elk."

"I beg your pardon?"

He lunged at her and began reaching beneath her skirts to pull down her pantaloons. Lovey Doll pushed against his shoulders. "Leo, what are you doing ...? Leo, kindly allow me to attend to it.... Leo!"

There being no whip available, he used a length of silken drapery cord.

He was a home-loving man by inclination, but sometimes Smith wanted to mingle with his fellows in a saloon. On those occasions, generally no more than two or three times a year, he would visit a bathhouse for a slow soak and send his clothes across the street to the Chinese laundry for a quick cleaning. It was understood that he would pay double for these services, since the presence of himself or his clothing tended to be bad for business.

On this night, made presentable for inclusion among the public, he entered the bar of his choice and began tossing drinks down his throat with a machinelike regularity. He did not want to drink at home because Nevis and Winnie both were irritating him, Nevis by way of his long face and fretful manner, and Winnie on account of her told-you-so smirk. To hell with them both. He wanted rough company, and the Big Bear Saloon was the place to find it. While he drank, Smith wondered if he would be fortunate enough to be included in a fight. He would never pick a fight solely to give himself satisfaction, since that would not have been an honorable thing to do, but he knew that if he lingered long enough among the drinkers of the Big Bear a fight would be thrust upon him, and Smith dearly wanted to push his fist into the face of anyone who deserved it. He was not a violent man as a rule, but recent events had soured his temper considerably.

"Smith."

He turned. Two men unknown to him had slid along the bar. The one who had addressed him wore a smile Smith found offensive.

"What of it," he said.

"Heard about you and the other feller's Injun getting stole. Too bad about that."

Smith turned away. He didn't want to discuss the Sleeping Savage with anyone.

"Worth money, they say," said the second man.

"Most likely still worth it, if you could find the dang thing again, I figure," added the first.

"Find it?" Smith asked. "Find it where?"

"Wherever it's at, friend."

"And would you be knowing that place, *friend?*"

"I might."

"We both might," said the second man. "For the right price, like they say."

"I'd give money, sure," said Smith, "but only to fellers that made me believe they're not just looking to take my dollars for nothing, see."

"Oh, that ain't us."

"We know, we do."

"Know what?" insisted Smith.

"Where it's at."

"And where might that be?"

"Can't be telling without a sight of some green."

"Can't expect us to give away what's for sale, Smith."

"Not interested," Smith told them, creating consternation on the faces of both men.

"But ... don't you want him back?"

"You fellers don't know beans about that old Indian, now do you. Get away from me. I don't like fools."

The two men retired to a corner and spoke between themselves, then returned.

"Smith, we figure if we tell you who told us to take it, you'll believe us about knowing where it's at."

"That way you wouldn't have to be trusting us so much," said the second man.

"Who was it?" Smith asked.

"Well, it was a woman, a lady."

"She had herself a carriage. Took us inside of it to talk it over about robbing you and your partner."

Sensing that Smith had begun to believe them, and sensing also that he was becoming angry, the first man said, "It was cash money she give us, and we both of us been looking for work lately and not finding any, see, so it was hard to say no."

"We couldn't say no," agreed his friend, "but now we feel badly about what we done, we do."

"So we're wanting to make it up to you and your partner about the Injun."

"What woman?"

"A real fine looker, she was, with feathers in her hat and fluffy stuff all around her."

"I never seen a better-lookin' piece."

"She's big man Brannan's whore, they say."

"Is that right," Smith said. He laid some money on the bar, but kept his meaty fingertips on top. "Where's the Indian?"

"A couple miles outside of town. We know where exactly."

"We put him there, we did."

Smith set the money free, and it disappeared.

"The same again when I see the Indian in one piece."

"Sounds like a square deal to me. You ain't mad about the taking, are you? You're gonna get him back."

"She give us plenty. It was temptation."

"We spent it already," admitted the first man.

"Drunk it, mainly," confessed the second.

"Gentlemen," said Smith, "we're going to go fetch that Indian right now, and when we get him we'll bring him back to town where he belongs, and then you'll tell my partner what you told me, and after that you can go get yourselves a fresh bottle of the best, on me."

"Square deal, all right. I reckon you're a gentleman yourself."

"Amen."

The Sleeping Savage, when delivered by wagon to Smith's yard after midnight, was unrecognizable and unusable. Nevis and Winnie stared at the pitiful remnants while Smith explained, and the two strangers confirmed the story. Smith paid them and they left. Nevis felt close to weeping. Wolves had torn apart the ancient but well-preserved flesh of the Savage, devouring most of it and separating the skeleton into disparate sections that could never be reassembled, given the missing leg and arm.

Even worse was the revelation of Lovey Doll's perfidy. Nevis wanted to disbelieve, but could not; the halting and shamefaced sincerity of the body snatchers was too credible for that. Lovey Doll, his special friend, the very one who had persuaded Leo Brannan to include an article on the Savage in his newspaper. Why had she done it? Smith and Winnie were watching him, aware of some shocking betrayal behind his grief, yet too polite to inquire after its origins.

Smith poked at the remains. "It's rotten now. Even if he was all there we couldn't use him."

Nevis turned away and went inside. Winnie said to Smith, "He's hurt bad about this. What's the woman to him?"

Smith shrugged. "Best not to ask, I say. I'm taking this mess out to the shit dump."

When he had driven away, Winnie went inside, fully expecting to see Nevis with a bottle and glass before him at the table. She found him instead with a look of great concentration ridging his brow, and a revolver she had never seen before in his hand.

"Where'd that come from?"

"Her."

"Brannan's whore?"

Nevis said nothing. Winnie fetched a bottle and glasses and poured two shots of whiskey. Nevis ignored his.

Winnie said, "That man, he had a good woman for a wife, and he trampled on her. He never should've done that to Zoe. What other woman would have given him a chance that way, gone off and let him make up his mind if he wants her or not. How many wives would do that, do you think?"

"Most of them, if their husband has the kind of money he has."

"That wasn't it with her! She gave him the chance to come to his senses because that's the kind of woman she is!"

"You talk as if you know her."

"I ... just know how she feels. This other one, this Imogen Starr, what a shitheel. She's the one wants Brannan's money. Zoe Dugan's a woman in a million. She's better off without him now. He's welcome to the slut he's got. Don't look at me that way. That's what she is. So I've been a whore myself, but I've never been like her, not for anything. There's whores, and then there's *real* whores, and that's her kind, and I don't care if you think her asshole smells like petunias. What's she to you anyway? Do you love her or something stupid like that? She's a shitheel, and now you know it. You believed those two, didn't you, that it was her as had them take your precious Indian? Well, did you believe them? Don't go all sulky and childish—you're a grown man."

Nevis slowly nodded his head. Winnie poured herself another drink.

"Don't waste a bullet on the likes of her. She's not worth the trouble. Her and Brannan, they'll make each other miserable. Two bad people together, that's my recipe for hell on earth. You know how many good people I ever met in my life? Three, that's how many. You and Smith and Zoe Dugan. Oh, and a boy back in Galveston, he was a good boy, so that's four. That's not many, Nevis. Did you think the shitheel was one of the good people in your life?"

Nevis nodded again, his mouth turning down.

"It's better to know the truth," said Winnie, "even if it's hard." She came to him and put an arm around his narrow shoulders. "Don't you be sad over someone like her."

"How could she have done it? *Why ...?*"

"Shitheels are like that. Don't ask me to explain it."

"She encouraged me...."

"Lovey Doll, that's her real name?"

"Yes. I suppose it is. It's the name she used to use anyway. I painted her picture years ago. Everyone used it, but I never saw a cent.... I was so disappointed, Winnie. I think ... I think that's what made me turn to drink, I really do. I turned into who I am because of her...."

"Not her; the painting that no one paid you for."

"Reproductions of it," corrected Nevis. "But all this time she was ... special. I thought about her so often ... and now, after I found her again, she did this to me. I did her no harm, Winnie, none at all."

"She'll get hers in hell, if there's such a place, and if there isn't, she'll make one of her own when her looks go, you rest easy about that."

Nevis swallowed his whiskey, and two whiskeys after that Winnie cajoled him into bed, where they spent a sorrowfully pleasant hour until Smith's return.

CHAPTER

46

The order had been placed, Imogen's brass elk sent along with it to a foundry in Pittsburgh, with instructions to reproduce the beast in all its magnificence to actual scale. Gold for the casting process would be forwarded to the foundry at the last moment for pouring, and the entire project was to be shrouded in the utmost secrecy for obvious reasons. When the golden elk was ready for public display and transportation to Colorado by rail, then would be the time to make the world aware of its existence, not before.

The train carrying the finished statue would be guarded by a contingent of handpicked Pinkerton agents, all heavily armed; Leo even considered requesting a unit from the army for additional protection, but Rowland Price convinced him this was not a good idea. "You're a man of the people, Leo, and not beholden to Washington for any favors. You can supply the necessary gunmen for your elk out of your own pocket. It's so much more impressive that way."

Leo agreed, and the creation of the elk had begun, all conflicting projects at the Pittsburgh foundry having been set aside for this most prestigious of commissions.

While a mold was assembled far away in the east, Leo enjoyed Imogen in any way he pleased. The elk had been a wonderful idea, a stroke of self-indulgent genius, but he would make her pay for her extravagance. He had promised her, after a severe beating that left her plump buttocks quite bruised, that when the golden elk caught the first rays of sunshine outside his home, he would make Elk House her home also, by way of marriage in the front garden, with her shining brainchild in splendid attendance. Leo reasoned that by then, his first wife would have passed on in good time to allow the taking of a second. Zoe was in fact his ex-wife now, the necessary time having elapsed since Leo's attorney filed the papers of annulment, but he saw no reason to mention this to Imogen.

Leo was not as happy as he should have been. A letter had arrived, marked for his personal attention, and in it he was informed that his unofficial fiancée was in fact a whore by the name of Lovey Doll Pines, whose portrait in a state of brazen nudity could be seen in half the saloons in the country, if he cared to look. Leo did not care to look. He summoned Rowland Price instead, and showed him the letter.

"Can there be anything of substance to this allegation?"

Rowland paused a moment, to phrase his response in the correct manner. "As a matter of fact, Leo, the name has already been mentioned to me, by accident, as it were."

"Are you saying Imogen is who this ... filthy document says she is?"

"As a matter of fact, Leo ... yes."

Rowland had already begun an investigation into the identity of a woman called Lovey Doll a week earlier, when Nevis Dunnigan let slip the very name Leo was now confronted with, and Rowland's cohorts among the Praetorians had promptly sent back by express mail the information he sought. Not only was Lovey Doll Pines the ex-mistress of a former Praetorian—one Walter Morrow, whose task of recruiting Leo Brannan had fallen to Rowland after that gentleman's unfortunate murder—but she was known to have been the mistress of several wealthy figures in California before then. In short, she was soiled goods of the most self-serving type. Rowland had been pondering the approach he should take with regard to his findings, and now, as if orchestrated by the gods of fate, had come independent accusations of a similar nature.

"Explain yourself," demanded Leo, and Rowland did, by producing the letter he had received from Denver. He poured a stiff drink for Leo while it was being read, and handed the glass over as the sheet fluttered to the floor.

"Oh, Rowland ...," Leo said. "What have I done?"

"What many a man has done before you, my friend."

"This is ... monstrous."

"That may be something of an exaggeration, but an embarrassment ... yes, I believe it could be so termed."

"What am I to do with such a creature? She has her hooks deep into me, Rowland.... "

"Pay her off. She'll leave without a murmur once she knows you've learned the truth about her."

Leo was assembling in his mind a larger picture than that suggested by Price. He knew now that he had sent away a good woman to be replaced by a whore, a professional temptress for whom he must have presented the easiest of targets. The way she had introduced herself to him aboard his private car; the way she had succumbed to his advances with pretty confusion and maidenly blushes; the way she had manipulated him into providing her with more than Zoe had ever asked for; the way in which she had suggested to him that the crowning glory of the home that was to be theirs would be a life-sized elk of solid gold ... The impudence and cunning of this Lovey Doll Pines were beyond comprehension, beyond the natural avariciousness of the average whore, were in an unnameable class all their own. He had been a perfect fool, the most willing of dupes, a plaything in her practiced hands.

And he had dispatched an anonymous assassin to find Zoe and kill her, because he had preferred the charms of the liar. He had once accused Zoe of being just that, but her lies of omission were as nothing in comparison to the monstrous deception wrought by this Lovey Doll Pines. A whore for a wife. The truth would have emerged sooner or later, possibly while he was seeking political office; it would have been a disaster of tremendous proportions.

"Pay her? Rowland, she has already cost me too much ... too much, you see."

"Then a little more won't break you, Leo. You gave your wife one million dollars."

"But she was a virtuous woman, despite her shortcomings. This one ... How dare she attempt such a tactic against me! I won't pay her a single cent!"

"That is your choice to make."

"How dare she!"

"A devious minx of the worst kind."

"She won't get away with it, Rowland."

"Indeed she will not."

"And she won't tell anyone how close she came to succeeding either; you'll see to that, won't you?"

"I don't quite follow your line of thought, Leo."

"The fellow you sent to Durango, the one with the dagger—have him take care of Miss Pines at the earliest opportunity."

"Are you sure such a move would be wise? Send her away, and that will be that."

"It will not! She has attempted to make a fool of me ... she *has* made a fool of me, and I can't forgive her! Set him onto her, I say, and be damned to all liars!"

"Leo, that will be difficult. Our man has left his usual haunts to pursue your wife. He could be almost anywhere. I have no way of reaching him until his current work is completed."

"But I don't want it completed! I want Zoe left alone, do you hear!"

"It's too late for new instructions now. I have no means of conveying them, Leo. Try to understand.... "

Leo slumped in his chair, face flushed, a light sweat gleaming on his brow. Rowland had never seen him so distraught, so clearly without control over himself. It was an unnerving sight. Leo Brannan had never seemed less like presidential material, and Rowland experienced the first faint shudderings of some great collapse in the making, the popping of nails from timbers strained beyond their natural strength. If there was no change in Leo soon, the edifice he was an essential part of might very well come crashing down. Rowland would do what he could to prevent that, since Leo's fall would bring about his own, so closely were they bound.

"Leave it to me," he said. "The Garfinkles once were a problem, and then they were not. There are surely answers to all this."

"Fix it, Rowland, and quickly."

Availing herself of the funds Leo had set aside for her was a daunting prospect. Since Leo had already attempted to have her killed, Zoe was sure the million dollars in Denver was set up as bait, to lure her into revealing her location. She had withdrawn a small amount through a bank, in Durango, and that had been the thing that drew the killer to that town, she was sure. If she withdrew all or part of the remaining funds by way of some other bank, in anoth-

er part of the state or the country, Leo would again send his assassin along the path taken by those funds, and this time strike without warning, probably by sniper fire undertaken at such a distance
as to render Omie's inner alarms useless. Zoe could not risk that,
and yet she needed every dollar of the million, to take herself and
Omie beyond Leo's reach.

They were living in a cabin near Telluride, having abandoned
most of their belongings for the sake of greater mobility, faster
flight. Zoe did not want to leave the cabin's comforting isolation for
anything but the best of reasons. She knew they could not stay
there forever; her physical appearance, and that of Omie, were bea-
cons for local gossip. The woman who had rented the cabin to them
was unable to keep her eyes from Zoe's stump and Omie's face;
eventually the population of San Miguel County would know they
were there, and word would be passed along Leo's clandestine
grapevine to the killer in a dress.

She discussed her quandary with Omie, there being no one else to
talk over such matters with.

"Go directly to Denver, Mama, and have them give the money to
you there. He won't expect you to do that."

Zoe thought it over. The idea had merit.

"But what if the bank manager there has been given instructions
to delay giving us the money, so that the awful man with the knife
can be set on our trail while we wait."

Omie had an answer for that too.

Mr. Blye was informed by the head teller that a woman calling herself Mrs. Poe wished to discuss with him in private the opening of a
very large account. Mr. Blye, the director of Denver National Bank
and Trust, had the woman ushered into his office immediately. Mrs.
Poe was accompanied by a small girl wearing a heavily veiled hat
that concealed her face completely. Under one arm Mrs. Poe carried
a large satchel, presumably stuffed with cash to invest at Denver
National; her other arm was in a sling, presumably sprained or
broken.

"Please sit down, ma'am, and you too, young lady."

Zoe and Omie took chairs facing Blye's highly polished desk, and
he sat opposite them. "May I order you coffee, ma'am, and a soda
for you, miss?"

"We are not thirsty," Zoe told him. "You may bring to me my
money instead."

"Your money, Mrs. Poe? I understood it was you who had brought money to me, ha ha!"

"My name is not Poe, Mr. Blye, and I should like to have the rest of my one million dollars, without delay, and without discussion between yourself and any other person."

"Mrs. Brannan ...?"

"Please begin the counting now, Mr. Blye."

"Mrs. Brannan, such an enormous amount, and in cash ..."

"Bills of large denomination only, thank you, since I have only one hand to carry it with."

"This unnecessary disguise, Mrs. Brannan ... I don't understand."

Omie was removing her hat. Mr. Blye stared at the half-blue face revealed as the veil was set aside. He had heard about Brannan's daughter and her birthmark, but there was more to the child's face that disturbed him than the simple fact of her blemish. Under her intense stare he felt sweat beginning to trickle from his armpits, and the woman's voice came to him as if she spoke from a great distance, through a thickly swirling mist. When she produced from inside her sling a heavy-caliber Smith & Wesson he could not even be afraid of it, or her, so great was the power of the girl's eyes; everything beyond the eyes was blurred, every sound faintly echoing. Mr. Blye experienced sudden pain in the forehead and stomach, and hoped he would not be sick.

"Proceed as directed, Mr. Blye. I say again, you will not discuss the money with your staff beyond telling them to assemble the cash. Is that clear?"

"Yes ..."

Mr. Blye attempted to strike the bell on his desk to summon his secretary, but was unable to move his arms. Amazingly, the bell rang anyway, without human assistance. Mr. Blye began to wonder if what he was undergoing was some strange and discomforting dream; had he eaten too much lobster the night before?

"Yes, sir?"

The secretary had entered, and Mrs. Brannan's pistol was shoved inside her sling.

"Begin counting out the balance of the special Brannan account," droned Mr. Blye. "Large bills only."

"The entire balance, sir?"

"Put two tellers onto it right away."

"Yes, sir."

"And ... "

"Sir?"

"Soda," gasped Mr. Blye.

"Soda; yes, sir. For three?"

"One ..."

"Very good, sir."

The secretary departed. Mr. Blye felt quite faint. He had not wanted a soda, but the girl did, and he did not know how he knew, any more than he could fathom the unseen hand that rang the bell. It was almost certainly a dream. Zoe Brannan, or Dugan, or whatever she was calling herself since Leo Brannan threw her out, would certainly not have had the gall to walk into Denver National Bank and Trust coolly to withdraw the money he had been instructed to hold against the revelation of her whereabouts. This could not be happening. *It is too happening!* came a shrill voice inside his head, and Mr. Blye grew frightened; what if it was not a dream, but madness of some kind.

His secretary knocked and entered, bearing a soda bottle on a tray. "I've organized everything, sir," he said, setting the bottle down before Mr. Blye.

"Oh, good," said Mr. Blye. It was not his usual mode of address at all, and the secretary studied him briefly. Blye was red in the face, his eyes unfocused.

"Are you unwell, sir?"

"Feeling fine, thank you," Mr. Blye assured him. The secretary went out again, and as the door was closed behind him, the soda bottle slid across Mr. Blye's desk and was snatched up by Omie, who began taking greedy swallows from it. Interestingly, Mr. Blye could taste it also—sarsaparilla, a flavor he detested.

As he waited for the dream or fit of madness to pass, Mr. Blye reminded himself of the obligation he would have been betraying if the events in his office were real. Leo Brannan would be very angry to learn of the unanticipated withdrawal. Mr. Blye was a member of Big Circle, a fact that Leo Brannan knew; he was also a Praetorian, which Leo also knew. What Leo did not know was that Mr. Blye was a spy for Mr. Jones of The Six. If the dream was reality, Mr. Jones would have to be told, along with Leo Brannan, but since it could not possibly be real, Mr. Blye did not worry much about the consequences. He would not even tell his wife. The taste of sarsaparilla was clogging his throat with its cloying sweetness. He wished the girl would hurry up and finish drinking the damned thing. He wished the money would arrive so his unusual customers could leave; perhaps then the dream could end, and he could treat himself to a shot of the fine bourbon he kept in the cabinet by the window. Oddly, the cabinet door swung open as he thought of it, and the decanter rattled on its silver tray; then the door swung shut again, then open, then shut, then open ...

"Omie, stop that," said Mrs. Brannan.

Mr. Blye closed his eyes. No more lobster—ever. Behind his eyelids there formed an interesting series of pictures, tableaux that moved, but slowly, much slower than in life: a woman with a long knife (yet somehow this was a man, how interesting, thought Mr. Blye); a mountain view as seen from the window of a train; a tall man in a long coat, his face pierced by holes; a sailing ship of the old-fashioned kind; a burial at sea; robbers taking valuables from train passengers; a huge stone house overlooking a valley blackened by mining and smelting; the face of Leo Brannan, a barely recognizable caricature of the man, with devilish horns sprouting from his skull; himself, sitting straight as a poker behind his desk, eyes closed, mustaches quivering ...

The door opened at the same instant as his eyes. The money was carried in, tightly bundled, tenderly cradled in the hands of his secretary, and set down on the desk.

"Sir, the head teller is anxious. He's unsure we can conduct business in the usual manner with so large and sudden a depletion of bills."

"Plenty more where that came from!" Mr. Blye assured him breezily, and the secretary departed once more.

Zoe scooped the money into her bag and stood up.

"Is there a private entrance?" she asked.

Before Mr. Blye could answer, the mother was following her daughter toward a concealed door in the oak paneling through which Mr. Blye took the pretty thing who visited him on Wednesday afternoons while the office door remained locked. The door led to a windowless private chamber, and from there to the street. The girl turned once before they passed through it, and the liquor cabinet danced on its legs like a thing come alive, spilling out the bourbon decanter. Mr. Blye watched its precious contents empty onto his Persian carpet with a melancholy glugging sound. There was nothing he could do about it.

* * *

"The thing is," said Smith, pouring himself another drink, "if your first Injun goes to the dogs, you get yourself another one."

The opening date for public revelation of the Sleeping Savage was already a week overdue. Since they had paid rent on the store until the end of the month, Smith and Nevis simply placed a card in the window that read: DISPLAY POSTPONED DUE TO UNFORESEE CIRCUM-STANCES.

"Another one? I don't understand."

"What I mean is, we dig up someone out of the ground and dress him up in Injun rig and put him under the glass and who's to know the difference?"

"Us," said Nevis, with some alarm. "We would. That's an outrageous proposal, Smith."

"Sounds practical," offered Winnie. "How much money did you sink into this already?"

"Too damn much. This way we can get it back."

"It's dishonest," protested Nevis. "Are you both pretending it isn't?"

"I'm all for pretending," Smith said, "especially pretending the new feller we dig up is the Injun. It could work if we did it right, but we need to work fast."

"Those fellers that stole him," Winnie said, "won't they open their mouths when they see a new one laid out?"

"Not if they don't want to get arrested for thieving the first one."

"Stop! This is absurd!"

"No it ain't."

"And just where do you expect to find a newly deceased corpse? Will you have us become grave robbers? I refuse!"

Smith was used by now to such outbursts from Nevis. The shock of having been betrayed by a woman had come down hard on him, and a certain lack of reasonableness was to be expected.

"Doc Pfenning's place," explained Smith.

"Pfenning? He's no doctor."

"Used to be, but anyway, you don't need to cure folks to run a funeral business. Good doctors are bad for Doc Pfenning's business now, I figure!"

"Sure," said Winnie. "He could tell you where a nice fresh one's been buried recent."

She was becoming excited over the scheme for a bogus Indian. The original investment in a genuinely ancient body had never struck her as worthwhile, but deliberate deception of the public contained just enough risk to make her blood run a little faster. Writing the letter of denunciation to Leo Brannan had excited her, but was not enough; she wished to see Lovey Doll's attempted sabotage turned upside down.

"I don't know." Nevis sighed. "I really don't."

"What's there to lose if we don't? We already lost everything, pretty near."

"Nonsense. The ice and sewage businesses will support us for some time yet, until Brannan kills them off."

"Dunnigan, sometimes you strike me as fainthearted."

"I certainly am not!"

"Then shake on it and we'll take ourselves down to see Doc Pfenning."

Nevis hesitated. "Go on," urged Winnie.

Pfenning's Mortuary and Funeral Parlor was located two blocks west of Brannan Boulevard, in an area not known for its excellence in architecture or the sophistication of its inhabitants. Pfenning buried miners, for the most part, and terminal drunks and sickly children. Himself an alcoholic, Pfenning was able to show a steady hand at all times to his clients, and paint the faces of their dead with expert skill, "so as to render the deceased as they were in life, joyously present among us," as his sign declared. There hung about him in equal measure the sharp reekings of whiskey and formaldehyde, and many who saw the permanent despoliation of his waistcoat were unable to determine the precise nature of the greasy film that clung there; was it merely the spilled meals of yesterday, or was it the grim exudations of the departed?

Long since removed from the ranks of legitimate M.D.s for his role in the deaths of Philadelphia women sent to him for abortions, Pfenning tended to view all representatives of higher authority as a bunch of upstarts in cahoots, a cabal of manipulators who had ruined him out of personal hatred for his reckless nature and nonconformist ways. He was, therefore, more than interested to be offered inclusion in the scheme Smith and Nevis brought to him. Pfenning saw the reborn Savage as an apt symbol for all forms of commercial enterprise, including his own; doctors pretended to know what they were doing, but very often knew nothing; he himself pretended to embalm the bodies brought to him so they might lie beneath the ground in a state of permanent incorruptibility, but he pumped only as much formaldehyde into them as would keep them fresh until church services were over and the deceased safely buried beyond the reach of their loved ones' noses.

"A capital idea, gentlemen, deliciously inventive, and a rare challenge to boot. There is, though, an insoluble problem inherent in the plan."

"What problem?"

"The nature of mortal flesh is your enemy. The Indian as you've described him to me seems indeed to have been a frozen remnant of the long ago, and his appearance will be impossible to duplicate in a body of more recent vintage."

"So we can't just use a dead man dressed Injun style."

"I regret, you cannot."

"Damn! We were kind of counting on you, Doc."

"And I appreciate your trust. Fortunately all is not lost with regard to this proposed venture. There is one way that presents itself, but the chances for success are slim indeed, I fear."

"Trot it out."

Pfenning took from a shelf along the wall a large can, and handed it to Smith, who deciphered its label.

"'Carlson's Pat ... Patented Mort ... Morterary ...'"

"'Mortuary Putty,'" Nevis said, reading over his shoulder.

"What is it?" Smith asked, wishing Nevis had allowed him to finish unaided.

"In essence, a means of filling in the holes created by accident and disease. Marvelous stuff! I had a fellow the other week, complete syphilitic, no nose at all to speak of, like something from a leper colony, you know, and I gave him a nose the Duke of Wellington would have been proud to own."

"It's modeling clay?" asked Nevis.

"Of a highly specialized kind. With this, a sculptor of great talent might fashion a figure in replication of your Indian, were he familiar with its characteristics, alas now gone."

"A sculptor," said Smith. "That's a feller as makes statues?"

"The same."

"And one of them fellers, he'd be called an artist, I guess."

"Assuredly."

Smith was eyeing Nevis. "Dunnigan, you listening to this?"

"I won't," said Nevis. "I won't profane the gift that was once held precious by me."

"Why the hell not?"

"Are you of artistic inclination, Mr. Dunnigan?" asked Pfenning.

"You bet he is," assured Smith. "Why, he done a picture of a lady friend you could see right off was her. Oh, he's artistical, all right, you bet—aren't you, Nevis?"

"I refuse. This will not happen."

"It'd work if you done the Injun in this morterary clay. He'll be under glass, all sealed off. Won't be any way someone can touch him and see it's a cheat."

"I will not cooperate."

"Winnie, she'd be all for something like this."

"Smith, you can't possibly ask this of me. The past is gone beyond retrieval, and with it my artistic aspirations. I will not revive so personal a side of myself for fraudulent purposes. I absolutely will not."

"Aaaww, now that's no way to be thinking. Doc here, he'll supply the stuff, and you can just shape it into the Injun all over again. You studied him enough when we had him to do the job blindfold. You don't have to put your name on it or nothing, just make the Injun over again so we can put him in the case where he belongs, so folks can see him."

"No."

"Hey now, don't you think it'd make a certain party as did you wrong go all white around the lips to see us open up the Sleeping Savage like she never intended should happen? Know who I mean? Don't that make it worthwhile? She'd be the loser, see, and you'd be the one had the last laugh, by God, don't you think?"

Smith and Pfenning waited for Nevis to make up his mind.

Leo surprised himself by being unable to stay away from Lovey Doll Pines, despite knowing of her past. He hated her for the ease with which she had inserted herself into his life, and for the relentless pressure she had applied to make him send his wife away and propose marriage to Lovey Doll instead, and for inveigling him into ordering for her a life-sized golden elk to be placed on the front lawn of what she assumed would soon be her house.

The woman's gall was truly staggering, yet recognition of the wrongs perpetrated against him by her could not erase Leo's need. He wanted her still, in the ways he was fast becoming addicted to. The humiliation he experienced, knowing himself incapable of stay-

ing away, was assuaged by the simple expedient of beating her
often in the course of their lovemaking. Imogen (he still thought of
her as having this name) would submit without more than a modicum of complaint to the increasingly bizarre demands he made on
her, without being aware that Leo must do what he did in order to
forgive himself for remaining silent over what he had learned.

He would not confront her with Rowland Price's report, would not
accuse her of mendacity and false pretenses, but he would whip her
with a silken cord, and manhandle her breasts so as to cause visible
bruising, and demand that she utilize for his pleasure certain
objects capable of insertion into the vagina. Lovey Doll did all this,
not knowing it was deliberate punishment. Leo felt himself
absolved of weakness—was he not punishing the woman who lied
to him?—and at the same time was able to despise Lovey Doll a little more with each outrage upon her body, since it made plain her
willingness to endure shame and bodily hurt for the sake of the millions she believed would be her reward. A whore in the truest sense
of the word, thought Leo, as he carefully slid a sash weight into one
orifice, and his index finger into the other.

47

There was a woman with them now, despite Lodi's often-stated maxim that females and felony never mix. Her name was Ellen Torrey, and she was the widow of one of Arch Powell's men from the Montana days. She had been something of a mother to Lodi when he rode with Arch, so he broke his own rule and allowed her to cook and clean for himself and his men in their new hideout near the Utah line. Ellen was forty-eight years old and past her prime, so Lodi didn't expect there would be any fights over her.

The new place had been purchased under a false name with a small part of the proceeds from the Brannan Mining payroll holdup. That job had proven to be Lodi's most successful work ever, and the gang had dispersed to spend their shares. Drew went with Levon on an extended vacation to Chicago. Nate accompanied Lodi on a shorter break from outlawry to Saint Louis, where they chanced to meet Ellen Torrey in the street. Ellen was down on her luck, having lost her job as a cleaning woman. Nate was opposed to hiring her on out of sentiment, but Lodi overrode his protest. "There's not one of us can cook worth a damn, and my stomach's getting older than the rest of me. She's coming back with us."

Drew and Levon returned to western Colorado by rail and stage and were met by Lodi, who informed them the new place now came equipped with a woman to meet their needs. "An *old* woman," he stressed.

"They're the kind that make the best food," said Levon.

The spread had a few head of cattle to lend an air of legitimacy, but Lodi was not expecting any company that had not been invited. The place was so distant from civilization no stranger could approach without announcing himself as the sole speck of activity in a landscape largely inert. The place sat high above country composed largely of wind-carved rock ledges and broad expanses of alkali flats. The view from the main cabin's front door commanded many miles of impressive nothingness, baked nine days out of ten by cruel sunlight. It was a harsh place, and lonely, but it was safe. Lodi planned on lying low there for some time, until a job worthy of his attention should present itself. The days were peaceful, uneventful, and remained that way until Ellen declared herself running low on supplies.

It was Drew who went with her in the buckboard to Cortez, twenty-three miles away. Ellen had picked him for the job, and Lodi said he had to go. Drew didn't mind; his existence had become so tedious that even a routine trip for supplies was an opportunity to ease the monotony of life between holdups. They started out at dawn, and made their own trail across sagebrush and red earth to town. Drew knew Ellen favored him above the rest only because he was the youngest, the most ready to listen politely while she talked of inconsequential matters.

Arriving a little after noon, Drew left Ellen to organize their purchases at the store while he went to the post office to see if any mail had arrived for Mr. Sampson, Lodi's alias as a landowner. Living in temporary isolation as he was, Lodi relied upon a tight network of outside informants to apprise him of work that might appeal to his talents. There was not a single letter, to Drew's disappointment, and he wandered back toward the store, but was diverted from his path by the smell of beer wafting from an open saloon door. Ellen could handle her end of things without him, he decided, and went inside.

"A tall one," he said, and the barman produced a foaming brew from the spigot behind the counter. Drew drained it quickly and ordered another. A young woman sat by herself at a table near the window, using its light to knit by. Drew had known whores to knit patiently while awaiting the attention of customers, but the young woman appeared uninterested in the few drinkers there. Drew ordered a lemonade and sauntered over to satisfy his curiosity.

Approaching the young woman's table, he asked,"Miss, could I get you a cool drink on a warm day?"

"Looks like you already did," she said, glancing up without allowing her needles to pause.

"Mind if I sit with you while you drink it?"

"I didn't say yet that I'd drink it."

She talked a lot harder than she looked. Drew was intrigued, certain now that she was not a whore. He set down his beer and the lemonade, and pulled out a chair for himself.

"Don't sit in that till you've been told you can."

"I already asked, but I didn't get an answer. I'll ask again, if that's what it takes."

"Go on and sit."

Drew pushed the lemonade closer to her side of the table. She ignored it and him.

"You live in Cortez?" he asked.

"Not if they paid me to."

"Me neither. I work on a spread a long ways from here. We're in for supplies."

"Take that stuff away and get me a beer, if you don't mind."

"Be happy to oblige."

"Be happy if you want, but be quick."

Drew got her what she wanted and sat down again.

"See how every man here's keeping his back to me?" she said, after a long pull at the beer.

"I do, now that you've pointed it out."

"They don't want me in here unless I'm for rent."

"That's generally how it is."

"Well, I don't care for things in general. The place I'm at is hot as a stove, and there's no beer to cool it down."

"What place is that?"

"Hotel across the street. Don't bother remembering where; I'll be gone before you get back in town."

"You talk like I've offended you."

"I talk the way I talk. You'll know when you've offended me."

"I'm John Bones."

"Do you rattle when you walk?"

"No, I don't believe so. What's your name?"

"Fay."

"Pleased to meet you, Fay."

"I can't see what you're so pleased about."

"That's because you're in that chair over there, and I'm in this chair over here. The view from this chair's better."

She laid her knitting down and took a swallow from her beer. Drew admired the movement of her long throat as the beer went down. He liked her more with every passing minute, even her hard talk, and found himself unwilling to accept that she would be gone from Cortez the next time he came by.

"Bones," said Fay, "you're trying hard to be a gentleman, and not doing too bad of a job, but I'm not for rent. Thank you for the beer."

She picked up her knitting again.

"That going to be a shawl, or what?" Drew asked.

Fay began to laugh, then stopped. "Only a persistent man asks a woman about her knitting. You must be serious, Bones, to make yourself look so foolish."

"I don't feel foolish, so that doesn't mean a thing to me."

"Doesn't it? You're blushing."

"I am not."

"Yes you are. You look about fifteen right now. No, it's not a shawl, it's a comforter, or will be someday if I care to finish it. You're red as a fresh-pulled carrot."

"I don't believe I've ever been compared to a vegetable before."

"Then this is a day to remember. Do you know a Mr. Ferguson who runs the livery stable?"

"No; I'm new here."

"He was supposed to have a horse ready for me before noon, and I still haven't seen it."

"Riding somewhere today?"

"No; I just like horses for their company."

"Fay, I'm beginning to see why all those fellows have their backs to you, and it doesn't have a thing to do with not being for rent."

"You can go away, then, if you don't like it."

Drew wished he could, but her needles had him hooked. He would no more have willingly left the table by the window than poured a cool beer into the dust outside. She was right about the blushing, though, only now it was caused by a slowly rising anger, with her and with himself for sitting there and being talked to that way. The best thing would be to deliver a stinging remark capable of setting her face afire like his own, but "Another beer?" was all he could say.

"If you want to."

Drew went to the bar again and returned with two glasses and a pitcher. "I only want one drink," said Fay.

"I'll take care of the rest. Where were you intending to ride on Ferguson's horse, if it's not something you'd prefer to keep secret?"

"Some place called the Rim. Do you know it?"

Lodi's spread was immediately below the Rim, a mile-long red and yellow sandstone ledge that jutted like a frozen wave behind the cabins and corral.

"Believe I've heard of it. Can I ask what it is you want to do there?"

"I'm looking for my mother. She works there, or somewhere near there."

"What might her name be, if you don't mind my asking?"

"Ellen Torrey."

"From Saint Louis?"

"Do you know her?"

"She's just down the street right this minute, at the store."

Fay dumped her knitting into a tote bag and stood up.

"Thank you," she said, giving Drew a quick smile, then she was out the door. He watched the foam slowly settling on his pitcher, then poured himself another beer. Lodi wasn't going to be happy about this, but Drew felt good. She had called him a fool and a carrot, but had also called him serious, so although there was much room for greater friendliness between them, he was fairly sure Fay Torrey liked him. He wanted to leave the saloon and go down to the store, but that would have made him appear too eager for Fay's company, and in any case, mother and daughter would appreciate his thoughtfulness if he kept out of the way while they became reunited. Ellen liked him, and Fay liked him; his prospects for advancement were better than fair.

Some time later, mildly drunk, he went to the store. Ellen was waiting on the sidewalk, but Fay was nowhere to be seen. "About time," Ellen said. "There's a pile of goods inside for you to bring out."

"Didn't the store man help you?"

"I told him I had a strong young man with me and not to bother. That was before I found out the young man was work-shy."

"I'll get it."

He began loading sacks and cans and kegs onto the buckboard. Where was Fay? Ellen was in a bad temper, and he felt it was more than his absence that had stoked it.

"Young lady come along looking for you, Ellen?"

"You hush up and keep working so we can get back before dark."

"Said she was your daughter."

"Just you get things loaded, that's your business, and let me mind mine."

"Seemed like a nice young lady."

Ellen ignored him, and Drew couldn't help but notice the resemblance to Fay when she did that. When everything was aboard he asked, "Is that all that's coming?"

"What else would there be."

Drew climbed up and took the reins.

"Where is she?"

"Mind your business. She's where she's best off—away from me, that's where."

"She's your daughter, and she came all this way. How'd she know you were here if you didn't let her know?"

"It wasn't me, it was a friend of the family. Now get going, or I'll drive myself."

They were a quarter mile from town when Drew looked behind and saw a rider following. The angle of her hat told him it was Fay. He decided to say nothing, but Ellen turned also and saw her daughter.

"Stop right here."

Drew set the brake. Fay caught up after five minutes.

"Go back," her mother told her. Fay looked past her and said nothing. "I'm not going to let you come after me," Ellen warned. "You turn around now and go back."

"You can't make me do anything."

"If you follow us you'll never find your way back after dark, and then the liveryman will have the marshal go after you for stealing his horse."

"It's my horse. I bought it. Bones, you might as well get moving, because I intend sticking right behind you."

Ellen said to Drew, "You think he's going to let her go out there and see what there is to see?" She meant Lodi. Drew thought there might be difficulties if he brought a stranger back, but Fay was Ellen's kin after all, and so would not be too surprised by anything, her own father having lived and died an outlaw. He slapped the reins and started the buckboard moving again.

"None of my business," he reminded Ellen. "We need to move on and get there before dark."

"This is your fault, going in that saloon."

"She knew where to go anyway, more or less."

Halfway to the Rim, Ellen had to get down and walk some distance away to relieve herself, and while she was gone, Drew spoke with Fay, whose horse had never been more than a few yards behind.

"Woll, she's real happy to see you. I love these family reunions, don't you? So much affection in the air."

Fay borrowed his canteen and drank from it, then handed it back. "She'll come around. It's not often she doesn't get her way, that's all."

"I'll bet you take after her too."

"You could be right."

By sundown they were near the Rim. Fay had not spoken again. Ellen had fumed in silence, blasting Drew with her mood; he looked forward to getting down from the buckboard and away from her. He was unsure how much blame Ellen would assign him when Lodi began demanding answers.

Levon, on lookout, had alerted Lodi to the presence of a rider behind Drew and Ellen, and Nate rode out to make sure the stranger got no closer if the circumstances demanded it. He had not expected a woman, and after looking her up and down asked Drew, "Who the hell's this—some whore you brung back? You know you can't."

"Better watch your mouth. She's Ellen's girl."

"Hers?" To Ellen he said, "What for?"

"Ask her," said Ellen, not even looking at him.

"Well?" Nate demanded, his horse alongside Fay's.

"A woman in trouble, she goes where her mama's at."

"How'd you know where, huh?"

"I don't see that it's any of your business. Are we close?" she asked Drew. "I'm worn out."

"Pretty near."

"And right here's as close as you get," said Nate. "Take her back where you got her, Bones. Use my horse."

"I'll let Lodi tell me that."

"You'll do what you're goddamn told, is what you'll do."

"Not today, not by you."

He flicked the reins and drove on. Nate could do nothing but ride on ahead. Drew half expected Lodi himself to ride out, but they reached the cabin without additional escort. Lodi was waiting, flanked by Levon and Nate.

"Didn't tell me you were expecting family, Ellen."

"Well, I wasn't. She just came, that's all. I didn't tell her to."

"Peculiar how she knew where to come."

"I didn't tell her," insisted Ellen, climbing down from her seat.

"Must've told someone, I'd say."

"It was Reuben," said Fay, dismounting.

"Who's Reuben?"

"Friend of the family. Didn't my father ever talk about Reuben when he rode with you?"

"Don't recall the name," said Lodi, running his eye over her. The sun was behind the jutting sandstone ledge by then; he thought she might be pretty if he could just see her face, but he was prepared to kill her if he smelled a setup. Lodi had been turned in once by a woman he felt genuine affection for, and shot his way out of a trap; he had enjoyed female companionship on a limited basis since then.

"Better come inside and get this talked through. Levon, get that stuff unloaded and take care of the team."

Inside, Drew quickly told his story while Ellen lit the lamps, then Ellen told how she had tried to dissuade Fay from following them back to the Rim, but Fay had got herself a horse and come along anyway.

"But you told this Reuben where you were headed, before you left Saint Louis, didn't you?"

"I guess I must have, but I don't recall."

"That wasn't smart, Ellen. You should've known better than that, married to a man that rode with Arch Powell. You keep your mouth shut about where you're going, because the law could be listening. Don't you know that?"

"Yes," admitted Ellen. Drew began to feel sorry for her. She looked considerably older than her years, and he guessed she was afraid of being sent away for her carelessness.

"I'm the one that came," said Fay. "Blame me not her."

"All right," agreed Lodi, "I'll do just that. Tell me why you're here, and don't bother telling me lies."

"No big reason, except my husband died."

"What's that got to do with anything?" demanded Nate.

Levon was coming in with supplies and going out again, trying to make sense of the snippets of talk he heard.

"Mister," said Fay, seemingly unafraid, "if you had a mother you loved one time or another, maybe I wouldn't have to explain it to you. My husband died, I wanted to see my mother, and if that doesn't make sense to you, well then, it'll just have to make no sense."

"Did he die?" Lodi asked Ellen.

"She says he did. How should I know? He always got in fights, I know that. She says he was knifed. I expected he'd end up that way. I told her, don't pick that one, but she did anyway, and now she's here."

"I don't like it," Nate said.

Fay looked at him, then away, as if Nate's opinion was not worth considering. Drew saw a cloud of anger cross Nate's face. He had never liked Nate, and Nate had made it clear ever since Drew failed to kill the Pinkerton man that he considered him untrustworthy, even if Drew had dispatched one of the Bentine brothers with a merciful bullet and performed his role in their robberies with a skill that helped assure them of success. If Fay Torrey irritated Nate, it only made Drew like her even more. He was enjoying the situation more than he cared to admit.

"Well, now, Mrs.... what name was he, your husband?" Lodi asked.

"I'm Torrey again, and glad to be."

"Is that so. Well, Miss Torrey, the boys and I are not what you'd call happy to have you among us, uninvited as you are. Being that you know what your pa did for a living, you'll appreciate that we choose our company with care. I just don't see how we'd need two ladies to look after us out here, only being four of us to feed, so I'm going to have to turn you around come morning and send you back where you came from, dead husband or no dead husband—that is, unless you consider yourself a better cook than your mama here."

Drew could tell Lodi was unnerving Ellen deliberately as a punishment. Fay took off her hat and threw it on the table. "I don't like to cook," she said.

"Then tomorrow you'll go back."

"I don't want to, if it's all the same to you."

"But you will, because you don't have a say in things around here." Lodi smiled.

"Sleep on it," advised Fay, and Drew saw Levon's jaw drop at her nerve; no one addressed Lodi in that fashion.

"I'll certainly do that. You can share your mama's bed tonight. In the morning you'll do what I said."

Lodi was upset with himself; he had just said something he had not wanted to say, and one of the prime tenets of his life had always been to say only those things he truly meant to. He didn't want Fay Torrey to go anywhere except directly to his bunk. She was not as pretty as he'd hoped, but her sass and boldness made her desirable. He wanted her. Bones wanted her too, he could see that, and Bones was younger and better-looking, but Lodi suspected Fay was the kind of woman who wanted the top dog, the pack leader, not one of the curs running behind, no matter how sleek his fur. Lodi didn't wish to get into an argument with Bones, whom he also liked. With luck, Fay Torrey would make both their lives easier by leaving in the morning as requested.

Following breakfast, when Fay was not inclined to saddle her horse and go, Lodi did nothing. Levon said to Drew, "She's an all right kind of woman, don't you think?"

"I suppose. She keeps herself to herself."

"That's on account of Ellen. I heard her say to keep low and not stir nothing up."

"You like Fay, Levon?"

"Oh, I'd have her for mine, you bet, in spite of that mouth she's got. That's a spitfire there, boy, but not mean, not deep down. How's she strike you, Bones?"

"Hasn't struck me yet. Haven't offended her enough, I suppose."

"You know what I mean. Is she your kind of woman too?"

"Levon, I'm too shy to talk about such things."

"Nate, he can't stand her. I wonder about Nate sometimes—you know, whether he's got the same urges you and me have got for the ladies."

"Well, it's been rumored that Nate's especially close to his mare, which is reassuring, considering I once heard about a man who was real close with his stallion."

Levon doubled himself over and slapped at his boots. When he could speak, he said to Drew, "He'd kill you, he heard you say a thing like that."

"I know it, and I'd kill him right back."

"Bones, you know this outfit works just fine like it is. You and Nate start gunning for each other, Lodi and me'll have to start over with new men that we don't know. You be nice to him now, you hear?"

On the second day after Fay's arrival, Lodi still had said nothing, had made no move to enforce his edict that she take herself away, and Fay began walking around more. In the afternoon she walked past Drew and headed for the narrow pathway that led up to the Rim. Drew took this for the beckoning call of opportunity, and followed. When he caught up with her, Fay was admiring the view to be had from the ledge's upper reaches.

"Think God made it?" he asked.

"Him or someone bigger."

When his arm slipped around her waist she made no objection, but asked, "Are you always so slow?"

"I'm bashful," Drew told her, to cover his embarrassment; no girl had accused him of that before. He covered himself further by kissing her, and found the body bent against his own to be without the least resistance or inhibition. This made him wonder momentarily if Fay was too experienced in matters relating to men, then he decided he didn't care. He didn't even care about Lodi, and the looks Lodi had given her.

"What's the argument between you and Ellen?" he asked when they separated.

"Have you heard me arguing? It takes two to argue."

"She's got a bee in her bonnet about something."

"And you just have to know what it is."

"I'm curious, I admit it."

Fay took a few steps away from him. "It's over a man," she said, "a man Mama fell in love with, but he was too young for her. He was just stringing her along because she gave him money. Then he started in on me, and she saw him do it and blamed me, not him. He left anyway after that."

"That's the whole story?"

"That's it. She won't forgive me. She's stubborn, just like me."

"Then why'd you come out here to be with her?"

"I've been asking myself that. Seems I might have made a mistake, wouldn't you say?"

"Not from where I'm standing."

"Do women like the things you say to them, Bones?"

"Some do."

Fay pointed along the curved edge of the Rim. "Does that lead anywhere? Is there only one way out of here? My papa always said you had to have a back door, even if you're out under the sky."

"There's a way out along there, Lodi says, but you couldn't call it a trail, just another way to go if you had to leave in a big hurry."

"Do you worry about dying, doing what you do?"

"Not particularly."

"That's what my daddy used to say to Mama. It near drove her crazy. She wanted him to quit, but he never did."

Drew watched her face while she spoke. He liked the shape of her chin, squared-off like a boy's.

"I think I've had my fill of scenery for now," she said, and went back to the path. Drew stayed where he was. He couldn't be sure what kind of bird Fay Torrey was at all.

In the afternoon Ellen came to Drew beside the corral. "You keep away from her," she told him.

"Why?"

"She's no good. She's mine, but she's no good."

"I don't see her that way."

"You and Lodi both. You can't come up against a man like that and win, not a boy like you. She'll play you off against each other, just like she's done before. Men, they'd be a whole lot smarter if they cut their peckers off. You stay away from her and maybe you won't get hurt."

"I'll bear it in mind."

"What mind?"

That evening Drew went looking for Fay, and found her wandering near the natural path leading up to the spot he had followed her to earlier.

"Care to see it again?" she asked.

"See what?"

"The scenery up there."

"All right."

They went up onto the ledge under a darkening purple sky.

"I put a blanket up here before," Fay said.

"A blanket?"

"It's over there," she said, pointing to a hollow in the sandstone. They both strolled over, and there was the blanket, laid out in a double spread with rocks at its corners to prevent the wind from blowing it away. Fay sat down on it, and Drew sat beside her.

"Take your boots off," she told him."Take everything off."

When Fay returned to Ellen's cabin, Ellen could tell right off she'd been with a man. There was the look of feline satisfaction on her face Ellen recalled from other incidents, long ago, and the odor of lovemaking that clung to her as she moved with much swishing of her skirts around the place.

"You smell like a polecat. Go fix yourself. Which one was it?"

"You don't need to know," Fay said with mild scorn, and went to fetch her douche.

Fay had been assisting Ellen with the meals, but she did so with bad grace. Ellen made her wait till the men were done before dishing up food for herself. Ellen disliked eating with her daughter, but she would not serve her at the same time she served the men. It was bad enough that Fay had already opened herself to either Bones or Lodi (Ellen suspected it was Bones, judging by his face at supper), but if she began sitting down at the same table as them she'd drop enough hints over what had happened, without ever speaking a word, to get the men fighting, and Ellen would have hated to see a young man like Bones lying dead. She sometimes wondered if Fay had some kind of demon inside her from the fact that Ellen's husband had not been the actual father. Maybe she was stuck with a daughter like Fay as punishment for her own sins, but she wouldn't assist Fay in any of her scheming over men. Lodi hadn't followed through with his threat to send the girl away, so he was already beguiled, like Bones. Soon there would be blood between them; it was inevitable.

On the third morning, Fay announced she was leaving. Drew felt his heart shrink, and stared at her for some sign that she was joking.

"Fine by me," was all Lodi said, but he was watching Drew as he said it.

"I want someone to take me back to Cortez in the buckboard."

"You got yourself a horse," Nate reminded her.

"I don't like riding. You can keep the horse, just take me back to town in the buckboard. I'm already packed."

"That'll be a job for you, Bones," Lodi said. "You awake there, Bones? Get the team set up."

Ellen watched as Drew put the mules into harness and placed

Fay's bag under the seat. Drew wanted to ask her why Fay was doing this, but Ellen's expression told him she knew what had happened between them, so he said nothing.

Drew didn't trust himself to speak until they were on the flats. "Going to tell me why you're leaving?"

"I wasn't welcome there."

"That's strange, because I recall very clearly doing my damnedest to make you feel welcome. I kind of thought you knew that."

"It wasn't anything you did or didn't do. It couldn't have worked out, not with Mama there, and Lodi."

"What's he got to do with it?"

"He would've called you out sooner or later, and killed you."

"He wouldn't."

"He would, and you know it. That's why I wanted you to bring me back to town. You can keep going with me if you want. You don't have to go back."

"Everything I own is back there. Go where?"

"You don't own a thing that can't be replaced in a general store. Anywhere, that's where I'd go. Do you want to?"

Drew thought about it. Once again, it was Fay directing the course of events; she was the pushingest woman he'd come across since Vanda Gentles back in Galveston. Her offer was a tempting one, but he felt he couldn't simply leave the outfit that way, without any kind of explanation. Of course, everyone would figure out what had happened in any case, if he did what Fay wanted. He could picture their faces, imagine their comments. Nate would say, "She opened it, he sniffed it, he followed her." Lodi would say nothing, but would be scornful of a man who abandoned his partners for a piece of tail. Levon would agree with Nate, but think to himself what a cute piece of tail Fay had been. Ellen, he imagined, would be furious, but at the same time hardly surprised.

"Well?"

"I'm thinking."

"Don't think too long or you'll bust a vein in your head. What do you need to think about? Either you want to come with me and live like a regular man does, or you stay with that bunch and get shot out of the saddle somewhere."

"Let me alone for two minutes, will you?"

"Two minutes, sure, I'll give you two minutes."

When those minutes had elapsed, she said again, "Well?"

"I can't. I'm sorry."

"Oh, you're sorry, all right. You're the sorriest man I ever met. Couldn't even make up his own mind for once. Now I know what kind of man I almost got tied up with. You're a real disappointment to me."

Drew was glad she had become angry rather than tearful; it made his refusal easier to stand by. They drove on in rigid silence, and dust rose in a low cloud behind the turning wheels as Drew followed his own wagon ruts of three days ago.

He set down her bag outside the stage-line office. Fay picked it up and said,"One last time. Do you want to come with me or not?"

If she had given him time to consider another chance he might have succumbed, but the way she presented it to him, with contempt ready to flood her eyes, made him refuse again, this time without hesitation. Fay went inside. Drew turned the buckboard and drove slowly out of town, feeling miserable and used. He hadn't understood what went on in Fay's mind, and now he never would. It was all over, and he supposed he should have felt grateful not to have ended up a traitor to his partners. He most likely would have ended up firmly beneath her thumb anyway, a strong-willed woman like that.

No one referred to Fay on his return, and Drew was grateful for the lack of open sympathy granted him, since that made it easier to pretend he felt nothing at all over Fay's departure.

After a supper marked by a distinct absence of talk, Drew went outside. Nate strolled over to him. "She was a whore anyway," he said, and Drew punched him in the mouth. They fell to the dust in a stalemated scuffle that carried them both across to the cabin, and Lodi and Levon had to come out and separate them.

"I'll kill you ...!" growled Nate. "See if I don't...."

"Cool off, the both of you," Lodi said."Bones, make yourself scarce for an hour or two, why don't you."

Drew picked up his hat and went to the ledge pathway. He wanted to see if the blanket was still up there where Fay had placed it, and it was. He flung himself down and watched the sky turning dark. It had been at around this same time yesterday that she gave herself to him, right there where he now lay alone and in pain. He couldn't understand any of it. Drew fell asleep there, still puzzled.

When he woke up, the evening had become night, cool and black. The moon's curved edge hung low in the sky, and Drew found himself shivering. He stood and beat his arms back and forth to warm himself, wondering what time it was. Standing there, he could see across the flats he had admired with Fay, and on those flats several torches burned. Drew studied them for a moment before realizing their meaning. Men were coming for them: lawmen with guns, following the wheel ruts he had laid down for them four times in three days. That was why Fay wanted to be driven back to Cortez, so the ruts would be that much deeper, that much easier to see by torchlight. They wouldn't have come in the day, but Fay had given them a trail to follow. Sick at heart, Drew flung himself down the path and raced for the cabins.

Lodi was still awake and dressed. He sent Drew to wake everyone else while he went up to the ledge, where Drew joined him minutes later. The torches were noticeably closer.

"It was her," Lodi said.

"It was her," Drew agreed.

"Well, it won't work, not if they think we're snoring. I expect they'll want to put riflemen all around us in darkness, then open fire or parley come morning. They're in for a big disappointment. I wonder if she sold us to Pinkertons or federals."

"She offered me a way out, if I'd come with her."

"And you turned it down. Don't worry, Bones; you'll live to tell the tale."

Inside twenty minutes everyone was packed and mounted. Ellen sat nervously on their quietest horse; she had not ridden in more than fifteen years. "Stay together and stay quiet," Lodi said, and they began winding their way in single file up the same narrow pathway to the top of the Rim. Once there, they could all see the torches below, flickering like fireflies. "Figure she ain't a whore now?" Nate whispered, but Drew ignored him.

The night was too dark for hard riding over unfamiliar ground. They walked the horses along the sweeping ledge for its entire length, then descended its sloping far side, cutting off their view of the torches. On open ground they could travel faster. Ellen clung to her saddle horn as they galloped north for a half hour, then they eased their pace to spare the horses. Pursuit would not begin till morning, with the discovery of the empty cabins. Levon predicted they would be at Bigelow's ranch by early afternoon if nobody's horse threw a shoe. Bigelow was one of Lodi's comrades in crime, trading horses and cattle back and forth between the world of legitimate commerce and his more remunerative dealings with Lodi's outfit.

"Ellen, you still in one piece?"

"Just about. Who put an ax handle under my saddle?"

They laughed, and were still laughing when the first shots came from their left. Drew felt the impact of a bullet entering his mare's shoulder, and she began sinking beneath him. He jumped clear before she fell, and looked around to see who might boost him behind his saddle for a getaway. Nate's horse was almost on top of him. Drew readied himself to jump up, but Nate rode past at a full gallop, his face fixed on Drew's as he swept by, and Drew was left alone, the sound of receding hoofbeats coming to him through a cloud of dust. Gunshots were still whistling by, so Drew fell to the ground behind his fallen mare, yanked his Winchester from its scabbard and began crawling away. The mare was still alive and suffering, but to put a bullet into her head would let the attackers know he had not been picked up and taken along with Lodi and the rest.

The law had been smarter than anticipated, had set an ambush along the only escape route in case the party approaching from Cortez was seen. Drew had been the one to tell Fay about Lodi's back door, and now he was paying for his loose mouth. Nate had been right about Fay, but Drew would still call him out, if they ever met again, over the way Nate had made no attempt to pick him up. It was a worse betrayal than Fay's, because even if they had never liked each other, they had ridden together.

Soon he heard voices, and stopped his crawling through the sagebrush. The voices came from several directions, and Drew wondered if he had somehow turned himself around. He could be sure of nothing at ground level, and so raised his head carefully to see if some avenue of escape might present itself. If he could learn where the hunters stood, he might be able to wriggle through between them in the dark.

"Hold it there. You drop that gun."

The voice was calm, unhurried. Drew did as he was told.

"Be real still now. Hey! Over here! I got me one!"

More figures came toward Drew and his captor. A man who appeared to be in charge asked him, "What's your name?"

"Lodi," said Drew.

48

With more money in her hand than she had thought it possible for one person to carry unaided, Zoe found a kind of courage. She had intended to flee the state, flee the country eventually, to ensure the safety of herself and Omie. But the money changed that. The audacity and ease with which it had been obtained gave her confidence, and following close behind that came defiance. Riding out of Denver aboard a first-class car, Zoe felt a robber's surge of gratitude for an easy getaway, and then the heady rush of belief that similar crimes could be committed with impunity.

She fought these impulses, knowing them for the aftermath of danger they were, a false excitement threatening to carry her beyond prudence. She had Omie to think of. Actually, it had been Omie who made the feat possible. Omie was a kind of armor, a shield against ill fortune, uniquely potent. Had there really been any risk in their venture to take what rightfully was Zoe's?

"Does anyone in this car recognize us?"

"No, Mama."

Zoe wore her false arm sling, and Omie's face was hidden again by the veil. Their appearance had attracted some attention at the station, veils being uncommon in the wardrobe of children, but Zoe had anticipated this by knotting a black scarf around Omie's arm, making her a mourner. Omie said all was well, so Zoe could relax, if her humming bloodstream would allow it.

They changed trains several times, riding through the night, and all of the following day, choosing the next section of their railroad escape arbitrarily, Zoe allowing Omie veto over whatever decision she made at each changeover. They zigged and zagged on rails, heading south by west in awkward increments. Eventually they stepped off their latest train at a small town in northern Arizona. Omie declared the place safe to rest in, and they took themselves to a hotel for some much needed food and a room in which to be themselves.

Zoe ordered all available newspapers to be delivered to their room next morning, and scanned them for articles relating to the theft of so much money from the Denver National Bank and Trust. There was no mention of any such deed, and she asked herself if this was because it had not been considered a theft, since the money was in effect her annulment settlement, or if Leo had ordered the bank manager to tell no one when the incident was reported to him. That seemed the more likely scenario.

She read the newspapers in haste, and overlooked completely a small article concerning the discovery of a man wandering in from desolate country several days before, a man unable or unwilling to give his name, who credited his rescue from the rigors of the desert—bearing nothing in his arms but a sawed-off shotgun—to the timely intercession of his guardian angel. The story was barely fifteen lines of type, and Zoe's anxious gaze swept across it in a trice, in pursuit of news closer to her own interests.

Worn out with traveling, the inner ferment caused by their success fading now, Zoe began to wonder what her next step might be. Flight beyond Leo's reach no longer held the same appeal. She had bested his killer and his banker, thanks to Omie, and it would have seemed like quitting to give in now by sneaking away to foreign shores. Leo was not so all-powerful as many thought him. Who knew him better than Zoe? He was a pathetic figure, really, a straw man, all of his strength stemming from his position rather than his person. Should she and Omie be afraid of him to the extent that they must run as far as possible to be free of his influence? Should they instead try to make some kind of peace with him, on equal terms? She did not know; nor did Omie, for whom all the options were meaningless.

The tall man had been visiting her again of late, requiring her help, it seemed to Omie, although she could not recall with any detail the exact circumstances of his visitations and requests. She had been of use to him in some unfathomable way as they both passed through a landscape of redness and heat, and that pleased her, but the tall man's needs had to be set aside now in favor of her own and Mama's. Together they had done something bad, even if the money they stole was Mama's anyway, and Omie wanted to forget such things as theft and the tall man for a while, and concentrate her attention on the one rag doll Zoe had allowed her to retain.

His handcuffs were kept tight despite his requests to have them loosened a notch or two. The train ride across Colorado to Glory Hole was going to test his patience. Drew was escorted by four federal marshals and a host of deputies, all crowded into one private car provided free of charge by Leo Brannan. Lodi had stolen from him, so Leo was determined that the court which tried him should convene in Glory Hole. Drew understood from casual conversation between the lawmen that Leo Brannan would have to fight the state government for that privilege, since Leadville was the official county seat, not Glory Hole, even if Lodi's infamous payroll robbery had actually occurred nearer to the latter.

He had not expected his deception to be swallowed so easily. Drew was at least ten years younger than Lodi, and although he had regrown his beard, there really wasn't much of a resemblance. He suspected no one wanted to question his identity too closely, since the capture of Lodi was of greater importance, so far as newspaper headlines were concerned, than the capture of one of his men. Awaiting transportation in Cortez, Drew had expected a visit from Fay, who could have told his captors they had a much smaller fish than they thought, but Fay had not come, and Drew continued his deception, more from mischievousness than anything else. It helped him to know that the men surrounding him, the men who would not allow him a little comfort, were being made fools of.

The marshal opposite him, who insisted on blowing his cigar smoke directly into Drew's face, asked, "What the hell have you got to smile about?"

"Not a thing," Drew said, smiling even wider.

The marshal leaned forward and slapped him hard across the face.

"Then quit. I don't like to see it."

"Anything you say," Drew said.

Leo had several things to be thankful for now. The model for his gold elk had been prepared in record time by a Pittsburgh sculptor of some renown, with the assistance of a team of willing students, and preparations for the creation of a mold had begun. The gold for the casting was on site, guarded around the clock by a team of Pinkerton detectives, and reports of the golden elk already were becoming part of the nation's daily gossip. Most press articles on the fabulous beast erroneously stated that the elk would be made of solid gold, which had indeed been Leo's original intention, until he was informed it would weigh too much for competent handling. He had given permission by wire for a hollow elk, which would be far cheaper and more manageable, but had not passed this revision on to the general public. An elk of solid gold had about it the stuff of legend, and Leo was determined that it should achieve such status.

He had chosen to forget that it was his lying mistress who first proposed the creation of the elk; Leo took that role for himself, and on the one occasion when she sulked over the absence of her name in all of the press coverage relating to the elk, he had hit her very hard and told her to mind her business. He had seen fear creeping into her face more often lately, and that pleased him. Leo was still unsure what her ultimate punishment should be, once he revealed to her that he knew everything about her she had attempted to hide. It should be something interesting, unusual, original.

He also had the capture of Lodi to exult over. There was some difficulty with the state regulations over where Lodi's trial should be held, but certain members of Big Circle were working on his behalf to have the usually applicable statutes waived in favor of a trial in Glory Hole itself, the right and proper place in which to administer judgment and justice on the fellow, in Leo's opinion. Lodi was currently being held in the county jail in Leadville, while the necessary legalities for a transfer to Glory Hole were under way. Leo had been told it was a secure building, with well-armed men in attendance. News of Lodi's capture had received as much ink as the golden elk, and rightly so.

The one blot upon these prospects for imminent personal satisfaction was the outrageous manner in which Zoe had helped herself to her annulment settlement in Denver. The manager of Denver National Bank and Trust was under investigation by Big Circle for

possible complicity in the case. Blye's unacceptable excuse for having handed the money over was that he simply could not remember
the event with any clarity, a ridiculous defense. Blye had even been
so bold as to suggest that Leo was a fool to set aside a cash settlement of such proportions if he was not prepared to let the lady take
it, a statement of such obvious malice it served to implicate the fellow even more. No word of the incident had been made public, of
course, nor would it ever be. Membership in Big Circle certainly
had its compensations. Leo wondered sometimes if being a member
of the Praetorians was not foolhardy, given the conveniences of the
larger body. He felt a twinge of guilt over his association with the
revolutionary kernel slowly gathering strength to burst through
from within, but for the moment was content to wait and see what
might transpire. He shared none of his misgivings with Rowland
Price.

When Lodi robbed a train up in Montana less than a week after his
own supposed capture, there was consternation in Leadville. Within the space of a day it was ascertained that the prisoner being held
as Lodi was in fact one of his men. Confronted by marshals, Drew
told them he was John Bones. Two of the marshals held him while a
third beat him senseless. By evening the federal contingent had
withdrawn, leaving Drew under no more than the usual jailhouse
guard.
    Nursing a swollen jaw and a closed eye, Drew told himself the
ruse had been worthwhile, even if it left him bruised. He was surprised that Lodi had been able to organize a job so quickly, and
assumed the train had been stopped solely to let the world know of
the law's mistake. Drew could imagine the panache with which
Lodi announced himself to the passengers as he robbed them, and
he wondered if Lodi would take a chance and attempt to spring him
from jail before his trial began, in order to thumb his nose at the
law again. Drew wondered also how he might react to his next
meeting with Nate, if such a thing should occur. Nate had deliberately left him stranded, an outright violation of the outlaw code,
and could not be permitted to go unpunished. That alone was a
good reason to hope for escape. It was a hope worth nurturing, since
it was all he had.
    Otis Trevitt was a disappointed man. He had bragged to his girl
that he was part of the group guarding none other than Lodi, and

now that it was known a trick had been played on everyone, Otis was left in charge of a nobody. His girl wouldn't be impressed at all by that. The town marshal had said another deputy would be given double duty with Otis, beginning the next day, in case the real Lodi should attempt getting his man out. But for the moment, with Lodi having robbed a train less than twenty-four hours earlier in another state, there was no possibility of that happening, so Otis was on his own, and would be until dawn.

When the woman and the girl came in, he was not fully alert, having been awaked from a catnap by the sound of the opening door. Otis was aware of his own drowsiness and its cause, but he could not understand why it was that when the woman asked him for the keys to the cell containing Lodi, he pointed to the key ring on the wall without a second thought. Why had he done that? He was sleepy still, and the girl watching him had a blue mark on the side of her face, which should have piqued his interest, but didn't; he was just as tired as tired could be, and when he saw the prisoner walking past him with the woman, he couldn't raise a hand or open his mouth to let the woman know it wasn't even Lodi she had released, just some nobody that rode with Lodi, but by then they were out the door, the girl leaving last, and Otis felt himself slipping back into a comfortable sleep. Everything that had happened was probably a kind of catnap dream, so he had nothing to worry about.

For Drew also, the arrival of the woman at his cell door had a dreamlike ambience. She said not a word, had simply unlocked the door and beckoned with her one arm. He could swear he had seen her somewhere before, but the time and place eluded him. He rose, put on his boots and jacket and went with her out to the office, where a deputy sat with hanging jaw and glazed eyes, staring at a young girl who stared at him with equal fascination. Drew thought the girl was also familiar somehow, but again, he could not recall where he might have seen her, despite the blue birthmark on her face.

Then all three were walking along the sidewalk, the woman's arm through his, and his other hand in the clasp of the girl. They were the very picture of a family out for a late night stroll, and the citizens of Leadville gave them hardly a glance. When they came to a buggy and team hitched to a rail, the woman told him to get in. Drew was handed the reins. He drove slowly out of town, still dazed by the hope of escape that had been so promptly answered.

They were well beyond the last houses when the girl said, "Mama, it isn't him."

"Isn't who?" said the woman.

"It isn't the robber man."

"Sir, are you Lodi?"

"No, ma'am. I guess you haven't heard the news yet. Lodi's up in Montana, just robbed a train there last night."

"But ... you are a train robber yourself, are you not?"

"Yes, ma'am, I am. I just told them I'm Lodi for a joke."

"Well ... this is most disappointing, if I may say so, Mr....?"

"Bones, ma'am, John Bones. I'm sorry you're disappointed, ma'am, but I have to tell you I'm grateful, and not disappointed in the least."

"Yes, to be sure you are, but ... Oh, botheration, this is not what I wanted at all."

"His name isn't what he says, Mama; it's something else."

"Not Lodi, by any chance?"

"No, Mama, something else. He keeps hiding it. I think it's ... Doogle."

"Leave the gentleman alone, Omie."

"Well, he should tell us the truth if we got him out of jail, shouldn't he?"

"Uh, ma'am, she's right. Bones is an alias. My line of work generally sees a lot of them."

"It really doesn't matter to me what your name is. It was Lodi I wanted. Now I don't quite know what to do."

"Ma'am, it probably isn't my business, but are you kin to Lodi?"

"Certainly not. I've never met the man."

"I was just trying to figure why you wanted him out so bad, ma'am, excuse me for asking."

"I'm going to call him Doogle."

"Omie, be quiet. Mr. Bones, are you an expert robber?"

"Ma'am, I'd have to call myself experienced, but maybe not expert."

"I assume it was Lodi who planned the work you performed."

"Yes, ma'am, mostly. Ma'am, how did you get me past that deputy?"

"It really makes no difference now. Is it possible for you to make contact with Lodi, Mr. Bones?"

Drew understood then that his escape had been arranged by the marshals, so they might extract from him some code or meeting place by which he intended reuniting himself with the gang. Such a procedure did exist, but Drew intended to reveal none of it. The breakout should have been staged in a much more believable form than this, with masked men posing as sympathetic bandits, not a one-armed woman and a girl.

"Doogle thinks we're fakes, Mama." Omie laughed. "He thinks we work for the marshals."

"No, Mr. Bones, we do not, and my question is sincere—are you able to rejoin your friends?"

"I ma'am, I'm not understanding half of what I hear tonight.... Little girl, how do you know what I'm thinking? And ma'am, do you want a train robbed ... or something?"

"Yes, oh, yes indeed."

"Mama, look at his hand! He's the one that tried to take your ring!"

"Pardon me?" Drew was becoming more confused than ever.

"His pinkie, Mama, it's gone, and so was the pinkie on the man who tried to take your ring on the train that time, only I wouldn't let him."

"Why, so it is! Mr. Bones, what a small world we do live in. Was that Lodi's work, outside Buena Vista just a short time ago?"

"Yes, ma'am, that was him, and it was me that wanted your ring. Sorry about that, ma'am."

"You didn't get it," crowed Omie. "I wouldn't let you."

"Omie, stop this nonsense. Mr. Bones is our friend now, or so I assume."

"Yes, ma'am. I'm beholden to you both."

"It was Indians that did it," announced Omie. "They cut off his finger and laughed about it."

"Well, it wasn't exactly them who did it.... Little girl, that's three or four times now you've done that. Ma'am, can she ... see inside my head?"

"Omie, one more word from you and I shall be most displeased. You're simply showing off."

Omie snorted undaintily.

After another mile Drew was told to direct the buggy into a stand of trees beside the road, where three saddled horses were waiting.

His deception appeared to be working. The Sleeping Savage lay in eternal repose inside the casket of glass, a close facsimile of the original. Nevis was pleased with himself; not a single paying customer so far had done more than gape at the sight and declare himself amazed at the thing's ugliness. Carlson's Patented Mortuary Putty had borne out the faith Doc Pfenning placed in it, and had caused Nevis no creative difficulties whatever, even when the time came to stain the Savage with old coffee grounds. The color had taken well, and after several applications the twisted limbs of the artifact had darkened to an acceptable hue, with just the right amount of unevenness and mottling to grant it the appearance of the original. The horsehair wig was not quite acceptable to Nevis's meticulous eye, but nobody seemed eager to question its antiquity. The customers came rolling in, their dollars collected by a scrubbed and coiffured and smiling Winnie at the door.

A customer late on that first afternoon of the exhibition brought to Nevis's attention a small detail: the glass case was becoming misted, creating a haziness inside that made viewing the Savage less interesting than it might be. Horrified, Nevis went to the case and examined it; the glass was indeed misting over. What was causing it? The bogus corpse had been placed inside the case and all air extracted by a fine-nozzled vacuum pump less than twenty-four hours before. Had the process of extraction been performed inadequately? Where was the moisture coming from? It seemed to be spreading even as he watched, obscuring the object within even more.

"What's wrong with your Injun, mister?"

"I ... suspect the ... the ancient gases trapped in his tissues are ... are escaping, due to the ... unnatural state of airlessness in which he has been placed."

"Being in ice, though, ain't that the same thing?"

"No, sir, it is not. Examine ice closely and you will discern fine bubbles of air, usually of an elongated variety."

"He's fogged up pretty good in there now. Lookit that stuff crawl along the glass. Mister, I want my money back. I can't hardly see him at all."

The customer's demand was echoed by others pressing around the case, some of them rubbing on the glass in an attempt to erase the mist forming on the inside.

"Please, please ... no touching of the crystal casket, ladies and gentlemen! No touching, please ... "

"Well, we want our money back. That thing isn't worth looking at now."

"Give us our money back, mister!"

"Yes! Yes, you may all collect a refund! Certainly you may, one and all! Please return to the door and take back your money. I do apologize for this disappointment, ladies and gentlemen.... Please, no touching the crystal cabinet!"

When the room was empty and the doors bolted, Winnie came to Nevis with a pile of cash much reduced from its encouraging bulk a half hour before.

"What happened to it?"

"I can't imagine. Perhaps ... perhaps the putty has too much moisture in its content."

"But wouldn't having no air in there keep it dry?"

"I don't know. I have no scientific understanding of such things. It could be that the air seal is defective. What a disaster! Smith should be here to share this!"

Smith, having decided he would not take a bath to suit paying customers, was emptying shitcans as usual.

"Why don't you open it up and see what's wrong."

"I suppose I must. This shouldn't have happened."

As Nevis unscrewed the air seal he heard the *whooosh* of air entering the casket, so the seal had apparently been adequate. What, then, had gone wrong? He unlocked the clasps and lifted the lid with Winnie's assistance. The smell of Carlson's Patented Mortuary Putty was strong, and the emaciated limbs of the Savage, composed entirely of this substance applied to a stick-and-wire frame, was positively weeping moisture.

"He's crying all over," said Winnie.

Nevis began wiping the inside of the glass lid with his handkerchief, then began dabbing at the limbs of the Savage. The putty came away like sticky clay, and he stopped before further damage was done.

"No," he said. "Oh, no ... we're finished. This will never do. One more touch and he'll crumble. Damn that Pfenning!"

"Don't blame him. The stuff probably works fine on dead folks; it's just not right for what you used it on."

"Winnie, do you ... do you happen to have about your person a certain necessary item ...? "

"You need a snort?"

"Most definitely."

Winnie produced a hip flask from beneath her dress.

"Help yourself."

Nevis's adam's apple bobbed frantically until the flask was emptied.

"Well," said Winnie, "Brannan hasn't built his ice plant yet, or put in the shitters like he said. It's not like you don't have a job or anything."

"But this was so important, so unique, or at least I considered it so when we owned the genuine article. Oh, that woman, that false friend ...! What a despicable thing to have done! What a crime against comradeship! How could she!"

"She's a bitch and a rich man's whore, that's how."

"But what does she have against me?"

"Let me tell you, there's nothing like a whore that finally smells big money. Once it gets up her nose, you better watch out if you ever knew her before, because she won't give you the wind from her ass, and that's a fact. She wants you to go away, is my judgment on it. She knows her man's going to put you and Smith out of business, and she doesn't want you finding another kind of business that'll keep you around here. She wants you gone."

"And she has succeeded brilliantly," said Nevis, contemplating the sodden ruin before him. It had required four days to build the Savage, and it had all been for nothing. Lovey Doll Pines had killed what was, in all likelihood, his final creative endeavor. Hers had been an unforgivable crime against art, a slap delivered to the smiling face of friendship. Try as he might, he could not forgive her.

The following day, Lovey Doll Pines received by delivery wagon the empty crystal casket. Inside was a note: *This contained a corpse, and does so still.* Lovey Doll did not comprehend Nevis's intention at all. He had been referring, as he penned the note, to the death of their friendship. Lovey Doll read the note a second time, then screwed it up in exasperation, and asked herself if the casket, quite a beautiful thing in its own right, could possibly be included among the parlor fittings.

Clean-shaven again, Drew did not resemble the man who had passed for Lodi. He boarded a train with the woman he had learned to call Mrs. Brannan; he still called her "ma'am" among company, to protect her from unwanted glances. Omie seemed content to call him Doogle, and had ceased her maraudings among his thoughts.

They were headed for Carbondale, where Lodi had friends. Drew had already dispatched a telegram: MR. JOHNSON WILL PRESENTLY

ARRIVE. INFORM MR. LINDELL. Johnson was himself, or any other member of the lawbreaking brethren; Lindell was Lodi. The message would be passed on, and when he could manage it, Lodi would come, or else send word to Drew of a location where he could safely rejoin the gang. Mrs. Brannan had thus far been reluctant to share with him the exact nature of the work she wished Lodi to engage in, but Drew was not offended; he owed her too much to allow resentment of any kind to cloud the hours spent in proximity to this highly unusual woman and her even more unusual daughter.

"Show me the wobble trick again, Omie."

Omie placed a pencil on the floor of the car, and caused it to balance on its point despite the lurching and swaying of the train, then made its chewed end wobble in a circle while the point remained where it was, and then, to amuse Doogle to the fullest, she lifted the pencil into the air without physical assistance of any kind. Drew was fascinated.

"How can you do things like that?"

"I just can," said Omie, with a smugness Zoe found exasperating.

"Don't brag so, dear. Mr. Bones may think less of your gift because of it."

"No he won't."

"Really, Omie, you try my patience sometimes."

"It's all right, ma'am. I enjoy seeing the things she can do. I never saw the like, really."

"Well, so long as she doesn't become tiresome."

"No, ma'am, she couldn't do that."

Zoe had noticed that Omie's face shone when she was in Bones's company, and the mother did not resent it. Leo once had elicited that kind of adoration, and betrayed them both with his foolishness as time went by. Zoe intended never to remarry, once her vendetta with Leo was done with, but it would not have displeased her if a likable (despite his trade) and forthright young man such as Bones gave Omie the simple enjoyment of his closeness, his genuine friendliness. A male of character and integrity should figure in the life of every female, Zoe reasoned, and vice versa. The time for such opportunity with regard to herself was past, she truly believed, but Omie's life had barely begun. Let her be coy and brazen and demanding of the young man seated opposite; he was no enemy, no cruel deceiver, and his delight in such tricks and stunts as Omie could create for him was in itself a wonderful thing to see, even if Zoe had to hide her feelings of satisfaction behind a mask of rectitude and propriety. She was who she was, and could not change now.

"Mr. Bones?"

"Ma'am?"

"Wait, Mama, I want to spin it.... "

Her pencil spun up to the ceiling, hit the stamped tin and fell back to the floor. Zoe looked around to see if such doings had been observed by other passengers, but they had not; the nearest was several seats away, half asleep.

"Omie, kindly desist. Mr. Bones, I believe I may trust you. I have, perhaps, caused you to think I place my trust in no one but your friend Lodi."

"I'd call him my boss, ma'am, rather than my friend."

"Regardless, I know you, and not him, and so I wish to share with you the purpose of my actions."

"Ma'am, I'm listening."

Zoe took from her bag a newspaper clipping, and handed it to him. Drew read the article and handed it back.

"Ma'am, that's a piece of goods that'll be surrounded by more guns than they had anywhere since the war."

"I am aware of that, Mr. Bones, and there lies the challenge, don't you agree?"

"Challenge is one word for it, I guess. My own word, ma'am, would be suicide."

49

Clay had to laugh. He was drunk, but he would have laughed even if he'd been sober. The newspapers were filled with it; the law had captured Lodi at last, then found out it wasn't him, then even lost the fellow they did have, and couldn't explain how it happened. He was glad, in a way, that he did not work for the official forces of law, not if they made fools of themselves like that.

He poured himself another drink. The bar was one of Denver's lowest, and he felt quite at home there. He had lived in a room upstairs for more than a week. Meals were sent up, and liquor, and he sometimes came down to the bar to drink some more. He had run up a considerable bill, and was unable to pay it, but Clay was not bothered. Since walking out of the desert down in New Mexico he hadn't cared about very much at all. He supposed his life was effectively over and done with; all he needed to do now was drink himself into the grave and find some peace.

"Mr. Dugan?"

The large man before him was unknown to Clay.

"No," he said. "Go away."

"I believe I'll sit, Mr. Dugan."

"This is my table."

"It's the hotel's table, and you're drunker than he said you'd be."

"Who said?"

"My employer."

"Well, he's right; now go away."

"He sent me to find you so I might make a proposition, Mr. Dugan. I don't know why he'd want a drunk on the payroll, but that's his choice."

"You tell him you couldn't find me, all right?"

"That'd be a lie, Dugan. I'm not lying for you."

"Then say I turned it down, whatever it is."

"Don't you want work? You're broke."

"I'm not."

"Sure you are, and you owe money right here in this pisspot hotel. You take the job that's offered, you can pay your way out of here."

Clay contemplated his drink. "What job?"

"Lodi."

"Say again?"

"You know the one."

Clay laughed. "You want me to catch him? There must be a couple hundred laws after Lodi, and they can't do it."

"The pay's good. Interested?"

"You didn't say your name."

"John."

The office Clay was ushered into that afternoon was elegant, yet strangely bare. The gentleman behind the enormous desk seemed elderly and frail in appearance, yet he exuded the distinct aura of power.

"Please sit down, Mr. Dugan."

Clay lowered himself into a wing-backed chair.

"My name is Jones. I have been interested in you for some time."

"Why?"

"You're an interesting man, Mr. Dugan. Your career fits no usual pattern. Your calling, if that is the correct word, is for rounding up criminals, but you have never sought the sanction of a federal badge. I wonder why that is."

Clay offered no explanation.

"Are you a steady drinker, Mr. Dugan? Sobriety is important on work such as this."

"I can stop."

"Good. My colleague has told you what it is we require?"

"The moon. You want the moon, and you'll get it before I get Lodi."

Mr. Jones laughed dryly. "You're too modest, Mr. Dugan, and you also exaggerate the invulnerability of the man. Lodi can be had, like any outlaw. The trick is to get close enough."

"It's been tried plenty of times. There's nobody more suspicious of strangers trying to wriggle their way into a bad outfit than the men who run that outfit. You've got to have credentials, be known for doing what they do, then they'll trust you."

"Quite so, and you will have your credentials."

"I don't see how, being that I'm on the other side."

"Fakery, Mr. Dugan, playacting, if you will. And you'll have an ally."

"What ally?"

Mr. Jones rang a silver bell at his elbow; the door behind Clay opened and closed, and a young woman stood beside him.

"Sit down, my dear. Mr. Dugan, meet Miss Torrey."

She sat in a wing-back several feet from Clay's and gave him a brief nod, which he did not return.

"Jones, I'm not doing anything with a woman along."

"Allow me to explain certain matters first. Miss Torrey has recently had contact with the outlaws that concern us; in fact her mother is their chief cook and bottle washer."

"Is that right?" Clay asked her.

Fay said, "She's with them."

"Miss Torrey left just hours before the gang's hideaway was approached by federal marshals. A young man who has since gained some notoriety was captured in the ambush that followed."

"The one who said he was Lodi."

"The same."

Clay turned to Fay again. "You sold them out?"

"No, but they must think I did."

"Miss Torrey's brief visit with Lodi coincided, unhappily, with a plan hatched some time before by federal authorities. Lodi purchased property near Cortez under the name of Sampson, and an alert land agent recognized the name as one of Lodi's many aliases. That is how the attack was launched, but as Miss Torrey says, Lodi will certainly believe it was she who betrayed him."

"I don't see how that puts her or me close to him."

"She will seek him out to make her case for innocence. Would a guilty party attempt anything so foolhardy?"

"It's a stretch, but he might fall."

"There is another card to play. Miss Torrey is romantically involved with Bones, the young man who so recently was spirited away from the Leadville jail. That gives her story further credence."

"Maybe, but if she's in love with Bones, why would she want to bring Lodi down? Bones'll likely take the drop alongside him."

"Mr. Dugan, I have not made myself sufficiently clear. I have no intention of delivering Lodi or Bones or any of the gang to the law."

"Then what the hell do you want? Pardon me, miss."

"What I want are the woman and child who took Bones from Leadville."

"What woman and child?"

"Believe me, Mr. Dugan, that was the rescue team—a one-armed woman and her daughter."

"I didn't read anything about that."

"Nor will you. The story is too embarrassing for publication, but sources tell me that is how Bones was taken from custody."

"Who are they, this woman and girl?"

"Their name is Brannan. She's the wife of Leo Brannan."

"What's a woman like that doing springing someone like Bones?"

"I don't know, Mr. Dugan. I should like to hire you to find out, and when you have done so, I should like you to bring them both to me. If that proves impossible, bring only the girl. Her name is Omie, and she is an unusual child."

"She's the one you want, not Lodi?"

"You have it."

"Why do you want her?"

"That does not concern you. Omie is worth five thousand dollars, Mr. Dugan."

"Split down the middle with Miss Torrey here?"

"I have a separate arrangement with Miss Torrey."

Clay looked at his knees. He understood nothing.

"Count me in," he said, looking up. "How am I supposed to find them?"

"Your partner will provide the necessary information. John has funds for your immediate requirements. Thank you for accepting my offer, Mr. Dugan."

"Pleasure."

When Dugan and Miss Torrey were gone, Mr. Jones allowed himself the luxury of satisfaction over a plan successfully launched. Tatum was still searching for the same prize, but Mr. Jones was a believer in placing more than one iron in any fire that intrigued him. One or the other of two such determined fellows as Tatum and Dugan would bring back Omie Brannan. The involvement of Zoe with Lodi, by way of Bones, and the affair between Bones and Fay Torrey, all formed a web of improbable complexity. Mr. Jones did not comprehend the overall design, but did not worry himself over it; the important thing was Omie, who would place him in contact with his departed wife, if she could. That alone would be worth every penny he provided to the hunters now put on the scent.

Mr. Jones had not been interested in Lodi until Zoe Brannan and her daughter took the outlaw's henchman from jail. A member of Big Circle, whom Mr. Jones knew, was privy to the doings of federal marshals. This man learned that the deputy left in charge of Bones at the Leadville jail claimed a one-armed woman and a girl with a blue face had taken the prisoner away, causing the deputy to fall asleep somehow, both during and after the abduction. The story was ridiculous, and the deputy was himself imprisoned as an accomplice to the unlikely duo, but his story still had not changed. Mr. Jones's informant knew the one-armed woman and the blue-faced girl could only be the Brannan females, whom Mr. Jones had let it be known he was very much interested in. The same informant also made Mr. Jones aware of a coincidence he thought might prove diverting; following the botched ambush mounted against Lodi outside Cortez, a young woman thought to have had dealings with the outlaws had been placed in custody, but thus far had not been thoroughly questioned.

Mr. Jones had smelled the tantalizing odor of opportunity, and made arrangements for the young woman's immediate release and transportation to Denver. She was everything he required, a gift from whatever gods directed the affairs of men, and he hired her to his cause with a minimum of resistance on Fay's part. He wanted a man with her on such a potentially dangerous assignment, naturally, and by good fortune (those nameless gods again) learned of the presence in Denver of a man who was little known but reputed to be among the most dogged in his pursuit of outlaws. Though Dugan was an occasional drunkard, it was said, he seldom mixed liquor with business. He was not an ideal choice, but he was available, and broke.

Now the cards were shuffled and dealt. The game, or rather a new game within the larger, never-ending game, had begun.

Clay and his new partner rode out of Denver on a night train. Clay was uneasy in the presence of Fay Torrey, and did not entirely trust her; any woman who chose to love a man who was beyond the law was probably not reliable, yet he had to depend on her for the deception he intended using to worm his way into Lodi's exclusive circle of felons. He studied her with sideways glances. Her face had the appeal of a nervous vixen, alert to the dangers surrounding it. He was shocked when she offered him a drink from a silver flask.

"Don't look so flabbergasted, Dugan. You like a drink, I like a drink. Jones isn't here."

Clay accepted the flask, drank from it and inspected its quality.

"You've got expensive tastes."

"Jones's money bought it. He gave me plenty when I told him about Bones. That old bird scares me. You look in his eyes and you can tell he knows more about you than you'll ever know about him. Jones and Bones. Why would he want this little Omie girl, do you think?"

"Can't say."

"There's men that like girls that age."

"He's not that kind."

"I don't like him anyway."

"Then why'd you take his money?"

"I'll tell you, Dugan: I was scared not to."

Clay knew what she meant. He had formed the impression that if he refused Jones's offer, he would not have lived very long. He had no proof that the large man called John would have lifted a finger against him, but that is what he believed. Since wandering in the desert, Clay had virtually ceased to apply logic to anything, including the events of his own life. Whatever twists and turns appeared in the trail ahead of him, he would accept them all and travel willingly to whatever lay at the end of the road. It made no difference if he understood what was happening to him; the trail itself was his guide.

"Think Bones'll believe you about the ambush?" he asked.

"Not at first, but he wants me, so he'll come around."

Clay wondered what it might feel like to be wanted. Fay seemed a surprisingly blunt female; maybe he could get along with her. She swigged liquor like a man, and looked out the windows into the passing night like someone searching for something, and not expecting to find it. Clay suspected she was not so sure that Bones wanted her, and was whistling in the dark, prepared to confront him for the sake of Jones's money. Clay was in much the same position himself.

"You're sure about this place we're going?"

"Mama told me about it when Papa was on the owlhoot trail with Lodi and a bunch of others. She used it to pass letters along to him from time to time, just letting him know she was still alive and wanting the same message back from him. He even did that a time or two. Johnson, it was always Johnson, the way the letters were signed, like a code."

Clay had heard of such practices, letter drops that sometimes were a safe house, sometimes a hole in a special tree: the silent telegraph, the subterranean post office of the men and women who rode outlawry's dark horse.

They finished the flask and prepared to sleep in their seats. The lamp above them was turned down low, and the rocking of the car was soothing. Clay tipped his hat over his eyes and wondered what kind of reception such an unlikely couple would find in Carbondale.

Leo told her of the golden elk's speedy progress toward creation, but he did so in a voice curiously flat, as if the news was scarcely worth conveying. Lovey Doll had noticed something else about Leo of late—besides his coarsening tastes in acts of love—and that was a reluctance on his part to use her name. It had required several weeks for her to become aware of this new development in their relations, but once she did so, the frequency with which he avoided calling her by name became obvious. He sometimes would stop partway through a sentence and begin again, and it was clear that the re-forming of his thoughts was prompted by a conscious desire to hold a conversation, however brief, without allowing the name Imogen past his lips. What had caused this inexplicable reluctance, and why had he become so brutal when they came together in nakedness? Her allowance for dresses and so forth continued to be paid, but Leo looked at her with eyes gone cold: fish eyes, Lovey Doll called them, but only in her thoughts. To Leo's face she was sweetness itself, although this time-honored tactic seemed also to misfire. Whenever she smiled at him, Leo would smile in return, but with a twist to his mouth that made her think of sour lemons. What was wrong with the man?

"I think perhaps you love me less," she said to him, her face and tone forlorn.

"You do?" he asked, the question deadened by lethargy.

"I most certainly do, my darling, because you so seldom use my name anymore. Does it pain you, shaping your lips to my name? Have I done you some careless wrong? You avoid my eye and address the walls when we talk, and that isn't often anymore, my sweet. I ask you, what have I done to deserve such callousness?"

"What have you done?" echoed Leo. "My dearest one, what have you not done, is the question."

"I don't understand you. What do you mean, Leo?"

"Nothing," he said, turning his face from her in the same infuriatingly dismissive way she had begun to notice.

"Leo, you're hiding something from me."

"I'm doing no such thing, my precious darling."

"Is it the news of that fellow escaping from Leadville?"

"Not even who we thought he was," said Leo, his laugh brief and hoarse, "and the scoundrel got away anyhow. I ask you, what hope is there in this world for justice to prevail when a second-rate robber like this Bones fellow can walk free from custody without effort?"

Rowland Price had informed Leo that the breakout was effected by a one-armed woman and a girl with a blue birthmark on her face. Why, Leo had asked, would Zoe do such a thing? It was a puzzlement and a mystery, and it gave him no peace of mind, especially when his false mistress insisted on conducting herself like someone cruelly used, instead of the whore she was. He would confront her with her crimes when he felt the moment was appropriate; until then he would use her body as she had elected to use his wealth and fame—with a heart free of guilt and a soul without remorse. But he could not speak aloud the name she had given him, the name that was not true.

"It should never have happened, Leo. You should take steps to ensure that the people responsible are punished."

"Do you believe in punishment for wrongdoing, my buttercup?"

"Oh, yes, most certainly I do."

"And I am in agreement. The trick, though, is to inflict the punishment when the guilty party least expects it. There is nothing so shocking as surprise."

"How will you do this?"

"I haven't yet made up my mind. What is that object in your parlor, might I ask?"

"The cabinet designed for use as a coffin by the Sleeping Savage, my dear."

"Ah, yes, to be sure it is. Why do you have it here?"

"I truly cannot answer. The owner left it with me. I have heard the venture was not a success. I suppose he wished to thank me for my suggestion to you that his disgusting Indian be mentioned in your newspaper, Leo."

"How sad to see someone's plans go astray."

"Sad indeed."

"The thing is airtight?"

"So I have been told, to preserve the body of the object from corruption."

"Fascinating."

"Shall I refresh your cognac, Leo?"

"You may, and why not have one yourself."

"I'm afraid strong drink does not agree with me, dearest."

"A pity."

She handed him a brimming glass. He tossed it down and swiveled his eyes to rest upon her, those cold fish eyes she lately had begun to notice more and more.

"That's a lovey ... a lovely dress you have on."

"I believe peach is a color that becomes me."

"Take it off."

Clay anticipated trouble. Whoever it was in Carbondale that took responsibility for the Johnson messages would think twice before accepting him. He had no proof he was an outlaw; Clay's sole credential was his being beside a woman who had slept with one, and even this woman was under suspicion regarding the Cortez incident. Both of them were fools for Mr. Jones's money. It couldn't possibly work. If their bluff was called and they were killed, it was no more than could be expected for their having dared to enter a den of thieves.

Fay did most of the talking, asking at every saloon if she could leave a message for Mr. Johnson. Every barman told her he knew of no Mr. Johnson, and she was asked for her name and the name of the tall man who accompanied her.

"Fay Torrey, and this is Mr. Zeebub."

"Zeebub?"

"B. L. Zeebub," said Clay. "You tell Mr. Johnson that B. L. Zeebub wants him bad."

Some of the barmen laughed, but others did not; Clay's face encouraged no levity. "Fay Torrey and B. L. Zeebub, yes, ma'am, yessir, I'll tell anyone called Johnson that comes in you're looking for him."

"Do that," said Clay, and they went on to the next saloon.

By evening, every likely place in Carbondale had been seeded with the universal alias, Johnson. They ate a meal and paraded up and down the main street several times, aware of the glances their unusual appearance together created. No one approached them, and as darkness came, they were faced with the obligation to provide a night's shelter for themselves. Two days spent together on train and stagecoaches had not served to make the pair more intimate; Clay had asked no questions concerning Fay's past, and she was equally closemouthed. Sharing a hotel room was unthinkable, so they paid for two, and said good night.

Lying on his bed, Clay was inclined to think the Carbondale lead had been too much of a long shot. Fay's mother may well have sent letters here for the Johnson grapevine while her husband rode with Arch Powell, but that had been years before; everything could be different now, and even if it was not, their clumsy dropping of the Johnson name everywhere in town betrayed an unfamiliarity with the system, which doubtless would work against them. Chances were they both had been spied on for most of the day, but would not be approached unless bona fide credentials of true Johnsonship could be produced. It had been a poorly conceived plan, poorly executed.

He dozed for a while, but was awakened by the sounds of conversation heard through the wall. The room next to his was Fay's, but no matter how hard he pressed his ear against the wallpaper, Clay couldn't understand a single word that was said. He could distinguish Fay's voice, but that of the man she spoke with was less distinct.

Clay pondered his options; should he simply wait to see what happened, which might result in a second interview being held with him when Fay's was done with; or should he walk into the next room and see what was going on? Waiting was probably the more prudent option, but Clay was feeling reckless.

When she heard the knock at her door, Fay had assumed it would be Dugan; instead, she confronted John Bones, and stepped aside to let him come in.

Drew looked around. "Your friend's in the next room, they tell me."

"And he stays there," said Fay.

Drew went to the window and raised a hand to someone in the street below, then turned back to her. "I'll bet you've got a piece of explaining just busting to get out of your mouth."

"It wasn't me."

"Lodi thinks it was. I had the same opinion myself when I saw those torches coming for us."

"It wasn't me. They were watching you for a long time."

"And you just so happened to visit and leave before they made their move."

"Yes."

"How do you know they were watching?"

"Because they arrested me before I got on the stage, that's why. There were badges everywhere. They kept me there for two days."

"But you didn't tell them a thing."

"When I heard everyone got away except Lodi, I told them my mother worked for him, and I was visiting her, that's all. I said I had an argument with her and left."

"And they believed you."

"I don't know. I was put on a train with a marshal and taken away. That's when I met Zeebub. He walked right up and hit that marshal so hard over the head he just fell down on the floor. He might even have killed him, I don't know."

"And he swept you up and put you on a waiting horse and away you went."

"He had two horses. The train was stopped at a water tower just outside of Alamosa."

"And you were so grateful you brought him along with you to the place your mama told you about."

"What's wrong with that?"

Drew sat down and shook his head. "He's a federal man, or else a Pinkerton, one or the other. The whole thing was set up to get you free so you'd lead them to me."

"He isn't a law, I can tell."

"Oh, you can, can you?"

"Yes, I can."

"Why does he call himself that stupid name?"

"I suppose he has a sense of humor. He keeps it buried deep, though."

"Fay, you shouldn't have brought him here. You shouldn't have come here yourself."

"I go where I choose to go."

"Lodi won't believe any of this."

"Is he coming here?"

"Your friend Zeebub tell you to ask that?"

"No, but he wants to work with him. I haven't done anything wrong. I didn't sell out Lodi or you. God, Bones, why would I set the laws on my own mother!"

"Maybe you and Ellen don't get along so good, or maybe you figured they'd let her alone, seeing as she's nothing but a shirt washer."

"You're a fool if you believe that."

"And you're a bigger fool if you think I believe you."

"I asked you to come away with me. I asked you to choose, didn't I?"

"That you did."

"And why the hell do you think I did that?"

"I couldn't say, offhand."

"If you were standing closer, I'd slap you."

Drew stood up and came to her. Fay slapped him.

"Care to again?" Drew invited, and Fay obliged.

Drew grabbed her and attempted to plant a kiss on her lips, but Fay fought him off. That was when Clay stepped into the room without bothering to knock. Drew flung himself away from Fay and pulled a pistol from beneath his jacket.

"Put that down, boy," Clay told him. To Fay he said, "You all right?"

"Yes ... Bones, put it down."

"When I feel like it," said Drew. "Mister, sit yourself in that chair."

Clay went to the chair and sat. Bones was a good-looking young man, and he could see why Fay wanted him, and had been prepared to do something dangerous that might bring herself closer to him. Clay wasn't afraid of the gun in Bones's hand. Clay could tell when a man was willing to use a gun, and when he wasn't. Bones simply wanted the upper hand while they discussed matters that needed discussing. Clay would play along on his own terms. He felt calm, ready to lie without sprouting a single drop of sweat. He was being paid to seize a girl, not this nervous outlaw.

"B. L. Zeebub," he said, "and I guess you'd be Bones. Put that gun up, I'm not armed."

"When I'm ready. What's your line of business, *Zeebub?*"

"I do what I can, for the best money available, that's what I do. I'd appreciate it, Bones, if you could see fit to let Lodi size me up, kind of a thank you for delivering your ladylove here."

Fay snorted. "I'm not that," she said.

"Any problem you lovebirds have, I'm plain not interested. Lodi's the man I want to see. You set that up for me, Bones, and I'll be your friend."

"I'm not setting up a goddamn thing, mister."

Drew was not sure what to make of Zeebub. The man was ugly and scarred, and had named himself in acknowledgment of his appearance; he looked like one of Satan's lieutenants on earth, eyes filled with the pain of his duty there; a demon who consigned souls to hotter places than Colorado and maybe shed a steaming tear as he did so. Drew put his gun away. Zeebub intrigued him. If they became friends, Zeebub might take Drew's side in whatever show-down was looming between himself and Nate Haggin.

"Maybe I've heard of you by another name," he suggested.

"Might have," said Clay, "might not have."

"He helped me, that's all you need to know," Fay said.

"It's not all Lodi needs to know."

"Be happy to talk with the man," said Clay. "You let me know when, Bones."

He got up from the chair, went to the door and let himself out with no further word. Drew and Fay were left staring at the door, then turned warily toward each other.

"So I'm supposed to believe everything," Drew said.

"Believe what you want, only get out."

"You came all this way, and now you want me to get out."

"That's right, get out if you can't behave like a man and not a pig."

"Don't start calling me names."

"I wouldn't even want to talk to you."

"Remember us, up on the Rim?"

"No; did something happen worth remembering?"

Drew picked up his hat and went to the door. His hand was already turning the handle when Fay said, "I remember."

Clay had to listen to them through the wall for half the night. He had seldom felt lonelier.

By midmorning Drew had horses for them both, and led them away from Carbondale. They followed a narrow trail to the west for almost an hour before Drew stopped and produced two bandannas from his saddlebag. "From here on in you need to wear these; that's the rule."

It seemed a reasonable request to Clay, and he tied one across his eyes without protest. Fay was less inclined to cooperate. "Why do *I* have to," she said, and her tone suggested to Clay that, having slept with their guide the night before, she felt she should be counted among the trustworthy. He had to smile.

"Put it on," said Drew, "or we don't go any further."

A moment later, he said, "All right, just let your reins go loose and your horses will follow mine. Keep your heads down."

Clay appreciated the advice within minutes, when his hat was almost swept from his head by a low aspen bough already denuded of foliage by the crisp nights and breezy days of October. They continued on for what Clay estimated to be another thirty or forty minutes, before being told they could remove the bandannas.

The mountain meadow they were entering was less than three hundred yards across, an oasis of grass surrounded by uninterrupted thickets of pine. At the far side stood a log barn and corral and a cabin. A woman stood in the doorway, watching them approach, and Clay could see, even though she stood in shadow, that she had only one arm.

They dismounted in front of the cabin and tied their horses to the hitching rail. "They're friends," Drew said to the woman, then added with a grin, "That is, I hope they are."

The one-armed woman was staring at Clay, a look of consternation on her face. He attempted a smile to lessen his intimidating ugliness, and said, "Afternoon to you, ma'am," in his friendliest voice, but the woman barely nodded in reply, and kept staring.

Omie was playing among the trees, which grew around the cabin so thickly she had to walk only a little way to imagine herself lost in a vast forest filled with terrifying creatures and Indians. She amused herself by sending fallen pine cones bowling along the heavily needled ground, and when she tired of that sport she picked up nearly a dozen and set them spinning about her head like tiny planets in orbit around herself, until that, too, began to bore her, and she let them tumble to the ground.

What she really needed was larger playthings, so Omie concentrated with her inner eye on a tree nearby, and commanded it to lean over and fall down. The tree stirred not at all, and she resented its stillness. Her anger was a sudden heat inside her skull, like a fire-warmed blade slicing her brain in two, and the tree she had chosen as its target shivered perceptibly for several seconds. Now her head hurt. Omie accepted that the tree was simply too big to obey her, but she reasoned that her hidden eye might very well be like a muscle, which must be exercised often to develop its strength. The pain in her head was easing now. If she did the same thing again tomorrow, it might be accomplished with less of a headache, and if she practiced using her eye for such tricks, as other girls practiced at their pianos and violins, she fully expected that someday a tree could be brought down at her command, as if it had been struck by lightning.

Omie decided she was hungry, and set her eye to locating the cabin. It did this by seeking out the mind of Zoe, and when she felt its colors at the edge of her inner vision, Omie turned her body to face them. She was able to do this with subtlety nowadays, with barely any infringement upon her mother's brain. Her first panic-stricken attempts to locate Zoe after she wandered too far from the cabin had resulted in her finding her way home by following the direction of the scream her probing had caused. She had found Zoe on the ground by the corral, and been unable to revive her for fully ten minutes. Now she was able to perform the same task without Zoe even knowing Omie was searching for her colors.

But this time something different occurred. When she sought out her mother, Omie received a picture in reply; it came unbidden into her mind from Zoe, and Omie sensed immediately it was not a thing that Zoe was thinking of, but rather a thing she was at that very moment seeing, and the thing was a tall man with a broad hat and holes in his face. Zoe's fear of the man, whom Omie had several times described to her, both before and after their truncated ocean voyage, came to her along with the picture, and Omie felt her stomach begin to knot. The tall man had come for her, the figure that had chased her and been chased by her through the darkened corridors of Elk House, and waltzed with her on the tilting deck of a ship at sea, and more lately taken her with him on a strange journey through a desert; this man was here now, in the flesh, driving his awfulness into Zoe like a spear, and the spear went straight through her and through the trees to Omie, who felt it enter her heart and brain simultaneously and cleave her open like a butchered hog.

The one-armed woman was still staring at him. Clay knew Bones and Fay had noticed now, but he could think of nothing to do but stare back at her, the smile dropping slowly from his face as he watched blood drain from the woman's. Suddenly she threw her hand up to clutch at her head, and gasped as if struck hard in the belly. Her eyes rolled upward inside her head, and she fell in the doorway before anyone could move to prevent it.

"Mrs. Brannan? Ma'am ...?"

Drew knelt beside her and lifted Zoe's head.

"What happened?" asked Fay. "Oh, God, what's that ...?"

Clay turned in the direction Fay was looking, and saw a girl approaching from the trees across the clearing, running faster than he thought anyone possibly could, her dress flapping behind her. And then he saw the reason for her speed—her feet did not touch the ground, but were dragged behind her through the very tops of the grass; and he saw also that her face was familiar to him, the half-blue face of his guardian angel. Then Clay knew he must be dying; why else would she be rushing toward him so, her hair streaming behind her head like a galloping horse's tail, and he accepted the coming of death, just as he had accepted everything that came his way since his time in the desert. He wondered, as his knees began giving way beneath him, why he could not breath anymore, and why his skull was awash with flame, and why the face of his guardian angel was twisted with hatred of him and fear for the fallen woman; and he understood, before consciousness was whisked from him like a rug from beneath his unsteady boots, that the angel believed he had killed her mother. Clay's final thought, as he plunged into darkness, was that everything happening at that moment was a colossal mistake, an unfortunate configuration of stars, their unkind alignment set in motion long before the time of his birth, to herald the time of his dying.

50

Fay still was not sure, hours afterward, what had occurred. First the one-armed woman had collapsed, then the girl had come flying from the trees, and Dugan had collapsed also at the sight of her, and when the girl reached them she, too, fell in a heap, but not before Fay herself felt a pain within her head like no other she had ever experienced, and Bones had fallen against the hitching rail to vomit.

They all had recovered within a short while, but Fay, the least affected, was aware of feeling like some kind of outsider. Even Bones ignored her, and spent his time with the others. All three adults and the girl seemed unable to get enough of feasting their eyes on one another, but it was the Brannan females and Dugan who appeared most entwined. They held long conversations interrupted by longer silences, during which they simply stared at each other, while Bones hovered nearby. Fay wanted him to pay her more attention, but he apparently had become very attached to the Brannans following their rescue of him from Leadville. She, on the other hand, was still a suspect in the Cortez debacle, and would probably remain so until Lodi arrived to pronounce her innocent, if he chose to. It was irritating all the same, to see a man who had used her body less than twenty-four hours earlier concerning himself with others of less intimate acquaintance The scene in the cabin that evening reminded Fay of some awkward family gathering, a clan reunited after many years, a roomful of strangers who knew little or nothing about each other, yet were bound by blood.

Omie disturbed her the most. The blue birthmark stood out like a splash of ink against her white face. The girl spoke little after waking up outside the door, and could not keep her eyes off Dugan. Fay couldn't see why; he was no uglier than the girl. Strange things happened as the afternoon wore on and became evening; small articles inside the cabin moved about of their own accord, trembling and jumping in a nervous fashion that made them appear alive; a coffee can flung itself against the wall; Bones's pistol drew itself from his holster and leapt onto the table, where it spun in circles before coming to rest with its barrel pointing at Dugan, who seemed not in the least worried. A sampler on the wall flew across the room and its frame broke against the timbers; when Fay picked it up she read: THERE'S NO PLACE LIKE HOME. Sudden gusts of cool air swept across the cabin, but no window or door was open; the stove chimney pipe bent itself before her eyes, then straightened out again; Omie Brannan's hair unbraided itself without the assistance of human hands, and floated around her head like seaweed beneath the waves.

Fay could follow only a small portion of the elliptical conversations that erupted sporadically around her, and was frightened by the inexplicable occurrences taking place before her eyes. She beckoned Bones outside and said, "I don't like this place. Something's evil here...."

"No it isn't. It's Omie, she just does things that don't make sense. She doesn't mean any harm by it."

"But her and her mother, they keep saying things to Zeebub, like they knew him before, but they *didn't*...."

"I know; I heard some of it. I don't know what they're talking about, myself, but there's nothing evil in it."

"I want to go back to town."

"You came here looking for me, and this is where I live. You and Zeebub can stay here till Lodi gets back, or else you can damn well move on. I'll put the blindfold on you again and take you away and turn you loose where you'd never find your way back here. I'll do that if you want, but listen, I don't believe Zeebub would go with you. He's not scared of anything, that man, I can tell. So you tell me what you want to do."

"You don't care for me at all, do you?"

"That's not so. I just don't like the way you expect everything to happen exactly how and when you want it to. When I took you back to Cortez in the wagon, you wanted me to go with you then and there, no other way would suit you, and so I didn't go. Now you want something else, because you're scared of a little girl with a funny face and strange ways."

"You still think I sold you out down there."

"I don't know what to think."

"But you'll have me, meantime."

"I don't recall forcing myself on you."

Drew waited for a slap, but none came. He didn't want Fay to go away, nor did he want her to complain about the situation she found herself in. The dramatic meeting that afternoon between Zeebub and the Brannans had left Drew in mind of a play by Shakespeare he had watched while in Denver, after posing for an artist, a play in which the stage had been littered with dead bodies when the final curtain fell. He did not understand why it had happened, that cataclysmic coming together of Fay's alleged rescuer and his own, but he was not afraid of it, wanted in fact to question them all closely, so he might be made privy to the unusual circumstances existing among them. He had caught snatches of talk passing between them, but none of it made sense to him, and he was mildly resentful of the fact that Zeebub had somehow inserted himself between the Brannans and himself.

Drew had been getting along fine with Omie and her mother before Fay showed up with her friend, and he was not sure why it was that he now felt everything was different; a corner had been turned, but he did not know why, or in what direction. Zeebub was more than he seemed, but Drew could not tell what that hidden part of him might be; nor could he tell what consequences there might be in it for himself, but he did not doubt that change of some kind was heading his way, a significant overturning of everything he knew and could understand. He was waiting for it to arrive, as he waited for Lodi, but the changes that would come from the people already inside the cabin would make Lodi's return a minor event by comparison; Drew knew that much, although he could not have explained why.

"Walk me over there," Fay said, pointing to the trees beyond the clearing.

"All right," Drew said, knowing the kind of reassurance she

required. He took her hand and led her away from the cabin. Drew asked himself if he was using her, and could not decide; he would ask himself the same question afterward, with a mind less clouded by desire.

Clay could no more take his eyes off Omie than she could look anywhere but at him. He had attempted several times to raise the topic of his visions and dreams down through the years, but was afraid to appear foolish in front of Fay Torrey and Bones. With both of them gone, he began again to try and comprehend what it was that linked him to this girl with the blue face. Omie herself had been unresponsive, in the manner of a confused child, when he broached any mention of himself and her, so this time he asked the mother outright. "Ma'am, I've met your daughter before, but only in my thoughts, if you see what I mean, never in the flesh, as they say. Ma'am, I don't know what it means. Do you understand what I'm saying to you, Mrs. Brannan?"

"I do, and then again, Mr. Zeebub, I do not. Omie has said several times that she was pursued by, or found herself in close proximity to, an entity she referred to as 'the tall man.' His description matches your own, Mr. Zeebub. I do not presume to know why this should be."

Clay wanted to tell the woman, even the girl—who was much too young to hear, let alone understand, the things aching to spill from his lips—about his experiences: not only those relating to the appearance in his dreams of Omie, but the way in which she had assisted him in his search for the killer and maimer of the southwest territories known as Slade to the nation but known by Clay to be Wixson, the seeker after the soul, whom Clay believed to be Morgan Kindred, adoptive parent of his own lost brother, Drew Dugan. Clay wanted to discuss all this, but could not; it was too personal, too closely associated with Clay Dugan, and for the sake of Mr. Jones of Denver's money, he was, to all intents and purposes, B. L. Zeebub, whose job it was to bring mother and daughter, but especially daughter, to Mr. Jones, for whatever reason that frail old man saw fit. So Clay Dugan held his tongue, even if it hurt him to do so.

Even Omie was not without constraint. For most of the afternoon, and well into the evening, her head reverberated with the echo of her terror when first she'd seen the tall man who came to visit, and she could do nothing but cause pots and pans to clatter, and turn over and over in her thoughts the incredibility of seeing the tall man before her, an actual man of flesh and blood, with holes in his face, just as he had been in her dreams down through the years.

Then, with the arrival of evening, and the disappearance of Bones and the new lady, Omie became calm and cogent. She looked inside the tall man's head and saw there a desert, on the far side of which lay his true identity. His name was not Mr. Zeebub, which Omie knew already that nobody believed, but she could not see the real name either, so far away was it. Mr. Zeebub was a liar, but he was not a bad man, that much was clear to her, and he was fascinated by herself, Omie saw that also, so she was not inclined to confront him with his silly name, and perhaps put a pain inside his head, until such time as he saw fit to speak the truth and let them all know who he really was. Omie was prepared to wait. She was afraid still, yet every bit as interested in Zeebub as he appeared to be in her. She was a part of him, and he a part of Omie, for reasons neither of them could grasp.

"Are you ... a robber, Mr. Zeebub?"

"Ma'am, I've turned my hand to many things, and have no legitimate profession that I'd choose to share with a lady like yourself."

"I'm a fugitive from the law also, and cannot sit in judgment. I ask about your past not from any moral presumption, Mr. Zeebub, but to find out, if I can, why it is that you and Omie are linked in so unusual a manner. There seems to be more at work here than coincidence, I do believe."

"Ma'am, I do myself, but I can't give you any answers."

"Then it may be that we must simply wait for them to be revealed in due time, as dictated by ... shall we call it fate, Mr. Zeebub?"

"Good as any other name, ma'am."

He looked at Omie, who had not taken her eyes from him for more than a few seconds in the past several hours. "Can you tell us, little lady?"

Omie did not shake her head, or nod, or blink an eye.

"Guess not," said Clay, disappointed, but at the same time relieved. He didn't trust Omie not to blurt out something that would send Jones's promised money scattering in the winds of whatever revelation came rushing from her mouth. Clay had to keep reminding himself about that money, or else allow his thoughts to be consumed by curiosity over the girl, which would lead nowhere. She could destroy him with a word, he was sure. Omie silent was a sight better than Omie talkative. The girl's eyes were deep as mountain lakes, and just as dangerous. Clay felt himself balanced on epiphany's cusp, fearful of tumbling down into familiar darkness.

"Ma'am, why was it you got Bones out of jail?"

"I thought he was Lodi. Fortunately he's able to contact Lodi through some means or other. I expect he'll be here soon."

"And what was the nature of your wanting to meet Lodi, ma'am, if it's not outside of my business?"

"I want him to perform a robbery for me, Mr. Zeebub."

"Train robbery?"

"He seems to excel at such things, by all accounts."

"That he does, but I was wondering, ma'am, seeing as you're Mrs. Brannan, and Mr. Brannan's got plenty of what it takes, just why you'd need to be robbing a train."

"I'm no longer his wife, but in any case, robbery for profit's sake is not my intention."

"Oh," said Clay, and when Zoe said nothing more, he asked, "Well, what *is* your intention, ma'am?"

"That is for Lodi to learn. Bones says you wish to join up with his partners, and if you do, I'm sure the details will be shared with you."

"Yes, ma'am. Didn't mean to pry."

"No offense has been taken, I assure you. A man such as yourself, Mr. Zeebub, who has frequented my daughter's dreams, could never pry. I feel ... I almost feel that you have been a part of our lives for so long already. Do you have similar feelings at all?"

"Ma'am, I do, and I just don't know what to make of it."

Drew came back to the cabin first, and Fay slipped inside shortly after. Zoe went to her and suggested they begin preparing a meal from the ample supplies on hand, and Fay nodded without a word. Drew gave Clay the nod to come outside, and Clay did so. Drew led him to a nearby creek and pulled a jug from it. They passed it back and forth in the increasingly chilly gloom beneath the pines, then ventured out into the open again, to watch the sky and the softly glowing cabin windows.

"See that shooting star?" Drew asked.

"Missed it."

"They're good luck."

"Well, that's the story of my life."

Drew laughed. "Maybe your life's about to change when Lodi gets back."

"What's this robbery she wants him to do?"

Drew hesitated, then went ahead and told him.

Clay said, "We'll need to see a few more shooting stars to bring that off."

"Could be Lodi'll say no. He sticks his neck out to get what he wants, but never so far it'll get chopped."

"He'll need an extra man for it, is my bet."

"Most likely. Zeebub, I don't know why exactly, but I trust you, so listen. One of the boys coming back with Lodi is called Nate Haggin, and he's a low dog. He left me on foot down Cortez way when we were jumped, just rode on by when he could just as easy have picked me up. I'm going to have to call him out over it sometime or other, and I'd appreciate it if you'd back me up, if it comes to that. Nate's got Lodi behind him, I'll tell you that right now. Those two go way back, rode with Arch Powell when Powell was big news up in Montana."

"I know."

"I guess Fay told you about her old man being with the same bunch, and her ma being with Lodi now, or at least until Cortez. I expect he shucked her off fast after that."

"You don't take women along in this line of work."

"Tell that to Mrs. Brannan."

"You tell her."

The jug went back and forth several more times before Drew asked, "Zeebub, what the hell was all that when we rode up today?"

"Can't explain it," said Clay.

"I know Omie's a strange one. Why, she can make things move without laying a finger on them, and she can see inside your head, Zeebub, she really can."

"My head?"

"Anyone's head. It's a gift, her ma says."

"I got a gift like that, I'd wrap it up and send it back."

Drew laughed easily. Clay could tell Bones liked him, and although he found it flattering, never having been truly liked by anyone before, he saw Bones as too trusting, too openhearted to be an outlaw. He expected that any kind of a fight between Bones and Nate Haggin would result in Bones's death. It was generally that way with good men; they didn't have the meanness to kill when they needed to. He felt a paternal sense of concern growing in him, a sensation Clay had not experienced since the early years of his son's life.

The cabin door opened, and Fay stood silhouetted against the light. Clay felt a twinge of jealousy, knowing how completely she belonged to Bones.

"Are you men out there doing nothing?" she called.

"No," Drew called back. "We're drinking!"

"Well, quit right now and come eat."

She slammed the door.

"That's a harsh woman sometimes, Zeebub, but I like her."

"Do you trust her?"

"That's a horse of a different color, as they say."

They set the jug down, handy for later, and went inside.

Omie would not eat, but sat looking at Clay. Zoe could do nothing with her, and so stopped trying.

"What's wrong with your girl, Mrs. Brannan?" asked Fay.

"Oh, nothing new. Set your mind free of it, Miss Torrey, Omie will only baffle you as she does me."

The men made suitable comments of appreciation over the meal, even if it was, in truth, not especially tasty, and retired outside to their jug again as speedily as they could.

"Let them get their blanket set up," said Drew. "It hangs across the room and gives them privacy. I always go outside anyway when Mrs. Brannan wants to get undressed behind it, just to keep her happy."

"That's not a happy woman, Bones."

"Not till Lodi gets back, she isn't."

"How about Omie? Is she happy? Can you tell, with all her strangeness?"

"I'd call her happy, sure, till you came along, that is. I never did see her before like she is now. You've spooked her, Zeebub."

Clay wanted to discuss with Bones the mysterious dreams he and Omie had shared for so long, but could not. Even the jug would never crack his jaw to that extent. Bones, however, seemed eager to talk, and Clay assumed it was the company of females that made him want to spend time with another man. Bones talked of his boyhood in Galveston, living next door to a whorehouse, and his brief stint with the army. Clay was startled to learn how Bones lost his finger at the behest of Panther Stalking and Kills With a Smile.

"The hell you say! Why, I intended hunting those two down one time for the glory of it."

"You never would've caught them, Zeebub, but they would've caught you sniffing around and had your balls in your mouth before you could blink. They were crazy in the head, those two, but they weren't always that way."

"You knew them before?"

"I surely did, that's why they spared me."

He told Clay about the mission at San Bartolomeo, and the events there that took him eventually to Galveston.

"That's the wildest story I ever heard. Is all of this true, Bones?"

"True as my name's John Bones. Wait up there; it's truer than that. My real name's Dugan, but it got changed when I got adopted back when I was small; not changed to Bones—hell no. I picked that for myself at San Bartolomeo and kind of stuck with it, like it was a good luck charm, I guess. Care to tell me your real name? It sure as hell isn't Zeebub, now is it. Zeebub, are you all right? Hey, Zeebub."

"What's your first name?" Clay asked, his voice flat.

"Andrew. They called me Drew, though. Listen, don't tell Fay I'm not called Bones. I just know she'd be mad at me over it, you know how women always want you to share every little thing."

"What's the name of the folks that adopted you?"

"What for? I never called myself by their name after they died."

"The name," said Clay, his voice almost a groan.

"Kindred. Morgan and Sylvie. That was back in Illinois."

"This Kindred, was he dark-haired, with religion?"

"He had God so deep inside him he walked funny. Religion's what took us down to where Smart Crow found me. She died there, Sylvie did, and Kindred too."

"You saw him die?"

"Well, the last time I laid eyes on him he was walking around the wagon and spouting from the Bible like a crazy man. How'd you guess he had religion?"

"Pass me that jug, Drew boy, and let me tell you more about yourself, even further back than Illinois. The Kindreds got you off the orphan train, didn't they, and you got on that train back in Albany, just down the road from Schenectady, you and Zoe and me."

"You? You were on that train? You're joshing me ..."

"I was there ..."

"What's your name, goddamn it, Zeebub? Maybe I can recall ..."

"Did I change that much? Don't you know me, Drew? Must be the way my face is nowadays, the scars and all...."

"Clay ...?"

"The same."

It was the noise outside that made Fay open the door. Dugan and Bones were rolling together beneath the trees nearby, fighting, it seemed. She knew it must have been Dugan who started it, not Bones.

"What are they doing?" asked Zoe, hearing the commotion now that the door was open.

"Fighting. Can you make him stop, Dugan ... Zeebub, I mean? He's the one started it I bet. He'll listen to you."

Zoe thought Fay was addressing her when the name Dugan was uttered, and wondered how she knew her maiden name. She went outside with Fay beside her.

"I don't think they're fighting.... They're laughing!"

"Oh, they're blind drunk, the both of them."

"Best leave them alone. Men will be men."

"Boys, more like it."

They returned to the cabin. Omie had fallen asleep behind the blanket an hour before, still not herself, still silent. Zoe sat and looked at Fay. "How did you know my name was Dugan?" she asked.

"I didn't say it was. Your name's Brannan."

"But it used to be Dugan. What made you say it, Miss Torrey?"

"I didn't."

"Excuse me, Fay, but I'm sure I heard you. May I call you Fay? It seems silly to keep on being so formal, the situation here being what it is...."

"I didn't say it. I didn't say anything."

Zoe could tell Fay's denials would only become more adamant if she persisted. Fay's lie was obvious, yet Zoe could not understand why it was necessary. She tried to recall the context in which that one word had stood out so, and after a moment's concentration, realized Fay had been referring to B. L. Zeebub.

"So his name is Dugan," said Zoe, "the same as mine once was. I don't see why you felt you needed to hide it from me, Fay. I knew his name couldn't possibly be as foolish as he'd have us believe."

"I didn't say it was Dugan! I didn't!"

"Very well. I seem to have upset you, and I apologize."

"I just didn't say it, that's all. I'm not upset."

"No. Well, I believe I'll ask those drunken men to share the joke with us women. Would you care to know what it is that makes them act like schoolboys?"

"No."

Zoe stood up and went to the door, aware at every step that Fay's eyes were following her. The sense of relief she felt when the door closed behind her was like stepping into cool shade after the heat of the noonday sun. She did not know why Fay should have taken a dislike to her so abruptly, nor why she should insist on holding to her lie. Perhaps B. L. Zeebub was drunk enough to enlighten her. The men had separated, and were lying with their backs against a tree, catching their breath. She could smell the liquor on them as she approached.

"Mr. Zeebub, I wish to have a word with you if I may."

"Ma'am?"

"Mr. Zeebub, is your name Dugan, by any chance? I ask only because that happens to have been my maiden name."

Both men stared at her, then at each other. Zoe became irritated by the dumbfounded expressions on their faces, a look so broadly incredulous she could detect it by moonlight.

"Well, Mr. Zeebub? May I expect a reply before sunup?"

"No ...," said Clay, his voice like a sigh.

"No?"

"No, I mean ..."

"Zoe?" asked Drew. "Zoe?"

"Are you Zoe?" Clay asked also.

"Certainly. I didn't tell you so?" she asked Drew.

"No, no ... you didn't."

"Zoe Dugan ..." Clay sighed.

Zoe was startled to see tears dribbling down his ugly face. Liquor was disgusting stuff if it made grown men behave in so ridiculous a fashion.

"And yours?" she asked, a little testily now. "Is it Dugan or is it not?"

"Zoe ... it's me, Clay."

"Clay?"

"And me, Zoe ... I'm Drew," said her brother.

"What are you saying ...? You both are quite shamefully drunk ..."

"Zoe, it's *us!* It's really *us*...."

"No. Stop this!"

Clay attempted to rise, and fell over his long legs. Zoe stepped back from him. Drew sat with a smile of serendipity on his handsome face, a smile directed at Zoe, who felt as if she had somehow blundered into an asylum populated by cruel but prescient madmen.

"It's us, Zoe, truly ... Mr. Pigeontoes and Mr. Duckfeet!"

The ludicrous names from so many yesterdays ago hit her hard. The drunken men at her feet were declaring themselves to be her brothers, her wonderful brothers of long ago, but they could not be, could not possibly be Clayton and Drew, never, not these two with their jug and their whiskey smell and slurred beseechment in their voices.

"She doesn't believe it," said Drew.

"I don't blame her," said Clay. "It's not possible ... you and me ... then us and her. It couldn't happen, not this way...."

"But it did, Zoe, it did happen!" Drew was on his feet, surprising himself with the sudden lurch up from the ground. He wavered for a moment, then straightened himself and said, "Zoe, it's truly me, and he's Clay. Look at us! Remember the train? You were the first one to go, back there in ..."

"Indiana ...," said Zoe, belief coming to her now in small ripples of acceptance. "But how can this have happened ...?"

Drew shrugged, and pulled so exaggeratedly comical a face he made Clay laugh, and Zoe found herself laughing also, a nervous, skittering laugh that tripped glancingly across the improbabilities, the sheer impossibilities standing between the likelihood of such a reunion, at this time and place. All three had been utterly ignorant of one another, and then, in a trice, were laughing and crying and believing, accepting the bumptious miracle wrought, it seemed, by whiskey's loquacious tendency and whatever etheric stirrings the finger of fortune had contributed. It was them. They were hers, part of her missing flesh and blood returned to her. She felt her head might explode, and realized the thing swelling her from within like a balloon was joy, simple and unstoppable, eager to be let free.

She took several steps toward her brothers, and Drew put his arms around her thin shoulders. Clay found his feet and lunged at them with opened arms, so tall he swept them both up and held them tight. Zoe was ashamed of the mewling sound coming from her throat, but could not make it quit. The men lost to her were brought back. Brothers and sister, they stood together, their bodies held closer than the embrace of any husband or wife or lover, and they continued standing so until their heads leaned even closer, and they inhaled the breath of their other selves and wept.

51

For two days they talked, holding back nothing of themselves. Clay told for the first time of his experiences hunting down the killer mistakenly known as Slade in the desert, and of Omie's unwitting help in keeping him alive; Omie herself had no memory of it, and remained silent throughout most of the three-way exposition filling the cabin. Drew was stunned to learn that Kindred had not only survived but gone on to search for the human soul, first with a foolish machine, then with a hatchet.

Zoe confessed to having murdered a man who attempted to rape her on the trail across Missouri, and wished she had done the same to the man who gave her Omie. "Don't feel so bad," Clay told her. "I burned down his barn." She admitted also to having married Leo Brannan while being unsure if Bryce Aspinall still lived. "He's dead now, though," she added, and showed them the tattered newspaper clipping sent by her anonymous friend in Glory Hole. "I believe it was Leo who arranged it. He sent someone to kill us both in Durango."

"Does he know a fellow by the name of Jones in Denver?" Clay asked.

"I have no idea who his acquaintances are."

Clay apologized to Zoe before stating that he and Fay had been hired to steal Omie away from her, using Fay's line of contact with

Drew. Zoe said, "Leo has not expressed any interest in Omie for a long time, since she isn't his by blood. No, this man Jones must want her for other reasons."

"Well, he won't get her," said Drew, "and he won't get you either, not with Clay and me standing in between."

Delving into the finer details of their biographies, Clay learned that Drew had been among the visitors to the cabin in Wyoming where the Bentine brothers hid from the law and met their deaths at the hands of Lodi's outfit.

"God Almighty," said Clay. "We were within talking distance of each other when I snuck down to look through the window there."

Everyone laughed over the fact that Drew had attempted to take Zoe's ring during the Buena Vista holdup, and been prevented from doing so by Omie, who was called "my little watchdog" by Zoe for her defense against Leo's hired killer in a dress.

Feeling somewhat left out by so much revelation, Fay stated again that she had not betrayed Lodi, and had only joined forces with Clay under the direction of the mysterious Mr. Jones because she wanted to see Drew again. "I just can't get used to not calling you Bones anymore."

They discussed over and over the simple things that had separated them, and the complex things that had drawn them together again, and when the intertwining of their lives was fully comprehended, the Dugans were faced with deciding if it had been the workings of destiny, or sheer coincidence that effected the reunion; if just one small incident in any one of their lives had been different, the chances of their coming together as they had would have been impossible. It was the biggest question of them all, and the most imponderable.

"It happened the way it happened," said Clay at last, on the afternoon of the second day, "and we ought to be thankful it did, that's all."

"So now we have to ask—what next?"

Zoe understood Drew's comment; should they stay where they were and await the coming of Lodi, or should they leave and begin again, as a family, in some other place far from Colorado. She had told them of the money sequestered in a safe place, almost a million dollars, more than enough to support them for life, and yet she wished to stay and administer further vengeance on Leo, for his betrayal of her and his attempts at murder by proxy.

"He has not suffered an appropriate loss," she said, "and I intend that he should. I don't expect assistance from anyone, if they don't wish to play a part in what I have planned. That will be Lodi's job, if he accepts it."

"We're in it too," Drew assured her, but Clay was silent. He was being asked, despite Zoe's assertion to the contrary, to participate in a train robbery. He had spent all his adult life in furtherance and loose application of the law, and punishment for those who broke it. He did not imagine he was himself a perfect man, a moral exemplar above reproach, but he had never broken the law. Now his newly restored sister expected it of him, by way of a family obligation to redress the wrongs that had been perpetrated upon her. It was Zoe's fight, Zoe's cause, but he could not shrug off his own responsibility for a choice. Choosing right over wrong was implicit in his view of the world. Leo Brannan was a despicable man, and a robbery committed at his expense was probably no grievous ethical transgression, if posited within the larger picture, but the dilemma confronting him caused Clay several minutes of moral anguish. Law versus family: it was as simple as that. They were all waiting for his answer, but he could not give it, not yet.

"Think I'll take a stroll before sundown," he said, and went outside to be alone.

The pines were moving softly in a cool breeze, the whisper of their needles calming. Clay walked among them, debating with himself the course of action or inaction he should pursue, but no resolution came to mind that was not swept away again by powerful arguments opposing it. He attempted to solve the impasse by standing still, but that gave him no deliverance at all, and so he walked on, weighing his options—there were only two, as distinct as black and white—and asking himself for guidance, since he did not believe in seeking it from God.

Racked by his own weakness, still unable to decide, Clay sat on a fallen tree, its trunk turned to rock-hard grayness, and placed his long chin in his hands. Zoe was his sister, and had been wronged. Brannan was no friend of Clay's, a multimillionaire whose wealth was based on Omie's gift of second sight. He did not truly deserve what Zoe wished to take away from him, and it was not as though she wanted everything he owned, just one thing, the very symbol of his pride and his decadence. But Zoe's way was against the book of law, and Brannan's property was made sacrosanct within that same ponderous volume, not a single page of which Clay had actually studied. He sat in disconsolate thought, reaching for the courage to choose.

He became aware of Omie's presence through a discreet tugging at the left side of his brain. She stood a short distance away, her blotched face partially hidden by shadows and foliage. Clay smiled at her. They had not talked, face-to-face, since she had knocked him down with her waves of invisible rage two days before.

"Come on over and keep me company," he called, and she moved shyly closer, until they were separated by only a few yards. Clay felt she was still afraid of and confused by him, just as he had been of her.

"I will never hurt you," he said. "Those times when we saw each other before, in the dreams, that was another kind of seeing, and we didn't know then what we both know now. I'm your uncle, and I'm your friend. Drew's your uncle and your friend too, but just between you and me, I think we've got something special, because we knew each other a long time ago, at least to look at. So that's the way it is, and you don't need to be afraid anymore, not of me, because I'm blood of your blood, and there isn't a closer tie."

"Mama said so," agreed Omie.

"And she's right, the way mamas should be."

"You can't make up your mind," Omie said, "can you?"

"No, I can't. Do you know what it is I can't make up my mind about? Can you see it inside me?"

"Whether to rob a train for Mama or not."

"That's it. Any advice?"

"You don't need to."

"Don't need to what?"

"Decide. I saw you there already."

"Saw me where?"

"On the train, robbing it. Drew's there too, and the humming-bird."

"What hummingbird?"

"The one that's there."

Clay waited a moment to organize his question, then asked, "Have you seen the robbery that hasn't happened yet?"

"I just told you," said Omie, a hint of vexation creeping into her voice.

"Me and Drew and a hummingbird."

"Yes."

"No one else? You can't rob a train with just two men."

"That's all I saw."

"So I don't need to make up my mind about being there, because you've already seen that I will be."

Omie nodded. The dead pine needles around her boots were swirling slowly, like iron filings drawn by magnets into spiking arcs that crawled as if alive. Clay felt the hairs on his neck rise, and hid his consternation behind a crooked smile.

"It doesn't mean anything," said Omie, and he understood from her thoughts that she was referring to the parade of needles around her ankles. "It just happens."

"Yes, it just happens Sometimes I think everything just ... happens, only sometimes it looks like it was meant to happen, and maybe it is. You say I'll be there on the train, and I haven't even decided to be there, so maybe it'll happen because it was meant to, like everything else. Or maybe not. I don't understand any of it, do you?"

"No."

"But I'll be there anyway."

"Yes."

Clay laughed softly. The horns of this dilemma had grown around and joined, forming a circle, trapping him inside. "Maybe we should go back to the others," he said, and they did so, hand in hand, with a cold wind blowing around them.

Fay was left out. She knew the Dugans all were attempting to include her in their conversations, but what was there for her to contribute? Her own life had nothing to do with their lives; even her affection for Drew was the merest conjunction of lines on a page, crossing each other for an instant as they aimed themselves in different directions. This time, here at the cabin, was probably the centerpiece of those crossed lines, and even then she could not have him to herself, had barely spoken to or touched him since the first evening. Fay had once worked as a waitress at a fashionable restaurant in Saint Louis, and remembered the vague sense of dislocation encountered each time she approached a table of friends who were eagerly talking, one with another, her presence beside them barely noticed, an adjunct to the scene, not a part of it.

She listened now as she had listened then, and felt Drew taken from her by the voices of his kin. She supposed she loved him, but was worldly enough to know such feelings might change if he was forever at her side, whispering sugar talk into her ear. The further he was taken from her, the more she wanted his return, his eyes on her, his body beside her own again. But he was smitten by the past, by the springing to life of shadows left behind; he could not get enough of Clay and Zoe and his peculiar niece, spent every moment with one or another or all of them, and spared no part of himself for Fay. She began to mope, but he did not notice this either, and for a while Fay became angry, then she began sinking into a genuine sadness.

There had been a number of men who passed through her life and her bed without leaving much of an impression on either, but Drew was different. He was decent, without being the fool many decent men were, and he was not rough and uncaring when they held each other naked; in short, he met the minimum requirements for love. Fay had never allowed herself to love before, and now that she had found a man worth opening her heart for, he was swept away on tides of fantastic circumstance, of joyous reunion and the brighter light of rekindled family involvement. Fay had never shared anything of herself with her mother, and her father had been absent more often than not. She envied Drew his rediscovery, even as she became more jealous of the man and woman and girl who monopolized his days and nights with their remembrances and plans. She should not have felt that way, she knew, but could not stop herself.

For Omie, everything had changed. The sudden introduction into her life of two uncles, each very different from the other, was so disconcerting she did not know what to think, how to feel. It was clear Mama was made happy by what had happened, but Omie had grown used to being Zoe's only protector, was proud of her role, and saw it whisked away almost from the moment Clay and Drew revealed themselves for who they were. It was their job now to make sure no harm came to Mama, and that left Omie with nothing inside her but a forlorn kind of gladness over the smile creasing her mother's face with unaccustomed regularity. She felt abandoned, without fully comprehending why, and so she upset small things around the cabin to remind everyone she was still there, still a force in Zoe's life to be reckoned with.

She had liked Drew very much before learning he was her uncle, back when he was still Doogle, the man she had taken away from jail, but his true identity had distanced them, and Omie turned her awesome attentions to the other uncle, the one she had always called the tall man. Where Drew was handsome, Clay was fascinatingly ugly, the ragged scars on his cheeks where the holes had healed over a thing she caught herself staring at often, and Clay often caught her staring, but never by a word or a look let her know he thought her rude for inspecting his ugliness. Looking inside him, she saw a man of great and constant sorrows, a darkly flickering flame of a man, not so dreadful to look upon as his fleshly self. The hidden Clay was more to Omie's liking, and she decided he was her favorite after all, especially since the new lady who had come with Clay had eyes that followed Drew everywhere. Omie could have beaten her off if she chose, but was magnanimous in relinquishing Drew to Fay; she had the more interesting man after all.

Dogging his steps to the fallen tree had been a good idea. He talked to her and shared a little of his inner self, speaking of things inside him Omie already knew of. She had done her best to help him by sharing her own thoughts, the ones that came to her from time-yet-to-be, and he seemed to appreciate her comfort. She had, as she told him, seen Clay there on the train that would be robbed, and Drew also, and a hummingbird for which she had no explanation. What she did not tell Clay was that she had seen herself there too.

On the third day, Omie pointed to the east and said, "They're coming." An hour or so later, Lodi and Nate entered the clearing and rode across to the cabin. Confronted by strangers and the woman he thought responsible for his being chased away from the Cortez hideout, Lodi said nothing as he dismounted. He simply beckoned to Drew, who followed him to the corral. Nate unsaddled the horses while Lodi walked Drew further away.

"Where's Levon?" Drew asked.

"Stayed in Carbondale to visit with his uncle a few days. Bones, I know you've got a reason for having all these people here, and I'm curious to hear it."

"The lady with one arm and her girl are the ones who got me out of the Leadville jail."

"I heard about that. Who's the one with the face like death?"

"My brother."

"Never knew you had one. Is he someone we can use?"

"Ask him that."

"What's that bitch doing here, Bones?"

"She's not the one who sold you out. It was the land agent you bought that place from. You should've used a different alias."

"Land agent? Says who?"

"A man called Jones, some big wheel in Denver. He told Fay when he hired her along with Clay—that's my brother."

"Hired them for what?"

"To kidnap Omie—that's my niece."

"Your niece?"

"The one-armed lady's my sister," said Drew, unable to keep from smiling.

"Say what now? Your sister sprung you from jail, then your brother's hired by someone to kidnap his own niece? Bones, you don't expect me to swallow this down, do you?"

"It's true, and you can quit calling me Bones. My name's Dugan. My sister's married name, by the way, is Mrs. Leo Brannan."

"Keep talking, Bones."

Drew told him everything, and had to repeat part of it when Nate joined them. At the end, Nate said, "You're a fool if you think that whore wasn't the one sold us out."

"She wasn't, and that's the last time you call her that."

"She's a whore, and you're a fool."

"And you're a man that won't pick up a partner when his horse is down. The next time you do anything like that I'll kill you, even if I have to back-shoot you to do it."

Lodi watched Nate to see if Drew's charge was true, and saw that it was.

"You two boys better kiss and make up quick. I don't want enemies in my bunch, you hear?"

"Just remember what I said," Drew told Nate, then walked away.

"Get rid of him," Nate said, "and all the rest. What's he mean, bringing so many strangers here?"

"You heard him; they're family."

Lodi started toward the cabin. Nate followed him, then stopped when he felt pressure of some kind forcing him back. It was like walking into invisible molasses. He became scared, thinking he was losing control of his body, then saw the girl with the half-blue face staring at him, and knew somehow that she was causing his paralysis. The one-armed woman saw it too, and said something to the girl, who turned away. Nate was able to move again, but did not do so for several seconds, trying to figure out what had happened. The girl had done it because she didn't like him, but he could not understand how it was that he knew this.

Nate had had a bad feeling the moment he and Lodi rode into the clearing, and everything Bones, or Dugan, had told them made him feel worse. It was a crazy story and he didn't believe half of it. The girl with the birthmark was against him, as Drew was, and Nate didn't like the looks of the other Dugan, the one with the scarred cheeks. Nate didn't like having the wife of the west's richest man there either, and he still believed Fay Torrey had sold them out. He didn't like females in general, and these two in particular. There was not one thing to make him feel good. Nate had not even felt enough like his usual self to call Drew out over his strong words in front of Lodi. Today was a bad day.

Fay asked Lodi where her mother was, and he told her Ellen had left the outfit and gone to Butte, Montana, under a new name. "We gave her a fair cut from the job up there," he said, "so don't worry about her.

The saga of the Dugans was related again, in more detail, and Lodi still hesitated to give it credence. He was intrigued by Zoe Brannan's plan, but especially distrustful of the elder Dugan.

"I've heard your name before," he said to Clay.

"Could be," said Clay.

"I don't recall which side of the trail I heard it on."

Lodi wanted to know if Clay rode the lawful side, or the lawless. The man looked like an outlaw, but that meant nothing; Drew Dugan, when he smiled, looked like an overgrown choirboy.

Clay said, "I've been a marshal and a sheriff and a bounty hunter in my time."

"That's a truthful answer, but maybe not a wise one. Am I expected to believe you've turned bad, Dugan?"

"I haven't turned anything. It's all been explained to you. I'm here by accident, so to say."

"You won't leave the same way," said Nate.

Clay looked at him. "I'll leave when I choose to."

"I'm not letting no bounty man walk away from here."

"I believe you'll do what your boss says." To Lodi he said, "If I go, we all go, and we'll do what we have to on our own. If you want a part of the job, say so now, but keep your dog on a shorter leash or I'll kick his tail."

Nate's gun was in his hand, then spiraling across the room. He stared at his fingers, baffled; how could he have fumbled a draw so badly?

"Better teach him about guns too," Clay said.

"Everyone just simmer down," said Lodi. He took out his pipe and began stuffing the bowl. "I want to hear more about the train."

Nate retrieved his Colt. The girl with the mark was watching him again, this time with a tiny smirk on her lips. Nate didn't like the other females, but this one scared him.

Leo pored over the reports arriving daily from Pittsburgh. The elk was cast; the elk was cooling; the elk was stripped of its mold; the elk was flawless, an outstanding success despite having been created in record time. The nation's newspapers were talking of nothing else. The elk soon would be ready for shipment across half a continent, under armed guard all the way to Glory Hole and on up to the stone pedestal nearing completion outside Elk House.

He received almost as much pleasure from sharing the reports with Lovey Doll, who cooed and purred over them as if the sheets of paper in her hands were bank notes. Leo encouraged her to believe that the day of the elk's arrival was to be special in another, more personal way; that would be the day, he hinted, that a ring of engagement would be placed on her finger.

"But tonight," he said, "we'll indulge in something different, my dear."

"Yes, Leo?"

"Remove your clothing and join me by the crystal coffin, if you please.

"Cabinet, Leo, not coffin. You have such morbid thoughts."

"To be sure. Hurry now."

When she was undressed, Leo opened the glass lid and instructed Lovey Doll to climb inside.

"Leo, no ...!"

"Do it for your love of me, darling."

"Oh, very well."

She climbed inside and lay down on the velvet cloth, resting her head on the velvet pillow. She felt her scalp crawl at the thought of the dead Indian having lain where she lay. Leo's face appeared upside down above her own, frightening her; he seemed to have a mouth in the middle of his forehead, eyes beside his nostrils and a balding beard.

"You look so very lovely there," he said, "so deeply in repose."

"Well, I'm not. This is silly, Leo."

"No, no, it was made for you. How charming your white flesh would look under glass. One moment."

He closed the lid, and Lovey Doll became very cross.

"Leo, stop this silliness immediately! Let me out!"

Her voice was tiny, a voice from far away. The cabinet was indeed airtight. He raised the lid. "Don't worry, my pumpkin. I wouldn't leave you where I couldn't touch you."

He lowered his head and began passing his lips along her thighs. "Such wonderfully soft skin you have ... "

Lovey Doll watched the ceiling and waited for Leo's instruction to get down from the cabinet. When it came, in the breathless voice he produced when aroused, she did as he instructed, and while allow-ing him his pleasure, Lovey Doll thought about the golden elk and the golden ring that would arrive on the same day.

He couldn't stand to be in the cabin, so Nate moved out to the stable. He accepted food, but would not eat inside at the table with the rest. Lodi told him to stop behaving like a man afraid, but Nate would not change. "I don't like them, any of them, especially the girl. She ... does things she oughtn't to do ... "

"I've seen it. She's got a little chunk of Satan inside her, all right, but she's only a kid. Keep on the right side of her and you don't need to worry."

"She watches me! Every time I turn around, there she is, just watching. She don't do that to anyone else."

She didn't do it to Lodi, and Levon, when he arrived, was fasci-nated by Omie's talents. The girl was a trickster, some kind of changeling or elf. Growing up in Wisconsin, Lodi had heard tales of such beings from the Norwegians, without ever believing them, but the girl was definitely not a human being in the same sense as reg-ular folk. He was glad Omie had picked Nate to dislike and not himself.

Zoe Brannan's plan was the thing to consider, and a poorly orga-nized thing it was. She had not progressed beyond the basic notion, and mistaken that for an actual plan, but there was none, only a willingness to make her husband look like a fool, and that was why she had come to him, to let him work out some way of achieving it. Nate said, "I ain't going back in there while she's inside, nor them others."

"That's up to you."

"That Dugan, the tall one—I don't trust him."

"He's in it for his sister."

"Maybe she's not his sister and she ain't Brannan's wife either. I don't believe any of it, and Bones is in with them on this. It's a move to get us trapped somehow. They don't even look like each other."

"You never really believed he had a name like Bones, did you? Sure he's a Dugan, and chances are the others are too. Why would the bounty man tell us to our faces that's what he was, if he's not here to rob Brannan? Nobody takes chances like that. They're here for the reason they say they're here, and you better decide if you're in this game, or out."

"I reckon I haven't decided," said Nate, disappointed to find Lodi so easily fooled by the newcomers.

Lodi went with Levon back to Carbondale and arranged with Levon's uncle for the fast dispatch of any news relating to the train that was rumored to be leaving Pittsburgh soon. Levon stayed in town to act as messenger, should any hard facts be learned. Lodi wanted the timetable that would apply once the train reached the Rockies and began passing through the valleys up toward Glory Hole. He was already familiar with much of the Denver and Rio Grande track layouts in the region, having studied them for the Brannan Mining payroll robbery.

Zoe Brannan had made the point that her husband would not be expecting Lodi to rob him again so soon after the first job, and he certainly would not expect to be hit in the same place along the line, which was the basis for Zoe's so-called plan. The only good spot along the spur to Glory Hole suitable for such an attack had worked out well, but that had been against a train less well defended than the next one would be, and sacks of paper money were easier to transport across rough country than a gold elk weighing several tons. That was where Zoe's plan fell on its face.

"The trick to pulling this off," he said that night, "is to steal the train. That's the only way to carry something like this. We can't pack it out on muleback."

"There'll be dozens of hired guns aboard," Drew said. "How do we get them all off?"

"There must be something that would make them leave the train," Zoe said.

"They won't back down from bullets or dynamite. That's what they're being paid to face, not that I think they'll be expecting anything. There aren't enough of us to pin them down that way anyhow, even if we got the train to stop."

"Then what can they be made to fear?" Zoe asked.

"A rockslide," said Fay, "something that looked like it would crush the train. They'd all jump off quick if that happened."

"But we can't wreck the train, or we'd have nothing to carry the elk away on," said Drew.

"And assuming we do get away somehow," Lodi said, "what do we do with a thing that big and heavy and recognizable? Every state and territory around Colorado would be telegraphed within the hour, and we'd be stuck on that train with nowhere to go. You can't steal something and call the job a success if you don't get away with the goods. A thing big as that elk is said to be, you'd have to cut it into pieces and smelt it down into ingots for easy transportation. That'd take days we just won't have available to us."

"Are you the best train robber in the business?" Zoe asked him.

"I like to think I am, but part of what makes a successful robber, ma'am, is figuring out in advance exactly what needs to be done with whatever it is you've stolen. Cash is easy—you stash it or spend it. A gold elk, that's different, maybe a hundred times harder to work with."

"But there simply must be a way."

"I don't like to be personal, but if it's revenge you've got in mind, why not just rob Mr. Brannan of another payroll? The man has fat payrolls, one every month. Why not let this elk go by, and tackle something that's easier done?"

"I want that elk. I want nothing else."

"And I'm trying to think how it can be done, but if I can't, then it won't be done, no matter how much you want it. And one thing more—we don't have a lot of time on our side, not if this thing's already made and set for delivery."

Zoe laid her hand firmly on the table. "We must all think harder, that's all."

Omie listened to this and other equally fruitless conversations for two days. She understood that Mama wanted to rob Leo of a statue, a golden elk that soon would be brought across the country by train, surrounded by men with guns so it could not be stolen. Omie empathized with Mama's wish to steal the elk, but could see also that the man called Lodi had many reasonable objections and doubts concerning the robbery. It did sound impossible, given the size and weight of the statue, not to mention all the men with guns. Omie wanted very much to contribute to the planning, but could think of no scheme that might overcome Lodi's logistical barriers.

On the second evening following Lodi's return, Omie went outside to pee, and on her way back to the cabin paused a moment to look at the sky. Sometimes, if she waited long enough, she saw lights among the stars, always in pairs, one red and one green, with a flashing star in between. She had asked Zoe what these might be, and Zoe had suggested—with a wry smile that told Omie not to take her seriously—that the lights were angels watching over the earth, each bearing in one hand a red apple from the garden of Eden, and in the other hand a green apple from the gardens of the moon. Omie knew her mother did not believe any such thing, but it was a wonderful picture to hold in her mind. She sometimes heard the sound of the angels as they passed overhead, a distant whistling and rumbling that always seemed to lag far behind the lights of red and green.

But tonight there were no lights passing across the sky. She stood in the open grass before the cabin for some time before resigning herself to their nonappearance, and wondered, as her thoughts turned to other things, if the golden elk her papa-that-used-to-be was bringing to Colorado was the one that had visited her in a dream a long time ago. She had not recalled the dream until that moment, and assumed it had returned to her memory because everyone inside the cabin was talking about the statue and how to steal it. Mama had often told the story of how Omie saw a herd of golden elk beneath the ground at Glory Hole, and so begun the mining empire both of them had been thrust away from by Leo, but the elk she remembered now was different. It had told her (it seemed perfectly natural to Omie that the elk could speak) that it had been brought by her from beneath the earth, and belonged to her forever. Those had been its words, and Omie pondered them. She knew from what everyone had quoted from the newspapers that Leo's elk was made from gold that came from his own mines, and that might be what the talking elk had meant. So the golden elk belonged to Omie, not to Leo. She went over the details of her memory once again, to be sure she had not misremembered or misinterpreted anything. It seemed quite clear—the statue was hers. That meant she could stop listening to what the grownups were saying and tell them what to do, since it was her own statue they were planning to steal. It had spoken to her a long time ago, but time, in such instances, was without meaning. The golden elk of years before was the golden elk so recently cast in Pittsburgh, and he was Omie's by self-declaration. If she allowed him to, the elk might speak to her again, and let her know how he wanted to be stolen.

Omie closed her eyes and waited for the elk to appear before her secret eye, but he did not. Instead, she became aware of a blackness approaching her from behind, a kind of cloud in the shape of a man, and when she turned she saw Nate Haggin standing a little way off, his face white in the moonlight, and a smell streaming from him that made Omie feel slightly sick. He continued to stare, so Omie did the same.

"I ain't afraid of you," he said.

Omie knew this was a lie, but let it pass.

"You're the devil's child," he said, taking a step or two closer. "I see through you, little girl, I do."

Omie doubted that Nate could see beyond his nose, but again she let his words pass. He was a man of tremendous ugliness, not so much in his flesh as in his other self, the one that extended several feet beyond the body that carried him around. It was a dark and shapeless thing, more or less manlike, but it churned and wavered and re-formed itself into many shapes representing nothing at all that Omie could recognize. By comparison, her uncle Clay, who was indeed a homely man, had a shadow self even taller than his bones and hat combined, and the tallness of him was rendered in strong purples and reds that flashed and throbbed and rearranged themselves constantly, but always in the approximate shape of a man. Uncle Clay had been dark all over when first she peered inside him and around him, but since they both found out he was her uncle, Mama's brother from long ago, his colors had brightened overnight, it seemed.

Uncle Drew was not so tall, and his colors were much more varied, but not so strong. Mama's colors had improved also, following the revelation of not just one brother but two; Zoe was very nearly golden sometimes, when she was near them both. The other lady was insubstantial somehow, but she did brighten when Drew was near, and Omie knew Fay loved him, as well she might, because Uncle Drew was a nice man and very handsome when he smiled. Lodi was an unusual combination of colors and shapes, but none of them extended very far beyond himself. Omie tolerated him, but knew he would play no part in her life, or in the life of anyone else quite soon. But Nate was a shadow all his own, and she despised him for the reek he carried with him everywhere. It was a good thing he slept in the barn, or Omie would have had to make him do so.

"You and the rest," Nate whispered, "you don't belong here. You go on out of here now, all of you, before it's too late, and ... it'll be too late pretty soon now."

He was so far beneath her Omie found it difficult to care what he said. She gave him a nudge, and he stumbled backward several feet, then laughed. "How do you do that?" he asked. "Tell me how you do that, little girl."

He moved forward again, and she saw a picture in his head of Nate and herself doing something Omie could not comprehend, but it was an ugly picture, the two of them being so close, so she pushed him further away still, and he fell over, laughing softly, and she understood that he was drunk, and that was what caused his shadow to be so elusive and threatening. When her uncles had gotten drunk on the first night at the cabin, she had seen them glow like fireflies, but Nate was a bad man through and through, without hope of redemption through color. His heartbeat was small and mean, like a toy drum, and he picked himself up and backed slowly away from her, his drumbeat angry, made irregular by hatred and a partially hidden pulse of fear.

When he was gone, Omie considered the thing called fear. She knew that all people felt it sometime, in large or small doses, and behaved according to their color and shadow self. Fear was always dark; the greater the fear, the deeper the darkness, and the deeper the darkness, the more terrible the shapes that could be placed within it: terrifying shapes, without dimension, beyond description. Omie had never known the shapes to come out from herself, but she was aware of them deep inside her: tiny, squiggling things like demons trapped inside a magic bottle. In men like Nate, the demons were larger, more powerful when stirred to wakefulness, as irresistible as the need to eat, the need to empty one's bowels. The shadow world of fear. She skirted its slowly boiling perimeter, peering inside for answers among the swirling darkness. No golden elk ever sprang from so inhospitable a place.

She looked up once more, searching for the angels with the apples, but the stars were unattended, each one a tiny shard of glass from the shattered ceiling that once had covered all things. Omie shivered. The night was cold; she could smell snow somewhere beyond the horizon.

52

Winter came to the nation before fall had properly taken its leave, and Leo's train was stranded in western Pennsylvania for two days by unseasonable blizzards, then was dug out and began moving again.

Too tall to be placed inside any kind of rolling stock with a roof, the elk had been securely lashed onto a flatcar, at either end of which rode boxcars crammed with Pinkerton guards. The locomotive was manned by an engineer and a fireman, plus two Pinkertons stationed in the cab to ensure that no robbers attempted to stop the train; another two kept the brakeman company in the caboose.

The weather being as it was, volunteers for guard duty in the open cab could not be found, and the man in charge, Boysie Frazier, established a rotating roster of paired names to make sure that no one froze. The railroad men were replaced at approximately two-hundred-mile intervals for the same reason. The railroad companies whose tracks were used as the train passed across the land were sworn to grant the special duty only to their most trusted and experienced men. It had been Boysie Frazier who suggested to his superiors that only railroad men with established families should be submitted for inclusion, since they would be less likely to risk ruination for their loved ones. It was always possible, reasoned

Boysie, that some young and reckless fool might be tempted to cooperate with a bunch of bigger fools who planned to steal the elk
somewhere along its journey.

Boysie didn't actually believe that anyone, professional or amateur, would do any such thing, since an attempt against a body of
men as heavily armed as those under his command could only
result in obliteration by gunfire. He had made the proposal anyway,
since it always impressed the men at the top of the company to
know that one of their operatives was using his head to calculate
the odds for success. Boysie very much wanted to be promoted into
the upper echelon of the Pinkerton ranks, and shrewdly took
advantage of the Brannan elk assignment to thrust himself forward. If the delivery took place without incident, he would almost
certainly be rewarded with his own office and a substantial raise
in pay.

The train progressed slowly toward the midwest, its progress
delayed by storms that covered the rails with up to seven feet of
snow. The guards took turns at sleeping in the crude wooden bunks,
fed the cast-iron stove each car was provided with, and smoked and
talked and gambled to pass the time away. This last activity was
generally forbidden by the company, but Boysie allowed it, because
bored men quickly became disgruntled men, and men in that state
never performed their duties to standard.

The boxcars were filled with smoke and easy laughter and the
smell of gun oil. Boysie traveled often between the two, by way of
the flatcar carrying the elk. Special doorways and windows had
been placed in the ends of the boxcars facing the priceless cargo, the
better to keep an eye on it at all times, and Boysie passed to and fro
through these doors so many times each hour his men began referring to him as "Fresh-air Frazier." Each time he passed by the elk
he checked its hemp and chain moorings to assure himself they
remained secure, and then he would stare at the countryside for
several minutes, whether it was moving past or stationary. Watching him through the end windows, his men joked about Boysie
wanting to be a landscape watercolorist, else why stand out there in
the freezing cold, looking at nothing.

At night, lanterns with directional shades were lit and aimed at
the elk, to obviate any need for checking by hand through the hours
of darkness, but Boysie went outside anyway to stand alongside the
golden creature with its nose raised to the wind, antlers already

soiled by carbon cinders from the smokestack. Boysie had overseen the elk's loading back in Pittsburgh, and when the railyard foreman had been about to have it placed on the flatcar with its rump toward the locomotive and its head toward the caboose, Boysie had objected, and made the steam crane operator lift it up again so the elk could face forward, scenting its destination. Boysie's wife often said he was overly artistic in matters of arrangement, right down to the way table cutlery was placed before him, but Boysie knew he was simply unsatisfied with things being anything less than the way he felt instinctively that they should be. So the elk faced forward, and Boysie went out to keep it company as often as he could, and ignored such comments as he knew were being raised behind his back. He was being careful, that was all.

Sometimes, as he paced the flatcar at night, he pictured how the elk must appear to farmers near the tracks who happened to glance out their windows as the train rolled past. First would come the snorting engine, the blackness of its bulk slicing through a field of white behind the arrow-headed snowblade, and then the illuminated elk, gliding by on its clanging bed of wheels, a fantastic beast from another time, frozen now among mortal men. Boysie was sure that somewhere inside him there lived a poet, but detective work was far more rewarding than setting down words, and he did not regret that the poet must lie curled up and drowsing within him, since the detective was able to affect the real world in ways no poet could.

Levon came out to the cabin despite snow on the trail high as his horse's belly in places, to tell Lodi the train had started out from Pittsburgh. A conference was called to try and formulate the plan that thus far had eluded them.

"A week, that's all we've got," Lodi said, "unless the weather helps us out."

"Bad weather's a problem for us too," Clay said. "What slows the train down slows us down just the same. How far would we get on horseback in the middle of a snowstorm?"

"Weighed down by gold," put in Drew.

"The gold," said Lodi. "Does anyone have even the beginning of an idea on how to lift it off the train and take it away with us? I haven't."

The Dugans looked at each other.

Zoe said, "I have been thinking."

"I'm listening," said Lodi.

"What I have to say will no doubt offend a man such as yourself, whose trade is robbery for profit. The fact is, I now intend that we should make our escape with nothing but ourselves."

"I don't believe I'm catching your drift."

"I mean to say, the purpose of the robbery is to take the elk from my husband, not to retain it for ourselves."

"Not retain it? And do what with it instead?"

Zoe told him, and Lodi laughed out loud.

"It's not funny," Clay said.

"You want to take something like that, a thing made of gold ... and do *that* to it? You Dugans, you're crazy. Pardon me, ma'am, I guess I just don't understand."

"I expected that you would not," said Zoe. "Are you no longer interested in helping me?"

"I generally take chances for profit, ma'am, the old-fashioned kind of stealing. This notion of yours is just ... I guess I'd have to call it childish. It makes no kind of sense to me at all."

"It's a gesture," Zoe said, "and as such, it has great significance."

"To you, maybe, not to me. No, ma'am, if I'd known ahead of time what it was you planned on doing, I never would have bothered trying to figure a way to get the job done."

"But you have said yourself that taking such an object with us is impossible. If we do what I've suggested, our problems are halved. We need only to capture the elk, without worrying how we might make off with it."

"But ma'am, it's ... it's a damn fool thing to do in the first place. No one ever robbed a train just to go and do *that* with the thing that was taken, no one at all."

"Then we will be the first."

"Nothing wrong with being first," said Drew.

"History," said Clay. "It'll make history."

"The world already has a few thousand years' worth of that," Lodi said. "Me, I prefer something I can use."

"Sure would be a story, though," said Levon. "Folks'd sit up and take notice, a thing like that happened in the newspaper."

Lodi shook his head. "Fame generally goes right along with fortune, and it's the second part I like."

"Maybe you need time for getting used to the idea," Clay suggested.

Lodi shook his head. "You people are going to have to go through with this half-robbery on your own. I won't risk my neck, or Nate's or Levon's, on something so wild."

"That's your final word?"

"It is. Just two men against that kind of outfit? They'll gun you down like buffalo."

"Not just two men," said Zoe. "I shall be there, and Miss Torrey has offered her assistance also."

"Is that right. Well, you ladies are both crazy, and I don't apologize for using the word." He looked at Clay and Drew, and said, "Men that would let you go along on something like this are no men at all. And that doesn't mean I changed my mind. Go ahead and kill yourselves if you want."

After this unpromising confrontation, Clay took Drew and Zoe outside to assess their chances of success without Lodi and his men.

"He won't change his mind," said Drew. "I know him well enough to tell you that, flat out. It's us and only us in this now."

"But we still don't have a single thing you could call a plan," Clay said, "and Zoe, I appreciate what you said in there about taking part, but that won't happen. It's Drew and me, and unless we can win Levon over to our side, or find another couple of men someplace, Lodi's right—it can't be done."

"Clay, as my brother, I'll listen to anything and everything you have to say, but as your sister, I can tell you now that you'd better stop fooling yourself. I have my own mind, and I make my own decisions, thank you."

"Then I'm backing out of the whole deal. Drew, did Fay say to you that she'd be willing to come along and hold a gun?"

"She did."

"And you didn't tell her no? What's the matter with you! What's the matter with both of you, and Fay too! This is a train robbery we're planning, not a visit to the store. Nossir, I won't take part if there's women along. I mean no offense by that, but ... hell, if you can't see how stupid it is, I give up. I've got boneheads for family, seems like."

Clay was not prepared for their laughter.

"What?" he said. "What's so damn funny?"

"The thing is," Drew said, "Omie told us we'll all be there, including her."

"Omie? No!"

"You know she sees things ahead of time. You've heard the stories. How can you say it won't happen that way?"

"Zoe, you told me the predictions are sometimes off the mark by a number of years. It doesn't matter what Omie says, a plan has to be made ... consciously, by making decisions, not listening to what a girl says will happen."

Even as he said this, Clay was aware of his own hypocrisy; he had fallen in with the plan to rob Brannan's train without conscious choice, had simply accepted his place among the robbers-to-be after Omie told him he would be there. He should not have done it, but he had, and he could see in the faces of his brother and sister that Omie had shared with them the conversation she had had with Clay. It seemed that Omie was running things without even trying, and that was about as foolish as a situation could get.

Clay frowned at them both and marched away to cool himself among the trees. It was all a mess, a foolish mess, this notion of taking the golden elk. He should have said so from the start, and not gone along with everyone. Lodi was the smart one, backing out the minute he learned what Zoe intended to do once the elk was in her hands. But Clay couldn't do that himself, not now, even if his head was pulling him in another direction from his heart. Family was family, and he had thrown in his lot with Drew and Zoe, come what may. He was a fool to have done it, maybe, but he could not turn away from them. The glow inside himself that had come with the miracle of meeting them both in the same day had given way since then to a sense of obligation, of duty, the kind of thing he had attempted to master when he married Sophie Stunce and gave her a child. It had been a failure then, and he did not want it to be a failure this time. The Dugans would not separate again, ever, even if the thing that held them together was a wildcat scheme with no hope of succeeding.

He began to grow cold, out on his own, surrounded by snow and pines, and so Clay walked toward the cabin again. He was still some distance from it when he met Drew, following Clay's tracks, and when he saw his brother, Drew said, his face shining, "Omie's got it, Clay! She's got the plan, and it's like nothing you ever heard before."

Clay stopped and stared at his brother, and wondered what could be causing the terrible sensation of dread that suddenly emerged within himself.

* * *

From the moment Levon had come to the cabin from Carbondale with news of the train, Omie found it difficult to think of anything else. She pictured it making its way across the frozen fields of the east, then the open plains beyond the Missouri. Levon had said the elk was carried on a railroad flatcar for all the world to see, and Omie saw it skimming along as described, her very own elk of gold.

The trouble was, no one knew how to take the elk away from Leo. Mama had wanted the man called Lodi to take it for her, since he was very good at such things, but he had not liked what Zoe intended doing afterward, and said he wanted no part in the taking. That made everyone sad and irritable, and their feelings swirled around the cabin in jagged waves that made Omie go outside to escape them. Omie was not so sad as the rest, because she had seen that there would indeed be a robbery, with both her uncles taking part, so it was clear that a plan would be found in time. The elk was coming closer every day, but before it reached the high mountain passes of Colorado, the means to take it would surely be known.

The train would have to come along the spur line between Leadville and Glory Hole. Omie remembered that line well, having passed along it with Zoe when they left Elk House to begin their voyage across the ocean, and again when they came back, and a third time when Leo told them both to go away forever. Scenery along the Glory Hole spur was among the most spectacular in the world, and in the same newspaper Levon had brought to the cabin with details of the train's coming, there was an editorial piece, which Zoe read aloud, describing how the golden elk and the public interest in its owner (Omie had scoffed at that description of Leo) would soon draw many people from the east, wealthy travelers who would want to journey along the spur just to gasp at the majesty of its surroundings. Levon had expressed doubt that folks would come all that way just to look at a stretch of country; "They'd have better things to do, most likely."

Recalling the thirty-odd miles of track that twisted and turned and snaked its way higher and higher toward Glory Hole, Omie found herself wanting to think of nothing else, so she stooped and took herself beneath the low boughs of a spruce and went on her knees to its trunk. There was no snow beneath the tree, it hung so low, and she squatted on her heels in the dimness there, breathing the faint odor of sap mixed with the smell of burning wood from the cabin's stovepipe chimney. It was the perfect place in which to close her eyes, the better to concentrate on what she knew was something important.

Now she was an eagle, soaring many miles to the east, and below her wings she saw the Glory Hole spur, a serpentine scrawl meandering among the peaks and valleys, two fine parallel lines. There were no trains below her as Omie flew along the track. She saw in passing that sometimes the rails disappeared beneath banks of snow, but the snow was not deep, certainly nothing that a locomotive could not push aside and trample through with its mighty wheels.

But there was one place where the tracks could not be seen at all, and Omie recalled why that was so: they ran inside a long wooden shed that covered the line completely for almost three miles. Railroad men had built the snow shed to protect the rails from inundation along a section of the line that became blocked by drifts up to twenty feet deep every winter, which hampered the coal trains bringing fuel to the many furnaces of Glory Hole. Leo had insisted they build the three-mile shed, so his mining and smelting operations could continue without interruption all year round.

Omie had enjoyed her trips through the shed: the suddenly intensified rumbling from the wheels; the immediate darkness enfolding the train; the sense of speed intensified by the closeness of the wooden walls outside the car windows. The conductor had gone through the train, telling all the passengers to close their windows before the entrance to the shed was reached, to save them all from the filth and smell of the locomotive smoke and fumes that would sweep back along the train as it passed through. He had not said the fumes were poisonous, but Zoe had told Omie of a freight train that had lingered too long in another high-pass tunnel, elsewhere in the Rockies, and of the engine crew that suffocated in their open cab, overcome by the belching of the thing they tended. That had been a tunnel through rock, Zoe said, and the snow shed was made of wood, with sunlight visible between the slats, but Omie saw that with the shed buried beneath snow as it was, the interior would be darkened as surely as if it ran through solid rock. The three-mile shed would be a dangerous place now, because of the snow piled above and around it, and trains passing through could not pause for any reason, or risk death by suffocation for everyone aboard.

Her wings stiffened and folded, and Omie fell from the sky, plum-

meting back into her body, which promptly fell over. Her legs were
without feeling from having been held beneath her while she flew,
and as the blood returned to them in a prickling rush, Omie heard
her name being called. Mama must have become worried about her
being outside the cabin for so long, and gone outside to look for her.
Omie could not call out to her, so intense was the tingling fire
sweeping along her legs, but she smiled in anticipation of what
Mama would say when Omie crawled from beneath the spruce,
because Omie knew how to rob the train without her uncles having
to fire a single bullet from their guns.

CHAPTER

53

Rowland had brought the pictures to Leo's notice with some expectation of anger, but was surprised at its extent. Leo became outraged as he looked at the half-dozen skilled renderings of himself in gross caricature, mounting a voluptuously overblown Lovey Doll Pines. From his own inked lips came the words: *What a fine piece of flesh you are, Imogen;* and the woman beneath him sighed: *For such a wealthy fellow as you, Leo, I'd be a Lovey Doll.*

The sketches were signed: Rembrandt van Rubens.

"Where did these abominations come from!"

"Everywhere you look. Someone has gone around the town at night, pasting them up wherever there's a wall."

Leo gaped at another rendering of himself and Lovey Doll; this time he wore a crown, and was saying: *A whore, a whore, my kingdom for a whore!* Lovey Doll, her legs splayed like a tree hit by lightning, responded: *I have whinnying ways, and will never say neigh to you, my rich man love, for your lust is unbridled.*

"Find the person responsible, and bring his name to me!"

"Yes, Leo."

Another was examined; Lovey Doll gazed at herself in a mirror while Leo labored behind her, sweat popping from his brow. Lovey Doll said: *Mirror, mirror, in my hand, who's the richest in the land.*

Leo's reply was: *That must be me she's talking about. How lucky I am to own a whore who cares!*

"Don't just stand there!"

"Of course, Leo."

Rowland left, wondering again if he had hitched his wagon to a falling star.

Leo pored over the renderings again; was he really that big in the belly, that bald around the pate? Lovey Doll would pay for this. There was no one else to affix blame upon, so she would carry the burden. She sickened him in any case, with her servile acquiescence to his every whim; she did it for his money, as depicted by the anonymous caricaturist, and Leo was ashamed, humiliated that his private vice had been displayed before the public gaze. No matter how rich he was, no matter how people might smile to his face, he would never live down such biting sarcasm. He was not sure what he would do with the guilty party, when found. It was a shame such a distraction should arise when every fiber of Leo's being was concentrated on the nearing of his golden elk. That was the thing most suited to his thoughts, not the squalid snipings of some hate-filled individual out there armed only with only a pen and ink.

Could this somehow be the work of Zoe, he wondered?

When the Dugans and Fay left Lodi's cabin, few words were passed. Lodi wished them well in their enterprise, and Levon expressed a wish to come along, but without conviction. Nate said not a word, and set the seal on their departure with a stream of tobacco juice from his lips onto the snow.

A line drawn between Carbondale and Glory Hole by crow flight would have measured little more than sixty miles, but on horseback the journey was closer to ninety, and required four days. In Leadville, Drew gathered up every newspaper for bulletins on the progress of the train, and learned that it had been delayed again near the Kansas line by snowdrifts on the tracks too deep to plow through; it was at least three days from its destination, and probably five. There was time enough for the Dugans to visit the site of their ambush and perfect the details of their proposed plan to steal the elk away.

The original trail to Glory Hole that Zoe and Omie had traveled along with the El Dorado Engineers was now little used, all freight and most individuals preferring to travel there in comfort aboard the twice-daily train from Leadville. The Dugans saw no one as they rode along the winding roadway reaching for the mountain passes, and were grateful for the railroad and for the cold that ensured the aloneness essential to their plan, which was, they all agreed, Omie's plan.

When it was proposed to him, Clay was amused, then annoyed at so flagrant a denial of common sense being accepted by Drew and Zoe. "It can't work," he had told them, "because there's no guarantee she can do this thing she wants to. If she can't do it on demand, at exactly the right moment, then it won't work."

"And we'll ride away, sadder but wiser," Zoe said, "and live well on the money Omie and I have hidden in a safe place."

"It's pure foolishness to build your hopes on something so wild and unpredictable as her being able to do what she says, exactly the way she says. I'm against it."

And yet he went with them when they saddled their horses to leave. Omie had said he would be there, and somehow he could not fight against involvement so mandated, no matter how harebrained the scheme that placed him there. His mouth uttered misgivings, but Clay's thoughts were all directed to the atheist's prayer—naked trust and a pair of crossed fingers.

Omie knew the shack would be there, perched on a bluff overlooking the snow shed's western entrance. They assumed, after listening to her description of its appearance and location, that it was some kind of service shack, probably stocked with items necessary to maintenance of the shed itself, and Clay anticipated having to shoot off the lock he presumed would hold its door secure against thieves and unwarranted interlopers. But when they arrived at the place, the Dugans found it occupied by as unlikely a party as themselves.

Lovey Doll blanched as her eyes passed over the sketches. She knew immediately who the artist was. "Rembrandt van Rubens" was the name Nevis Dunnigan had used when he concocted funny drawings for her amusement back in Kansas City. She had not realized it was a joke until some years later, in the library of her San Francisco rich man, who owned an extensive collection of books containing reproductions of the world's finest art. The question facing her now was whether or not to tell Rowland Price.

"Outrageous, aren't they," said Price, but Lovey Doll was aware of the smirk on his lips. "Leo is determined to find the fellow who drew these. Do you have any idea who it might be?"

"No."

"If Leo is unable to find the guilty party, he'll be very angry. On the other hand, anyone assisting him will be rewarded. I might add that Leo is rather surprised that anyone in Glory Hole should know your real name."

"What do you mean?"

"Miss Pines, do you think Leo is such a fool as not to know everything about you. This is your name," he said, pointing to the words spilling from the mouth of the woman beneath Leo Brannan. "Lovey Doll. Please don't waste my time by denying it."

Lovey Doll felt faint. Could Leo's change of nature have been prompted by his discovery? Would he still be inclined to marry her now that he knew who and what she was? She felt tinglings of panic begin to swarm across her skin. If Leo abandoned her, where could she go, what could she possibly do? Nevis had betrayed her with his lewd drawings, turned her expectations upside down.

"Dunnigan," she blurted. "Nevis Dunnigan."

"Ah, the erstwhile promoter of the Sleeping Savage."

"Tell Leo I want him punished," said Lovey Doll.

Rowland's smirk deepened. "I advise you to make no demands at all on Mr. Brannan's tolerance of you; in fact I'll go so far as to warn you that he would consider it a favor if you were to pack up everything you own and depart Glory Hole as quickly as you can. You and your friend Dunnigan have attempted to make a fool of an important man."

"It wasn't me! It was Dunnigan! I won't leave ... "

Rowland placed his hat upon his head and began walking to Lovey Doll's front door. "That is a decision only you can make, Miss Pines, but bear in mind, you are not the owner of this house. You live here on Leo's sufferance. Do think seriously about what I've said, won't you. And by the way, Miss Pines, may I convey to Leo any news of the little one?"

"Little one ...?"

"You informed him some time ago that you were with child. I must say I can see no evidence for such an event. Are you too tightly corseted, Miss Pines, or shall I tell the father that he is not to be any such thing?"

"Get out ... *Get out!*"

When she heard the door close behind him, Lovey Doll fell to the floor and began to spit and scream, rolling back and forth along the carpet, utterly without control of herself. If she could have shot Nevis Dunnigan she would have, but she had no idea where he lived, and in any case, she had given him her only pistol some time ago, in the vain hope that he might become so distrustful of Rowland Price he would kill the man. That had not happened, and now everything was at risk—her marriage to Leo, even her continuation as his mistress; Nevis had destroyed it all. Only when she began literally to choke upon her own rage did Lovey Doll stop herself and lie quietly on the floor, listening to her galloping heart, listening also to the distant shattering of her dreams.

Rowland went to the offices of the agent whose store had been rented by Nevis Dunnigan for display of the Sleeping Savage, and was given the address of the lessee. Rowland explained matters to Sheriff Simms and his deputy, and all three went to Nightsoil Smith's residence, where they found no one at all, only the odoriferous honey cart, with a message chalked on its tank: LEO BRANNAN AND HIS WHORE BELONG IN HERE.

Clay and Drew watched from a ledge above the shack near the entrance to the snow shed. There were three people below, two men and a woman, and all appeared drunk. Their open wagon, with the legend ICE on its side, was nearby.

"They aren't railroad people," Clay said, "or they would've come on a handcar along the tracks, and what's a woman doing with them?"

"To keep them warm?" Drew suggested.

"There goes the bottle again. They're having a high old time. Well, we can't use that place, not with them in it, unless you want to pretend you're a railroad man and go down and tell them to leave."

Drew shook his head. "It wouldn't be smart to let anyone know we're here, even a bunch of drunks. Maybe there's a shack at the other entrance."

It was decided to ride further along the pass to see if such a shack existed. Drew volunteered to do this while Clay went back to explain things to the women. Everyone was cold and in need of shelter. The weather had been kind, without further snow, but temperatures at night were well below freezing. Drew returned after a difficult ride through deep snow, and reported that there was another shack at the far end.

"I saw wheel ruts too," he said. "Those drunks drove their wagon along the railroad tracks from Glory Hole, not along the trail from Leadville. They must've had lamps and come straight on through the shed."

"Bunch of fools. They're lucky a train didn't meet them halfway in."

"The shack's like the one at this end, big enough for all of us, and there's a draw just a few hundred yards from it that's protected from the wind good enough for horses, practically no snow at all in there. We can use it if we want to, Clay."

"Doesn't look like we have any choice. I went and looked at the drunks again, and they've unhitched their team and put them in the shack. They're not going anywhere."

"You don't think they're fixing to do what we're fixing to do?"

"Three drunks, rob a train? They couldn't be so stupid, liquored or not, and one of them's a woman."

"Most of our bunch is female too," Drew pointed out.

"But we've got Omie," said Zoe, "and they don't."

The fact that everything depended on Omie made Clay uneasy. It was a cowardly way to attempt such a thing, he believed, even if the plan would not place her in harm's way, if it came off as intended.

Once across the Colorado line, as the train began climbing the gentle slope that would carry it away from the plains, Boysie Frazier felt his nervous state enter a new kind of excitation. Perhaps it was the air, which grew more rarefied as the elevation of the rails increased, or maybe it was the reduced number of days and hours remaining for bandits, should they wish to attempt a robbery. This was so remote a probability Boysie tended to dismiss it, but he could not help but be aware of his own anxiety.

By the time Denver was reached, near midnight, nine days after the train had left Pittsburgh, Boysie was fidgeting unconsciously, making more outside inspections than before, and causing comment among his men, all of whom were heartily tired of the assignment by then. Boysie promised them all a change of clothing and as much soap and bathwater as they could use, once Glory Hole was reached and their work was done. The weather was fine, although cold, and it was estimated that, barring any sudden avalanches in the mountains, the train should arrive in Glory Hole sometime in the afternoon, the day after next. Boysie had received a clutch of reports from a representative of the Denver Pinkerton office. Telegrams from Pueblo, Salida, Buena Vista and Leadville all confirmed that the tracks were open and passable.

While the tender's fuel and water were replenished, Boysie looked across the darkened marshaling yards and attempted to reassure himself all was well, and would continue in that vein until the job was completed. He admired the way in which the local office had distributed false news that established the train's time of arrival in Denver at a little after dawn the next day, by which time it would in fact be approaching Pueblo. It was a precaution taken to lessen any chance of the train's being mobbed by the curious, and Boysie fully approved of the deception. Subterfuge practiced in the name of the law was a good thing, unlike its outlaw cousins, cunning and deceit.

He strolled around the train, along one side and back down the other. Like everyone else aboard, Boysie was irritated by his own grime and the uncomfortable bunks that had provided too little sleep. The company had considered changing the complete team three times during the trip, then lowered the cost of that plan by deciding to change the team just once, at the midway point, then finally calculated that it was far cheaper to keep just one team aboard the train, from Pittsburgh all the way through to Glory Hole. It would mean considerable hardship for those concerned, but would save the company a lot of money. The job of overseeing what would undoubtedly be a somewhat cantankerous crew by journey's end befell Boysie Frazier, who was known to have qualities of physical endurance few other men possessed. He had been instructed to set an example, and thus far was confident he had done so, despite the trying circumstances of having been delayed, for days sometimes, by the early onset of winter.

But he did wonder about one small yet disturbing thing. During those occasional moments when he was able to sleep, Boysie had experienced a recurring dream. He was not given to dreaming as a rule, and had never dreamed the same dream twice, so far as he could recall, and yet he had seen the girl with the blue face four times now. She had spoken without moving her lips, always the same message: *The tunnel. Don't go in.* He had come awake from each of these baffling visitations, shocked by the accelerated pace of his own heartbeat, the sweat covering his skin and the peculiar tingling of his fingertips. It had been the same each time, but it was not the repetition of the message that upset Boysie so much as the separate inquiries he had received from three other men aboard the train. In every case, the men had asked if there was a tunnel anywhere along the line to Glory Hole. Boysie had assured each man that there was not a single tunnel, no stretch of track that burrowed into rock for even a few yards, and had witnessed the relief in their faces. When asked by him why they wished to know, the men had said they were merely asking for the sake of it. Their replies were unconvincing, their manner shamefaced. How was it that four men (and possibly more) had dreamed identical dreams? Boysie did not dare raise the subject for fear of ridicule and a loss of general confidence in his ability as leader, but he could not forget the message or the messenger.

She still could not reconcile herself to being with the Dugans. If she had been with Drew alone, Fay might have been able to maintain her composure, but surrounded as he was by family, Drew was distant with her, even a little short-tempered. She had thrown in her lot with them for his sake, and she could not see why he chose to be so ungrateful. Nothing about being with the Dugans appealed to Fay, or led her to believe in the success of their plan. A robbery perpetrated by a girl was not something she could truly believe in, and Fay hoped, as they waited together for the train, that Drew at least would see sense and declare himself unable to proceed with so idiotic a scheme. Fay supposed the mere fact that Omie was herself a Dugan, or at least half a Dugan, gave the rest a kind of faith in her abilities, however remote from the business of train robbery Omie's talent might be. Fay was not a Dugan, and feared for them all.

Omie sat by herself in a corner of the shack, on a crate of tie spikes, her eyes closed. She had asked for silence, so she might "talk to the men," and silence had been granted. Drew and Clay played cards with a deck found on a shelf, and Zoe spent much of her time staring out the only window, a tiny yellowed pane facing a snowbank. Fay thought she might scream if no sounds were uttered soon. She wished she had never accepted Jones's offer of freedom from custody of the law if she would cooperate with him and bring Omie Brannan back to Denver, assisted by Clay. Once Clay recognized his siblings, any chance for honoring her agreement with

Jones was gone, replaced by a foolhardy scheme that could not possibly succeed. They occupied the maintenance shack solely on account of a rejected woman's desire for vengeance, and a peculiar young girl's whimsical vanity. Even if everything proceeded as Omie wished, and no one was killed, Fay knew she would still have to share Drew with all of them.

It was to be Nevis's final comment on Leo Brannan and Lovey Doll Pines before leaving Colorado. The golden elk was too great a target to ignore. Once Smith had been persuaded to take part, Winnie went along too. They had everything they owned in the wagon, and something else besides, a creation of Nevis's that had been hidden beneath baggage and a tarpaulin. Smith sold his honey cart to an interested party, and left it behind for the new owner to collect. He had emptied his last shitcan, he said, and so had Nevis, and all three got drunker than they had been for some time.

It was to be a new life for them, somewhere far away from Glory Hole, but before they departed the region for good, one last insult must be hurled at the man and woman who had ruined them. The scheme was conceived in a mood of alcoholic euphoria, and executed without a moment's sobriety to stand in its way. The ice wagon was loaded, and they drove it out of town to a place where the roadway began veering from the railroad tracks, at which point they drove up onto the tracks and proceeded by that route.

Arriving at the Sky Gorge bridge, they discovered that the mules were reluctant to cross. The bridge spanned a deep chasm with a torrent of water rushing far below it. Smith, who understood the nature of his beasts, unhitched them and led them across blindfolded, one at a time. He and Nevis and Winnie were obliged to haul the wagon across themselves, but the bridge had a downward slope to it, and they managed well enough. When the mules had been hitched again, they continued on to the snow shed, lit two lamps and proceeded through at a leisurely pace, drinking all the while. It was not until they reached the far end and pulled the wagon off the tracks that they considered what might have happened had a train come along during their confinement in the shed. The picture of disaster that came to mind, and their casual ignorance of danger until that moment, struck them as hilarious, and they laughed and drank some more, and fell into the snow and threw snowballs while the mules watched.

The shack at the Leadville end of the snow shed was perfect for their needs, and Smith broke the lock with a crowbar, then, in a fit of magnanimity, took the mules inside as well. "They're God's creatures too," he said, burying his face in the nearest mule's neck. The second mule shat on the earth floor. Winnie said she wasn't going to clean it up, so Nevis did. Dumping the dung, he looked across the valley and saw a train steaming along the tracks on the far side. The line formed an enormous loop before entering the snow shed, and everything that would pass through it could be seen at least fifteen minutes before it arrived, on the opposite side of the loop. Nevis watched two locomotives linked in tandem slowly hauling a long string of coal cars behind them. Their steady chuffing came to him clearly, amplified by the valley itself. They would be able to hear every train approaching the snow shed, and look to see if it was the one bearing the golden elk. When it came, there would be plenty of time to arrange things.

The reaching, as Omie called it, was different for every man. Omie knew where they were simply by directing herself toward the elk. She did not know exactly where the train was located at any given time, but could go directly to it by way of its cargo, which belonged to her. She neither understood nor questioned the means by which this was accomplished; day or night, near or far, her golden elk was easily accessible to Omie.

Once aboard the train, she could not feel its vibrations or hear the whistle, or listen to the conversation of the men there, but Omie was able to whisper into the mind of any man who was asleep or in a state of lethargy, and a surprising number were. The words she used were simple and unchanging, and the men sometimes came awake instantly, as if her breath had tickled their ears, and sometimes they slept on, but she knew the message had been planted inside them anyway.

Between western Kansas and the central valleys of Colorado she had visited every man at least once, and thrust herself into the thoughts of their leader many times. Drew had instructed her not to bother with the engine drivers until the last, since these would be changed at regular intervals, whereas the same roster of guards would most likely be maintained throughout the trip. "Pinkertons," he said, "they'll do a job cheap if they can." Omie told Drew the same men were always there, and he said that was good.

The train was closer now, much closer. There was something in the mood of the men aboard that told Omie they were becoming both excited and anxious; the end of their ordeal was near, but they feared a tunnel ahead that was not even there. A kind of jagged fog filled both boxcars at either end of the elk's flatcar, a nervous flux, something unspoken.

Omie had done her work well, taking dozens of catnaps throughout the thirty-two hours the Dugans lived in the shack. Omie hated her blue face, but she fairly strutted when she considered the gift she had and was able to use with such skill. She would make a piece of history without lifting a finger; how many other people could do that. Everyone was depending on her to prepare the men aboard the train for her final onslaught, the thing for which Omie was holding much of herself in reserve.

The bottles were running low. Smith was drinking more than his share, Winnie complained, and when Smith denied it, she began to rant at him, blasting her words directly into his face, until Smith shoved her away. Winnie fell against the mules. She launched herself at Smith, who fended her off easily, laughing. Nevis witnessed their wranglings with a bleary eye; they really should not have been treating each other with such contempt, he thought, especially since he was so very fond of them both, but it was difficult to intervene; he had attempted it several times while they lived together in Glory Hole, and been told to mind his own business. Winnie in particular was adamant that no man should come to her rescue, and Smith, admitted Nevis, saw him as nothing that a strong man such as himself need worry about.

"Stop it ... " he said, but they ignored him, and Nevis was too drunk to be sure he had spoken with sufficient loudness. "Stop it!" he yelled, and the protagonists both looked at him, distracted from the sound of their own voices.

Smith said, "Huh?"

"What ...?" said Winnie.

"You *mustn't* ...," Nevis told them. "We're all *friends.*"

Smith and Winnie began to laugh. Nevis thought they were laughing at him, and when they saw his features begin to crumple, they laughed even louder, but let him know by much waving of the hands that their laughter was for themselves, or for no reason at all. Nevis began laughing also. That was when the whistle across the valley sounded.

"Train ...," said Nevis, and the other two began laughing again. "Train!" he screamed, and picked himself up to yank open the door. He fell into the snow after a few steps, but was able to see the train toiling along the far side of the loop, a short train, just two boxcars and a caboose, but on the flatcar riding midway stood the unmistakable shape of the elk, sunlight burnishing its flanks.

"There ...," breathed Nevis, pointing. "There ... "

He heard Smith and Winnie struggling clumsily through the snow behind him. The whistle sounded again.

"That's the one," said Smith. "See it shine?"

They watched the train, a toy moving of its own volition a mile away, carrying its precious Christmas tree bauble. Nevis was immobilized by its arrival; the train brought with it uncertainty that his plan would work as he wished it to. It seemed, now that the time had come, a silly kind of thing to do, but he had swept up Smith and Winnie by proposing it while drunk with his own belief. Now, seeing the train, he was less sure, and he found himself shaking from more than the snow that had passed into his boots. If he had been alone, Nevis would have hidden behind the shack until the train had followed the loop around to the snow shed, entered it and passed him by; then Nevis would have gone away, and never mentioned to anyone a single word concerning his silly plan. He could still do that, if he chose.

"Better get started," said Smith, and Nevis felt his heart squeeze itself into a knot. It was too late. He was afraid, but could not imagine why. The plan was nothing more than a prank, one last thumbing of the nose at Leo Brannan, a poor man's revenge, pitiful, inadequate, but necessary, or so he had felt when first he thought of it.

Winnie was pulling him up from the snow. "Come *on*...."

Nevis rose and followed his friends to the wagon. The tarpaulin there was stripped away, his creation laid bare.

"Pitiful ...," he whispered, looking at it.

"Not beautiful," said Winnie, misunderstanding, "but it's not supposed to be, is it?"

Smith climbed into the wagon. "Take that end," he said. Nevis took it. "Lift," said Smith, and Nevis lifted.

When Omie's skin became white and her breathing slowed to a series of shallow gasps, no one touched her. She sat in the corner, her eyes wide open, seeing what the other Dugans could not. Even Zoe had never seen her in so intensely physical a trance before, and for a brief moment considered shaking her to bring Omie back from the brink of whichever psychic pit she was approaching. Only Drew's hand on her shoulder prevented it.

Clay was outside the shack, watching the train crawl around the loop that would bring it to the long snow shed and the trap laid inside, an invisible trap no man could anticipate. He was tense, his skin twitching, even if he had to do nothing more dangerous than wait and see if events transpired as Omie had said they would. He did not feel brave; he did not feel at risk of physical harm; he was not girding himself for gunplay or confrontation. Clay admitted to himself, as the train passed from his sight at the loop's far end, that he felt superfluous, a man pretending to be doing a man's work. A girl was doing a man's work that day, and he was aware of not only his noninvolvement but an unsettling shame. He should never have allowed Omie to persuade any of them to be a part of this. It was for Zoe's sake the trap was laid, and for no one else's. Clay wanted it to succeed only because its conclusion would allow them all to go somewhere else and begin again together. The trap inside the snow shed was a settling, an act of reprisal, anything but a conventional robbery. He had to remember that.

54

Lyle Ingalls and Pat Cullen had taken over the locomotive in Pueblo shortly before dawn, having been granted the honor of taking the elk train, as it had come to be known, along the final stages of its journey to Glory Hole. The job was theirs because both men had exemplary records for safety and punctuality, and were model citizens to boot. The Pinkerton agency's criteria had been well met by the Denver and Rio Grande Railroad.

Their mood, as the train began gathering steam on the run west to Canon City and Salida, was one of satisfaction and professional pride. This was their reward for years of diligent service for the company. They had stared at the elk in the predawn light and been awed by its frozen majesty. This was to be the run of their careers, both men were sure. Their wives had already begun treating them differently, and when the elk was delivered safely to Leo Brannan, and Lyle and Pat came home again, their lives would have been changed forever; it was a certainty. Pat shoveled coal into the firebox like a demon fueling the atmosphere of hell, and Lyle squinted into the cone of light the Baldwin 4-6-0's powerful acetylene lamp cast along the track ahead. Nothing could be allowed to go wrong, or their status within the D&RG would be tarnished forever.

Sunlight from the east soon allowed Lyle to switch off the lamp.

The Baldwin's firebox roared hungrily, and the first leg of the trip
was accomplished in perfect time, but soon afterward, somewhere
between Canon City and Salida, both men began experiencing
vague sensations of disquiet. Neither mentioned it to the other,
since no specific thing was the cause, but as the run proceeded
through the morning, they found themselves thinking of tunnels,
deadly tunnels, the kind that had killed men over the years, not
only during their construction, but afterward, when locomotives
were stalled inside them, resulting in asphyxiation of the crew.
These thoughts were irrational, both men concluded, still not having voiced their fears, because the line from Leadville through to
Glory Hole had no such tunnel, just a three-mile snow shed.

No one had ever died in a snow shed that Lyle and Pat had heard
of, but both men began considering the means by which a snow
shed might be compared with a tunnel, and both, by the time Salida
was reached and the train turned north toward Buena Vista, had
reasoned that the one thing that might render a shed as potentially
deadly as a tunnel was the presence of snow all around and above
the timbered structure. Snow was not as dense as rock, but would
that make any real difference if a train became stranded halfway
through such a thing? Lyle and Pat had been through the shed during winter many times, when it was completely covered by snow,
and they knew that those three miles of travel, even if accomplished at a steady speed, generally resulted in a throbbing
headache before sunlight was seen at the far end. Once out in the
open air, such pain as they had was wiped away by deep inhala-
tions of fresh air. No train had ever stalled in the shed. There was
no reason to surmise that one ever would. But they could not stop
thinking that one might.

Boysie Frazier had to spend more time on the flatcar simply to
draw a full breath. The air in both boxcars was ripe with the odor of
unwashed males, but that was not the reason Boysie needed to be
outside; there was something else filling his chest, a sense of dread
so intense it clutched at him like a claw around his heart. And he
was not alone; other men came out onto the flatcar, and made comments on their need to be away from the stale air they had lived in
for too long. Their talk was mild, apologetic almost, but their faces
were drawn with fatigue and some other emotion Boysie could not
decipher, a kind of trepidation that lurked so far beneath the surface of their usual selves they would not acknowledge it, or discuss

it with others. Boysie recognized himself in them all, but was likewise constrained from asking any man what it was that troubled him. Chances were they had simply become bone-weary. It had been a difficult assignment for everyone, despite the lack of actual danger. Before the day was out they would be in Glory Hole, freed from responsibility for Brannan's elk, able to wash themselves clean in oceans of hot water, able to shave again, and dress in fresh clothing. They would eat the best food that town had to offer, and become drunk if they wanted, and sleep the sleep of the just on soft mattresses. It would be heaven. Their nearness to such luxury and indulgence should have rallied the spirits of his men, but all Boysie could see were faces made taut by fear, as was his own.

After Buena Vista was passed, the inner turmoil of the engineers worsened. They still did not speak of it to each other, or to the two miserable-looking Pinkertons sharing their cab. Pat had begun to fill every minute with thoughts of his eleven-year-old daughter, but found he could not hold her steady in his mind; no matter how hard he tried to picture her as she was, one side of her face became darkened by a swirling blueness, like ink poured into clear water. Pat could not erase the least part of it, and came to realize it was not his daughter at all, but some other girl who insisted on crowding aside anything else he might wish to see while he worked, and it was she who made him consider the deadly ways of railroad tunnels, even if her lips were motionless.

For Lyle, the trip had become fraught with inexplicable moments of anxiety. He kept turning his face away from the track his locomotive traveled, expecting to see inside the cab someone other than Pat and the two Pinkertons, but there was no fifth person there, and after he had performed the same check a dozen times, Lyle began wondering if his mind had not somehow become addled, although there had never been any indications of madness in his family. He would have become angry over his own foolish behavior, if only the overwhelming fear of tunnels had receded and allowed him access to any emotion other than the foreboding that held him so tightly in its grip. His fingertips inside their heavy gauntlets were growing numb, and he knew it was not the cold that made them so.

She was out of the shack now, had stepped outside as if in a trance and positioned herself at the end of the snow shed, her feet set firmly between the tracks. No one had stopped her; Omie was a law unto herself, her blank face and rigid walk the very badge of her independence. She stood in the place of maximum danger, and began filling the snow shed with a viscous wave invisible to anyone but herself. Primeval fear, raw and shapeless, poured into the shed, an inky darkness thrust by willpower into the long and narrow receptacle prepared for its storage. Deep snow covering the shed made it impervious, a natural containing element. The waves of fear eddied along it without being dispersed, without losing any part of their strength, eventually filling the shed. In the process, Omie became weak, although her weakening was not of so obvious a nature as to alert Clay or Zoe or Drew, who stood nearby, waiting for what Omie had told them would happen.

As the final curve of the familiar loop ran beneath the wheels of the locomotive, Lyle Ingalls felt a lifting of his spirits, but when the Baldwin faced the entrance to the snow shed, Lyle's hand reached instinctively for the brake lever. Ahead, blocking the entrance to the shed, stood something the like of which he had never seen before. The Baldwin come to a halt, its nose less than ten yards from the object, and the Pinkertons and engineers stared.

Boysie knew no stop was scheduled, and was immediately alarmed. He ordered all guns at the ready, knowing this must be the preamble to an attack. Peering through the rifle slits cut in the boxcar's side, he could see no one near the train, but indistinct voices came to him from the locomotive's cab. Warning his men to remain on alert, Boysie climbed up onto the tender, and saw what it was that had caused the halt. In the entrance to the snow shed stood a mockery of Leo Brannan's elk, its body a rain barrel, its legs taken from a table, the neck a piece of bent pipe, the head a narrow wicker basket, the antlers two broom heads.

Boysie watched the area around the train, anticipating gunshots. Rifle barrels protruded from both boxcars like porcupine quills. Boysie wondered why the barrier was such a flimsy thing, when a stack of railroad ties would have been more difficult to plow aside, then realized he was confronted by intelligence of a high order; the wooden elk was so unexpected, so bizarre, it had done what ties and boulders would not have—caused the engineers to stop the train.

"Keep going!" he yelled. "What the hell did you stop for ...!"

A snowball hit him in the neck. Turning, Boysie saw three figures advancing from behind cover, and barely had time to notice that one was a woman before the first rifle was fired, at which signal every other rifle on that side of the cars began firing. The three figures spun and fell, the larger of the men rising again before being cut down by so many bullets parts of his clothing disintegrated.

No answering fire came from any part of the mountainside near the tracks. Still atop the tender, Boysie asked himself how anyone could be so foolish as to mount a robbery with only three persons, and one of them a female. And not one of them had been carrying a gun. It could not be reconciled with his past experience of criminal mentality, and he did not know what to do next. The four men in the cab were looking at him, their faces blank with shock.

Boysie waved his arms frantically. "Go ahead! Go ahead! Keep going!"

Lyle did not want to go ahead. The comically grotesque wooden elk stood guard over an entrance to some kind of hell, as surely as Saint Peter stood by heaven's gate. Despite its flimsiness, Lyle knew the thing facing his locomotive was a warning not to proceed further. The snow shed was a trap. Disaster lay waiting inside. A creature of darkness lived in the shed, a serpent three miles long, wanting them to enter its square mouth and pass willingly into its belly. Lyle was afraid of the serpent, and dismayed that a woman had been shot down before his eyes, and could not think straight anymore, only express by his inaction a reluctance to do anything but wait for an instruction to throw the train into reverse.

"Go ahead!" screamed Boysie. "What are you waiting for! Go ahead now!"

Boysie's legs were trembling. He had no understanding of the events that had followed the stopping of the train, and was aware of his own reluctance to enter the darkness presided over by the outlandish creature planted on the tracks. He tried to think of a reason why he could legitimately order the engineer to return everyone to Leadville, but no reason came to him. The engineer and the fireman were not moving to obey him, and his own men in the cab were standing as if turned to stone. Boysie aimed his pistol at the driver, and when this was not enough, he thumbed back the hammer. Lyle released the brakes, then eased open the throttle.

The Baldwin edged forward, and its snowblade shoved aside the elk, whose legs broke off instantly. Boysie jumped from the tender down into the cab, and was immediately surrounded by smoke

forced down by the shed's low roof. As the train moved further
inside, darkness gave the oily smoke a sinister thickness. The engineer switched on a carbide lamp that washed the cab in white light,
and ignited the acetylene lamp on the engine's nose. Boysie saw the
tunnel walls ahead slowly moving to engulf the train. Every man
aboard was being swallowed alive. It was a fantastic thought, but
he could not rid himself of it. Heat from the firebox was making
him sweat. He wanted to think about the three fools who had done
what they did. Boysie was unsure now if they had intended anything more threatening than some kind of stupid prank. How would
he explain this to his superiors? It had not been his fault that someone in the first boxcar had opened fire without orders to do so, but
ultimate responsibility for everything would devolve upon his
shoulders, he knew; that was how the company operated.

The man beside Boysie was whimpering. Boysie knew he should
have been shocked at such unmanly behavior, but he was not. All
accepted laws governing reality had been left behind with the sunlight. Replacing them were causeless fears, an intangible sense of
being drawn toward the locus of some dreadful event beyond imagining, a thing that lay in wait up ahead in the darkness beyond the
engine's beam of yellow light. Whatever its nature, it would happen
soon, Boysie was sure. His order to proceed into the tunnel was
what made the thing a certainty. He could have avoided it by deciding on a return to Leadville, but he had chosen the way ahead, and
now must face the event his decision had made every man aboard
the train a part of.

The smoke thickened even more. The engineer and the fireman
had slipped bandannas up across their noses and lowered the goggles from around their caps to shield their eyes. Boysie and his men
had no such protection, and all three began to cough. The smoke
was visible in the carbide lamp's intense light, coiling and streaming around them like phantoms. The engine crew were like masked
demons from some mechanical netherworld, and the sound of the
locomotive, laboring to make up the speed and momentum it had
lost by being stopped on a two-percent grade, was amplified by the
wooden walls sliding by until it became the panting of a great
beast. The air itself was exhaled breath, noxious and repellent. The
train was moving too slowly, crawling to its own extinction in the
gut of the beast. Boysie heard vomiting nearby, and saw one of his
men collapse on the cab floor.

"Go faster!" he called to the engineer. The sooner they were through the snow shed, the sooner they could all breath again. The man at the controls ignored him. Boysie grabbed at Lyle's arm to make him pay attention. The arm was like rock, made rigid by some inner tension Boysie could not shake loose from him. The fireman collapsed suddenly, muscles in his neck jumping like trapped fish.

The train seemed to be slowing down, and there was another sound now, of screaming from the boxcars. Boysie knew there was nothing wrong back there, nothing that could be seen and shot at; it was the same in the engine cab, where an encroaching terror without form or substance was being inhaled along with the greasy smoke, choking reason, swamping the senses with panic. Boysie felt it too, this nameless force, and made himself resist adding his voice to those reaching him. The men were going crazy; he should have been back with them, calming them, assuring them it was a trick of some kind, this mania gripping them all, a result of smoke inhalation. How, he wondered, could railroad men pass through the snow shed on their scheduled runs without experiencing such waves of dread; did their bandannas and goggles make a difference? But the man at the controls was frozen with fear, and his fireman had lost consciousness. Boysie now thought the thing that had attacked the train had been set loose by the three fools who had thrown a snowball at him. They had somehow laid a trap that went into effect even without their presence, maybe a gas of some kind to distract the senses and derange the mind temporarily. Boysie liked the notion, and wanted to tell someone, explain away the disorientation they all felt, but he could not move, and for the first time became aware of his own body's response to the gas; his fingers were locked hard around a handrail, as if he anticipated being swept from the cab by terrible winds. He tried to remove them by willpower, and failed, and knew then that he could do nothing whatever to assist or lead his men through the terror entering their bodies with every breath, growing stronger inside them minute by passing minute as the train continued to crawl forward.

Eyes streaming with tears he could not forestall, his lungs filling with smoke and shame, Boysie set aside a small part of his mind to contemplate the end of his career. He was finished with the Pinkerton agency if he could not deliver the elk and his men to Glory Hole without mishap, and he doubted now that any such thing was possible. He could not be sure how far into the shed the train had come, but it could not have been any more than a mile; another two miles of the same unique assault would result in someone's death. Boysie thought the fireman might already have died, he lay so still on the metal floor.

Gunfire came from the boxcars, the men surrendering to the enclosed space and the miasmic gas and their own confusion. They were shooting at invisible presences. The shouting and screams that followed, and the increased rate of fire, a fusillade of gunshots from within both cars, attested to their wild aim. This was the event Boysie had anticipated once the shed was entered, the disaster that had given him a foretaste of itself as the first coils of smoke licked around the cab. He had denied the feeling, and taken everyone inside to meet with disaster. It was his fault entirely, and he would eat the blame like a man, if he survived.

The gas, he thought, his hands still clenched around the rail, the gas was killing them with their own bullets, and the smoke, if they didn't pull out of there into clean air, would finish them all off with carbon monoxide poisoning. But the train was moving at an even slower pace, the firebox unfed, the engine driver frozen at his controls, unable to build up speed against the grade without additional power.

At last the shooting stopped. Boysie felt himself begin to pass out, but the smack of his forehead against the wall of the cab ran a steel rod of determination through him. He signaled to the two men on their knees nearby, jerking his thumb toward the tender. "Cut it loose ...," he gasped, "loose from the engine! Let it all roll back ... back out!"

One man was able to understand, the other was not. Boysie and the first man began climbing up onto the tender and across the piles of coal. The smoke was thicker there, near the roof of the shed, and they climbed down onto the front blind of the first boxcar with a sense of relief, even if the air at that level was also fouled by smoke and fumes. Together they yanked at the coupling pin, but it would not shift. "Back to the next one ...," said Boysie, and they entered the boxcar.

Several bull's-eye lanterns had been lit, and the scene revealed in their glare was like some lurid illustration from the *Police Gazette*, a tableau of twisted bodies with terrible gunshot wounds, and the staring, frightened faces of the witnesses to what had happened.

Even here the smoke was a visible presence, swirling around the living and the dead in eddies created by the still-open doorway.

"Jesus ...," breathed the man with Boysie.

"Everyone who can move," said Boysie, struggling to keep his voice calm, "get back onto the flatcar. We're cutting it loose and rolling back out of here. Move, damn you!"

His order resulted in a sudden surge toward the rear door. Men who had been afraid of the nameless things assailing them from the darkness outside now clawed at each other for the privilege of being first onto the flatcar with the golden elk. Their bull's-eye beams jabbed across its flanks and antlers, granting the elk illusory movement, a stag caught wide-eyed among streamers of smoky darkness at the edge of a forest fire.

"Pull the pin ...! Wait!" Boysie commanded, but no one would. Every man rushed past the elk and began crowding through the end door of the second boxcar. Boysie attempted pulling the pin himself, wanting to take the flatcar and elk with him, but again, the coupling would not part. He yanked at it, swearing, damning his men for their cowardice and panic. The metal bar and chain attached to the pin jerked and jangled, but would not dislodge the one thing coupling the flatcar to the boxcar ahead. Pausing to catch his breath, Boysie heard similar janglings and curses from the rear of the flatcar, and knew that his men were attempting to separate the second boxcar and the caboose from the rest of the train, regardless of his orders and his presence on the section that would be left connected to the still-advancing locomotive. Boysie could stay with the elk and risk asphyxiation, or run back to join the rest. He heard the rear pin fly out of the coupling, stood, and ran.

The second boxcar was already separated from the train by several feet as he reached the flatcar's end. The men were stepping back from the doorway, giving him room to land safely if he chose to jump, and Boysie jumped. Hands grabbed him and hauled him inside. The boxcar and the caboose had almost stopped moving by then. Boysie turned to watch the flatcar receding into the darkness ahead. He had tried to take it with him, but had failed. He was no less a coward than his men, and his career was over. The boxcar stopped completely, then began rolling slowly backward. One man was left in the locomotive cab, along with the engineer and the fireman. If any of them died, it would be on Boysie's conscience forever.

* * *

Drew had already begun his walk into the snow shed with a lantern when the sounds of shooting came to him, echoing along three miles of snowbound tunnel. He stopped and tried to count the shots, but there were too many, a staccato barrage without distinction, blurred and softened by distance. Something had gone wrong. Nothing was supposed to happen until the train was well inside the snow shed. Could the three drunks at the far end somehow have been responsible? They had seemed unlikely robbers when Drew and Clay spied on them, but there had to be a reason for such a multitude of shots.

He began walking again. Drew's part in the holdup was to meet the train as deep inside the snow shed as he could, by which time Omie's special magic would have rendered the Pinkerton guards insensible. Drew was himself affected by the aura of fear swirling in the darkness around him. He knew it was baseless, that the only thing he need be fearful of was the narrow space between the shed walls and the locomotive when it passed him. Clay had said to him, before Drew began walking, "Whatever strange things you feel in there, ignore all of it, and concentrate on not getting run down by that train, understand? There's nothing in there, but you'll think there is. It's just empty space with railroad tracks through it, remember that, and don't panic."

Drew had to remind himself of those words every few minutes as he advanced. The shooting had probably lasted no more than fifteen seconds. He could not hear the sound of the locomotive, which should have been inside the shed by then, and his concern over its precise location along the track was magnified by Omie's manufactured waves of terror into a worry that gripped at Drew's innards like an invisible hand. He told himself it was nothing; the train would soon be coming toward him, gunshots notwithstanding. He told himself the darkness around him was benign, unpopulated by demons or goblins; it was a man-made cavern he hurried through, not some underground place of bats and stalactites. He had only to keep walking, board the locomotive when it approached him, and his job would be done. Drew knew what levers to pull, what handles to grip in a locomotive cab, having brought several to a halt during his work with Lodi. His task was simple, and would be successful if only he could continue to ignore the leering darkness around his lantern's inadequate glow.

Now he could hear the engine's steady chuffing, and knew it was well inside the snow shed. Encouraged, he began walking faster toward the sound. No matter what had prompted the outbreak of shooting at the shed's far end, the train had proceeded according to schedule, and every man aboard it would begin to experience what Drew was obliged to wade through on foot, a kind of terrible molasses in the air, unavoidable, inexplicable, a thick soup of nameless terror that would go straight to the heart of any man who was not cognizant of its source.

Drew was aware that his niece had filled the shed with formless dread, but he was obliged to stop anyway, a half mile in, and vomit. He was in awe of such ability; Omie was the possessor of powers beyond Drew's comprehension. Clay had explained as best he could the peculiar relationship he had shared with Omie for years on some other plane of existence, but Drew had not fully appreciated the nature of the family gift until now. Zoe had told him of their mother's ability to see things from afar before they happened, Drew having been too young when Nettie died to remember any of it, and he accepted the fact that even though he was not himself gifted, Omie certainly was, to the extent that Drew was prepared to believe in her plan for taking the golden elk with a minimum of risk to everyone. He had elected to go into the snow shed himself, fearing that Clay, who had proven himself overly susceptible to Omie's etheric emanations, might succumb to the atmosphere within and fall down on the tracks, to be killed by the train when it came through.

He could hear it with more clarity now, a constant chuffing of steam pistons, but it was slower than Drew expected, and he wondered if the engine driver had been overcome too soon by Omie, before having built up a sufficient head of steam to bring the locomotive all the way through. He calculated he had come more than three-quarters of a mile into the shed by then. The plan called for him to rendezvous with the train at least a mile inside, allowing a full two miles for Omie to have worked her influence upon the men aboard. If the train was proceeding at a slower rate than anticipated, he might have to go further to meet it. Drew increased his pace, his high-heeled boots stumbling across railroad ties in the semi-darkness.

The sound of more shots reached him, reverberating with greater volume than before. This time there were fewer, and these were more widely separated. Drew could hear screaming also, and this made his skin crawl; was Omie's spell too powerful, too terrifying? He had left her staring into the darkness he was now penetrating, her features molded into a mask that aged her face twenty years; Omie was a little woman with a need to punish her erstwhile father for his misdeeds, and she had made herself a conduit for other-worldly influences to that end. Drew doubted that any amount of shooting or screams could penetrate the veneer of invulnerability Omie had fashioned about herself. She would continue pouring mortal fear into the shed until she saw the lamp of the approaching locomotive; only then could she allow herself to let the effluvium of fear passing through her begin to ebb away.

Drew saw the light himself now, a dim glow reflecting poorly around wooden curves, suggesting the source was not far behind. Drew paused and listened to the sound of the engine; it had slowed even more, almost to the point of stalling on the track. He had suggested this might happen when Omie presented her plan; with an engine crew paralyzed by fear, the boiler would very likely not be attended to, and the train would come to a halt long before it could reach the end of the shed, especially since it would be laboring against an uphill grade. "Then go in and meet it before that happens," Fay had suggested, with a touch of sarcasm; Fay was not inclined to look upon the Dugans with favor, not when they had money to burn, yet insisted on doing what they intended doing. "You Dugans," she had said to Drew, "you think you've got the right to do what you want. Well, you haven't. Don't do this stupid thing. I won't help you do it. You're a bunch of crazy people even to think of it." Drew was aware that Fay simply wanted to hold greater influence over him than his brother and sister and niece did, and he knew there was no real chance that Fay would succeed, not against those odds.

The light ahead was growing brighter. Now the lamp on the engine's nose shone into his eyes, and the walls either side of Drew were suddenly less threatening; he could see thin white lines between the boards where snow had pushed through. He could smell the smoke that spilled occasionally into the lamp's beam, diluting its glare, and with that smell came another, which Drew recognized instinctively as the rank odor of human panic and fear. He could not tell what might have happened aboard the train, but it was clear that Omie's fog of panic and distraction had penetrated as deeply as planned, and wrought some fundamental change. Drew turned out his lantern in case someone aboard the engine was still peering ahead with his hands on the throttle, although that seemed unlikely, given the sluggish progress it was making toward him. He kept on walking, keeping his head tilted slightly down so the loco-motive's lamp, blindingly bright now, was hidden by his hatbrim. The smell lurking behind the smoke was thick in his nostrils, and Drew was forced to stop and vomit again between the rails. He leaned against the shed wall, stomach lurching in dry spasms, his head suddenly filled with a need to be still, for fear of encountering some deeper morass of pure terror. The train would have to come to him.

And come it did, at an increasingly slower pace. Eventually the snowblade slid past Drew's knees, and he readied himself for a fast climb up the iron ladder into the cab. The drive wheels went rolling by; the ladder was visible in the light spilling from the cab, and Drew reached for it. Climbing inside, he saw two men on the floor and one at the controls, but that man appeared to be as dead as the first two, despite his upright position on the driver's seat. Drew attempted to take the gauntleted hand from the throttle, but it seemed to be frozen there in some kind of death rigor, so he maneu-vered the man's entire arm instead, and fed more power to the wheels. That done, he opened the firebox and began shoveling coal inside to keep up steam pressure. The locomotive responded gradu-ally. Drew kept feeding the firebox until he could see daylight seep-ing along the snow shed walls.

Clay picked up Omie and carried her aside when it became clear she had no intention of moving out of the way. The engine rolled past while she was still in his arms. Clay saw Drew wave from the cab window, and set Omie down on her feet beside her mother. The tender came next, then a boxcar with a number of bullet holes in its sides, holes that had been blasted from within; and then came the flatcar bearing the golden elk, its glory tarnished now by oily smoke. The rest of the train was gone.

Drew applied the brakes, then jumped down to apprise Clay of the three men in the cab. "I thought they were dead in there, but they're all still breathing." Together they entered the boxcar and found seven men dead of gunshot wounds, and one other, without a scratch, who sat facing a corner, muttering nonsense to himself. "All the live ones get put off here," Clay said, "before they wake up and start shooting." Three of the four living men were lifted down and placed in open sunlight beside the track, but the driver could not be prized from his throttle. Clay said, "All right, let him stay. I'm not going to break a man's arms."

Throughout these preparations, Omie stared wordlessly at the elk. It had come to her as it said it would, but now that the creature of her dreams was made real before her eyes, she experienced a pang of disappointment. It was only a statue after all, even if it was made of gold, and in no way resembled the splendid animal that had stepped through her mind so long ago, leaving its cloven prints there. When her uncle Clay had stepped forward from her skull and into her life, Omie's reaction had been intense, a rush of fear and anger, but even though the golden elk now stood within touching distance at last, she felt almost nothing. Clay and Drew had talked of dead men inside the boxcar; Omie supposed she had done that, and did not want to see them. There were not supposed to be any dead men aboard the train, only men who had fainted out of sheer dread. It had all gone wrong, even if the object of the plan had been delivered.

Zoe stood gazing at the elk also, seeing in its greasy flanks the sorry spectacle of her husband's hubris. It was a magnificent yet pathetic monument to Leo's aspirations, a thing that rightly belonged to a girl, and now the girl had taken back what was hers. The cost, though, was high. Zoe went with Fay to examine the box-car, and both got no further than the doorway. The dead lay sprawled in their own blood, surrounded by the fallen weaponry that had brought about their deaths. It was impossible to see Omie as the cause, but difficult to exonerate themselves, the adults who had permitted, and even encouraged, Omie to do what she had done.

Zoe and Fay and Omie climbed into the engine cab, and Drew set the train rolling. No one spoke as the miles between the snow shed and the Sky Gorge bridge were covered. The final act in Zoe's revenge would be completed with an air of somber detachment, one last move necessary for the public humiliation of Leo Brannan.

Drew stopped the train midway across the trestle. The women remained in the cab while he and Clay let themselves down onto the narrow walkway alongside the rails and carefully made their way back to the flatcar and began releasing the ropes and chains binding the elk to its wooden bed. Far below, the cataract tumbled and roared. No man knew its depth, but the waters raced so swiftly through the narrow defile they were never able to freeze, even in the coldest months of winter. The elk would be held forever beneath a foaming maelstrom of whiteness.

"Hold it," said Clay.

Lodi and Nate were walking along the bridge between the rails, approaching them from the rear. The last of the elk's bonds had been thrown aside by then. Drew had his pistol; Clay's shotgun was back along the line, with the horses, since gunplay had never been anticipated. Lodi was smiling, Nate was not.

"Seems I didn't give the little lady her due," said Lodi, swinging up onto the flatcar's end. Nate joined him.

"Seems like," said Clay. "Want to give us a hand tipping this big fellow over the side?"

"Be glad to, but we'd like to take what you might call a souvenir first."

"Nobody takes anything," said Drew. "It goes into the water just like it is."

"That's a waste of gold, don't you think?" reasoned Lodi.

"No, I don't."

"Here's what we want, Nate and me. We want an antler each. That sounds kind of strange, don't it, but that's what we want. We figure they can be taken off easy, being small at the base. We even came prepared. Show them, Nate."

Nate produced a heavy blacksmith's hammer from beneath his coat. Clay noticed the hammer was in Nate's left hand, leaving his gun hand free.

"Nobody takes any part of the elk," Drew said again. "We took it, so it's ours to do with as we please."

"Ordinarily I'd agree with you," said Lodi, still smiling, "but there's nothing ordinary about any of this, not to my mind, so we'll just be taking a small chunk of that crittur, if you please. Why don't you two take a leg each yourselves, maybe? Nate'll lend you the hammer, won't you, Nate?"

"Sure will."

"Get off this train," said Clay. "You never wanted any part of this deal, so no part of it is what you'll get."

"Where's Levon?" asked Drew. "Is he out there somewhere with a rifle on us?"

"Levon went to Carbondale. He's not in on this."

"And neither are you," Clay said. "Get going."

"Can't do it," said Lodi, drawing his gun. "I'll thank you both to let us do what's right. Throwing a million-dollar elk into eternity, that's just plain wasteful, so step back now and don't make trouble where none's needed."

Drew pulled his Colt fast, but Lodi shot him faster, and Nate stepped forward to put three more bullets into him. Drew felt each one slam into his body. He should have kept his gun holstered and tried to reason with Lodi, or waited until Nate was on top of the elk, hammering at the antlers. He had been hasty, and soon he would be dead. He had not been smart. This was what happened to a man who was not smart enough. He had always considered himself smarter than most, but here was the proof that it wasn't so.

He felt pain in his chest and stomach, but the pain was not close to him. The pain was happening to some other man. Instead of pain, Drew felt the tiny breeze created by a hummingbird's frantically beating wings as it hovered before his face. He had seen the hummingbird inside his hat while the gang waited to rob the payroll train, but he had seen it one other time before that, years ago, but only now recalled the incident. He had gone fishing along the Mohawk River with Clay, back in Schenectady, before their father left the Dugans on their own. It had been a warm August day, and Drew had fallen asleep on the riverbank, to be awakened by the hummingbird. It had hovered before his slowly opening eyelids, a shimmering bauble suspended in the air on blurred wings, just inches from his nose, and Drew had marveled at its loveliness, its body an exquisite ornament held before him like some impossible promise. He had stared at the hummingbird and felt his heart fill with an emotion that could not be named, and when the brilliant creature suddenly dived away and was lost to sight, he felt a sense of loss that could not be borne. Clay had asked why he was crying, and Drew had been unable to answer. Now the hummingbird had returned to fan him with its tiny wings again, and peer at him with the jet beads of its eyes, and assure him there was nothing to fear, just a long sleep on the riverbank, and an eventual awakening that would surprise him very much. Drew gave the hummingbird his thanks, and fell into an inexorable vortex.

Clay felt his limbs turn to lead. His brother lay on the flatcar with a curious smile on his face. Drew looked very young, younger than he had in life. He was a boy again, a dying boy, too young for death but dying anyway, and Clay, unarmed, could do nothing but watch him die, and feel inside himself the beginnings of a hole, that familiar hole he had always known since the orphan train separated them, and now, on this other train, he was parted from Drew again, this time forever, and there was nothing he could do, nothing to halt the separation, nothing to punish the separators, whose crime against the brothers was magnified by the smallness of the time they had shared together before flying apart again. It was more than a crime, it was a sin, and Clay could do nothing to punish the sinners, could only look at the handsome face of his brother, lost, then found, only to be lost a second time, and feel all over again the opening of the hole within himself that only a living Drew could occupy. He felt the hole growing inside him as Drew's eyes closed upon the world, until the hole was everything, without dimension or end, a yawning emptiness beyond calculation or reconciliation, simply a hole wherein he would have to spend the remainder of his days.

"You get back now," Lodi warned, "or you'll get the same. I mean it. Nate, get working with that hammer."

Nate holstered his gun and leapt onto the back of the elk. The hammer was drawn from his coat and raised to strike a first blow against the unsullied golden head, when the side of his neck blew out in a fountain of blood. Nate fell slowly from the beast, his hammer falling onto the flatcar near the golden hooves. Lodi raised his own pistol too late; a bullet took him in the chest, and he staggered several steps backward, bumping his spine against the elk's hindquarters before the second bullet tore away his temple and he slid down the elk's back legs onto the flatcar's bed and lay still, his head inches from Nate's left boot.

Clay turned. Zoe stood atop the fuel tender, her arm and pistol still outstretched.

There seemed nothing else to do but follow their plan, though it had gone disastrously awry. Clay set about using the firebox shovel to try and tip over the elk. He could not bear to think of Drew, lying nearby; the elk had to disappear, be gone from the flatcar, or Drew had died for nothing. Lodi had been right; it was a robbery committed by fools. Now there was nothing to do but finish things off the way they had planned, and be done with it. The women helped him, shoving at the elk's belly, but it did little more than rock on its hooves an inch or two each way. With Drew's help and a couple of long crowbars, the job might have been accomplished. Without him, it seemed hopeless.

Now Omie had only one uncle. The handsome one was gone, lying in a sprawl no different from those of the men who had killed him. She kept thinking of a hummingbird, but did not understand why. No one else was looking at Drew. They were all trying to push the statue off the train. It would tumble down and splash into the roaring waters so very far beneath them, and be lost forever. But they could not move it. Omie threw the weight of her inner self at the elk, and saw it shudder. The others felt it too, and without being aware that it was Omie who caused it to shift, they leaned against it with all their might. Omie had to smile crookedly at that. They were not capable, all three, of doing with their bodies what she knew she could do without even touching the elk. She poured hatred into it, for the death of Drew, and for the men who had done it, and for the fathers who had left her, and the man dressed as a woman who had come to kill her, and for all that was not good among the teeming pastures of the earth.

And the elk began to lean outward, its antlers like toppling trees, its hooves on the near side lifting free of the flatcar's planks. It trembled on two legs, perfectly balanced, until Omie gave it a final contemptuous shove. The elk fell stiffly over the edge without even touching the bridge, and by the time everyone but Omie had rushed to see it hit the water, the elk had already vanished, the commotion of its landing whipped away instantly by the rushing torrent below. It was as if the statue had disappeared into the very air of Sky Gorge, disassembled its own trillion atoms for dispersement on the wind.

With its passing came an end to the misadventure. They returned to the cab, and Clay mimicked Drew's various manipulations of the engine's levers until he discovered how to throw the train into reverse. The driver sat as before on his seat, eyes fixed on the tracks ahead even as his train returned to the snow shed. He was not aware of the passengers in his cab, nor of their careful removal, as the locomotive stood and panted steam, of a young dead man from the flatcar. He did not react when Clay climbed back into the cab and set the throttle for a slow climb up the grade again, this time with the intention of reaching Glory Hole.

Clay jumped down when the wheels began to turn, then lifted and carried his brother away into the trees where the horses were tied.

55

L eo was waiting at the station when his train arrived more than an hour late. It was in fact just half a train, and its engineer rammed the locomotive slowly into the barriers at the end of the line. The man was found to be in some kind of trance, from which he was not to recover for several days, and even then he was unable to recall anything, including the two dead men on an otherwise empty flatcar that should have carried a golden elk. The ropes and chains were there, but the elk was not.

The boxcar contained more dead men. As the crowd that had gathered to see the elk milled about the train, a telegram from Leadville was handed to Leo. It explained the missing boxcar and caboose, but contained no word on Leo's elk. Subsequent investigation along the track before the day was done found three men by the Glory Hole end of the snow shed. These men, like the engineer, were without coherent memory of the events that had left them where they were found. Three bodies, one female, were discovered at the Leadville end of the shed. The circumstances surrounding their deaths were explained by the Pinkerton agent in charge, although he could not deny the three had attacked the train with nothing more lethal than snowballs.

In the days following the arrival of the half-train, Lovey Doll waited with some trepidation for Leo to make known to her his wishes concerning their future together. She drank heavily while waiting, knowing he must have been driven almost to the point of madness by the disappearance of their precious elk, as was she. When finally he did arrive at her door, he bore a bottle of champagne tied about the neck with a red silk ribbon.

"I'll hear not a single word tonight about The Mystery," he said, employing the term the newspapers had coined. "Not a word, do you hear?"

"Yes, Leo."

"One of those fellows they found, he was your friend, the one who gave you the casket. Can you tell me what in heaven's name he was doing out there?"

"I understood you wanted no mention of the incident, Leo."

"Answer me!"

"I ... have no idea why he was there...."

"So you had no part in this business, *Lovey Doll?*"

It was the first time he had used her real name. Lovey Doll wondered if this represented a new and more honest beginning for them, or the end of whatever it was that Leo felt for her. But if he had come with finality in mind, why had he brought champagne?

Noticing the direction of her gaze, Leo said, "To celebrate our betrothal, my sweet." His smile was meager, but she forgave him. Despite his concerns over what already was being referred to as "The Theft of the Century," he had come to her with a message of love and reconciliation. She was forgiven her lies, and Lovey Doll decided at that moment she would forgive Leo his deplorable physical assaults upon her person. Now everything would be different, she was sure. Maybe, in some perverse manner, the inexplicable theft of the elk had summoned in Leo the lineaments of a better man, the man he once had been. Lovey Doll smiled with genuine hope as the bottle was uncorked.

"Glasses," Leo said, and she fetched her finest.

He poured generous measures and they sipped, bubbles touching their noses.

"Please dress yourself in the red gown," Leo requested.

"Of course, my darling."

Lovey Doll hurried to her room, and returned wearing Leo's favorite. She found him standing by the crystal casket, and began to doubt that he believed her claim of noninvolvement. She truly could not understand how a man such as Nevis Dunnigan could attempt so foolhardy a change of profession as to become a train robber, she truly did not.

Leo said, "I wish to see you beneath the glass."

"Dearest, you know I find it uncomfortable."

Leo thrust a full glass of champagne at her. "Not with more of this inside you, my darling." He smiled. "Indulge me, do, just this once."

"Very well, only for you, my dearest one."

She quaffed the champagne in one unladylike gulp, then looked at Leo to see if he disapproved of such unfeminine conduct, but he was smiling, this time with conviction, and so she stepped up and laid her body down on the casket's velvet bed. It was less irksome to perform this task than it had been the first time; scarcely had she arranged herself comfortably than Lovey Doll felt a ring slipped onto her finger. "This," said Leo, "is the seal of our betrothal."

Now it was real. Lovey Doll raised the beautiful object to her face and watched the sparkling lights that leaped from Leo's diamond. The flashes of white fire were beyond comparison with any other thing that might have excited her blood. It had been worthwhile after all, the deceptions and the personal humiliations; Leo wanted her for his wife. Her new ring shone with a splendid radiance, and the hand supporting it became heavy even as she gazed with enraptured eyes. Lovey Doll felt her arm fall to her side, but was not alarmed, since Leo attended to it by arranging it along her thigh. He wished her to be without discomfort. How very kind he was this night, as if determined to atone for his wrongdoing. She forgave him all over again. There was a taste at the back of her throat that Lovey Doll found puzzling, but she could not bring her thoughts to bear upon it. Her eyes were closing with languorous ease. The casket really was a fit place for her to take her rest after all.

Leo watched with detachment as Lovey Doll slid into a narcotic stupor. He had been troubled by the possibility of her detecting the strange taste of his powders, but she had said nothing, had drunk it down like a child her medicine, and now she slept. His doctor had assured him that his troubles of these last few days would be pushed aside by the drug of his prescription, and Leo had given Lovey Doll a week's dosage.

When she began to snore, he lowered the lid, and made sure that the vacuum screw was tightly in place. As Lovey Doll peacefully exhaled, moisture began building inside the casket, hiding her form behind a fine misting of the glass. Leo watched as her features became lost, made vague by her own breath. It required almost a half hour before the building up of mist inside the casket ceased. He would leave her in the casket's poisoned air until morning, just to be sure she was really dead, and would sit beside her until then. To maintain a solitary vigil by the deceased was the least he could do, Leo thought.

Drew was buried along the great divide, his grave left unmarked, and the remaining Dugans proceeded to Provo, where Zoe had left her money in a bank vault. Fay left them there, declaring herself sickened by the entire family, their foolishness in allowing a girl to set up a robbery, and their arrogance in throwing away the thing they stole, a thing that had cost Drew his life. She would accept no money from Zoe, and returned to Carbondale, for want of any other place to go. There she met again with Levon. Fay persuaded him to retire from outlawry, and within a month was married to him. They swore a wedding oath never to reveal the location of the elk. Levon did relent and tell his grandson in 1927, but was not believed.

The Dugans moved to Washington state and found a large house for themselves by the ocean. Clay walked often along the shore. Zoe invested her money carefully and was able to support them all. Her one indulgence was a small sailboat, which she handled with dexterity despite her missing arm. Omie became uncontrollable during her puberty, and was thought to be connected somehow to the death by unknown means of a handsome boy from the nearest town, whom she had fallen in love with and been rejected by. There being no direct evidence of implication, Omie was not officially charged with any wrongdoing. She refused to discuss the matter with her mother and uncle. The Dugans had always held themselves in isolation, and the rumors drove them further from society.

Omie waited for Drew to appear in some ghostly guise, but he never did, even when Omie begged his spirit to manifest itself. His brother's nonappearance greatly disappointed Clay; he had somehow expected more of Omie, who thereafter spent much of her time alone. She did, however, warn Clay of a dangerous woman traveling from the east to do him harm. Clay knew who that was, and began carrying a pistol. He would not shoot Sophie with it, just make her go away and allow the dead to sleep apart from the living.

When he was approached on the beach several days later, he knew the woman with her hands buried at her waist inside a fur muff was his wife, come to attempt vengeance again on behalf of their son. Clay intended asking her if the controversy over Omie and the local boy had been the thing that set her on his trail again, but before she had even come within speaking distance, the woman pulled a pistol and began firing. Clay fired back, despite a bullet in his left side, and killed her with his third shot, by which time he had received another wound, to the thigh.

Stooping to examine the face of his attacker, Clay detected a faint shadow of beard growth along the jawline, and took himself up to the house, bleeding steadily, to berate Omie for having got it wrong. Tatum was taken out to sea in Zoe's sailboat that night, and dumped overboard with a sack of stones chained around his ankles. Nobody in the town believed Clay Dugan had shot himself accidentally, twice, as he claimed, and further notoriety was heaped upon the family. Zoe suggested they move to another state, and Clay agreed it would be wise. Omie said nothing; she knew they would be living in California within a month.

When Clay was able, he resumed his lonely walks along the beach, and one day was surprised to see a man come down from the cypress trees along the shore to join him on the sand. The man waved in a friendly manner, and Clay stopped out of politeness, wondering who he might be. As the man came closer, Clay thought he detected a face beneath the straw boater that was familiar to him, but could not be sure; he must get new glasses, he reminded himself. The man was only a few steps from Clay when a gun was pulled. Clay stared at it in surprise, and watched the muzzle jump and flash as he was shot five times by Sophie, who then turned the pistol on herself and sent the last bullet into her brain.

The two were found later that afternoon by Zoe, who knew now that she had delayed too long in moving. They could have gone elsewhere to live before the house was sold, but she had insisted on waiting, and this was the result. She felt as guilty over Clay's death as she had over Drew's, and Omie's silence on the subject as she assisted her mother to dispose of both bodies as they had done with Tatum, convinced Zoe that Omie considered her guilty too. As Clay and his wife disappeared beneath the moonlit swell, Zoe was tempted to throw herself in after them. Omie broke her silence with one word—"No"—and mother and daughter returned to shore.

* * *

The Praetorians gradually succumbed to massive subversion by Big Circle, and the roles of both bodies were subtly reversed, the greater absorbing the lesser, rather than the intruder taking over its host. Rowland Price was among the last of the holdouts who still believed that Leo Brannan might one day be in the vanguard of a new political force in the land, until Mr. Jones took pity on his foolishness and showed him a report detailing the extent to which his dream had become a joke. Rowland had been instrumental in disposing of Lovey Doll Pines's body after Leo told him the woman had committed suicide, and he expected some reward for having been so invaluable an aide. He hurried back to Glory Hole to plead a sudden need for cash, but Leo, having received the same report by mail, would not involve himself further with a man who had brought him into so inept an organization. Price wished he were able to set Tatum on Jones and Leo both, but the man had disappeared some time before. Rowland Price moved east to protect himself from possible reprisal instigated by these wealthy men, found himself still frightened on Cape Cod, and so took ship for England.

When Zoe died of a heart attack in San Bernardino in 1905, Omie destroyed the inside of their home while sitting in an armchair. She explained the destruction to her cleaning lady the next day as the work of vandals. These vandals struck again several months later, and at regular intervals after that, but by then the police department was not interested in apprehending them. Omie Dugan was a pariah.

Four years after the death of her mother, Omie received a visitor, who arrived in a gleaming automobile. A man of great age, he introduced himself as Mr. Jones, but before he could state his business further, Omie told him his wife was inaccessible to his need for an interview, having already been reborn as a male in Idaho. Mr. Jones turned away, and suffered a fatal stroke less than five minutes later, while on his way to the train depot.

When Omie was forty-three she was judged to be insane. She had neglected to wash her person or care for her property in any way for a number of years, following the departure of the last in a lengthy roster of maids and cooks and gardeners. Omie had driven them all away with her strange behavior, except for the last, who left her when it became known that Omie had no money left to pay for hired help.

When county officials came to inform her that she was to be taken to the asylum, Omie laughed at them, and pushed them off her porch while standing behind her screen door. They returned the following day with several large men, but when they attempted to break down the front door, a sudden gust of flame from an instantaneous fire in the hallway drove them back. The fire appeared to ignite spontaneously in all parts of the house, upper floors and lower, and although two fire engines soon were at the scene, it was generally agreed that the best they could do was set their hoses to spray the roofs of the houses on either side. No one saw Omie Dugan alive, and her bones were never found among the charred rubble.

The mystery of the golden elk's vanishment took hold of Noble Burgin's imagination and was rendered into a play, *The Shining Stag,* in which Noble proposed that the statue had been removed from the train by a hot-air balloon. This aerial theft, perpetrated by a brilliant madman-inventor of the Jules Verne type, was Noble's most audacious stage effect, and was itself hailed as the work of a genius. The production proved to be even more successful than his two previous offerings, *Red Hellions* and *The Man-eater!* Noble retired from the theater a happy man, believing he had won a permanent place for himself upon the stage of high art, and he died some years later of a ruptured appendix. In time, Noble's great works would be forgotten completely.

In 1900, Slade's arm was broken when he fell against an endless belt and pulley system while harvesting wheat in Alberta. The break was not set properly, and his usefulness as a worker diminished from that time. He was angry over the incident, and angry over the incompetence of the horse doctor who set the break so poorly, but there was nothing he could do about any of it. Slade had been proud of his strength and his ability to outwork men half his age, and now the source of his pride was gone. The harvest was in, his term of hire was finished in any case, so he moved on, as he always had.

Riding an empty boxcar across the emptiness of Canada, Slade saw that his life was effectively over. Unable to perform work with an arm that grew steadily weaker, he was good for nothing. To be a cripple and a beggar was more than Slade could endure, yet that was the future awaiting him. He could not recall his past with any certainty beyond a year or two, and always thought in terms of what he did with his life in the present. No past, no future, and now the present had become a burden to him. Slade found a measure of his old pride in being able to consider the facts without flinching. He had never wanted sympathy, had no use for love, but would have surrendered his other arm to know who he was.

For a time he begged for food and such work as a man with a crippled arm was capable of performing, but not enough of either came his way, and Slade despised himself for having to ask anything of anyone. Whatever the nature of his life had ever been, it had not included groveling for charity, of that he was sure. As winter came on, Slade decided he would not live to see the spring. It was the only choice available to him that did not gore his pride, the one thing remaining to him, and he took no food into his body from that moment on.

A slow death by starvation was not what he wanted for himself, so at the first opportunity, Slade took himself away from the world of men and entered the world of snow. It was the season's first heavy fall, a blizzard of whiteness, perfect for Slade's needs. He walked out of the town in which his decision had been reached, and within minutes had no idea where he was, so thickly did the falling snow surround him. He walked as long as he could across open prairie, his extremities beginning to lose feeling, and when he was certain he had become completely lost, and that the snow would continue falling for at least another day, he sat down and closed his eyes to await the coming of old man death, whom Slade was prepared to greet as an equal.

The process of dying by cold took longer than he had anticipated, but was far easier, once he was genuinely reconciled to quitting the earth. The warmth left his body steadily, and was replaced by a comforting numbness. He congratulated himself on having chosen wisely. This was the way to go, on his own terms, in his own company. It was a shame that he could bid a silent farewell to no one, since no one but himself existed in his memory, and even that man was reduced to one name only. His leaving of life was an anticlimax to its living, he felt, even if he could not recall who and what he truly was. It was better to end such an empty life, since it was the remembrance of his years that provided satisfaction to a dying man, assuming those years had been well spent. Slade had no idea what he might or might not have done, the attacks of memory loss had become so frequent in recent years. Sometimes it had taken an entire day to remember his own name, and in the end he had assured himself of that one thing by having SLADE tattooed onto his arm, lest he forget himself entirely.

It was slipping from him by degrees, his notion of aliveness, as the snow began burying him beneath its blanket of neutrality. He began to doubt the arrangements for his own demise when he saw a woman approaching him. What was a woman doing out in the cold and snow? Slade sat very still as she came near, hoping she would pass blindly by and leave him to die in peace, but the woman came directly to him, and stood before Slade with a look of great pity on her face.

Staring at her, trying to conceal his annoyance, Slade found himself attempting to give the intruder a name, and the name came to him at the same instant that he recognized her as his wife of long ago. It was Nettie standing before him, of all people. He asked her how it was possible that she had found him amid all the swirling and frigid emptiness of his chosen place, and she told him it was easy; she had been told to be with him at the last, to remind him of his life, the thing that he had chosen to leave behind. His decision would be respected, Nettie told him, but before he would be permitted to depart, he must remember everything he had forgotten.

And as she told him this, Slade remembered it all, the life of his younger self sweeping back into him like air into an unstoppered vacuum; the courtship of and marriage to Nettie; his work in the railyards of Schenectady; his gradual souring of temperament when the children came, three of them, and his love of liquor, which smothered the obligation to Nettie and the boys and girl they had produced. Slade felt shame overcome him as the night of his escape aboard a freight train was depicted before his eyes; he had ridden it west, exultant to have evaded responsibility at last. Then he saw the wreck in Ohio that cracked his skull and cured him of any need to drink by robbing him of his identity.

James Slade Dugan was his name, and Nettie Lamb had been the woman he gave that name to, as sweet a girl as he could have wished for, and he had treated her like a dog. She stood before him now, neither sad nor exultant, as young as she had been when they met, and if the freezing air would have allowed it, Slade would have wept for what had been his and he had thrown away out of sheer foolishness, to embrace an empty life of drifting and forgetting and careless murder. He saw the face of every victim, relived every blow delivered by the stranger with his face, the monster that had been himself.

"Why did you have to tell me ...?" he asked his wife, and she said it was to punish him, since punishment must come from within himself, and that could not happen without a reckoning with his past, a mirror held before him like a sheet of ice, in which was reflected his weakness and folly and loss. And when it was revealed to him, the agent of his restoration of self began immediately to fade, her slender form melding with the snow, white upon white, until she disappeared.

Slade was left to stare at the great nothingness he had engendered, and into which he now plummeted like a stone, the first of the Dugans to die in the new century, the first of the last of the line; and that fact was shown to him also as he fell, so that he might know that the blood freezing in his veins would never be passed on. They all would die, the blighted Dugans he and Nettie had made, without any offspring but virginal Omie. When he had swung aboard the train so long ago he had taken himself away from his past, away from his future, and the future of the Dugans. It all would come to nothing, the passing of the blood from his father's fathers, and it had been he who let fall the precious chalice. It had been Nettie's blood that died the most, since she had stayed behind to do what was right. They were her children more than his; Slade had done nothing more than dilute the blood of Nettie Lamb. Now he understood his crimes, understood also that there would be no absolution. He knew, as his soul was shredded like mist in sunlight, that none was due.